SLICED
from LIFE

CHUCK GUIDOTTI

Copyright © 2020 Chuck Guidotti
All rights reserved
First Edition

PAGE PUBLISHING, INC.
Conneaut Lake, PA

First originally published by Page Publishing 2020

ISBN 978-1-6624-1570-8 (pbk)
ISBN 978-1-6624-1571-5 (digital)

Printed in the United States of America

Dedication

My heartfelt thanks to my lovely wife Lynne and good friend Rich, whose support and encouragement allowed me to put into words what my heart felt. Also my grandchildren, who I populated into some of my stories. Above all, my humble thanks to God, without whom, I could never have created the bond of love and sacrifice displayed by my characters. Enjoy.

Contents

The Gift of Giving 7
The Violin 16
Friendship 31
The Castle Keeper 43
Going Home 64
True Blue 82
Man of Honor 97
The Magical Paints 120
Remembrance 141
Long Distance 164
    (A Love Story) 164
The Fisherman 193
A Slice of Life 216
    Part One 216
    Part Two 265
    Part Three 308
Brothers 335
Cleared for Takeoff 364
The Little Ones 393
Forever 404
Fraternity 421
Passing Tribute 444
The Visitors 458
Mustang 484
Cycle 497
Tau of the Emporium 557

The Gift of Giving

It was a sunny but chilly day in the fall that saw two children frolicking through the park. Mom was just ahead of them, allowing their youthful nature to explore while keeping a furtive eye on them. Maryn was the oldest, nine years old and full of the enthusiasm that us older ones tend to lose as time goes by.

Mason, a precocious five-year-old, struts about like a band major, inquisitive or nosey, as you may prefer. Maryn is like a second mother to the little one, which pleases her mother extremely so. It's not that she tends to his bathing, feeding, and other distractions that a five-year-old can invent, it's the genuine love that binds her to his needs. Content with this knowledge, Mom knows there is nothing to worry about. When she decides to rest on a bench, there is no such need for these two windmills, and she chuckles to herself that they have so much pure energy to spend, some of which she could only wish to garner for herself.

Mason would run after a butterfly, and Maryn would watch with delight at his frustrations at not catching it. Maryn in turn would stop to smell the last of the blooming roses and toy with the prospect of plucking several for the vase at home. While they cavort, Mom becomes somber, staring into her mind's eye at what waits for them at home. Dad has been out of work, and finances are an acute worry. What savings they have are quickly drying up. His job as a financial analyst was terminated when the company was sold to an organization that stressed thrift over compassion.

On the other side of the park, a Mr. Joshua Cordivan was resting on another park bench, although resting would be a kind word for it. His company had provided all their employees to a lavish celebration the night before and had instructed that all who attended come dressed in any outfit they chose as long as it was colorful and not conventional. As CEO, this was his edict, and he was fond of flouting the conventional. Mr. Cordivan's attire was that of hobo, those roaming free spirits who traveled the country by any means and subsisted on handouts granted to them after some type of labor. His clothing was rumpled and in need of a patch here and there. He hadn't shaved in a week to give him the air of a true roamer. The festivities had wound down to the wee hours before concluding. Offers were made to take him home, but he chose to walk, something that was part of his daily constitution.

However, this time, Mr. Cordivan felt the tug of sleepiness and while crossing through the park, meandered to the nearest bench. Needless to say, it was not long before his prone body covered the entire bench, accompanied by some searing nasal affectations one would call snoring. Blissfully, he whiled away the night. The dawn or rising sun did nothing to disturb him from his tranquility, and his sleep continued without disruption.

Mom called to the children, and after feigning resistance to suspend their exploration, off they trotted, a slight distance behind the good shepherd. As they walked, a slight distance behind Mom increased to a larger but manageable one, and she was cautious about being to restrictive. The children's antics prevailed as before, but Maryn ensured they would not get out of hand. There was a slight rise ahead, and before it on the side of the path was the bench that Mr. Cordivan had adopted as his temporary bedroom.

Mom disappeared for a moment over the rise as the children were about to pass by the slumbering gentleman. Prior to this, Mr. Cordivan had awakened somewhat but was still in a dozing state. As the children approached, Mason stopped and eyed the prostrate man with his soft hazel eyes. He reached into his side pocket, which Mom had pinned to protect its contents. His small hand wriggled by the obstruction and grasped the object that lay at the bottom of the lining and extracted it. It was a five-cent piece Mom had given him for performing some obscure deed, which in itself didn't merit any more than a "Well done." Walking close to the man, he placed the nickel in an open pocket. Maryn questioned him about what he was doing, and the boy replied, in a sweet innocence not tarnished by what we call *experience*, that the man was poor and maybe the money would help him. Maryn was about to scold him when Mom called to the children. They both scooted off to join her, Mason turning his head to eye this "poor" man before passing over the rise.

Although he had been dozing, this did not prevent him from experiencing one of the most touching and warmest acts of kindness he had ever witnessed. A mere child stood as a witness to the most desired act that one could wish for—charity. What could this little boy have bought for himself with that paltry sum, which to him would have been a treasure? And yet, he forwent a self-fulfilling notion to grant that treasure to a stranger!

He was a decent man, and although he wasn't very religious, he recalled a story in the Bible where a Pharisee had donated a large sum to the temple and looked with scorn upon an old woman who gave of her last two coins. Which gave the most? The old woman for she gave from her want, while the Pharisee gave from his surplus. Surely, to the little tyke, this was no surplus, but the man thought that in his giving, the little boy had no awareness of his generosity, only that someone was in need.

While meditating on this, he suddenly became aware that the children had gone. It was his intention to thank them and maybe do a little more, but it was too late. Did they come to the park often? Maybe then he would meet them again, but there was no way of assuring this. He grasped the nickel as if it were the only source of income he had and gently placed it in his pocket with a slight pat as if to properly secure it. Up he rose from the bench and thought of having some breakfast. He remembered a stand at the end of the park where a good cup of coffee and maybe a Danish could be had. All during this walk, thoughts of the children would not desert him. He had eyed the little girl as she guided her brother away and saw the loving look in her eyes. Truly a family blessed and this could only come from loved ones at home, her parents or other family members. As he neared the stand, he caught a glimpse of the children and what may be their mother. She was fumbling through her purse, trying to extract the proper amount of change to pay for a sweet bun that the boy and girl were sharing. The look on her face betrayed an embarrassment at not having the right amount, and in fact, her purse was empty.

She grabbed the bun before the children had torn it apart and offered it back to the vendor. Mr. Cordivan caught the eye of the vendor and discreetly signaled that he would take care of the tab but to not let the woman know. Mr. Cordivan was a frequent customer of the vendor and had been so for many years. Without skipping a beat, the vendor explained to the woman that he was sold out for the day, and because he did well, the bun was on the house. The relief and thankfulness of the woman mirrored her own goodness, and Mr. Cordivan knew he had guessed correctly as to the kind of parent or parents the children had. Happily she returned the bun to the children, who, as children, promptly tore it apart, Mason being given the larger portion by his sister. When they had left the stand, he approached the vendor and thanked him for his quick reaction in saving the woman from grief. He gave him a large bill and refused any change whatsoever, asking if he knew the family.

He replied he may have seen them before but wasn't sure. With that, Mr. Cordivan proceeded to hop a cab to his residence. After showering and a much-needed shave, off he went to his office. As head of the company, he could choose any time to show up, but as an example of dependability, he chose to arrive before any of his employees. Although devoted to profit, an underlying theme of his operation was fairness and that a loss was preferable to profiteering. As a result of this principle, the business thrived and was able to develop a reputation that heralded its accomplishments. Still, the thought of the little boy and his family would not leave him. That cherubic face and its infant sincerity clung to him like a tight sweater. And the girl was that sweet counterbalance which completed the picture. Would it be possible to ever find them? What would he do if he did? He reluctantly surrendered this trend of thought and returned to his task of running the company.

Several days passed, not one of which went by without a thought of the mystery family. Finally, his department heads notified him of several openings in the financial department. He placed ads with several papers to fill these positions, and the company's reputation assured that there would be no lack of applicants. One of those was a man whose only desire was to care for his family, that pinching pennies would be a thing of the past. Nervously he filled out the forms and waited for an interview with Mr. Cordivan. When his name was called, he rose quickly and patted down his jacket to smooth out the many wrinkles it had accumulated. Walking into the office, he was asked to be seated, which he did in the fashion of a schoolboy who had been sent to the principal's office, apprehensive but also hopeful of a positive outcome. As he watched Mr. Cordivan studying his application, his eye caught sight of a nickel embedded within a picture frame that was to the side of the desk. His stare was very focused; why was a nickel considered so special? His trance was broken by Mr. Cordivan's voice, who had glimpsed the gentleman's rapt attention to the frame. To relieve his puzzlement, the director, rather proudly, explained the course of events that brought the coin into his possession.

As he related the story, he described the family that was the source of this display. A mother with two young children, a seemingly devoted woman with a frayed green-and-black checkered coat. A little boy with a rather tight-fitting brown overcoat and a girl with a very bright-red sweater.

What touched him the most was the young lad's unbelievable generosity and sincere concern for the "poor man" lying on the bench. That nickel, he exclaimed, will always remind him of that day and will stand as an example of selflessness. When he had finished, he turned his attention to the man's application and nodded with satisfaction to the many pluses he had read. Where he had gone to college, his standing upon graduation, and the fact that he had worked many years for the same company. That showed a degree of dependability which he sought the most from his employees. After some further questions meant to learn the ground on which this man stood, Mr. Cordivan said that he would be in touch with him. At least this was not a firm rejection, and the man took some heart in it. He shook the director's hand, which impressed the latter, for it was a grip of iron, a transfer of true character. The walk home was lighter than it would have been with a firm rejection. He took in the trees and bushes in the park, the birds fluttering and chirping, and even the occasional unleashed dog that ran up to him with a wagging tail, a sign of friendliness. When he reached home, he paused for a moment and closed his eyes, a slight movement of his lips portraying thanks to power beyond equal.

Stepping into the hallway, two young children ran to greet him, yelling, "Daddy! Daddy, you're home." The boy had a tight brown overcoat he had failed to remove, and his daughter a bright-red sweater. On the hat rack was a green-and-black, frayed checkered coat. His children followed him into the living room, and as he sat down, he gazed into the faces of his two angels, who returned his look with one of near adoration. He grasped the boy by both shoulders and drew him close. He asked his son what he had done with the nickel given to him so long ago, a nickel he had held so lovingly because his daddy had given it to him. The boy's eyes looked down, and he grasped his little hands together, twisting them about and trying to answer a question he thought was about him doing wrong.

Finally with as much composure that a five-year-old could muster and with just a tinge of justification, he said, "Daddy, I gave it to a poor man." With that, the father pulled his son to his breast and hugged him tightly, so much so that the boy protested that he couldn't breathe. "Daddy, did I do a bad thing?" he responded.

"No," said the father, "you had done the right thing."

Several days passed, and with each day without a word concerning his job prospects, hope dimmed a little. Returning home from several interviews and contacts, he was greeted by his wife, who had in her hands a letter addressed to him and bearing the company logo. With a raised anticipation, he clawed open the envelope and unfolded the harbinger of his fate. As his eyes danced across the neatly typed words, his mouth moving in unison, he erupted with a yell, "We got it! We got it!" The little boy couldn't understand why his dad was jumping up and down, swinging Mom off her feet into a circular dance.

Maryn was old enough to understand, and she competed with Mom for hugging rights. He showed his wife the letter, and she read where there would be a yearly orientation for all employees that was to be held at the Sherman ballroom, a stylish but inviting center of recreation. But, she uttered, her only coat was frayed, and she didn't want to embarrass her husband, and the children's clothing was barely passable. "You silly woman," was the term shot back with, "I married you, not your taste in clothing." Delighted with knowing her husband would soon be working again, she went to the bedroom closet to sort anything that had a chance to see the light of day. Next she sorted through the children's clothing. A boy was a boy, and he could make do, but a girl had to look fresh and dainty, a difficult task with what was at hand. Money was a problem, or else they would all be sporting new wardrobes. Necessity is the mother of invention, so the saying goes, and invention was put into full force within that joyous household. What emerged was a testament to a determined mother and wife. While not Fifth Avenue, they would suffice for what lay in store.

The ballroom was beautiful, a sight the children had never seen. Mason was so caught up in all the lights that shone around the room. The multimirrored ball that hung down from the center of the ceiling twirled, reflecting the stationary lights that played upon it, with the little boy chasing after them, laughing with delight. Maryn reflected the conservatism of her dress and maintained a very adult composure while at the same time envying Mason and his unrestrictive antics. Light refreshments were available at the side tables, and the children soon abandoned any pretense of self-control. Mom and Dad soon joined them, the children picking through the cookies and cake and ignoring all else.

The employees, new and old, mingled and exchanged pleasantries, getting to know the recent hires and reacquainting with the established ones. The mood was light and airy when a smattering of applause grew louder and longer. Mr. Cordivan had arrived and was sauntering across the floor. As he made his way to the table where Mom and Dad were, he stopped abruptly, eyeing the man and then his wife, confirming her identity of the woman in the park. Then the children appeared from under the table, where they had been playing tag when both of them froze in their tracks. The boy gulped, grabbed his daddy's hand, and whispered up to him, "Daddy, that's the poor man."

"I know, son, I know," he replied, his tone reverent. Maryn's face appeared from behind her mother's side, confused by the poor man's appearance. "Sir," said the father, "may I introduce my family, which I believe you have some acquaintance with. This is my wife, Jennifer." Jennifer was enthralled when her husband had related to her the meeting he had with Mr. Cordivan and the history of the framed nickel.

"I'm honored," she said.

"No, the honor is mine, ma'am," her husband's boss retorted. He walked over to Maryn and placed his hand on her face, caressing her cheek, which promptly turned red. He mentioned as to how he noticed the care she exhibited with her brother that day in the park, which spoke volumes of her fondness for him. Then, approaching the boy, the gentleman knelt down, placing both hands on Mason's arms, and drew him close. Mason was bewildered for a moment until Mr. Cordivan addressed him.

"Son, I want you to know that the gift you gave me that day will always have a place on my desk and in my heart to remind me of the sacrifice you made. Do you understand me?" Mason may not have known the exact meaning of those words, but he understood the tone, and he nodded in the affirmative. "I want you to be my friend always, as I wish that for your entire family." The boy stepped closer and wrapped his arms around the man's neck to signify his approval and acceptance. A small crowd had gathered to witness the exchange, and a round of applause bounced around the walls, a sign of tribute.

After his wide-eyed experience, Mason, along with Maryn, returned to the refreshment table for some unfinished business, the seriousness of the moment passing into history, but not from their hearts. Mr. Cordivan motioned the parents away from the table and made a request of them. He wanted to fund their future education and would accede to their wishes. Jennifer said that it was much too generous and that they would not be able to repay him.

"My dear, payment has already been rendered. My wife passed way some years ago, and I lost a son in the service of his country. His presence, your whole family's presence, has revived the joy I once had. To deny me the privilege of doting on them will deprive me of that joy. But as I said, I will go by what you feel is best."

For a moment, the father hesitated, looked at Jennifer for support, and said, "Sir, I am humbled by your proposal and know from what I have that which you have lost. We accept."

During the following years, the father, by his exemplary work, rose in the firm, and when the time came, he would succeed Mr. Cordivan as head of the firm, a promise that was solemnly kept. Maryn became a gymnast and later a renowned writer of children's stories, never losing her zest for life and its rewards. Mason, dear Mason, eventually lost his boyishness but not his boyish charm. He went to college and became a lawyer, an excellent one, and soon joined his father at the firm as chief legal counsel. When clients or business associates were entertained at the office, invariably one would inquire about the framed nickel. The story was related with relish, not a detail lost. When they discovered that the neatly dressed and courteous counsel was the moving force and central figure behind it all, pray tell, what did he receive that justified his generosity? He simply pointed to the frame and said, "Being so young at the time, it was not until I grew older and looked back that I was able to know and fully appreciate what I did. It was the blessed gift of giving."

The Violin

The cool March evening reflected the easygoing pace of those who strode the pavements of the bustling city. For the most part, it was an exercise in unfettered indulgence, just aimlessly strolling for the sheer joy of it. The many storefronts would attract not a few to scan the offerings displayed with colorful attractions, some beyond their means to purchase, but nevertheless fulfilling. Others would seek any of the many eateries that would sate their hunger. The mood of the throng was generally amiable, and strangers would nod to each other, smiles passing back and forth. There was no real agenda, only an unconscious effort to enjoy the delights of the evening after a day of work. The old and young mingled without discrimination, sometimes remarking upon the differences in their ages, though in thought only, the older ones chuckling at the energy of the younger ones.

In the downtown venue, along the broad avenue, several facades boasted names familiar to the populace, famed for their entertainment. The Palace, Princess, or Savoy were famous for their plays or musical offerings. It was from the Palace that Arturo Agrimonti mounted his carriage after a brilliant musical presentation this evening. Known as one of the preeminent violinists in the world, he had appeared before royalty throughout the world and for those appreciative of his talents. Having finished his engagement of over a week, he was en route to the city harbor port, having booked passage for a return to Europe. Arturo was in his late seventies but still retained a certain vibrancy that mesmerized his followers. But his outward look of confidence obscured a nagging mood that caused him enormous discomfort. An intelligent and thoughtful person, he wrestled with a not-finalized decision, a decision that would shake the musical world of the very early twentieth century.

The coachman spurred his horses onto the thoroughfare, encountering the bustling traffic of competing cabs. Diverting to side streets, the lack of congestion bode well for him as he sought a speedy arrival at the docks and a quick return for more fares. His experienced handling of the reins ensured a swift passage, but in his haste, he failed to negotiate a rut in the road, the carriage violently lurching, jostling his occupants from one side to the other. Chagrin more than injury elicited a reprimand from his fares. Unseen and unheard was the tumbling from the rear boot of the master's violin case, a result of the carriage's misfortune. Onward the cab sped, no one the wiser for the loss that now lay in the gutter perhaps to be trundled upon by another carriage.

Arriving at the departure gate and unsuspecting of the missing case, the handlers at dockside loaded the remaining luggage onto the shuttle carts, which were brought to the ship's cargo conveyers and hoisted aboard. Somewhat tired, the master and his entourage boarded the ship, promptly heading for their staterooms and a night of rest.

The street where the violin lay was thankfully deserted, the case partially hidden and protected by a fallen trash container. It lay undetected for several hours until a small figure, a young boy, approached from a side alley. Mason was heading for his morning station near the thoroughfare to accept his consignment of newspapers. As a ten-year-old, he had cheerfully assumed the role of second provider for his family's needs. Over the mild objections of his father, he had felt the need to supplement the family's small income, derived from his father's job as an assistant printer. Actually, Mason's father was rather proud of his son's actions, which signaled an emerging maturity. The amount he earned, which was really small, didn't matter so much as the gesture. The family lived on the third floor of a tenement building in a modest neighborhood. The tenants were of low to moderate means, and most were friendly, as if they were in some sense a family. This fostered a degree of community where the needs of some were filled by the others. Of course, it was always a two-way street and seldom abused.

Stepping off the curb, Mason noticed a shadowed form lying on the ground next to the trash container. His curiosity piqued, he stooped down to better examine the object. His eyes widened, momentarily startled by the sight of a violin case. What was it doing here, how did it come to be here? The loss of such an instrument surely would have spurred a strenuous effort to recover it. But here it lay. Nervously, he opened the snaps and raised the lid. In wondrous amazement, his eyes bathed in the glory of the most beautiful violin he had ever seen. To Mason, this was manna from heaven.

The violin was not alien to the boy, as for two years he had been taking lessons from an old Italian neighbor, Pietro Falchetta, who lived on the second floor and had nurtured his interest in the instrument.

It came to pass when Mason was heading to school and was descending the stairs when he heard the soothing strains of a violin wafting from the apartment next to the staircase. His curiosity as well as his appreciation of the music moved him to peer into the room. Having just moved into the building, there were few people that the family knew. The short man with his back to Mason was, to delicately describe him, plump and balding. He swayed back and forth, in harmony with the delicious notes leaping from his magical hands. Frozen in place by the captivating melody, Mason was startled when the man stopped abruptly and turned to face him.

"Ah, my little one, you like?"

Not knowing what to say or do, he stiffly nodded yes.

"You are new to building, I no see you before."

Recovering some composure, he replied that his family had just rented their apartment. Gaining a little more composure, Mason stared at the violin in the gentle giant's hands, his eyes suggesting a need to know more about this wonderful instrument he had never seen before.

"I tella you what. You like, I teach."

When Mason returned home from school, he related his encounter with the rotund man living on the second floor and his offer. His excitement about the prospect of learning to play a most marvelous instrument prompted his parents to inquire of the other tenants as to the character of this benefactor. It seems that Pietro had been a fixture here for as long as the tenants knew, possibly being here even before them. Satisfied that the offer was genuine, Pietro was allowed to tutor Mason and adamantly refused any payment for his efforts. "He play well, dat isa my payment," he intoned. Clearly, Pietro loved children as evidenced by his unbounded charity that was lavished upon them during special events and holidays. "Uncle Pietro" was their live-in Santa Claus. In Mason's case, it was different. Here was a total commitment, not just an endearing gesture, and Pietro's deft handling of the lessons and his kind demeanor enamored Mason to the task.

Mason was not a quick learner, but what he did learn he mastered as well as any young student could. Mason was no genius, but he did have a flare for unexpectedly turning a standard rendition into something more. There was promise, but it would take time. With each advancement, Pietro's pride was evident.

Taking the violin case in his arms, Mason continued to his newspaper pickup and took his standard amount of issues and proceeded to his usual corner location. Keeping the case close-by and eyeing it to the point of distraction, he was relieved when all the papers were sold. With his pockets loaded with cash and a beautiful violin in his possession, Mason felt as light as a breeze as he hurried home to tell his father of his find. Looking at the violin, Mason's father let out a whistle of appreciation, acknowledging the value of the instrument. He turned to his son for a brief moment. His eyes locked on to Mason's, silently asking him as to what he would do now. The boy understood his father's intent and replied, "We have to find the owner and return it to him."

No father would be prouder than he was as the youngster vindicated his honest upbringing. Together, they left the tenement and proceeded to the news building that Mason worked for. There, a notification ad was placed, listing a violin and case recovered in the general area of its find. Care was taken to be vague on the description and actual location of discovery so that any possible claimant would have to provide the exact details needed to verify ownership. This was not an easy thing to do financially, but honor must be served and the cost absorbed. Leaving the building, Mason looked up at his father and asked if the owner would be found, hoping secretly that maybe he wouldn't but soon regretting that impulse of selfishness.

"If I had lost it, I would hope someone would return it to me," he mused.

Back at home, Mason asked his father if it would be okay to show Pietro the violin. Permission was granted, provided he was very careful, telling only Pietro of the find. Expecting Mason for his usual lesson, the teacher was deeply impressed when shown the instrument and the story of its discovery. He duplicated Mason's father's reaction by letting out a shrill whistle, to Masons's amusement. Did all adults react like that? Pietro asked his pupil if he was thinking of using this wonderful instrument for his lesson.

"Do you really think I should?" the boy replied.

"Why not," the jovial man replied. It was made to be played.

Assured that no harm would be done, he grasped the violin and slowly raised it to his shoulder and under his chin, pausing for a moment to savor the electricity it generated, the anticipation of the melodious notes he would hope to generate. Alas, his first strokes of the bow only brought about a screeching sound that caused his teacher to first cover his ears in mock pain and then to burst out into laughter. At first Mason flinched in reaction to his mentor's antics and then broke out into a chuckle himself. He had assumed that the magic of the violin was sufficient to ensure a flawless performance but all too soon realized that the magic could only be unlocked by an able hand. Placing the the bow in position again, and with a more composed mind-set, he again stroked the strings with a measured movement, only this time a sweet flowing melody wafted through the air. Pietro closed his eyes and clasped his hands prayer-like against his chest, a gesture that rewarded Mason's efforts. Truly, this fine instrument could elevate any competent player to a higher level of accomplishment. No wonder the master was so renowned. His skill and the qualities of this musical creation were a combination unequaled.

When he had finished, Mason looked to Pietro for some sign of approval, which was so evident he need not bother.

"Mason, I wanna you to play inna park tomorrow evening."

The park. This was where an evening of entertainment was provided by whoever chose to perform. The invitation was a badge of honor for Mason, and his chest puffed out just a little. Although informal, the venue offered a chance for aspiring artists to display their talents. Now he would find out how far he had progressed and was more than a little nervous.

A week had passed before the master's ship docked in France. His entourage headed to his favorite hotel, his reception rivaling that of royalty. Escorted to his quarters, he dismissed his aides and settled upon a favorite armchair, a glass of sherry in his hand. He stared through the closed window pane of ornate glass, not looking at anything in particular, as if searching for something. Alas, the search was within himself, and he questioned whether he could find what he was seeking. Sipping the golden-brown liquid, he confronted his fear, a fear harbored for so long he wondered how he could have contained it. The man had convinced himself that despite his continued excellence, his abilities were on the wane. After all, he was in the winter of his life. What more could he give? This was more of self-doubt than of any physical shortcoming. Nothing seemed to divert this path that would lead to musical exile. Soon, when the time came to pass, he would surrender his position of virtuoso, never again to grace the halls of music. At this critical moment, the doors to the suite burst open, his aide Marko stumbling into the room, a look of sheer horror upon his face.

"Master, Master, it is gone, gone, missing from the luggage."

The old man replied, "What are you talking about, Marko? What is missing?"

Falling to his knees, his head down and voice quivering, the shaken man replied, "The violin, Master. It's gone. We searched everywhere, in the ship, on the docks, even the streets themselves, but could not find it. Oh, Master, I have failed you."

Grabbing the shaken man by the shoulders, he softly replied, almost in a whisper, the soothing tone bringing some degree of relief to this faithful servant. "Marko, nothing can be gained if you revert to a total wreck. Violin or not, I still need you and have always valued your service. Go now and compose yourself. We will talk later."

This stunning news brought about a conflicting assessment by the old master. The loss of his violin could be the vehicle upon which he would ride to retirement, explaining to his loyal fans that the engine of his greatness was lost. Without which, further pursuit of his craft would be unthinkable. On the other hand, the instrument had been in his family for generations, and the familial as well and the monetary value could not easily be discarded. This conflict only aggravated his original dilemma, and he became morose and unsettled. He refused to pursue the matter for the time being, content to sequester himself in his quarters.

Mason was thrilled. His performance was fairly good, as evidenced by the applause and the affirming smiles of his family and Pietro. His sister, Maryn, pretended to swoon as he played, almost distracting him into an uncontrolled belly laugh, but he was able to resist the urge. His mother, Jennifer, showed a proper decorum while he played but transformed into a jubilant and avid fan when he finished, grabbing and hugging him, to his embarrassment. The reception heralded future appearances by this novice to the world of entertainment. He wondered, however, what the reaction would have been if he had used the master's own article of fame. He could not risk it, but the thought was tempting. He asked his father if anyone had inquired about the violin, but there were no inquiries. He had mixed emotions on that score, visualizing that perhaps no one would claim it, and in that case, it would be his. How could that be? It was too valuable to not be sought out. Whatever the outcome, he had to be content to let the course of events flow.

Mr. Agrimonti's travel agent had stayed behind to tidy up any loose ends and to schedule future appearances. His office was not far from the theatrical district and close to the corner where Mason hawked his papers.

In fact, he may well have purchased a paper from Mason on occasion. Having returned from lunch and without anything urgent to do at present, he relished the free time he had. Yesterday's paper, which he hadn't read, was at the side of his desk. Glancing through the various articles, his interest was drawn to the classified section. He marveled at the various things that were offered for sale or the situation section of people seeking work or offering their talents for hire. How well he remembered an item he had purchased which turned out to be a steal. This favorable experience had fostered an interest in the section, although more out of curiosity than a need. One article that provided a dramatic bump was the effort to contact the owner of a lost violin.

Poor slob, he thought. *How can you lose a violin? Serves him right.* His secretary tapped on the door and entered.

"Josh, overseas phone call."

Grunting an affirmative, he walked to her office, wishing that someone would invent phones that could be picked up anywhere, and identified himself to the caller. After several moments, he stiffened and motioned for his secretary to bring him the paper lying on his desk. The caller was an aide to Mr. Agrimonti, relating in a troubled and labored recitation about the loss of the master's violin. A vain hope was to contact the American agent in slender hopes that inquiries could be made to locate the precious item.

He tore through the pages until he found what he had derisively panned only moments ago. "Could it be? Could it be?" he murmured to himself. "Yes, yes, hold on a minute, I think I'm on to something. You're sure it hasn't been found? Listen, let me get back to you, I may have something, only don't tell Mr. A in case it's a false alarm."

Oh my gosh, he thought, *could the poor slob be Mr. Agrimonti?* He surely hoped so. Hastily scribbling the address listed in the notification, he grabbed his coat and hat and sped through the door. Coming onto the street, he glanced around until he spotted a police officer. Since street signs were few and far between, perhaps he could provide directions.

Scribbling the instructions on the back of an old envelope that used to carry his paycheck, he made his way to what he hoped would be the pot of gold. Arriving at the tenement, he glanced at the envelope to confirm the address. Now to find the apartment. Anticipation started to well within him, an unusual sensation for a man trained to deal with all contingencies.

Racing up to the third floor, he stood before the door behind which he hoped his prize would be found. He was about to knock when the door suddenly opened, startling both parties. Jennifer was just leaving to buy groceries and, composing herself, asked the stranger if she could help him. After identifying himself, he asked if this was the family that had found a violin. Caught off guard by the straightforward question, she called to her husband, who had come home for lunch. After a few preliminary queries, the man was invited into the apartment and ushered to the kitchen table, which served double duty as the family's community center. Satisfied that the man's credentials were valid, the discussion centered on the events that led to the discovery of the violin. The agent seemed most impressed in the manner in which the whole episode was handled, especially the part played by Mason.

Now came the proof of the pudding. Could he see the instrument so that he could verify its authenticity? Surely, and Mason brought the case to the table, looking as if he would be losing a friend, which in a sense would be true. The agent exclaimed that as the master's booking agent, he had seen the violin many times and would know if this was it.

In all the excitement, no one seemed to ask a most important question. Mason seemed to be above the momentary rush of excitement and pointedly asked, "Sir, who owns it?"

"Good heavens," he replied, "how could I skip that? Well, young man, it's none other than Arturo Agrimonti. You've heard of him?"

Mason's mouth opened wide in abject surprise. Had he heard of him? He was his hero. Pietro had often mentioned him and regaled Mason with all kinds of stories, even the one time that he had met the master in earlier times, just as he was coming into prominence. He often joked that he should have gotten his autograph.

"Really, sir, it's his?" The moment would forever be etched in his mind, something surely to be passed down to future generations.

What would be called high drama was evident as the lid was raised. The silence that ensued strained the nerves of Mason's parents until "That's it" gave release. Holding the violin in his hands, turning it over and over and examining every facet to be doubly sure. The agent's broad smile seemed to bring closure. Mason, softly and with eyes welling, asked the man if he would be taking this treasure away. What transpired was both heartwarming and a sign of trust. Facing Mason and peering into the boy's inquiring blue eyes, he said that as of now, it was in good hands. And quite possibly, but not a certainty, perhaps the owner might wish to extend his personal thanks. When further information was obtained, he would contact the family and make arrangements for the turnover. He marveled that at no time was any mention made of any reward or compensation, a fact that stung him a bit, as he was used to seeing the avarice that accompanied fame and fortune. Warmly he bade farewell and looked forward to contacting the master with the good news.

The phone call to France awakened the master from a fitful sleep. Told about the recovery of his beloved instrument, he immediately made plans for the return to the States. Marko was instructed to learn every detail about the find and to instruct the agent to meet them when they disembarked. It would take several days before leaving, several tortured days, for the master had yet to reconcile his joy at the recovery with his own self-doubt.

It was a beautiful day and one anticipated with great expectations. Mason was to perform again at the park. The joy in him went beyond self-adulation; it was pure, a gift to be shared, hoping only to please others. Pietro talked encouragingly to the boy, a slight nervousness apparent. Nothing that a few swipes of the bow could not cure. However, other things were in play. The agent had dropped by the day before and informed that the owner would soon arrive and that a formal meeting would be arranged, something proper for the occasion. Gee, Mason thought, a meeting with the master! What could top that? A knock on the door aroused the normal curiosity, and Mason raced Maryn to the entrance. Arriving first, and jostling her out of the way, he swung the door open. A well man of medium stature, salt-and-pepper beard, shocking white hair, and a very expensive-looking cane draped over his wrist stood before him. No need to ask who he was. His picture was on Mason's dresser.

"Master, Master!" the boy shouted, at first alarming his parents, who then understood their son's reaction. "It's really you." Being young forgives many errors and presumptions as witnessed by the youngster's rush to embrace his idol. Arturo, so used to adulation, relished this innocent sign of affection. Jennifer began to apologize for her lad's familiarity but was stopped by the wave of his hand.

"Madam, so seldom have I received such a welcome. Let me bask in it for a little." He chuckled, extending his hand forward, grasping her dainty hand and raising it to his lips. Her face blushing, she invited him into their flat. After the introductions were completed, and a refreshment offered, Mason brought forth the reason for his visit.

"Come, sit beside me," he motioned to the awestruck boy. "I thank you for what you have done."

"Oh, no, sir. It was my father who knew what to do. All I did was find it."

"Well, son, that was the most important part, but you are right, there were others too, and I hope to acknowledge them all."

Mason was in a dream world, and in a dream world, all things are possible. There was no wall of pretense between him and the master, as if they had known each other far beyond Mason's years.

Glancing at the clock, the youngster noted that the park would soon open for the day's entertainment. Turning to Mr. Agrimonti, he asked, "Sir, we are having a talent show in the park today. Would you like to go with us?"

Jennifer interrupted, "Mason, he may have other plans."

A little crestfallen, his fortunes revived when Arturo replied, "Why, I would be delighted."

"Oh, great! Mom, Father, he's coming." His delight was all-consuming and infected everyone in the room. He grabbed the master's hand and literally pulled him from the sofa and led him to the door, picking up the case that Pietro had lent him.

"What are you doing?" the old man asked him.

"Getting my violin," Mason replied.

"No, no, no," echoed through the room.

The boy was startled. Had he done something wrong to offend the master?

He need not have worried. "Bring me my violin, son." A little confused, Mason complied and presented the jewel to its owner. "You will play with this," the smiling man replied, thrusting the case into a surprised boy's arms.

"Oh! Master, for real?"

"For real, son."

Mason wrapped his arms around it and brought it to his face, caressing it with his cheek. The magic was complete and the magician thoroughly enthralled by the boy's uninhibited response.

The day was sunny, reflecting the mood of the crowd, a gentle hum of conversation running through the throng. A small platform doubled as the stage with small steps on either side. The family seated themselves in the first row, the master between them.

Offerings from the various performers delighted the crowd. Their amateurish presentations were a combination of polished skill or mistake-filled efforts, but all was taken in good stride, and the applause rewarded the accomplished and erased the misgivings of those who weren't. Soon it was Mason's turn, and Pietro walked with him to the stage, whispering encouragement. Although he had performed only a few times, he had somewhat of a following, their cheers echoing through the crowd.

As he raised the violin to his shoulder, he glanced at his family. And to Arturo, he silently mouthed, "This is for you." The master responded with a nod and a broad smile. Mason.'s hand guided the bow across the dormant strings, releasing the sweetness of the notes.

His benefactor, eyes closed, swayed in cadence to the vibrant strains, a sign of approval. While the piece was standard, the presentation delivered a new twist that even a proven artist would have found novel and most acceptable. Innovation was beginning to reside in the skills of the novice, a trait that the master noticed. He shook his head and thought, *So young, so young*. The finale brought a wave of applause, the assemblage rising to their feet. Bowing to the crowd, Mason acknowledged their tribute and, for several long moments, bathed in this most luxurious experience. *This is how the Master must feel,* Mason thought.

Eventually the lauding died down, and instead of walking off the stage, he held up his hands to gain attention. Stepping forward, and coughing to clear his throat, the boy spoke in a determined voice, its tone meant to instill abject attention.

"Friends, today you have honored me, as well as the other performers. I would like to repay your kindness. Present with us is none other than Mr. Arturo Agrimonti."

The mention of the name brought a swelling sound of ohs and ahs as heads swiveled back and forth to catch sight of this star. Pointing to the master, Mason implored him, with a sweeping gesture of his arms, to accompany him on the platform. Caught by surprise, he nonetheless heeded the lad's summons and joined him, feeling slightly awkward. What could the boy want? Turning to the white-haired figure, Mason lifted the violin and placed it softly against the man's chest.

"Sir, will you play for us?"

For a moment, the master was speechless, thoughts of his perceived failings flooding his consciousness. His misgivings tore at him, and he was on the verge of walking away when Mason, noticing a reluctance, again urged him to play, surprised at his hesitation.

"My son, you can't understand. What you want, I may not be able to give. I am an old man and may have seen the best years of my life." There is something about the innocence of a child that separates them from the most learned of us. Failure is not always evident to them, only a temporary setback. They seldom find refuge in moaning about their fate but cheerfully challenge the odds against them. Of course, this is an innate trait not consciously realized but pursued nonetheless. Mason looked at the master and in a way chided him, as would an elder to a child when sensing self doubt.

"Sir, I have always wanted to be like you when I came to love your work. It has not always been easy, but whenever I thought I would fail or fall short, I thought of you and what you must have gone through to become what you have made of yourself. No, sir, you have much to give. Please?"

The words stung, not in a way that would elicit resentment. He peered into the imploring eyes and staunch resolve of an unyielding figure, and quite possibly an angel. He grasped his jewel and slowly raised it to his chin, nestling its body against his broad shoulder. With great deliberation and mixed emotions, a practiced hand rode the bow over the chords, the sound a soothing mixture of tones and sequences. The deeper he went into his offering, a feeling of resurgence overcame the man who would have ended it all.

Notes responded to this reawakened sense of achievement, his body stiffening in a pose of defiance to his previous surrender of will. Although he had not lost his skill, he had recovered his resolve, and the music reflected this miracle. Mason stood by, awash in the glory projected by his mentor, the joy on his face unbounded. The finish was received with a standing ovation and calls of "Encore, encore!" or "Bravo!" Acceding to the crowd's inviting demand, several more pieces were played, every movement devoured by an adoring audience.

With the last note, the master raised his arms in mock surrender, a sign that all too soon, his presentation was over.

The day ended with the departure of the Master for his return trip to Europe. Before leaving, he spoke privately with the boy, explaining that while appreciative of his support, there were many things that he needed to resolve. He vaguely excused his reluctance to perform for fear of disheartening the youngster who had relit his flame of passion for the art. But still, he must determine whether this was an emotional response or a genuine revival of his talents. How many years did Mason age in this exchange of mutual admiration? The parting was manly and straightforward, the affection for each barely concealable. The family, Pietro, and Mason waved a farewell as the carriage faded from view: he was gone.

Returning from school, Mason was surprised to see a large package lying on the community center. Jennifer read the question in his eyes and responded that the parcel was delivered earlier that morning by a bonded deliveryman. It was addressed to her son, and she resisted Maryn's nagging to open it, her daughter pouting with disappointment.

His curiosity piqued beyond containment, the covering was ripped open, revealing a wooden veneer. Taped to the top was an envelope addressed to "The Maestro." Putting it aside for the moment, Mason flipped the catch on the container and raised the lid. His voice responded to the sight of the contents with a scream of delight, turning to his mother and hugging her tightly. "Mom, Mom, it's beautiful. Look at it!" Nestled in the surrounding felt covering glistened a violin of exquisite color and finish. Grabbing the letter, he abandoned formality and ripped it open. Silently and then aloud, he read the contents:

> My Little Maestro,
> You may not understand fully what I have lived with these past few months, except to say that I allowed it to fester within me to the point of despair. Your belief in me has convinced an old man that he still has much to offer, and when we meet again, we will talk. I am resuming my tour of your country and will be returning on a new liner making its maiden trip. I will be sailing on the *RMS Titanic*.
>
> Your friend,
> Arturo

FRIENDSHIP

The sky was overcast, muting the competing colors of the landscape and casting a pall of gloom. A tall figure, resplendent in his now pale blue uniform, stood with a rigid pose before a grave marker, its whiteness challenged by the subdued lighting.

His face was as firm as chiseled granite, and his steely blue eyes, fixed intently upon the face of the headstone, moved over the letters that identified the remains interred beneath the lush, close-cropped grass at his feet. His lips moved, making no sound, but in cadence with the thoughts of his mind, reciting the name etched out in neat lines. Every letter evoked a twinge of, what would you call it, sadness, remorse of what might have been? These competing emotions did not lessen his gaze or his resolve to pay tribute to the one laid below the earth. Slowly his right arm swung in a slow, deliberate upward motion, his hand forming a perfect flatness, with the tip of his index finger caressing the side of his temple.

He stood motionless for a while and then lowered his arm to his side. His eyes watered slightly, as thoughts of past adventures flooded his mind. How a friendship was formed and lost, how plans made together went unfulfilled. But not because of indifference or neglect or any of the vices that plague any friendship. No, it was the unforeseen, an event not anticipated but nevertheless which happened.

Reluctantly his mind raced backward in time, feverishly trying and failing to stem the tide of thoughts and images that cascaded like a rogue wave against his consciousness. He knew the pain that it would inflict, but nevertheless, his efforts were to no avail, so powerful were the forces of memory, even a reluctant one.

The drone of young people laughing and talking, accompanied by parents and guardians, wafted over the school's courtyard. Friends, renewed acquaintances, new students feeling slightly nervous, and the yard monitors strutting about with a assumed importance out of proportion to their actual role. A pile of snow that had only a few weeks ago covered the ground with its fleecy whiteness had been plowed into mounds that challenged the boys and even a few girls into acts of derring do, much to the chagrin of the adults. Oh, their new clothes, wet and wrinkled. These and other minor outrages, at least in their parents' eyes, occupied the throng until the bell, much to their relief, would signal the first day of learning.

Mason, a lad of ten, always loved school and waited impatiently to begin his class. He was a fairly popular boy but was an earnest student, hoping one day to fly with the Air Force. Hopping from one friend to another, he enjoyed swapping summer tales, not above embellishing a fact or two, but that was the game most of the boys played. If anything, there was no resentment but a challenge to see who could pull off the best whopper.

As he waited near the entrance, he caught sight of Ryan, an older boy he knew only too well. He didn't like what he was seeing and hearing. Ryan was standing in front of a smaller student, his voice demanding and hard and his body language threatening. The boy looked cowed and uncertain, looking about as if seeking protection from the harangue he was enduring. New to the school and apparently very alone, he seemed ripe pickings for the bully. Not on Mason's watch.

Ryan's size and weight advantage had no deterrent on Mason's determination to confront him. "Ryan," he uttered with a tinge of coldness, "leave him alone." The glare of his eyes and a stance that signaled a confrontation was more than enough to cause a gulp of surrender and a hasty retreat.

"Thanks, I owe you."

"No, you don't, I just don't like bullys pickin' on people. Name's Mason, what's yours?"

"Jeff, but I go by Scooter, guess it's 'cause I can run pretty fast."

The bell rang, and both boys entered the school, heading for their assigned classrooms, which had been designated by mail to the various families. Mr. Richard's homeroom was Mason's destination and was slightly surprised that Scooter followed him in.

"This your room, Scooter?"

Scooter nodded with a big grin, and Mason slapped his arm around the new boy's shoulders, a sign of acceptance. Seated next to each other, it would be difficult not to see that the seed of friendship had been firmly planted.

The morning's routine rolled into lunchtime, and the bell signaled the awaited breaking of bread. The boys strolled to a bench and plopped down, relishing the break from their morning's lessons. Mason unzipped his backpack and grabbed a bag, his mouth watering. From a side glance, he noticed Scooter eyeing the bag, only to avert his eyes when Mason looked directly at him. He also saw that Scooter had nothing with him to eat. Pulling a heavily loaded pork sandwich from the bag, he offered it to his friend.

"Mace," a contraction of his newfound friend's name, "it's your lunch."

"Naw, I got more than enough. Mom's always afraid I'll starve to death."

This wasn't entirely true, but Mason saw a greater need in Scooter than his own. There was some fruit and a piece if pie, so his hunger was somewhat sated. The day went fairly well, until the yelps erupted when homework was assigned. "How could they, we're only kids" was the usual mock refrain. Leaving school after the final class, Mason and Scooter waited for their parents to pick them up. Mom was there, but Dad was working and getting into the car. Mason noticed that Scooter was still alone and offered to wait with him until he was picked up. Head down, he replied, "We ain't got a car, I'm hoofing it, thanks." Although that wasn't unusual, there were other things about Scooter that pried at Mason's sense of compassion. The boy's clothes, although clean, were threadbare, and his shoes looked as if the soles would soon depart this earth. His frame was very lanky, and not just because it was dictated by his build, but he suspected from lack of proper nutrition. Perhaps his pork sandwich provided some relief. Hopefully.

"Aw, come on, Scoot, let me get a star in my crown by being a do-gooder."

After a little more coaxing and chiding, and a compliant Mom, off they went.

Three miles south of town, they turned onto a dusty side road for another two miles.

He walked all this way? mused Mason. He had to; the school bus didn't reach this far.

"Right over there," chimed Scooter, pointing to a house whose siding had seen better days and a roof that sagged in the middle. Paint was obviously a victim of neglect and the windows dusty. Opening the car door, Mason observed a silent embarrassment on Scooter's face and a refusal to look at his house, head and eyes down. The ride home was more than enough incentive to outweigh the negative observations he was afraid others would share at the sight of his home.

Hurrying to leave the car so that Mason and his mom, Jennifer, wouldn't have to dwell on it too long, Scooter uttered a sincere thanks and raced up the walk.

"Mom, okay?"

"Sure."

"Hey, Scoot, pick you up for school tomorrow, okay?"

"Wow, you bet."

During the next few days, Mason learned more about his new friend. Scooter lost his mom several years ago, and it struck the family pretty hard. Other than his father, whom he loved as dearly as Mason loved his, he was alone. For many years, his dad had worked at a printing firm but was laid off the past year and, finances being what they were, was forced to sell their home and rent what he could afford. Mr. Powell was a self-reliant man who neither sought nor asked for any type of assistance, a quality being a detriment to Scooter's well-being. This was an age where many looked upon aid as a sign of personal failure and therefore refused to accept what they perceived to be handout. He looked for work, but jobs were too few and far between, mostly temporary and paying very little. He was not an uncaring or harsh man but failed to see the needs of his son in a more practical light.

During recess, the boys talked the talk of youngsters, trading their secret desires and hopes.

"I'm going to join the Air Force," intoned Mason matter-of-factly while holding his gaze upon an airplane that was passing over. "Yep, I'm gonna be a fighter pilot and become an ace."

"No kiddin'," chimed Scooter. "That's what I want to be too."

Thus, America's safety was assured and secured in minds that dared to dream.

The following weekend, having slept over, Scooter devoured Jennifer's pancake, inhaling being the better word to describe his animated ingestion of this prized meal, much to her delight. Maryn, Mason's older sister, sat mesmerized as each layer disappeared, causing Madden, old enough even at five years, to appreciate the seeming miracle he was witness to. Scooter took a great liking to the family and Mason's dad, Bernie, who showed a keen interest in the boys' activities. Having demolished a record somewhere in the world for consumed pancakes, Scooter thanked Jennifer before being yanked out of his chair by an impatient Mason.

"What's the hurry, Mace?"

"We got business to tend to, and to phrase a hero of mine, 'we're burning up daylight.'"

Riding double on a bicycle, the boys neared Macky's junkyard, what today would be called a recycling center.

"Mr. Macky, okay to look through the junk?"

"Yeah, but be careful." Mr. Macky had known the boy for several years and his father for many years before that. He was always impressed with what they could do with the refuse that people discarded.

"What are we lookin' for, Mace?"

"Well, Scoot, Mom can't be picking you up every day, so maybe we can do somethin' about it." As he foraged through the myriad piles of metal, after some length, he let loose with an "All right, I think this is it." Yanking a frame from the tangled pile of nondescript scrap, he showed it to Scooter. "We got a bike. It's missing the front wheel, but I got one in the garage I think will fit. Tire's soft, but looks okay. A little Brillo on the chrome will shine it up just pretty and maybe a little paint." What Mason described in such basic terms belied the artistry wafting through his mind as to what a jewel it would become.

The joint effort at restoration revealed a side of Scooter that demonstrated his ability to work mechanics almost as well as Mason. Together, they secretly competed with each other to assemble, revise, or improve their design of the once-derelict bicycle.

"Hey, Dad, come and look."

Bernie stepped into the garage knowing that he would not be disappointed but was floored by the complete transformation of what was once a wreck only a junker could love.

"Boys, this is a great piece of workmanship that deserves an appropriate reward."

Off to the local diner they went, the boys ordering their hearts' desires.

It was episodes such as this that cemented the bond between the boys and Scooter's semi-adopted family. In school, they tried out for the basketball squad, though their talent was moderate. Making the team as subs, they were content, since they were able to watch the action from the prized position of the bench. In one game they were actually allowed to show their prowess on the court, several of the players needing a breather. As Mason dribbled down the court, Scooter secured a position near the basket without being guarded. His buddy looped a pass to Scooter, which, in his best imitation of a practiced warrior of the court, hurled toward the basket. His serious face soon broke into a deep-throated laugh as the ball missed the net completely! That's why they were subs.

These and other forays into the magical age of youth, with its challenges, pitfalls, and other elements that could not be defined until they occurred, served as the standard that tested the mettle of these adventurers. Those that came to know them would believe that a stranger would not be far wrong in thinking they were brothers. Scooter's hair was darker, his eyes blue, and his form slightly smaller than Mason's, but their characteristics and personality began to mirror each other.

Saturday was a day of adventure for the boys, a day to explore the woods around town and to search for any treasure abandoned by people who were too lazy to head for the town dump. After some time, Mason started to fidget. Where was his buddy?

The phone rang in the den, and Bernie began talking in a rapid series of questions interrupted by stretches of somber silence, all the while staring at Mason.

"Yes, yes, I understand," he countered to the caller, grabbing his keys from the table and ending with "We'll be right there."

"Jennifer, Mason, grab your coats. Maryn, keep an eye on your brother until we return."

"What's up, Dad?"

"Tell you when we return. Have to go."

Perplexed by Bernie's rush to the car, Mason could only guess by his father's determined motions that something very serious had occurred. Once on the road, he related the contents of the phone call to Mason and his mother. Earlier this morning, Mr. Powell was rushed to the hospital with severe chest pains. Having no other family to turn to, Scooter asked the admissions clerk to contact Mason's parents. The plight of the poor lad and his need for moral support was the sum total of the phone call.

Mason felt a hollow pang in his chest, a feeling of helplessness. He needed to be with his friend, as any true friend would feel. Parking the car, they proceeded down the hallway to admittance, but before reaching it, Scooter raced toward them and grabbed Mason in an embrace of consolation and reassurance, muttering, "Mace, he's gone. My daddy's gone." The words were barely audible, his faced buried against Mason's shoulder, but the tone was understandable even if the words were not. Speaking to the doctor, Bernie learned the details of Mr. Powell's passing.

They left with a shaken and subdued young man, Mason doing what he could in a quiet way to be a rock for his friend to cling to.

Friendship always seems to breed a maturity of action all out of proportion to youth. It is this quality that allows one to forge through the emotional valleys never experienced before, an innate quality that many never knew they possessed. Mason had that quality.

The following week was difficult indeed. For all practical observations, Mr. Powell was considered indigent. This in itself was not insurmountable, for although Huntsville was a small town, it prided itself as a caring community. There was a plot of ground that many would consider a potter's field, but in all the history of the town, there was not one grave to be found there.

A group consensus deemed that no poor soul would be abandoned to obscurity and forgotten. In many cases, through the benevolence of the local churches or fraternal organizations, a place could always be found that a poor soul, alone in the world, could find eternal sanctuary.

Even with this outpouring of support, there still remained the question of cost. The children at school raised some cash with various fund-raising schemes, and various business concerns contributed what they could. Still, there was a considerable shortfall. After the burial, Bernie wrestled with the remaining debt and how it would be resolved. To him, this was a burden unsought but nevertheless looked upon as the right thing to do.

A day after they had returned from the hospital, Jennifer received a call from the state child services unit. Notified by the hospital concerning Scooter's status, they asked if they could meet with the family to determine a future course of action. A week later, a representative visited the home. Bernie and Jennifer, not to mention the children, were fearful as to what would become of Scooter. Both boys were on the second floor landing and could hear the conversations that would determine the boy's fate.

Because the system was overloaded at the moment, the agent asked if the family would be willing to keep the boy temporarily as a foster child. A sum would be paid to maintain him until a placement could be found. Bernie's reply resounded in the boys as if a megaphone had been used.

"I don't want the money. What I want is to adopt the boy. Can I do it?"

Both boys turned to each other with mouths wide open, grasping arms entangling each other in wild mirth, but cautious to remain quiet. The reply from the agent was qualified but seemed to hold promise of an affirmative decision. The family would be notified in due time.

No sooner as the door closed, the joyous yelping, of not only the boys, but Maryn and their parents, erupted throughout the house. Entangled bodies defied any effort to define whose arms and legs belonged to who. Even Madden had a somewhat appreciation of the merriment, although he couldn't figure out why. An angel had alighted upon this household.

With the addition of a new member to the family, a different but enticing fabric was being woven into the everyday activities that the members indulged in. Scooter's merging into the daily family life was seamless.

Even Madden was taking a shine to the hopefully permanent presence of Scooter. He thrilled to the attention and small gifts that were showered upon him by a boy who had known very little of this himself. Granted, he dearly missed and still loved his father, but the tenor of his life began to change gradually into one of material satisfaction and emotional security. School was now a lark, an adventure to be relished, in spite of homework and the admiring glare of geeky girls—ugh!

The boys weren't off scot-free. They had chores to do and small jobs that gave them some spending money. They came down with colds, or bruised a limb or two, but this was the currency gladly paid, although for them this fancy notion was coined in a more pragmatic way. Hey, you get what you get.

The weather was turning colder, and the daily parade of clouds hinted at what most adults shunned—snow! The boys were ecstatic. Mason couldn't wait to show off his skating abilities to Scooter, hoping to teach him the fine points of skating so that both would be able to join the pick-up hockey team, a sort of sandlot on ice. Sure enough, the weather obliged, and Skully's pond iced over. Fortified by hot chocolate, the future Gretzk's or Howes would work for hours, tumbling, laughing, or getting a little frustrated when failing.

On occasion, Bernie would bring Jennifer and the other children down to the pond as a breather from the daily routine, as he did this day. Those who could flouted their skating skills, while those who had none collided with whoever was unfortunate to be in their way.

The boys were just putting on their skates. A curdling scream echoed from the far side of the pond. Somehow, a figure had crashed through what was thought to be a solid sheet of ice.

"Oh my god, Madden! Madden!" screamed Jennifer. The boy thrashed wildly, clawing the air with his mittened hands, as if to lift himself from the freezing cauldron.

In a move that mirrored each other, Mason and Scooter raced to the broken ice and watched helplessly as the little boy slipped beneath the surface.

"No! No!" they yelled, both plunging into the forbidding water.

The pond wasn't very deep, and they must have wondered how Madden could have disappeared so quickly. Back and forth they weaved, trying to find him by touch, the water being very cloudy What air they had was quickly being consumed, yet they persisted in their efforts, not wanting to waste a moment, lest a second or two spelled the difference between success or failure. Their courage could not stem the gray veil that started to shroud their minds, consciousness slowly slipping away. Miraculously, one of the boys, then the other, felt a limp form and tenaciously held on, pushing it to the surface. As Madden broke free, he was pulled out by his father. The arms of the boys stood out, slowly receding beneath the surface until clutched by anxious rescuers. Their limp forms were covered with blankets and hustled to waiting cars that sped with wild abandon to the hospital.

The room was silent, interrupted by the pulsing sounds of the heart monitor. A small form seemed dwarfed by the large bed in which he lay, the white sheets almost matching the paleness of his face. Hovering over the still lad was a somber youngster. He grasped an outreached hand with both of his, caressing it tenderly and peering intently at the drawn face.

"How'ya doin'?"

"Okay, I guess. How's Madden?"

"He's fine. We done good, real good."

"Glad to hear…Boy, I feel tired." Eyes closed.

"Yeah, well, you need your rest."

"You know, I feel like I was flying, just like we're goin' to do when we become"—cough—"pilots."

"You'll probably be the best we have. You…you…"

"Will you help me if I come…up…short?"

"What do you mean?"—sniff—"You'll probably have to help me, ha!"

"I knew you would say that. I'm glad we're buddies."

The words were coming harder and harder to say and even harder to hear. His hands squeezed tighter as he saw the peaceful look of his friend, which only served to reduce his ability to hold back the wall of anguish that mounted with each exchange. He turned away for a second, hoping to collect himself.

"We make a great team. When I…get…home…I'd like to…"

The words, though soft, stung like an angry bee. There was no power that could be found, save prayer, to ease his breaking heart as he listened to the hope that would never be fulfilled.

"You bet. You're my brother, and brothers do all kinds of things. We'll study like mad"—sniff—"and read all kinds of books and…and…" He couldn't go on; the wall holding back his grief began to dissolve. It didn't matter. It was at this moment that the stricken boy's eyes seemed to convey a sense of finality, without fear, without regret.

Wait! No! He was talking about coming home. He wants to be a pilot, he…he…

Then the realization struck home, and there was no more to do or say.

It almost seemed as if it was bedtime and time to sleep. The boy looked at his comforter, his pal, his heart, and so very slowly slipped away.

These many years later, he knew that it had been a blessing of friendship that had blossomed into brotherhood, one that could not or would not be broken in this life or the next. How many times had he returned to this hallowed ground, to relive what might have been, wondering at the great potential they both had and what could have been achieved? This self-torture was in itself a salve to his aching heart, an effort to never forget, for to do so would dishonor his friend. With all the pain he endured, he would not surrender one second to oblivion. With a final salute, and as if on parade, he smartly wheeled to one side and proceeded down the path, his eyes gazing upward as two fighter jets streamed overhead, a leader and his wingman. He followed their flight until they disappeared into the clouds. He smiled, knowing that one day they would be reunited in flight for all eternity.

There is no greater love than greater love than to lay down one's life for one's friend. (John 15:13)

The Castle Keeper

The day was bright and sunny, its fall-like coolness chasing away the last vestiges of summer. A group of young boys pranced down the sidewalk, a clutched football signaling the end of baseball as they headed for the park. Maddy, being ten and slightly older than the rest, was their acknowledged leader, a mantle he wore with unconscious acceptance.

"Hey, Mitch, go long," he uttered, and as the boy darted forward, Maddy assumed his best posture of a Joe Namath or Peyton Manning and flung a spiral toward the fleeting receiver. That he missed his mark didn't faze him one bit, but the taunts of his buddies did.

"Hey, deadeye, when are you going to learn how to throw?" was one of the taunting quips, and Maddy's reply was low-keyed but definitely required.

They were like any group of boys in any of the small towns that dotted the country; brash, joyful, a little irreverent, and most of al, noisy. Truly a youngster's life, and they meant to make the most of it.

As they ambled along, each contributing his share of acceptable mayhem, their journey took them past a house that perched on a small rise. The exterior was gray stone on a fairly manicured plot of land, surrounded by a low wooden fence. A few weeping willows gave it a sleepy appearance, as their drooping branches caressed a small gazebo at the rear.

The boys had nicknamed it the Castle, although it did not quite live up to the description. But their imaginations dictated it be called such. As they passed by the gate leading to the house, Seth, in a nervous whisper, called out, "Hey, Maddy, he's looking from behind the curtains," nodding his head toward the direction of the front window but keeping his eyes straight ahead. The form made him uncomfortable, the boy not wanting to surrender to eye contact.

"Whatcha afraid of, the bogeyman?" Maddy snickered in reply. "Come on, let's get to the field before we lose squatters rights."

The house was previously occupied by an elderly couple by the name of Yates. Sometime ago, the building became vacant. Being a small town, there was not much that was not known about anyone, not that gossip was rampant, but because most everyone knew each other and tended to talk freely. Maddy's father had returned from the municipal office and was told that the Yates were involved in a fatal auto accident while visiting a relative who lived out of state. Maddy had run some errands for them and had liked them for their kindness and the delicious cookies Mrs. Yates would heap upon him. He recalled how the couple displayed a loving compassion for each other, something that touched Maddy in a moving way. He would miss them.

Only recently had the house shown any signs of life, and one could only guess who the new occupant was. Well, the grapevine would soon provide that answer, so off to the field.

Maddy had a mixture of youthful exuberance and vitality, conflicting with a mild streak of scorn or indifference, something that was not conscious to him, although his young mind would grapple with what he did and wonder why he would react that way. Being a basically good youngster, it was a thorn in his character that he did not relish, something he refused to relinquish to a youthful allowance but nonetheless not knowing how to deal with it.

When possible, the youthful gridiron hopefuls would trek to the park and pass the old Yates residence. And almost every time, Seth would nod toward the window, and the image of a person could be seen peering from behind the curtain.

Curiosity began to gain serious currency, but fear of the unknown tempered any urge to resolve the issue. That is until the most unthinkable happened. Being the leader, willingly or not, had grave consequences for he who wore the crown, and Maddy was it.

Finally yielding to an unfulfilled desire for answers, the group, urged on by Seth, double dog dared—would you believe it, double dog dared—Maddy to confront the unknown person in his lair.

"Hey, guys, are you nuts? What am I going to say, 'Hey, mister, who are you, and why are you staring at us?'"

The pressure was on, and no amount of backing off was going to satisfy the gang. This went on for several days, and finally, like a dam that was overwhelmed with flooding, he broke. Girding his resolve, he nervously marched through the gate and strode up the path to the door.

He glimpsed at the curtain, and the figure behind it disappeared. This was a relief to the boy, thinking the resident too shy to respond to the inevitable door knock. Wishful thinking. A creaking door signaled the approach of impending doom, and the thought of appearing as a coward to the guys kept Maddy from hightailing out of there.

"Hello, what can I do for you?" uttered the resident. He was stocky but not overly so, with jet-black hair and piercing hazel eyes. His voice and stature did not compete with the visions the guys had imagined of him as the unseen ogre. This was more of a disappointment then they would have believed.

Oh, where is the monster to be slain?

Composing himself in a manner that suggested complete control over his shaking body, he blurted, "Er, hi… ah…I…er…we—"

"Speak up, lad, cat got your tongue?"

"Er, my name is Maddy, and I used to know the people who lived here. I, er, we, saw you behind…we wondered who you…gee, mister, let's forget the whole thing."

This was the emergence of the scorn and indifference that had plagued Maddy, and he felt helpless to combat it. As he hurriedly turned to leave, he stopped when the man replied, "Hey, I'm Ron Yates, the Yates boy."

This discovery erased the mysterious image forged by unfettered youthful imagination and relaxed the tension in Maddy's tortured body.

"No kiddin'? Wow, we thought you were some…" Maddy caught his tongue and recovered unconvincingly, but Ron's chuckle conferred an informal and welcomed absolution.

"That's okay, kid, I was curious and young once." The manner of his reply spoke volumes to Maddy's instinct for sincerity, and a trickle of liking started to replace the previous impressions, now openly refuted.

"I'm sorry if I bothered you, but I'm only a kid, haha."

"No offense, lad, glad to have met you."

As Maddy began to turn, he caught sight of a small figure just inside the door. It was a beautifully carved image of a seal, the wood left natural to give it more artistic authority.

"Wow, what is that?"

"You like it? Here, take a better look at it." Ron handed the hefty figure to Maddy, whose eyes were afire with admiration.

"Man oh man, this is great. Where did you buy it?"

Ron saw the deep appreciation in the awestruck boy's eyes and replied, "I didn't buy it, Maddy, I made it." The unseen enigma, now redeemed, was a master wood-carver?

"Mr. Ron."

"It's Ron, Maddy."

"Thanks. Gee, this is great." Maddy had tried different hobbies but failed to connect on any. While absentmindedly whittling on a derelict piece of wood, he resolved not to waste his time needlessly and determined to create something other than shavings.

Although rough, it satisfied his search for a hobby he could embrace. Now, seeing this beautiful animal, his resolve was cemented. This was what he would like to do.

"Thanks, Ron. It's great. Not to make you jealous, ha, ha, but I do a little carving myself, not like this, but maybe one day." That one sentence would forever alter this budding relationship.

As Maddy returned to the now excitedly expectant group of awestruck urchins, they badgered him with all kinds of questions.

"Who is he?"

"What did he say?"

"What did *you* say?"

The nervous nellies slobbered over every tidbit Maddy offered. In a way, it was a partial letdown, as now the veil of mystery had been lifted and replaced with, what, a normal guy? No more would the stroll past the house elicit visions of impending doom but become another mundane effort on their part.

During dinner, Maddy related his encounter with the new occupant of the Castle. His dad, Bernie, was surprised that Maddy had made such a forward approach and mildly admonished him. Not that he believed the boy was in any danger, but that it may have been an intrusion on the man's privacy.

"Son, you have to realize that not everyone is as outgoing as you are."

"I know, Dad, but this guy is really cool. He carved this animal, and it was great. I hope you can get to meet him."

Jenn, Maddy's mother, was a little more stringent. "Madson Charles, I hope you will be more thoughtful in the future. We can't just go about bothering people."

Oh, how he winced when he heard his formal name, knowing that was a shot across the bow. Funny how parents can get very formal when lecturing their brood. Changing the subject forestalled any other admonishments.

In the days that followed, Maddy was tempted to visit Ron and possibly see some of his work. That would be great and would be a way of picking up some pointers.

One thing bothered the now enlightened youth. It was easy to miss unless you looked for it. How come he had never seen Ron around town? Surely at the supermarket or even at the movies, which he frequented with the gang. Come to think of it, he noticed that there was no car in the driveway. How did Ron get around?

Finally, with his father's permission, Maddy would visit Ron and ask to see his work. Having known the Yates, and hearing about how nice Ron treated his son, he had no qualms in allowing the boy his wish. After school and his chores done, Maddy rode his bicycle the short distance to the house on the hill. He knocked on the door and waited a short time before a familiar creak announced a response.

"Boy, those hinges need some oil," he muttered to himself.

"Well, my new friend. What can I do for you, Maddy?"

"I was hoping to see some more of your work, if that's okay?" The slight pleading in his eyes might have been the charm that induced Ron to show him in.

"What do you want to see?" Ron remarked with a little teasing, as he sensed the urgency in the lad's manner.

"Well, how about your workshop and the tools and the paint and—"

"Whoa, buddy, I get the idea. Follow me." Ron could barely keep ahead of Maddy, as if he were trying to walk right through him to get to the mother lode.

They passed through the door that led to the basement, or in Maddy's eyes, the treasure room.

He stood transfixed as his devouring eyes fell upon the workbench, assorted tools and projects in progress, along with many finished articles.

"Man, Ron, this is just great. Boy, you sure can work with wood."

"Well, Maddy, it does keep me busy."

Ron showed Maddy things that his eyes feasted upon, delighted that such a young person could savor and reflect the joy that he himself felt whenever he laid tool to wood. He noted the specific areas that Maddy showed an interest in, which in itself validated his opinion of the boy's desire to take up the craft.

For several hours, the boy grilled Ron as if he were a suspect in a crime, his attention to detail impressing Ron as to the seriousness of Maddy's inquiries.

Looking at the clock, the youngster let out a small yelp. "I'd better get goin', Ron, or Mom'll skin me alive if I miss supper." Smiling, his mentor swooped his arm in a bowing motion toward the door and followed the hurrying kid to the landing. As he was about to leave, Ron thanked him for the visit and asked Maddy if he would like to work with him on some of his projects. *Oh my gosh,* mused the youngster, *Babe Ruth is asking me to carry his bat.* Ron had attained legendary status.

"I'll check with Dad, but I think it'll be okay. Gee, thanks, Ron."

It took great concentration to pedal home without running into anything as Maddy's mind swirled with the thoughts of coming projects and the chance to improve his skills. *Wait till the gang hears about this.* Fortunately, nothing or no one was the recipient of any wayward collisions or contusions.

The leader of the pack reveled in his newfound fame as the boys wanted to know everything that happened. Although overwhelmed, Maddy maintained a fair level of modesty, knowing he hadn't really accomplished anything yet that deserved the fawning attention he was getting. For a boy of ten, that revealed a maturity on the rise.

At Mass the following Sunday, Maddy scanned the pews, hoping to catch sight of Ron, without luck. Maybe he went to evening Mass. As the family left the church, the boy approached Father Al and asked him if he had met Ron yet.

"Yes, I have, son."

"Is he okay? Not sick or anything, I hope. I didn't see him at Mass."

The priest paused for a moment and, with a measured voice, said that Ron was okay and that he shouldn't be alarmed if he was not in attendance. It was an answer that could be taken many ways, but Maddy didn't press the issue.

On the days that Ron's protégée was learning the dos and don'ts of woodcarving, a familial relationship developed. As they would grapple with certain problems that surfaced at the most inopportune times, it was these tests of problem-solving that cemented a bond of friendship and trust. A trust that would be tested.

One day, after several hours in the sweat shop, as Maddy kiddingly called it, he asked Ron if the two of them could go to the corner diner for a soda or ice cream. Digging into his pockets and pulling out a few crumpled bills, he uttered, "My treat."

Ron's reaction, though slight, signaled a reluctance as did his voice. "Er, well, Maddy, it's not…I mean, there're things I have to do." All the while his eyes resisted looking directly at the boy. Not picking up the nuances and slightly disappointed, the apprentice bid adieu and clambered on his bike.

"I'll see you Thursday!" he yelled as he pedaled away. "Call me if anything changes. See ya, Ron."

"See you, Maddy," Ron softly intoned to himself, his head lowered. He so wanted to go with the boy but couldn't. Soon he would have to reveal an important part of his life to this trusting person. He dreaded that day.

Progress had been fairly good. The youngster knew how to follow instructions, and while mastering that phase of his training, he tried to match that with the actual application of the blade to wood. Fineness of detail was the paramount goal of any artistic endeavor, especially this one, and Maddy struggled mightily to achieve it. Ron was doubly impressed that when the boy stumbled or failed to execute properly, he redoubled his efforts so that on the fifth or sixth attempt, he came nearer to his own personal goal of accomplishment. That didn't mean it was to Ron's satisfaction, but all in all, progress was being made.

"Hey, Ron, I know you have a lot of stuff that needs doin', but maybe we can catch a flick at the Strand."

"Sorry, kid, but you're right, I do have a lot of work piling up. Some other time." Hardly had the last word slipped out, then he bit his lower lip, perhaps as penance for lying to the boy. The kid was giving his all, but Ron knew he wasn't, and the inner pain became more than a nuisance. Soon, very soon.

Christmas was not too far distant, and the work in the shop reflected the joyous occasion. Little elves, fairly easy to make, became a pet project for Maddy, although he made other items that required only a little more talent. Still, his production was impressive. One of the exceptions Ron made was in deference to the season. He lavished the work with color, festive colors of acrylic paint. Maddy enjoyed that part thoroughly, sometimes applying more paint on himself than to the figures. Both he and Ron laughed quite a bit over these antics.

Every year, the church would sponsor a bazaar and rent out tables for other entrepreneurs eager to sell their creations. Looking at his haul, the novice carver wondered if they were good enough to sell. Ron, looking over the items very seriously, and turning some around in his hand to exam it more closely, exclaimed, "They stink," followed by a rip-roaring belt of laughter. Infected by this outburst, Maddy rose up in mock anger, betraying this outward disillusionment with his own contribution of mirth and merriment.

"Seriously, Ron, what do ya think? I don't care about the money so much as I will about their likin' what I did."

"Don't worry, sport, you'll do fine. Didn't I teach you?" The student will always try to please the teacher more so than others, if only because he made it possible to reach this plateau.

The rest of the evening was spent selecting those items that would go on sale. Ron was donating some of his work, which, gauging from his perfection, would bring in quite a haul.

"Okay, pal, help me pick something out."

"Oh, Ron, I can't. They're all so beautiful, it's hard, and besides, if they were mine, I don't know if I would want to lose them."

"Remember, buddy, if you can make these, you can make others. You may lose the sculpture, but you never lose the skill that made them. God's gift should be shared, not hidden away." The way Ron spoke resounded in Maddy like few other things had. It was like a parent who would give up something for his child, knowing the joy it would bring, but also recharging the charity in his own heart to do it again. Sharing and giving never go out of style.

"Ron, if I sell anything, I'm going to donate it to the poor people, okay?"

"Only if you don't outsell me, partner." He chuckled, tousling Maddy's hair. Then came the moment that Ron dreaded would come, and he had no answer for it. Nonchalantly the future artist rattled off how he would set up his part of the table, asking Ron for advice and then inquiring as to how he was going to set up his section. "I'm sorry, Maddy, I won't be able to make it. I'm sending this stuff ahead. You can make sure it's displayed properly, but that won't be too hard for you."

The jolt was enough to make Maddy wince. "You won't be there? But, Ron, I can't do this alone, and besides, we're partners." A small glistening of moisture started to well in the boy's eye. "We're a team, you gotta be there," he lamented, grabbing Ron's shirt.

"Maddy, I'll make you a promise. If I can break away, I'll be there. It's something I can't avoid, okay?" The moisture, now a stream, stained the face of the crestfallen boy.

"You really mean it? You'll come if you can? Will you double dog dare promise, and you know if you double dog dare promise, you have to come?"

"With all my heart, I double dog dare promise and will try my best." Ron grabbed the boy and held him tightly, a tear caressing the side of his face too. The hurt he may inflict on this boy was more than he anticipated. Can he keep his promise? He could only hope.

Crestfallen, Maddy said that his dad would come over a day before the bazaar to pick up the figures. He looked at Ron with a searching glance, hoping it would be enough to elicit a change of heart. Nothing.

"Okay, I'm off. See ya." The parting words would have been the standard exchange during other times, but this was one that was drained of endearment, the hurt crowding out anything other than the pain he felt. He couldn't fathom why it would be so difficult for Ron to be there with him.

After dinner, he spoke to his father and bared the letdown he felt.

"Son, there are many reasons why people do what they do. It's only afterward, when and if they care to explain themselves, that we then see what we couldn't before. Then it makes sense and we accept it. I think you should give Ron the benefit of any doubt you have and wait for him to satisfy your search for an answer." While he said this, his manner was more than a father comforting his child. Maddy could sense something else but couldn't nail it. The only other consolation was that at least he unburdened his heavy weight upon a loving dad. He was always there for Maddy, and he was there now.

The days preceding the bazaar were hectic ones, so much that Maddy was unable to visit Ron, not that he had much desire to do so. His feelings were still in flux, but he held on to a glimmer of hope that the double dog dare promise would do the trick. In his world, it was a badge of honor not to be tarnished. So young and so many conflicts. How do the grown-ups do it? he wondered. Gone was the scorn and indifference, replaced by a youthful maturity that could see value where he had not seen it before. In the same manner as before, it was not so much a conscious thing but a natural reaction to an elevated sense of honesty to himself and to others.

The buzzing drone of the wandering crowd echoed across the walls of the gymnasium, the din making it hard to hear much of anything in a normal tone of voice. But the enthusiasm of the shoppers and the variety of items for sale made for a happy turnout. Maddy tended to his display while assisting the woman who had taken over Ron's portion of the table. The boy's artwork was admired, and several pieces were sold, but his attention was riveted to the entrance, a silent prayer urging whoever the angel was of longshot prayers to answer his.

Many times the door would open, and an expectant swell would rise in his chest only to deflate when it wasn't Ron. *Come on, come on, where are you? You made a double dog dare promise... You can't break it.* Repeatedly, the boy was teased so many times by the hoped-for arrival of his friend that he surrendered.

Maddy did fairly well, but money was the furthest thing from his mind. The pride in his work was diminished by not having his mentor witness the appreciative comments of the buyers; he had justified to some extent the investment Ron had ploughed into him. When the festivities ended, Maddy's dad arrived to pick up his son and pack up what was left. Noting that only one elf remained, he commented to his solemn son, "You did pretty good. Maybe I'll charge you cab fare." The attempt at levity fell flat, and in silence they left the hall and headed home. "I know you're disappointed at Ron not showing up, but you may not know all the circumstances that may have caused it. You have to give him a little slack." Again, Dad's words aroused in his mind the same sense of omission that he experienced when he had first confided in him the disappointment he felt when Ron refused to attend the bazaar. Was there more to it than just the words and, without saying so, an implication that a measure of trust had to be forthcoming?

The weekend saw the boys heading for the field again. Maddy had still maintained his chairmanship of the group, and being a kid, the lure of sports beckoned.

"Hey, Maddy," Seth remarked, "I heard you hauled in some heavy coin at the bazaar."

"Yeah, right, I'm goin' to retire."

One of the smaller boys, Vince, piped up with his nasal twang, "Yo, boss, Mom bought one of your elves. Gee, it's cool, Maddy."

Ah, the adulation. Small as it is, I will bask in it, coursed the unspoken thoughts of the leader. Onward they trudged, mouthing things of little meaning, except among themselves.

As they approached the Castle, Seth finally looked directly at the window, only because no one was peering at them. "No one's there," he chimed. Maddy stiffened for a split second then motioned the guys to go ahead. "I'll catch up with you. Gotta do somethin'."

The creak of the door responded to his knock, and Ron motioned the boy in. "Let's go to the kitchen, we can relax with some hot chocolate."

"Hey, Ron, look, I talked to my dad, and he kind of made sense that maybe there was something you had to do and—"

Ron interrupted, "Son, I owe you a very belated explanation, one I hope you will accept. That and an apology. Let me see if I can say this right." The chemistry that had developed between these two kindred souls made the statement sound less ominous than it would have been otherwise. But it was the mystery that was killing Maddy.

"When we first met, I saw the interest you showed in my work. Out of courtesy, I encouraged you to pursue that interest, quietly holding to the thought that eventually it would just be a passing thing. Kids today have the attention span of a gnat."

Maddy let out a little guffaw, quickly covering his mouth, but reassured when Ron did the same. *Hey, this isn't too bad.*

"While this went beyond what I intended, it brought me a certain amount of joy. The fault doesn't lie with anything you have done but with what I've put you through. I have limited my personal life for reasons that you may have difficulty understanding. It's something that I have lived with for some time now, something I felt was unfair to inflict upon you."

Gee, is he wanted for some crime or somethin' like that? mused Maddy, only to quickly disavow the thought. *Not Ron, no, not him, but what?*

"My parents were on their way to visit me when they were taken. I had been living alone, and they would visit from time to time, health permitting. In the aftermath of the tragedy, I was now completely alone."

Alone, how could Ron be alone? thought Maddy. *He's a great guy. Who would not want to be his friend?*

"I assumed ownership of the house, wanting to keep it as a remembrance of their lives and memory. *Content* is not the word for it, but the way I would be living would have to do. You see, Maddy, I'm afflicted with what is known as agoraphobia."

Huh, what the heck is that? The statement was bewildering only because he didn't know what it was or if it was infectious. Ron saw the look in his eyes and tried to reassure the confused boy.

"Maddy, it means I can't go out into the streets or movies and anyplace where people are. It's associated with panic attacks. When I did try to leave my home, a fear gripped me so tightly it was all I could do to get back to what to me was safety. I didn't choose this, it happened."

The thoughts that cascaded through Maddy's mind weren't so much that he now had his answer but that this gentle soul was the victim of something he could not fight, something that was cruel.

"Gee, Ron, that has to be sour milk in the cat's dish."

Ron, relieved by the comical remark, broke the tension with a genuine belly laugh. "Where do you come up with such ridiculous lines, although I truly appreciate that one."

The boy walked over and hugged Ron, a supportive hug that only a child could give. "Look, big guy, that ain't gonna mean anythin' to me. We're buddies, and if you're glued to the ranch, so be it. I can still work with you? Will you still teach me?" As far as he was concerned, the questions were rhetorical, as he had no doubt of the answers.

Heading home, Maddy never went to the field but instead wanted to speak to his dad. What he learned shed light on those instances when he could not understand the well-intentioned but vague counsel of his father or Pastor Al.

"Son, way before you were born, I knew the Yates and Ron. He was an energetic little guy with a lot of ambition. His parents were good friends of mine. I didn't know the circumstances of when or why Ron moved away until they confided in me. They were heartbroken and honored Ron's wish to live independently.

"After the accident, I learned Ron was taking possession of the house, and I dropped by one day to renew acquaintances and to offer him my help if he ever needed anything. He also had called Father Al and asked him for his spiritual assistance after explaining the restrictive situation he was living in."

Wow, Maddy mentally quipped, now he finally understood the noncommittal way in which Father Al and his dad spoke to him.

It was not up to them to reveal Ron's predicament but Ron himself. It was at this time that the value of trust, that which binds one to an ideal of informed acceptance of a person or cause, tugged at Maddy's conscience. Did he place his trust in Ron? It was something he couldn't answer convincingly, but a self-doubt he vowed would never happen again. He also learned that things were not always what they appeared to be, such as the images the boys cultivated about Ron before they even had a chance to meet him. What other times in his young life had he made the same mistake? He thanked his dad in showing care for Ron and for revealing the past history of the Yates family. The future looked a little brighter.

On the outer limits of the town, a series of low hills rimmed the border of a small creek and then meandered to a central point where the height culminated at sixty-five feet. Along the crest, a rustic wooden railed fence was in place to prevent the uninhibited from getting too close to the edge. Surrounding the heights, a wooded plateau of evergreens and hardwoods provided entertainment and solace to nature lovers and adventurists, the latter being Maddy and his crew. Parking their bikes about a half mile from the stream, they meandered through thickets and what weeds survived the early frost.

Climbing trees was mandatory, though more often than not, a few bruises or lumps accompanied the brave tykes returning home from their conquest. These were badges of honor not to be lightly dismissed but causing dismay to protective moms.

The early morning soon was spent, and gradually the throng of youngsters diminished as hunger preyed upon them, many leaving for home as informally as they had gathered. Maddy stayed and began tracking through the open areas and copses, covering a good amount of real estate, before beginning an upward stroll from the base of the hill line toward the crest.

He had developed a fair appreciation for the beauty that could be found in nature, although his perceived manliness could not be revealed to the guys, lest they tease him. Oh, well, their loss. The effort to ascend to the crest brought on heavy breathing and a little sweat. Pausing at the top, he scanned the view below and away, unconsciously thinking about how small the houses and what people he could see looked. Moving closer to get a better view, he approached the wooden rail, replete with a warning to be cautious, an obvious admonition that caused him to roll his eyes. *I think they get it,* he thought. Maybe, but not all.

A smattering of leaves conspired to conceal a loose rock on the downward sloping section of ground. As Maddy approached, his foot kicked it loose, the sudden jerk causing him to fall backward. His forward momentum lunged his prone form toward the lower rail of the fence, the quickness of what was happening preventing him from latching onto it with his flailing hands. Unbelievably, horribly, his helpless form slipped over the edge, his mind a jumble of fright and confusion. He sensed immediately that his preservation was in jeopardy, an afterthought that needed no conscious acknowledgment.

If any saving grace could be gleaned from this potential tragedy, it would be that nature divined that the evergreens present below—Douglas firs, junipers, blue spruce—had grown in a thick and crowded mass. Most notable was a white pine that grown for ages and was at least forty feet in height. As he plunged earthward, the seconds it took to reach the bottom seemed endless, pronounced more so by not knowing when he would abruptly impact the ground.

The needled branches of the pine slowed his descent somewhat, the limbs being wrenched from the trunk along with a host of others.

He disappeared into the greenery as if being swallowed by some mythological creature. A hard bump here, a jolt there, all in rapid succession, jostled his limp form until he crashed to the ground. He uttered a loud groan, the result of a sharp pain coursing through his right leg. It was broken. In pain, he closed his eyes and wondered what happened. *You fell, you jerk* was his immediate comeback. *Nice going.*

The pain increased to the point of nearly blacking out. Barely lucid, he was able to vaguely see that he was close to the base of the hill. He noticed an indenture, like a half shell hollow or small cave near his foot. Maybe, bearing the pain, he might drag himself into its shelter. If not found soon, he would be at the mercy of the elements. He was glad that Mom insisted he wear flannels under his outer garments and that his fleece-lined jacket was fairly warm.

That would last for the short term, but beyond that, he feared that any plunge in the temperature might be tough to handle. The combination of the cold and hunger increased his drowsiness, his eyes succumbing to the lure of sleep. For the time being, the pain was held in abeyance, a welcomed relief, although the sleep was fitful and did not last too long. In a way this was another blessing, in that any prolonged inactivity might induce hypothermia and possibly death.

How long he lay there could only be guessed at. On some occasions, he thought he heard the muted sound of a siren or a howling yell of voices. His now delirious state of mind was becoming very compromised by his condition and the weather, and it was difficult to know what was real and what wasn't. A rare dream would have him in the comfort of his home before a roaring fire, while another would have him shivering in ice-cold water.

At times the silence surrounding him became a noise in itself, what one would experience while traffic passed continuously and then stopped altogether, the absence of sound itself becoming a form of disturbance.

When able to think clearly, he tried to remember his Boy Scout training tips on survival or the TV show *Survivorman*. Do not wander from your position—*Fat chance of that happening.* Gather what you can to protect yourself from the elements—*Good thing there are lots of pine needles and boughs that I can use for bedding and warmth.* Light a fire—*No can do, no matches.* Carry food to provide energy—*How 'bout a pack of gum and a Peppermint Patti?*

The dense evergreens prevented him from knowing if it was afternoon or evening. His stomach, however, signaled the passing of some form of dining, whether it be lunch or supper. He remained hopeful of rescue, but it was wearing thin as time went on. However, he would not let the unthinkable enter his mind, that he would not be found—or worse. *C'mon, guys. Get out here and look, for Pete's sake.*

Plainly exhausted, the gray haze would cover his eyes, and he would curl up into a fetal position despite the pain and drift off for a short while.

Two hands reached around his body, one snaking under his shoulders and the other cradling his legs. The movement was slow and gentle, but the pain of his leg awakened Maddy, but only in a hazy way. His curiosity was tempered as he had no desire to relinquish the warmth of the blanket that cloaked him or the delicious sleep that now enveloped him. *Good for him, whoever he is.*

"Hey, sport, how're doin'?" The voice sounded concerned and hopeful, as well as it would be. A stressed but grateful father sat on the edge of the hospital bed, with his wife beside him, clutching Maddy's hand and staring at the serene face.

Aw, shucks, let me sleep, growled the boy's inner mind.

"He's still out," Jennifer remarked. The delightful voice of his mom parted the protective veil that had embraced his fragile consciousness. His eyelids slowly opened and widened as he verified the source of maternal concern.

"Mom, Dad, I…" Still a little weak from his ordeal, he fell silent as his mother placed the fingertips of her cool hand upon his lips.

"We'll let you rest and come back later. For now you need more rest," she purred, the softness of her voice almost defeating his attempt to remain awake and to find out what the heck happened.

"I'm okay, honest. I'm just a little woozy, and that darn pain in my leg won't let me get some rest for a while. So tell me, what went on?"

Leaning close to the boy, Bernie related how he and Jennifer had become concerned when the boy hadn't returned to complete his early afternoon chores. Questioning some of his passing friends, they couldn't shed any light on where he was. Maddy had been late before, and no undue concern was felt, but as dusk began to creep over the town, however, this soon became a real worry.

Calling Seth's parents, Bernie was filled in on where the kids had specifically gone that morning.

Gee, thought Maddy, *did I stir up a hornet's nest.*

Driving to the woods behind the hill line, a nervous father found his son's bike where he had parked it. Yelling his name a few times, in hopes a forgetful son would reply and sheepishly appear, the silence instead ignited fear. With his cell he called Jennifer, trying to keep her calm while offering benign explanations. The word was spread throughout the neighborhood and beyond, countless friends and even some strangers responding to a call for help.

Hour after hour the search spread through the wooded area, which was extensive.

The thick undergrowth and thorn bushes didn't help any, impeding the effort and burning up precious time. Into the night and early morning, bands of searchers would yell the boy's name and scour wherever they could.

I did hear them! Maddy thought. *I did hear them. It wasn't a dream.*

Pausing his narrative, Bernie sighed and remarked, "We didn't expect to find you where we did. Everything was centered on where we found your bike. Noting the broken boughs and other debris where you were found, we concluded that you had fallen from the crest. Ironically, if you had crashed through the fence, the broken rails would have been a signpost that may have led us to you earlier. As it turned out, your groaning was a key factor in finding you. The trees and shrubs made it near impossible to see where you lay, so I guess pain wasn't such a bad thing after all.

"Well, it turned out okay, son. We gotcha back." A tearful face pressing and kissing the boy's hand, a mother and wife equally moved.

"Dad, it was an accident, honest. I didn't do any double dog dares or stupid stuff like that. You'd have to be an idiot to take that chance. The only part of the mess that felt good was when some guy wrapped me in a warm blanket. Boy that felt good."

"I'll tell Ron you approved."

"Huh? Ron? No way. You're messin' with me, Dad."

"No, son, it's true. But I'm glad it is. He probably saved your life."

"But, Dad, he can't go nowhere, how could he...but he did, didn't he? Wow!"

"You know, son, it took a great deal of courage, maybe more than we'll ever know, to overcome the fear he has been living with.

"Unless we compete on that same ground, we can look at someone and never know the angels or devils that abide within them. When word got out, groups of volunteers passing Ron's house caught his attention. Seth's father, Lou, filled him in and was surprised when Ron hesitated in joining the them." In truth, Ron was frozen for the moment, fear generated by the unknown fate of his little friend and the sickness that had governed his life. He was helpless.

"I knew the challenge that faced Ron and wasn't surprised with what Lou had told me, nor could I pass judgment on him. What I do know is, that whatever demons he faced down, he did so for you and only you."

Maddy squeezed his father's hand in acknowledgement of what he probably had come to conclude himself. His worth had been determined by the tremendously selfless act of another, and not for personal gain or satisfaction, but by and for pure love.

A few days later, the oft-visited leader of the pack was back home, bored to death by all the inactivity he was forced to endure.

"Easy does it, sport, let's not break the other one," his mother would chide when she saw her son's impatience. "Some of your friends will be visiting today, but you can't go blasting off. Take it easy and just enjoy not having to go to school."

School? Maddy cringed that his mom would spoil the day with such a callous remark. School?

Ron called and spoke to his friend for quite a while. The words weren't as important as the bonding they generated; for a ten-year-old boy, he had grown ages in the past few days.

The following Sunday, the family attended Mass. Before services, the well-wishers paid their respects to the lad and parents, Maddy beginning to feel like a celebrity. Afterward, a quiet reflection in prayer and thanksgiving to God for the miracle he had wrought, a resolve to do better in all things, and a care for the needy. These were already the attributes of this fine family but reaffirmed anyway.

Maddy, eyes closed, his silence a prayer in itself, felt a light presence upon his shoulder.

"Hey, guy, got room for me?"

Eyes wide open, he looked up and nearly shattered the contentment of the parishioners with, "Hey, Ron, it's you!" The chorus of chuckles from among the faithful signaled approval and understanding of his outburst. Looking around and somewhat embarrassed, Maddy motioned Ron to sit beside him and whispered his delight. "Man, oh, man, it's really you." He entwined his arm around his friend's shoulder.

Quietly the older man received the eye contact of thanks from the boy's parents, equally surprised by his appearance. As Mass begun, a feeling of spiritual content flowed through all who had experienced and been a part of this family's plight.

Mass ended with Ron carrying his friend from the vestibule in his best imitation of Tiny Tim.

"Home, James," chortled the boy, so alive with delight.

Invited to lunch, Ron accepted but with a slight reluctance. His surprise appearance and show of self-confidence had been a monumental effort on his part.

He had battled with the rising surge of panic from the moment of his decision to attend Mass, not to mention his rescue attempt. Only his inward courage and determination helped to temper the ever-present possibility of a relapse. Focusing primarily on his little friend, he was able, for the moment, to hold his own. How does one overcome this disability? What treatments are available? The questions are as numerous as the people inflicted with this pain.

While Maddy's parents were setting up the dining room table, Ron and his buddy rested in the enclosed porch, which gave him an opportunity to talk to the boy.

"Look, I know you must feel great that I came to Mass, and I feel the same way, only a little differently. What I am going through is a battle for every moment when I'm not feeling, well, afraid. I don't know if it's something that will ever be overcome. But at least I have understanding friends."

The look in his eyes spoke more knowingly than his words. Sensing a need to be a rock for his friend, Maddy hobbled over to him and slapped him on the back, a sign of understanding.

"Hey, pal, I think I get what you're telling me, but we can pull it off." His energy started to pour out as only an unfettered child could produce. "There's too much you have to teach me, and I'm going to hold you to it." In his amateurish way, the student was now becoming the teacher—a teacher on how to live with what you have and to make the most of it. On and on he cited this and that, waving his arms in excited motions, creating visions of future endeavor, slaying the imaginary dragons, saving the fair princess. Whether it worked was not as important than the sincere effort by the little guy.

"Time to eat, guys." Jennifer's voice turned both heads in her direction. Maddy, hoisted onto friend's arms, continued his litany of things to come, a smiling Ron nodding his head at every utterance.

"Yeah, and I got some ideas that I think are going ta be great, when we start to…"

Going Home

The day was exceedingly beautiful, the sun shining ever so brightly as a gentle wind bore the aroma of the many flowers that lined the walkway. All this was but an added bonus to the exhilaration that Bernardo Alvarado was experiencing as he made his way past other students who were leaving school after completing the latest semester. His foray into higher learning had been an adventure and the challenge he hoped it would be.

"Yo, Bern, wait up, compadre!" one of the students shouted. Those Americans. He relished their slang and the personal intimacy it conveyed, along with the nickname Bernie that they bestowed upon him. It was different than what he expected when he first arrived at the Institute, not knowing anyone and feeling a little lost. It wasn't long before he was adopted by these impetuous Northerners and made to feel like one of, to use their term, the gang.

"What are your plans?" Pete piped as he threw his arm around Bernie's neck. He, along with Sam, Josh, and Vito, had formed the five Musketeers. This had to be explained a little to Bernie, never having heard of the famous original trio created by Alexander Dumas. He had chuckled, noting that he had never used a foil in his life. The gang would laugh at his innocence, which made him more likeable to the group. And he relished the friendship given so freely to him.

"I am going home to my father's farm. I would also like to see my friends in the small town not too far from there." Since he started his studies, lack of money had limited his return home and then only when the gang chipped in to pay for his bus fare. The last time was when a devastating flash flood hit the town and surrounding farmlands. They also journeyed with him to render moral support and to do what they could to help.

The young men formed a circle, interlocking their arms across each other's shoulders, and muttered a soft prayer. As they broke up and wished each other safe passage to their destinations, Peter grasped Bernie close to him and, with a deep look of concern and care, spoke quietly.

"My compadre, if you need me for anything, I will be there."

"I know, Pete. Thank you."

With that, all the young men went their separate ways, Pete looking over his shoulder at Bernie in a final glimpse of brotherly concern.

Bernie had decided that his journey home would be through the countryside, a trip that would consume less than a week of travel. Several factors dictated this Louis and Clark approach.

Not the least of which was his lack of money. What he had was barely enough for the bus fare. But money wasn't the only fly in the ointment. He dreaded the roads that skirted the high hills and the manner in which the driver negotiated them. More than once he winced when peering out the window and seeing only a deep ravine or chasm below and no sign of the roadway, as if the bus was floating on air. All too often he would tightly shut his eyes, sometimes arousing laughter from children who were seated with him. To them it was hide-and-go-seek, a notion of theirs that relieved him of profound embarrassment.

Another point was that the meandering road really turned away from his town at the end, the distance much farther than the cross-country trek he favored. Besides, the beauty of the countryside was an alluring prospect.

Money was a factor, but because he had so little, it didn't really figure into his plans that much, the exception being to buy some food if need be.

Hoisting his backpack upon his shoulders, he headed away from the campus in a direction he determined would be the best route to take. His pack contained several sandwiches, a few cans of beans and vegetables, and some pieces of fruit. His only concern was hopefully they would hold him for a while, perhaps living off the countryside when he had to. A large plastic bottle was his source of water, but its weight added a necessary burden to his soon-to-be aching back.

Another piece of gear, but the most important to him, was a soft leather cylinder, much like a map case, of medium size with attached straps. This he hung around his neck. He eyed it with a protective gaze and clutched it tenderly.

The stillness became very evident as he entered the rolling hills and fields. He thought back when he was bombarded with music in his dorm room. Pete and the others would have "study" meetings, and how anyone could learn anything with all that racket was a miracle. Still, he enjoyed some of it, as it was very different from what he had heard growing up. The style and customs of his friends always provoked animated comparisons, and the friendly putdowns on both sides were a source of enjoyment. Even now, the absence of this enjoyment was beginning to make itself felt. He was truly alone.

He thought about his childhood and how his father, Edwardo, would take him into the fields to learn how the crops were grown. His father was a hardworking, loving man who didn't dote and also didn't ignore his son's needs. He knew that work had to be balanced with play, but in an informational way. Pointing out different plants, jokes would be made about how they looked or, in a serious vein, the importance of their need. He welded the son's appreciation of what the earth could provide if treated with respect.

Coming to stream, he wasted no time drinking his fill so that he wouldn't have to lighten the water jug. He fingered the line in his back pocket, to which he could attach a fishing hook, but not being particularly hungry, he passed on it. This was one of the lessons he learned from his father: take what you need and only when you need it. He had witnessed too much waste at the Institute from those who never had to worry about sacrifice or want.

Resuming his trek, he hummed a little, perhaps his way of keeping himself company. Of this he would probably laugh. Pulling his machete from its scabbard, he loped off a portion of a sapling to use as a staff not only for balance but as a defensive measure in case he should run into wild game, or worse. The area he will explore is part of the Braulio Corrillo National Park, and within its confines one can find, if not first sought out by, some very exotic animals.

With sadness he had learned that the beautiful jaguar is almost gone, although there were ocelots and pumas to be had, if they had a mind to accommodate those who trespassed upon their preserve.

The real benefit of this excursion was the knowledge he acquired of the various plant life in his country of Costa Rica. Looking at various trees or plants triggered the recognition of their species, subspecies, or other orders of their existence. His nimble mind floated with pride that he could actually distinguish certain plants from others, this aspect of accomplishment dulling when confronted with something he couldn't identify. This was all taken in stride, for as his American friends used to say when lagging behind on one project or another, "Rome wasn't built in a day." How strange, of course it couldn't be built in a day. It was this unfamiliarity with the concept that brought great amusement to the young men, and they had even more fun trying to explain it to Bernie. Oh, how they would laugh at the seriously questioning face, which then would light up as the meaning became apparent. Those Americans!

Oh, how he missed them, even though it had been such a short while ago that they went their separate ways. He wondered if they would feel the same way as he did, reveling in the freedom and adventure that would open up to him. After all, he was born to this way of life, the rural way of life. Without exception, the boys had grown and lived in the city or suburbs. Would they feel the mood of the vibrant growth that now stretched before him? To them, it was an honorable pursuit that, hopefully, one day would be as profound to them as it was to this sole sojourner. Oh, how he missed them.

He gathered various plant samples that piqued his interest, especially the unknown ones. His actions would serve him well, as this was the foundation upon which his craft would rest. Knowledge had to be pursued more so than having it delivered, and this was the impetus upon which his pursuit thrived.

As the sun began tilting toward the horizon, Bernie began to look for a place to camp. A grassy knoll, fairly flat, would serve as his bed for the night. A small and controlled fire was set with rocks forming a protective perimeter that would contain the flames and also impart some heat by their radiation. A thin blanket would suffice to ward off any chill, and his backpack provided support for his now weary head. He clutched the leather case and held it to his chest in a paternal fashion, looking at it while seeing into the future. This was his precious gift that he was taking home to his family.

Away from the fire, he stared at the sky, now very black. The stars resembled diamonds scattered across velvet. The lack of any ambient or competing light left him with the impression of being inside a very large cave. He thought back to the years when his father had taken him on journeys to various towns, and walking was the only means of getting there. They, too, would lie on the ground and look at the sky, his young mind marveling at such a display by nature and God.

Learning to be a farmer was the course he was to have taken, but his father wanted more for the boy. What little money that could be spared was set aside in a fund for a higher education. At that point, it was just an aspiration of a parent wanting to do more for his son. He was the eldest, Umberto being a younger brother, and Marisol, his sister, who was even younger. Bernie had shown that he cared for the earth and what it could provide. This was the incentive for his father to search for the proper education his son would need.

The University of Costa Rica had established a satellite campus just outside the National Park some miles from the farm. It placed a strong emphasis on agriculture and animal husbandry. Learning of this, the patriarch knew that this could be a path for the boy to follow. Easier said than done. The boy had to excel at the local school and, if successful, travel a bit to attend high school. Bernie knew what his father's wishes were, and with his own enthusiasm, he eagerly applied himself to his studies. That alone would not be enough. The financial burden would be even more than what his father could have saved over the years.

To say that Edwardo was a simple farmer was an understatement. It was he and countless others like him who tilled the soil, learning how to coax from the earth its bounty. Improving strains of seed or applying common plants for medicinal use were legend but barely acknowledged by the world at large.

Resting his weary body, Bernie began to slip into a welcome respite of sleep. The fire hopefully would keep any predators at bay and warm his bones. As with anything the mind will come up with to amuse or befuddle oneself, it did so in a very funny way with Bernie. Just before surrendering consciousness, he remembered Vito in an animated conversation, urging his friend to be careful during his travels.

"Watch out for those Indians, the head-hunting ones!" He smiled to himself, for now he turned the tables on his friends and, with authority, explained that as far as he knew, there were no head-hunting Indians.

"There're not? Boy, are you lucky."

He laughed but appreciated the sentiment. Vito was mildly surprised that there were Indian reservations in the country as in America, although sadly, the population of some were diminishing in number and, along with that, their culture.

His father had ventured to several of the encampments and learned a great deal as to how the tribes were able to produce not only food but other uses that science was only now catching up to. With that, he went to sleep. He didn't realize how tired he was, for at no time was his sleep disturbed, despite the cries of the different nocturnal inhabitants.

Having been raised in farming, his regimen reflected that. Before the sun had yet dared to crease the surface with its brilliance, Bernie was up and ready for breakfast. His friends at the dorm would protest at his early rising, Josh roundly assailing him with accusations that he was sired by a rooster. His body could only obey what had been nurtured in him since he was a boy. This was an unconscious acceptance on his part, just as breathing was, never really questioning it.

He opened his backpack to grab a sandwich and, at the very bottom, sighted an unfamiliar brown plastic container. Knowing that he hadn't packed it, curiously he pried the bulky lid off and let out a curt yelp—"Yes, yes, yes!"

As if uncovering treasure, he eyed the contents with delight and read the small note folded to the side, "Hey, compadre—enjoy, the Five Musketeers." His smile was so broad it also cracked the crease at the corners of his mouth. The treasures uncovered were three Twinkies, something he equated with fine dining; two packets of cashew nuts, which Sam received regularly from home; a slightly melting giant Hershey bar; and some dried cheese clusters.

Many of the things the boys received from home were shared with each other, especially Bernie, as they knew of his circumstances and also that some of these were alien to him. But the Twinkies really ignited a sense of comradeship. To think, they would give up such a tasty delight and think nothing of it. Oh, those crazy Americans!

Gulping down a portion of his "treasure," he would save the sandwiches for later. Making sure there were no fire embers, he covered the area with soil and retrieved his backpack.

"Where is it?" he worriedly muttered as he scoured the ground and the foliage. "Ah, there you are." It was the leather case that had rolled down a slight slope and was hidden from view. "No, my sweet. You will not easily get away from me," he murmured, as he lovingly eyed the soft tan container in his hands. Placing the strap around his neck and grabbing his staff, he proceeded through the undergrowth to a clearing and began his trek again.

With the sun now displaying a respectable height in the sky, he sighted a beautiful Tucana, with its display of brilliant colors. What a sight to behold.

He regretted not having a camera, although Sam had volunteered to loan him his. Not familiar with it and not wanting to lose it, he thanked him but refrained from taking it. Still, maybe he was too hasty. Now all he could rely on would be his memory. The day passed uneventfully, no dangerous animals crossing his path, although from time to time he heard faint growling in the distance; he was hoping they weren't growling from hunger, a joke he played on himself. *I'm too skinny anyway.* Not so. He was just under six feet and had a fairly developed torso, with strong legs, the result of his years of hard labor in the fields. His jet-black hair was complimented by his very dark-brown eyes. "Hey, olive eyes," Josh would quip, when Bernie reacted to an exciting incident, displaying a stare that stood out for miles. He reveled in the fun, and he had his share of comebacks as well, the least of which was "You Americanos."

As the day wore on, Bernie never ceased to be impressed by the naked beauty surrounding him. Any fear of predators was non-existent, the calmness and quiet casting a trusting acceptance of the countryside. Inevitably, the pangs of hunger soon stirred within him. As he was deciding on his "menu" from the backpack, he strode into a small clearing by which a small stream meandered. Lunch! Unloading his backpack, he took the line from his pocket and quickly attached a pair of hooks. Using a broken portion from a tree limb, he fashioned a float. Digging into the soft earth at the edge of the bank provided several large worms which he hoped would be the attraction for his desired lunch.

Casting the line into the water, he angled over to the base of a shady tree close to the water. Using his pack as a pillow, he reclined, grasping the line securely in his hand and pulling his cap over his eyes. A little snooze would be in order. Being totally relaxed and drifting off, the line tugged aggressively on his hand. *Whoa, this soon?* He pulled hard, but whatever was on the other end was not going to surrender so easily. It was a losing effort for the poor fish's efforts however, and soon Bernie was hauling in a rainbow bass of about two pounds.

This is a popular freshwater game fish in the country. With hungry eyes, the great fisherman first started a protective fire, then cleaned and hoisted the delicious treat upon two forked branches just above the flames. As he waited for the fruit of his labor to cook, again he rested on his pack and began to think of past days when his mother, Joanna, would cook the evening meal of fish, rice, tomatoes, and homemade bread. His mouth watered, and he could almost smell the fresh scent of the fish, which was really coming from his own meal.

Bereft of any condiments, it nevertheless was a banquet for our explorer.

Washed down with his bottled water, his content was so great that he fell asleep. The rest was needed, and after several hours, he was up again and on his way. If his good fortune continued, he would not have to use up his sandwiches, although his was seeking an excuse to munch on the Twinkies.

Wherever he looked, his vision was not jaded by the continuous exposure of the flora around him. How his friends would have appreciated this raw introduction to nature. Walking along, his mind raced back to when he was working in the fields. Umberto and Marisol were yet too young to really do much of anything, but they put forth as much effort as their young bodies and will could produce. Edwardo would smile at their faltering efforts in trying to dislodge a growth of heavy weeds that competed with the crops, cajoling each other to pull more or to just do something, anything. When they succeeded, they would go before their father, bearing the results in their hands.

"See, Father, we have saved the fields." His mock seriousness in reply indicated to them that they had contributed mightily, and off they went to Bernardo.

Taking a break, he would lead them into a small grove of trees and brush adjacent to the field. There they would look for anything of interest, as Bernardo had convinced them they might find hidden treasure buried somewhere.

Occasionally, Marisol would squeal with delight upon finding something different. In this instance, she came across a bird's nest laden with two eggs, nestled in the crook of a tree limb. It was the nest of a band-tailed pigeon, whose low-pitched owl-like voice could be heard as if to say, "Leave my children alone." At least that was what her older brother had convinced her was gospel.

When the day's work was finished, they would join together and head for the farmhouse, the younger children racing ahead for some imaginary award at being first. Was it that long ago?

His attention now caught the sight of a clump of flowering bushes, very small in height but expansive in breath. They were at the edge of a small ravine, below which flowed a stream, possibly the same one he had fished earlier. The flow was rapid and turbulent, its racing movement creating a din of its own.

Wishing to get a better view of the flowers, Bernie leaned over the growth.

As he did so, the leather case wriggled from his neck and fell to the edge of the ground. "No! No!" he screamed as it vanished from view. Throwing his pack down, he leaped over the crest of the ravine and, trying to keep his balance on the steep slope, attempted to snare the straps with his flailing hands. His head crashed into an overhanging branch, causing pain and delay, but with a vengeance he resumed his pursuit. Downward he raced, but the case seemed to have wings of its own, and then it disappeared in swirling waters as if invited by some mystical siren.

He stood transfixed, unbelieving of what he had just seen. His treasure was gone, gone. This was for his family, and now there was nothing. Head aching, but not really noticing or caring, a dejected young man made his way back up the slope. He silently cursed the flowering assembly that had led to this disaster and picked up his pack, forlornly gazing at the stream and what it took from him.

For several days, his mind would not let him rest from the gloom that shrouded his every waking moment. His strides were now mere exercises in mechanics, the exhilaration of discovery severely tempered. What would he do when he arrived home with nothing to offer? In the near distance, he saw the curling of white smoke floating upward and then dispersing on the wind. This could be dangerous if it were a fire among the trees and shrubs. As he made his way forward, he caught sight of a small shack, the source of the smoke.

Coming closer, he saw the construct of the hut, a combination of canvas, what appeared to be animal skins, and brush and branches. At once he froze. *No! No! Is it?* There, hanging on a spar that supported part of the dwelling, was a familiar brown leather case, hooked by its straps. Instantly he rushed forward and grabbed the source of his misery and now joy. *You're here, how?*

"May I help you, my son?" Startled, Bernie turned and was confronted with the sight of an elderly man, maybe eighty years or more, slightly bent over, with shocking white hair.

Stammering a response was the best Bernie could do.

"Father, er, I saw…I…I…thought I had lost it."

"You mean the leather case?"

"Yes, Father, it is mine, I lost it several days ago, and it means so much to me."

"I know it is yours, my son."

"How could you know that, Father, we have never met."

"I saw the look in your eyes, my son. No honest person could have that look if they were going to steal."

Relieved, the boy grabbed the man's gnarled hand and kissed it. It was an instinctive effort that brought gratification to the old man's eyes and a smile on his face.

"How did you come to find it?"

"I went to the stream nearby to fish for my dinner. I saw it caught in the branches of a tree that fallen partly in the water, which was swirling angrily like it always does. Not being as young as I wish I could be, it was difficult to kneel down and reach for the straps, but I did.

"Come, my son, let us go inside and be comfortable. Your case will be safe on the hook."

Bernie cast a last glance as if to reassure himself that it was really his lost treasure, entered, and sat on a small cot, the old man reclining in a battered folding picnic chair that had seen better days.

"Now tell me, what had happened to you and your possession?" The boy related how his curiosity caused its loss and the ensuing effort to regain it. That he despaired of ever seeing it again. "Your efforts were painful, were they not, my son? I see the dark bruise on the side of your face."

"Not only that, Father, but I almost broke a rib or two, and that part of my body is marked as well."

Rising, the old man shuffled over to a chest and removed several vials from it. "Lift up your shirt, my boy," he instructed and then proceeded to moisten a cloth with the contents. "Let us see if this helps." After rubbing the affected areas, he sat down, lifted up a jug that was at his feet, and poured a brightly colored liquid into a tin cup. Handing it to Bernie, he motioned with a sweep of his hand.

"Drink up, boy, it won't kill you." Not really a drinker, he nevertheless would not insult the generous man with a refusal. Surprisingly good. "It is made from different fruits that I have blended, plus a tomato, if I am ever fortunate to get one."

Gradually, Bernie felt a reduction in the soreness where the old man had applied his remedy. Seeing the relaxed mood of the boy and the apparent relief he felt elicited a sign of satisfaction on the grizzled face of his benefactor.

"For years, my family and those before them sought out the secrets of the plants. It is magic to some that certain things can be cured or made whole, but it is only with constant searching and trying different ways that anything can be made to work."

"May I take some with me, Father? I am a student at a school that teaches growing many things, and perhaps this can be used to make more to help others."

Painfully bending down near the cot, the old man retrieved a bottle with the precious liquid and placed it in the young boy's hands.

"May this be what you hope it will be."

"I pray that it will be, Father, and bless you."

They talked at length about many things before the exhaustion of the day betrayed itself in the many yawns Bernie could not contain.

"Now we will sleep. The cot I must have for my old, broken body, my son, for that I am sorry."

"No need, Father. I am used to the ground." With that, and a steady crackle of the stove fire inducing a calm, both fell asleep, content with the day's offerings.

The delicious smell awakened the youngster, his mouth beginning to water for an expectant breakfast feast. The old man was quietly humming as he tossed the contents of the pan into the air and catching them with a practiced motion.

"Come, my little one, we eat." The elderly one motioned his head toward the small cabinet near the cot, indicating to Bernie a couple of crumpled aluminum plates, or what appeared to be. Taking each one in turn, he ladled the sweet-smelling meat in equal portions. The smell alone was captivating, would the taste be equally so?

Finishing their breakfast, Bernie remarked, "Father, that was delicious. It is a taste that I cannot compare with to anything else I have eaten. Was it pork or beef, maybe even some fowl that I have not heard of?"

"No, my son, it was just snake."

Snake? The beginnings of a stomach revolution began to stir within the boy's stomach, but with great restraint he quelled it, much out of respect for the hospitality he had received.

"I hope you enjoyed it, what do you think?"

"It was different, Father, I have never tasted anything like it." That part was true, but not the implied meaning of it.

The day wore on, but it soon came time to bid goodbye.

"God go with you, my son, and may he bless you."

"He has, Father, he has, many times."

The old man placed his arms around the boy and grasped him tightly, burying his face into Bernie's chest. This must be how a grandfather embraces his loved ones, he imagined, as he had not known his own but believing he would have shown the same endearment.

Walking away from the hut, and turning his head occasionally for a few last glimpses, he wondered if he would ever see him again. Probably not. And he would be the poorer for it.

Examining Bernie's life, one would learn that he was the recipient of many blessings. His family was loving, he was a good worker and student, and his outlook on life was no different from many other youngsters, but his love of the fields fostered a desire to learn more, and through his family's efforts, a start was made to afford his way into college. As a result of his academic record, he secured a partial scholarship from the state. This and the other forms of finance would just enable him to squeeze through his first year. After that, who knows?

His studies were challenging, as was to be expected, but his professors noted his avid and intense devotion to whatever the studies entailed. His innate intelligence was fine-tuning with the structure of formal instruction. His goal was to help establish a way to feed the world by growing the best crops possible, with all that entailed, along with reforestation, the renewing of areas where logging and mismanagement had reduced the great rainforests.

The institute had received news from the main campus that a food processing and research facility would be locating near the SoapUI River. Not only would they be served by the company farms, but to the individual farmers it would be a boon, as distance and transportation problems weighed heavily on any income they could realize from the sale of their produce. The company managers had contacted various officials to negotiate how future operations would best serve this goal and also to recruit workers.

Of prime interest would be those who offered skills not only in the processing of food but also in the research and improvement of food development. A small program was instituted to provide onsite training and allowing the trainee to exercise his/her expertise. They would still be able to continue their studies under a structured schedule and also receive a stipend. Encouraged by this outreach, the institute supplied the company with student records of those they felt were qualified, Bernie being one of them.

His spirits soared, receiving backslapping and high-fives from the gang. Their joy for him was almost greater than his. At the end of the month after school let out, there would be interviews scheduled for the candidates at the town hall. This was one of the goals for Bernie, besides family. He also realized that there were no guarantees, but his optimism shielded this reality.

Lost in thought, he was startled as a figure emerged from the bushes, reeking of alcohol, probably rum, which competed with the stench of his clothes.

"Hey, my friend, where are you going?" he slurred as he tried to put his arm around Bernie's neck. Shrugging him off, and repelled by the odor, Bernie answered that he was going home. "Where is that, my friend?" the stranger replied while gazing over the boy's head and making a pronounced head nod. Before he could answer, he felt a crushing blow from behind, pain shooting into his head and neck. Another blow, and he was on his knees, his vision clouding rapidly.

Before passing out, he heard a voice instructing another to grab the pack and case which hung around his neck. Although on the point of collapse, this last order stirred a renewed resistance on his part to save his treasure, but he was unable to overcome the effects of the assault and slumped to the ground. How long he lay there he could not tell. On regaining consciousness, it was well into the afternoon, and the pain was unbearable. His water bottle nearby, he doused his head and gulped a few swallows to rid his mouth of the dust he ingested when he struck the ground. What to do now? He didn't know the direction they took, and if he thought of going after them, what would he use to attack them, much less defend himself. His machete was gone also.

Picking himself up, his best course of action would be to continue straight ahead, so at least he would be nearer home, the best option he could up with. Again his heart had been seared, this time not by nature but by fiends from hell. He was not a vindictive person, but the hot coals of emotion would belie that.

The afternoon light receded as the sun began to dip beyond the horizon. Soon it would be dark, but he would continue on nevertheless. The nocturnal sounds began as if on cue, and his searching steps probed for any obstacle that might hinder or injure him. Not having eaten since morning, his stomach joined the cacophony of sounds so natural to these surroundings, that being the least of his worries. Abruptly he stopped. Something alien to this natural habitat tugged at his senses. Of course! Rum! The aroma was very faint at first, but cautiously he moved forward ever so slowly until it penetrated the air about him, an alcoholic cologne. Then he heard an almost welcome sound—snoring! Could it be?

Advancing in the direction of the slumbering-induced drone, he parted a bush and froze. There on the ground, beside a small fire, were two limp forms, fast asleep—he hoped. At the foot of the larger one was his pack and next to it his prize. Steeling himself and lowering his body to the ground, he crawled the crawl of a desperate and totally frightened young man. This did not prevent his determination, however; his eyes fastened on his goal. Slowly, slowly, then a crack! His knee had crushed a small dried limb, and the snoring stopped. It seemed his heart stopped too, until mercifully it resumed again, along with his breath.

He reached the straps of both the case and pack, pulling them toward his body with agonizing slowness, the sweat inundating his body from every pore conceivable. He glanced at the man's companion, sleeping with his back to the fire. At his feet was the machete, and that also was retrieved with the same deliberate caution. Now to remove himself and flee as swiftly as possible.

A small dark rounded object caught his eye—a fist-sized rock. He grabbed it and looked at it, then glancing over to the prone figure of his tormentor, he squeezed it as if to ignite a life in it that would do his bidding. He stared at the now helpless figure he once was and, although not consciously contemplating it, wondered if his skull could survive a crushing blow. He closed his eyes and banished the thought that now became real to him. No, he would not become like them, men lost, probably without redemption. Were he to succumb to the temptation to exact revenge, his who life would have been pointless.

This spark of resolve tempered the flaring anger that had consumed him. No, he would not be like them. Slowly, but with more confidence, he backed away into the surrounding bushes. Threading his way through the dark, he hurried as fast as reasonably possible, not wishing to make the slightest sound. Feeling that he was a safe distance away, he increased his speed, his path now lit by a full moon. His pace increased as he began to run, not daring to look back, but only because he did not wish to tempt fate. In any event, he now had his machete.

Danger or no, he eventually had to rest. He lay down among a group of saplings, concealing his body with their fronds, and took a short nap. Feeling refreshed and listening carefully for sounds that threatened danger, he emerged from his ad hoc bed and continued his journey. Hours later, the rising sun revealed a line of hills in the distance, hills that lay north of his farm. He was almost home. He stopped and rummaged through his back to see if any food remained. Unfortunately, those louts had consumed everything, even his cherished Twinkies. Now that was enough for him to cause bodily harm, he laughingly mused to himself. He looked with relief at his recovered case, fingering the leather as if to caress it. The position of the hasps indicated that the flap had not been opened. The treasure was safe.

After refreshing himself with water from a small stream, he now had sight of the countryside that was so familiar to him. Not too far ahead would be the small rise of ground that overlooked his family's fields. With a nervous tension that screamed for release, he quickened his pace, relishing a return to his birthplace. A stumble here, a trip there were nothing more than a mere delay from eventual satisfaction. He paused ever so briefly, lifting his eyes to the sky to mouth a silent prayer of deliverance. Truly, God had looked over him.

At last he reached the top of the rise and…yes! Yes! There they were. He bolted forward and began a mad dash down the slope.

"Father, Mother, I am home." His voice was unrestrained as he belted out another familial chorus, "Umberto, Marisol, I am back, your brother is back!" With each stride, his pack rose and fell with a thump upon his shoulders, its remaining contents inflicting a small amount of soreness he was oblivious to. His wanton eagerness also allowed his scabbard to drift between his legs, causing him to stumble forward and crashing to the turf. Ripping it from his belt, and now adorned with the sod of the earth, he renewed his flight undaunted, until at last he reached his goal.

He paused momentarily to gain his breath, closing his eyes and again intoned a silent offering. Then with the excitement of a child about to open Christmas gifts, he started to recount what he learned in school, the different projects he was involved in, the great friends he had, and of course the pending interview. Its success would justify his father's faith in him. What had seemed endless to him, but in reality was a short dialogue, came to a close. With that, he took the case from around his neck, unhooked the hasp, and lifted the flap.

Gently he withdrew a moisture-logged roll of cotton and began to unravel it on the ground. Uncovered was a slender, pliable sapling, but no ordinary sapling. In his quest to achieve, and at the bidding of his instructor, he worked at trying to graft two flowering specimens that would produce a most distinct floral appeal. The result was promising, but there was no guarantee it would take. It was in a semidormant state that allowed it to survive so far, embraced by the moisture of its wrappings. This was, he hoped, a sign of survival.

Kneeling down upon the earth, his hands scooped away the loose, damp soil until he had excavated a hole large enough to receive its burden. Gently lowering the slender plant until its roots rested upon the bottom, he pushed the mounds of soil down and around the base, until he had gained a level slightly higher than the surrounding ground. Rising and standing back, he envisioned the future when this infant would one day flower in a majesty all its own and cloak his family with shade serene.

He glanced around the field, at the small wooded grove, then down the trail to the family home. It seemed as if the flash flood had never happened, everything looking quite normal, but it did, and it was bad, very bad. With that, he knelt down and wove his arms around his father's headstone, placing a gentle kiss upon his inscribed name. He did the same for his beloved mother, Umberto, and Marisol. He had come home.

TRUE BLUE

Ever since she saw her first rerun of *Drag Net*, being a police officer was all Maryn ever wanted to be. Often, with pad in hand and pencil in the other, she would mock Sergeant Joe Friday's famous comeback line, "Just the facts, ma'am." Being just six insulated her from any derision by her siblings but also left her open to the feigned resistance of the "suspects," whom she usually corralled into being interrogated. Her mind being quite sharp for her age, she soon learned to cope with "unruly and uncooperative" persons of interest by cajoling her dad to act as Officer Gannon. His paternal credentials usually demanded submission by the culprits.

Being a young, active tyke, her interests were varied, although anything to do with the people in blue always attracted her undivided attention. Reading the crime section of the paper had her vying with Dad for first dibs. As youngsters are prone to do, they will pursue any subject of interest to the point of exhaustion and then move on. Not so with her. While she enjoyed dolls and tea parties, they competed equally as well with any law enforcement or criminal activities that made the news or were included in a magazine or newspaper feature.

Growing up steeped with this accumulated knowledge forged a determination to become more than just an active bystander.

Every now and then, she would remember her youthful zeal and how it resulted in the fruition of her dreams, becoming a police officer. But today, she had a different goal in mind. She arrives a short distance from her prime target and leaves her cruiser, package in hand. Walking a defined and planned route, she cautiously approaches her target, an innocent-looking small bungalow, scanning the environs to ensure secrecy. Approaching the railing of the rear porch, she places the package securely atop the support post, ready for a quick retreat if need be. Satisfied, she moves slowly away, keeping a wary eye out to avoid discovery. Obtaining a position of concealment, she eyes the setup with a focused view. Some might call this entrapment, but she doesn't care.

What would compel a dedicated and honored police sergeant to violate her oath of upholding the law? The question is soon answered.

She watches intently as a figure emerges from the rear door. Her quarry is taking the bait as the package is retrieved. A satisfied smile crosses Maryn's face as she hears a shriek of delight. Mrs. O'Mally has received a gift that has mysteriously appeared every month, on the same date, for over a year, signed, "Your Secret Admirer."

Her task completed, she returns to her cruiser and continues her patrol. Over a year ago, she responded to an emergency call for assistance at this very home. Receiving no answer to her knock on the door, she carefully entered and found this gentle woman on the floor cradling an elderly man in her arms, her husband. Awaiting an ambulance, Maryn assisted as well as she could, trying to determine the man's pulse and heartbeat. She noticed the loving embrace of the woman, holding his form as if to prevent its flight from her arms.

Upon the ambulance arriving, Maryn relinquished her responsibilities as the team placed the man on a stretcher and carried him out. Maryn volunteered to transport the woman to the hospital, reassuring the frightened woman that all was being done that could be done for her husband. Somewhat consoled, she related that they had just celebrated their fifty-second anniversary that day. He always left a present for her, signed, "Your Secret Admirer."

Maryn was touched by the gesture and recalled when her husband, Dave, would do something similar. How many bumps in the road were smoothed over by little touches like this? The lost look on the woman's face spoke reams about her concerns and worsened, if possible, when informed her husband had passed on. Maryn later returned to transport the bereft woman back home, the latter praying softly and looking more composed. Thanking Maryn and heading into her house, she turned and hugged the police officer and placed a kiss on her forehead.

What had started as a onetime gesture matured into a monthly endeavor, a rewarding one, as the reaction to the gift was worth repeating. It didn't replace but reinforced the tender attention that her husband had showered her with. Maryn believed that a police officer should always uphold their calling with the most professional manner possible, but this did not preclude compassion where possible and to be just plain human. She had traveled quite a distance in terms of accomplishment from her first inkling of police work and later at school.

Life doesn't always give you what you desire, because if it did, why would you strive for anything? It's the pursuit that adds seasoning to the result. Maryn did strive to achieve what she could or anticipate certain roadblocks when they appeared. But in reality, there are some things that cannot be negotiated without pain. It came in the predawn hours of her shift when an emergency call routed her to a quiet neighborhood. Lights flashing, her cruiser approached a group of milling people at the side of a fenced-in yard.

"In there!" they shouted. "In there!" She approached a wailing woman cradling a small child. The boy was wet and still, his mother crying and yelling for him to wake up. Seizing the child, Maryn noticed the pool and began to initiate resuscitation. Agonizing minutes passed before rescue arrived and took the child. Before that happened, the lad opened his eyes and smiled, a swell of relief passing through Maryn's chest. *Damn, I did good.*

Escorting the ambulance to the hospital with the frantic woman in tow, she waited while the ER doctors worked on the still form, comforting the child's mother. She wondered how long they would have to keep him before his release to his parents, the father just arriving after being notified of the accident at his night job. Preparing to leave, Maryn saw the doctor usher the parents into the treatment room and close the door. Through the observation window, she saw the woman grab her chest and scream then try to claw her way past the doctor to the limp form on the gurney, her husband restraining her against his body with a desperate embrace.

What Maryn believed was confirmed when the physician shook his head slightly, side to side. She stood transfixed, numb, knowing that just a short while ago, there was hope, now so brutally crushed. Sadly she left the hospital, a small hole in her heart created by an unknown angel whom she may never have met in any other circumstance. There were many boys and girls she would never meet, but this one she did, and it revealed her humanity, not just her professionalism. Her drive back to the station was hindered by the moistness in her eyes.

When attending high school, she formed a forensic club called Sherlock, after one of her favorite fictional characters. The youngsters loved it and created school plays based on the whodunit premise. For the majority of the students, this was a lark that didn't require any real type of commitment. Not so for Maryn. Avid reading and studying the strides made by authorities in law enforcement procedures, equipment, and social interaction bolstered her decision to be a part of it.

Her decision to apply at the police academy did not sit well with her parents. After fruitless efforts to persuade their daughter to attend college, they finally gave in to her resolve, knowing that her stubborn determination would not be in vain, if anything, it would be an asset. She was the only female candidate, but that didn't faze her, not even the doubtful looks of the other candidates. Her lack of airs or that the world owed her a living impressed the instructors almost as much as her abilities to master the curriculum. Familiarity in this case did not breed contempt but a oneness with the other aspiring would-be officers.

Continuing her patrol, she reflected how fortunate she was. Having been on the force since she was eighteen, ten years later has found her a wizened, seasoned servant of the public. Her keen abilities at ferreting out clues or the handling of evidence resulted in her promotion to the ID Bureau. She would always refer to herself as a CSI, or crime scene investigator, made popular by TV shows. A little conceited, she thought it sounded more sexy. Nevertheless, her performance resulted in several commendations and the granting of her request to combine this position with that of patrol duties. She felt a need to be "out there" rather than sequestered behind a desk. It was a choice that benefitted all concerned.

That was still in the future. When she graduated from the academy, while not the top cadet, her standing was still impressive. A storybook ingredient was meeting Dave, another applicant who accidently knocked her down when rushing to class. Initially cross at rudely being upended, Maryn struggled to her feet, resisting his assistance. Brushing herself off, she began to walk away, Dave apologizing and asking if she was okay. She turned to give a sarcastic reply, but call it what you will, the look each gave to the other sealed their future. They became inseparable, sharing lessons, quizzing each other, and generally being a support group.

That Maryn placed higher than Dave became fodder for needling and generally good-natured mayhem. She would refer to him at times as "semi-intelligent," eliciting laughter and a pulled punch to her shoulder.

A year later they were married, police fashion, with a phalanx of fellow police officers raising their batons to form a bridge over the exiting couple from church. Their being posted to different squads presented a problem, but it made their reuniting more savory after finishing separate tours.

Called into the station to process evidence, she was met by the submitting officer, Barry Morrison.

"Hi, Bar, what'cha got?"

"Ah, some dirtball stole clothes from Maggie's shop and was hauling down the street. From the way he was moving, I knew somethin' was up and stopped him. Maggie came running up, hollerin' and screaming, 'He's the one, he's the one!'" The chastened suspect, a sixteen-year-old boy, was sitting on the outer bench, waiting to be processed by the juvenile squad. "He deserves some real time if you ask me, the crud." Barry, for all intents and purposes, was really a fine officer but prone to be crude at times. This made it difficult to relate to him, Maryn seeing a lack of formality a drawback.

Having partnered a few times with him, she saw the turn-off he exhibited when dealing with complainants. One thing learned quite early was, no matter the problem, even if it was beyond the officer's ability to rectify it at that moment, a show of concern and a small dose of consolation usually brought a sense of closure to the problem. How often she was profusely thanked for her efforts, an effort she had tried to instill in Barry.

"Hey, Sarge, how 'bout coffee after the shift?"

"Sorry, Bar, have to pick up Jennifer from school."

That really wasn't the case. Barry, for all his crudeness, had a likeable quality about him, if you looked for it. Maryn believed his crudeness was a crutch for, how would she put it, self-confidence? He was fairly good-looking, with a dark-brown curl that floated above his eye, giving him a younger look. His six-foot frame easily contained two hundred and fifteen pounds of bulk. Punctuating all this were two very blue piercing eyes that secretly caused Maryn to swoon. No, there was too much baggage.

Dave and Maryn were soon blessed with a baby girl. Rather than complicate life, it made it a source of commitment that they relished. The challenge of different shifts energized their solutions. When both were working, Marcy, their next-door neighbor, would accept the child. Being alone, it brought joy to the older woman to have fresh life in her care.

When Maryn was promoted to sergeant, the guys and girls on the force teased Dave that they knew now who the smarter one was. A celebration at Howie's bar capped off a great day. Was there any more to life than this? The following day, aglow from the continued well-wishing of her fellows, she reported for the day shift. Mounting her cruiser, she set out to prowl the streets, stop at different locations to pay respects (for which many citizens commented to the chief), and in general, being as visible as possible.

"Car 31," blared her radio.

"Car 31," came the response.

"West and Haven. Report of car accident, possible injuries."

Not too far from the location, Maryn switched on her rooftop lights and, siren blasting, headed for the accident. As she approached, she saw that it was a dreadful head-on collision and prayed it was not worse than it appeared. Alighting from her vehicle, she approached, ready to render any assistance she could. Fred, one of the officers, stopped her and said, "No, Sarge."

"What do you mean 'no'?"

"Sarge, please, no!"

An icy feeling shot down her spine. One of the others officers draped a covering over the front end of the vehicles to conceal their contents. It was than she focused on the red car and the tag, and her world fell apart.

"No! No!" she shouted as she struggled to get past the officer trying mightily to hold her back.

Dave took any and all exams to further his career, being a detective his prime goal. "With my charisma, they'll confess to anything," he would joke. He, like Maryn, had issues with Barry and would try to wean him from his faults, but without success. His John Wayne syndrome was deeply imbedded, and what it would take to mollify it was a question unanswered. As a whole, the department of Hillview functioned with a fair amount of efficiency. Maryn, through grants and charters, attempted to upgrade the equipment used by the personnel not only in the ID Bureau but throughout the force.

One piece of equipment would one day be a source of vindictive satisfaction. A special digital 35 mm camera was procured, its features delighting Maryn to no end. Gone are the days when she had to sweat out film development, hoping she had the right settings and bemoaning her lot when some of the shots didn't pan out or were somehow compromised. This provided a safety net, and she would exploit it to the limit. How proud she was of herself. When Maryn was leaving for work, Dave surprised her with the news that he had made detective. Wow, two promotions. Tonight they would celebrate. Only they wouldn't.

Dave had been on his way to buy flowers and a bottle of wine for his favorite girl. The driver in the approaching car had suffered a heart attack and, unconscious, veered into the path of Dave's SUV. Neither survived. The gloom in the department matched the black drapings over the entrance. Flowers inundated the foyer, and numerous people paid their respects, much of it, not only for the loss of a defender of their safety, but for the personal sorrow felt for Maryn.

Life moved on, albeit with an added urgency, for who knows when their time will come? Being a police officer doubly affirmed that conviction. She moved on also, but very slowly, not wishing to relinquish the slightest iota of her past, but keeping it in perspective so that it didn't affect the daily needs of her job or child. It was some time before she paid even the tiniest of interest in Barry. Strange, he was so different from Dave, and yet there was something about him that attracted her. All in good time.

Harvey Atwater, a seventeen-year-old, was a thorn in the side of the department, more so to Barry, as the misfit lived in his patrol sector. More than once, Barry had the misfortune of encountering him on many occasions where his conduct, though not criminal violations, were a nuisance and affected the quality of life to many in the neighborhood. Counseling or one-on-one by the pastor were to no avail. He smirked openly at authority, helpless to do anything more than shake their heads and hope one day for deliverance from this pest. Of course, Barry's handling of the youth in no way engendered any modification of his conduct. In fact, a hidden hostility had brewed a frothy soup of vengeance inside one so young.

Maryn had been called out on several break-ins. The burglaries all had the same signature, or MO, that would seem to tie the crimes to a single person or group of individuals. Wanton destruction seemed to be the paramount objective of the burglar. Valuable items were taken, but the mindless carnage left one speechless, no plausible reason for it. With her newly obtained camera, detailed photos of great clarity visually described the mayhem wrought upon the different concerns broken into. It helped her develop a profile on who the perpetrator could be. Young, brash, no scruples were among her observations, but these were not the hard evidence needed to apprehend or convict, only a signpost that could lead to an arrest. Physical effects were taken to the station and examined for any trace evidence, particles, hair strands, soil, or other accompanying indicators. It was grueling work. Hopefully something would stand out.

Maryn was assigned to the evening shift, and the balmy weather would spark a flurry of calls. People did not want to stay indoors. One particular person was Atwater. Roaming the back streets and casing anything that provided him with a chance to acquire illicit merchandise, he came across United Glass, a company specializing in all types of glassware, mostly windows and tabletops. Having been schooled in the art of alarms by several adults he had worked with, it was with no difficulty that he disabled the side door unit.

Upon entering, his first goal was to locate the office where electronic equipment would be ripe for the picking. He stashed his stolen pickup on the next street to deflect attention away from the company. Using a dim flashlight, none too bright for picking his way through the floor displays, his body jostled a glass frame which crashed into another, shattering both. While trying to move past the debris on one of the tables, his arm was sliced severely by a projecting piece of glass protruding from the pile, causing a massive blood flow.

His fear was heightened as he saw his life's blood painting the floor with its inherent red hue. Sighting a table covering in the available ambient light, he snatched it and wrapped the cloth tightly around the wound, finally stemming the outflow of blood. His coarse and vile nature now let loose his wanton rage as he smashed almost every glass display around him until it formed a mound that covered a large part of the floor.

His presence hadn't gone unnoticed. A night watchman on his way to work observed a figure forcing his way into the building and called the police from a payphone. The response was quick and silent. As there were many calls that night due to the weather, Barry's unit was the only one available in that sector. Hearing the assignment over her radio, Maryn called in and volunteered as back up. Given permission, she headed to the scene, lights flashing but siren off. Unfortunately, she had been cruising on the opposite side of town, thereby increasing her arrival time.

Parking a short distance away with his lights off, Barry approached the half-opened door with caution then proceeded to discard that safeguard by entering the building before his backup arrived. If there were more than one suspect, he would be in dire trouble, but in this instance, he was fortunate. Slowly moving, with only the dim lighting as illumination, he spot a figure crouching behind a desk. Focusing his flashlight on the form, Barry barked a commanding order, "Okay, sleazeball, get over here," while unholstering his automatic.

Rising, the boy walked toward the officer, growling, "I ain't done nuttin'."

"Ya, I can see that," Barry quipped back at him. "Turn around." As Barry was cuffing the suspect and turning to leave, Maryn, also with her weapon drawn, confronted the two.

"What happened, Bar?" she asked as she scanned the floor piled high with broken glass. Jokingly she says, "A hurricane must have passed this way."

"He did this, he cut me!" shouted the cuffed youth. "I gave up like he wanted, and he sliced my arm real good with a piece of glass he picked up. He said punks like me ain't nuttin' and cut me, cut me real good."

"Why, you slimey—"

"Enough, Bar, we'll figure this out later."

"But, Maryn, he's a ball-faced li—"

"I said enough, now's not the time. Get him over to General, I'll notify the shift lieutenant and Juvy to meet you there."

A little shaken at not having his version considered, a slightly chastened but angry officer left with his charge. Communications was notified to contact the owner so that he could take inventory to determine any loss.

Being well drilled in crime scene processing, Maryn proceeded as if a memory card had been inserted into her lobes. Methodically she covered every angle that could produce fruit of the crime. She especially was thoroughly captivated by the ease and completeness of her new camera. Gone were the worries that would pop up after processing and wondering if she got all the shots needed or if they would turn out. What bothered her, however, was the nagging thought, although she tried to suppress it, that perhaps there was some truth to the boy's accusations.

Barry's personality and crudeness at times did not lend itself to any form of endearment or consolation, which with another officer may have lent more credibility to their claims. Liking a person always outweighs not liking them. This may not be fair, but it's a fact, and it may well turn out to be a pivotal element in Barry's case. Ever the professional, she still had conflicts and tried to put them aside. In the police profession, as it possibly may well be in others, once you're hung with a tag, whether good or ill, you're going to be stuck with it. Case in point was Maryn. With double *M*s in her name, she acquired the nick name M&M, something harmless and a source of jibes. Barry's tag was bought by his past behavior, in itself not fatal, but hardly a yardstick to dispel his present complication.

The boy's father, a person almost as unsavory as his son, filed a complaint against the officer. It had to be honored, and a hearing would be held in court the following Monday. Barry was suspended with pay pending the resolution of the charges. The change in his demeanor was striking. Gone was the haughtiness, replaced with a somber, sober manner that fostered the impression of submission, something totally alien to his character. While turning in his weapon and shield, a glance around the squad room revealed officers turning away, failing to make eye contact or just generally ignoring him. They too had tried to make him see the light, so to speak, and now it had come back to bite him.

I'm one of them, why are they treating me like this? he silently asked himself.

Barry wasn't totally without hope. It still was a case of he said, she said and how the evidence was presented. Two prior complaints of being heavy-handed didn't help any, but there was no violence associated with it. A crap shoot.

Then he felt a slight touch on his arm, Maryn's hand resting on it, and a soft, sad smile on her face. His descent from Mt. Olympus was all she needed to dispel her assumption of his guilt. Disproving it would be another matter. "Go home, Bar. I'll do what I can." Hearing that gave him a lift, for whatever else he thought about her, paramount was her stature as a top-notch investigator.

Monday came, accompanied by all the second-guessing attendant to these types of things. A few off-duty officers were in court, either convinced he was innocent or there to see him get his due. Barry was a man almost all alone. After court was called into session, with admonitions from the judge for proper decorum, the prosecutor began to present his case. In many proceedings, a municipal hearing was held to hear the prosecutor's charges and to examine evidence. A lodge attorney represented an anxious and fidgety defendant, almost on the verge of chewing his nails off.

In the presentation by the prosecutor, the defendant will not be required to testify, as the burden of proof is on the State. His duty will be to lay out the case against the defendant, along with any and all evidence pertinent to its outcome. A determination will be made by the justice to refer the matter to the grand jury, hear the case as a misdemeanor, or dismiss it outright.

The first witness called was the treating physician at the hospital. His testimony was dry and bland, not worthy of a TV script, but nonetheless required. The severity of the wound had consequences, as to what level had yet to be determined, although it was testified that fifty-two stiches were required to bind the wound. A noticeable wince crossed Barry's face on hearing the total, and his body slumped slightly in the chair.

Next, the obnoxious plaintiff took the stand, dressed in a mismatched suit and tie, his wardrobe mirroring his incompetence. Asked as to what happened that night, he tore into a tirade of being persecuted by the officer, citing many examples of the run-ins he had with him. This perhaps undercut his own credibility, the number of instances implying a certain amount of initiation on his part. Several times the judge admonished him to tone his testimony down and to stop filibustering.

Maryn was seated in a side venue, going over her notes and photos. These would surely be addressed to the court in testimony and photo documentation. How she dreaded her part, for it could end the career of a colleague, but her duty was preordained. As cold as it was to say, the chips had to fall where they would. Ignoring the testimony of additional witnesses, she scanned her written report, assuring that what she wrote was correct, then looked over her photos. Sheet after sheet—then she froze! Slapping the side of her head, verbally she muttered, "No! How could I have missed this?" To doubly verify the significance of what the photos revealed, her practiced eye pored over every photo, each conforming to the original discovery.

Her elation was difficult to control, and before she could do anything else, the prosecutor now called her to the stand. Nervously she was sworn in and was seated. The prosecutor then continued with the usual protocol of stating her full name, rank, position in the department, and years of service and commendations. This was standard practice to establish the credentials of the witness.

"Sergeant Madson, did you assist in covering a burglary at United Glass on the date in question?"

"Yes, sir."

"Tell the court, if you will, what you encountered."

"When I entered the building, the complainant was in cuffs, amid a glass-strewn floor. He claimed that the defen—Officer Morrison had inflicted wounds on his person."

"Was there any visual evidence to that effect."

"Yes, sir."

Barry silently groaned, and with both hands cupping his face, he lowered his head.

"How severe were the wounds?"

"I did not have the opportunity to see the wound, only that copious amounts of blood were visible."

Again Barry was struck with the proverbial punch to the gut.

"Did you witness the assault?"

"No, sir."

"What did you do next?"

"After instructing Officer Morrison to transport the suspect to the hospital, I made all pertinent notifications and proceeded to process the crime scene."

"What did you do?"

"I processed the scene to obtain any latent prints, to document any theft after the owner arrived, and photographed all aspects of the location, inside and out."

"Did you uncover any latent prints?"

"Yes, sir, on a pane of glass from the side door. They established the then suspect's identity."

"Anywhere else?"

"Some partials were recovered, but identifications have not been determined yet." With that the prosecutor thanked Maryn and was about to address the judge, when she interrupted, "Sir, Your Honor, I believe I may have evidence that can shed more light on this case."

With a slightly puzzled look, almost signifying a suggestion of "What else is there?" he bade her to continue.

"Notwithstanding the then suspect's claim of being deliberately cut by Officer Morrison, after examining my photos, I noticed a curious and very telling composition of the blood and glass. In every photo, the preponderance of the blood, which covered an extensive area, was *beneath* the broken glass. The then suspect accused Officer Morrison of injuring him with a shard that he had picked up from the pile. I contend that if that were the case, why was there an absence of blood upon the top of the pile that would have been commensurate with that below?

"That, plus the fact the then suspect's arm had been bandaged with a table cloth, something Officer Morrison did not have and stated in his report that he had not administered. If he did, his person would have been covered with the then suspect's blood also. This precludes the fact that if the cutting was as the then suspect claims, deliberate by the officer, he surely would have been covered with blood at that moment. In fact, I found no blood residue on him, which would have been difficult to not see. Again, it was stated the officer picked up the shard from the pile, broken glass already in evidence, glass beneath which lay the then suspect's blood."

To say Barry was reborn was an understatement. His posture livened with the rejuvenating testimony heard. He held back a little. There was still adjudicating to be done, hopefully in his favor.

"May I see the photos?" the voice of the judge breaking the silence. Poring over the file, pausing here and there, wrinkling his brow, which may have denoted doubt, he closed the file and said, "You believe this to be the case, Sergeant?"

"Yes, sir."

"After reviewing this evidence, I hereby dismiss the case of the state. I am convinced of its veracity, and I also recommend that the juvenile bureau institute charges of false swearing and filing a false police report against the complainant. Mt Atwater, I hope the outcome fits you better than that suit." A suppressed smile creasing his lips.

Not wishing to press his luck, Barry refrained from a stand-up whoop but quietly thanked his attorney and looked back at Maryn. She waited for him at the rear exit and shook his hand as he came up to her.

"Maryn, I now think what a butt off I may have been. In fact, I know it. Growing up, my father would criticize many things that I tried to do. Nothing ever pleased him. Mom wasn't always on my side either. How it came to be, I don't really know, but I figured, hell, before anyone tries that stuff on me again, I won't take it. Over the years, I guess being this defensive got out of hand, and my hardnosing was more of a reaction, a barrier to any assault upon me in any way."

Maryn could see the innate hostility melt from his eyes. Would this be a turning point in our bad boy Peck? One could only hope. Maryn then said, "You owe me."

"What do you mean?"

"Dinner at seven, and don't be late."

Man of Honor

The bitter cold tore into the face of the disheartened and angry men of Easy Company as they trudged their way through the snowdrifts. Disheartened by having to endure the miserable weather and angry that they weren't able to hold the Germans that assaulted their line. That they were able to even mount a coherent retreat was a miracle in itself, but retreats don't win battles, at least that's what many of the boys, not yet really men, felt in their hearts. This was supposed to be a quiet sector where exhausted troops could rest and refit and newer units could acclimate to the weather and the additional training where possible. What happened? This question not only plagued the men in the field but of each echelon of command. What happened?

Confusion reigns supreme when an unexpected challenge clips your chin and knocks your rear end into the dust. This was no different because it wasn't really expected. Didn't the krauts know they were beaten? Hadn't we pushed their butts back into Germany? What did they think they were doing? What they were doing was smashing the American line and forcing a hasty retreat in many sectors. Heavy armor, supported by equally heavy artillery bombardments, had woken the cows and the sleeping Americans in the early hours of December, 16, 1944. Not only woken them, but decimated their ranks.

Desperate attempts were made to form fire brigades, but without knowledge of what they were up against, it only increased the damage, as tanks that the enemies were not supposed to have roared through the lines like stampeding dinosaurs. Hesitation meant a final day on earth, and to flee might ensure another day to live through. These men weren't cowards; they were human, and their natural instinct for survival shifted into high gear. Some men shed that instinct, as individual or group reactions were heroic, many unsuccessful. When the American soldier had parity, he was unequalled, and it was this quality instilled in these brave men that drove their spirit and desperate efforts.

PFC Ernie Greene was a live-and-let-live guy. You didn't bother him; he didn't bother you. The Germans made the sad mistake of doing just that—they bothered him. A constructionist in civilian life, Ernie had engineered his dugout to satisfy his creature comforts, drawing envy from his fellow grunts. If he was going to fight, he was also going to enjoy his downtime and spared no effort to achieve it. Forced to leave his domicile by the ill-tempered Krauts fostered a resolve of retribution, partly supported by his being Jewish.

Ernie may have been self-indulgent, but it didn't detract from his fighting abilities. On the contrary, content soldiers usually performed better when coddled to some degree, and in combat, having a blanket or a hot cup of coffee was being coddled. Racing from his dugout with a group of other refugees, he made for a stand of trees and flattened himself to the ground. His companions raced on, believing their comrade had lost some semblance of sanity by remaining behind. No, Ernie was sane but also vengeful, and he intended to vent that emotion for all it was worth.

The cause of his quick evacuation was lumbering up the field, a monstrous tank, a king tiger, as he recalled from squad briefings. *Tiger, hell,* he thought, *more like an elephant.* As big as it was, it was also slow, its tonnage a detriment to its speed. To his surprise, no infantry accompanied the behemoth, a no-no in combat when even these giants could be assaulted if not protected a covering force. As the tank swung by, Ernie leaped to his feet and grabbed a rung on the side of the hull and hoisted himself onto the rear deck.

Glancing around to ensure he was not spotted, and using his helmet, he pounded the commander's hatch cover. The confidence of the enemy that they held the upper hand was demonstrated when the hatch slowly opened and a voice uttered, "Vat is los?" apparently believing the uninvited guest was a comrade in arms. Quickly Ernie ploughed his rifle butt against the tanker's skull, causing him to collapse from sight. Ripping a grenade from his chest strap and pulling the pin, he hurled it into the darkness of the interior and slammed the hatch shut. A moment later, the cover assumed the status of a pressure cooker lid, as the force of the explosion nearly ripped it off its hinges.

Rifle at the ready, he waited for some movement within the smoke swirling upward. Nothing. He jumped down and ran toward where his buddies had headed. These were the types of individual actions that would play havoc with the enemy, but would it be enough? In some cases, the retreats were well managed as the commanders were able to provide rear guards that allowed the main bodies to escape reasonably intact. In this instance, it was Easy Company that drew the short straw and moved into blocking positions, allowing the rest of the Second Battalion to move out.

How this all came to be was startling. As the allies moved forward on all fronts, the Ardennes area seemed to be blessed with a relative degree of tranquility. Here, various units of the US Army were set in place, to rehabilitate or acclimate to the conditions. Hitler had other thoughts about the matter and believed in his warped mind that he could mastermind an offensive that would at the least cull the enemy into negotiating a separate peace if successful. Through the months preceding the assault, he gathered, scrounged, or scraped up anything that presented an offensive threat. Secrecy was tightly enforced, as a quarter of a million men were concentrated in the area, and for all intents and purposes concerning military intelligence, they did not exist.

Scarce armor, supplies, and a very limited supply of fuel were husbanded in the designated areas. It was a crap shoot, but the ex-corporal, still gripped by the ghost of past fading victories, relinquished reality. If anything can be said that was positive in all this, it would be that these harebrained adventures would end the war sooner. Hitler despised his generals, except for his ruthless SS commanders, and routinely brushed aside their complaints or downright opposition to his schemes. To some of the skeptical senior officers still holding commands, and defying their hard-earned experience gained through intense on combat, it seemed possible if only because nothing else promised victory.

Fog, that which the enemy had used to their advantage, was now used by Easy to disengage from action and retreat along the path Second Battalion had taken. Radio communications were sporadic, and their location was uncertain. Continuing westward was the only option of finding support and coordination. Fortunately, fuel problems by the pursuing Germans prevented them from making any headway in closing the gap, and for several days, their slim luck held out, although the cold and hunger were a constant reminder of their dilemma. Eventually, radio contact was established with Battalion HQ, which had been diverted from their line of march by harassing assaults, the enemy attempting to pin them down for larger follow-up units. In fighting off these attacks, it caused them to veer away from their planned route, which by now prevented any support for Easy Company.

Until any type of relief could be offered, problematic at best, they were ordered to a map reference which pointed to the small Belgium hamlet of Bizory, just outside Bastogne. Here they were to set up defensive positions while desperate efforts were being made to scrounge up additional support. Regiment had been notified as well as Division. At least everyone knew where to claim the bodies. After several grueling and exhausting days, with nothing but cold rations and melted snow for water, the sight of a church spire signaled the presence of a village, hopefully their designation. It was. Point men returned with independent reports that the town was clean, a welcome piece of news.

Still, the tired men entered cautiously, not quite believing they were, as some would use the pun, out of the woods yet. A small group of civilians approached the commander, a little bewildered to see troops that, days earlier, had passed through in such excellent condition but now looked bedraggled and gaunt. The mayor in the group approached the commander, naturally concerned by their presence.

A few moments after a quick explanation, the captain was ushered to a small residence, the mayor's home. He offered that all radios had been confiscated by the Germans and any outside news could only be passed by word of mouth, village to village. After giving orders to his sergeants to mount a small defensive perimeter outside the town and the posting of sentries, with orders to be alerted instantly if anything broke loose.

The tired but imposing form answered to the name of Captain Lacy Smith, twenty-nine, a graduate of West Point. This resumé emboldened the younger troops, but the older ones held their assessment until he proved himself. Six foot five, a deceiving one hundred and ninety-five pounds filling a form-fitting uniform, he would do a recruitment poster justice, especially when donning his net-laced helmet, through which a pack of butts was entwined. After graduating from the Point, he was given scattered assignments, mostly in the Quartermaster Corps. Severe battle attrition of combat officers hastened his posting to a combat unit. He was confident, had the knowledge, but lacked the experience.

He was smart enough to lean on the very few veteran noncoms that he had, usually deferring to their assessment on a particular situation. This had garnered some respect from them, but only because they had never really been in such a spot like this before. Now would be the proof of the pudding.

"Your Excellency," he said with a deference that swelled the form of the old man, "the enemy has broken through our lines and may be here soon. Our orders are to defend this town. However, I would suggest you send your people away. I cannot guarantee your safety or that of this beautiful village."

"*Mon Capitan*," the old man angrily replied, "this is not the first time we have had to deal with the Boche. The last great war revealed their cruelty." His eyes flaming with passion as he spoke. "No, we will not be put to shame by running away. Our cellars are deep, they will protect us. If you have a spare gun, I will take it and fight alongside you."

What courage, thought the captain. *I wish I could bottle it.*

"Very well, sir, we will do what we can. Also, will it be possible to bring a little food to my men? They are in poor shape and near exhaustion."

"*Capitan*, what we have is yours. Do not worry, these brave young boys will be cared for as if they were my own sons."

"And if possible, sir, could I use your house as a command post?" To which the mayor agreed. "But before anything else, *Mon Capitan*, I must tell you something very interesting. There is a man who lives in a small hut not far from here. He is an American."

"An American?"

"Yes, when the Great War ended, he appeared in our village. He was polite and quiet but had a much damage to the side of his face. The children at first were afraid of him, but his gentleness soon calmed their fears. The uniform he wore was American and had three stripes on each arm. He asked if he could stay, but not in the houses. He chose to live on the edge of the village, on a small piece of ground near a small stream and a few standing shade trees. It's just beyond that small hill." The old man pointed to the north. "He never asked for anything but would work for anyone who needed help, especially at harvest time. Over the years, he became one of us and was always willing to share his labors."

"What's his name?"

"To this day we do not know. He answers only to a funny word called Sarge."

"Thank you, Mayor, I think I'll pay him a visit."

"I think he knows you are here already, my friend. He is smart like that. When the Boche were here, they never discovered him, but he knew where they were. If he had been discovered, I fear they would have shot him. Those devils have no soul."

Checking the perimeter and seeing to the feeding of his men, the captain surveyed the lay of the land and the possible approaches the enemy could take. It was a daunting exercise, as each contingency plan he could mentally form was dashed by the lack of personnel. Doing all that he could, he decided to check on this unknown American, leaving his very young lieutenant in charge, himself barely able to shave. What he had was what he had.

Driving through the small plaza, now alive with the frenzied competition of the women, old and young, to feed their newfound charges, he headed toward the small hill, negotiating the soft ground with the aid of his jeep's four-wheel drive. Approaching the crest, he observed a man sitting by a fire roasting something, the smell reminding him that while his troops were being fed, he himself had not eaten. The natural result was a watering of his mouth that was difficult to conceal. Leaving the jeep and approaching the man, who had risen, his gaze betraying what his stomach already knew.

"Can I offer you something, son?"

"Boy, that smells delicious, but it can wait."

"Wait, hell, you don't eat now, it'll all be gone. I'm hungry too."

The backhanded invitation was quickly accepted, and the captain's taste buds were rewarded with a tasty delight. Whatever it was, it brought closure to his culinary drought. Offered a glass of wine, it was quickly consumed, bringing on a mild remonstration from the host that it deserved to be sipped to gain the full flavor. Offering his glass for a refill, he repeated the same rate of consumption, to a mild grunt by the irritated man. No class.

Offering a cigarette, which was quickly snatched, the captain engaged in small talk to learn more about this stranger who was accepted by the villagers.

"What's your name, friend?"

"Sarge" was the dry reply.

"Where ya from?"

"The States, I thought that was obvious."

"What state?"

"Nowhere in particular."

It seemed that any further probing in this area would be futile, so he went in another direction.

"What outfit were you assigned to?"

"The US Army."

Again there was a reluctance to open up. The commander gave up any other attempt to pry into what seemed to be a fiercely held privacy.

"What ya up to, Captain, other than having a bunch of guys down there digging holes all over?"

"To tell you the truth, Sarge, I was only curious, but as I was talking to you, I overlooked the obvious."

"And what was that?"

"That I was talking to a man who probably saw a lot of combat. Not that I'm trying to enlist you, but your knowledge of the surrounding turf and lay of the land could be useful to me in what I have to do."

"I'm not in this war, son. I had my share."

Momentarily stunned by this abject refusal, ignoring the needs of his fellow countrymen, the captain stared at the man's downcast eyes, wondering how he could be so cold.

"I'm not asking you to violate some religious principle, or whatever else you're hiding behind. Look, I have one hundred seventy-three souls that depend on my making the right decisions, supported by very few veterans and even fewer noncoms."

He saw a slight wavering in his opposite's demeanor, his head looking away as if to chase away any thought of surrendering his refusal.

"Do me a favor and I'll let it go at that."

"What do you want?"

"Hop in the jeep and take a small ride with me. I promise I'll bring you back."

"I guess I can do that."

As the jeep headed down the slope, he remarked to Sarge that the hill position offered a great view of the surrounding area and would be an ideal forward observation post.

"Never thought of it that way, Captain, but you're right, it's ideal."

As they reached the plaza, the drive was deliberately slow so that the reluctant passenger could see the face of the kids that heroically posed as soldiers. Their cherubic faces, the self-conscious taller boys, the pugnacious shorter ones, ingrained themselves on one who had not seen his own kind for over two decades.

They may have been scared, unsure, or many other distracting reasons, but they were also determined. Whatever the shortfalls, they would not go quietly into the night, and if indeed they were to go there, they would drag the enemy along with them. The captain sensed this, but that alone was not enough to develop even a moderate defense. More was needed, even if it wasn't a bonanza.

"Look around, Sarge, and tell me these kids don't deserve even the slightest bit of hope or help." You couldn't really know what the old man was thinking, his scarred face concealing any real signs of expression. For several minutes, he swung his head around slowly, watching the boys in khaki.

What could be his reason for hesitation? Slowly he turned to the Captain and spoke.

"Cap'n, I don't like the idea of being responsible for your boys."

"You're not, I am, so get that out of your head."

"But you don't know a danged thing about me."

"What I do know is that I need help, and if I think you can help, just let me live with that responsibility. Crap, that should take some of the load off you. Remember, I'm only asking you to be a scout, to give me the best way to set up my guys, to give them a fighting chance. You don't have to be John Wayne."

"Who?"

"Never mind."

Again the old man looked around then faced the hopeful officer.

"Okay, son, I think I can handle that for you. But let me be clear, I ain't goin' to be some hero."

"John Wayne?"

"Who?"

"Forget it, let's go to my HQ and look at some maps. You do know how to read maps, don't you?"

"I had three stripes on my arm that didn't jump there from some zebra, so don't you fret."

In his intense concentration to persuade the old Sarge to climb on board, the captain only now was aware of a small gaggle of children, shouting, "Sargie, Sargie." Their mirth and giggling was contagious, igniting a teeth-baring grin from the veteran officer. The way they tugged at the older man's arms and the embrace they wrapped around him signified a relationship of an endearing community. In effect, these were his children by their choice, especially several who could not have been more than two or three years old. His smile and interaction told it all. All the more so after gazing into a face that would have been more appropriate for a Halloween mask.

"Thanks, Sarge, I was hoping you'd say yes. Would you like to join me at HQ? I've asked most of my officers and noncoms to convene so that I can get some input on what we're going to do."

"I'd like that, Cap'n."

The house being moderately small could barely contain the assembled men, but eventually they crammed into any space available. Not being shy, the savvy Sarge broached a question before the captain could even begin his evaluation of their dilemma.

"Cap'n, may I ask what our assets are?"

"Good question, Sarge, I think all of us should know what we have and what we need. Four M3 half-tracks, right, Smitty?" a side remark to a lieutenant responsible for any mobile equipment. Nodding in the affirmative, Smith continued.

"Three mortars, four machine guns, some land mines and a bazooka. Hal, how many rounds for it?"

"Twelve, sir," came the reply. "Rifle ammo is ample if carefully husbanded, and each man could be allotted two or three grenades."

"Cap'n, can I make some noise here?"

"That's why we're here, Sarge. Oh, by the way, guys, in case you're wondering who the mystery man is, I'll fill you in later."

Sarge continued, "What you have in the way of firepower ain't goin' to cut it all the way. You're goin' to haft'be sneaky and dirty. Maybe I can help you there." Already the men were warming to ole Sarge.

"I look forward to your suggestions. What I have in mind that may give us some sort of edge is a mobile reserve. One or two half-tracks mounting one of the mortars and two of the machine guns. We can only spare half a squad for each unit." A murmur of approval and then another question from the grizzled man.

"Capn, with your permission, I'd like to take a couple of yer fellers wit me on a quick survey. I think I know where to place some of the udder units for the best results."

"That's why I recruited you, Sarge, although I can't guarantee a pay boost." The gleam in his eyes and the smile on his face reflected the growing confidence in his new recruit.

"Another piece of news, not all good. We were able to reestablish communications with Battalion. They ended up just outside Bastogne on a defensive line which is not too far from us. The bad news is that we're being used as a blocking force that will alert them of any assault by the Germans. It stinks, but they said that any support they could scrape up would be sent to us. I didn't like the 'scrape up' part, but orders are orders. Okay, get back to your units and dig in as well as you can. We'll alter our dispositions after recommendations from the scouting party. Dismissed."

"Sarge."

"Yes, sir?"

"You don't have to salute, Sarge."

"But it's comin' back to me, sir." A small guffaw pierced his gruff beard.

"Okay, okay, but don't get too used to it, you might irritate my guys with that spiffy put-on. Do you think you can really give me something?"

"Sir, it's okay to call you sir?"

"Don't be a smart aleck, what's up?"

"Well, I've roamed this area almost all the time I have lived here, and I think I know where we can place the remaining machine guns and mortars. Look at where we are. Our right flank buts up against a fairly deep stream, and our left almost melts into that wooded ridge. That's some protection and wouldn't take too many men to keep an eye on it."

"Sounds good. Took that into consideration earlier, but we're on the same page."

"True, Cap'n, but I have some ideas on the frontal situation. I don't believe the krauts can really get behind us, unless it's some small scouting force, so we're basically okay there."

"What do you have in mind?"

"It don' take no genius, no disrespect."

"None taken."

"To see that our frontal coverage can be maximized by the placement of our guys and weapons in those areas that can produce the best effect. But first I have to find them. Will tomorrow be too late? We're losing daylight."

"We can risk it, but at first light, get out there."

"Yes, sir." With that the newest faux member of Easy Company traipsed off to his hut, throwing off another of his salutes to the delighted captain.

Some things in life will either jolt you, amuse you, confound you. The next morning brought a mixture of all three.

"Captain! Captain!" shouted the HQ aide. Having slept on the overstuffed chair by the fireplace, the startled commander shot to his feet, grabbing his carbine.

"What? What?" he shouted, racing toward the door, while the messenger gestured restraint with outstretched hands.

"What's going on?"

"Look for yourself, sir."

Curious would be an understatement as he brushed aside his corporal and anxiously stepped to the doorway. There, facing the startled captain, was Sarge, standing perfectly as any soldier, but perhaps a little better, in rigid attention, festooned with web belt, puttees, and canteen on a wrinkled uniform, crowned with a doughboy helmet. His right arm shouldered a Springfield rifle.

"Sarge, what the hell is this?"

"Sir, I'll feel better if you let me do this my way."

"But you're a civilian."

"You're confusing me, sir. It's okay to get killed in civilian clothes, but not in my uniform? Makes no sense."

For a moment, Smith pondered what the ole Sarge said and burst out laughing.

"Too much Point protocol, I guess. What I'm doing is illegal anyhow, so what the heck, let everything fly, with reason of course."

"Yes, sir, within reason." With a snappy salute, he bid his still-laughing captain and with two other men, who also were laughing, set out beyond the perimeter. Passing a checkpoint and establishing a password, he declared, "Now you guys look at what I'm wearin' and remember it. I don' want no holes in it, or me for that matter." Several point men went ahead to ensure that no surprises would beset the scouting party. At the end of the day, after assessing the terrain and what could be done to utilize its features, he returned to the command post.

"Well, Sarge, what good news can you give me?"

Spreading the map and looking at his scribbled notes and drawings, he pointed out the ideal locations where effective fire could be brought on any assaulting force, basically if it was predominantly infantry. If tanks were included, he pointed to a section.

"Here, sir, would be the best place for, what'cha call it, a bazooka?"

Lacy studied the map and the drawing and agreed with the ole man. "I guess you're right, Sarge. You sure you're not an officer in hiding?"

"Heavens forbid, man, I don't like to be insulted." His turn now to break out a belly whopper. Regaining his composure and looking at the vast area to be defended on the map, he asked, "I'm wondering how we'll be able to coordinate our defense, sir."

"Well, sarge, I know you guys had communication problems in the Big One, but we kind of have a little bit of an equalizer. Let me show you." From a canvas bag, he pulled out a rectangular object that resembled a miniature pay phone, an aerial protruding from the top rear.

"This, Sarge is a walkie-talkie, you might say a portable telephone without having to drop any quarters in it. By pressing this button and using the selected frequency, you can contact anyone with a similar unit. Right now, we have at least eight, if all the batteries are working. I'm going to dole them out to the most critical units."

"Well, I'll be," intoned the amazed warrior. "What won't they think up next?"

"You'd be surprised, Sarge, you'd be surprised." Instructing those units using the radios, the captain pointedly instructed, "Forget the formal designation and just tell me who you are and what post, don't waste time, and if you're going to be overrun, say so and destroy your radios."

"Well, Sarge, now we wait. OPs are instructed to alert us when they see the slightest movement that indicates an impending attack."

"Well, you can wait, cap'n, I'm goin' back out, if you don't mind."

"Sarge, you've done your bit, and you're not a combatant. I can't put you in harm's way anymore than you've been. I've stretched the limit."

"Sir, as you say, I'm a civilian. As such, you can't order me to do anything."

Before he could reply, the defiant old goat was gone. Shaking his head, Lacy could wish he had a dozen, or hundred, men like him. He could lock him up for his own safety, but he couldn't lock up that darned determination, and damned if he was going to.

Battalion had warned Easy that the weather prevented air support, so they shouldn't look for it. One bright bit of news was that the Third Army, under General Patton, was making an effort to relieve Bastogne, so it was vital that Easy hold back any attack coming their way.

"Sure, Colonel, we'll throw snowballs at them" was the sardonic, under-the-breath reply by the radio operator, who left that segment omitted when relaying the message to the captain. "All units, stay alert."

Man, that was redundant, thought Lacy. *What else are they going to say?*

"HQ, this is Murphy, out post one. I see movement. It looks like infantry coming over the rise supported by armor. I count, one, two…six tanks."

"Pull back and rejoin the defense perimeter."

"You got it."

There followed a lull, with periodic reports on the progress of the dark-clad enemy. They appeared to be wary but unaware of the force opposing them. What force? A pitiful thorn in the side. HQ didn't have to receive any transmission when the firing started. The usual artillery fire plastered the area in support of the attacking force. It was heavy but indecisive. The placement of the machine guns and the work of the mortars, however, proved damned effective in halting and turning back the first wave of infantry. The first supporting tank was knocked out by the bazooka team, which justified the position that Sarge had plotted out for them. As additional tanks rolled up to bypass the burning wreck, first one, then another got mired in the soft, wet, snow-covered ground and stalled. Sarge had picked the right point to channel the armor advance so that it was ineffective and vulnerable to antitank weapons.

Then it was quiet. The Easy grunts were buoyed by their efforts but were quick not to crow about it. This was only round one. Sarge was seen to move from one position to another, giving moral support or picking off the enemy with his rifle. He rescued some wounded men and pulled them to safety as the youngsters cheered him on as if he just scored a touchdown or smacked a homer. This was their Superman. Returning to HQ, he informed the captain of the situation firsthand, although communications beat him to it. But this lent more validity to the claims being made by the different outposts, and by all accounts, they were holding. Night brought an uneasy peace, the burning tank casting an eerie light across the landscape. Round one to the good guys.

With the coming of dawn, a renewed assault hit the line. This time, the enemy was not deterred and pierced the perimeter. The precaution that the captain had included in his defensive preparation paid off as the mobile reserve raced to the threatened areas and threw the enemy back with a ferocious counterattack all out of proportion to their size. The retreating enemy were mowed down by the flanking units, and peace prevailed, at least for the time being.

"Captain," one sergeant quipped at the aid station, "can we find out if Sarge has any relatives out here? That man is unbelievable. He was all over the place."

Lacy was silently grateful for letting him loose, hoping that he would make it through the carnage.

Outpost after outpost reported running low on ammo. Their determination had held the beach, but without ammo, they wouldn't survive.

"Cap'n, I know it's not kosher, but tonight I'm going out and see if I can round up some booty from the krauts lying out there. I've seen a few MG 42s that would come in handy." He was referring to that nasty but deadly machine gun that spat out rounds faster than you could count.

"It's risky, Sarge."

"So is trying to hold without ammo, what choice do we have?"

"You're right, but I can't ask you—"

"You're not askin', I'm tellin' ya." And with that he disappeared into the wooded area. The fighting had petered out as the sun was sinking below the skyline. A stillness, but for how long?

Before the light disappeared, the scene outside the perimeter was that of total, all-out war, bodies and equipment strewn about, mostly German. But his little force was being whittled down, little by little, prompting a pleading, *Patton, where are you?* The respite was grasped with caution, allowing for the unexpected, as these green troops had suddenly ripened to some degree and took nothing for granted. Part of this resolve was due to Sarge, as he moved from one post to another, instilling a fighting spirit. His foray onto the field produced some weapons that could be used along with an ample supply of German grenades, the potato masher, called that by its shape. But not much that would turn the tide if pushed to the wall.

Even this Superman needed to rest, and he flopped in a foxhole to regain his wind. One of the young grunts looked at him with a perplexed look and, ever thankful for his help, wondered why he would be putting his skin on the line. Sarge had a choice; the teenage soldier didn't. Still, this endeared the crazy old fool to the impressionable boys he encountered. The night passed quietly, except for probing patrols. If Jerry really knew how thin the line was, it would be kaput. Lacy kept up to tabs on his remaining units, relieving where he could to provide some rest and food. He marveled at what these "amateurs" had achieved. *Where are you, Patton?*

As the dawn replaced the night, a barrage of artillery, more intense than before, crashed among the positions and the village. The push was on, and as Sarge looked out over the field, the mass of troops attacking was frightening. This was for all the chips, everything. He grabbed a walkie-talkie from the observer and screamed into it.

"Cap'n! Cap'n! This is Sarge, bring everything you got up here. This ain't no probing attack, this is it!"

The noise was a cacophony of sound that dulled the senses, as shell bursts and automatic fire competed with one another for prominence. Sarge watched helplessly as the fingers of the plunging fire engulfed one position and then another. Being helpless only exaggerated his feeling of being useless, unfair though it may be. There were many that day who felt helpless.

Eventually, Captain Smith arrived at Sarge's hole, although crashing into it would be a more accurate definition.

"What's it look like, Sarge?"

"We're dead!"

"Good, for a minute there you had me worried."

An exploding round terminated any attempt at a profane reply.

"Any word from battalion? Any word from anybody?"

"Zilch, Sarge. Right now we're orphans."

Another close round caused a fit of cursing, something that vets will always concede reduces the tension, but don't bet on it.

Casualties among the German were horrendous, but they continued to push forward. These were no ordinary troops but Waffen SS, the most feared soldiers in the German Army. They started as a military offshoot of the Nazi political organization and became almost an army within an army. Regular units, especially in Russia, welcomed any SS unit that fought alongside them, even though they may have despised their cruelty, because of their doggedness in accomplishing any goal they pursued. They usually got first dibs on any new or special equipment, and now Easy Company was the recipient of this preferential policy.

Slowly, resignation crept into the subconscious of the Allied soldiers, even as their outward demeanor indicated nothing but confidence. Desperation will color any situation to what you would prefer rather than what exists. At some points, hand-to-hand combat resembled a bar brawl with the GIs usually prevailing, and to their credit, they could and did fight dirtier than the enemy. These local victories did nothing to forestall the inevitable, however. Facing a delayed reality, Sarge quietly said to the captain, "Now I appreciate how Custer felt."

Preparing for the end, he attached his bayonet to his rifle and girded his body f for the final effort of his life.

Lacy winked at him as if they were going on a double date, only it would be a date with destiny. Okay, as previously briefed to his men, if any were still in any condition to perform, he would fire a red flare, and all remaining troops would charge the enemy from their positions. Yes, it was desperate; yes, it was callous; and yes, it was war. How would history view this sacrifice?

Easy Company prepared to join the Light Brigade into historical and military lore. As the captain raised the flare gun upright, Sarge looked at him and gave a nod of approval. *Let's get it on.* As his finger began to squeeze the trigger, black geysers tinted with orange flames began to erupt among the charging troops, cutting huge swathes in their ranks. At first the effects were shrugged off, but the repeated hammering was more than even these fanatical troops could endure. The ranks broke slowly, then cascaded quickly toward the rear, being chased continuous with death-dealing strikes.

Turning to his rear, Sarge saw the implements of their salvation—tanks, gloriously beautiful, heavenly sent tanks. Tanks of Patton's Third Army, tanks of the Ninth Armored Division. A roar rose up from the men, wildly cheering at these chariots of deliverance and their crews. They formed a steel phalanx in front of the perimeter, while in the distance, additional tanks closed in behind a now surrendering regiment. Men were throwing all discipline to the wind, racing from their positions and embracing the tankers. Sadly, the numbers were few, but the energy more than made up for that. Sarge rose from his foxhole and was eyed skeptically by the crew of a nearby tank as they viewed his uniform.

"It's okay, I'm one of you guys. They forgot to tell me WW I was over." He received a slap on the back from the tank commander and a cigarette.

"I'm Sergeant Joe Hewitt, looks like we got to you guys just in time. The old man Patton wouldn't have approved of you guys being overrun."

"Hell, we had them just where we wanted them," boasted Sarge.

"Yeah, sure." Big grins were plastering every face within sight. "Be right back, have to get my gear." A reasonable calmness now prevailed, amplified by the lack of a feverish resistance that had dominated the senses only moments ago.

What appeared to be his grave was now simply a tortured piece of earth as he grabbed his gear and rifle. Small groups of men were hailing him and spouting all kinds of sentiments. To better participate in the revelry, he leaped upon some sandbags and began to yell and scream himself. They did it, they di—*crack*. The piercing sound caused a momentary hush of silence as hundreds of heads turned to the source. A burst of automatic fire signaled the termination of the problem, a foolhardy sniper.

The revelry was beginning to roll again until a voice shouted in disbelief, "It's the Sarge!"

He stood motionless for a moment, his eyes looking in bewilderment at the crimson stain that began to expand on his lower chest. He said nothing but appeared as if he had just awakened from a deep sleep, his eyes opening and closing as if to focus on what he could not conceive of. That he had been shot. Slowly he began to sink to the ground but was taken into the arms of his comrades, who had rushed to his side.

"Medic! Medic! Where the hell is the medic?"

It soon became apparent he was beyond the help of any medic, as his life's blood stained the snow-covered ground. The silence again was pronounce, but only because of the heartache that gripped his comrades, some breaking into uncontrollable sobs. The captain defied the mood by sternly ordering the men to collect the wounded and dead, the infantry with the tankers dealing with the prisoners. His was not an uncaring act but an effort to avoid a numbing that could impair their duty. He too felt the pain and loss, but now was not the time to address it. Besides, other brave boys lay like Sarge. He justly felt Sarge would not be lonely or alone in his journey to wherever warriors like him would be consigned. He ordered that all personal effects from the fallen be collected and brought to HQ for subsequent release to families and kin.

The next day saw an outpouring by the villagers as those who made the ultimate sacrifice were honored. Not yet buried but shrouded with colorful blankets that the women had donated to give more dignity to their forms, the youth of America were arranged in impeccable order. Upon learning that the boys were to be buried on a desolate and barren stretch of ground, the mayor had protested to the captain.

"But, sir, we have to do this, we have no alternative."

"No, no, *Capitan*, you misunderstand me. There is no honor to put these men in a place without name or history. They belong to us. Their youth was lost so that we could continue with ours. No, *Capitan*, I will not hear of it. They will be buried in our cemetery, and God be willing, it will be forever."

As usual with such an event, the sadness was barely containable, especially toward troops these people had never met before. But one thing that was not a stranger to them was sacrifice, and they too had sacrificed. Among the Easy guys were those villagers who also went to God, and the joining of these two groups before God would be celebrated for years to come. They were family, now and forever.

Back at HQ, Lacy now prepared to work into the night and beyond if necessary to draft the letters to the families of those who would not be returning home. His aide came in during a brief break, an urgency in his voice.

"Sir, I think you will want to see this." He handed the captain a worn, smudged gray envelope that bore traces of blood on one side.

"Where'd this come from?"

"From Sarge's personal effects, sir. It was in a side pocket of his tunic."

Grasping the last vestiges of his friend, he stared at it for a while and wrestled with whether he really wanted to know what it contained. Sometimes it's better not to dig too deep, especially after cultivating the feelings he had for this man, not wishing it to be tarnished by something less than the man himself. It was an irrational sentiment, but so is war, and he tossed it to the side of his desk, returning to his letters of condolences.

After each letter expressing sorrow for the families' loss, his eyes were drawn to the inert form with the force of a magnet. Eventually, he convinced himself that practicality dictated he read the contents, if only to determine if he had any relatives. They would deserve to learn of this hero.

He retrieved the envelope, a twinge of remorse awakened by the presence of the blood coating the envelope. Within the envelope was a smaller one, which he placed aside as he unfolded the letter. He leaned back and allowed his eyes to roam over the poorly handwritten words.

> Son,
> How I miss you and your mother, oh, how I miss your mother. You were just a squirt of two when I had to leave to serve my country. Your mother would explain to you as you got a little older why I had to leave. I had planned to tell you all about my travels when I got home, but things happened. You may not even get this letter, but I have to write it to keep my world from disappearing completely. This letter is my conscience.
> I had to fight bad people, and it was something I hope you will never have to do, it ain't good for the soul. I fought the bad people many times, and for being so good at it, I was promoted to sergeant. Being a sergeant meant that I had to take care of other young soldiers. It reminded me of you wearing my soldier's cap and playing with a wooden sword. We fought the pretend enemy and always won. I will never forget your laughing and hugging me after we won a battle.

One day I got hurt bad and was in the hospital. They fixed me up as much as they could, but my face, you would not know me if you saw me. Anyway, they were going to send me back to fight again when I got the letter, and they told me your mom had passed away. My world was hurt, but I still had to think of you, to care for you. You were all that I had left to remember your sweet mom. The men who were my bosses said that soon I would be sent back home to take care of you, but I still had to fight the bad people.

I wish I could live that day again. We were after the bad people, and they were fighting back hard. The people that I was boss of were getting hurt terrible, and they were crying and yelling. The noise of the fighting made me scared, and seeing my boys getting hurt caused me to stop and fall to the ground. I didn't want to die. I was scared, so scared, I got up and ran away. Nothing could stop me, and I kept on going. I don't know how long it was before I stopped, but when I could think a little, I realized that I was yellow, a coward.

Young men who depended on me died because I was not there for them. It is a shame I will live with forever. I won't bring that shame on you, because one day people will know what I did, and you will suffer for it. Know that I love you and will always remember you. Perhaps I will have the courage to mail this letter one day, but until then it will be a reminder of what I became.

Oh, God, forgive me. May I one day make amends for my faults.

Your loving father

Placing the letter on the desk and drinking in the emotions of its contents, Lacy closed his eyes and recounted the many acts of heroism this "coward" afforded to his young boys. His actions toward his son were extreme, but to him they were honest. Would he have done the same?

He eyed the smaller envelope and picked it up. Lifting the flap, he withdrew a tattered photo of a young boy, about two years old, wearing a soldier's cap and hugging a handsome man in uniform. He looked at it for some time, a remembrance of a joyous time for Sarge. Reaching into the breast pocket of his jacket and withdrawing his wallet, he retrieved a photo of a young boy, about two years old, wearing a soldier's cap and hugging a handsome man in uniform.

"O God, forgive me. May I one day make amends for my faults."

I think you did, Dad, I think you did.

The Magical Paints

After a leisurely lunch, Rocky, as he was known to his friends, retired to the den for a moment of relaxation and reflection. He was a widower and at an age where many of the things that interested him had become jaded. Not because of age, but because society had changed the value on many of the things he held dear. He was no activist or campaigner for reforms that flooded his consciousness via the papers or the air waves. His revolt was silent and confined to his acceptance or rejection of the latest cause du jour.

He had a tall build, his close cropped hair resembling frosted topping. The face was kind and angular, imbedded with two piercing eyes that eternally twinkled, inviting a collaboration of friendship. To shake his hand revealed a genuine strength of character, its grasp total and all consuming. His status was well known at the charitable events, fund raisers and other gatherings, especially among the widows and single women who deemed him a handsome catch.

Sitting in the sun lit room, made cheerful by the careful appointments made by his late wife, he scanned the walls where many awards hung in precise order. These were accompanied by other numerous forms of recognition defining his talents, placed on shelves and racks. These were not as neatly arranged as those on the wall, because they had to be dusted from time to time and his skill as an organizer fell woefully short of his wife's.

All in all, it was an impressive display of his talents, one that years before would not have seemed possible. He often dwelled on those early years and wondered, if he had taken another step on way or the other, if all this would have come to pass. The confidence he nurtured carefully was absent in the beginning, something that only grew as he made his way through the thorn bushes of life. He still marveled at those who plied their talents against odds striving to overcome the impediments that never occurred to them, or if they did, had not prepared a defense against them.

These were the ones who suffered the most, believing their fortunes were made by what they believed to be a singular talent, only to be confronted with the sorry fact that they were mundane efforts at the most and garnered little attention or acclaim. This was the weeding process that presaged an emerging group of accomplished practitioners, and rightly so, for mediocrity is the bane of perfection.

Anyone looking at his awards would think he had achieved perfection. While not the case, it pleases one to think so. As he scanned over the display, his eyes always settles upon a special certificate of accomplishment. It was his very first honor, won so many years ago. No, it was not perfection, far from it, but receiving the award was perfection in itself. He cherished it above all the other accolades he collected. It was hard earned and he remembered well the path that he had taken not only for that initial triumph, but for the many that followed.

The veil of time can be lifted to view how all this came to pass, and it began in the last decade of the 19th century when our soon to be aspiring candidate was born. His family life in New York City was similar to many other families living and working to sustain their way of living. There were no notable events that distinguished them from all the others except the common thread they all possessed, to just make it through day by day. The small house they lived in was warm and inviting, due to his mother's touch, while his father brought home the bacon.

In those days, a woman's home was her domain without question, any attempt to compromise that claim meeting with a sharp rebuke or disdain. It was a different world, where the pace was slower and more manageable, the day's events being in most cases a normal routine. In Rocky's case, his mother Rose turned the routine into an adventure on many occasions, surprising son and husband with delightful antics and cheerful singing. Her glow could only be matched by the sun at high noon. From this Rocky learned how to create a haven for himself in times of dismay, by emulating his mother's optimism.

His father Fred was no less an influence, possibly more so than his mother. He worked for a museum of art as a restorer and display coordinator.

When he was old enough to understand, Rocky's father would enthrall him with the magical properties of the beautiful art work that he was privileged to work with. Wide eyed and anticipating wonders beyond belief, he drank in every word that described a vision to behold, his mind reveling in the colors described and the impact they must have had on those fortunate enough to see them.

He was proud of his father, a kind man, a gentle bear of a man whose family was paramount in his life. His large hands belied his ability to handle and treat the artwork entrusted to him. His social graces a magnate to all who worked with him, not to mention those he just met in passing. The boy learned, little by little, the world of art and yearned to be a part of it. His parents indulged his appetite by buying him crayons so that his active mind could gallop across the spectrum of colors.

What he created brought him pleasure and no amount of carefully screened smiles or laughter from his providers. His brightened face reflected their benevolence. There was no thought of a lofty goal for him to attain, just the pursuit of adolescent indulgence.

From time to time, his father would take him to the museum. Even at this young age, his eyes filled with wonderment at the collection of paintings and sculptures. It was manna from heaven. There was a small area in the room where his dad worked that contained a desk. This he was allowed to sit at and given materials available, or those brought from home, he applied what skill he had to create art. The results weren't important at that time, just the sheer joy of putting paint or chalk to paper.

At evening dinner, he was a chatter box, inundating his mother with all the sights he had seen and the smattering of "art" he had created. Even then, there was no inkling of how this would progress, only that he was content.

School was another issue. When he began fourth grade at the age of nine, his intellectual awareness started to emerge. Things began to take shape in a more recognizable order of things, starting a process to explore the best way to express his vision of them. To this end, a pivotal figure emerged that would mold his formative talents. Miss Hurley was his new teacher, a middle aged women with a spry demeanor and a tolerance for many of the improprieties that young children are wont to commit.

Her winning smile equally matched an opposite display of disapproval when needed. This was avoided at all costs by most of the children, her presence and maternal influence cherished by her brood. Most, but not all. Perhaps in every age, in every classroom, in any school, there will be someone not in sync with the order of things. And his name was Kurt Grimes. Not a truly bad person, but enough of a challenged child of discipline that many avoided his companionship. There were efforts by some of the kids to form a friendship, but they were turned off by his crude or selfish attitudes.

Good kid that he was, Rocky was among those that failed to strike up a relationship with the boy. Children want to please, to be friendly; that is the nature of most young people. They are also quick to leave a sinking ship, but not Rocky. He would persist, always failing, but still trying, to win over a troubled soul. Kurt knew this and would manipulate Rocky countless times, his innocence blinding him to the subtle abuse.

Miss Hurley picked this up, but was reluctant to interfere, wanting the boy to solve it on his own terms. If needed, she would intervene. As the routine for the class developed, she established a free time. This was offered to the class so that they could exercise their imaginations with whatever they chose to do, within reason of course. The flurry of repetitive hand motions by Rocky caught her attention. Sensing a foolish animation on his part, she was surprised as she approached his desk, to see his hand whipping across a sheet of paper, applying a colored pencil with flourish, pausing to view the effort, and continuing with another application.

Not that the rendering was particularly appealing, but that he was so intense in what he was doing. She marveled at his single minded drive, even to the point of ignoring her as she stood by his desk. When finished, he was slightly startled at her presence, thinking he may have done something wrong. Sensing a concern on his part, she commented on a fine job he had done, relief easing his initial fear. "Thank you, Miss Hurley, it's not very good," he honestly replied. "You'll do better." "Thank you, Miss Hurley, I hope so."

So began a relationship that would chart a course toward eventual fulfillment, something not envisioned at the time, only the need to reassure a youngster that his honest efforts were appreciated. She knew the inner needs of children and addressed them when she could.

During dinner, he would relate the many happenings at school, wound up like a spring and releasing the events with just about the same speed. His parents were pleased that his new teacher met with his approval, so much so that they determined at some future date they would arrange to meet her.

Gulping down his food, his attempt to leave the table was halted by his father's shot across the bow. "Whoa, buddy, what's the rush?" "Gee, dad, I want to do some practicing with my crayons. Miss Hurley said that I would do better after I told her that I didn't do too good." His father grinned, a comfort in knowing that in this teacher, his son had struck gold. "Okay, sport, but not too long. You need to get some rest." "Okay, dad, I won't be too long."

The parents in the neighborhood volunteered shepherding duties. A mother or father walking with the children to school. On one occasion, Rocky's mom had the pleasure of meeting Miss Hurley and came away reassured that her son was in good hands. His teacher related to a thankful mother that it was important to encourage his fascination with art. Commenting on that, Rose fascinated the teacher in describing how her husband had taken Rocky to the museum one day. When the little boy entered the restoration room, he was caught up short by several discarded frames that had been reused to display some of his drawings.

"Gee, dad, those are mine. I didn't think they were that good." "As good as I want them to be, sport," was his reply to a blown away kid.

Miss Hurley was moved and allowed that she'd continue to nurture his interest as long as he wanted to. The fly in the ointment was Kurt. Finally, Rocky saw the light; his efforts with the boy were going nowhere and decided to keep his distance. Kurt soon became aware that he had become persona non grata with Rocky and this inflamed him; he would be the one to dictate relationships, not the other way around, and so he harbored a growing resentment toward his one-time benefactor.

The troubled youth had an innate sense of guile that disguised any spiteful initiative, which served to forestall corrective or punitive measures against him. He would verbally tease or taunt his classmates in such a clever way, that only he knew the sting he had inflicted. Rocky could sense the insult, but was powerless to respond, not knowing how. He could live with it and did.

Truth be told, Rocky wasn't too happy with his progress. His drawings appeared to lack a certain lock on his imagination. Try as he may, his efforts would fall short, such a daunting dilemma for a nine year old, but it was real. "Miss Hurley, am I trying too hard? I know I can't do real good pictures like I see at the museum and I know that, but I try." "Maybe it's time for you to try paints." "Paints? You mean like the real painters?" "Almost. These are not oil paints, but close enough. Here, try these vials the next free time and see what happens." "Gee, miss Hurley, thanks a lot. I can't wait."

The switch in mediums proved to be a moderate success. The easy flow and application of the paints brought a certain calmness and more studied approach, changing his former style. For such a young person, what could you expect or demand.? In his case, this new approach toward painting energized his anticipation of achievement, but only marginally his talent. Still, with every small step he could see some improvement and in an adult way, accepted that. One of his great strengths was patience and patience he would need.

Kurt noticed the collaboration between Rocky and Miss Hurley. What a teacher's pet he thought. Well, I'll show him. He convinced his parents to buy him paints similar to what Rocky was using. His design was to show him up as much as to compete with him. In fact, some of his work was better than his rival's, but not satisfying. They were cold.

How could one so young be so possessed of such animosity? Miss Hurley happily announced to the class that the assembly next week would feature the presentations of any children wishing to display their projects. Any subject would be entertained. Wow, thought Rocky, I'm goin' to get in on that. At free time, he mused on what he would paint as his project. Having decided on his subject matter, he dove into his task, but concealed the work from miss Hurley who usually strode the aisles eyeing the children as they labored. "Miss Hurley, I want to surprise you and my family, so if you don't mind, will you not look at my work?" His earnest and polite request was acknowledged with a concealed smile as she turned away.

During the next few days, his free time was a bee hive of activity. Trying different color combinations, and different formations, he slowly began to achieve a real sense of achievement. He stopped, looked at the work from different angles, resumed painting and repeated the process several times.

The day before assembly, he proudly informed miss Hurley that he was going to submit his painting to miss Peach, the coordinator of the arts and crafts award program. "Why, Rocky, that is wonderful. May I see it?" "Well, er, I want it to be a surprise. Maybe if you saw it for the first time when they showed it, you would bring me luck." "Of course, I understand, and I'll be rooting for you." "I'm goin' to bring it to miss Peach after recess." The secrecy that Rocky maintained would come at a terrible price. Later, placing the painting in an oversized folder, he made his way through the hallway toward the coordinators office.

Kurt had been eyeing Rocky all week long and was miffed at the secrecy he observed. Who does he think he is, some great painter? What's he hiding? Since he had also decided to enter the competition, mostly to upstage Rocky if he could, he trailed behind the boy as he made his way down the hall. The hopeful artist was carefree and jaunty as he walked along, almost whistling, but remembering it was against the rules. The folder under his arm was not sealed, and its largeness contributed to the painting gradually slipping out and falling to the floor, unnoticed by the lad.

There was one who did notice; Kurt. Waiting until the unsuspecting boy had entered the office, he scooped up the painting, put it in his folder and retreated to an empty room, waiting until Rocky passed by on his way back to class. He then presented his folder to miss Peach, and left. All folders would only be opened on the day of the assembly, as Kurt had learned, so Rocky could not know until then that his work was missing.

The room was buzzing with the normal drones of children vocally cavorting and a few adult words of admonishments. The atmosphere was joyful, mostly because there wouldn't be any class work for a while. On stage were several rows of the children's contributions; paintings, wood works, smalls quilts, which of course were the efforts of the female persuasion, and other items of interest. No thoughts of winning anything crossed Rocky's mind; just the participation alone was enough to enthrall him with thrill of the hunt.

The usual pronouncements were made by the principal after the Pledge of Allegiance, the singing of the national anthem and a passage from the bible. Then the room became quiet as miss Peach mounted the stairway to center stage. She had been the school art director for decades.

Her bulk caused a few thoughtless children to giggle through their cupped hands. A stern glance from a teacher brought a silent rebuke which chastened and silenced them. Miss Peach had taught for over thirty years, but was only in her early middle ages. Her girth made her seem older as did her bun style hairdo, the once golden brown tarnished with traces of gray. When she spoke, her voice was that of a mellow songbird, which dismissed any previous perceptions about her size or do.

Well liked, she returned this attribute with the same warmth in which it was received. Now she got down to business, silently urged on by the breathless contenders. One by one she introduced the various entries and its authors. Expectantly, Rocky held his breath as she reached his painting. "This entry, is a painting submitted by Kurt Grimes." Kurt Grimes? This has got to be a mistake. Look for the name on the folder miss Peach. It's mine, not Grimes'. She continued on, praising the work, then moving to the next entry.

He was frozen to his seat, and then he caught sight of Kurt. He was sneering at Rocky, a giveaway that he had pulled a rotten stunt on his competitor. He was helpless, what is he going to do, scream "that's my painting, he stole it?" What proof could he provide? He was a boy, a young boy, what did he know of deceit and what's more, how to combat it? After the assembly was over and in the hall, he sought out miss Peach. "Miss peach?" "Yes, Rocky, what can I do for you?"

"Er, well, didn't you mix up the names on the paintings?" "Which one are you referring to?" "The one you said was done by Kurt." "Oh, that was a lovely painting and it was in his folder. How could I mix that up?" "But what about my folder?" "I'm sorry my boy, but it was empty. I didn't have time to follow up on why. You did make an entry didn't you.?" "I guess not, sorry to bother you miss Peach." Rocky knew he couldn't pursue this any further and returned to the classroom where he immediately sought out miss Hurley. She too had been troubled by the fact that Rocky's painting had not been in the exhibit.

A crestfallen youngster, on the verge of sobbing, quietly related the empty folder and the suspicion that Kurt had a hand in it. "Well, Rocky, I believe you, but since you didn't sign the painting, you'd have difficulty in linking this to Kurt. I know you've had problems with him, but promise me that you will not retaliate."

A sign of his true innocence was when he inquired, "What's that mean, miss Hurley?" "It means you will not make any effort to attack him for what he did. You are the one who will suffer." "Oh, my dad taught me never to fight unless I had to defend myself, but don't worry ma'am, I won't make any trouble," She fought back a well tide of emotions, this from a nine year old going on thirty. He was being a man without realizing it. The trust in his eyes spoke volumes about the conduct she could expect from him, and she did everything in her power to resist the despising she felt toward Kurt.

To his credit, Rocky didn't confront Kurt and in not doing so, infuriated him to a point that a certain vengeance was exacted. In the aftermath of what he had shamelessly done, he received no satisfaction whatsoever.

Kurt was a child from a good home, his parents as devoted as any; somehow a disconnect from a stable home was hard to justify. He was of fair size, so that didn't enter into the equation, as were his features, which showcased a handsome boy. His intellect was sound, he was a quick learner and he understood many things not evident to the other children. So why a character so at odds with his god given gifts? Overtures were made by the children to befriend and understand him, but to no avail. He seemed to be fighting himself as well as some object of his scorn.

As the now very old Rocky reflected back to those times, he thought about Kurt and learned years afterward what became of him. The Great War was in progress and the United States eventually became embroiled in it. For whatever reason, Kurt enlisted and after training, was sent to France as part of General "Blackjack" Pershing's American army. Through news reports and because he was a native son of New York, Kurt's battle actions made headlines. During an enemy assault, Kurt and several other soldiers were manning a machine gun when a grenade landed among them

Pushing his colleagues aside and without hesitation, he flung his himself upon the deadly ordnance, smothering the ensuing blast with his body. He was fatally wounded, but refused any medical treatment until those wounded by the explosion were taken care of first. A firsthand account by one of the survivors revealed the nature of Kurt's service. He constantly volunteered for dangerous assignments and was a close comrade to those he served with. He shared what he had with them, be it rations, water and especially liquor. His buddies weren't surprised by his actions that day; he was a boon to them and would be missed dearly. He did not lose his life, he willingly sacrificed it, so said the citation on the award; the Medal of Honor.

Rocky was content that his nemesis had redeemed himself, but at such an awful cost. What turned him around so that his life now had meaning and commitment? The why didn't matter so much as the result.

Again his mind drifted back to those days of trials, setbacks and the occasional triumph.

Trying to move on, Rocky resumed his painting and as the months wore on, some improvement became apparent, but not enough to satisfy the effort expended. Painting after painting was displayed before miss Hurley and this time he signed each one, but she sensed his frustration. Was she like that at his age? Possibly. We tend to forget the hurdles that hindered us and only remember crossing the finish line.

"Rocky, after class will you stay for a few moments?" "Sure, miss Hurley, is everything okay?" "Nothing to worry about, I won't keep you long." After the other students had left, she asked the boy to have a seat near her desk. He was compliant and sensed no urgency, so his mood was relaxed—for the moment. She opened her desk drawer and retrieved a compact leather case that was fairly large. Rocky eyed the article with interest, wondering what it was. He soon found out.

"Rocky, you have tried so hard to improve your art skills and that is the heart of what we all do-effort. I have something here that may be of help to you." "Gee, miss Hurley, what is that?" Without any preamble, she replied, as a matter of fact, "Magical paints!" "Huh! Magical paints? You're kidding me, right miss Hurley?" "Not really. When you're ready, I'll explain it to you. For now take my word that these are indeed magical paints." The boy had grown close to his teacher, beyond that of a student and mentor and she felt the same way.

It was this forging of a trusting rapport that persuaded Rocky to take her word; something he would ordinarily have dismissed from a lesser person.

As she opened the case, a transfixed youngster rose and with widened eyes, looked upon the most beautiful set of painting vials he had ever seen. "These are for me?," his voice trembling. "Yes, they are. But you are not to reveal their power to anyone, not even your parents. You may keep them with you at all times, take them home if you want, but maintain the secret. Now mind you, the magic doesn't happen all at once. It has to be nurtured."

He stood there as if a magnate held him to the spot, not moving, only looking at his new found treasure, his eyes devouring every brush, vial, stencil or any other items they fell across. "Miss Hurley, I…I don't know wha……" Not finishing the sentenced he wrapped his arms around her neck. He lingered for a short while and then stepped back, his posture upright and rigid, head held high as he displayed a manly posture that indicated a resolve to hold true to the secret at any cost. She saw the bravado and in her heart she was moved by the gesture.

"Remember, patience and the magic will slowly work." With that the boy hungrily grabbed the case, nodded to his benefactor and whisked himself out the door. Just think, he said to himself, magic! Wow!

He couldn't wait for the next free time, but was a little disappointed at the scant improvement. Still he remember what miss Hurley had said about patience. The burden of youth is not lightened by worry, but only by positive pursuits. So he continued, day after day and with each endeavor he began to see a little improvement. Hey, this thing about the paints is true. It really works, he thought. Miss Hurley agreed that he was making gains and continued to encourage his progress.

At home his dad noticed the improvement. "Hey, sport, how come you're becoming a Rembrandt?" He almost spilled the secret when he impulsively answered, but caught his tongue in time. "It's the mag——better paints I'm using dad." Whew! But this confirmation of his progress propelled him to a higher esteem of what he accomplished. He began to explore more daring compositions and the colors were striking in their various combinations.

The comparisons when he first started with crayons with what he was now producing could only be rated as a dark dawn surrendering its gloom to the light of the sun, if only in relation to a young boy's abilities. No Rembrandt, how could he be?, but with a promise of something in the future.

The time flew swiftly as each day gave him a satisfaction truly earned.

Before leaving class at the end of the day, Miss Hurley asked him to stay for a short while. Noting that things were going okay and he hadn't ruffled any feathers academically speaking, there were no questions to ponder. He smilingly sat at the desk while Miss Hurley looked up from a file on her desk. "How brave are you?" "Eh, er, brave?" Oh, oh, what have I done now, he thought? "I don't mean brave in facing lions in the coliseum. I'm talking about a competition. "A competition, like what?" "Well, starting in two weeks, the schools in the city are invited to present the works of their students for a competition, an art competition to be held at the convention hall. Are you up for it?"

It was a stunner. He was being asked to showcase his talents. Was he good enough? "Miss Hurley, are you sure you want me to enter?" "Yes, I think you can give a good account of yourself, or I wouldn't be asking you." That was it he thought. If his teacher could vouch for him, then he must be ready, or good enough. "What do you think I could do?" "I'll leave that up to you. Your talents will shine in whatever the subject matter is, I know it will." "I'm not worried, I have the magical paints." Patting the case with his hand, he smiled as if it were a foregone conclusion.

His parents were ecstatic. How wonderful. He was on top of the world. Now he had to settle on a subject to wow the judges. Over and over he would pick one, discard it and pick another until the final selection was approved by his parents. Given his abilities, it would take at least a week to create the painting. Wait 'till he sees miss Hurley and tells her.

She agreed with his choice and that the free time would be used as well as any home painting to accomplish his goal. The end of the school day saw the happy and ambitious boy heading toward the stairs to meet his father waiting outside. As he was about to grab the railing, Margaret, a fellow student, stumbled and careened down the steps, screaming in pain. Instantly, he dropped the paint case along with his school books and rushed down the flight to help her. "Are you okay Margaret?" Sobbing, she could only nod no.

While attending to the injured girl, he was unaware that Kurt happened upon the accident, but instead of helping, he saw a chance

SLICED FROM LIFE

to get at Rocky. Knowing that the case was a source of pride to him, he snatched it up and in the commotion was unnoticed as he left the school.

After Margaret was taken to the nurse's office, and a little shook up, Rocky went back to retrieve his paints and books. It wasn't there! Oh my goodness, it's not there. Where is it? Turning to the dispersing students, he yelled, "did anyone see a black case?" Not getting any replies, he thundered aloud the same question, "did anyone see a black case," the desperation in his voice alarming the children. With no replies, he scampered around the landing and hallways, thinking perhaps someone picked it up for safekeeping, waiting for the owner to retrieve it. No such luck.

As a last recourse, he went back to his classroom, but miss Hurley had left for the day. He hoped that if someone did find it, it would be returned, since he had stenciled his name and class on the flap. Joining his father and relating the events that occurred, he was soothed, but not by much, when his father insisted that it was probably a misunderstanding. A good Samaritan probably had it so he shouldn't needlessly fret about its return. Oh, how he wished his dad was right.

The following morning, a quick stop to the principal's office and lost and found cast a gloom; the case not being in evidence. Upon entering class, he nervously approached miss Hurley, a sense of guilt hanging on his attempt to explain the loss of the case. "You looked everywhere?" "Yes, miss Hurley, the principal's office, lost and found, everywhere." His obvious discomfort and apparent self-inflicted wounds reduced his ability to look at her eyes. Miss Hurley surmised the heavy burden he was carrying and to his credit not trying to excuse it away.

Placing her hand on his shoulder and lifting his chin up with the other, she placed the value of the case extremely below that of her student by the kind words she uttered. "A thing like this always happens Rocky, it's not the end of the world." "It is for me, miss Hurley. Now I can't go into the competition, the magic is gone way, if it ain't returned." "After lunch, I want you to join me in the conference room, okay?"

"I guess so, but how is that goin' to do any good?" "We'll find out together."

Hoping that someone would relieve his weight of worry, he plodded through the morning and into lunch time. His sandwich tasted like cardboard and the milk like chalk. It's a wonder he even ate at all. And still, no return of the case.

Dejectedly, he entered the conference room and took a seat next to miss Hurley. "Now then, what's this nonsense about not going to the competition?" "It won't do any good, the magic is gone. I won't be able to paint. I don't feel it anymore." Placing both of his hands onto her silky smooth palms and gently squeezing them, she looked deeply into his eyes, feeling his body surrendering to failure. A more dejected person she had not seen for ages. "Look at me," she said quietly, "and listen carefully." Her words while soft, struck a cord in him and he stiffened, a sign of submission.

"The only magic is you! What force do you believe could have forged the creativity you possess? Magic? There is no such thing except that which you make with your own desire and will. The talent you have was always within you, hidden by inexperience and trial. Your own will to create the beauty you did was the magic, not something from a fairly-tale. If it were magic, why stop at what you painted? Why not become a Rembrandt or Michelangelo? You couldn't, because it wasn't magic."

The boy was almost in shock. Me, I created all that without magic? No way, I'm not that good he protested. While he believed that his teacher was trying to ease his pain, the dye was cast, his skill lost. Seeing that he was not convinced, she produced another black case. "You found it," he blurted out. "No, Rocky, this is a different one. I have several." "Several?" "Yes, and I want to prove something to you, if you'll let me." She placed a place sheet of linen paper on the table and opened the case.

There were the vials, the same ones he had in his case. She withdrew several of them along with a brush and placed them before the wide eyed, uncomprehending student. "Now, I want you to take the vials and dabble some of the paint on this mixing board. Grab the brush." He just stared at the assembly of items as if in a trance until she spoke again. "Do as I say, Rocky, do as I say." Reluctantly he poured some of the contents from each vial onto the board and grabbed the brush. His eyes silently asked her what to do next.

"Paint." "Paint?" "Yes, paint." "But I can't." "Yes, you can. Close your eyes for a moment and go back to when you first started using the colored pencils." This he did. "Do you remember how you felt?" Rocky searched his young mind, going over all the emotions he thought he may have had when he first embarked on his journey of artistry. "It's hard, miss Hurley." "Let me help. Did you feel excitement?" "Yea, I think I did." "Did your mind explode with visions of making something colorful." "Eh, er, I think I did." His resistance was soon dissolving in the mental roadway that was being laid out for him. "And I tried to do something, even if I didn't know how," his voice confidently retorted. "Was there any magic then?" "No, only what you gave me later." "No, Rocky, the only magic I gave you was your own slumbering confidence."

"Don't you see, what you started was yours and yours alone, brought alive by your own desire to explore a new world. Now, take the brush and prove me right." "Slowly, studying the brush, paints and paper, he move his hand, dabbled his brush into the soft ooze of color and move it across the virgin surface. The first strokes were tentative, then they began to have rhythm, each following effort gathering more definition and preciseness. What barrier he had conceived in his mind was now being shattered, refuting the doubts that had consumed him.

"Miss Hurley, look! I can paint, I can paint." He thrust the brush to the side and wrapped his arms around a compliant witness and believer. His head buried in her chest told her all she needed to know. The ghosts of doubt had been vanquished, and a new spirit born. "I'm sorry, miss Hurley, I didn't mean t—"

"No need to apologize," she said, wanting to stem a flow of moisture conspiring to escape from her eyes. "We have very little time. I want you to spend the rest of the week working on your presentation. You are going to compete I hope. Any ideas?"

"Well, I had this one thing which I wanted to do and now I think I can do it." "Fine, you can use the conference room during free time so that you won't be disturbed. If you wish can work at home also." The relief on Rocky's face mirrored that of his teacher. Her silent prayers were answered and a trusting heart had been renewed. He returned to the classroom, where Kurt gave Rocky a sneering smile, as if he had achieved some great mischief, which was true.

To the boy, it was another insult he suffered daily by the bully and dismissed it as he did with all the others. The following days were filled with expectations as he worked on his project. The sole use of the room was a blessing and at home his parents added additional support.

Although Rocky didn't actively try to hide his painting from Miss Hurley, she harbored a respect for his privacy and rarely entered the room. His face was like the beacon of a lighthouse at night; a constant glow of brightness. Several days before the showing, the boy leaned back, focused on his composition and sighed with relief—done! He walked to the door and just eyed his teacher, his silent manner indicating an invitation. She rose from her desk and approached Rocky, looking over his shoulder and then at him. "Finished?" "Yea, finish. Want to see?" Being so reserved, she almost dismissed her self-restraint, anxious to see the completed presentation.

Content to see a competent work of art, she was unprepared for the image that almost captured her breath. "Oh, Rocky, it's beautiful." Running to the door, she called out, "Janet, run and bring miss Peach, right away." Returning to the beaming boy, she placed her arm around his shoulder and gave him a squeeze, feasting her eyes again on the jewel before them. Miss Peach then entered the room. "Anne, is there any trouble, Janet came runn—," her words stopped abruptly as she joined the other two in front of the painting.

"Lord, its moves my heart," her words barely audible as she stood transfixed. The reaction by the two adults prompted Rocky to respond to their almost silent and static presence, just glaring at the canvas. "Thanks miss Peach and miss Hurley," pride swelling his chest as he saw the approval.

What the boy had done was not so much in the art as what it conveyed. A pure innocence. Two small boys, playing as soldiers. They wore mismatched clothing resembling uniforms with homemade ranks adorning their sleeves. On their heads were triangular hats made of newsprint that served as helmets. In the best possible pose that they could conform their small bodies to attain, they stood at attention, cherubic faces raised upwards, and small hands professing a salute across their brows. Their eyes gazed proudly toward the object of their consummate attention—the American flag.

Rocky had done more than just a painting he had enshrined patriotism. "My boy," miss Peach's trembling voice breaking the silence, "I will personally see to it that this work will be taken to the competition." Miss Hurley smiled at him and they chatted for a while after the director had left, carefully cradling the framed source of jubilation.

"You were right miss Hurley." "Oh, I was and what might that be?" "Well, this magic thing. I ain't got it all figured, but what you said made sense. But, I'm only a kid," she had to suppress a smile at his adolescent reasoning, "and it was when I started with the brush that it started to hit me. Oh, miss Hurley, thank you for being my friend." As a teacher, the instruction and guidance of a student are paramount for any teacher. To receive lavish praise and gain a confidant from any student is a bonus not to be dismissed or frittered away.

In that this dedicated teacher had been an inspiring and tireless instrument in Rocky's life, he would perpetuate her memory by rendering a portrait that hung among his collection of awards. When troubled, he would speak to her likeness, rationalizing on the counsel he felt she would have given him, the same counsel that revived his ambitions those many years ago. He later learned that his affection for her was love, love like that for a parent. Her passing rent his heart and bolstered his resolve that he would never entertain failure, but use the "magic" she gave him, to succeed.

He now drifted back to those years of his youth, to the day of the competition. Excitement abounded as he half dragged his parents to the horse trolley stop. Saturday, was a busy day, as throngs of people flooded the streets. He always enjoyed the trolley, being able to view the buildings and people in relative comfort. As they left the trolley and walked the short distance to the hall, his brisk pace gave evidence of his desire to get in and grab the best seats possible. This was tempered by his father's restraint. "I'm sure we'll be able to see everything quite well." Surely his dad wasn't as pumped up as he was. Adults!

Securing a relatively good set of seats by leaving their jackets on the arm rests, the family approached the stage where all the exhibits were on display. Wow, he thought, there's a bunch of them, and they look pretty good. The yells and screaming of the younger kids, chasing one another, bumping or pushing each other into harm's way, failed to distract the boy's enthusiasm or the search for his painting. "There dad, mom, there it is." They had not seen the completed work and their reaction was a replication of miss Peach's.

Standing behind his son with both arms draped across the boy's chest, Fred's face beamed with pride as did his wife's. They stood and stared, being jostled by the human traffic, but standing their ground.

Nothing elevates a sense of satisfaction more so than that of parents pleased by the accomplishments of their child. Rose leaned over and kissed her son's cheek, he slightly rebelling at this awkward sign of mush, especially if seen by the other kids. Ugh. Still, seeing his work on the stage meant that he belonged to whatever fraternity governed these things. It was another world he never visited before, a subdued rapture that tingled his body.

Children in the main are still children, but a few manage to rise ever so slightly to another plane, many not even realizing it. Because of this, they maintain a balanced ego. In Rocky's case, he knew that he had achieved something dear to him, but refused to surrender to the lure of celebrity. It was not his nature. He was devoted to family, made friends, and tried to be charitable; things that he embraced with a common attitude of selflessness. Being gifted as a painter was but an added addition to his trove of self-worth, not an end in itself.

An announcement from the stage brought some semblance of order to the mild chaos and the seats began to fill. When a degree of order was evident, a familiar face appeared at the lectern. Miss Peach, with her warm appeal, thanked the families and the students for their contributions. She explained that three prizes, 1st, 2nd, and 3rd, would be awarded to the winners along with several honorable mentions as well. The presentations had all been judged the night before, a convenience afforded the public, as the process was lengthy but also very dry. Those who wished, would be allowed to circulate among the paintings afterwards, providing an opportunity to observe close up the wonderful expressions of the children.

With all the entries, Rocky was a realist and resigned to whatever choices the judges had made. Of course it was in his nature to win something, but he satisfied himself that at the very least he was competing.

The first three prizes ignited tumultuous applause and cheering that graced each honoree as they received their certificate. The honorable mentions fared as well. As each returned to their seats and the welcomes of their families, Rocky and his parents prepared to leave. Fred slapped his son on the back, not so much as a consolation for not winning anything, but to acknowledge his pride for the boy. They were caught short by a belated announcement by miss Peach, who had scrambled back to the lectern.

"My dear friends, the youth of our city have served us well, as you can see by their efforts today. I never cease marveling at what these young minds can conceive of. What we have seen today is a harbinger of their future, a future holding great promise. The awards today were truly earned, a tribute to the talents of our children. It's in this vein that the judges have ventured on ground never before considered." Walking over and placing her hand on Rocky's painting, she continued.

"Every now and then, the art community is rewarded with an example of work that belongs in a class by itself." Rocky started to shake, wondering what to make of her words. His father squeezed his shoulders and seemed equally tested as well. "She's talking about me; dad, my painting," he whispered over his shoulder. He gulped hard, trying to stabilize the beginning of a roller coaster ride his stomach was entertaining.

"As judges, this is an honor and privilege very few of us will ever again entertain in our lifetimes; that it will portend a continuing effort by the artist to build upon this exquisite offering. The beauty of art is its ability to reach into our souls and to satisfy the yearning that it invokes. This painting does that and more. Let me say now………"

He didn't remember the exact words she said years ago, only that they held his family in place for the few moments that mattered. He closed his eyes and visualized as best he could those final words he did remember……… "that one day his name will be recognized as a salute to excellence. May I present to you………"

His eyes floated down the face of the yellowing certificate to the name inscribed in the legend and mouth the name miss Peach did years ago………

Norman Rockwell

Remembrance

Jennifer Alvarado, a name that invokes praise and adulation from the professional community of artists. Her chosen pictorial profession has garnered honors and attention throughout the world. The contents of her commission book are crammed with avid admirers all vying for her talents. The only exceptions she allows are those for assignments already contracted for by magazines such as, National Geographic, Archeology, Wild Safari, and other noteworthy issues.

In some instances she will forego a scheduled photo shoot to cater to a worthy charity, the disappointed customer usually allowing the postponement graciously, feeling fortunate to have been on her list in the first place and knowing delayed appointment would be honored at a later date. Alvarado was no prima donna, which allowed her to reign with good intentions and to regulate her work accordingly.

Her passion was wild life over that of the domestic scene, but that did not detract from one because of the other. To see her work was to see a personification of absolute beauty and detail, often compared to the work of the famous Ansel Adams or Mathew Brady of Civil War fame. She truly would brush aside the comparisons with the modesty of one picking out a frozen TV dinner. But she would not compromise on her work. All or nothing.

It was this attitude along with professional accomplishment that provided her with a commission several months before. Africa Today, a magazine spotlighting the continent's varied treasures, offered to underwrite a lucrative photo safari. This was manna from heaven, not only for the opportunity to display her talents, but because showcasing these varied animals and the threats that they face, including extinction, was a driving force.

This was not her first foray into Africa. A year and a half ago, she had negotiated a short term photo safari and had brought her two children with her. Mason, a ten year old wide eyed and eager to see the wild, and Maryn, a twelve year old in used with the same artistic ability as her mom. Oh how excited they were, awaiting the adventures they would share with each other and the fine people they would come in contact with. She remembers the first day and how it would shape their future. And this is how it began.

* * *

"Gee, mom. I can't wait to get out into the bush, is that what you call it?" "You'll get your chance honey, but for now I want to see this wild animal refuge center and what they do. It looks interesting."

Before setting out for her assignment, she made time to visit this intriguing establishment. Mark and Sue Watson had been heartbroken at the sight of injured or sick animals from the wild cast aside like cord wood. Determined to do what they could to help these unfortunate and beautiful creatures, they received permission from the Tanzanian government to set up a camp for their rehabilitation. Having some business contacts in the States, a campaign to raise start-up funds was started, with wide publicity aimed at the heart as well as the pocketbooks. Gradually, a foundation was formed and all proceeds diverted to this magnanimous cause.

They were delighted when meeting Jennifer, hoping any publicity generated by her would be a boon to the refuge. Although not her designated assignment, she said that it would be her privilege to do what she could. The prior photo shoot would not be compromised by a week's delay and she looked forward to exhibiting the work the Watsons had been doing.

"Mom, I think that's cool. Boy, just think of all the animals that are going to be famous because of you." "Well, honey, not that they would be famous as much as being noticed; how they have suffered, and what these kind people are doing to help them." "I guess that's what I mean, Mom. Somebody ought to know what's going on here." Maryn had the same read on these creatures as her mother and didn't need much to reconcile their views. If fact, Maryn had started to take up photography with an inexpensive digital camera Mom had bought for her birthday. "One day I'll be as good as you, Mom." "I have no doubt of that, honey."

Mason was more of a down in the dirt type, who liked to take on any challenge as long as his mother made sure he didn't bite off more than he could chew. Where Maryn was a sedate, lovely, light haired girl with beautiful brown eyes, Mason was a prototypical stevedore product. Slightly shorter than his sister, he had a diminutive build that was not typical for a boy of his age, being muscular, but not overly so. His darker brown hair complemented his equally dark eyes. Brother and sister, while competitive, were not combative, and in many ways, supportive of each other's endeavors.

The Watsons led the family through the compound, which was divided into screened sections, where same type animals could be housed. The areas were generous, allowing a certain amount of freedom for the occupants. Ostriches, various birds, a multitude of gazelles and other wounded or ill denizens lived almost as if they were on the free range. The scope of this enterprise duly impressed the family, the energy to keep it operating a seemingly daunting task. The attendants were chosen for their commitment to and knowledge of the animals in their care. Living on site, the Watsons were able to ward off any problems or emergencies within reason.

The children were enthralled to say the least. Any seemingly tame animal that nuzzled up to the fence and with a nodding permission by their hosts, the children delighted in petting or feeding them. The various types, and colors were contrasted against the drab ground and pale ground foliage that managed to survive the penned in tenants attention. The variety of trees provided shade for the ground bound while the primates delighted in hopping from one branch to another. "What happens to them, Mrs. Watson?" asked Maryn, clearly drawn to the condition of some that begged for sympathy. "If they survive in good condition, we transport them back to their native area, or an area that will support that type." What about the others? "You mean the ones who may not make it?" "Yes, Mam." A momentary pause reveals a brief sadness in her eyes, her mind's eye recalling the countless moments when there was no alternative but to put an animal down. "We can't save them all, but we try to ease their passing."

She changes the subject for the children's sake, their lives will have their own share of down times soon enough. "You may be surprised to know we have a baby rhino." "You do?, oh may we see it?" "Of course, follow me." The joyous expectations of the children were infectious to the accompanying attendants, a break from their worthwhile, but at times, mundane chores. Lawani, a woman employed by the refuge was a sort of guide/chaperone to the children, and could hardly keep pace as they pulled her along to the enclosure where the baby animal was kept. Wani, as she was called, caught her breath and with a nod of approval from Mark, brought the children into the enclosure that housed the young animal.

"She," "He." "Oh. He is so sweet," squealed Maryn as the uncertain animal backed away slightly. "Here." Wani gestured, take this vegetable and offer it to him. "Slowly, the little tyke approached the pro-offered morsel and began to contently consume it, all the while with Maryn gently rubbing his head. "What's that little bump near his nose?" Mason asked. "One day that will be his horn," Sue volunteered. "You mean like I see in the movies?" "You bet. And I'll bet you can't tell me what it's made of," a sneaky smile crossing Mrs. Watson's lips. "It's like cow bone, ain't it?" "No, believe it or not, it develops from a protein, much like what your fingernails are made of, or your hair, even hooves of animals." "What?, no way," the boys voice challenging years of experience. "It's true Mason, most animals have horns that are covered with a thin layer of this covering, but they are true horns, not so the rhino's."

These and other revelations had the children's minds swimming with visions and wonders that so captivated them, it was a wonder they could calm down at all to eat lunch. "Later," Wani, said, "I will show you a nice surprise." That was the wrong thing to say to children who had just settled down and were supposed to eat, but an aroused hunger won out, and only then just by a hair.

The lengthy lunch did nothing to dull the anticipation of Wani's "surprise." "Come, children. I will show you a wonderful thing." Wani's voice was light and flowing, the children won over to her maternal care. "Mom, Wani's going to show us somethin' cool, okay?," knowing a refusal was as distant as the nearest galaxy. Dashing to the woman's side, each clutching a hand, they were steered down a path that led to an enclosure not much different from the others. A well of excitement was bubbling in the young adventurers when Wani said, "Look, over there, at the bottom of the tree."

Eyes suddenly opened in wonderment, they saw three lion cubs. One was a little bigger than the other, but all were of a sand, tawny color. Their ears were so large as to make them look like stuffed animals, as did their tails. Their faces reflected a cuteness that just spelled "hug me." Surprisingly, Wani swung open the gate and motioned the still mesmerized children inside. The attention of the baby cats, as to be expected, was diverted to their guests. Two were younger than the larger one, he being about nine months old. Slowly they approached the strangers and the smaller ones after a few circles of the group, just sat on their haunches and yawned. The larger one seemed more adventurous and approached the kids, who backed away slowly, unsure of what to expect. "Do not be afraid, my little ones, harm you he will not." As if to prove that point, the cub nuzzled his face into Maryn's hand and ran his body across her legs, almost toppling her.

Satisfied that he earned her attention, he then turned toward Mason. Somewhat startled, the boy froze, not knowing what to expect, when the juvenile cat then plopped to the ground at his feet, rolled onto his back, and raise his paws outward. "He wants you rub his belly," quipped Wani. "He what,?" shot back Mason. "He wants you scratch his tummy." Disbelieving, but wanting to see if this was true, the boy slowly bent down and cautiously placed his fingers on the exposed abdomen, flinching as if to pull back if he sensed any danger. His scratching motions soon sired a purring reaction from the prone and completely comfortable would be predator.

The docile response emboldened Mason to increase his massage and the cub reacted with a sound that sounded as if he were snoring! "He likes you, boy. A friend you now are." "I hope so." Maryn had taken the opportunity to photograph the interplay, adding these shots to the others she had started to accumulate. "I want eight by ten glossies, girl," shot the lad, as if he had proven his bravery and wanted it recorded for history. "What a ham. I was shooting the cub, not you," she jokingly replied. "We come back tomorrow," Wani said, for now they have to be fed and cleaned." "See you tomorrow"……the words halted abruptly. "Hey, Maryn, what are we going to call him?"

Remember the story mom used to read to us long time ago, about the bull?" "Oh, you mean, Ferdinand?" "Yes, Ferdinand." "I think that's sissy, how about Max or Killer?" "Oh, shush, Ferdinand is perfect, right Wani?" "Whatever you call him, listen he will." "Okay, then. It's Ferdinand." "Oh, I pity him when his friends find out what we named him," chimed in a chagrined Mason. With no opposing support, he relented and grunted his approval. For the rest of the day, Maryn, observed proudly by her mother, exercised her camera to the limit, her posture in composing a prospective setting revealing the promise of a future paralleling her mother's.

The day was fulfilling, but tiring. As the sun began to set, they retired to austere, but comfortable quarters to await a new dawn. The sounds of the night, not only from the enclosures, but beyond, signaled the variety of life not seen during the day, stirring the imagination to couple each roar or grunt to some perceived animal creating it. An exercise in futility, but entertaining, as nothing sirs up the intellectual appetite as does the unknown.

The children were up before the sun, but had to be tempered in their anxiety to explore anew. Wani was still asleep in her hut and any exploration would have to await her good services. Impatiently, but allowing mom to sleep without bugging her, the children could not help but marvel at the lion cub. Would they be able to see him again? They so wanted to. Their desires were fulfilled, when after breakfast, Wani appeared at their threshold. Jennifer had agreed to accompany the Watson's to other sections of the refuge to record several exotic animals. She allowed the children free reign, with moderation, meaning no wild antics, such as would give Wani the reason to regret her services.

Their first choice was to revisit the cubs, really Ferdinand. The close and personal touch of this animal was like magic and perhaps it would vanish as quickly as it had appeared. Their fears vanished as soon as they stepped into the enclosure. Romping up to them, the amiable feline again nuzzled Maryn and fell prone to receive a belly rub by the boy. Seeking a more active partnership, they began to run and enticed "Ferdy," as they now called him, to chase after them. He would pounce on Mason with a still cub-like growl and wrap his paws around the "victim's" shoulders, all along keeping his claws retracted, his paws giving the appearance of old fashion catcher's mitts.

They would roll around the ground, the cub allowing Mason to fend off his attacks with pulled punches and clenches. The result was fun beyond anything they'd ever experienced, not to mention the smell that accompanied their return to quarters. Boy, did life get any better than this? Day after day saw the affection increased along with the trust that it engendered. While the other animals garnered some of their attention, the lion's share, as the pun would go, went to Ferdy.

Still, what they did get to see was not entirely overshadowed by their closeness to the cub. Maryn was captivated by the Thomson and Grant gazelles, those that had been healing and would later be released. Her future album would contain their images as well as that of Topi and Hartebeest. Ostriches and Secretary birds provided a welcomed contrast with the mammals. But a medium sized bird caught her eye and she asked Wani what kind it was. She didn't know the formal name, but it was a Yellow Billed stork, adorned with a pinkish white body and black wings and tail, coupled with a dull orange face. "Why is it here?," asked Maryn. "This bird is wading bird and much it eats comes from ponds or not so deep water. It no can do that." Looking closely, the youngster saw that the lower half of a blunt yellow bill, was damaged. The poor creature could not fend for itself and had to be force fed.

Eventually and sadly for the children, it was time to move on. They knew it had to end sometime, but young minds always find a way to put into seclusion those things that are not tolerant of their youthful desires and so are accepted only at the last possible moment. Jennifer thanked the Watson for their hospitality and the chance to discover the humanitarian effort carried out by such a dedicated group of people. And they hoped that the efforts of Jennifer would translate into world and financial support, so desperately needed. The children hugged both hosts as only children can, the Watsons relishing every embrace.

"Mom, Mr. Watson, we have someone else we'd like to say good-by to. Is it okay?" Everyone knew who that was and they nodded in the direction of the now familiar enclosure. Upon seeing his friends approaching, Ferdy raced to fence, pacing back and forth as if to say, "c'mon, let's play." He sensed their lack of motivation and was puzzled. Both children knelt at the base of the barrier and placed their faces into the wiring. The cub came up and nuzzled against their noses and mouths, again pacing back and forth as if to encourage them to come inside. There would be no further games or play and for a while the saddened pair just were content to pet him through the fencing. The cub then sat in front of them and with mournful eyes, seemed to know that their time was over. As they walked away, their feline friend just sat there as if he would never move again.

Returning to the waiting group, more heartbreak was in the offing. Standing off to the side was Wani. With no hesitation, they bolted to her outreached arms and folded their bodies into hers. She held them tightly, lowering her head to the top of theirs and planting a prolonged kiss, first on one than on the other, each signaling a love of the heart and mind. There was no effort to speed this good-by, for it would be the last. With muffled sobs, and moistened eyes, both refused to disengage, until Wani, knowing that her own reserve was quickly melting away, grabbed their hands and placed them to her lips. "Remember me always, my little ones as I will remember you."

With that she turned and walked away. Yes, she would be remembered. Always.

* * *

The children were excited. A new adventure awaited them, but this would be more extensive than their earlier experience. Mom was going to capture the great migrations of the Serengeti plains. They loved the flight over and the water transport to Musoma, a town on the lower end of Lake Victoria. From there they would travel by convoy to the Mara river, and using two boats, the party would travel to a point where the borders of Tanzania and Kenya to the north nearly meet. To envision the great mass of Wildebeest, driven by their needs for water and feed, crossing boundaries of two nations, is a spectacle not to be missed or forgotten.

It's this exploitation of nature by its creations to heed their instinctive drive that compels one such as Jennifer to capture every essence, every motion, every nuance of survival so that the beauty and sometime desperation can be experienced. With electricity in the air, the party leaves the town by transport to a location on the Mara river, where they will board the boats. Loaded with camping equipment, including tents, survival gear, food and water and a dozen other necessary items, they will journey along the waterway to a location that will avail them of the best possible vantage point for observation of the expected migration. The children are ecstatic, and their mother more so, but maintains a modest restraint. It wouldn't do to allow an over active emotion to dictate photography.

Maryn of course continues to emulate her mother's art with the still trusty digital camera she first possessed. Mason just gawks and whistles at the newest thing that catches his interest. Because the Tanzanian authorities have restricted any but the most limited tourist activities, it was with the greatest difficulties that Jennifer was able to secure a permit for her photo shoot. As with keeping with this permission, a Maasai Morani or warrior familiar with the area had been assigned to the venture. His word would be law. There would be no abuse of the privilege and indeed this was a coveted privilege that had to be honored without exception.

Among the novelties carried on board was several packets of MREs, Meals Ready to Eat that had been obtained from military surplus back home. While not ideal for extended durations, when coupled with traditional food, fresh game or packaged commodities, they were a source of quick nourishment without the fuss of an extended meal. The kids kind of yucked at the prospect of eating foiled food, ugh.

The night before leaving, a torrential downpour from the north caused the river to receive an abundant addition to its already swollen condition, the waters roiling as if angry as the hissing and crashing waves seemed to say. Other than the soaking they received, all arrived safely at the designate point and began to set up camp. The boats were only partially unloaded as the day was almost gone and the sounds of the night sentinels made themselves known. Assured by the warrior that there was no danger, the camp was set up quickly, Jennifer hoping to get a good night's sleep and the children likewise. "Mom, I left some of my gear in the boat, can I go get them?," Maryn pleadingly asked her mother. "Make it fast, and take Mason with you. You need your sleep, so hurry it up." Taking the warrior at his word, they had no fear of something happening to them and jaunted down to the river bank.

"What now?," chimed Mason. "I left my camera here and my nighties. You know how cold it can get at night." "Huh, nighties, you mean those heavy flannel bloomers." "Oh, Mason, you are so crude." Then, as so often happens, there's always the exception that proves the rule, in this case, the mooring rope that had seen better days and due to age and decay, began to part at the pull of the river's currents. Strand by strand, it soon parted, the boat being torn from its mooring and into the fast moving stream. Their screams were blotted out by the thrashing noise of the waves, their destination now unguided to who knows where.

Abject terror would be too mild a description for what the children were experiencing. Clutching each other tightly, their options next to nothing except to pray that their boat didn't overturn or sink.

After several hours unbroken by any relief, eventually their fears surrendered to the power of fatigue and sleep. Still in embrace, they slumped to the floor boards and lay still for many hours until a sharp jolt aroused them. The swift current had rammed the unmanned craft onto a boulder strewn bank, almost clear of the raging water, and enough to prevent further movement. Wide eyed, the first instincts of the children was to flee the craft and this they did without pause.

After several steps, Maryn grabbed Mason by the arm and shouted, "stop, we're okay now, but we won't be if we just run.

"What do ya mean," replied the still terrified boy. "Okay, we're away from the river, but we have nothing, nothing but what's in that boat." The boy's eyes traced the direction of her arm pointing at the stranded craft. "Gee, Maryn, you're right. I was too scared to think. Boy am I glad you're my sister." She felt a sense of calm come over him and shared in that emotion as well. They would need all their wits to survive until rescued, a given, bolstered by a supreme confidence that their mother would find them. Carefully, they climbed over the gunwale and made their way to the stern where a canvas covering stretched over a mound of supplies.

"Look for those MREs that mom bought," the instant reply from the boy being an "ugh." "Look picky, its food and where else are you going to find it? There's no 7-11 around that I can see." His carping was automatic, not reflecting his true acceptance of what his sister was stressing. Fortunately, the food packs were secured in plastic bundles, and after gathering quite a few, back packs were loaded with the haul. "Grab a couple of those jump suits, we're going to need them in this bush." This proved to be a wise move, as they were sturdy and could withstand rough treatment. The material also provided some warmth which would be needed at night when the tempcratures dropped.

Several canteens were added to the pile and with each one carrying a load, Mason of course volunteering to take the heaviest, they moved inland. If the boat stayed where it was, it could help a search party find them. That was soon dashed as a rogue wave swept the inert craft into the roiling current yet again. Mason gulped hard at the sight. "Gee, Maryn, we're really lost now." Resorting to his Boy

Scout training, and partially to impress his sister, he began to arrange the rocks and boulders from the bank to spell out SOS. "What do we do now?," he said, looking hopefully at his sister. "I think we should move inland a little in case the river decides to ruin our day by flooding. We can look for anything lying around to build a shelter.

Hauling the supplies was a little difficult, but manageable and they proceeded to a plot of ground where some stilted trees provided some shade and a bounty of broken branches littered the area. Being an avid subscriber to the Survivorman TV show imbued Mason with the same sense of improvisation that his hero displayed. Could he duplicate, at least in effort, what the survivalist had demonstrated in his shows? Only time would tell. Gathering a bunch of branches with Maryn's help, he proceeded to construct a skeletal frame work over which he draped a plastic tarp. This provided some protection from the sun, but what about the night? They would have to brave it through—no matches.

The night was uncomfortable, but the jumpsuits helped to some degree. Holding each other for body heat gave some relief, not so much for the temperature gain as for the solace each gave to the other. Truly brother and sister. The night echoed the familiar sounds heard so long ago. Sleep was fitful, but eventually the draw of strain and tension induced a welcome release.

The benefit of the MRE meals beside their nutritional value, rested in their ability to self-heat. A chemical reaction eliminated the need for a fire and so our hungry duo indulged in sorting out the packs to suit their particular tastes. "You know, Mar, maybe I was too quick to dis these things. Not bad." Hunger has a way of transforming the bland to the delectable. "We have to be careful and ration. We don't know how long it will be before they find us." 'Before they find us.' That alone was enough to inspire Mason in the belief that indeed they would be found. What a few words can do.

After breakfast, a stroll around the area to see what the land had to offer, which wasn't much by the sight of the vegetation, dusty ground, a few hillocks and some dense bushes. Maybe they could find some eggs in the clumps, but quickly nixed the idea. Raw eggs did not fit on their menu. Hand in hand, casually as tourists on vacation, they walk her and there, even back to the river bank which was still angry it seems. Not to be denied, Maryn used her camera to capture a few shots, but more so to boost her confidence. A bird here, a lizard there, it seemed so natural as if meandering through the park.

As the day lengthened, the heat began to tell on them. Frequent visits to the river for replenishment of the canteens were many, but dangerous. Crocodiles were known to infest the river at certain points, especially during the migration crossings. This was a known fact, their mother listing that as a point of interest for the photo ops and the kids recoiling in feigned horror at something they could only imagine. This ignorance was a disaster in the offing, but their good fortune allowed them to avoid the unthinkable.

Back at the camp, a hysterical Jennifer was at her wits end, not knowing the fate of her children. That a boat was missing at least grounded her and the warrior's belief that somehow they had been swept downstream, the rotted rope adding confirmation. The second craft had been damaged and would take some time for repairs to be effected. Only then could they pursue what they believed was the only course that seemed logical. Time wears a snail's disguise as the party worked frantically on repairs. But urgency could not replace skill in eliminating the damage. It would take precious time, time for Jennifer to torture herself with all kinds of fates that could befall her loved ones.

As night came on, the duo repeated their previous night's efforts to get some sleep. Occasionally they would hear a growling or roar that frightened them, because it seemed to be closer than before. Oh, for a fire. Mason tried turning a pointed branch into a piece of wood and spinning it with a bow string with his laces, but without success. The night was pitch black, the stars as bright as they had ever seen, but it was what they couldn't see that was their main concern. If anything, they were trying to be brave for each other, for if one faltered, so would the other. Again, sleep overpowered their fears and the fates deemed that no voracious animals would contend with them.

The sleep, while helpful, could not give them the refreshment they needed. They had breakfast and decided to explore a little further from their shelter. Maybe, just maybe, they could spot something that might help them. Heading inland, they approached a dense growth and were on the verge of circling away from it when a tremendous roar froze them in their tracks. They looked at each other as if the answer was in each other's eyes. Then they saw it. Masons eyes opened so wide that the irises failed to touch both upper and lower lids. Maryn squeezed her brother so tightly he could barely breath.

There, emerging from the clump, was a male lion. But this was the largest that either had ever seen, either at the zoo, at home, in animal books, or at the movies. They could run, but to where? Instead they stood rooted to the spot, knowing that any resistance would be futile. As if to confirm their fears, the lion charged, and Mason, trying to protect his sister in a feeble way, cast her aside and stood in her place. There was no stopping the feline brute as his course was plotted and aimed directly at the frightened boy. At the moment of contact, the lion cast his quarry to the ground and straddled him, his fierce eyes focused on the prone form. Closing his eyes, Mason murmured a quaking prayer and prepared for the worst. The animal lowered his head and Maryn turned away, not wanting to witness her brother's end.

The boy closed his eyes tightly as the big cat opened his mouth and proceeded to……whip a slobbering rasping tongue with a slurping motion across the boy's face and neck several times. "Help," Mason's mind screamed, "he's tasting me before he eats me." "Get away from him you brute," Maryn yelled, as she threw a rock into the animal's flank. Unperturbed, the hulking beast turn his head and stared at his attacker, slowly moving away from the boy and walking slowly toward a petrified youngster. She too closed her eyes, hunching her shoulders in anticipation of a gory demise. After what seemed like a small sliver of eternity, she felt a slight, moist pressure against her hand. Startled, she opened her eyes to see that the lion was nuzzling her fingers and licking them. His mane completely engulfed her, only her legs being visible.

* * *

As night came on, the duo repeated their previous night's efforts to get some sleep. Occasionally they would hear a growling or roar that frightened them, because it seemed to be closer than before. Oh, for a fire. Mason tried turning a pointed branch into a piece of wood and spinning it with a bow string with his laces, but without success. The night was pitch black, the stars as bright as they had ever seen, but it was what they couldn't see that was their main concern. If anything, they were trying to be brave for each other, for if one faltered, so would the other. Again, sleep overpowered their fears and the fates deemed that no voracious animals would contend with them.

The sleep, while helpful, could not give them the refreshment they needed. They had breakfast and decided to explore a little further from their shelter. Maybe, just maybe, they could spot something that might help them. Heading inland, they approached a dense growth and were on the verge of circling away from it when a tremendous roar froze them in their tracks. They looked at each other as if the answer was in each other's eyes. Then they saw it. Masons eyes opened so wide that the irises failed to touch both upper and lower lids. Maryn squeezed her brother so tightly he could barely breath.

There, emerging from the clump, was a male lion. But this was the largest that either had ever seen, either at the zoo, at home, in animal books, or at the movies. They could run, but to where? Instead they stood rooted to the spot, knowing that any resistance would be futile. As if to confirm their fears, the lion charged, and Mason, trying to protect his sister in a feeble way, cast her aside and stood in her place. There was no stopping the feline brute as his course was plotted and aimed directly at the frightened boy. At the moment of contact, the lion cast his quarry to the ground and straddled him, his fierce eyes focused on the prone form. Closing his eyes, Mason murmured a quaking prayer and prepared for the worst. The animal lowered his head and Maryn turned away, not wanting to witness her brother's end.

The boy closed his eyes tightly as the big cat opened his mouth and proceeded to......whip a slobbering, rasping tongue with a slurping motion across the boy's face and neck several times. "Help,"

Mason's mind screamed, "he's tasting me before he eats me." "Get away from him you brute," Maryn yelled, as she threw a rock into the animal' flank. Unperturbed, the hulking beast turn his head and stared at his attacker, slowly moving away from the boy and walking slowly toward a petrified youngster. She too closed her eyes, hunching her shoulders in anticipation of a gory demise. After what seemed like a small sliver of eternity, she felt a slight, moist pressure against her hand. Startled, she opened her eyes to see that the lion was nuzzling her fingers and licking them. His mane completely engulfed her, only her legs being visible.

Flabbergasted, Mason saw that it was Ferdy, jowls clamped tightly on the snout of a crocodile that had ventured toward the unsuspecting boy. With great strength, the lion whipped the reptilian form back and forth until it was thrown back into the current. He eyed the floating reptile, dead or alive, until the water's movement took it away. Ferdy approached the boy, planted a very moist tongue across his head and returned to the comfort of his shade. From that moment onward, neither child had any more fears for their safety.

As night approached, the day's events had proven exhausting. The chill was beginning to wear on the castaways, but they were also inventive. Mason cuddled up to Ferdy and Maryn soon followed. Oh, the warmth was delicious, less so the smell. An uniformed observer would have been hard put to define the scene of two children firmly entrenched on the form of a predator.

Again the ritual of the morning routine entailed the usual MRE breakfast, which when offered to Ferdy, resulting in a quick sniff and avoidance. But Lions have to eat too, and it was still early in the morning when the overnight visitor disappeared. It was not noticed until they called to him and there was no reply. Had he abandoned them? Well, he was wild, it's not like he was a house pet. This brought little consolation and fostered a feeling of renewed abandonment. This was dispelled when their friend appeared and strolled beneath the tree, promptly dozing off. There were trace of red around his mouth and on the tips of his paws. It soon became obvious—they had their breakfast, he had his.

Somewhat later, and contrary to what lions usually do, Ferdy began walking away from the camp, occasionally looking back. With no understanding to what he was doing, the children just looked and thought he was leaving the again. He returned, nudged them, and again walked away, looking back at them. "You think he wants us to follow him?, Maryn asked. "It could be," Mason replied. "What the heck, let's give it a go." People always seem to think that when they talk to an animal, it will understand what they're saying. True or not, it displays a bond and trust unique in this type of relationship. Witness the following. "Hey, Ferdy, hold up while we get our gear together." And that is exactly what he did, resting on his haunches and only moving when the pair started the trek from the camp.

Being their protector, they could only pray that what followed would be a step toward rescue. If only mom knew that they were okay. She must be a wreck, but they knew she would fight Hell to find them. Mom never let them down and they held that feeling even now. Oh, how they missed her. But these kids were resilient and a lesser display of fiber may well have resulted in a far different outcome.

After several hours, their thirst eased by a few watering holes, the scenery became more hospitable, the grasses thicker, the shade of the trees darker. It even seemed cooler. Then there came a view only seen in the movies or magazines. A pride of lions, laying in the shade in various forms of contortions. Flitting back and forth were the cubs, biting a stray tail here, or engaging in mock combat. Ferdy's presence and his loud roar left no doubt as to who was boss.

To get a prospective on what the children were going to experience, the social makeup of the pride had to be examined. Aside from the dominant male, the lionesses are the most permanent members. Lesser males may come and go but the females are the glue of the group. It is the females who do the bulk of the hunting and work as cohesive teams when cornering their prey.

There also may be a predominant female among the family as there is with the male. Together the pride is the only permanent social group among cats, similar to the social compact of elephants, the females again the bonding force of the group. All other cats are solitary. The survival of any animal or pride is the availability of food. The great migration of the Plains provides this source, as over a million and a half Wildebeests and half a million zebras, make their annual trek to and over the Mara river. This had been Jennifer's and the children's destination, and perhaps it could still be if dame fortune smiles upon them.

It was no wonderment that Ferdy was the king. His sheer bulk precluded any challenge to his authority and the females were submissive to his demands. As the newcomers made their way among the pride, several cubs approached and not having encountered humans before, easily ingratiated themselves with their guests. A mother began to rise to challenge these strangers when Ferdy's roar of admonition forced her to retreat. With his presence, the children felt somewhat secure and blessed with having a ring side seat among these wonderful creatures. Whipping out her camera, Maryn will one day proudly show her mom that she lived the life of the wild. The matrons were beautiful subjects, regal in their postures, the cubs adorable in any attitude. Ferdy stood royally at the center, surveying his domain, his form majestic and powerful. Gee, mom, I bet you never had pics like these.

There have been instances where humans have co habited with packs of animals in the wild, proving that there is a certain degree of acceptance. Whether the social compact of the pride contributed to the strangers' acceptance is debatable, but the debate is secondary to the accomplishment. With the night coming on, the huntresses, leaving the cubs with the older ones, left the refuge and stole into the night. Ferdy again became a favorite toaster oven and except for the usual audible nocturnal interruptions, a quietness settled upon the sleeping denizens.

When a kill is made, the game is usually consumed by the hunting group on the spot. If a male is present, he will usually get first dibs and in this case there were only two younger males that shared in the bounty, no threat to the pride's leader. The returning females would now be able to nurse their cubs, and the males reverting to their sleeping modes. Even a young lion was valuable. Females faced certain danger from hyenas and a male lion could prove to be a deterrent to any hostile action by these tenacious predators. They would scavenge, but attacking for a kill was not alien to them.

Again, the waking pair had their usual breakfast, even sharing some with the not so discriminating cubs. Ferdy would take his leave of absence, possibly finding the remains of the night's kill. His absence did not emboldened any adverse acts from any of the pride, but they kept their movements limited, not wanting to tempt fate.

* * *

The camp was buzzing with activity, the repairs to the boat finished. The anxiety of Jennifer could only be measured by the worry creases in her face, her demeanor steadfast and determined. They would cast off hopefully for a rescue mission and not a recovery. To broaden their chances of success, another boat was employed to troll along the opposite bank, expanding the chances of locating them. She refrained from even thinking that the boat may have sunk, relying only on her hopes and prayers to boost her resolve.

It had been almost three days and time was the enemy of this expedition, but to race pell-mell could prove disastrous; speed could obscure clues and had to be moderated. All this hung heavy on a mother as it would on any mother. Relief swelled within her as they shoved off at last. Along with the warrior were veteran trackers and others familiar with the terrain. As the banks slipped past, lookouts, with years of experience in reading the countryside, scanned with great intensity. If something was out of the ordinary, it would stand out as clearly as any object illuminated by a flashlight.

* * *

"Maryn, do you think they'll ever find us?" The boredom had begun to cause Mason to think too much about their predicament, despite the novelty of living among wild animals. "Hopefully before our food runs out, but yes, I know mom will find us." "You know, I wonder if anyone will believe that we actually lived with the lions." "I don't see why not," Maryn said, "how about that lady that lived with gorillas. Would you have believed that?" "How 'bout Tarzan?" "That doesn't count, it was fiction." "Oh, yeah, your right." Ferdy was a source of comfort, and they couldn't have made it this far without him or indeed been able to be accepted by the pride. But they couldn't stay here forever. Their options of movement and entertainment was severely limited, prompting them to wonder how individuals lived solitary lives like this.

After hours of cruising, a lookout shouted to the pilot. "Over there, I see something on the bank." The rush of bodies to the gunwales caused the boat to list sharply and almost swamped the craft. Turning toward the sighting, the bow crunched upon the beach and hung fast. An anxious Jennifer was helped ashore and the warrior pointed to the assembled rocks that spelled out SOS. Hope soared, but only in that they had found where to children had landed. Jennifer knelt to one knee and grasped one of the rocks, bringing it to her cheek, a reminder and substitute for her cherished ones.

"Missy, Missy," exclaimed one of the trackers, "look, I find." In his hand was the remnant of a MRE packet. "They were here, they were alive. Keep looking, they may be close by." Calling over the other boat, all available persons were ordered to fan out and look for anything in the immediate area that could point to the missing children. Several more packs were found indicating a movement to the south. With the warrior's agreement, pursuit in that direction was mounted.

The dawn had barely subsided when the hulking lion dashed to the side of the sleeping pair. His growl, though somewhat muted was enough to stir them to a drowsy attention. His pacing was more urgent than they had ever seen before and he repeated the same back and forth motion that convinced them to follow him days earlier. Grabbing his mane, Maryn was pulled from the ground, and along with a bewildered Mason, headed in the direction the lion had come from. Was there a danger he was protecting them from? Was he taking them to a safer place? All they could do was follow and the pace was brisk, causing them several times to pause for breath, not so the lion, as his actions indicated an impatience with their progress.

Whatever their questions, they precluded any doubt as to the motives of their furry benefactor. Their trust in him was absolute, an innate quality of young people, lacking the cynicism of older ones fostered by years of unpleasant or hostile situations or betrayal. Perhaps Ferdy sensed this from their very first meeting, their innocence a prime factor in his affection for them. But where was he going? If only he could talk, but his actions were the only language he could convey. After a tortuous march, they approached a rise that afforded a wide view of the shallow valley before them.

Here the animal stopped, surveying the land before him. He turned to Maryn, then Mason, and emitted a low growl, something he did at times to gain their attention. It was his way of "talking." "What is it, boy," Mason asked as he stood along side the hulking form, his arm draped across his mane. Ferdy shook his head up and down and growled again. Finally, he looked straight ahead as if pointing and held his gaze.

During his morning foray to obtain "breakfast," some distance from the communal assembly, Ferdy detected a faint but familiar odor. It was not too long ago where its presence was overwhelming. It wasn't that it was obnoxious or threatening, but just another element that he had to consider among all the other challenges or factors he faced as leader of the pride. Cautiously following this invisible beacon, he abruptly stopped; voices, wafted from behind a small hill. Concealing his bulk among palm fronds, he lay motionless as the voices melded with a group of emerging forms. His mind quickly and instinctively arrived at one possibility—a hunting party.

With few exceptions, most of these people did not have the dreaded long sticks which barked fire, causing death or injury to many inhabitants of the wild. Why are they here? The concept of a rescue party was not a concept fathomed by his animal's mind and for long moments he watched as they passed by. He sensed no imminent danger, as he had many times before, when groups like this killed many of his kind. No, they seemed different, and a certain passiveness on their part awakened a dormant memory where people like this had saved his life after his mother had been slain.

Now he began to understand in his own logic that maybe they could "save" his adopted castaways. They did not belong to his pride as such; they were not of the wild. They needed to be with their own kind. Stealthily, he retreated from his hiding place, and when safe from discovery, he legs pumped with the fire of desperation, fueling the muscular pistons with untold energy. He had twofold goals, although as an animal it couldn't be reconciled in human terms. First, he wanted to bring his children back to their own kind. Equally important, was the protection of the pride. If need be, they must move on to avoid contact and possible conflict with the searchers.

The children also searched the horizon, noting nothing of any interest to validate their friend's concentrated stare. Nothing, exce——wait, what's that? Movement, undetermined shapes emerging from undergrowth. Little by little, they start to jell into cohesive shapes—people, real, honest to goodness people!!! The diminutive figures grew larger as they steadily moved forward. The jubilation of the siblings was barely containable as they jumped up and down, crying and laughing at the same time. Then reality hit hard, very hard. It was the end. The end of an ordeal and a wondrous adventure. And the end of something else.

Turning toward their friend, his baleful eyes could not conceal that he too knew that the end had come. Both flung themselves onto either side of his massive head, grasping his mane and the brow of his forehead tightly. Their embrace would be the last, as would ever seeing him again. With their faces, buried in his soft warm fur, all efforts to disengage were thwarted by the seductive contentment of the moment. They would never have this again.

After filling their hearts with this moment, they freed the giant reluctantly and backed away. The cat approached Maryn, planting a slobbering, rasping tongue with a slurping motion across her face. Turning to Mason, he repeated the same tongue lashing, the boy not even bothering to wipe his face, but accepting the ritual as a final act of bonding. With a final growl, possibly a sign of his own heartbreak, the king of this or any other jungle stole away into the lifting morning mists.

It took the voice of a yelling tracker to jolt them to attention. Wheeling around, they could see that some of the group had spotted them on the hill and began to hail them. Hand in hand, the boy and girl began a mad dash down the gentle slope, running as fast as the slowest one would allow. They stumbled a few times, scanning the various faces until they saw and heard the one that meant the most—mom! Into her arms they charged, all three tumbling to the ground in a joyous heap, kissing and hugging in abundance. The trackers and the warrior gathered around and in their own customs, chanted a hymn of recovery.

What a tale to be told. It would be one for the books, or magazines, or newspapers, or any of media outlet that cared to bring to the world a miracle of survival. As they gathered together for the return to the boats, an unbelievably loud roar echoed through the air. "What was that?," a relieved and happy mother inquired. "It was a good by, mom, a final good by."

In the years that followed, Maryn fulfilled the promise she had shown as she teamed with her mother to produce some of the finest visual art admired and coveted by many. She garnered awards and trophies as one who might collect stamps or bottle caps. In a room devoted to the acquired items of esteem, one wall contained only the enlarged photo of a magnificent beast standing proudly on a hill, tawny brown, beautiful in strength and truly the inheritor of the phrase,——King of the Jungle.

Long Distance

(A Love Story)

As he entered his office on the third floor, Chris Mason was whistling with content. He was cheerful and happy, no doubt by the success his small firm had achieved in the world of dog-eat-dog. The year 2000 started with a bang. When he first founded the firm, along with several shareholders, there were many hurdles that were successfully negotiated, and the company thrived, defying the startup doldrums that had crushed many other enterprises. The key to his level of operational survival was the ability to tap into any and all sources of business leads that could prove beneficial. That did not mean he took reckless chances, although chancy might be a conservative definition.

All in all, things looked rosy, and he meant to keep it that way. Attempts were made by competitors to diminish his enterprise through competition or underselling, most ending in failure, but educating him with the knowledge to avoid ruinous tactics. His multifaceted array of products and how to improve on them were key to his productivity. On the move constantly, his business acumen was reflected in his company's profitability. All business people strive to improve and increase their lot, and he was no different. Unlike others, he was not a business snob and catered to any outlet that promised growth.

Confident and handsome, these were assets that stood him well, especially when dealing with female counterparts. Courteous and professional, he never intentionally used this advantage to chart the course of any discussions, the natural effect of his persona being all that was needed. His standing with the few office employees he had was a benefit that allowed him to operate without intrigue of inter office interference, as it may have done in other firms. How many failed, not just because of bad policies, but because of behind-the-scenes rivalries that were poisonous and corrosive?

An article in *Business Today* caught his eye. Always looking for a new way to improve, he was interested in an article centering on United Technologies. As a consulting firm, it had scored many successes, as profiled in the article. Similar to an auto mechanics manual, it brooked no speculation or wild opinions, only the bare facts and results obtained from various enterprises, their cutting-edge innovations and other attributes that made them profitable. This is what he wanted, unvarnished appraisals that revealed the true worth of any firm. If he wished to expand, an ever-occurring impulse, what better way than to tap into an organization showcasing the best and brightest?

"May, please look up the number of, er, what was the nam—oh, here it is, United Technologies."

"Okay, Chris, be right back." Hanging up, he rolled his chair over to the wall-to-ceiling window, leaned back, and with hands clasped behind his neck, surveyed the towering buildings that invoked an image of the petrified forest. Hard to believe, but in almost every room, on every floor, and in all the buildings were competitors, winners and losers in the constant challenge to convince the public that what they had was what they wanted or needed.

Answering the intercom, he wrote the number on his schedule pad and thanked May. She had been with him from the start, a perky woman that just drooled confidence and optimism. The coffee shop he frequented harbored many souls of different pursuits, and hearing her speak to one of her friends, her discourse was funny and to the point, avoiding any putdowns on the subject she was referring to. She displayed a certain sensitivity that spoke volumes about her character. Without hesitation, he approached her table, introduced himself, and flat out asked her if she was interested in a job. Startled for a moment, which was unusual for her, she invited Chris to take a seat. From there the discussion crossed many Rubicons before she was convinced the offer was legitimate and not a pick-up ruse.

Truth be told, it was her energy and positive attitude that smoothed many a rough spot and kept all the hair strands on Chris's scalp intact. She soon knew his moods and dislikes, a true Girl Friday, and Chris knew it. Romance was kept at bay, although that could always be a consideration as she was a beautiful young lady with a not-too-shabby figure. No, Chris needed a working partner, not a working girl. It was one of his most pivotal hires, not only in what she accomplished, but in knowing others whose talents Chris could utilize. Her circle of fraternity proved bountiful in securing brains that could master the different levels of his requirements. In truth they became friends with the deepest commitment for each other's welfare.

So now to take the plunge. He flicked off the numbers quickly, waited a few seconds before a profound screeching sound tore into his ear. "What the…" he quipped. "What was that?" Seconds later, as if to soothe his jarred senses, a melodic voice confirmed the connection he had sought.

"United Technologies Consultant and Product Development Department, how may I help you?"

"That's quite a mouthful, young lady."

"That's why they pay me the big bucks."

Chris couldn't help but smile. That's something he probably would have said.

"Please forgive me, I have been waiting ages to say something like that, and I finally I got up enough nerve to say it. I'm Ellen Landry, assistant to the product development chief. How may I help you?"

Chris immediately liked this woman, displaying some of the same irreverence he concocted at various times. Casting a certain amount of business decorum to the winds indicated a person of confidence, who, if needed, could correct any misgivings her jocular approach generated.

"My name is Chris Mason of Mason Industries, but before I bare my chest, I think you'd better have your phone lines checked. My brain almost leapt out of my skull after dialing your number. The noise was horrendous."

"My apologies, Mr. Mason, I will have it looked into. Now what can I do to soothe your chest, er, I mean answer your questions?"

Oh, he was going to like working with this girl, he thought. "You probably have my firm listed in whatever who's who database you have and am interested in contacting production facilities that are similar to my own. My aim is to have a shared development program on new and emerging consumer products."

"Hold on a minute please, Mr. Mason, while I check."

He could hear her chair rolling, stopping, and a file drawer being pulled out, followed by the flapping of what sounded like pages in a book. Moments later, she reported to him that there must be an oversight as his company wasn't to be found in the directory.

"Look, that happens, but let me fax you my info and you can formulate a licensing agreement for me to sign. I really would like to use your services as your reputation for success is admirable. I would email, but the fax is just as good."

"Email? I don't—yes, the fax will be sufficient. I look forward to it, Mr. Mason. Your contract is just what we are delighted to honor. It helps us to grow too."

Grow? he thought. "Any more and there wouldn't be room in the city to hold them." Whatever it was, even briefly, he was caught up with this encounter and couldn't explain to himself why. Sometimes first impressions are obscured as time passes, and you can't recall what kindled them in the first place. He looked forward to the next conversation, the voice of Ellen firmly entrenched in his mind.

"How did it go, Chris, any luck?"

"Don't know yet, faxed my request and am waiting for the reply. I think we'll do okay."

Ellen's pluck reminded him of May, and that was a good gauge by any standard. Before the day was out, Ellen called confirming the receipt of the fax. With these in hand, he would pursue the ones with the most promise. There was that certain attraction gnawing at him again, and Chris abandoned to some extent his business posture. After a few days, he contacted United not so much to express thanks but to talk to Ellen, determined to see if the same attraction was there. Waiting expectantly for the connection to manifest itself with the age-old ringing sound, again that hellish static resounded against his ear. Apparently, the problem hasn't been corrected yet, he thought, when a serene voice prompted a relaxation in his demeanor.

"United Technologies, may I help you?"

"You must have caller ID, 'cause you didn't splat out the rest of your title."

"Caller ID? Is this Mr. Mason?"

"Yes, Ellen, just wanted to let you know I contacted several leads that may produce good results. Thanks."

"It was my pleasure that we were of some help. Oh, by the way, Mr. Mason, on the several occasions I've called for updates, there's been a terrific racket each time on the line."

"I've experienced the same problem, and they say they are checking," he replied. "Keep your fingers crossed."

There was something in her voice he could not resist. Oh, how he wished he could see her. As of now he could only tread lightly, trusting that an opportunity somehow would invent itself.

Content with the flow of business, he still could not resist revisiting in his mind the voice of what must be an angel. May noticed his distraction and questioned his new mood.

"You're a woman, May."

"I hope so, or nature's been fooling me all these years," she snapped with a crackle.

"You know what I mean, smarty."

"Okay, buster, what's up?"

"It's that assistant, or whatever title she uses. I can't shake her."

"Oh boy, am I seeing a meltdown?"

"Seriously, May, what do I do? I'm not really a ladies man, I mean, I just can't spin a line like some girl chasers do."

"You don't have to. Just be yourself. That's how you hooked me." A smile, a wink, and she walked back to her office.

Being preoccupied with this matter of the heart would be too strong a definition, but it was a mild source of distraction. After several days of the normal business grind, May walked into his office to discuss the new leads.

"Hey, Chris, scanned the companies Ms. Landry provided. What's your take?"

Looking it over, Chris hmmmned a few times before commenting to his Girl Friday. "Loomis Specialties, very interesting, but puzzling." He thought to himself that Ellen said it was a company on the rise. How could she have missed this?

"Have you looked at the bottom line, boss?"

"Yeah, but it has possibilities."

"Chris, it looks like it might being tanking, why bother?"

"We don't know the reason for that, maybe something that can be flipped, but on the positive side, there's product recognition and market share to consider."

"You could find a silver lining in a coal mine."

"Well, this is no coal mine, but it could indeed have a silver lining. Call the CEO and set up a meeting, will ya?"

"Yes, keemosabi, I go." What a girl and what would he do without her; he didn't want to know.

With that, he now had the perfect excuse to call United. Again, the ear-shattering noise almost caused him to hang up.

"Mr. Mason, so nice to hear from you, and how may I assist you today?"

"I'm thinking of pursuing an interest in Loomis Specialties, thanks to your info."

"I called to confirm if the listing was sufficient and am gratified that it met your expectations," she said.

"I truly appreciate your efforts, and I do believe that there will be more transactions between us, unless you're transferred to Siberia." A muffled laugh signified a receptive ear.

"What do you have in mind?"

"Well, er, I don't know how to, er, pose this request, being that we are fairly new to each other and, er, well, oh, let me just spit it out. Would it be okay for me to address you by Ellen, Ms. Landry, and you can do likewise?"

"I really don't think I could address you as Ellen, Chris." A deep-throated spate of laughter tingled Chris's ear as a signal of permission. Oh, how she could turn a vocabulary misstep like that to her advantage while at the same time amusing her victim.

"I feel a lot better calling you Ellen than Ms. Landry, it is 'miss,' isn't it?"

"Last time I looked, no ring adorned my finger, and yes, it is 'miss.'"

Great, Chris thought, *at least I won't have to beat my chest because of lost opportunities.* "Nice talking to you, Ellen, and I will keep you apprised of any results from your contact information."

"No need to, Chris, but it would be nice to know if we helped you and your company. I'll look forward to your calls, have a good day."

"You too, Ellen, bye."

"Chris," piped May as she entered the office, "I've set up an appointment with Rick Loomis, head of Loomis Specialties, for tomorrow at 1:00 p.m. He suggested you meet him at Carlo's for lunch."

"Carlo's? That's a great restaurant. He must really want to impress. I've been there several times. What a place."

"Tell you the truth, Chris, I talked to his secretary, and she's worried that the company may hit the rocks. This was secretary to secretary, so you know it's for real."

"I'll know more and what to do about it after we've talked."

* * *

"Ah, my young friend, what a pleasure to see you again."

"Hello, Andre. I believe you have a reservation for Loomis?"

"*Oui,* monsieur, he is waiting for you." The affable maître d' led the way to table, made a slight bow, and retired. Rick Loomis rose to greet him as Chris introduced himself, shook his hand and seated himself. His counterpart looked a little haggard, his blue eyes dull and his brown hair slightly mussed; nevertheless, his greeting was warm. His demeanor suggested a vulnerability, a search for a release from his obvious discomfort of company misfortune.

"How about a drink to get the flow goin'?" suggested Loomis. "And please call me Rick."

"Okay, sounds great, Chris is mine."

"I was surprised when my secretary informed me that you were interested in some type of working agreement. With the shape of my business, I thought it was going to be impossible to attract any investment whatsoever. Honestly, Chris, I need an angel right now, and I'm not too proud to admit it. We've had this company for two generations. I can't let my family down."

Over the course of the lunch, snacking and gulping like two dorm students, Rick laid out a proposal for Chris that seemed fair and rewarding. But Chris had to know more.

"Rick, how could such a solid company as yours come to grief? I've read the financials and find it hard to believe you're heading for a hole."

"The truth is we made an investment that backfired on us, and we couldn't recoup. I fired my financial officer after discovering his inept handling of our revenue sources and debt payments. It was a near-total disaster, and I blame myself for not keeping on top of it."

"What do you propose to do?"

"Look, you know or can find out that we're pretty solid. I just need to get off the floor."

"Rick, I have a crackerjack assistant who can process all the pros and cons and give me an idea of how far I can go. Will you let me do that?"

"If it will save the company, why not."

Chris looked at a man who was decent, something he valued in any person. The haunting look first observed disappeared, dissolving into a hopeful, expectant display that seemed to lift the weight of disaster from his shoulders. With both hands grasping Chris's, Rick thanked him for the opportunity to reverse his misfortune. Chris may have been a tough businessman, but he was no shark, and he felt the better for it.

"Well, what happened?"

"You, my dear, are going to his firm and look over any and all financial records."

"You what?"

"May, take whoever and whatever you need and please help this guy. If it can be done, fine. If not, then that's it. Please?"

"Wow, you really are Santa Claus, but okay, I can't really give you an argument. You put up with a lot of mistakes I made and that of others but still were decent to us. That I grant. I'll do what I can, I promise."

Feeling somewhat elevated at his monumental task of trying to save the world, or at least Rick's world, this was a perfect excuse to call Ellen. This time he held the receiver away from his ear until the connection was made.

"United, may I help you?"

"I see you've shortened your intros."

"Oh, Chris, it's you. Stop teasing, or are you messing with me?" A slight laughter dismissed any hint of annoyance.

"Just wanted to tell you I met with Loomis, and if things work out, we may be partners. His fortunes are pretty low at present."

"They are? But all the info I have indicates a going concern. I'll double-check. And how are you, causing trouble?"

"Not with you. I know better." His heart was racing as he wished so much to be able to do more than just talk to her.

He hesitated to push their association beyond what it was at the moment, not wishing to scare her off so soon in their relationship. Any encouragement on her part would change that in a heartbeat, but he had to be patient. Little by little with each phone call, contrived or genuine, a certain chemistry was developing. Something both couldn't ignore.

Ellen Landry came from a moderate-income family, and as such, in order to attend college, it required financial sacrifice. This was not alien to her, for early in life she knew nothing was just handed to anyone. She had been a pert little thing who loved life and lived it to the fullest. At times she tended to fret when things didn't go her way but never took it out on anyone, an endearing quality she always maintained. In school, from grade to high and even in college, friends were easily made, and her goal to excel was matched equally if not more so by her determination not to fail. Being petite, it disguised her ability to fend off many misconceptions about her vulnerability, which surprised anyone foolish enough to test her.

Ellen's story was not much different from others striving to succeed and paid the price in doing so. Fortunately, her career in business flourished as she competed with others for the plum positions to be had. Being attractive, while an asset, played no role in the hard-based strategy to do well, for the bottom line dictated who stayed and who was let go. One intriguing feature that always garnered stares was her beautiful full-length red hair, which by itself was an attention getter. Accentuating the flowing locks was a streak of pure white strands that formed in a wide ribbon from the left part, down to the end of the tresses. Her recognition factor was never in dispute and at times made her the center of unwanted attention.

If Chris had to make a comparison, while May was his Girl Friday, Ellen would be his Girl Saturday. Their growing friendship did not conceal her consummate skills as a professional and indeed portrayed her as a reliable partner in any relationship that could develop.

While the possible merger with Loomis was still on hold, with May sorting out the financial mess, Chris still had to maintain an ongoing search for business opportunities, and of course, this meant calling Ellen. Oh, how he loved these excuses, reasons, whatever you would call it, even if he had to make up a new definition to justify the call. Again he withstood the angry barrage of hissing static as the connection was made.

"United, may I help you?"
"Guess who."
"Ahhhh, Rumpelstiltskin? Ivan the Terrible?"
"Oh, you couldn't come up with Frank Sinatra or Brad Pitt?"
"Who? Never mind, what's up, Chris?"

"I need some distributor outlets to service my products. Things are picking up, and I'm afraid the existing outlets will not be enough."

"I think I can help you there. Other than that, how are you? Hussy that I am, I missed you the last few days."

The longing between both of them had been brewing for a short while, and now it approached the boiling point. Chris could only envision the moment he would actually see her, to hold her, to dismiss this ache that could only be removed by her presence.

"Chris, I have to leave town for a few days, a company retreat, so don't go hitting on my replacement."

"Ouch! That hurt," he grumbled. My girl—wait, his girl? He finally admitted to himself what he only hinted at. His girl. Was he her guy? He had to be and that would be settled when she returned. The rest of the conversation was intimate but disguising what was in reality a foregone conclusion. To convey it on the phone would only dilute the very personal nature of their feelings, left to be fully exchanged only upon that delicious moment of encounter, face-to-face, lips to lips. Hanging up, he turned to see May sitting on the edge of his desk.

"Got it bad, huh?"

Chris didn't think her presence an intrusion and in fact welcomed her being there.

"Yeah, I guess so. Is it possible, May, to fall in love with someone over the phone?"

"Why not? I've heard stories of people going gaga over each other just by letters. Can you believe giving your heart away by mail?"

The question he posed wasn't even real, for he knew he loved her and wanted to share it with someone, someone like May, whose endorsement truly made it real.

"Okay, I've wallowed enough at the love trough. What do we have in to look at?"

Business proposals, sales records, and other essentials integral to the operation of the firm were examined, validated, discarded, or just filed way. But not his innermost longings, which were put in abeyance only for as long as he could practically ignore them.

Time and events moved on, and to ignore them invited unwanted consequences.

Chris was his own man. Charitable to a certain point, he was no pushover. In his drive to succeed, he thought of others, respected convention, but until now was a pretty much stay-at-home guy. Arguably, the input of romance was the one ingredient he had not foreseen or sought but now was unavoidable.

The days to follow can only be described as torture, and to lessen its pull, he delved into his work with a passion equal to that which now tore at his heart. Was it enough? He probably would be unable to answer that with any degree of reliability, so conflicted were his emotions.

Dealing with the Ellen's replacement was conventional enough to ward off any bad behavior reports that he would have to defend, he joked to himself. Inquiring when Ms. Landry would return to work, he was told it would be the next day. Thanking the receptionist, he hung up, elated that now he would put in play his next move, taking her to dinner.

"Chris, that's such a nice gesture."

"Yeah, I counted my money, and I think I can afford you."

"What, with hotdogs?" Again the mutual laughter.

"Look, I want this to be a banner day. Tomorrow, Thursday, June third, 1:00 p.m. at Carlo's."

"What bank did you rob?"

"Hey, smarty pants, I'm independently wealthy, what do you say?"

"Okay, Chris, but I have a late conference, so I'll meet you there, is that all right?"

"Sure, I understand."

"There is something else I want to say and was going to wait until dinner, but I have to say it now."

Oh, no, thought Chris, *the gentle letdown is coming.*

"These past few months have made a great change in my life, especially because of you. I can't explain it any more than how the stars are there or how the sun shines, but I've experienced something I've never felt before."

"Wow, is this the real deal?"

"I can't wait to see you and share with you what I hope you have for me."

"Ellen, you can believe it. Your desire is my desire."

Can a dream be real? In this case, it was, and Chris has soared to the lofty heights that only clouds can reach.

"May, guess what? It's on, a date with Ellen."

"No wonder you look so loopy. I'm glad for you, Chris."

The rest of the day was a blur, his concentration consumed by a promise of fulfillment. What would he say, how would he say it? Would he stumble or shine? These were delightful conflicts, reveling in prose that would probably sound ridiculous, something a lovesick teenager would try to compose.

The next would have been better spent on Mt. Vesuvius, the work accomplished negligible. The clock seemed to conspire against him as the ticking seconds seemed like minutes and the minutes hours. May steered as much activity away from him as possible, until he donned his coat and headed for the elevator. May gave him a grin and a thumbs-up. He returned the uplifting gesture and rode down to the first floor, the doorman at the front hailing a cab for his use. He dared not be late and constantly checked his watch. He held a bunch of roses that Ellie the flower woman always was selling outside the building. Let's see, tie straight, nails clean, shoes shined, these and any other contrived threats to perfection were addressed in detail. Why was the cab moving so slowly? Good thing he didn't bite his nails. Finally…finally, Carlo's.

He overtipped the driver, almost stumbled from the cab, and nearly steamrollered a pedestrian, profusely apologizing while backing into the doorman. Yep, he had it bad.

The maître d' returned an informal salutation and escorted a very nervous Chris to his table, leaving two menus and asking if he would like to have something.

"No, thanks, I'll wait for my party, Andre." As he seated himself, facing the entrance, he began to ponder while eagerly expecting her appearance and remembering Ellen's words. "There won't be any trouble recognizing me. Just look for the sharpest dame you can ever dream of and add a lustrous mop of red hair with a side dish streak of white." How could anyone miss that? At least it wouldn't be him. Again and again he peered at the entrance, and every time the door was opened, he tightened in anticipation only to be disappointed. Glancing at his watch, Ellen was twenty minutes late.

Did the retreat last longer? Could she find a cab? More disturbing, was she injured in some way? If physically indisposed, why didn't she call or have someone call for her? Another twenty minutes cruelly crawled by, his concern not knowing in which direction they should be focused. Tortured enough, he decided to call her office, but this time, instead of the harsh crackling that had plagued him before, he was greeted with a professional inquiry.

"United Technologies, may I help you?" This wasn't Ellen's voice, but that wasn't unusual if she was attending the retreat.

"I'm sorry, but could you have Ms. Ellen Landry paged, please?"

"What name is that, sir?"

"Ellen Landry, she works in the Consultant and Product Department."

"I can't place the name, sir, but I've only been employed for a week. Let me check the department roster and I'll get back to you."

Can't place her name? Department roster? What kind of incompetents did they have working there? Chris was not only unnerved, he was furious.

"Sir, I checked, and there is no such person employed at United. Are you certain that this is the correct company?"

"I called, didn't I? I'm no child. If this is some game, there will be hell to pay. I'm coming over."

"That will have to wait until tomorrow, sir, we're shutting down for the day. An exterminating company will be here soon, and everyone is being sent home. However, we will open as usual in the morning. Thank you for calling United."

Chris was stunned. What was happening? It was like a scene from a movie thriller, only this was no movie. He summoned the maître d', handed him a handwritten note addressed to Ellen along with two twenty-dollar bills, and implored him to give the note to the lady that hopefully would show up asking for his table.

The man could see the anguish in Chris's eyes and responded with a comforting assurance that he would see to it, while returning the money. "Your relief will be my payment, monsieur. Besides, I make too much money as it is." He patted Chris on the back as he left. "Good luck, my friend."

Following a hellish night with no answers, no solace save to gulp down several glasses of scotch, a disheveled and confused man headed to his office.

"May, May, come in here, hurry."

She had never heard a summons like this before but knew it wasn't just an arbitrary demand for her presence.

"Chris, you look like hell, what's going on."

As Chris related the previous day's events, she fell back into the plush customer chair, wide-eyed and disbelieving.

"What are you going to do?"

"Do? I'm going over there now and find out what the hell's going on."

Entering the building, he approached the information desk, identified himself and his company, and explained that he wanted to locate an employee. The courteous receptionist begged his patience while she placed a call.

"Sir, I'm directing you to Personnel and Records on the fourth floor. Ask for Ms. Clovis."

Somewhat mollified by the polite interchange, Chris proceeded to the elevator, entered, and impatiently waited while the floor-indicating bell tolled each level, finally displaying 4. As the automatic doors parted, he stepped out and paused for a second.

Let's see, he thought, *right or le—oh, this way.* Walking the corridor, he was struck by scores of photographs lining both walls, men and women in relaxed postures, some smiling, some taciturn.

What a legacy, to have your pho—

Abruptly Chris froze. His eyes conveyed what could not be denied, the color alone a banging drum of recognition. A beautiful woman, half seated upon an office desk, a smiling face, the whiteness of her teeth contrasting with the mellow tan of her complexion. This indeed would have been enough for anyone to be attracted to an inviting presence, but the lightning bolt was her hair. Red, gorgeous red hair, with a white streak coming off the side. Glancing to the legend at the lower right, his eyes rested upon the name inscribed—Ellen Landry!

This can't be real, thought Chris. *But it is. I've found her! Now who's crazy. Not listed in this department, huh? Hogwash.* Resuming his journey and refreshed with a righteous vindication, his strides were now determined as he entered the designated office.

"Ms. Clovis, please."

"And you are?"

"Mr. Mason of Mason Industries."

"Of course, I'll page Ms. Clovis. If you will have a seat—"

"That won't be necessary, Gladys. Mr. Mason, nice to meet you. Will you step into my office?" The department head was in her late sixties or early seventies and displayed a matronly look, although with a pleasant aura. She seemed pretty spry and moved quickly, which almost left Chris behind. After seating himself, Ms. Clovis addressed him informally.

"You can call me Anne, if you prefer."

"Chris here."

"Chris, I took the liberty of pulling up your account. In the past, before computers, it was a dogged task to maintain the paper trail. Thank heavens most of that was transferred into digital data. I say that because your firm's initial application with us was in 1958!"

That has to be a typo, 1958? he questioned to himself.

"Your company requested business contacts for a month and a half and then went dormant for quite a while."

Wait a minute, how is six weeks considered dormant for a while? But he left that enigma aside to get to the heart of his visit. "Miss, er, Anne, I'm trying to locate an employee by the name of Ellen Landry. I believe her photo is displayed in the hall."

"Oh, Ellen? It's funny you should mention her name, it's listed as the processor on the application of your company. Also a Chris Mason. Was he your relative?"

"You might say so." A stabbing, ice-cold shock gripped his body and if possible his soul. *What is she saying? What in heaven's name is happening?*

"Did you ever meet her?"

He honestly answered that he never had, but the shock was numbing his responses.

"Maybe the director or the CEO of your company back then?"

Desperately seeking to unravel this mystery and keep his sanity, he replied, "I don't think so, but I'm curious. That photo, is that Ms. Landry's daughter?"

"Oh, no. She never married. That's a company photo portrait done as the firm was growing and employees that excelled were granted Hall of Fame status."

No, it can't be. It's impossible. His mind was reeling to the point of total collapse.

Now grabbing at straws, he asked if anyone could tell him about her. His ruse was that she looked so beautiful in the picture and wanted to know more about her. In truth, he always wanted to know more about her, what kind of life she wanted, if it was with him, and what they could be together. Yesterday's date was to fill in all the blanks. Now it appeared larger blanks were emerging. He wanted, no, he needed an answer, something to make sense of this mental turmoil.

"I was hired by United as an intern after graduating from college and successfully passing the usual interviews," volunteered Anne. "Assigned to Ellen's department was a great break for me. She was very instructive, and our association was mutually rewarding. I tried to emulate her work ethics and in doing so made strides leading to eventual promotions. As girls, we shared the usual gossip making the rounds and who was doing what to who. Of course, office romances were not unheard of, although frowned upon as being disruptive. I guess that's why I remember a certain change in her persona. She usually shied away from any involvements and made that clear many times to me. 'Mixing business with romance will only screw you up,' she advised me, and for the most part, she held to that. There were many suitors she could have snagged and easily too. She was a great catch."

Chris's comforting reaction was knowing that against all improbable odds and against her own prohibitions, she had chosen him. Did Anne also know this?

"You say she changed. How?"

"Well, it's so long ago, difficult to remember all the details, only that she became more lively. At lunch breaks, where all the ghosts are given up, she began to speak about what the future held for her. I asked her what she meant. She only hinted that a man had come into her life."

"Did she identify him?" asked Chris nervously.

"Oh, no, I don't think so, and if she did, I can't remember. Several weeks later, she confided that her person of interest had made reservations for dinner, and they were finally to meet face-to-face. Oh, it sounded so romantic."

"What happened?"

"From what I remember, especially by the way she responded the next day, it must have been a disaster. She was sullen and also seemed very apprehensive, about what, I don't know. She never divulged the results of the engagement, and I never sought to pry it from her. You never mess with a person when they are in that state. It took quite a while for her to even approach the carefree way she had lived, and I don't think she ever went much beyond that. Pity, she was such a doll. And I don't ever recall her dating anyone, at least she never confided in me if she did."

At no time did Anne speak as gossip, her narrative one of quiet reflection and of a consolation she couldn't provide for Ellen. Chris felt the hurt in his heart and felt betrayed by his inability to do anything about it.

Indeed, Ellen did go to Carlo's, tingling with excitement and the expectation of finally seeing her man. She was slightly puzzled that a reservation was not evident when she spoke to the maître d'. He assured her that it was no problem and had her seated. The restaurant had only been open less than a year and wanted to appear as friendly and considerate as they possibly could. She eyed the entranceway, not knowing what her shining knight would look like, although she solved his problem by describing the color of her hair. *He won't be able to miss or, as a matter of fact, resist me,* she laughingly murmured to herself.

The moment was dying down as it was evident he was late, woefully late. She had allowed for traffic or a late business transaction, but not even to call? A little annoyed, she asked for the use of a table phone, which the waiter immediately brought her. Preparing to hear that hideous static, she instead was solicited by a ringtone, much to her surprise. The connection was followed by a monotone impassive declaration that the number dialed was not in service!

What? She dialed again and then a third time with the same result. The phone company would be hearing from her tomorrow, she vowed. Not satisfied with an apparent failure to meet the needs of the public, she dialed information and provided the operator with the name and number of the party she had tried to contact.

After a few moments, the agent replied, "Sorry, ma'am, there's no such listing for the name and number you gave me."

Are you kidding me? Ellen screamed to herself. "Operator, please check again, there must be a terrible mistake or your gear is out of order."

The reply was the same, "No such listing." Slamming the receiver, she rose, tears streaming down her cheeks, suddenly afraid, but what of? His not appearing, discontinued phone service, or no listing of the company? She ran from the restaurant and nearly ran into the street, so blinded by her now clouded vision. Hailing a cab, she directed the driver to Mason Industries. A screenwriter could not have conceived a more chilling scenario than that which confronted Ellen. The address was an empty lot!

It was at this point she felt totally lost, unable to comprehend this nightmare. Slowly, she began to withdraw, a measure to keep her mind from snapping. It would be her saving grace, for in her present state, she couldn't cope. She needed time, plenty of time. What transpired was beyond sharing with anyone, and she never did.

"Anne, what happened after that?"

"Well, she continued to work until retiring in the early eighties. I hated to see her leave. Eventually, I was promoted to her old position, and it was mainly due to her tutoring and unselfishness. You know how some of these ole crabs can get." The last part elicited a joint laughter from the both of them.

"Anne, I enjoyed sharing your story about such an intriguing person. Thank you."

Leaving the office, he retraced his steps to the framed figure with the enticing smile. *What happened to you, what happened to us?* He fingered her face lovingly, a slight moisture evolving from the corner of his eyes. He stared at her for what seemed like hours, burning the portrait into his mind with such determination that if all else faded, that would still exist. Sadly he walk away and exited the building, knowing more about her but not knowing what happened to her.

Hailing a cab, his first impulse was to return to the office but lost any interest in dealing with any transactions, which he probably would screw up in his present state of mind.

"Carlo's please."

"Yes, sir." A return to the scene of the crime, for that's what is was, a crime. He had been robbed of what may have been a life fulfilled. Chris was approached by Andre, who displayed a quiet manner and apparent sympathy for the young man.

"Sir? I hope you were able to locate your friend."

"What, oh, er, no, I didn't."

"Please excuse my impertinence, monsieur, you seemed beside yourself yesterday, and I was concerned." Chris was impressed with the overture and responded with a warm handshake. "Will you take a table, sir?"

"Might as well."

As Andre led the way, Chris was about to follow when something caught his eye. It appeared briefly than disappeared, the result of the waiter moving through his line of sight. Appearing again, it was a red color, not of clothing, but something else.

He veered from the path Andre was charting to get a better look, and when he did, he stood stark still as if flash frozen. Seated by herself was a woman crowned with red hair, a white streak flowing from the left part!

No, it can't be. It's against the laws of nature or physics or any law that exists that has to defy this impossibility.

Andre halted and noticed the rapt attention given by Chris to the seated patron. "Do you know her, sir? Sir, are you all right?"

Chris stared at the woman but became self-conscious and turned to Andre. "Do you know who she is?"

"Why, sir, that's Ms. Landry."

"Landry? Are you sure?"

"Yes, sir."

"Andre, this is very important to me. I need to know everything you can tell me about her."

"I take it this is the woman you wished me to give the note to?"

"Yes, yes."

"Not knowing this was the woman you were concerned about, I still have the note. Do you wish I convey it to her?"

"No, but I need you to tell me everything, everything." The imperative in his voice was shaking the maître d'.

"Well, I've been here for twenty years, about the time I first noticed her, I mean, the hair and all. Her patronage was confined to two days or so in June, which is why she is here today. She is very pleasant and easy to converse with. Once, she confided very vaguely that she occasioned an anniversary on these visits, the details of which were never revealed to me."

If this was truly her, she would be in her midseventies, Chris thought. Yesterday was to be their first date, and now, years later, she still celebrates a nonevent? He was deeply moved that such a cherished memory could survive all these years. He had to find out; failing to do so would haunt his conscious being to no end. Thanking Andre and indicating his desire to be alone, Chris pondered his next move. He gazed upon a serene being, oblivious of his presence, wanting to touch her, to speak to her, to consummate their belated date. There was no profit in what he planned; what future could there be? But rationality took second place against his innate need to relive, if only for a short time, a promise of love. Revving up his nerve, he approached the woman leisurely sipping coffee, sitting erect, with her left hand resting on her napkin-draped lap.

"I beg your pardon, ma'am."

Looking up with a smile on her face, she replied, "May I help you?"

"Well, er, I'm waiting to be seated, and until then I just can't stand in the aisle. Would it be an intrusion for me to ask that I join you until then?"

"If that's the best pick-up line you can come up with, you need practice," a grinning face retorted.

Yes, yes, that's her, the spunk, the challenge in her voice, it's her! Chris was elated but not so carried away that he could dismiss the impossibility of this encounter. How? Why? He had no answers save for the question. The charming face revealed the wrinkles of her years but could not conceal the beauty that still remained.

"And young man, if I am to keep my reputation from being soiled by a stranger, you can remedy that by introducing yourself."

This woman hadn't changed. Whatever hurt she endured, apparently she had made peace with herself.

"Call me Chris Ma—er, Majors."

"Ellen, Ellen Landry."

"Thank you for allowing me to join you."

The light in her eyes convinced him that he was on firm ground. What trepidation he first had faded with each passing moment of light banter. There was no serious inquisition, just the normal give-and-take of two strangers enjoying what would have been a brief encounter. But to Chris, he wanted more. To know more about her, her life, to find out the things about her that were denied by a cruel fate.

He had to tread lightly, not wishing to dredge up anything from the past that would incur a flashback of pain.

"And now, young man, tell me you're not married or else I will feel responsible for breaking up a happy home." The laughter of both aroused the diners close-by, their looks displaying disapproval of the rowdiness. "Let them gawk," a feisty Ellen whispered, "they must lead dull lives." Again a chorus of laughter erupted, the diners shaking their heads. "What type of work are you engaged in, Chris?"

"I have a small company and dabble in different products, very boring really."

"As long as you can pay this tab." Again that easy smile, so enticing he wanted to hug her.

"I worked at a consultant firm about a hundred years ago, and retired, oh, about twenty years ago."

Already knowing she hadn't married, he didn't pose the question, unless she brought it up herself. He did however want to plum her depths of commitment that would have been shared if they had the future he envisioned. He felt some guilt asking her, "Anyone that stole your heart?" Almost instantly he regretted the question. Her eyes had a pensive look, as if peering into the past. There was no display of overt sadness or an indication that he had gone too far. She had resigned herself long ago to the heartbreak and the mystery of a union never achieved, although there was never a satisfactory answer as to how or why. What remained would always be entrenched in her being and savored as long as she lived. Many would have looked upon her as a one-man's woman.

She felt a kinship with Chris that ignored their brief association. "Yes, long ago. It was something that crept up on me, both of us really, and promised that fairy-tale ending. What makes a relationship? I don't know, I only know that it happened. It was only a few months, but enough time to know that my future was with him."

A lump began to creep into Chris's throat, hearing what many crave to hear from a loved one and finally having it realized. He couldn't help staring into her eyes, the pathway to the soul, and what he found would never be duplicated again.

"We had arranged a rendezvous, oh, I like that word, it sounds so romantic, here at Carlo's. It never happened."

Why not, Ellen, why not? What conspired against us? Chris challenged silently.

"Let me just say that I never met him or heard from him again. Did I feel abandoned? You bet, but as with the ocean's tide, time began to flood out my hurts, but only slowly, painfully slowly. Despite all this, I never harbored the thought that he deliberately shook me off, ignored me, or maybe found somebody else better than me." Chris was on the verge of disintegrating, the moving narrative filtering his every fiber. *She was mine, but I could never claim her. What cruel fate could do this to us? Why? Why?* He almost bit his tongue trying to remain impassive but respectfully attentive.

She paused to sip her coffee, gauging Chris's reaction. Perhaps she sought consolation for her plight, or maybe it was something that had to be released after being pent up so long. Levity was cast aside as Chris took both of her hands in his. What he couldn't do before, he would try to make up for it now, as best he could. There is no flight manual to access when flying into virgin territory, and this was no exception.

"Ellen, if we were birds, we'd be of the same feather. I too lost someone, and to this day, the reasons are as obscure as a cure for cancer."

"Was she beautiful?"

"Yes, she was." His mouth almost uttering, "She is."

"Can you talk about what happened?"

"There's not much that I understand about that, even today. It made no rhyme or reason. Our rendezvous, as you like to phrase it, never came off. Of course, it was a bitter experience, but amazingly, it led me to discover more about her than I could ever imagine." Anne had filled in many pages of the blank book labeled Ellen Landry, for that he would be eternally grateful. "I tried to locate her, but that proved fruitless."

"Do you see any fault in her?"

"Oh, no. You had to meet her to know what a considerate person she i—er was. I truly believe what occurred was beyond her control."

"You sound just like my Chris. He was like that."

The amazing interchange between these two star-crossed lovers defied the odds of probability simply because they had never met in person. And yet, it proved that love truly knows no boundaries or some set of arbitrary rules.

There was much to think about, now and later, when in the solitude of his apartment, Chris would delve into everything that occurred. He needed to sort out the various conflicts that had clung to him since the day before. Also the realization that soon he would have to leave. The temptation to scream out loud and release his pent-up burden was approaching the red line.

Again taking her hands in his and gazing at so sweet a face, he chose his words carefully. "Ellen, from our shared experiences, I think I can truly, if you let me, speak for him."

"If that's a proposal, I accept." Her eyes were twinkling in delight.

"Don't temp me, young lady." Welcoming the tension breaker, Chris resumed. "The cherished love that you harbor could never have been cultivated by a one-night stand or a casual adventure. These things stand the test of time and trial. It would be easier to destroy a brick wall with your fist than to cast into oblivion that which God has gifted to you. Hold that in your heart, and every doubt you have will and must melt away before that truth."

There was no more to say. She knew that also and nodded her head in acceptance of Chris Mason's speech.

"Say, young man, how 'bout a date next year, same time, same place?"

"Your treat?"

"Sure."

"It's a date." Rising, he walked to her side, her face looking up at him, rendering a silent thanks for his comfort. He leaned over and placed a gentle kiss upon her head, feeling a love, their love, something that transcended the physical attributes of carnal love. Perhaps this was the greatest of the two loves. He walked away, her eyes following his every step until he was out of sight.

"Mademoiselle, Ellen?"

"Yes, Andre."

"Excuse my intrusion, but that gentleman who you entertained had given me a correspondence that I was to convey to you. At first he demurred, but after I observed that most delightful relationship, it may well be that he would wish you to receive it." He handed her the note and excused himself. Ellen, like a child on Christmas morning, eagerly tore open the envelope and began to feast on its contents. As her eyes drank in every letter, every word, a new spirit began to flow through her aged body. When finished, she grasped the note to her chest and uttered a soft thank you. Then, she was quiet.

Chris opted to return to his apartment in hopes that some solitude would provide him with a chance to sort out what had happened. After calling May to excuse his absence, he settled upon his well-worn sofa. With a scotch in hand and the TV providing a comforting white noise background that always seemed to induce meditation, he embarked on recounting the day's events. His being was still charged with the electricity of seeing a dream, for how could it be otherwise, until he reminded himself that he had touched her. Oh, that he might forever cling to that memory of bliss. But that wish could not answer the questions of how or why. He would never know, as hard as he tried to rationalize the day's events, never know how it came to be. How could he?

Fate, or nature, whatever the definition that charts our course through life, can be capricious, and in Ellen's and Chris's cases, no one was minding the store. The bridge that connects past and present has a barrier that prevents a comingling of either entity. Somehow, this barrier was pierced, affecting these two and setting up the creation of a cross-generational romance. The phone static was the agent that established the link between them, and until it was eliminated, a bond was established. Why these two and no one else can again be laid at the doorstep of an erratic force. But even so, this force is not without its correcting measures, and in due time, the breach was closed. That was signaled very simply when the respective calls were answered sans the static, albeit not to the parties desired. Cruel it was, but who would pay for it? Of course you know.

An interesting avenue to explore were the clues, if given the proper context, that may have given Sherlock Holmes a run for his money. These were manifested in Ellen's questioning replies, such as who Brad Pitt was or the term *email*. Of course, neither existed in her time. Nor did Chris's office building. That shock alone almost sent her over the edge. The fax with the licensing agreement was never put in force because the financial arrangement with the bank had no record of Chris's firm. The irony of all this was that despite all heavenly odds, or maybe because of them, a love for the ages was born.

Meditating to the point of dozing off, an interrupting voice from the television awakened Chris.

"And the city council will take up the proposed tax issue tomorrow. And just in, a report from Man on the Street reporter Gayle Curtiss. Good afternoon, Gayle. Please share with the viewers what seems to be a human interest story."

"Thanks, Janet. It's one that will tug at your heartstrings. While interviewing various people about the city's new tax plan, I was a short distance from that fabulous restaurant Carlo's. The sound of a siren far off grew in intensity as an ambulance raced through the traffic and screeched to a halt at the front entrance. It took me a while to finish with my interviews, by which time I decided to investigate with my cameraman. Here's the feed just moments ago."

"The ambulance crew is exiting the restaurant with what appears to be an elderly female strapped to a gurney and covered with a blanket. As with any emergency call, they are moving very fast, no doubt to rush the stricken person to the hospital. And following the rescue personnel appears to be a waiter with a grave look on his face. They are racing off to the hospital now, so let me see if I can get to him. Sir, sir, can you give any information about what happened?" His eyes glued upon the retreating ambulance, his concern was interrupted by the reporter's query. "Oh, it is so unfortunate. I didn't know what happened, until I went to speak with her."

"And you are?"

"Oh, I'm Andre, Andre Aumont, maître d' at this restaurant."

"You seem very upset over this patron."

"*Oui*, I have known her for many years. She is one of my most favorite customers, a friend, if you will. She is a woman of purpose."

"What do you mean by that?"

"Every year at this time, she has made it a ritual to frequent our establishment, to observe some anniversary or other."

"Do you know what kind of anniversary?"

Chris was mesmerized. *Anniversary? It's her. Something's happened to her. Is she okay?* All he could do was listen and feel the total helplessness that welled within his throbbing chest.

"No, I do not. It was very personal and special. I never imposed on her privacy. However, today she dined with a handsome young man, and in all the years I have known her, she displayed a glow that I've never seen before."

"Was it her lover?"

"Oh, please, mademoiselle, nothing like that. She was too old for that."

It hurt Chris to hear that, but he knew differently. In his heart she would always be young despite her years, for love never grows old, only better.

"Then what happened?"

"After he left, I delivered a note to her that had been given to me by the young man. I then returned to my station. She usually would have left after her coffee but did not do so. Concerned that she may have been having some difficulty, I returned to her table."

"What did you find?"

"She was sitting erect, with her hands clutching the note to her bosom. She seemed content as if she was sleeping and enjoying a wonderful dream. Gracing her face was a contented smile, and thinking she was enjoying a pleasant memory, I waited discreetly for a proper moment to intrude. However, after a reasonable observance, I noticed that her position and expression had not changed at all. I approached and asked, 'Mademoiselle, mademoiselle, are you ill?' She did not respond, and I knew something was wrong. Immediately I summoned for emergency assistance. When they arrived, they checked the fine woman and then transferred her to the mobile stretcher and thence to the ambulance."

The note, thought Chris, he gave her the note. He had completely forgotten about it. That was meant for his "other" Ellen, unconsciously not recognizing the absurd distinction.

What he didn't know or could not know was that the hastily scribbled message was above the norm, the words so immediate and universal that if written a thousand years before, the impact would be no less. This was the balm that healed an injured heart and brought solace to a woman shorn of a love that was promised and then cruelly snatched away. Chris had done more than he could have imagined, inadvertently though it was. Her pain was now gone, the emptiness a thing of the past. But what of him? How would he address the same emptiness? Who or what could ease his pain?

Time. Time that was a partner to his perceived happiness and time that stood in the wings during his despair. That intangible force that infects every aspect of what we do, unable to alter or stop its march. Its passage eroding the conscious like a waterfall eroding the rock it cascades against. Still, he will not relinquish, even though the pain will be a constant companion, the author and source of his improbable journey. From time to time, he will visit that hallway, silently contemplating what might have been but, more importantly, grateful for the experience, unfulfilled though it is.

He traces his fingers across her face and lips and touches them to his own. One day he will meet another, not to replace what is firmly entrenched in his heart, but to join with it. True and lasting love can never be reduced, only built upon. He can't see that now, but it will come to him. It will be traditional and rewarding, and finally the pain will be gone—forever.

The Fisherman

The beautiful lake mirrored the color of the azure sky. It was the largest in the county, its size almost comprising the total area of the jurisdiction. The hills on one side provided protection from the northern winds, while the groves of trees on the southern shores granted shade and relaxation to the visitors who swarmed the beaches. In between, the land was inviting to owners of the lakeside properties that were in continuous use all year-round, with some being available for rentals.

An occasional deer, or black bear would entrance the visitors as much as producing disdain from the regulars. Their feeding habits were not too well accepted, as the gardens would attest to. All in all, it was a friendly setting for any who wished to avail themselves the pleasure of the day or months, as some retreated to this area regularly. One such person was Chuck Madden, an elderly gentleman who lived not too far from this fluid body of delight.

Truth be known, Chuck would not be with us in the next few years as time was seeking a reckoning of his existence. This said, he had so much to live for and to give. He lived with his daughter, Jenn, and husband, Bernie, and their two sons, Mason and Scooter. After the passing of his wife, the caring couple insisted that he come to live with them. The clinching incentive being that the boys adored him and wanted to know all kinds of cool stuff he could teach them.

Chuck was lonely and, after being convinced that he wouldn't be a burden, accepted the offer, much to the delight of the kids. One of the things he had a passion for was fishing. However, he was no ordinary fisherman. In fact, a true fisherman would define him as a wannabe, a fake, or some other description that may have applied to him. You see, he was no conventional devotee of the line and reel. More often than not, he used the wrong gear or bait or line or some other flouting of the conventional approach to bringing in the big ones, or for that matter the small ones.

Using his 1964 Ford pickup as locomotion, he would pull his sixteen-foot boat named *AMY AM.* and trailer to the lakeside ramp. When sighted by other fishermen, their sighs and resignations were carefully hidden from the master of perceived ineptness. They were true fishermen in that the proper equipment was used and the correct application of such was adhered to with almost religious observance. Not so with Chuck, and this rankled them. Their gripe was not that he was so wrong in what he used or did but that, darn it, he was so successful! Many a time he would come back to the ramp with a mess of fish, while his peers would hardly have a bite, or what they did catch was meager. Not all the time, but enough to ruffle a few feathers.

His love of fishing was so profound that the freezing weather would not be a deterrent for him, although his catches were limited due to ice and rain and other factors. He was also inventive. Using the aluminum from discarded beach chairs, he was able to fashion the framework of a shelter half over the stern of his craft. This provided protection from the sun and those nasty northern winds. Along with a small jug of "medicinal" liquid, he made out pretty well. When asked by the infrequent visitor the secret of his success, he truly answered that he couldn't tell them, not out of secrecy, but because he didn't know himself. He was truly a contradiction in terms.

Though fishing was his obsession, it didn't detract from the love for his family, especially the kids. He thrived on their attention, as any proud grandfather would. Their constantly poking of questions and their responsive expression of awe from an answer gave him no end of satisfaction.

Mason was six and the older of the two boys, with light hair and twinkling brown eyes. His mouth still retained the piehole appearance so noticeable in newborns and toddlers. He grinned constantly, which matched perfectly with his inquisitiveness, the questions shooting as fast as that of a machine gun. When addressing Scooter, the boy, while not really understanding the impact of what he was hearing, would bob his head back and forth in unison with his grandfather's animated delivery. He would ooh and aah at things, not quite comprehending them, but reacting to the theatrical and gyrating descriptions. The boy's hair was stubby, his black eyes shining like polished lumps of coal. Both lads were wiry in build but could absorb most of the mayhem they would mete out to each other in brotherly combat. As with the young wild animals developing their skills among themselves, this was their testing time. The violence was minimal, with a scrape here and there requiring only the soothing caress of their mother to heal.

He was known to them as Poppy and, when returning from a day at the lake, sought comfort in their company, nestling with them on the sofa. While Scooter was too young, he promised Mason that one day soon, he was going to take him to the lake. The kid flipped as if Christmas morning had arrived. The anticipation of the duo charting the high seas, or lake in this case, was one of those instances that formed the bonds of kinship and future memories to look back on. Chuck had only to retrieve the folders of his mind to recall the little girl he had on his lap when reeling in a big mouth bass, her shrieks of delight reflecting her unbounded joy. These and other times had seen him through the sad periods of his life when things had turned against him. In later years, she bore him two grandchildren to assure the continuance of memories to come.

The passing of his wife before the children were born deprived them of the sweetness only a grandmother could impart. How he wished that the kids would have known her and reveled in her consummate wisdom and nurturing. With this, he doubled his efforts to provide that missing element, sparing no effort to guide and entertain the two squirts that tugged at his heart.

Anticipating the day that he would brave the open waters in the quest to land a whopper, Mason asked his grandfather to again recite the tale of the Ghost. When the tyke was old enough to understand,

Chuck would weave a tale about a fish reported to be a giant that thwarted all efforts to land it. It was called the Ghost because those who claimed to have snagged it were denied the honor of hoisting it at the scales because it always threw the hook. All too often, he told a mesmerized Mason, fisherman after fisherman were astounded that what they thought was a sure thing turned out to be an empty line.

The fish in question was reputed to be a giant sturgeon. Somewhere in the neighborhood of three to four hundred pounds. The river to the north of the lake harbored this species and on occasion through the years, flooding would cause a number of them to inhabit the lake. Their fighting qualities lured many an angler to this inviting area to test their skills. Those caught were of moderate size but held the promise of larger ones, even the Ghost, which would provide years of storytelling for the lucky one who landed him. Alas, it seemed that as hard as they tried, very few were able to even hint at getting him to nibble. Still, hope yearns eternal, and there was no dearth of hopefuls.

He then spun a tale that ignited the boy's imagination with visions of near conquest by his infallible grandfather. On one occasion, mused the elder, his line tugged with such force that it began to pull the boat, going faster and faster with each second. His mouth frozen in awe, Mason hungered for the desired result, the capture of the Ghost. This was to be denied as the storyteller announced that his filament had been a mere ten-pound test line and could not support the inexorable strain.

"Bang," he uttered, and the boy's eyes blinked involuntarily at the unexpected sound effect, recoiling slightly backward before grabbing his grandfather's hand.

"Gee, Poppy, what happened next?"

"Well, son, all I could do was stare at the frothing water, and I thought to myself, 'If he had a nose, he'd be thumbing it at me.'" Both of them had a good laugh.

"Will you try again, Poppy?"

"I don't go out there just to get him but to enjoy myself. If he happens to run into me again, sure, I'll try to land him. I've run into him before."

"You did? I didn't know that."

"It's not the greatest thing in the world, like winning the lottery, so I would tell a few friends but not make too much of it. Still, there were some nice head butts. It seems like we were getting to know each other, like sparring in the boxing ring, not really wanting to hurt the other guy."

"Is it like Buddy, our Lab, I mean having him for a friend?"

"I don't know if you would call him a friend, more like respecting him and how he has lived all these years."

"How old do you think he is, Poppy?"

"It's hard to say, Squirt, but from what I saw of his size, about seven or eight feet, he could be real old. Do you know that in Russia, they catch sturgeon and sell their fish eggs."

"Huh, fish eggs? That don't sound too good to me."

"Well, to some people, it's delicious and costs a lot of money for the good stuff. But some of these fish used to grow to fifteen feet or better."

"Wow, Poppy, these must look like whales."

"It's a shame too, because the overfishing has kept them from making more babies. That's why, when I catch a fish like that, I throw the runts back in so that they can get bigger and mate up with a girl fish."

"It's like they get married or somethin'?"

"Yeah, somethin' like that." He chuckled, barely audible.

The following day saw Chuck again plying his almost daily hobby. He landed a fairly large catfish and put it inside the barrel at the front of the boat. He believed in keeping all his catches in their natural environment until time for cleaning. Not too long after first coming to the lake, and wanting to slake this thirst and fill his belly, he came across a building housing the community center/shelter. A small section served food, a wonderful variety which filled his needs. Meeting the manager, a fine woman who went by the name of Maggie, he learned that the center tried to accommodate anyone in need of food or a bed. Their source of income depended mainly on what the dining room would bring, donations and a partial stipend from the county.

"Do you take fish?"

"What?"

"Do you take fish, you know, those things with scales and fins on 'em?"

Laughing, she replied, being unprepared for the question, but yes, any donation of fish would be appreciated. She raved that her cook was a whiz at preparing any dish listed on the moderate menu, and the inclusion of fresh fish would be a godsend.

"What will you take for them?"

"I'm no mercenary, so I'll tell you what, if I bring in any amount that suits you, I'll take a breakfast, is that okay?"

"More than fair, er…"

"Just call me Chuck…ah…"

"Maggie."

"Okay, Maggie, it's a deal. Whatever I catch, it's yours."

So for the next few years, Chuck and Maggie became good friends. She was in her midsixties but looked younger, her spryness giving wings to her feet. If dejected, the doctor would order one dose of Maggie, followed by a smile and conversation. Being only five-foot something was a point that generated jibes and jokes by the regulars. Strangers had better bite their tongues if they ventured into that territory. Maggie had an eye on Chuck but knew he was a one-woman man and just left it at that, although their friendship sufficed for all occasions. On one such day, with the weather so bad, Chuck deigned to hole up at the center. At the counter with a steaming cup of hot coffee, he would entertain the regulars and the newcomers with stories of his encounters with the denizens of the lake.

It was here that they became acquainted with his encounters with the Ghost. With a captive audience, Chuck would, with his customary zeal and exaggerated hand motions, spin a tale that may have rivaled Captain Ahab's encounter with Moby Dick. He would crouch, indicating the prowess of a hunter and describe the lure being taken by his elusive quarry. The rod would bend under the prodigious strength of his nemesis, and his arms would ache at the strain of maintaining his grasp upon the yielding vinyl link to his adversary. The line would play out as rapidly as he would allow and then abruptly would halt its travel, reeling it in. To weary his prey, he would repeat the process over and over, but the weariness was also gaining on him. With each sentence, the gathered throng seemed to pull with him or retreat or tire, his words so overpowering. Then when it seemed victory beckoned, the disappointing climax sucked the emotion from their bodies. Cruel fate intervened; as he was ready to land the giant, a passing and careless speedboat cut across his line, severing the only hold he had on the creature. The women gasped, and the men uttered unkindly words for the miscreant who thwarted the holy grail of fishing from their friend. Even if they didn't believe him, they were thrilled by the expansive tale and relished them whenever he offered them up.

But this was no fairy tale, even if it made good fodder for the listeners. Still, Chuck was not ingrained with the overpowering desire for revenge. It was a good battle, something he always sought in a fish, but no rancor at having lost him. Maybe in the future his fortunes would turn. Maggie would always pour him another cup of coffee, and they would talk about many things. Her golden-brown hair always brightened up the room and her blue eyes reminded him of the lake on a sunlight day with the sky reflecting the same color from its surface. He was deeply fond of her and learned that she had lost her husband not too long ago. The center gave her a purpose, and she took it. They made a handsome couple that some of the biddies secretly hoped would lead to romance. She encouraged him to continue his storytelling; it gave great pleasure to the older ones whose movements were limited and who relished his experiences.

He brought the kids in several times, and they were treated like royalty.

"My Poppy is the greatest fishman there is," Mason would sternly attest. He was so proud of his grandfather that this alone vanquished any shyness he may have had. Scooter made the same type of statement, but at three years old, his syntax labored a bit. There was no shortage of pie or ice cream, and the older people thrived on their exuberance. Their manners were, well, like that of a six- and three-year-old, mixed but honest.

"When I go water, Poppy?" Scooter would quip.

"When you're a little older, that way you can steer the boat, but I need you to be bigger and stronger." It was these fatherly assurances that won the hearts of the boys, and true to their species, they would never forget a promise. And Chuck would never break one either.

Leaving the center one day, he was approached by two men, one of which toted a camera of some sort.

"Hi, I'm Greg Pritchard, channel 6."

"Well, what can I do for you, Greg Pritchard, channel 6."

The response sprung a laughter that was always available for encounters like these. He liked Chuck right away, and his attitude made it easier for him to continue.

"Chuck, I've been hearing a lot of stories about a fisherman who seems to be charmed, and the locals pointed you out."

"Well, if I'm charmed, I'm still single and not very wealthy." Fortunately, the cameraman was getting every bit of this in digital. His openness made the interview fresh and real, especially when Chuck refused to look at the camera but carried on his discourse with a convincing ease. "What can I do for you, son?"

"Would it be possible to ship out with you, that is the proper term, isn't it?"

"If you mean you want to take a hike in my boat, sure, why not?"

They proceeded to the dock and boarded his boat.

Of course, on the way to his fishing spot, the questions were many and varied.

How long had he been fishing, what he caught, where he lived, and so on. Chuck didn't mind the questions; he was not in search of fame or whatever else others would strive for in a case like this. This was just being courteous and maybe enlightening for the reporter to what fishing was all about. Not being self-conscious was a bonus for both parties, and in fact, some of the exchanges were mundane or lacked any urgency. This relaxed atmosphere contributed far beyond what Greg had sought.

"Chuck, the name of your boat."

"What about it?"

"I get the *AMY*, what is the *AM*?"

"Oh, that. I named it after my wife, and she got a kick out of the *AM*. She asked, 'What the heck does that mean?' Being withdrawn as I am"—causing a muffled laugh from Joe—"I wanted it to be our private joke, so to speak, *A* stands for *and*, the letter *M* for *Me*. Amy and Me. I get a lot of questions about it, love it."

Finally, Chuck killed the motor and cast his anchor into the water, a plume of spray dousing the cameraman, who, with foresight, had covered his camera. Grabbing his favorite pole, the older man cast a line yards away into the water and sat down.

"That's it?" chimed the reporter. "Not unless you want to dive in yourself. Fish can't read invitations, only react to them, the hook that is."

"I kind of had a different idea about this."

"Oh, and what might that be?"

"I thought it might be more movement, action, that sort of thing."

"Well, let me put it this way. It's like a date with a nice woman. Things start out slow with all the proper show of interest, doing things that are required to keep the flow going, and just waiting for the right moment to be more intimate. Just like fishing. You cast the line, make sure the boat is anchored, and wait for the tug on the line. That's the intimate part."

"I never thought of it like that."

"Some days are just lazy, which I don't mind. It gives me a chance to doze. But at other times, I'm reeling in five, six, seven fish in a row. The waitin's 95 percent of fishing, but the other 5 percent more than makes up for it. Tell ya what, Greg, grab that extra pole and throw a line in."

"For real? I've never fished before. What do I do?"

"Nothing really. Just wait for a nibble, and *poof*, pull the line hard."

No sooner had the words left Chuck's mouth than a sudden pull bent the newcomer's pole, startling him. Half frozen, he yelled, "What do I do now?"

"Crank the reel, you dipstick."

Regaining some composure, the novice followed the advice, and soon he was battling a big mouth bass.

"Stay with him, son. You have a nice one there." The battle was on, and to Chuck's delight, the coached angler was holding his own. "Let him fight a while. See what he has. Yep, he looks mighty fine." Eventually, sweat drenching his forehead, Greg concluded the contest and hauled the fish aboard, a five pounder; Greg's grin was a sign of realizing the appeal of fishing.

"Wow, now I see what you mean. Watching others doesn't begin to convey the excitement or the challenge fishing can give you. That was mighty kind of you, Chuck."

"Yeah, I'm known for that," he deadpanned, causing Greg to laugh and slap his mentor on the back.

"Look, you know I'm doing a story, but would it be okay if I continued to fish with you. Joe won't mind."

"If he's not going to film anymore, I have some hand lines he's welcome to use."

It seemed Joe was infected with the same inclination that his boss had succumbed to and eagerly snatched a line and joined the fray. If one didn't know any different, it would seem the trio had been friends for ages. The cache of beer at the stern was readily consumed amid chatter of this and that. The tally for the day was eleven different fish of various sizes, the winner being Joe, who hauled in a ten-pound catfish.

With the sun on the decline, it was agreed by all to head back to the center. As Chuck began to lift the pole from its holder, he felt a vibration and paused. Another bite! Anticipating the jolt on the line, he was taken aback by the extreme pull that almost tore the rod from his hands.

"Joe, grab your camera." He had deep suspicions as to the origin of the new challenge, and it wasn't long before they were confirmed. Broaching the surface, a torpedo-like object reflected the waning light off its silvery body. "The Ghost! Joe, get every bit of this, you may not have another chance."

"What do you have, Chuck?" questioned Greg. It indeed was the legend of the lake. For years his landing had been the goal of anglers seeking the ultimate trophy, perhaps today. "I don't believe I heard of it."

"You had to be from these parts to know about the story, so don't beat yourself over it. It's a local thing and pretty well confined to this area."

"Wow, are we going to make fishing history or whatever notoriety that will come from all this?"

"Don't believe so, Greg."

"Why not?"

"Well, I use a lot of hand-me-down stuff, just enough for me to enjoy what I do. I really wasn't gunning for the Ghost, so all I had was a lighter test line to serve my needs. It was to supply Maggie and the center with tomorrow's meals. I expect the line to go at any second, but until then, let's have some fun."

For a while it looked like the battle would not end well for the elusive prey, and Chuck was back and forth along the boat, tracking the fish's movements and almost sending Joe into the drink. He had no illusions about landing the battling adversary, but in the back of his mind, there just may be a chance. At one point, he had pulled the animal within an arm's length of the boat and was toying with the idea of hooking him with the gaff. This notion was quickly discarded as he would not relinquish his sportsmanship to an artificial, if not unfair advantage. He was not willing to change what he was to become something he was not. Sensing an opening of escape, the Ghost turned and sped from the boat with lightning speed, the drag on the reel acting as a pivot point to supply the resistance necessary to break the line.

"Gee, Chuck, you lost him. What a shame."

"Don't fret over it, Greg, it was a good fight."

"Don't you feel bad about it?"

"Not really. It was a good struggle, and he won fair and square, so I may be a little disappointed, but not by much. There's always another time."

"How's that?"

"This is not the first and probably won't be the last time we'll tangle. I don't count hem, but we've been in each other's hair quite a few times. And if the lines were the right strength, we wouldn't be here today."

Greg could not be but impressed by this home-spun philosophy that revealed the true decency and honor of his host. What was an assignment had turned into an adventure and a lesson in character.

Leaving the dock, the reporter thanked Chuck for a great day, something he and Joe had never anticipated. It sparked a resolve in him to approach any new assignment with a more studied outlook and to look for those variables that instilled inspiration rather than just accommodation. Chuck was quite taken with the experience and couldn't wait to share it with his family and, later, the crowd at the center. Unloading the bountiful catch at the kitchen and grabbing a quick cup of coffee, he kissed Maggie on the cheek and left for home. Driving along the darkening roads, his mind traveled back to his younger days when he sought an outlet for his restlessness.

A smile creased his face as he conjured up the image of Amy, who would one day be his wife. His attempt to court her was futile despite his best efforts. He was good looking and at six feet had a fairly imposing physique, and his gray eyes were appealing. What manners he had were acceptable if not overwhelming, for in her presence he was as helpless as a pup and just as dysfunctional. They were not neighbors, but there were many occasions when their paths crossed. The tipping point came when he was purchasing an item at the general store and overheard her responding to the clerk about some fishing gear she was interested in. Using that as a shoe horn, he casually interrupted the clerk, asking for the best rod he could get.

"You fish, Chuck?"

"It's in my blood, Amy." The sheer terror of a bald-faced lie paralyzing him for the moment.

"Maybe you can help me, I'm trying to get something for Dad to celebrate his birthday."

If ever there was an opening, he was going to go for it. Her angel-like face, framed by her blond hair, so captivated him that it was difficult to think straight in her presence. Chuck wasn't a ladies' man and lacked the guile and suaveness of a practiced suitor. He was all thumbs but gave it a good try.

Peering into her blue eyes, wondering what they saw of him, he attempted to showcase various items that might interest her. It became apparent to her that he really didn't know what he was doing.

She was observant but not dismissive of his fumbling and was pretty kind to his efforts.

"Tell me, Chuck, you really don't know a thing about fishing, do you?" Embarrassed, he nodded and started to walk away. "Wait, where are you going?"

"Ah, I…er, I'm sorry about misleading you. It was my chance to impress you and maybe get to know you. I guess that blew it." Again, he started to walk away until she placed her hand on his arm and halted his movement. With a softness in her eyes and a redemptive voice, she replied, "Anyone wanting to do something this bad can't be all bad." She laughed at the double use of bad. "Come on, buy me a cup of coffee."

To say he was flying would only be tempered by the fact he was actually soaring. From that moment onward, their association grew not only by being in each other's presence but by what they shared. He had no other outlet for his energies other than his job at the leather works where he was the product manager. She sensed that he needed something to relieve the stress of the day and surprised him by suggesting he take up what he had used as a ruse to meet her.

"Me, fishing? I don't know the first thing about it."

"Leave it to me, Cyrano," she said, referring to the fictional character who tried to win his lady by subterfuge. And leave it to her he did. At first the learning curve took a little getting used to, but he managed to survive, albeit in unorthodox ways. He never learned all the proper usages or gear, but that was immaterial to the joy he suddenly experienced.

Her passing tore at his heart, but he maintained his focus by continuing what his wife had brought to him. Now he had a tale to tell Jenn and Bernie when he got home.

"Dad, that's exciting. You are famous." She laughed.

"Oh, I don't know about that, but we did have a ball."

His son-in-law, Bernie, was a great booster in anything Chuck attempted and was blown away by the story. The squirts were in bed so had to wait until a new day to learn what passed on the lake. The elder couldn't wait to see the excitement in Mason's eyes as a new saga awaited to invigorate his imagination, especially the tug-of-war with the Ghost.

After breakfast and preparing to go to the lake, the phone rang.

"Chuck? This is Greg. Good morning."

"Same to you, guy, what can I do for you?"

"Hey, I have to tell you, yesterday was something I'll never forget. You brought the boy out of me. Anyway, I showed my station manager and the producer some clips of our adventure, the whole works. The center and those wonderful folks, that beautiful lake, and of course the angling we did. Joe got some super shots, and your persona just leaped off the screen. They're not going to run it as a filler tonight." The news didn't exactly ruffle Chuck's feathers, but what followed came as a pleasant surprise. "Instead, they're going to feature a whole half hour on the 'Personalities' segment with our stuff. A whole half hour!"

"Is that good?"

"Chuck, that's like being called up from the minors to play for the big club."

"Then can I get a raise?"

"If I had it, you'd get it, my good friend. It's be on at seven, so don't forget."

Pulling Greg's chain, Chuck retorted, "Hey what channel is it on?"

A few more exchanges, and then they signed off just as Jenn entered the den.

"Who was that, Dad?" After detailing the conversation, she became all a twitter and squealed with delight, embracing her father more so for the recognition he was getting than anything else. "Oh, Dad, you earned this. Wait till Bernie gets home. Better yet, I'm going to call him at work, and he can tell all his friends."

Being fairly modest, if only for himself, he would as soon chuck all the fuss and just go fishing, but the thought of exposure for the center was a prime consideration. The hope was that it would translate into a positive exercise of support and recognition for this oasis of charity. Maggie deserved it. The uproar was expected after he informed the gathering of the pending program. How many times he was slapped on the back had to be calculated with an abacus or some other counting device. This was a family if not by blood, then by golly, by name and love. Eventually, he squirmed through the well-wishers and boarded *AMY*. Trolling out to his spot, it took a while, in the solitude that was always his partner, to truly comprehend what had happened. With no diversions other than the water lapping at the waterline, his mind's eye replayed the salient events of the day before, and this morning's throng filled with gaiety. He marveled at the ease in which such joy could be encouraged by just doing what he had always done.

No, it wasn't him, but what others made of him. He was their shining knight in armor, but what he failed to realize, he had *always* been that, something he never conceived of for himself.

His humility wouldn't allow dwelling in the heights reserved for notables. He was content with his lot, and that alone personified his qualities.

That night, the family gathered in the den, Mason and Scooter ensconced on either lap of the patriarch. Jenn and Bernie were noisily admonishing the commercials to hurry up and get out of the way. Chuck seemed a little more involved than normal, but at last he was about to relive and bask in the glow of yesterday's outing. He secretly wondered if he would look photogenic but slapped that notion down as a sign of vanity, well, almost vanity. His curiosity won that argument. Finally, the opening credits to "Personalities," a weekly address to some person or other warranting their fifteen minutes of fame, so to speak. Then Greg, opening with a short monologue describing a thumbnail sketch of the following production.

As the scenes appeared, the kids were screaming, "Look, it's Poppy!" Their eyes brimmed with amazement that their grandfather was on TV. "Poppy, Poppy, that's you!" screeched Scooter, duly impressed by the fisherman and his activities; his riveted attention and lunge for the screen almost caused him to fall from his perch.

All through the show, Chuck felt a certain surrender to the lure of notoriety, no matter how hard he tried to suppress it; who could blame him, he was human. At the conclusion, the phone rang. It was Greg.

"How'd you like it, Chuck?"

"You didn't get my good side, I'm going to sue. Hell, Greg, it was a great job. My family, especially the kids, think I'm a hero."

"You're already that in my book, Chuck. Listen, if ever you want company, I'll be glad to fish with you, and I'll bring the beer."

"You better. Thanks, I'll give you a call when I'm desperate."

Going to bed, he paused for a moment like he always did, thanking the Lord for the life that had been given him. He also thanked his wife for the wonderful gift that transformed his normal outlook from existence to excitement.

No need to describe the next day. Frank Sinatra couldn't have been more received than Chuck was at the center. His resolve of modesty was somewhat eroded by the warm-hearted attention and fawning so generously showered upon him. Maggie giggled as she told him about the pledges of financial support pouring in from all over and that the county was going to increase her funding. He shook his head in faux disbelief that what he was a part of could produce such results. As things ground down to a somewhat routine morning and having had his precious cup of coffee, he was informed by Maggie that the local fishing club was sponsoring a fish-off, whatever that was. On the date mentioned in the flyer, all comers were invited for a one-day fishing competition, involving two categories. One for the most fish caught by weight and the other for the largest single fish by weight. The prize: one thousand dollars. Wow.

It was as if a red flag had been waved before the bull. Dang, he was going for the gold. On that day, loaded with goodies, sunscreen, and a plush cushion provided over his objections by Jenn, he set out from the docks, the kids cheering him on with no doubts that he would emerge the winner, hands down.

This time his approach was more serious, and he reinforced that bent by the inclusion of a heavier test line, this one he specifically looked for. He discarded the nonchalance that was his hallmark and was more determined than he ever remembered. Did fame change him? Was he becoming what he disdained? No, not really. He now felt that instead of just being lucky, he was going to work at being what the true fisherman had to endure: disappointment, hoping for a good catch, a reward for actually accomplishing what they set out to achieve. These and other things made him realize the sweat and tears that the others had endured and, maybe in no small way, fueled their resentment toward his successes.

Having accepted that self-imposed examination, he was still determined to enjoy whatever the day would bring, be it success or failure. As the morning wore on, his fabulous luck still held, and he landed some nice specimens. Into the barrel they went. Their size precluded being entered into the contest, but not Maggie's kitchen. Now he quietly thanked Jenn for the cushion, its softness taking the edge off the hard slat he sat on.

His part of the lake was empty of other craft, which wasn't that unusual considering its size. It also eliminated any distraction from talkative anglers who would invariably recite "the ones that got away," or some other irritating behavior. He settled comfortably under the shelter half, shaded from the warming sun. Occasionally, with the pole in its holder, he would pull out a length of line and hold it between his fingers. If he happened to doze off and got a nibble, the vibes would instantly awaken him. Settling in, content that Maggie would have a load for tomorrow's lunch, he closed his eyes. Not having a watch, he couldn't tell you how long he was in stasis, but his body shot erect when the signal on the line was felt.

"Okay, pal, give me what you got," he muttered. One jolt, then another. This guy was really making his presence known. Then the line went slack. *Well, yah can't win 'em all.* The thought barely receded when another forceful yank nearly plucked the rod from his hands. *Yeah, that's what I want. Come on, baby. Give me a fight.* If this baby was as big as he thought, Maggie was goin' to have a feast for a week. Again the pause, but Chuck would have none of it. This guy was playing possum; the comparison made him grin, and he relished the moment of levity. True to his suspicions, the line went taut again, prompting him to reinforce his grip. The reel started to protest the action by the unwinding of its spool, the speed increasing by the second.

Go, baby, go. Tire yourself out, I got all day.

The reel went silent. With this he started to crank the line in. As strange as it may be, Chuck reacted only out of his own sense of instinct, not knowing if what he was doing was correct or not. It had been his hallmark all through the years of fishing and as good as anything else he may have tried. One could only wonder how the pros would have shaken their collective heads if they had been privy to his style. That was speculation; this was real. Again the line played out, but the captive decided to make a circular course turn and head under the boat. If that happened, the line could foul, and he might lose the catch. Quickly he started the electric motor and brought the craft in the opposite direction that would nullify the fish's intent.

It worked, and the line was again away from the *AMY*. For the next hour, it was cat and mouse, another comparison that broke the tension somewhat. He had a chance to quickly gulp a refreshing bottle of beer, cupping the container between his wrists while holding the rod.

This guy really wants to battle it out. It'll almost be a shame if I net him. He wants nothing more than to go home.

So intent was he on the competition that he overlooked the obvious; this was no ordinary fish. The struggle alone should have been a tipoff. Could it be—yes, all the signs were there. No other fish could have done what he did. The stamina, the strength. He was a pro. It had to be the Ghost! Armed with that conclusion, he knew that what was to follow would take all his guile and energy. This was one of his hardest outings, the sweat penetrating his jersey and turning the light color blue almost black. His admiration for the finned fighter promoted a conflict. Did he really want to end the rivalry? He considered his age and health; he may never have another chance.

Too much was invested not to continue, and his sporting nature would not let him concede a release for his valiant opponent, as a moment's weakness almost suggested. So the struggle continued. Recognizing the Ghost as his adversary, he heightened his awareness and what tactics he could apply. Paramount was preventing the hook being thrown, but that was largely out of Chuck's hands unless he made a huge blunder. He pressed his mind to recall some of the fishing episodes he and the kids would watch on rainy days. Mostly it was to remember when to let the run occur or when to apply the drag. Regrets surfaced for not paying more attention, and now he may pay for it.

So far what he executed bore a surprising level of success even he didn't know how he was achieving it. If only the backbiters could see him now; they would swim the sea of "I told you so." He was committed, no turning back even if he wanted to. That thousand bucks was a great incentive, but here was a need for more than incentive, as he began to feel faint. For almost two hours he had tackled his greatest prize and wondered if he could continue. He needed to rest if the fish would allow him to do so. Sighting a partially submerged tree, he angled the AMY to the large-surfaced branches and limbs. Securing the boat to the floating flotsam, the rod was lashed to the biggest limb, freeing his tired arms.

Exhausted, he slumped to the deck and let out a rush of air. Oh, that felt good. Basking in the exquisite relaxation since bedtime, he wasn't in any rush to resume the contest. In fact, the fish was probably thankful for the respite too. The silence was eerie, as if a truce had been declared between combatants. No broaching the surface, no birds squawking for bait, just the gentle lap of water against the side of the AMY. Chuck just wanted to lie there forever, an understandable if not very practicable desire. Yielding to the inevitable after about twenty or so minutes, he lifted his sore and aching body and ambled over to the rod. A tug on the line confirmed that the Ghost had not hightailed it to the hills.

Okay, what do I do now? he thought, something alien to his fishing experiences. *Shucks, I'll just shove off and see what happens.* No sooner had he cleared the tree then the Ghost answered for him. Thank heavens for the layover, it was enough to counter the pull exerted by his captive. The speed, while still impressive, was slower than before. Was the Ghost tiring? Chuck made no effort to reign in his quarry, depending on the exertion to work for him. After another half hour of different tactics that failed to throw the hook, it appeared that a surrender was in sight. Could this be it? The end of a legend? There was very little resistance as the line was reeled in, bringing the compliant and exhausted battler to the side of the boat. Yes, it was the Ghost.

Chuck was held in awe to see this beauty close-up, but he wanted more. With the shore of the lake close-by, his intention was to reach a shallow spot, with the line secured, and join the fish in the water to fully appreciate its bulk. Mooring successfully, over the side he went, carefully sliding into the calm surface gently, hoping to avoid anything that might spook the giant. Here was the culmination of years that saw battles and defeat on his part, but enjoyment nonetheless. It was as if he were going to interview a renowned star, the prominence of the Ghost that powerful. There was no movement by the still form, only the seeming acquiescence that his fate was sealed. Chuck ran his hand across his length, stroking him gently then pulling back abruptly. Just behind the dorsal fin was a deep gash, probably the result of an outboard motor prop. As with any wounded animal, the man's heart was rendered with deep sympathy. Oh, the pain it must have and is enduring. All this and still its fighting heart would not surrender the fight until its energy had ben sapped. He caressed its flanks gently, noting that he was even bigger than the unofficial reports had pegged him. There was no effort to flee, a posture that garnered sadness. This was to be the end of a magnificent creature, and it made no effort to avoid it. Chuck may be a pseudo fisherman, but he was a genuine human being. Cupping the fish's head in his hands, he spoke to it as one comrade to another.

"No, my friend, you won't be hoisted on the scale to determine your weight, or stretched out to list your length.

"You won't be the subject of gawkers who could never know your true worth, or the fighting heart that some men could only hope to emulate. We've had our time, and it's best to let you have your own. Go, enjoy your home and stay away from people like me."

The ghost stayed motionless, and if there was any way to read the mind of an animal, especially this one, what would it reveal? A dog wags his tail, a cat purrs against your face, what does a fish do to reveal its innermost feelings, if indeed it has any? One would like to think that indeed there was a connection between the two, especially on the part of the Ghost. Let us say actions speak volumes, and in this case it was the refusal of the sturgeon to move.

The hook had been removed, the line set aside, and yet the giant just held his position, looking in Chuck's direction. Was he looking into his eyes? One couldn't really tell, but how could one not surrender to this romanticism? Finally, with a gentle push, the silvery object moved to the side and turned outward. Having gone but a few yards, it turned toward Chuck, paused, then resumed his journey to the depths of the lake, kicking up a froth of water, then disappearing.

No thought of the money he had lost weighed on him. If held to that standard, a quarter of the Ghost's weight would have been sufficient to win the competition. And that would have been the end of the countless stories his existence generated.

Returning to the dock, he grossly understated his reply when asked how he did. Fair. That was the sum total of what he would share with questioners. His catch came in third, but the catch he gave up would always top the charts. Congratulating the winner and tying down *AMY*, Chuck headed home, with lots of memories of the day's actions to occupy his thoughts. He would never try to catch the famous legend again; it had earned its freedom, if only from him.

With no school to worry about, Mason flipped when his grandfather told him to grab his fishing gear.

"For real, Poppy? We're goin' fishing?"

"You bet, squirt. Mom has a lunch packed for you."

On an impulse which he rarely acknowledged or reacted to, he called his daughter.

"What's up, Dad?"

"I'm taking Scooter fishing."

"Dad, he's too young."

"He'll be okay. I'll strap him onto the seat. I want him with me today." Why he would bring him against his previous concerns for the boy's safety was something even he could not reconcile. Why the urgency? Nevertheless, the boys were ecstatic, impatient to sail the high seas. Maggie, who loved the kids, saw them off, entrusting each tyke with a muffin and a cup of chocolate. Could life be any better than this?

The AMY puttered through the water as the anxious brood occupied their grandfather with all kinds of chatter, the favorite being, "Are we there yet?" Finally, he dropped anchor and handed Mason a smaller rod, the boy's eyes glistening with excitement. Scooter was a little less than thrilled at being hot tied to the seat, but Chuck mollified him somewhat by handing him a fishing line. He looped a farther section around a cleat, knowing that a free line taken by a fish of good size could injure the boy's small hands. He gazed at his charges with the satisfaction that comes with knowing what fine men they would one day become. He hoped to see that.

Getting ready to cast his line, he was struck with a sharp pain on the right side of his chest. The sudden bolt of discomfort almost caused him to stumble.

"Poppy, what's the matter?" an alarmed Mason shouted. Regaining some composure, he assured the frightened boy that it must be the heebie-jeebies, a term he frequently used to describe some setback or other. This calmed Mason as he had heard it so many times without the result of dire consequences.

This was no harmless heebie-jeebies. Chuck knew something was seriously wrong. Not wishing to alarm the boys, especially Mason, who could understand better than his brother, he feigned a problem with the boat's motor.

"Hey, squirt, we have to go in. The engine didn't sound right, and we don't want to be caught out if it broke down."

"Aw, Poppy." Disappointment written into a pleading face wanting to stay out there. "Do we have to?"

Fighting the creeping pain, he tried to answer in the usual confident manner he always projected. "Yep, but we'll go out again."

Fortunately, Maggie was still on the dock when she saw the boat coming in. As it neared, she saw the discomfort in Chuck's face and his hands and arms waving to her to take the boys right away.

Tying up, and knowing a serious situation was in hand, she scooped up the boys with a promise of more chocolate and some doughnuts.

"Yah comin', Poppy?"

"Go ahead, I'll be right there."

Once inside the center, the frightened woman called for an ambulance and then notified Jenn. With the staff looking after the children, she raced back to the dock. Her hero was nearly unconscious.

"Don't let the boys see me like this."

Cradling him in her arms, she held him until the ambulance arrived and took him away. Jenn arrived soon after and left for the hospital.

The following day, the center was devoid of the chatter frequently abundant throughout the hall. The *AMY* lay at her berth, quietly moving from side to side as the swells washed her sides, her motor silent. The lakefront was shrouded with an atmosphere that competed with the gray skies overhead. The knight in shining armor had ascended to Camelot.

A few days later, one the fishermen who had been frustrated by Chuck's successes came across the final chapter that ended the legend of the lake. A huge silvery form, with a large gash behind its dorsal fin, was found floating, as if wanting to be discovered. No more would it promote the desire and competition to ensnare it. No more would it invite all comers to accept the challenge its existence created. Was it a coincidence that its demise, the cause of which was never determined, came so soon after the passing of his greatest pursuer? Could it have been a surrender from a life fully lived and which now had no focal point of contention? Some would deride this comparison that only humans are invested with, that when a loved one passes, another will follow not far behind. Can we dismiss this? We'll never know, but the hint of possibility will always fuel the debates that surely will flourish around these two icons.

A Slice of Life

Part One
Introduction

Pineview. A small town like hundreds if not thousands that dot the landscape of this country. Its census numbers less than nine thousand souls which inhabit a settlement that is bordered on one side by a rolling countryside of trees and meadows coexisting with rich farmland. On the other side is the encroaching phenomena of suburbia. Its existence is permeated by a closeness borne of its size, enjoying a moderate business community and a thriving social network. The apparent sameness of its construct is ignored by the attitudes of those who have lived here for years, the familiarity engendering a contentment and appreciation of what a small town breeds. They may lack the sophistication of their larger counterparts or the bigger cities, but to them, they could do without the hustle and bustle, settling on a more docile lifestyle. This is not to say they lack entrepreneurial skills or are devoid of some industrial or manufacturing capabilities. They are just tucked away, by design or happenstance, in areas that don't compete with the almost pastoral ambiance they enjoy. In such a setting, there are small clans, families who have lived here for decades and newcomers with a shorter claim. Crime is no stranger but manageable. The low-key of daily life mutes any serious rivalry that could disrupt the harmony that eludes other municipalities. Many might gauge the success of any town by its affluence, but in this case, they would surely be wrong. Its strength is its community, a community that shares and cares. Smallness breeds a certain maternal sense of embrace, a trait so entrenched it has become innate, if not consciously acknowledged. This is the setting awaiting Richard "Richie" Murphy, a product of this town.

Okay, Richie just finished his semester for the year and was home, looking forward to the downtime before resuming his education. Pop promised him a car if he did all right with his grades, and he couldn't wait to see the spiffy girl magnate that awaited him. Gulping down his breakfast and encouraging his father to do likewise, they left the house and drove to Pete's Garage. Pete usually had some neat and cool cars that, if not new, were clean and affordable. Oh boy, the excitement welled within Richie's chest as they drove into the lot.

Pete is an affable guy who smiles a lot and impresses his customers with a trusting façade. It's not easy to accomplish this as many would be car buyers have been burned or disappointed.

"Pete, you remember Richie?"

"Yeah, he was about as big as my beagle last time I saw him." The laugh that followed was joined by the other two. "Well, what have you got for me?"

"Over here, just got it in. Everything works, good engine and nice interior." Richie was almost drooling, for this has got to be a knockout.

Pete ushered them to the rear lot where a tarp had been draped over what would be Richie's dream college gift.

Hurry, hurry, I'm dyin'! screamed the young man's mind. As the tarp was removed, his heart sank.

"How do you like it?"

"Like it? Like it?" he muttered to himself. "It's a dog." A 1989 Buick Century, hardly a chick chariot. Then a moment of reflection. *Okay, if this is what Dad got me, then that's what'll be,* he thought. After all, his father wasn't rolling in dough, and he vowed to make the most of it. Some guys didn't have cars; he did.

Thanking Pete, Richie told his dad that he would be home after a trip to the DMV to register the car. Hugging his dad, and slapping

Pete on the back, he headed out. Along the way he saw a friend of his from high school days, Jooster.

"Hey, Joos, want a ride?"

"Well, I'll be, the prodigal son returneth."

"Yeah, on the way to register my 'new' car."

"Need company?"

"Yeah, hop in."

It's great meeting a school chum after months of rubbing elbows with strangers and wannabes. Man, how the past trials and errors surfaced without too much effort, causing some embarrassment and a lot of mirth.

"What are your plans? Work, loafing, Foreign Legion?"

"That was my first choice, but I don't speak French."

"Hey, chowder head, that's why they call it the Foreign Legion, don't they teach you that stuff at school?"

"I know, I know, just wanted to see if you were alert."

A wandering fly or casual observer would be hard-pressed to separate the serious from the hijinks that these two perpetrated on each other. It didn't have to make sense, because not making sense was the sense in itself. These were kids' minds inhabiting young men's bodies. After taking care of business, a casual drive down what in many other towns would be considered a side road, but in Pineview, it was the main drag. How familiar the different storefronts, quite a few to engage the daily shoppers or transients.

Jolly's barbershop was always a source of amusement, as the kids would press the snouts against the glass and make faces at the customers. Being ensconced in a chair with the barber cropping the hair or shaving the neck prevented any retaliation by an irate patron lest he shed some blood or receive an unwelcome crew cut.

These and other memories needed no further stimuli for them to relive the bygone days of their youth. Dropping his friend off at home, Richie had a taste for some pizza and where best to go, then to Marco's, who had the best offerings in the world, or at the least the county. Upon seeing the young customer, the Italian owner gave him a big embrace and inquired about his absence.

"Hey, Marco, didn't I tell you I was going to college?"

"Mamma Mia, I forget, yousa was a here one a day and den yousa gone. How 'bouta I make a you a bigga pie?"

"Just a slice, Marco, I have to get home."

A small town like this was an incubator for many relationships, great if they were cordial, disastrous if they were not. Richie was fortunate to have the former. He then stopped at the park and strolled over to the pond. The geese always pleased him, and reaching for a portion of the pie he had secured in a bag, a throng gathered at the morsels he threw into the water. Lying on the grass revived a sense of gradualness that was absent from the hectic days of study, going from one class to another. He drank it all in, for soon, in the fall, another rat race would commence.

A ball bounced his way, and he grabbed it before it could go into the water, disturbing the gorging fowls. A tyke of about three breathlessly approached and, displaying an absolute, total disregard for age or protocol, sternly demanded that his ball be returned.

"You know, my friend, I usually charge money to give back things that I save."

Taken aback, the now subdued toddler said, "All I have is one penny. Please, can I have the ball back?"

"Well, let's see. I usually charge three pennies when I save something, but let's see."

Reaching into his pocket, Richie withdraws two cents and, while doing so, noticed what appeared to be the boy's mother, who had witnessed the exchange and was smiling.

Giving a wink, Richie turned to the boy and said, "Guess what? Two more pennies appeared in my pocket, and that makes three. I guess you will be getting your ball back after all. And since you were so good, I'm going to give it to your mother to save for you, okay?" With that, the peewee threw his arms around the shining knight's neck and hugged him. "Bye, man." Off went another satisfied customer.

The small things that he missed were larger because of their absence. The only thing that made being away from home an empty experience was the thought of returning. No big expectations, just the unvarnished life of everyday encounters enriched by whatever motivations were subscribed to. He drove home and began to think of supper. Ah, supper. His mouth almost succumbed to drooling as he thought of the different meals Mom could whip up from scratch. What would it be tonight? Meat loaf, which was his heart's passion?

Or Stromboli, which she created as deftly as a magician pulling a rabbit from a hat? Whatever it was, his stomach would not feel cheated.

Before dinner, he sat on the front porch swing, waving at passing neighbors who welcomed him home. His sister, Jenn, came out and handed him a glass of iced tea. They were pretty close and had lots of fun together. He would cause her face to redden when he asked if Clifford was still making eyes are her. Ah, young love. She had missed him and curled up on the swing beside him. She placed her head on his lap as she always did, and he stroked her curls. Being fourteen, there was plenty of time for her to grow up, and he relished his place in the stages of her life.

"Supper's ready," came a call from inside the house.

"Race ya."

"You always win."

"Okay, I'll make it easy for you. I'll count to three, and you can shoot out on two."

The girl was now going to take down her big brother.

"One—"

And with that, Richie shot into the house.

"Hey, no fair."

"Sure it is, I said you could go on two, and I always keep my promises. I didn't say anything 'bout when I would go." With that he gave her a big hug, and she kissed his cheek. Big brother was home, and he showed it.

After a scrumptious meal, the family retired to the living room, where Jenn plopped on the floor, head on pillow and earbuds blasting the latest music. Mom relaxed on her rocking chair, knitting something, the origin of which would not be known until presented to the recipient, something she did regularly. Dad was engaged in the latest world and local events, which were gleaned from the *Daily Bugle*, the county paper.

And Richie, surrounded by the greatest wealth anyone could ask for, just sat there for a while, counting his blessings. Satisfied that his appreciation of life had been acknowledged, he flipped on the TV to watch a game of baseball. They could have been a better team, but what the heck, it was something. After a few innings, he drifted into another world. A new day would be in the offing.

The morning sun had a sneaky habit of finding that tiny space between the window blind slats and his face, annoyingly beating the snooze alarm to the punch. After offering forgiveness to sol, he donned his clothes and marched down to the kitchen.

"Hey, sleepyhead, were you gonna stay in bed all day? It's seven thirty." His dad would always needle him, but Richie would always come back.

"I need my rest to put up with all you deficient people." With that his dad flung a damp kitchen towel at him.

"What's your plans?"

"Think I'll just play it by ear, Dad. So many people to look up."

"Does that include Steve?" Ouch, that one bit him. Steve was a good friend of his, the two growing up together and sharing many of the hijinks kids often indulge in, with each blaming the other when caught doing something wrong. Just before leaving for college, their exploration of the political scene fostered many a debate on the qualities and commitment of several candidates. Not intended as a point of conflict, it nevertheless devolved into a point-by-point heated discussion as to the acceptability of one particular candidate. The dust was flying through the air, neither one surrendering any point of contention. At its height of acrimony, Steve stalked from the house, slamming the door so hard a pane of glass shattered.

"Heavens, what was that?" cried out Richie's mother as she ran to investigate.

"Nothing, Ma, just a little disagreement with Steve."

"Good thing it wasn't a big one from the commotion I heard."

"I'll take care of it, Mom." Which was what he hadn't done before leaving for college. It festered on him and hadn't really been forgotten. But he guessed that both their prides would be a barrier to reconciliation until one of them saw the light.

"Well, Dad, if he doesn't slam the door in my face or something more dramatic, I'm going over to see him."

"Aren't you that sixteen-year-old son I had that knew everything?"

"Well, he thought he did. Now he has to find out if he learned anything after five years."

With that, Richie laid his hand on his dad's shoulder, who in turn placed his hand on top of it, a sign of silent support. It felt really strange, not knowing how this was going to work out. They used to fight a little, but the punches weren't as hard as the knot he felt in his stomach. Oh, well, onward to the execution. Alas, poor Richie, I knew him well—or well enough to know that this day was not going too well already, not at 8:00 a.m. Driving the Buick with the stain of original sin, er, dislike—oh, it's a dreadful car—he headed to Steve's house.

Now I know how Marie Antoinette felt before she got her short haircut, Richie mused. Getting out of the car, he spotted Steve in the side yard. At first, his look was one of surprise, then, to Richie's amazement, he started laughing so hard he doubled up. Incredulously, the bearer of reconcilability could only gawk at what seemed to be a display of directed humiliation. And it was. Steve shouted out, "And *that's* your dream car?" Again he let out another round of stomach tumblers. Somewhat chastened by this assault upon his vehicular acquisition, he sucked in his gut and walked toward his onetime, maybe-never-to-be-again friend and muttered a "Hi, Steve."

Growing a different and serious face, the young man strode toward Richie, silent and determined. Was he going to spit at him, kick him in the shins, or lay a wallop on his head? Reaching with both arms, causing Richie to withdraw slightly, he embraced the startled friend, or non-friend, that to be determined by the next move.

"Hey, pal, we both messed up."

The air drained from Richie's lungs in relief, and he returned the arm wrapping scenario with the same passion.

"Boy, that was dumb of us."

"On your part, dummy, I was corrupted by you, it's your fault."

With that, both now-friends-again buddies tumbled to the grass, rolling over and over. Oh, how exquisite the scent of forgiveness.

"And what was that crack about my car, punk?"

"You mean that refugee from a scrapyard?"

"Yeah, I know what you mean, Steve, but Dad could only afford that."

"I'm pulling your chain, Rich, I know if he could afford anything better, it would probably be a Jag."

"Yeah, it would be small enough so that I wouldn't have to lug you with me." Another round on the grass, their laughter uniting their past friendship with more to follow.

"You got plans for tonight?"

"Hadn't thought about it."

"Think about this. Ever since you came home, Vicky's been asking about you."

"She has? I mean, we never really connected."

"That's because your brain is disconnected. Didn't you ever notice her mooning eyes whenever she got within adoring distance of you?"

"Not really. In case you have forgotten, I was enmeshed, or should I say messed up, with Gloria."

"Yeah, whatever happened to you two?"

"Beats me. She said I wasn't serious enough. For Pete's sake, I was heading for college."

"Don't make no difference."

"Well, let's see what's on for the summer while I'm still single and free."

The drive home provided Richie with the solitude to appreciate the mending of a very broken fence. *Throw at me what you will, world, I am ready. Almost.* Stopping at the traffic light, the wafting odor from Marco's excited the gastronomical juices in his stomach. No further invitation was needed. Parking in the lot, and hurrying to satiate his palate, he almost knocked over a slim beauty with auburn hair and hazel eyes—Vicky!

"Oh, Richie, you didn't have to clobber me to get attention." She was giggling at her self-imposed attempt at humor.

"Ah, sorry, Vick, was in a hurry. You okay?"

"Not that a slice of pizza can't remedy."

Oh, boy, what next, he thought. "Yeah, I guess I can spring for that, college didn't take all my money."

Vicky was a nice person to begin with, and her infatuation with Richie had not subsided one bit. Her only change was to be more reserved, and this had an effect on the boy. He didn't feel he had to run for the hills, with Daisy Mae on his heels. In fact, they were very much in sync with each other as both spilled their respective tales. Time fosters maturity in many surprising ways, and it showed with her.

"Rich, there's a dance at the high school Saturday. Do you think you'll go?" An invitation if ever he heard one.

"Could be, would you like to go with me?"

"Oh, I'm sorry, Dave, you remember him from science, is taking me."

Bummer. Oh well. "Maybe I'll see you there if I go."

They spent a little more time together, then he took her home.

"Oh, what a lovely car." On the other hand, maybe she hadn't matured enough.

Okay, one save, one near miss, not too bad for the second day home. What else? Being a small town didn't provide many opportunities for diversity, but he was used to this life. It had treated him well. Seek and ye shall find.

He thought about the differences in Gloria and Vicky. Both were pretty, but their makeups were different. The latter was cheerful and outgoing, but her earlier personality was just a little too flighty for him. Maybe that was why he paid scant attention to her. Gloria knew what she wanted, and her self-confidence needed no additional support. While pleasant, she always seemed to possess an inner drive that demanded near perfection. Maybe that was why they couldn't make it together. Oh well, win none, lose all.

Dinner that night was the magnet it always was, at least for Richie. It was his alcohol, so to speak, to relieve him of the small disappointment with Vicky. Why did it bother him so?

He looked at Jenn, hoping her approach to boys would fare better than his to women.

Decisions, decisions. If he was going to the dance, he'd need some new clothes. After breakfast, he decided to walk to Earl's Department Store. While not very large, it stocked quite a few items that someone or other always needed. In his case, a new sports jacket and a pair of slacks. Acquiring his new duds and bidding farewell to the clerk, his attention drifted and—*pow*. He slammed into a solid chunk. Facing the stationary and possibly crippled object of his careless meandering, his eyes widened with surprise in sync with his mouth.

"Ben, you ole dog, hope I didn—"

The words trailed off into silence. Before him stood a well-filled-out US Army uniform, medals on its chest not only attesting to the honors received in combat but its result as well, an empty right sleeve. Ben had been a classmate of Richie's during high school, a personable person whose athletic ability was demonstrated on the football field. His running skills had earned him many honors, but he was also a mentor to the younger players. How he would allow them to almost dominate his time because he was a caring person. One did not have to go far to figure that out; in school, he was the bane of bullies who tried to cow the younger or defenseless students with their fear tactics.

His presence alone ensured that those days were over. He was tough but not a wise guy or someone who took advantage of a bad situation. He was the boy next door, and many a girl in the senior class knew it. After graduation, he and Richie and a few of the regulars hit the circuit of post day school parties. They had a good time, sans any alcoholic overkill, beer being the choice of poison. Mellowing and feeling good, the group lay on the grass in the park, each describing his future intent. Ben was going to join the military. What? He doesn't have to. It's all volunteer, you dope, no drafting. Of course, they knew that but had fun needling him. They also knew of no one more suited to defend the honor of this county than Ben.

Now Richie faced his friend, battle scarred and still imposing in his stature.

"Darn it, Ben, I feel dopey."

"You always were, you clod, come'ere." With his right arm, the damaged warrior drew the mute collider into as good an embrace as one limb could manage. Richie made up for it with a deeply heartfelt crush with both his arms. "Hey, don't get sloppy on me, I just hand this uniform pressed."

"Gee, Ben, it's great seeing you again." Richie's embarrassment fading with the outreach of his buddy. "What's up?"

"Well, I want to go to the dance Saturday and was figgering on civies but changed my mind. In fact, a lot changed my mind."

"What do you mean?"

"I don't want a repeat of what happened when you saw me for the first time."

"Ben, that was only because you caught me off guard. Listen, hero, plenty of people would love to see ya there."

"Hey, pal, in case your eyes have conked out, I'm not all here."

"Well, in that case, Freddy Sinclair, the nerd shouldn't come either, because he's not all there either." Richie emphasizing the statement by pointing his finger to his head.

"You're a cruel man, but I get your drift. Will you be going?"

"Yeah."

"Good, I'll need all the support I can get."

Richie felt a pang of sadness. Sadness that a selfless person could think that he'd need supportive strength when that's all he ever gave to others. *No, my friend, I'll be with you to fend off those fears that I know will never materialize.* They left Earl's and had a bite at Marco's before the soldier was driven home. The Welcome Home banners were still fluttering in front of the house.

"I'll pick you up at seven, and be sure you wear that uniform. That way they won't notice the rags I'll be wearin'." His voice a soothing assurance.

On the way home, Richie remembered Dad telling him that Ben had returned from overseas and that he had been wounded but didn't know the extent of his injuries. The boy had just shipped in a few days before the errant son had come home from college, so there wasn't much info to go on. Oh, how he wished he'd known, not only to avoid the scene in the shop, but to have gone to see him.

He stopped at the park, again to disfigure the grass with his bulk and to taunt the geese with his faux honking sounds. The ground was cool, and he spread out, hands clasped behind his head, staring up at the clouds, trying to find people or animals in their formations. A tiny head impeded his gazing by bending over his face.

"Hi, man."

It was the little boy who conned two cents from him. *Maybe he thinks I'm his bank,* a sarcastic thought that was an attempt at humor. The tyke was a cutie all the way, what with dark-brown hair and green eyes, his diminutive size so endearing. Mom was right behind, smiling an acceptance to the encounter.

After their first meeting, the lad had pestered his mother with all kinds of things to say about the man who saved his ball. Now he had another chance to meet his hero and made no bones about it.

"Hey, big guy, what's up?"

"I like you, man. Are you my friend?"

Oh, that the world would be populated by the untarnished mind of the innocents. Children are one of the best gauges of the human character. They have no guile or even know the definition or usage of the word. Sparkling they are and in many cases are avoided by the less pure because they are reminded of what they lack.

Richie introduced himself to the mother with the admonition, "We have to stop meeting like this, people are starting to talk." The boy looked at him quizzically, not understanding the humor inherent in the statement but looking intently at his new friend. Talking to the woman, it was learned the boy's father had passed away, and he pined for the companionship his father had fostered. The chance meeting the other day brought a new light into his eyes that had been drifting away, little by little. Learning of this, Richie felt a new appreciation for the leprechaun-like bundle.

They visited the park on a regular basis, and he made a point to scour the grounds when in the neighborhood so that he could hook up with his new friend. Recalling his years as far as he could remember of his youth, he too was caught up in the fatherly interest that his dad showered upon him. The many mock battles that he "won" by defeating the "evil" prince of darkness. He smiled, the belief at that age that he was victorious because of his combative skills. Bless the innocence that was reinforced by the kindness of his parents.

Dinner that evening held a certain withdrawal on Richie's usually animated tabletop conversation.

"What's up, son, you look a little down, as if someone stole your car."

"That would be an impro—" He caught his tongue in time. "An improper thing to do." Whew.

"That's an odd way of saying it, and you're right, but what's eating you?"

"I met Ben at Earl's today and afterward a little boy who lost his father."

"You can't save everyone on the world."

"I know, but I just want to save the ones I know."

Mom peered at him with her maternal look, and her smile conveyed her approval.

Instead of watching the game, he decided to plop on the porch, inviting a chance to snooze. The sandman cast his granular residue upon the compliant recipient, a receipt for payment his fluttering eyelids. No sooner had they closed then a startling summons encasing his name rang out.

"Richie, you're home."

Oh, no, that voice. It could only be one person, Gloria! Reluctantly rising from his cherished prone position of comfort, and very grudgingly, he saw the source of his discomfort. A very shapely woman, with jet-black hair and eyes to match. This was a discomfort? He walked to the door and stepped out, waving his hands to indicate a seat on the steps. Side by side they sat, Richie uncomfortable by her sudden appearance and what it might portend. They hadn't left on the best of terms, so what was her game? Her overture caught him by surprise.

"I'd like you to take me to the dance, Richie, if you're going."

Oh, boy, that came out of left field, but I'm going to make a shoestring catch. "Er, look, I don't think it's a good idea."

"Why not?"

"Well, we didn't leave on the best terms, and I'd rather not test the waters again." Disappointment merged with the welling in her eyes.

"That was my mistake, a big one that I've regretted even before you left."

Wow, she means it, but how can I take a chance? he thought. "I believe you, but I have to resolve my misgivings about this. I wouldn't be comfortable just diving in again."

"I understand."

"Besides, I'm takin' Ben to the dance."

"Is he prettier than me?"

"He needs moral support, ya know?"

"I think that's great of you, Rich. Listen, I'm going to take off. See you at the dance?"

"Sure." He watched her moving down the steps, graceful as a cat. Yet there was no desire to ignite a romance, her veiled invitation an offer to be had.

The next morning was bright and helped dispel the partial gloom of yesterday. He would stroll again through the neighborhood, unconsciously adding names to the houses he passed. Mr. Herman, Sally Marsh, and so on. Then he saw a thundering yellow streak heading for him, unavoidable but welcome. The thudding crash established a union that was absent since the start of college.

"Buddy boy, how are you?" The lovable yellow lab belonged to Ms. Fricke, a sweet elderly woman who reminded him of the term *pixilated*, attributed to a character in a film he saw. The dog was her constant companion and protector. The animal nuzzled his snout into Richie's face, lapping it with his tongue in joyous delight.

Labs usually give their friendship openly, but he had a special relationship with his now returned friend. Richie had a sense of guardianship for Ms. Fricke, who at times seemed to be in another world. Not that she was truly deficient, but had an air of floating through each day, harmlessly going about her routine, alive with spirit and a purpose, infecting others with her zest for life. As a young boy, he ran errands for her, cut her grass, and delighted in the home-made apple pie she used as payment for his services. At times he would sit with her and revel in the fairy-tale stories she'd weave, engrossing his mind with the visions she planted.

This was no hit-or-miss thing but a truly developed relationship that he cherished. Her ability to fend for herself was evident, but Richie and his family always kept close tabs on her. Knocking on the door brought a frail-looking woman with the typical bun hairstyle of a school marm to the entrance. Upon opening the door, her sight of Richie propelled her down the steps, almost leaping into his arms.

"Oh, you're home. How I missed you, and so did Buddy. My, you look so handsome. Come on in, I have some apple pie made fresh."

He relived the old days, the pie a mere reminder of all the kind things she had done for him. Especially the cookies she mailed to the college and for which he was the envy of anyone he shared them with.

The knitted scarves, the woven sweaters, fleeced-lined gloves. Many of these things he still retained if only to remind him of her, since many didn't fit anymore. This was the benefit of a small town where familiarity need not breed contempt and which contrasted sharply with the community of college students whose loyalties were varied but not as hardened as this town's. Here was a permanence typical of a close-knit, unofficial family found nowhere else. This was so demonstrated by the way she fussed over him like a hen with her chick. She almost wiped his face, which had managed to smear itself with the golden goodness of her delectable pie. Buddy's head lay on his lap, eyeing the intake of the baked morsel, hoping somehow that a misdirected forkful would manage to escape the clutches of the fork and find its way to his mouth. Alas, Richie was more hungry than careless, although in recognizing the loyalty of his K-9 friend, he slipped a portion into his mouth when Ms. Fricke had turned away for a moment.

His affection for the woman was as firm as a boulder in a hurricane, and he tried to ease any loneliness evident in her solitary life. As he left, she loaded him with all kinds of goodies that almost embarrassed him, as he had nothing to offer. But in fact he did; his presence was a gift magnified by their years of friendship, her eyes gleaming with a content dispelling any fears for her well-being. He placed his arms around her tiny form, which disappeared into the folds of his arms as if a magician had made her disappear. The union lingered for many moments, each reluctant to surrender the delicious embrace so quickly. Walking to the door, she bade him goodbye with a kiss on his cheek and a smile of thanks.

Do they have many people like her in the world? He hoped so. It would be a pale existence without them. Noting the time, he scurried back home for lunch. Dad was at work, and Mom was just finishing what he hoped would be the usual feast. He looked at his mother as she did her labors in yeoman fashion, almost never complaining, unless it would be to rankle Richie about his slovenly kept room. But that was in the old days, and he, having reformed, she had to search high and low to come up with a convincing gripe. Now she had one, something inbred, inborn, or innate in every mother throughout history—was he ever going to get serious about any women? Sure, he had college, but that didn't mean the foundation couldn't be laid down.

What is it with mothers who want their kids to give them babies? It was like the Chinese water torture—drip, drip, drip.

"Mom, you worry too much."

"I don't want to come down the aisle in a walker."

Laughing, he quipped, "Mom, you're not an old hag—at least not yet." To which she slapped him with the kitchen towel. Born Lynne Carol Carlucci, the year being unimportant, she grew up as an only child. This had some effect on her as she was very outgoing and friendly. There was no lack of love or happiness in the family, but somehow she sensed an absence she'd only recognize when she grew older.

Knowing this, she was determined that when she married, children would be plentiful. Her dark-brown hair, straight and shiny, mated perfectly with her delicate figure, prompting some to urge her into a modeling career. By her own words, she was not a "paper doll." Working as a sales clerk at Earl's, she met her future husband, Brian Murphy, who was so taken with her that he forwent the jibes from his friends that he spent too much time at the cosmetics department.

It was this determination to absorb the barbs from his friends that convinced her of his sincerity. His persistence was rewarded when she accepted an offer of a Coke at the soda fountain at lunch.

Lynne was no starry-eyed female, having her feet planted firmly in reality, but she left a little room for romanticism. Brian supplied that in spades. He was fairly handsome with a prominent jaw paired with an angular face, blue, blue eyes, and as curly a mop of light brown hair that crowned his head. His effort to woo her went very slowly, not wishing to turn her off with his impatience. On the other hand, she was a little miffed that he took so darn long to do anything. A match made in heaven. A roadblock to the developing romance was that they both worked day jobs, and the only opportunity for him to see her was during his lunch hour. Evening rendezvous were limited due to various commitments, frustrating both parties. This torturous separation of bodies and mind intensified their desire to be with each other, which in some ways was sated during the weekends, but not enough.

Finally, the Irishman staked his claim to her future by proposing, the words barely out his mouth when she pressed her lips to his in the affirmative. Ah, love, young love. Now she was older, but her youthful looks never deserted her, although being called pleasantly plump would elicit mock rage and another thrown towel. The "old man" still maintained his virility, despite a frosting of white at the temples. His jaw still radiated strength and determination, which revealed itself quite well when he'd be challenged on any issue with which he disagreed.

Their pairing was ideal but suffered the same pangs that all marriages endure. It was the resolutions to these bumps that were the secret to their harmony. They had it nailed. Lynne made the first installment on populating the household with the birth of Richie. The labor was difficult but rewarding with his entry into the world. Difficulties delayed the next entry into the family, Jenn, who came almost eight years later. It was later discovered that the birthing process had damaged Jennifer's chances for any more children. She mourned quietly the news but was thankful for the two angels she had. At least they wouldn't be alone.

Brian was a good a provider as any and surprised his wife from time to time with flowers.

"Are these 'not for any reason' flowers?" she chided.

"I don't think I did anything that had to be forgiven," he replied with his arms around her waist and kissing her neck from behind. As the breadwinner, he could always find comfort that his family enjoyed what his wages could support, "Keeping up with the Joneses" a concept never entertained. Working as foreman at the mill displayed his competent skills and garnered the respect of his charges. His intelligence was inborn, and what he didn't know he learned by the expedient practice of questioning, trial by error, or just plain common sense. The only chink in his armor was a temper and impatience; while not excessive, the kids knew better than to cross swords with him, while Jennifer always stood her ground. No one is perfect.

The children loved him as they did their mother. They didn't incite competition to judge who was better or who would relent to incessant requests for privileged treatment.

Lynne or Brian never lacked for love and respect from their children. Since Richie was the first to enter college, he set the standard that Lynn would hopefully match when it was her turn. This was yet to come, and Richie wound his arms around his mother, hugging her affectionately before setting off on another jaunt.

"Where to, Magellan?"

"Gee, Mom, I didn't know you knew anything about those fancy GPS gadgets." Again the towel soared toward his head, the dampness weighting the cloth enough to give it distance and effect.

"You know what I mean, you escapee from Count De Sade's castle."

"Ow, Mom, that hurt."

"Serves you right, crybaby."

There was no shortage of antics at the Murphy house, and in truth, they added considerably to the closeness that prevailed. Joy and happiness are as good at bonding as mortar is to masonry.

"There are a lot of people I want to catch up with. I'll be back before supper."

"You better, we're having ham steaks, sweet potatoes, tomatoes, and chocolate pudding." No better incentive than that.

"You bet, Mom." A fast cheek kiss and out the door.

He knew many acquaintances, but only a handful were special friends. These were acquired just being who he was, and the mutuality of the kinship served to highlight his early years. It was in these formative times when he could count on their assistance in time of need, and they could rely on him to do likewise. Like the time his baseball rolled into the culvert and his buddies helped him lift the heavy wrought iron grate to recover it. Or the time Timmy lost his pooch, and the guys spent hours looking for and then finding the little fur ball. So many instances through the years, no doubt mirrored by other Richies and other kids in other Pineviews.

Heading toward the ball field, he felt a need to smack a few into the outfield, hoping that some of the kids were playing pickup as he used to do. As he approached the grounds, the sound of youngsters yelling and cajoling, screaming and laughing, signaled the presence of our future—kids. No hurrying, random actions, miscues and hits, camaraderie, all these totaled up to the abstract and total joy freed from their young bodies. He paused and sat down on the remnants of an old bleacher seat, surveying the conflicting colors and styles of the boy's uniforms or clothing. He grinned. *Did I look like that? Most probably so.* Clothing etiquette was not a high priority, only fun.

His mind drifted back to a scene similar to this and recalled a not-so-pleasant memory. The morning chores were left unattended because of his eagerness to join any pickup game at the diamond. Having taken his position on the field, a blue Chevy pulled up, his father exiting the vehicle with a piqued expression on his face.

"Richie Murphy, here and now!"

The sound of his father's voice almost froze him in place, not to mention the embarrassment he felt. While Richie was basically a good kid, he was a little rebellious and at times would be prone to sulking. His youth could not fathom the many natural calls for freedom that his lively spirit thrust upon him, only that he had to answer them. And this was his problem, separating those urges from his responsibilities. While able to indulge in many youthful activities, they were wisely parceled out by his parents so that his time was well managed. He couldn't or would not see this, only that it infringed on what he and he alone wanted to do.

This probably happened with many youngsters at so tender an age, but to Richie, it was a form of solitary confinement at the Big House or a tour with the chain gang. Surprisingly, the normally good-natured boy developed a sullen attitude when he felt put upon. This was not going well, and his father laid down the law—sort of. Grounding or depriving his son of privileges didn't seem to be going anywhere, so how do you straighten him out? This was unchartered territory for the concerned father. Taking his son aside, he searched for a way to reach him. "Son, I want to talk to you, man to man." This was unexpected but resonated in the boy. He was being placed on even ground with his dad instead of being relegated as a mere bystander.

It wasn't so much what his dad said, but how he said it. A soft voice, an expression of deep concern, an offer of help in trying to overcome whatever problems he identified with. The boy saw the earnestness in his father's eyes, not a demanding parent, and his defiance softened considerably. All he knew was that maybe his dad was right in what he was trying to tell him, although he would not concede completely his own erring ways. Still, it wasn't something that corrected itself automatically but only with the continued efforts by both the boy and his parents.

As time wore on and growing responsibilities were assumed, voluntarily or otherwise, the youngster began to sort out the wheat from the chaff, so to speak; a different lad was emerging.

"Hey, Mister, watch out!"

Alerted by the warning, Richie instinctively raised his arms across his face. Wrong place. The ball squarely plunked him in the stomach but had no real punch.

"Gee, we're sorry."

"Hey, pal, happens all the time. I'm okay."

"I know who you are, Mr. Murphy, isn't it?"

"That's my dad, I'm Richie. Wait a minute, you're Douglas from March Street, aren't you?"

"Yeah, you have a good memory."

"Remember you when you and your uncle helped my father put up the side fence last year."

"Man, that was a tough one. Thanks for the sodas, it sure was hot that day."

There were just enough youngsters to field teams of seven each, and Richie managed to enlist in their ranks. Being bigger than all the rest incurred quips of unfairness by the opposing side, but his errors and lousy hitting more than atoned for his perceived advantage. All in all, it was great fun and an even greater release. The afternoon sped quickly but enjoyably. For the briefest of time, he was a kid again.

Have to do that more often, he thought to himself on the way home. The lure of a home-cooked meal again agitated his gastronomical environs and caused him to quicken his pace. He compared the expected feast to the fast-food joints near the campus that did no more than fill his stomach rather than excite his taste buds. *Better enjoy it while you can, you still have to leave in the fall. Bummer.*

"Hi, Mr. Rosen." A neighbor.

"Hello, Frankie." The newsboy.

"Still have it, Art." Remarking on the deft set shot that always cleared the net on the pole-mounted hoop. These and other people he encountered revealed no paucity in acquaintances and, to some degree, relieved his mind from the tantalizing and mouth-watering thought of food. Not just food, a banquet.

"Wipe your feet" was his normal greeting from Mom, a routine anticipated and observed lest the wrath of Kahn be visited upon the unwary. "And behave yourself."

"What for?"

"Clifford is our guest tonight. He and Jenn have a homework assignment and thought it would be nice for the both of them."

Oh boy, here was a chance to do a little teasing, but a stern look from his mother put ice on that idea. After washing up, Richie followed the scent wafting from the kitchen and took his seat at the table. Jenn was seated with Clifford, who sat very stiffly as if waiting for an inspection. Richie sat opposite and in perfect position to intimidate him. Jenn sensed the mayhem, mild though it be, that her brother may perpetrate against a helpless victim.

Looking at him, she silently pleaded by her facial expressions to forgo any acts of intimidation as this would surely bring chaos. *He's a kid, leave him alone, please?* In his heart, Richie had no intention of embarrassing the youth but wanted to pull his sister's chain to let her know what she'd owe him by his restraint. Let's see, car washed for a month, his laundry for two weeks; oh, the selection dazzled him as if he were in a treasure room trying to select the most valuable bauble. Clifford looked like a stray pet that had been found abandoned, his eyes darting from one member to another as if seeking acceptance or absolution for some sin he might have committed.

If it was just the studying part, no problem, but his discomfort was compounded by the fact that everyone at the table knew he had a sweet spot for Jenn, try as he might to conceal it. *Heck,* thought Richie, *he's suffered enough. Let me put him out of his misery.*

"Hey, Cliff, what's the project you and Jenn are workin' on?"

"It's about the solar system and all the planets, sir."

"Richie will do. In my room I do believe I have an atlas or some sort of encyclopedia on space and the planets. You're welcome to it, if I can find it."

Jenn smiled, her lips pursing a silent "Thank you."

The dinner was as expected and the chance at deviltry stifled by his now emerging sense of honor, or the fact his sister would entertain dismembering him. In any event, he retired to the porch to catch a few innings of uninspired baseball. Again the sandman intruded on his conscious state, and he disappeared into the realm of dreams. These unconscious interludes defy reason or order as the mind has unfettered reign over the menu of visions and experiences. In one episode, our hero is hurtling at over a hundred miles an hour in an attempt to evade pursuers, while in another instance, he is slinging lead at the OK corral. These dreams don't convey safety in any form while the sleeper is engaged, for to him or her, it is real, or as real as they believe it to be. Then came a moment of sweet release as a beautiful starlet heaped moist, unrelenting kisses upon our sleeper, the reality of which would not be relinquished until, suddenly, his eyes opened.

Buddy?

The lab was joyously salivating over his friend's face while Richie reacted with rejection, not of his faithful friend, but for what he interrupted. At least no one would know what he had succumbed to, and Buddy wasn't talking—he hoped. When a certain degree of lucidity penetrated his dome, he realized that he had fallen asleep on the porch. He learned that his mother didn't have the heart to disturb him, and for that he was thankful. All in all, it was a very restful sleep, the culmination of which would remain a secret. Ah, breakfast, he could smell the bacon and pancakes wafting through the air, and so could Buddy.

Okay, sport, let me bribe you with some strips and you remain dumb. That ludicrous thought imparted an intelligence to the animal which Richie subconsciously assumed could be bought off with a piece of bacon.

Hey, dummy, dogs eat, they don't tattle. Tail wagging away, the faithful canine followed his friend into the kitchen.

"Hi, Ms. Fricke, how are you?"

The small women interrupted her conversation with Jennifer and replied, "Fine, young man. I see Buddy found you."

"Indeed he did, he'd make a good alarm clock, provided he had a towel."

"A towel?"

The breakfast put starch into Richie's frame of mind, as each morsel descended into his stomach with fulfilling contentment. So much so that he couldn't take advantage of several pies that Ms. Fricke had brought over. That would wait until later. Excusing himself, he went to his room to change. What would he do today? He'd wing it as usual; routine was not for the free-ranging young man. As he headed out of the house, Jenn caught up with him.

"Hi, kid, what's up?"

"All my chores are done, and I'm bored. Would I be an anchor if I were to tag along with you?"

Richie cherished his sister, and they were as bonded as any could be. He recalled the time a miscalculation on the ball field cause him to break an arm. She fussed over him like a nervous Nellie and tried to cater to his needs. Being a five-year, her frustration when failing to do so filled his heart with laughter as the determined angel of mercy would reprimand herself for any miscues or omissions. As siblings, they shared many pitfalls and successes with an eye toward each other, comforting when needed, joyous in celebration.

As they grew older, Jenn developed a stubborn mood that defied her character. At times it was dark and caused concern to her brother and in some cases promoted an estrangement. He carefully stepped away until it passed but knew that while it existed, trouble loomed. Youngsters can be headstrong, making it hard to set them on the right course, their inexperience an obstacle to understanding what they themselves see as a failing in their persona. It's not something that can be corrected by punishment or cajoling but by a persistent input of love, and this Richie provided by example and closeness, always letting her know he was there for her. It was not fawning but just being who he was that eventually set her straight.

Her dark-brown hair meshed beautifully with her hazel eyes. With thin lips, her face framed a perfect set of teeth, and along with her petite figure, it wasn't long before another chapter of life emerged—boys. Too young to fully embrace the attention, nevertheless there was always a welcome acknowledgment of the compliments and interest shown in her. Clifford, a gawking, awkward would-be suitor seemed to harvest a more than passing notice in Jenn. The other girls gave him little attention, and falling under the spell of this beauty only worsened his hope for anything more. It was the impossible dream. But Jenn saw something in him the others failed to see.

By nature he was shy, quiet, and studious, which had the effect of nullifying his nice face and courteous manner. He didn't stand out in a crowd and therefore melded into the background. During class, students were paired together for a particular exercise, and Jenn drew Clifford, the other girls giggling under their breaths. What a loser! Not being judgmental, Jenn ignored the rudeness and smiled at Clifford. His lowered eyes signaled an obedience to whatever her will desired. Surprisingly, as they worked on the project, like scales on a fish, his rigidness began to scrape off, no doubt due to his partner's enjoyable company and manner.

Working seamlessly, chatting back and forth, the project was satisfactorily finished and budding friendship established. Jenn truly enjoyed his company, and he felt this, more so because of his general exclusion from his classmates. This experience in due time would produce a different young man.

"Okay, pipsqueak, we're off."

"Where to?"

"I'd like to drive over to the farmer's market on Mill Road."

"Oh, goody, do ya have any money?"

"Hey, I'm home from school, do I look like a bank?"

"That's okay, I'll shoplift." Lifting her up and swirling her around, he made for his car. "Ms. Fricke left you a pie."

"And you better leave it alone."

"Too late," she squealed, cupping her hands to her mouth to stifle the taunting laughter. Back and forth they verbally jostled each other, an ingredient indelibly etched into their manifest of sibling jousting.

They strolled along the aisles and examined, handled, or just eyed various items of interest or not.

"Look, Jenn, there's Clifford." A quick turn of the head, eyes locked on target, and a "I'll see you later." Dumped by his sister, oh well. He was glad, for both of them, so he didn't mind her quick departure. Anyone who's been to a farmer's market can enjoy the variety offered and maybe a good price here and there.

A sudden tug on his jacket caused him to turn and look down at the perpetrator.

"Hi, man." It was his good little buddy.

"Whatcha doin', pal?"

"I walk, Mommy look fer toys."

"And what kind to you like?"

"Choo-choo and"—making a sound like a jet—"whoosh." Looking at the boy's mom, and indicating a direction, off they went. "Bye, man." He really liked this little urchin, so devoid of all the things that have made adults pale in comparison. One day, he hoped to take the little tyke out on the town.

Resuming his leisurely stroll, he contemplated buying things that he knew were silly and unimportant, but the variety of colors and forms dulled the senses as they did for many shoppers.

Reaching for a nondescript item, he glanced over the table and saw a potential fly in the ointment. Gloria! Attempting a U-turn was negated by the winsome sound of his name wafting over the steady drone of the myriad throng—"Richie, Richie."

"Oh, hi, Gloria, what's new?"

"Just shopping. Are you still going to the dance?"

"I intend to."

"Alone?"

Wow, she never gives up, does she? "No, taking Ben."

"Will you save me a dance?"

"Yeah, I guess I can do that."

His efforts to extricate himself from an uncomfortable situation was resolved by an angel sent in response to a subconscious request for deliverance.

"Hi, man, look, Mommy got me this." His little guy saved the day. The mother of the boy was fairly pretty, and the familiarity of the pair gave Gloria the impression there was more than met the eye.

A quick introduction, a few words, and Gloria begged off, other businesses that needed to be attended to. Still not giving up, her eyes on the older woman, she said, "I'll see you tonight." Breathing a little easier, Richie picked up the lad and gave him a big squeeze. Turning to his mother, Richie gave no inkling as to the romantic intrigue that was interrupted.

"She's a very pretty girl, are you two a two?"

"Nah, we used to date, but not anymore, and while I'm at it, please excuse my denseness. I've never introduced myself. Richie Murphy."

"I'm Donna Glass, and this is Pip."

"Well, Pip, what did Mom get you?"

A face replete with an unbounded effort to unload a pent-up store of excitement exploded with a "Look, airpane."

Richie made the prescribed amount of fuss and exhilaration over the model. Now he knew how his dad or mom felt when they gave him something that he so wanted. Giving the boy a hug, he set him down and, kneeling beside the boy, told him that he was his best friend.

"Real?"

"Real." Another hug set them both on their way.

There was a lot to think about on the way home. How would he handle Gloria at the dance? What of Vicky? The unknown was filled with mystery, and he had no desire to tempt fate or to divine what may be in store. Oh, boy, this he didn't need. Maybe Dad would give him some pointers; after all, he was an old hand at this stuff. Richie forgot that Dad was a left thumb in a right thumb world, that Mom was his only foray into matters of the heart.

Saturday morning and that sneaky sun did it again! Right through the opening in the Venetian blind slats. His own private alarm clock. Tonight, tonight…he was trying to mate the words to the tune his mind was fixating on. Was it a movie or stage play?

Not that important—why can't I shake this tune? Ah, breakfast, another treat in the offing, only this time it was a note instead of eggs and bacon. Seems Mom had gone to Ms. Fricke's for something or other, so it was toasted strudel or some other conglomeration to that he had to scare up. Jenn was no help; she had to keep her figure and just gulped orange juice and had a piece of toast. Dad was off somewhere.

This reminded him of the many mornings at college when his nutrition was a hit-or-miss proposition but was endured for the greater good—getting an education while starving to death. He settled on toast and peanut butte—*ugh*—and coffee. Now at least he had time to catch up on the latest in the newspaper, which, discounting the national items, wasn't much. A small town tends to bare its warts because there's no way to hide them, but he chuckles at the stories that would have been fillers in the bigger news rags.

"Cat Missing For Two Weeks Comes Back Home."

"Man Drives Car Forgetting To Put The Tire Back On After A Flat."

You just can't make this up. Then, "Hero Returns Home From Battle, Making A Sacrifice."

The story was about Ben and did him justice, not like the big market papers that were political to the extent of turning him off completely. The story resonated with his bravery and decisive actions in combat. It was an Ernie Pyle piece, and that alone gave it a prominence that demanded attention. Mr. Pyle was a war correspondent during WWII who won the hearts of the troops he wrote about and from the nation that read his homespun accounts of the boys fighting and dying. So revered was he that when he was killed on a small island off Okinawa, the unit he was covering erected a plaque to his memory. "This Unit Lost a Buddy."

He saved the article and looked forward to the dance that night. Hopefully it would be a source of welcome to the wounded warrior. To while away the time, he washed the car (at least it would be dark, and they may not see it), got his clothes sorted out, and in general just loafed. What a forgotten sense of casualness that had been lost at college. Now it hung on him like a long-lost relative and just as happily received. Eddie, the postman, delivered the usual junk mail and some fliers better suited for the recycling bin. He had delivered mail to the house for years, and for a short while, he shared some iced tea with Richie.

The informality of the town tended to blur lines of distinction between those serving the government, be it local, state, or federal. Many were known for so long that their titles were secondary to who they were. This may be why the political aspects were debated with more civility than that practiced on a higher level.

Some had foresworn public service to avoid the stamp of cronyism or biased partisanship which seemed to be dividing the nation. Eddie was glad that he was near to retirement so that that assumption could never be applied to him, which was never a consideration due to his years of loyal service and dedication.

"Ed, being around town a bit, have there been any changes due to the economy?"

"Funny, but I've seen an increase in some areas. Percy's old hardware store is now a boutique, and someone fixed the run-down Harris house and made a bed-and-breakfast."

The amiable chatter in the shade mirrored that of other low-keyed towns; the word of mouth almost always seemed to surpass the normal channels and was more the intimate for it. A person in need, the local charity seeking funding, kittens rescued from a culvert, all stem their resolve because of the intimacy involved. Moments later, Ed hoisted his mailbag and thanked Richie for the respite then resumed his delivery of the mail. Richie marveled at his dedication, which had to be exercised in all types of weather. Hearing the phone ring, he scurried to the kitchen extension. Ben called to confirm the time he would be picked up.

"Ready to go, pard?"

"A little nervous."

"Hey, big guy, no sweat, they're your friends."

"I know, but it's been a long time."

"Like riding a bike."

"Have to get used to that with one wing."

Richie almost bit his tongue, only intending the phrase to reassure his friend.

After finishing the call, he was concerned about the reaction of those at the hall. Not too many heroes attend dances. It was a touchy proposition, one that required a different kind of bravery.

The day went pretty fast, along with taking care of his personal chores and helping Dad with a few things. A quick shower, getting dressed, and a personal quality check by Mom and Jenn.

"Nice jacket, son. Trousers are okay, but no tie?"

Assuring all that the death penalty had been revoked by the clothing convention, a quick kiss for Mom, Jenn's hair manually mussed, and out to the chariot. Ben was ready at the door and quickly hopped in the car.

"Like your uniform, Ben. It fills out real nice." *Another shot across the bow. When are you going to think before you shoot off your mouth? Fills out nice! Man, look at the empty sleeve!*

"Hope it doesn't draw too much attention."

"So what? You earned it."

"Rich, you can say that because you're my buddy, but others might think I'm showing off."

"Not to worry, you'll be among friends."

Parking the car, both men headed toward the school's main door, greetings from several people returned with a nod or a thanks. Inside they made their way down the corridor to the gym's entrance, which had been festooned with crepe paper rolls and hand-made signs. Ticket stubs were given out for the end-of-the-night door prize. Grabbing their stubs, both entered the large hall. At that moment, a crescendo of shouts and applause descended upon the startled figures.

"Benjy, Benjy, Benjy, our hero, hero," and many other accolades swamped the uniformed recipient.

"Richie, this your doing?"

"Nope, had no idea. Enjoy it, bro."

"What am I supposed to do?"

"I don't know, maybe you should bow or something."

A swarming crowd solved that problem as well-wishers relieved the soldier of any fears he may have had. Backslapping, cheek kisses, and handshakes combined to remove any doubt as to his place among them. The band struck up a few patriotic tunes in keeping with the event, Ben trying mightily to be modest.

It took more than a few minutes for the scene to gain some semblance of normalcy, but the glow remained undiminished. Several girls fluttered around the overwhelmed star of the evening, and he ate it up. Richie decided to move off until it was safe to be within artillery range of his friend and scouted the assemblage for acquaintances. The swirling mix of bodies and music made it difficult to zero in on any…oh no! Gloria, and she was walking straight toward Richie.

"See you made it."

"Yeah, almost got crushed in the process."

"C'mon, let's dance." They squeezed onto the floor with the girl squeezing even tighter.

The fragrance in her hair teased the senses of the reluctant partner, and he felt a certain wilting of his determination to keep her at a distance. Darn their secret weapons. Fortunately, the number lasted only a short while, and when the music stopped, Ben approached them.

"Hi, Gloria, how are ya?"

"Fine. How about a dance?"

"Yeah, Ben, show her your moves."

Thank goodness for the eleventh hour reprieve. Without a shred of vanity, Richie felt that Gloria hit on Ben to stir some jealousy, perhaps hoping to reignite their past history. Not a chance. He moved along, leaving the pair behind. After more than enough sets, they seemed glued to each other, an unexpected turn of events. If she's trying to induce jealousy, she's pulling out all the stops.

Eyeing the couple several times as they moved along the floor, Richie began to sense that this was no put-on for his benefit. There seemed to be a genuine attraction between his former flame and her partner. Well, I'll be, he mused. He smiled and hoped that this would be an end to his battle against involuntary servitude, of the female persuasion that is. Feeling a little lighter and hoping all the best for his friend, his attention focused on finding a dance partner.

Turning, he slammed into a small figure and apologized. "Gee, Rich, all you do seems bent on crippling me."

Oh, gosh, Vicky. "Gee, I'm sorry."

"No harm done."

"Where's your date."

"Doug? I ditched that clod. He was making eyes at every skirt he saw and wasn't shy about hiding it."

She was fuming but soon cooled down when Richie asked her onto the floor. Okay, now he had her, what does he do with her? It wasn't difficult to meld with her. The soft music created a mellow frame of mind, and her closeness was more than that required for casual dancing. It was an invitation he began to address with his cheek nestled against hers and a response to her particular fragrance, a perfume so light but tantalizing. The movements were slow, as if dancing was secondary to just holding each other. He was awakening to the possibility that what was captivating him was not just a hormone surge but a real attraction. Was she doing the same? Feelings of substance do not turn off or on like a faucet; they are either accepted or discarded, depending on the desire or lack thereof. Richie felt the desire and was fully ready to exploit it. Was it mutual? Only time would tell.

Every dance was theirs. As the evening drew to an end, surprise! Gloria walked over to them with Ben in tow.

"Ah, buddy, do ya mind if Gloria took me home?"

"Are you nuts? Look at her and look at me. Even I wouldn't go home with me if I had your choice."

The resulting laughter was affable, and as they turned to leave, Gloria responded with a cryptic "Nice knowing you" followed by a discreet wink. Can you believe it? Her and Ben? Now that the anchor seemed to be released from his concern, Richie felt a new lease on life, or at least a reasonable rental. Vicky seemed pleased by the matchup, believing the competition from that quarter seemed remote for the time being.

So elated was Richie that the Buick in no way was a source of visual embarrassment as he seated the young girl next to him. It was getting late, so any intention of a soda or burger was passed. She apologetically asked if it would be okay if she was taken home. No problem, he had things to do himself in the morn, but the drive was deliberately slow, both wanting to savor these moments of solitude and future expectations. Her home was a modest rancher, with a bevy of greenery that seemed to cast it into a virgin forest, with an anticipation of wild animals appearing and bounding away. Vicky had developed a green thumb and was enthused in keeping the grounds abundant with various plants and bushes.

Pulling into the driveway, he turned his lights off. Interior lights provided the only illumination as he opened the door, menacing shadows mimicking their movements as he escorted Vicky from the vehicle. They walked along the paved path and reached an enclosed front door, brightly painted and with the family name prominently displayed on a rustic plaque. The night would end but with a promise of more to come. They turned toward each other, their eyes intently holding each other's face in a visual lock, as if seeing each other for the first time. Richie gently put his arms around her, an embrace that drew them closer. He planted a light kiss on her cheek, a good-night peck, not wishing to blow the whole evening with an assumed right to do his own will.

She brushed off the effort and mated her lips to his. His head swirled, the sweetness rivaling any nectar he had known. A dormant emotional and intellectual response captivated his whole being, with myriad sensations coursing through his body. Whatever the reason, he didn't want it to end, and neither did Vicky, until. The overhead door light flashed, breaking the trance and bringing both down to a more earthly level.

"Darn, Mom does that every time I come home."

"You mean with every guy you have in tow?"

"No, silly, she's a light sleeper and can tell when I'm coming up the walk. But in case I'm with a ruffian, it comes in handy." A quick peck on the lips, and she disappeared through the door.

Oh, now I'm a ruffian, he laughed to himself.

The drive home refused to acknowledge the bumps and jarring from the rutted road, as Richie was floating on cloud nine, or whatever number suited him. Just like that, he was hooked and gladly reveled in the prospect of a blossoming relationship. She had always been there for him to snatch up, but Gloria was the fly in the ointment. No more.

Buoyed by a romantic night, his morning joust with the sun was contested feebly; all was right with the world. He lolled in bed for a while, savoring the magic of her kiss, which didn't last long as Jenn yelled for him to get up. Time for church. He loved going to Mass with the family, but today an incentive was added to the mix—Vicky. Arriving at the church, the family greeted many friends and ascended the steps to the main doors. The sun shone brightly, mimicking Richie's mood, his gait light and face purposely searching for the cause of his stimuli. Ah, there she was. Departing from the family, he made a beeline toward the source of his new enlightenment, suddenly pulling up short by what appeared to be the actions of a fickle woman. Vicky was being escorted by a handsome young man, his arm cradling her waist, while she smiled at him in a very determined manner.

Quickly he assessed that the kiss last night didn't make a union, and perhaps it was just too good to be true. Okay, he floated on the cloud of romance during the evening, but there are many instances where fruition is never achieved. All this occurred so quickly he had scant time to sulk, accepting the perceived rejection while trying to backtrack quickly, but too late.

"Richie, over here." Her voice was clear and a feigned bout of deafness would not suffice to extricate him a confrontation with the couple.

"Ah, hi, Vic. Nice to see you." Her face was puzzled by the overly polite or aloofness he displayed.

"Richie, I'd like you to meet Tom."

Boy, he thought, *she throws it right in your face, and in church of all things.*

Her escort responded, "Glad to meet you. Cousin Vicky described you so well, I almost think I would have known you without the intro."

Is there such a thing as eating crow mentally without choking on the bones and feathers? He felt guilt while maintaining a smile and rebuking himself for such a jump to a very ill-timed and undeserving conclusion.

"You mean warts and all?" he replied, a little self-forgiveness rising to the fore.

"You're right, Vic, he does want to make you laugh." The young man shook a very-much-relieved Richie's hand.

Jenn matched Richie by sighting Clifford on the far aisle and informed her parents they would be bereft of her presence if it was okay. Joining the boy, his parents smiled as they sat together, rather closely, and avoided mooning over each other, the awkwardness a sign of affection. After services, the families indulged in the usual warm-hearted banter. Tom excused himself to attend to a previous commitment, leaving Vicky totally in the hands of Richie. Clifford was invited back to the Murphy home for lunch, priming Richie's penchant for mischief. This was averted by the preemptive stares of Mom and Jenn. There's nothing like a Sunday lunch with mixed families, and the din was only secondary to the animation of waving hands and bodies while trying to translate an idea or thought.

The food of course took preeminence on the list of compliments, Lynne trying to maintain a modicum of modesty. A total success of dining and conversation.

After lunch, Richie and Vicky headed to the park and the pond where the geese flocked to his pro-offer of bread he'd snatched from the table. They laughed and frolicked, free of any dark clouds or demons in the closet. Hand in hand, the couple walked, pausing for a pecking kiss, and moving on, her running ahead and he chasing her in mock frustration. Grabbing Vicky by the waist, he lifted her and swung her around, her head tilting back and arms outstretched as if flying, and flying she was, right out of his grasp. Her descent was abruptly halted by smacking the ground on her rear end. "Ouch, that's a lousy way to break the spell," she laughingly spouted as a concerned Richie picked her up.

The concern was rewarded with a lingering kiss. They looked into each other's eyes with the time-honored silent vow of commitment, words being null and void. Walking back home, hand in hand, they appeared as if they had been together for years. Other couples in the park somewhat compared with them, not noticing the similarities they shared with each other, having eyes only for themselves. Romance will do that.

Richie had promised Clifford he would drive him home. As they prepared to leave the house, Jenn accompanied them to the door. Richie mumbled some excuse about bringing the car around, a deceitful lie since it was in the driveway, so that an intimate goodbye would be private. He sat in the car for a few minutes, confident that any attempt by the two to enrich their circumstances would be fruitful. Waiting longer than he anticipated, he was glad when he saw the boy smiling as he entered the car. "Treat her right or else." The bot froze, then Richie grinned and said, "I know you will."

"I promise sir."

"Richie."

"I promise, Richie, sir, er, Richie." A tap on his shoulder relieved any tension, and the trip home was filled with the usual stuff younger boys ask older men, at least that was how he viewed Richie. They were a cute couple and something Richie felt would not be a childhood fling; maybe, somewhere in the future a real bond. Only time would tell.

Driving home, he thought, *Was I that young? Of course, stupid. Young and stupid.* His self-chastisement ended as he pulled into the driveway, and Vicky exited the house, sharing goodbyes with his parents. As she sat closely beside him, a sense of contentment warmed him. Was it too soon to think of any permanence, something beyond what they already had? The thought was intriguing and romantic, but all this was subconscious to both as they bathed in the here and now. They were silent, their minds creating the words they wished to share and the visions that seemed promising. As the sun started to set, a detour onto the outskirts of town brought them to the meandering country roads that crisscrossed the rich farming community.

The overwhelming green of the crops, interspersed with the color of the various fruit trees were enhanced with the concentrated rays of the sun as they began to withdraw over the horizon. Then the dusk surrendered to the pitch-blackness unique to the sprawling, unlit vastness before them. Turning on his lights brought a quick flicker of adjustment to his eyes. Vicky's arm was entwined around his as he maneuvered with his left. The markers raced past as if to avoid capture, and the odd creature or two avoided premature demise by their swiftness. There was really nothing to see, but the point was isolation, a world of their own, beholding only to themselves. The sweet hum of the detested car lolled them into a trance-like mood and, if not for the occasional rut in the road, may have put them to sleep. Eventually, the solitude was terminated by the bustling traffic as they reentered the town's environs. Others also had taken up the delights of a road trip to cap the day.

The anticipated good night's embrace fully occupied both eager supplicants, and neither was left wanting. The overhead door light cooperated by either malfunctioning or more, due to a mother's consideration for privacy. For a while they clung to each other, immersed in the sensation unique to lovers, something they were becoming aware of, if not by words, then by their physical attraction. Too soon for Richie, the spell was broken. A parting cheek peck, a whispered good night, and Vicky leaves a swooning suitor at the door.

Entering the house, Mom and Jenn were cleaning up, and Dad was reading the newspaper, a comfortable conclusion to the day's events.

"You're back early, what did you do wrong this time?" Jenn teased.

"Oh, the same thing you did with Clifford." A reddish glow began to cover her face as she stammered a "Mom, he's being mean to me." He mussed her hair, gave her a squeeze, then kissed his mother and retired to the porch. Oh, so much to think on, but he succumbed to the now oft-repeated ritual of dozing off. The dreams were compliant with his conscious romantic desires, and through the night, on and off, he was a hero, lover, rescuer, or any heady fictional character that imposed itself on his dormant mind. Reality would be a comedown, but hey, as Bogart said, "We'll always have Paris."

Supposedly intelligent, our hero again allowed sol to paint his face with the morning's early rays. He popped up very refreshed and, after a quick shower, headed for a morning's repast, hunger tugging at his innards.

"Morning, Mom."

"I'd ask how you slept, but that mushy moaning and groaning and 'Vicky, Vicky' kind of sums it up." A restrained smile creasing her face. "Pancakes?"

"And sausage?"

"You bet."

A knock on the rear door and Richie leaves the table to answer the summons.

"Hey, Ben, c'mon in."

"Hope I'm not disturbing you."

"Naw, you're just in time. Mom, another customer."

"Pancakes and sausage okay?"

"Yeah, my mouth is watering, thanks, Mrs. Murphy."

"What's up, Ben?"

"I guess you know I didn't just come here for breakfast."

"Well, we always got together elsewhere, so my Sherlock Holmes training is coming in handy, but I enjoy you being here regardless. Spill."

"Well, Gloria. We've only seen each other a few times, but is it okay, what with you going with her and all?"

"Hey, pal, that's history, knock yourself out."

"I wasn't sure, you being my friend an' all." The relief was evident but unnecessary, the result of a strong friendship.

"You're good, buddy, always have been."

"Another thing is, ever since I've been home, the praises and well-wishing is starting to wear on me."

"Enjoy it while you can, pal. A week after I got home, people would ask 'Who?' when I greeted them." A bellowing laugh confirming the jest. "No, Ben, these people know your sacrifice, and they have nothing comparable to it, so in a way, they offer what their hearts tell them to offer. It'll pass, but never forget it."

"I didn't look at it that way, thanks." A pensive look signaling an effort to fully absorb the town's tributes and to relive the many instances of lavish praise. He had received so many and became somewhat jaded by the sheer numbers. His reflection brought a certain amount of discomfort for allowing such a cavalier attitude to repay those that saw him as a true hero. That would change.

"Hey, pal, you goin' to eat that sausage?" broke his concentration.

"Oh, yeah, lost in thought for a moment. You touch that morsel an' you're dead."

"You and what army?"

Raising a clenched fist, Ben retorted, "I don't need an army to handle you, lightweight." A faux combat and grappling sent a few utensils and empty plates to the floor.

"Land sakes, what are you two crazies doing? Get out of here and let me be in peace." The words were not as harsh as the stare she gave them as she looked at the mess.

"Sorry, Mom, but I had to put this guy in his place."

"I think the place for you two is in jail, scoot."

Both quickly grabbed the remaining sausages, sans bread, and quickly beat a retreat.

Sitting on the steps, the old friends chatted about what the future held for them. "If I can pass the requirements, I'd like to stay in the military. There's precedent for it. I've read about quite a few guys who've lost limbs and remained in the service."

"Gee, Ben, you must really like it, I mean, to go all through that trouble."

"Not if the draw is there, and believe me, it is. I want to do it for my country."

"I think you already did."

"That's not it, Rich. I knew the dangers, but these pale in comparison to what I see as a mortal threat to our country. I can't ignore that, and there are thousands of others who feel the same way. Not all people are meant to be soldiers, just as those who aren't meant to be accountants, policemen, or any other civilian pursuit."

Richie was deeply impressed with his friend's philosophy, a changing of the guard so to speak. He paraphrased in his thoughts a passage from the Bible that seemed appropriate: "When I was a child I spoke as a child, then I put away childish things." At least that's as close as he could remember it. He just hoped that both of them would never completely put away childish things. It would be too darn dull if they did. They sat quietly for a while, arms draped across each other's shoulders, a silent tribute to their enduring friendship. Eventually, the spell was broken when Ben asked Richie if he had any plans for the day. Feigning destitution, Richie mocked a plea for financial salvation, as he was broke, broke, broke.

"Seriously, I'm goin' to my dad's plant to see if they're taking on any part-time help. Could use the rubles, 'bout you?"

"Still getting paid I guess until they determine what they want to do with me, so I'm pretty set." Ben had an appointment with Gloria, so Richie was on his own again.

"See ya later."

"Okay."

The drive to the factory had Richie thinking how blessed he was. All limbs intact, a family, an education, and no health problems. And best of all, Vicky. The plant manufactured a host of home appliances, and Brian was the floor manager. He couldn't see his dad's face but could pick him out as he strode the floor barking instructions and gesturing to a crane operator for the placement of his load. His dominant posture and lack of hesitancy were hallmarks fully ingrained on his son.

"Hey, Dad." Without breaking stride, his father held up his arm in a swinging motion to stop his son, concentrating on the overhead load until it was secured. Turning, with a broad smile on his face, he walked up to his son, asking, if everything was okay.

His face clouded a bit when Richie inquired about any part-time openings. "Son, right now, things are getting hairy."

"Gee, Dad, look at all the activity. Doesn't look slow to me."

"Those things were in the pipeline and had to be moved, but I think the pipeline's sprung a leak. Orders have been falling off." Brian wasn't a person who rattled easily, but a departure from his usual nature signaled a concern that was difficult to conceal. "It could be seasonal, but with the way the economy is goin', it's tough to tell." Richie placed his hand around the back of his father's neck and brought it forward to a gentle head butt.

"No problem, Dad. See you later."

He had concerns for his father, but it was a wait-and-see proposition, something he certainly could not control. It wasn't fair, not for his dad or the people working there, but what was fair today? The free time he enjoyed was fast turning into a guilt trip. Okay, he indulged in the activities that the downtime afforded him, and now he had to flesh it out with something more responsible, and this effort to effect a job fell flat. A small town like this just didn't breed overemployment. Driving past Earl's Department Store, he noticed a sign, "Part-time deliveryman wanted." Wow, if ever a guardian angel came through, it was now.

A quick inquiry to Mr. Rosen, the owner, secured the job, and the pay wasn't too shabby, although Champaign was out of the question. The really good part would be running into people he had known for ages, not to mention the handsome tips they'd bestow upon their well-known, if not favorite son. He'd start tomorrow, so tonight was a night to celebrate.

Calling Vicky in hopes of celebrating, she told him that her Aunt Ruth was ill, and she'll be attending to her for a few days. It was out of town, so seeing her would be a problem until she returned. Sharing their anticipated loneliness, the young lovers overdid the dramatics, as all young people do, but that is the coin of the realm. It was not forever, although to both it might have seemed that way.

"What's up, pup? You look a little down."

"Ah, nothin' really, Mom. Vicky's goin' to be away for a few days, ya know, and I'll be a little boring."

"Why don't you go to the county bazaar tonight, take Ben."

"I don't think he'll be wantin' to go with me, Gloria and all."

"Go anyway. Here's some mad money, I know you're strapped."

"Aw, Mom, I can't let you do that."

"Shush, yes, I can. Now eat some lunch."

Richie always liked the bazaar, what with all the attractions and cheap tickets for any event or contest. He and his dad used to come home with armloads of prizes, with Dad being the primary winner and he the pack mule. Oh, it was great.

A full stomach can do wonders to a person's outlook, and Richie's was no different. With blueberry pie anchoring the foregoing feast, he perked up a little and began to muse about the day's possibilities until he left for the bazaar. Ah, the dreaded Buick. It needed and received a car wash, with a wish that the water could impart some magical properties that transformed it into some grand and eloquent conveyance. No such luck. At least it was clean, with no one to impress but himself, his friends either not going or pairing up with significant others. He offered to take Jenn, but Clifford and his family were taking her with them. Bummer.

Drifting through the day, helping Mom or waiting for dad to come home from work, he whiled away the time with minutiae, his mind on Vicky and how he missed her. This was different than when he was going with Gloria, a strange but wonderful emptiness. It signified something that was hard to categorize, but he knew it was special.

After dinner, another gastronomical triumph by his mother, Richie tried to encourage his dad to accompany him, but to no avail.

"I'm too old for that stuff, you enjoy yourself," was the reply from behind the newspaper.

"Me thinks thou hath losteth his toucheth" was the sarcastic reply, but it elicited no compromise from the elder. "See you later, Mom."

"Enjoy yourself."

The drive to the county grounds was a short hop and a skip away, and in no time he parked the quasi beast and walked to the main aisle where the different attractions were arrayed. Considering the economy, the mass of offerings were substantial. The colors of the multitude of items seemed to be the main draw, as the throng would gang up on a booth or stand like moths to a flame. He marveled how something bright could outweigh its practical value or use, but that was what the fair was about, letting loose and being frivolous.

Busting balloons with darts separated a few bucks from his pockets with nil results. Ditto with the milk bottles. Still, he was enjoying himself. The air was moved with a slight breeze that carried a welcome coolness with it. The crowd produced the inevitable bumps and "Excuse me" apologies, the "Hello" and "How are you?" ingredients that were part and parcel of the enjoyment they engendered, for no fair should be placid and sterile, despite the warts. Ah, the raffle booth. Now he would try his luck at dame fortune.

There were chances for a cruise, a getaway to the mountains, a fishing trip, and best of all, a raffle for a 2013 Ford Mustang! One ticket is all anyone needs to win, and that's exactly what he bought for a buck, along with the cruise raffle. That he would give to his parents if he won. Not overly confident of his luck, but in the mood they generated, he stuffed them in his pocket and continued down the aisle to the other beckoning attractions. He parceled out his remaining funds quite frugally, wishing to enjoy the night while being solvent, a difficult task what with all the fanfare and enticements bellowed out by the persistent hawkers.

He paused at a table when he felt a tug on his jacket. Instinctively, and without turning around, he knew who it was. Pretending to not notice, he continued on until another, sharper tug brought him to a halt.

"Is some animal trying to attack me? Or did I fail to pay someone at the last table?" he quipped in a mocking tone of surprise.

"Hi, man, it's me."

"Of course it's you, c'mere," Richie spouted as he grabbed the happily laughing boy and swung him in a circle. The lad quickly wrapped his arms around his friend's neck and hugged him as tight as he could.

"Pip, you're strangling him," his mother playfully chided the child.

"Hi, Donna. You feeding him spinach? Boy, he's got a grip."

"Heavens no, he abhors it. But he does like cauliflower, go figure."

"I bet he likes pizza, right, sport?"

"You bet, man."

"Off we go."

The pizza concession had tables for the diners to use, and it was a cozy trio that feasted on the fare offered. Pip thoroughly ate his slices, all three of them. Donna and Richie were more reserved but enjoyed their treat and the conversation that a sated palate generated. The boy had been excited for days, anticipating the fair and all the treasures his imagination could conjure. There's a magical aura that a young mind can project and mostly for them as adults tend to lose that quality as they get older. The mystery and joy is there but not as pronounced and in some cases easily dismissed. Richie was on the border line, an unconscious attribute that thankfully remained dormant, his present state of mind a companion to the youngster's delight.

The evening flew in pure enjoyment, the antics and reactions to newfound discoveries by Pip generating laughter and amusement. Donna was appreciative of Richie's attention to her son and allowed him to indulge in spoiling the child at many of the stands they visited. Stuffed animals, only one or two, picking the numbers on the roulette wheel, and a host of other distractions filled the boy with unbounded responses, most of which were "Thank you, man" or "Wow, I win?"

Finally, the slow reactions and drooping eyelids signaled an end to the youthful foray, and Richie had his limp form draped across his chest in a gentle caress.

"Ready to go?"

"Yes, but I'll have to call for a cab, I don't have a car."

"You have one now, and I'd be pleased to take you and the little guy home. It's little enough payment for the fun we've enjoyed tonight."

"Thank, Rich, I'd like that."

With Pip snug in his mom's arms, Richie set out for Donna's apartment. As they traveled the short distance to her apartment, she casually glanced at her benefactor and determined he'd be a fine father one day. Her admiration for his kindness bled over into a personal attraction that was hard to suppress. Nothing overt, just the natural draw that someone of Richie's character would promote. Small talk was exchanged, the usual fare when larger issues were ignored or not relevant to the occasion. The car pulled into the driveway adjacent to her apartment building, which was a two-story affair. Taking her keys, he opened the door and ushered her into a well-furnished unit. The warmth of the room was a welcome contrast to the chill that had begun when they left the fair grounds.

"As soon as I take care of Pip, I'll make us some coffee."

"Sounds great. You have a nice place here."

"Yes, we…I've found it to be very suitable."

The room was cheery and the furniture attractive, the layout very functional. The kitchen was at the far end and seemed to be fitted out. He was glad she wasn't living in a dump, being single and all. He eyed the whole room, and several framed pictures caught his eye, the subjects obviously being Donna, the child, and a man, presumably her husband.

As Donna lay Pip on the sofa and turned, she stumbled against Richie and emitted an apologetic laugh while turning to face him. As she did, the laughing abruptly stopped, and her smile disappeared as her eyes locked onto his, the moment rife with an expectation that could not be avoided. It couldn't have, shouldn't have happened. But it did. On his part his only excuse was a sudden impulse of youth;

with her, a crushing loneliness relieved only by the presence of her son.

The kiss was tender and compassionate, not denigrating into a tawdry display of unrestrained lust. In fact, the full realization of the sensation was overridden by an emerging sense of betrayal. He on his part because of Vicky, her because of a mistaken belief that she dishonored the memory of her husband. She pulled away, saying, "Oh, I'm so sorry, Rich, I shouldn't have, I had no right." But Richie grabbed her arm and brought her back into another embrace, an embrace not for any amorous intention, but to soothe the guilt that was evident on her face. She was no hustler, the pain was real, but that one moment of weakness signaled a need he could not fulfill.

With her in his arms, she felt a sense of comfort as he spoke to her. "Hey, listen, we made a big mistake, but the world didn't end. You're human, and I'm human, and sometimes we act like that." Injecting some humor to lessen the somber atmosphere, he rejoined, "Do you think I would have kissed you if you were homely?" She sniffed a smile, looked at him, and then lowered her eyes, resting her cheek on his shoulder.

"Richie, I miss him so much. Jerry and I were so much in love and now he's gone." The tears were a little heavier now, and Richie held her tighter. He bit his lip, furious he could not have restrained himself, instead giving in to a moment of weakness. *Darn it, why does forbidden fruit have to taste so sweet?* he questioned. Not only that, but the more reality set in, the more the guilt over his betrayal of Vicky became all consuming.

Being a very young man whose worst violation of human decency amounted to teasing his sister or the pranks he played on his friends, this was a new and terrifying experience. Now he had to summon every bit of self-confidence and outward assurance to ease the conflict Donna was experiencing.

"Rich, you're great, and if you'd let me, I'd like to talk to you. Let me put Pip to bed, and I'll be right back." His heart reached out to this woman whose loss could only be imagined. Without recognizing it, his emotions were chivalric, wishing only to shield her from the misfortune of the occasion. It was like the times his sister had been hurt by a cross word or some stupid altercation, and she'd relied on him for solace. He would hold her like he did Donna.

Richie searched for the coffee and proceeded to have two cups ready by the time Donna returned.

"I didn't put anything in them."

"That's okay, I take it black."

A little more composed, she reached across the table and took his hand in hers. "Jerry and I were high school sweethearts and married soon after graduation. He didn't go to college because the company he started to work for liked his dedication, and he began to move up after a while. He reached a point where he became management, with the pay that goes with it. Believe me, we needed that boost, what with just starting out. Soon, Pip entered our lives, and it was a dream come true, a complete family. I guess we were like a lot of other young families, with all the good and bad that we came with it." As she spoke, Richie could feel the squeeze of her hand, as if highlighting each phase of her life as she described it. Her gaze was steady, and there was no hurriedness or excitement in her commentary.

"Jerry was asked if he would take over the plant near Pineview. It would mean relocating, but it gave him a chance to move up the ladder. He wanted to know if I was willing to move, if not, he would refuse the position. It wasn't easy to pull up stakes and leave behind everyone we knew, but I wanted what was best for my husband." This woman's commitment to her husband was evident by the way she spoke of him and the occasional glance at the framed photos. Several times she suppressed an understandable catch in her throat, relating their involvement with the community and the progress being made at the plant.

"Oh, he would come home and, like a kid with a new toy, explain how the day had gone and the way the workers were responding to their boss. There were glitches, but by delegating responsibility to those who showed an understanding of what needed to be done, the pieces were falling into place. He listened, they acted." She recalled how the hours were long at first and the loneliness was only tolerated because of the goal being pursued. How high can any man climb with this kind of support? Still, it was a burden. Pip suffered the most, not understanding why his father was always away. He loved the rough housing and mock battles that so bond a boy and his dad, the make-believe world that children thrive on, knowing that they really didn't exist but wish they did.

Donna, being the good wife, never faltered in her support, nor did she ever display any discontent. There would be ample opportunities for the good times, and she'd be patient.

She'd made few friends, but not for lack of trying. For a young mother, her prime concern became her home and family.

"Then one day, a police car came to the apartment. My husband had collapsed at work and was rushed to the hospital. The officer was a veteran who probably had gone through this many times, and his concern for us was comforting, but naturally, it did little to calm my frittered nerves. The doctor in the emergency room greeted me and briefly explained that Jerry had suffered a heart attack and was being moved to the ICU. That was the last time I saw him, you know what I mean." Her eyes began to well, and the squeeze of her hand was harder, the white showing brightly on her knuckles. What followed was heart-wrenching, as she had to bury her husband, all alone in this world. Her mother, the only family she had, was unable to travel, and what acquaintances she knew provided some support, but there was a giant hole in her life, and she had no way to fill it.

"The company was grand. They paid all my expenses, and the insurance issued to all employees was generous. But I didn't want money, I wanted Jerry." She bowed her head, a few drops from her eyes staining the lap of her dress. Quickly wiping her face, she continued. "While it was hard for me, how do you explain to a little boy hat his father is gone, that he'd never be seen again? Whenever there was a knock on the door, or he heard a man's voice, my heart crumbled hearing him say, 'Dadee? Dadee?' That's why I'm so grateful to you. The glow on his face when you greet him, the love he has for you, is slowly replacing the emptiness he's had to endure these past ten months.

"It tickles me to hear him call you 'man.' I've tried to get him to say your name."

"No, don't, I get a kick out of it. The little squirt will learn names soon enough. This is our little connection, and I wouldn't trade it for anything."

What had been a three-cent down payment had been parlayed into a priceless personal entrenchment beyond any means of calculating its worth.

"I've wanted so badly to tell you how you've made our lives better and that you will continue to be part of it."

Why not? he thought.

"My mother wants me to move back with her. It's a decision I've wrestled with. I know she'll need help, and Pip will have another new friend to make. I've had to think of him, so I know you'll understand." The sudden jolt in his stomach beat the thought that suddenly raced across his mind. No more "man"? No more runs in the park or going to the fair or for ice cream? These were trials for older people, not freshman graduates. These were heart-tugging experiences for those who've gone down this road many times, not for a wet nose like him. If it's bad now, what happens when he gets older?

The compactness of these thoughts encompassed no more than a pinprick of time before he responded.

"No need to tell you how I feel about that, I just pray that it works out for everybody. And you know that I'm always here for you guys." Richie believed that this might have been the only time that Donna bared her soul to anyone. If she had, he probably never would have known any of this. It was comforting to know she thought so highly of him in sharing her troubled past and attendant heartache. "I still want to see you and the kid. I'm addicted to three-year-old gumballs and his mother." She laughed as they walked to the doorway. A mutual embrace ensued that embodied their new relationship and was more so satisfying because of what it signified and what it revealed about themselves. A gentle kiss on the forehead and Richie was out the door.

Driving home, the solitude settled upon him like a Past Due notice slip; an accounting had to be made, with his conscience. What could he tell Vicky? Should he tell Vicky? His concentration so immobilized his senses that he almost collided with another car.

Pulling over, he breathed deeply and exhaled with the same energy. What were the pros and cons? Telling her the truth and risk losing her, or keeping it locked in his mind's vault and moving on? His innate honesty made it a battle that soaked his shirt with sweat. Making a decision that he could live with was not just to avoid the problem by doing so but to earnestly believe that it was in the interest of all concerned. He would confide in no one. The truth can be just as damaging as a lie, maybe more so, because a truth presupposes that all factors were weighed before acting, a daunting indictment of one's faithfulness. A lie concealing a harmful truth has more merit if designed to avoid inflicting pain.

Even with these considerations, where you can argue for or against, the taste of betrayal still lingered. Richie had decided to live with his choice, a choice that originated by a lapse in judgment. Yes, the drive home would be far from peaceful, and a troubling night awaited him.

Part Two

The following few days were not kind to our troubled young man. Refusing to accept the premise that what he felt was not a betrayal but an unexpected moment of weakness that many would've found difficult to control, he cloaked himself in a mantle guilt. While not overtly baring his soul to family or friends, his questionable body language or stilted conversations signaled the distress he was enduring. Others of a lesser quality of character may have shrugged everything off as a passing fancy and thought none of it.

However one looked at it, whether a blessing or a curse, it was solely on his shoulders, a burden he refused to share with others. A young man, shorn of the experiences of older contemporaries, has no yardstick to truly measure his responses or solutions to what besets him. Perhaps this was his learning time, but it was brutal. Without someone to confide in, the abscess of his mental wound was torture at its best and hell at its worst. If one constant could be applied to him, that would be his persistence to fight it through, no matter the penalties he was incurring. One of those was the eventuality of being with Vicky again. Here was the true torture or hell, take your pick, for it would happen, and what could he do?

Dinner was bland, not because of the food, a tasty pot roast with baked potatoes, carrots and onions and tomatoes, custard pie, and delicious coffee. Richie exerted a valiant and fairly effective effort to disguise his dilemma, although his quips to Jenn about Clifford were nowhere to be found. She'd been accustomed to and secretly enjoyed the barbs her brother routinely showered her with. Tonight was different, and she had trouble reconciling his polite countenance with his usual almost irrelevant pigtail-pulling antics. Mom and Dad were also aware but shrugged it off as a tough day somewhere along the line.

Following dinner, Richie holed up on the porch again, the TV playing to a self-consumed, nonattentive audience. What scenarios that played across his mind had all the elements worthy of novels, but this was real life, and each scenario brought no relief as to what he would eventually do. Thankfully, the sandman, faced with a challenging subject, was able to secure a pathway to the land of snooze, and the young man drifted off, a welcome reprieve. A blessing was the tranquil visions that he encountered, a release from the dreariness which he would face soon enough.

Ben was there, only this time he was waving both arms, or Ms. Fricke weighing him down with a monstrous pie and Jenn laying her head on his lap. Oh, this seemed so real, the disjointed figures and contradictory scenes so familiar to anyone who dreams a lot. Then Vicky appeared to him, and he reached to embrace her, but his actions were mimicked in real life and caused him to awaken. Just as well, he started working at Earl's today. The smell from the kitchen was inviting as he entered the room. He planted a kiss on the neck of his mom and sat at the table, still a little wooden from his conflicts. "Tell Mr. Earl to hold that fabric for me." Her words fading as she left the kitchen.

"Where're you goin', Mom?"

"Ms. Fricke needs some help, and I'll only be gone a few hours. Don't forget about the fabric." Reentering the kitchen, she placed her arms around her son's shoulders and planted a kiss on the top of his head. "Things okay? I'm a little concerned about you."

"I'm fine, Mom. It'll straighten itself out." She didn't pursue the matter and left him with a pat on the back. Idly he eyed the far end of the table where he smiled at the sight of a half-filled coffee cup. His dad always had a cup of coffee but left the second up half-filled. No secret here, just a habit that became a familiar and expected family idiosyncrasy. He wondered what his legacy would be to confound the curious. The smell of his breakfast lost out to his lack of hunger and a partially eaten piece of toast along with a few gulps of coffee rounds out his morning fare. On to work.

"Hey, Rich, glad you're here," welcomed him as he entered the store. Mr. Earl Rosen, the owner, was chipper as usual, and it would be difficult to find someone he didn't like and vice versa.

"Thanks. Mr. R. Oh, Mom asked about some fabric you're holding for her."

"You can pick it up at the end of the day. Nice material."

"Mom always has something goin' on. What do you have for me?"

"Oscar Perkins has some boxes to be delivered to his farm. Needs 'em right away."

"No problem, Mr. R, I'll head right out there."

Fortunately, they fit in his car, precluding the use of the store's decrepit pickup.

The drive to the farm was short but cut through some pretty countryside, which helped relieve some of Richie's anxieties. How often he walked these fields and woods as a youngster, only now realizing the bliss enjoyed at the time. Oh, to return to yesteryear. Turning into the meandering driveway, various mechanical creations lined the borders. Some were restored vehicles or farm machinery, and others were so-called modern art culled from various parts and assembled to form a particular animal or other form of representation. How cool! Sighting Mr. Perkins near the barn, he tooted his horn and accepted a wave as the man eagerly headed his way.

"Hi, Mr. Perkins, got some stuff for you. Anything good?"

"Hope so, fixin' the tractor and had to replace some parts. C'mon in."

The interior of the barn almost looked like a museum in waiting. Various constructs in odd shapes and forms, some identifiable and some totally lost on the imagination, festooned the walls and ceiling. Some believed the man was in his second childhood, while others thought he was bonkers. This had never bothered Richie, as the man was a saint. His generosity was well-known, his support for many causes legend.

"Earl called and said you were on the way. Here, have some coffee, fresh brewed by Martha." The saying goes, not until you've tasted Mrs. Perkins's coffee, you hadn't tasted coffee at all. It's a wonder her fame had not spread throughout the land, when other claimants to a special product received more attention and profit than was warranted.

This never bothered the couple. It was enough to share what they had without a profit motive. This aspect was what endeared them to their friends and neighbors.

"Golly, this is the greatest. What's her secret?"

"I tell ya, an' I'll have to bury you out on the north forty," the ebullient farmer replies, with a wink and a twinkle in his eyes. Some years ago, he and his wife bought the farm as an investment, but also to work it. The small head of cattle, some milk cows, chickens, and eggs provided a nice source of revenue. The real killing came from his creations. Many sold for outrageous sums. Richie wondered what would've happened if the self-styled entrepreneur had been born in a junkyard, a small chuckle escaping from his mouth.

"What's so funny, Rich?"

"Aw, nothin', Mr. Perkins, just picturing you in a different location."

"Good or bad?"

"None of that, just somethin' that teases my imagination. You are one of a kind."

"Martha says that all the time, but with any women, it can mean anything." His laugh competed with Richie's. Opening the boxes satisfied the man's concerns about the parts he ordered, and while examining them, Richie asked if it'd be okay to stroll through the barn.

"Why not? Help yourself." Whatever he looked at, whether he could divine their nature or not, his appreciation for the artistry was evident by his comments, a whistle acknowledging some impact or just the consummate attention he showered upon the creations. Then he froze. A tarp covered what appeared to be the front end of a car, a 1971 Ford Mustang by the looks of the partially visible front end. His heart jumped into his throat then his mouth.

He always had a fixation on this particular Mustang and couldn't believe it was in front of him, if indeed it was what he thought it was. Yelling over his shoulder, he called to the farmer, "Hey, Mr. Perkins, is this a '71 'Stang?"

"Hold on, let me see." Coming over to the far end of the barn, he made a quick glance and replied, "Yep, sure is." Richie's riveted attention to the dormant apple of his eye elicited a remark from the older man. "Interested in it?"

"Yeah, but I couldn't come up with the coin for it."

"Well, let me show you what's here." Removing the tarp revealed the car had seen better days but was a good candidate for rehabilitation. No better demonstration as to the admiration this man had earned through the years was by his next pronouncement.

"Rich, I'm getting a little long in the tooth. Some things I can't do like I used ta."

"Like what, Mr. P?"

"Stuff around the farm that requires muscle. The little I can hack, the bigger things not so much anymore. I got a proposition fer ya."

"I'm all ears, sir. What can I do for you?"

"Give me one day a week, here at the farm, and you can work on the car, I mean it's yours."

"I'm sorry, sir, but even not knowing what it might be worth, I couldn't take advantage of your offer. I don't think I could do enough to earn it."

"Dang you, Richard Murphy." These formal words signaled a storm cloud heading the namesake's way. "If I want to give that heap of junk to you, don't you dare question me, ya got that?" The reprimand was accompanied by a forgiving smile and a nudge of his body against Richie's, a sign of paternalism.

"Gee, Mr. Perkins, I'll do whatever you need, short of murder, that is. It's a generous offer. I won't let you down."

"I know, son. Besides, I don't have time for that crap." This was revealing to the recipient of what he had always craved; for if anything, the farmer always had time for anything he cared to do, and this was his way of sharing the blessings he had. The look on the boy's face was payment enough, as would be whatever labor he provided. "I have to get the tractor fixed, you look at it all you want."

He couldn't believe what was now his. He had some mechanical ability, and what he lacked could be weaned from some of his friends. Money would be the sore point, but one thing at a time.

Recovering the car, he retraced his steps back to the where the tractor was being repaired. "I'll be leaving now, Mr. P. Thanks again."

"Give my regards to your folks."

"I sure will."

What gloom that still clung to him evaporated with this surprising windfall. He couldn't wait to tell his dad or anyone else for that matter. His mind wandered over all the fixes he imagined would be required to restore this gem to its former glory.

"How'd it go, son?"

"Oh, great, Mr. Rosen. He's a great fellow. Did'ya see his works? Man has talent."

"I used to go near his farm when I was a kid, talked to him some, but I'm sorry I missed the opportunity to know him better." The rest of the day was business as usual, and Richie felt very involved in his duties. Many of the people he'd deliver to were known to him, which of course spurred the tips he received.

Near the end of the day, a late delivery had him on the streets. Winding down the main drag, he stiffened slightly when he spotted a familiar form—Vicky! Oh no, not now. He hoped in vain that she hadn't spotted him. No such luck. Her cheerful wave could not be ignored, and he pulled to the curb.

"Hey, tiger. Missed ya" greeted him as he exited the car. Embracing Richie, she planted a peck on his lips and squeezed him tightly.

"Missed you too. Just get in?"

"About an hour ago. Listen, you have any plans?"

"I have a delivery to make, then I'm free." Free. If only if that was really how he felt at that moment. The gloom had taken up roots again, and he gamely tried to conceal it.

"How 'bout I meet you at Marco's and we can catch up, tiger." Her buoyancy and pep almost erased his present concern and allowed him to maintain a facade of intimacy.

"Sounds good. See ya later." Planting a smooch on her forehead, he smiled and returned to his car, dreading what the near future would bring. Not because of her, only what he had harbored for the past few days. The delivery gave him too much time to relive over and over his past indiscretion and how he must deal with it. But each scenario provided no solution, only consternation and uncertainty.

Did Mom or Dad ever have to go through what he was now embroiled in? If so, how on earth did they handle it? He now began to realize the fairly sheltered life he'd led, at least up to now. Growing up was sure a pain in the—

Whoa, he thought, *why are you so down on yourself? Sure you have a problem, but problems can be solved.* He tried to buckle up his resolve with this new assertion of confidence, if only he believed half of it. Right now that was the only lamppost shedding any light, so he clung to it.

Parking in the rear lot, Richie entered Marco's, greeted by the aroma of fresh bread combined with the mouthwatering essence of pizza. He glanced around and sighted Vicky sitting a booth fairly secluded from the rest of the floor. Rising, she greeted him again with a by-now-accepted puckered pair of lips.

"Order anything?"

"No, waited for you."

"Pizza?"

"Sure, why not, my hips won't complain." She needn't have made that venture into satire as her form was ideal and not subject to the unwanted forces of nature that caused many a female to gain unwanted poundage.

The order placed, small talk ensued, as it dud with those firmly committed to each other, their feelings known, not needing elaboration. Still, the void must be filled. As Vicky recounted her stay at Aunt Ruth's, her words droned rather than floated, Richie's attention superficial. As when the pressure on a dam becomes intolerable when its confined elements threaten to burst forth, so too did the pressure on Richie's predicament finally reach its limit. Words flooded abruptly, words he vowed to conceal, words that seemed to be coming from another person, as he seemingly stood outside himself, witnessing this from afar. He was so mentally removed from coherence that it was a wonder he could function in any capacity.

"I kissed a woman."

"What?"

"I…I-it was, er, what I mean is….ah."

"Okay, you kissed a woman, what else?"

Not the usual "How could you?" "You betrayed me," or "You monster, I hate you."

No, fortunately for Richie, Vicky was not a reactionary person. She listened with interest but without judgment, at least not right away.

"Honest, Vick, it was just that once. It was an accident, sort of." As he spoke to her, alternating his eyes from her gaze to the floor and back, looking sheepishly and lost, he wished for a hole to appear so he could drop into it. Sensing Richie's honesty and contriteness, she spoke with a casualness opposite of what he expected.

"Was she pretty?"

"Huh?"

"Was she pretty? If you're going to cheat on me, she better not be a dog." Was she cynical or comical, Richie couldn't tell until she grabbed his hand in hers and smiled warmly. "Hey, tiger, if I thought you were the cheatin' kind, this chair would've been empty three seconds ago."

"Oh, Vick, you can't know what I've gone through these past few days. I dreaded seeing you again, having this burden in my heart." The unexpected reprieve lessened his anxiety and instead prompted a full recounting to Vicky of what happened. There was no need of this on her part, but allowing Richie to bare his chest seemed to be a welcome catharsis. As he spoke, gesturing wildly with his hands to stress certain points, she eyed him with silent acceptance, not once interrupting his dialogue. Better to squeeze every last drop of remorse by the expedience of revelation than to let any iota remain and fester.

The relief was evident, and Richie felt a newborn sensation. He mouthed an endearing term to his sweetheart, who nodded and then moved closer to him. She knew what she had and, if anything, was more convinced of their relationship than ever.

"Hey, good-lookin', how 'bout we head out?" The mood had now evolved from a somber exchange to one of brighter prospects. Off they went to the dreaded Buick and scooted out of town to a more pleasant and romantic arena, wherever that may be found.

During deliveries the following day, Richie had run into a couple of his high school buddies while having a bite at Marco's. Gordon Sullivan, working at Pete's Garage, was a master mechanic, and Harvey Metcalf, a metal worker and handy with a paint gun.

"Hey, guys, got a few minutes?"

Both took a seat with their friend, all of them then inquiring and sharing about their present goings-on and past escapades, the latter wringing some humor and not a little guilt.

"What's up, Rich?"

"Have a proposition for you guys." He then laid out the trip that uncovered his sainted Mustang.

"Wow, you've been in love with that dream for as long as I can remember," Gordy said with elevated interest. He had a fondness for unique cars, and this certainly filled the bill.

"Whatcha have in mind, Rich?" chimed in Harvey.

"Well, guys, I work half days on Saturdays and plan to take advantage of Mr. Perkin's offer to do some serious work."

"How far you willin' to go, Rich?"

"That's the tough part, I really don't know. Have to feel it out and see what it's goin' to cost and the time needed."

"Look, I can give you some time, but I'm short on dough."

"Thanks, Gord, your skill's what I really need. You can look at what's there and tell what we can and can't do.

"Harv, you're the best at fabricating anything made of metal. There may be parts we can't get and may have to make them. Plus, if we ever get it moving, I'll need a bang-up paint job." The enterprise stirred up the imaginative juice of the trio, and the future venture seemed off to a good start. "I'll let Mr. Perkins know what we've planned so that your coming and going will be expected. Shouldn't be a problem, he's a great guy."

"Must be, if he gave you that jewel." Gordy marveled at how dame fortune smiled on his buddy.

"What's the end game, Rich?"

"Well, if we get any kind of decent restoration, maybe enter a few car shows, and who knows, might even win some cash."

"Dream on, pal, do you know how much dough those people throw into their pets?"

"That's not the point, Harv, it's the effort, and if we can make it happen, why not? C'mon, we're going to be the Three Musketeers."

"Wasn't there a fourth?" spouted Gordy.

"Yeah, but they left him out of the title." Richie was belly laughing at what he thought was a good play on words.

"Don't go on the road with that act, Rich." The atmosphere was festive and charged with expectation. This was a challenge all young people relished, regardless of the obvious obstacles. They acknowledged that if it was easy, everyone would and could do it, so what was there to compel them to even try? No, this was not easy but welcomed.

They rehashed their days growing up and parted knowing that a new chapter was added to their books of life. Driving home, Richie almost felt a pang of sorrow for the Buick. While not elegant or flashy, it had been dependable, a feature overlooked by his distaste for the model he'd been given. Being older had dividends of revelations not apparent while growing up. Glitz did not always serve one well and in fact obscured sterling qualities nestled inside the less than glamorous. Practicality was one measure of worth, as well as durability and longevity. These qualities were not always evident with a wide-eyed youngster craving with his heart and not his mind.

Strange as it may have seemed to him, his hostility toward the Century lessened and even in some ways turned to admiration. Hey, not everyone had a Buick Century although there probably were not as many who would want one. Do cars accept owner apologies? He laughed and tapped the steering wheel as if to solicit forgiveness. Pulling into the drive, he saw Clifford leaving through the side door.

Ah, another young lover. Jenn was waving him off when she saw her brother and quickly ran to the car.

"Rich, he's taking me to the school dance." Her voice was shrill with excitement.

"Are you guys an item?"

"Oh, Rich, stop that, we're too young for that."

"Like when he left the other night with a smile on his face?"

"Oh, you dirty old man. Stop that." Then with a supplication in her voice, "Will you take us, please, please?" Refusal was not an option, and in fact, he got a kick out of being the chauffeur du jour.

"Okay, rug rat, you're on."

Brushing past the smothering hugs and kisses, he entered the house through the kitchen door. The choice was rewarded by the fragrance of another feast in waiting.

"What's the commotion with your sister, Rich?" His mother's question was idle curiosity as nothing really fazed her anymore concerning her children, as long as it didn't entail murder, theft, fraud, or any other assorted acts of mayhem.

"She's in heaven."

"Oh, you mean Clifford."

"Yeah, young love."

"Well, you seem a little chipper. Everything work out?"

"Yeah, Mom, sure did."

She knew enough not to probe deeper and was content that he seemed back on an even keel.

"Dad's late tonight."

"Yes, he called, something about a company reshuffling, and being the union board, he had to find out what's happening."

"I'm worried, Mom. When I went there for work, things seemed to be on the down swing."

"Me too, sweetie, but let's not break any eggs until we find out how big the omelet has to be."

"Ha, that's a new twist on eggs, I like it." Just then, the door swung open as if a tornado was sweeping through the area. The force was hard, and as it banged into the doorstop, a pane of glass was dislodged and fell to the floor, fortunately remaining in one piece.

"Brian, what on eart—"

"Damn idiots. Damn them to hell." Richie's father was livid with rage, his face pinkish and growing redder. He threw his coat to the floor and rushed to the cabinet, removing a bottle of Irish whiskey and gulping down a few draws, sans benefit of a glass.

"Brian, as I started to say, what on earth are you doing and why?"

He paused, stared at her, not really wanting to put into words what ripped at his guts, at least not until he calmed down, if indeed he could. He walked to the table and pulled out his chair, lifting it by the back strap and slamming it into the floor, again accentuating his anger. Richie had never seen his father like this, and he guessed it was true that an Irish temper best not be summoned from its sleep. Lynne held back, not for fear, knowing nothing on earth would move her husband to harm her. Brian needed time to compose himself, and a series of questions would only irritate him more. She'd wait, and so would Richie.

With a calculated and careful move, she walked over to the table and gently took the bottle from his hand. He glanced up with a weak smile of assent, folding one hand over the other and just staring ahead. She poured a cup of coffee, placing it before him and seating herself beside him, rubbing his neck with her soft hand, watching his color change and his mood soften.

"How long have I worked for them?" he rhetorically asked. "Twenty-two years, that's how long. Old man Garrison was a good egg and treated us well. Anything within reason he granted. Now he's gone, and his sons have taken over. Didn't think too much of it since everything kept goin' as usual these past few months. Now these know-it-all with their college degrees want to cut the staffing 10 percent on all three shifts. Me and Paul, the plant manager, argued till we were blue in the face." He paused and took a deep gulp of the refreshing brew, ignoring the scathing heat of the black liquid, causing Lynne to wince. "We told 'em that they were cutting the muscle from the production and assembly crews. How the hell are we going to maintain what little revenue we were getting, what with the slowdown. These numb nuts think that reducing payroll is the answer, but I tell you, Lynne, things are goin' to crash."

She looked at him sympathetically and mouthed a few words of encouragement, but they were hollow compared to the jolt he was slammed with. He cared for his men and would go to the wall for them, but it was a battle that was lost before it could begin. The new owners proved later that their position was unalterable, and it proved devastating. Brian apologized to his wife when he had cooled down, but the deep resentment could not be erased from his face. Richie had never seen his father this angry, although there were times when he had committed a no-no that the Wrath of Kahn was visited upon him, but not with the fury he had witnessed tonight.

Eventually, normalcy returned to the gathering, and a subdued supper was served. The next day dawned bright and warm as Richie headed to Earl's. A list of deliveries were waiting, and he plotted the best routes to eliminate overlapping and waste of time. Mr. Rosen was very liberal in his requirements as to how his employees performed their duties. He was a kindly soul, and this alone was sort of a shield against being exploited by his workers. Roly-poly, with thinning hair, and short of stature, he reminded Richie of an oversize leprechaun, but not with any malice or derision. The man had emigrated from Israel and landed in this country practically penniless. His determined mind-set and willingness to tackle any job offered put him in good stead with his employers. He soon discovered that he was adroit at managing any potential prospect into a monetary advantage.

This of course allowed him to be increasingly independent and build his confidence to the point where he started his own little business. Learning the ropes was a bit tough, but he succeeded in overcoming many hurdles that all entrepreneurs face. In fact, the challenges only whetted his appetite to succeed. Outgrowing his present business, he looked for a way to expand and, while on a business trip, landed in Pineview for an overnight stay. The following day, when preparing to leave, he was attracted to a building not too far from his hotel that seemed ideal for expanding his business. Having a service that provided a variety of items eliminated the failure associated with specialized products, something he learned through trial and error.

His take on the good citizens convinced him that while being a small community, there would be a need for the various merchandise he would stock. He had a knack for understanding how his variety of offerings, good prices, and fairness would parlay into a winning combination of loyal customers and profitability. Foremost, however, was the training of his staff so that all were treated in a manner to encourage satisfaction and repeat patronage.

Richie really liked the little guy, and the fact that many of his customers were known to him made the job more likeable. This also generated some nice tips. Who said familiarity breeds contempt? At lunch, which was always the same place (Marco's), he would meet Gordy and Harve on their breaks. The pair had gone out to the Perkins' place to check out the dream car.

"Have to tell you, Rich, it looks pretty darn good. Under all that crud, you have a fine piece of machinery. Still, a lot of work, but when we get together Saturday, we'll put her up on jacks and really see if anything's out of whack."

"Thanks, Gordy, can't wait to work on her."

It was these interludes that provided the variety that put at bay the sameness one would expect in a small town. While fairly free of the crime that dogged the larger towns and cities, the placidness was almost like an ether extract, although not all were prone to a sedentary or unhurried existence; it just seemed that way. Still, it was pleasant enough. His one constant was Vicky. Her presence in his mind was placating and soothing, as well as addictive. There were occasional instances where he arrived at a destination without consciously knowing how he got there, being so preoccupied with his thoughts. People have been known to be conscious but so absorbed in something else that one might believe a guardian angel had to have been guiding their movements. It was like looking at something, seeing it, but your mind was fixating on something else, both at the same time.

Surviving his errant mental meanderings, and his deliveries done for the day, all that remained was supper and Jenn's dance night, not that she would let him forget it.

"Now be nice to him," she implored at the dinner table. He smiled and winked at her to ease her well-founded fears. Having called Vicky earlier, she happily agreed to accompany the group to the dance. Perhaps Richie would glide the floor with her, something she recalled from the high school dances. Back then, the girls would group on one side of the gym and the guys on the other. It was comical, the expectations of the girls peering over to the shy, nervous, or disinterested boys. Then the peel off one or two and then finally a flood of guys, brazen only because the numbers concealed individual self-consciousness.

Richie hadn't been a real ladies, or in this case, girls man, groping with his youth and inexperience to strike the right cord in any encounter. This was evident when he asked Vicky to dance. They knew each other from classes, but not much more. One thing about the boy, he knew how to dance. Watching Fred Astaire movies and with a little coaching from his mother, discreet of course, his flair for guiding his partner resulted in a near perfection of movement. Strange, it was the one ingredient that could have fostered a greater involvement with the young girls, but he never exploited this gift, much to the dismay of those he danced with. And this was the case with Vicky. The dancing was fulfilling along with the hesitant small talk but nothing more.

A perceptive young lady, she resisted the temptation to encourage a more meaningful relationship. That would be up to him. As was the case, his limited approach to the opposite sex was just that, limited. Still, Vicky had a thing for him, but proper decorum restricted any overt act on her part to egg him on.

During the latter part of his senior year, Richie finally felt the tug of romance while dancing with Gloria. The sensation rocked him into the realization of what he had been missing before, how like a dolt he just festered on the vine instead of pursuing love, at least that was how he saw it. The coupling was mutual, and much to the dismay of Vicky, he was taken. Hearts break easily and mend just as fast. Maybe one day, who knows?

And one day did come. As they entered the gym, Jenn and Clifford went their own ways. Nothing changed. The boys still grouped together like mallards and the girls like swans, causing Richie to mentally laugh. Was he that bad? Vicky reacted to his broad smile, wanting to know what was so amusing. She too then laughed, aloud, when he pointed out the unchanging habits of the woos and wooers. It never dawned on them that not too long ago, they too were like this. As they moved around the gym, they caught sight of Ben and Gloria, looking more like a couple.

"Hey, guy, what's up?"

"Hey, Rich, nice to see you and Vicky. Well, truth be told, we were asked to chaperone tonight. I guess they figured nobody'd start any trouble with a decorated war hero riding shotgun." His satirical comments showed a lighter dimension to Ben, and that was good, thought Richie. And the way Gloria was holding on to him didn't hurt either.

"Well, I for one, and Vicky, promise not to start any rebellions."

"I'm countin' on it, buddy," Ben remarked with a wry grin and subtle chuckle.

A few words later, they parted with Richie guiding Vicky onto the floor as a tune blasted over the loudspeaker. Gee, he hadn't felt like this for ages, or at least the last dances at school. Tucked firmly in his grasp, the feeling of Vicky against his chest and the inviting aroma of her perfume heightened his affection for her. In the short time since they came together, their learning curve of commitment had soared for such young people. They were still kids, their older ages from those they were dancing with having no appreciable difference. They had yet to reach that level that truly separated them chronologically from the gawking boys and flighty girls that surrounded them.

There's something about a school dance that each one there will remember later in life, and this was true to Richie and Vicky. Friends made, advances rejected, swooning over handsome boys, or pretty girls turning guys into mush. This would be true to the throng of youngsters in their midst. Oh, how they will enjoy looking back on these days when they have to face the realities of real-life demands in the future.

The evening flew by, and the last dance, appropriately titled "Good Night, Sweetheart," serenaded the milling couples into an "eyes closed, head-to-shoulder" embracing where movement was barely perceptible, the close contact sufficient for gratification.

Our starry-eyed couple was not immune to this but were eventually jolted to an awakened presence when the music ended. The lights came on, and the loud speaker destroyed any semblance of romanticism by barking a good night in a scratchy, annoying, juvenile twang. Like magnets, Jenn and Clifford appeared, slightly subdued no doubt by the magic of the occasional songs they danced to. Ben and Gloria bid good night, and the gym emptied for the evening, having created memories for more than a few, some dear, some not so much, each one gaining another perspective on life.

The short drive back home couldn't prevent the youngsters from falling asleep, their heads resting against each other. The older pair smiled in accord at the innocence they projected and wondered if their future would be as promising as theirs turned out to be.

"Okay, buddy, you're home." This snapped Clifford to attention.

"Thanks, mister, er, Richie, it was a great night." He turned to Jenn and quickly planted a kiss on her cheek, exiting the car, and waving good night.

"You guys have a good night?"

"I think so. We danced some nice songs. You know, Clifford is a good dancer." With her head in the clouds, she'd naturally think so, but from what Richie saw, he wondered how long Jenn would have to soak her feet to reduce the swelling.

No pain, no gain. At least they enjoyed each other. Richie dropped Jenn off first, wishing to be alone with Vicky. Driving her home, she snuggled close to him, a comforting and telling gesture which filled the car with a serene satisfaction. No words were spoken or needed to be, just the secure feeling of closeness. Again, the walk up the path, the lingering goodbye; a compliant mother who again forsook the illumination over the doorway. Their kisses weren't ravenous but deliberate and tender, portending a greater fulfillment of their emotions to be had but realistically far in the future. While not set in stone, enough had been shared to hint at something more permanent when the time was right. They gazed into each other's eyes, confirming this unspoken desire.

Feeling reluctant to release his hold, the lateness of the hour did it for him. "I'll call." A quick peck on the cheek and she scooted through the doorway, leaving him mellow and wanting but satisfied.

The next day found him at the Perkins farm. His work schedule had been reduced to three and a half days due to the light demand. This worked out well for Richie as he had an itch to begin work on the car. A bracing cup of Mrs. Perkins's coffee set his mood in motion. Peeling back the tarp, he began a meticulous survey of the forlorn car and after an hour or so found it to be in fairly good condition considering its long hiatus. He listed some salient points that he'd pass on to Gordy to get his read on how they'd proceed. Thanking Mr. Perkins, he drove back to town and to Pete's Garage.

"Hey, Gord, here's what I found, but I'll need you to confirm a lot of this stuff. Available Saturday?"

"Yeah, I can make it, and I'll give Harve a call, I know he'll want to help."

"Thanks, see you out there."

Like a kid anticipating Christmas, Richie could hardly wait to begin the long road to rehabilitation for his dream car. That Saturday, Gord showed up with a tubular-framed two-wheeled trailer hitched to his station wagon, and Harve was already there when Richie arrived.

"Pete said that if we got the wreck, er, I mean the remains out, we could use the rear of the shop to work on it."

"That's great, but I think we're goin' to have a slight problem. All the tires are flat."

Mr. Perkins, who had joined the group, volunteered, "Hell, son, I'll get the tractor, and we can just lug it out." What would have been a laborious and strenuous task was made considerably easier, and soon the former glory of the road had been mounted on the trailer. "I expect to see Cinderella in her gown when you guys are done," the farmer spouted.

"You bet, Mr. P." With that the little entourage proceeded to town and eventually nestled the fallen angel into her berth to await a new beginning.

Pete was as caught up in the venture as the boys and, where possible, would make any effort to help them in their daunting task. Parts, if he had them, they could use, and as long as the routine of the garage was not compromised, they had free reign. Pete was one of those guys that upon meeting him for the first time, a sense of familiarity ensued. Many an encounter was soaked in accommodation; he had a thing for radiating a connection that caused a customer to return if needed. He'd been a master mechanic with his armored division during the conflict in the Middle East some twenty-odd years ago. The section he commanded knew better then to slack on any vehicle that had to be serviced, not that they would, but his direction was iron clad and unforgiving. If he couldn't participate in the action, he darn well made sure those that did had the best operating equipment. The tankers came to know this, as on many occasions they'd find him swimming in a sea of sweat during those suffocation days of heat, working on a vehicle that could have waited a day or two.

Just a small complaint about a malfunctioning piece of equipment saw it corrected immediately, regardless of the hour, and the guys under him emulated his passion for servicing anything that was brought to their attention. Being a sergeant, he turned down a field promotion as it entailed a transfer into an administrative position. No, his kids came first, and the word got around. He would find treats or booze in his tent, not knowing who his benefactors were, but he didn't have to, they were all his guys. He served three tours and had seen the gory side of combat when his crew had to retrieve a light armored vehicle that had been knocked out. The remains of the crew still inside stung him greatly as the casualty teams removed their bodies from the wrecks.

When the time came to return home, he felt he hadn't done enough. Since he was being individually separated, he felt strange as he headed to the transport that would take him to an airfield and home. As he left his quarters, the sight before him stirred a feeling of comradeship that you'd only expect in the movies.

Lined up on both sides of the sandy strip that passed for a road were many of the men of his combat unit. Not a man was out of line.

They even put on their best uniforms and stood at ease. It took the greatest of willpower to contain the knot in his throat or to keep his eyes dry. An officer shouted "Attention!" and the air was electrified by the sound of clashing boots brought together on the command. As he walked to the command Hummer, a colonel approached him and saluted, which he returned with a crisp and rigid motion.

"Pete, Sergeant Heerman, we'll miss you. Take care, Sergeant, and enjoy life." A warm handshake was interrupted when discipline broke down completely, and the men broke ranks. They rushed to and surrounded the vehicle, yelling their sentiments or slapping him on the back. He ventured into the amiable mob, trying to make contact with as many of them as he could.

Then it was time to leave. Driving away, his composure completely evaporated, and he cried the cry of a man shorn of his friends. There was no shame in this, and the driver maintained a steady stare on the road without comment.

Arriving home, he and several other returning troops were feted with a small parade down the Main Street, the small but vocal crowd appreciative of their service. Many friends showered him with the usual accolades and a drink or two. How different from what he'd just left. His mind conjured up the many faces he knew, even those who'd given their all. He silently prayed for them and felt just a twinge of remorse. They were there and he was here, something he knew didn't make sense, but the feeling persisted, and he accepted it.

He had no family, and after securing a small apartment, the next thing was to get a job. Not being a twenty-year man, his back pay and a few other benefits constituted his only source of revenue. The town's newspaper showed a small listing for employment, and his eyes were attracted to a listing for an auto mechanic at Lou's Garage. He entered what would be his own place one day and was interviewed by the owner, who was impressed with Pete's credentials, remarking, "How the hell did they let you go?" The fit was perfect, and so continued a good working relationship.

The day came when Lou wished to retire and asked Pete if he was interested in the place. He didn't have to ask twice, and after arranging a loan from the bank, Pete's Garage was formally established.

One day, a young woman drove to the front bay and asked him to check her engine. The red light had gone on, and she was very nervous that something terrible was in the offing.

"You did right, ma'am. But I can't do it today, tomorrow for sure."

"Oh my. How do I get home?"

"Tell you what, how 'bout I drive you home and call you tomorrow when I'm finished?"

"That's very kind of you. I hope it isn't an imposition."

"Not at all, only too glad to help."

The woman had blazing red hair framing a handsome face set upon a petite figure. She was a customer, and he treated her as such.

The next day, after a minor but important part had been replaced, he called the woman, indicating he'd finished the repairs, and if she wanted, he'd pick her up. She replied in the affirmative and soon was on her way back to the shop.

"Ah, let's see, here's the repair receipt and the work done, $19.20 will do it."

"That's it? I was really worried it could be more."

"Wasn't that much, ma'am."

Her name was Nancy Reilly and owned a dress shop right off Main Street. Without her car, it would be difficult to pick up supplies or deliver a finished order. Her satisfaction delighted Pete as he knew all too well what being stranded could mean. She waved goodbye and drove off.

A few days later, she again appeared at the front bay, complaining that the car shook too much.

"Maybe it's the shocks. I'll look at it and call you." He repeated the transit to her house once again, small talk generating a pleasant exchange of give-and-take. After an hour or two, Pete came up empty on any problems she'd described, and he repeated the ritual of notifying her. The routine followed the same course as before. It wasn't too long before Ms. Reilly, exasperated, parked at the front bay once more.

"The pickup is too slow. I don't want to get into an accident," she lamented, holding both of her hands against her chest in a praying posture. Dutifully, he got into the car and drove several blocks to assess the performance, returning with a shake of his head.

"Sorry, ma'am, can't find anything wrong."

"When?"

"What?"

"When are you going to do it?"

"I'm sorry, ma'am, do what?"

"Are you as thick as that concrete pavement?"

"Huh?"

"When are you going to ask me out? I'm running out of car complaints."

The usually sharp mechanic was blindsided. His attention to automotive concerns were so ingrained they dulled his otherwise acute senses on almost all matters except for one of the heart. Pete was only too aware of the hard realities of combat but was taken completely by surprise with this amorous assault. Armed only with a winsome smile, piercing blue eyes, and demure composure, Nancy had cast her line, but would he bite? He was a goner, and she reeled him in.

Within the year, they were married, and Pete had a new family to take care of with the same devotion he showed his troops. Life was good, and before long, a new addition to the family was expected. The expected arrival was signaled by an excited mother-to-be, exhorting her husband to get the car, fast! The short ride to the hospital was navigated by a nervous but careful expectant father in waiting. Into the ER he took his wife, who was then rushed to the maternity section. They took his preliminary information, smiled, and congratulated him, then directed him to the waiting room. There was plenty of time to go over the different names they'd choose from. John, William, Peter for the boys; Meg, Pam, Nancy for the girls. He was giddy with expectations, not wanting to wait one second longer to hold his little bundle.

Joining in with another father-to-be, they swapped stories and built unimaginable futures for their future children. Oh, he couldn't wait, but that was natural.

Sooner than he could have expected, the doctor entered the room. But there was no smile, a rushing forth with hand extended, only a face set in stony grimness. "Mr. Heerman, will you please come with me." A shock of fear penetrated his whole being.

What's wrong? Where's my wife and baby?

Led by his arm, the doctor took him into an adjoining room and set him down. His first words caused Pete to want to grab the doctor and stifle the words he instinctively knew were coming. *God, no, no. Don't let it be, please, Lord.*

"Mr. Heerman, please be strong."

Pete felt as if he was falling into a tunnel, his vision distorted by the supposedly comforting words the doctor uttered. *I don't care how many times he's said this, it's my wife and baby, not his. Oh my god.*

He grabbed the doctor's arms and held them in a grip to stave off the crush of what was to come. "She was in labor, and her system broke down completely, causing an adverse reaction to affect the baby. We tried to reverse and repair the cause, but it was beyond all our efforts. It happened so fast. We lost them both, her and the boy." The doctor, in his humanity, spared Pete the details. That would come later. Right now, he was a soul in pain. What was supposed to be the crowning point in Pete's life was now its nadir. A son, he had had a son.

The months drifted by with the sameness of a fog, his psychological vision dulled by the trauma no one should have to shoulder. Friends tried their best to ease the void in his heart, with little or no success. The sight of families with little children bore a hole into his consciousness, reminding him of what could have been. It took an innocent encounter to start Pete back on the road to normalcy. While at the drugstore waiting to pay for an item, he felt a small movement on his hand and looked down. A small child, no more than two, was grabbing at his hand. "Da, da?" He stared into the cherubic face and the complete trust the tike displayed.

"Oh, I'm sorry, sir, he didn't mean to bother you," a woman, the boy's mother, hurriedly offered.

"Ma'am, I welcome that type of bother." Kneeling down and placing a hand on the boy's shoulder, he talked kindly to him, asking his name and if he knew how old he was.

The sweet halting voice, trying so hard to answer things his young age could not hope to comprehend, captivated Pete. Perhaps he envisioned his son being like this, and that swelled within him a dream he could bear. A release from the morbid and an entrance into a new light, a light of comfort and lessening of sorrow.

"Ma'am, I know you don't have any idea who I am, but if you have any problems with your car, Pete's Garage will take care of you." She saw the kindness in his eyes as he eyed her son, a kindness that dispelled any notion of a hidden agenda. And she did bring her car to his garage and made it practice to bring the boy.

Time heals, and it did, slowly, but in the end, Pete surmounted his loss and rejoined the flow of life, with a memory of what he had and could have had, a reservoir of thoughts and feelings he was privileged to live.

"Hey, Pete, is it okay if I come in here now and then after hours and work on the car a little?" Gordy asked.

"Hell, yeah. You know the routine. Just make sure you lock up."

"Hey, Pete, thanks for your help," Richie chimed in. He really liked Pete and was gratified by his generosity. Now it was time to head home.

The next day was filled with more deliveries and the associated tips. Life was moving along fairly well, but he still had concerns about his dad's security at the plant. Why is it, he mused to himself, that the new operators of the factory would ignore the experience and advice of a tenured worker? It had to be arrogance, as neither sons had any practical managing expertise. Were they blind to the alternatives? Dad had remarked they held a view that the business would be fine, contrary to the dropping revenue stream. Oh, it was only a momentary slump, things would improve. Richie hoped so. Jenn was outside jumping rope with her girlfriend Maggie, a cute little sprite who had a secret crush on Richie.

A quick peck on the cheek and a tousle on Maggie's hair heralded his entrance through the kitchen door. The smell of the evening's fare wafted across his nostrils. His head tilted back and eyes closed, which was accompanied by an exhaled, "Ahhhhhhh." Baked ham! The watering of his mouth was unpreventable, the growl in his stomach signaling an urgency for relief. "Smells good, Mom."

"Oh, you received a call from DiPalo Ford. A Mr. Bookbinder. Know him?"

"Can't say that I do. What'd he want?"

"He didn't say, just to call him."

Richie knew no one by that name and surely not at DiPalo Ford. Oh well, probably a pitch to buy a car or something like that. It wasn't too late, so he dialed the number. After a few rings, "Hello?"

"Ah, this is Richie Murphy returning a call to Mr. Bookbinder."

"Oh, hello, Mr. Murphy, this is Ellis Bookbinder, sales manager at DiPalo Ford."

"Ah, Mr. Bookbinder, let me save you some time. I'm home from college, destitute, and I already have a car."

"Mr. Murphy, I have no intentions of selling you a car. In fact, I want to *give* you one."

"Is this Ben pulling my leg?"

"I assure you, Mr. Murp—may I call you Richie—this is no gag. They drawing for the Mustang at the county fair was held today, and your ticket was pulled, #1920 I believe."

"Wait a minute." Pulling his wallet out, Richie nervously poured through the assorted minutia until he came across a green slip of paper with the number #1920. "Yes, I have it. This isn't Pete, is it?"

"Again, Mr. Murphy, this is legitimate." Understandably, the young man was stunned. No, it couldn't be, how lucky could he be? After further conversation, it slowly became evident that this was the real deal. Richie asked if he could wait a few days before claiming the car. As long as he had the ticket or identification, he could do so at his leisure.

"Richie, you look as if you've had terrible news," his mother inquired with great concern as she saw his stunned-looking face.

"Oh no, Mom, in fact it's great news. Wait till Dad comes home."

His mother hugged him with shrieks of joy after learning of his good fortune. Jenn ran into the house thinking her mom had hurt herself, and she too shrieked with joy, knowing her brother had struck it rich. They stood like the great cat that ate the canary when Brian came through the door.

"Oh, oh, this don't look good. What did you spend that we can't afford, thinking I will like it?"

"No, Brian, it's not you, it's Richie. He won a car from DiPalo Ford."

Richie explained that Mom had given him some cash to enjoy himself at the fair, where he bought a chance for the car. "So your mother really owns the car," he deadpanned to his son, who was momentarily taken aback by the jest.

"Mom, is that right?"

"Oh, you beast, Brian, stop torturing your son. No, Rich, he's playing with you." As if to underscore his mother's assurance, his dad grabbed him with a big bear hug.

"Way to go sport. You deserve it."

His head swimming with the fulfillment of an impossible stroke of luck, Richie savored the prospect of cruising down Main Street with Vicky at his side. Could life be any better than this? At work the next day, he shared his news with Earl and with the customers he dealt with that day. Like a raging prairie fire, the news spread. The glow he felt was fueled by the anticipation of getting behind the wheel and talking off. He couldn't wait, but then he had to, there were several items of business to take care of.

"Hey, dude, nice goin'!" shouted Jooster as he flagged down Richie. "I'm jealous, partner, imagine a nobody like you winning something like that," he prattled as he mussed up Richie's hair with an energetic noogie.

"Hey, I can't help it that the gods on Olympus favor me over a lesser being like you." Wrapping his arm around his friend's neck in a gentle choke hold. "If you're nice to me, I'll let you smell the paint, haha." The mutual give-and-take displayed the intimacy developed over years of friendship that fostered the irreverence and putdowns. It wasn't always like this. During their preteen years, Richie first encountered Jooster Simmons in grade school. The boy was resentful and a handful for the teachers. He and Richie were often at odds and almost came to blows on occasions. His sandy tousled hair, green eyes, and gaunt face conveyed an image to be wary of. Being in the same class, the boy didn't fit in too well, but to his credit, he did make an attempt.

During recess, Richie made one more effort to communicate with the restive boy. At first he was shunned but persisted until the lanky lad suddenly turned, grabbed a handful of Richie's shirt, and blared at him. "What do you want, rich kid? Leave me alone." The boy's face betrayed a crestfallen look, as his eyes fell to the ground. He was silent as he released his grip and appeared subdued as if giving up fighting the demons that beset him. Kids have a way of tuning in on other kids, and Richie wanted to believe this was not the real Jooster.

"Hey, Joos, why'd you say 'rich kid'? I ain't got that much more than anybody else here. If you need a few bucks, maybe I can scrounge some." The offer seemed to mellow the combative youngster, and his demeanor took a 180-degree turn.

"After school. Need some time to think, okay?" he said with more of a pleading sense than a command. Most of the students lived close enough to the school that walking wasn't a big thing. The boys walked to the nearby park, where they commandeered a bench. Sitting with his forearms draped across the top of legs, hands clasped, head looking downward, Jooster hesitantly opened up. For a boy who had always demonstrated a hard facade and unyielding attitude, it was difficult for him to relinquish this self-protective barrier. In his young age, he learned to thwart anything that could be a threat to him, even if the intent of others were benign. He lacked trust.

"Rich, I'm tired. Tired of fightin', tired of running away all the time. I don't know what to do." He told how his mother, the love of his life, had passed away. His father, even on a good day, was of no support to his son. He drank, and quite often, the effects contributed to an undeserved shellacking for the lad. He had nowhere else to turn, enduring the miserable cards dealt to him. Eventually, his father decided to pull up stakes, but without the boy, leaving him with his aunt. While tolerant of the boy and even displaying kindness on occasion, the ingredient he sought most was absent—a little love. His jaundice view of life prevented him from realizing that friendship could be had, could be cultivated with his peers, but he had lost any trust he may have had and thus wallowed in self-pity and anger.

Now he was drained. Too mentally exhausted to resist anymore. Richie listened and realized how blessed he was, having what was denied to Joos.

"Hey, got any plans right now?"

"Naw, my aunt lets me set my own schedule as long as she knows where I am."

"How 'bout we shoot over to Marco's? Have a buck. We'll split a slice, okay?"

A little residue of defiance surfaced. "I ain't wantin' no charity."

"Hey, lunkhead, it's not charity. I'm full from lunch and may not be able to finish it." Although he knew it for what it was, the thinly disguised lie allowed Joos to accept while preserving his independence. In the days following, a gradual but marked change overtook the combative boy. His barriers began to fade, and his inclusion in all things boys did when grouped together showed a side of him that aroused surprise. "Okay, who are you and what have you done with Jooster?" would have been a popular exclamation if anyone had dared to exploit it.

No, he wasn't an instant angel, he still had issues with his temper, but they were mere ruffles on the sheet that had been terribly wrinkled before. His actions began to mirror those of the boys he classed with, especially Richie. Entering high school, one would have been hard-pressed to believe what Jooster's earlier life had been. His friendship with his youthful benefactor was borne of need and fulfilled by trust. The former disgruntled boy no longer existed.

"Really glad for you, Rich. Hey, does that mean you're goin' to put the kibosh on the 'stang at Pete's?"

"No, I'm goin' for it. Wanted that car for ages."

"Hey, remember 'rich kid'?"

"Ya want a poke in the nose?" He laughed.

"No, for real. Ya won the new car, Gordy told me yer fixi'n a 'stang at the garage, and yer drivin' Ms. Daisy in that Buick. Three cars."

"Okay, wise guy, get off my case." Jooster slapped him on the back, knowing he had tweaked his friend's funny bone. "Listen, jarhead, I have to finish my deliveries, I'm headin' out."

"Rich, seriously, it'd be kind of you to let me hang at Pete's and maybe do some stuff for the car."

"Sure, have no problems." This was Jooster's way of paying off some of the debt of friendship accumulated over the years.

Richie began to wonder if a Repair Richie's Car fan club was in the offing. He didn't mind that so much, because of the camaraderie it would engender. There were many of his friends he'd yet to contact after such a short time home. It would be great to remake lost connections and listen to the news that he missed out on. His delivery rounds were finished, and heading home, his head filled with those delights only an expected treasure could implant. Reaching his home, he was puzzled to see his dad's car in the driveway. His shift didn't end till much later. Was something wrong? A slight chill ran up his neck, and a quick silent prayer was automatically registered with the Big Guy. *Hope nothin' bad's happened,* he thought. Fighting an urge to avoid any unpleasantness he feared might be waiting, he gingerly fingered the knob and then just burst in, wanting to quickly get it over with.

His dad was seated at the kitchen table, with Mom standing beside him, as if consoling him. The elder was quiet and failed to look up when his son entered. Mom looked at her son, the grimness on her face only too evident. She had both hands on her husband's shoulders, a soothing rubbing motion interrupted by her son's entrance.

"Dad, what's wrong? Are you hurt? Mom, what's goin' on?"

Brian raised his head, his son's concern provoking a reply. "Sit down, Rich." He could hear Jenn in the next room crying, which instilled a greater chill to engulf his whole body. Did somebody die? Oh no, that was the worst fear he could imagine at that point, until his dad's next words put things in a better context, but not that much better.

"Son, I was laid off, me and about a dozen other guys. Seems the big cheeses figured that by cutting the payroll, they could save some money, but what they'd done is cut their own throats. Old man Garrison is probably spinning in his grave."

"What're you goin' to do, Dad?"

"Nothing much about the job, that's for sure. I'll go downtown tomorrow and see about unemployment, damn it." The last two words were accompanied by a fist slamming onto the table, the force causing the sugar bowl to spill its contents onto the floor. Anger and frustration were not to be denied, although Brian tried to restrain himself, lest he heighten his family's anxiety even more. Lynne wrapped her arms around his neck, her head caressing his, tears discoloring the blue of his shirt. Richie was uncertain as to what he could do or say to ease the tension in the room and just remained silent. Jenn came into the kitchen with no restraint and flung herself onto the lap of her dad, adding to her mother's embrace. The room, with the exception of the mourning sounds, remained quiet for some time as each were subdued by the shock. Eventually, life, greatly altered and disrupted, had to go on. Brian gently peeled his daughter's sobbing frame from his lap and, turning his head, gently kissed his wife's cheek in a consoling gesture, something she needed at that moment. She shared her husband's joys with as much fervor as he did and did no less with his disappointments.

Dinner that night for Richie didn't seem to be the usual draw, not surprisingly. The somber mood lingered until after dinner and the table was cleared.

"Okay, everyone, let's sort out what's going to be," Brian said calmly. Emotion would not rule the night, and only by a clear appraisal of all the facts would any future course of action be taken. "As it stands, even if I'm able to obtain unemployment compensation, we're still in a pickle. Your mother's medical bills from her surgery is still hefty, despite the coverage we had. The mortgage has to be taken care of, life and health insurance can't be avoided, and…" He looked at Richie with an apologetic and sad look. "And I'm afraid, son, that college is out. We still owe quite a bit for your first year, and now everything's out of reach. I'm sorry, really am."

"Dad," choking back his disappointment, "family comes first. You have to do it, and that's all there is to it." His initial emotion was replaced by the realization that whatever his desires, they now had to be placed aside for the sake of his family.

"You and Mom have taken care of us and given Jenn and me all we could hope for. This is real, and now I have to do what I can to help." Brian looked at his son with a pride evolved over the years by the togetherness and love that had withstood many other disappointments, although not of this magnitude.

"Dad, maybe I can get some work after school, you know, and chip in," Jenn offered, her squeaky voice from crying causing her father to first laugh and then choke a little at her innocence of sacrifice.

"You'll do no such thing, young lady," her mother intoned, also touched by her daughter's offer. "We'll manage. These are the years I will not have taken from you."

Richie had an off day from Earl's and pondered the bleak future. Money of course was the elephant in the room, a persistent pall of gloom. One thing the Murphy family had was pluck, and the gathering at breakfast indicated a resolve to find some way out of the family's predicament. The options weren't many, but these few were explored fully. First, Brian had to seek unemployment compensation, and the bank would be visited to see what allowances could be made for the mortgage if the financial situation wasn't eased. Jenn scoured the Help Wanted ads in the newspaper, and Lynne took stock of what ready cash was on hand or in the bank account or in the ready cash that she had squirreled away for a rainy day, not expecting a downpour. Determination can only hold desperation at bay for so long, and with this in mind, Richie made a decision, a drastic one.

The following day, after asking Mr. Rosen for a later start of deliveries, he drove to DiPalo Ford. Directed to the sales manager's office, he was warmly greeted by Ellis Bookbinder after identifying himself. The sales manager displayed a wide smile and enjoyed the mantle of a philanthropist as he eagerly shook Richie's hand.

"Please be seated, son. We have some business, some joyous business to conclude." He shuffled through a stack of documents on his desk, not finding what he was looking for until he opened a side drawer. "Ahhhh," he muttered, "there it is." Withdrawing several papers, he placed them on the desk and peered at them intently, holding the frame on one side of his glasses, magnifying the contents with its lens, as he scanned across line after line until he interrupted with a "Yup, all correct and ready for your signature."

The secretary in the adjoining office idly looked up and viewed the young man whose face was less than what she envisioned it'd be. He sat with his head down, looking up periodically at the manager, mouthing some words and showing no sign of ecstasy. Occasionally his hands would sweep in motion up or down as if explaining some complicated issue, the manager reacting with a somber and disturbed reaction. He rose from his padded chair and walked over to Richie, placing his hand on his shoulder and speaking to him in what appeared to be a consoling manner. Richie looked up and offered a weak smile and patted the manager's hand with his own, as if to thank him for his concern.

Returning to his desk, he retrieved a thick oblong ledger and opened it to a section that was partially fragmented, portions having been removed along perforated lines. He drew his pen across the document, marking it with the appropriate information, then carefully folding it along the punctured lines, removed it. Standing, he said a few words, then offered the green-colored article to Richie. As he stood to receive it, his hand hesitated slightly, perhaps not wishing to consummate the business at hand. Taking the offering, he shook the man's hand and turned slowly, with a perceptive sadness, toward the door. As it opened, the secretary heard Richie thank the manager for his understanding and compliance with his request then left.

Bookbinder walked to the door, watching until the young man left. With a sigh, he remarked to no one in particular, "He won a dream and woke up." Shaking his head, he returned to his desk, having been given an insight into an extreme act of familial love.

After taking care of a related errand, he resumed his deliveries, the task empty of the usual satisfaction promoted by the smile of his customers. The day was long, devoid of that essence of lightheartedness he was blessed with. Finished for the day, now he had to contend with what he knew would be a strong reaction from his father, something he didn't relish but was inevitable. Entering through the kitchen door and greeted with the accustomed fragrance of dinner being prepared, his dad was seated at the kitchen table. Mounds of paperwork surrounded him, his pen jotting down various combinations of numbers, its meaning known only to him.

"Hi, son. Done for today?"

His mildness comforted Richie, not wanting to see the worst side of his father. The man was his rock, and he dared not see him in any other light. But now he had to screw up his courage for what he'd do next. Approaching the table, his hand retrieved an envelope from his pocket and placed it on the table.

"What's this, Rich?" Opening the envelope, he looked at a bank receipt, his face reflecting a frown of uncertainty. "What the hell is this? Where did this come from?"

Richie was afraid of this. His dad was a proud man, but the boy wasn't sophisticated enough to know how to avoid the impact.

"I sold the Mustang."

"You what?"

"Dad, I had to. You need it, I don't." He closed his eyes, expecting to hear a violent comeback, something he didn't relish to see or hear. Instead there was silence, a strained silence. Where was the blow back? The "I can still take care of this family without your help." Nothing. He at last ventured to open his eyes, not knowing what to expect, and the last thing he did expect to see was his father holding both hands against his face, sobbing. "Dad, Dad, please don't." Brian grabbed his son's arm and drew him close, wrapping his other arm around Richie's waist and drawing him closer, an embrace of gratitude and acknowledgment of what his son had done.

Lynne had been silent during the exchange, unprepared for what transpired, but as a mother and wife, her benign presence, wisely refraining from injecting any comments or judgments, was a fortifying factor. She was Brian's rock, as he was hers. Drawing herself to her husband's side, she gently stroked his head and placed a gentle kiss on his temple.

"These darn allergies, did you change the filters on the furnace, Richie?" This impromptu ridiculous cover-up was greeted with a stoic reply.

"You bet, Dad, I wouldn't want you to sneeze all night." The meaning of the words was not in what was said but the relief they brought to two proud and loving souls. Potential embarrassment was muted by a simple act of semantics, something everyone did now and then.

"Rich, I know how hard this had to be for you, and I can't be more proud of you for doing it."

"Dad, it's a car, not my life. You, Mom, and Jenn are. I still have the Buick." With that a well-deserved round of laughter broke out. "No, seriously, Dad, it's not the flashiest bucket of bolts on the road, but its dependable. I get where I have to. Besides, I have a prince charming in the wings over at Pete's Garage."

"How is that coming, son?"

"Well, Pete has been great, and some of the guys are helping out. It'll be slow, but the wait will be worth it."

Dinner that night had a new flavor to it, a banishment of anything that conflicted with the harmony that prevailed during dinner. They would struggle, but in the end, it was each one's contribution that'd see them through. That night, sleep came easily to Richie. For the moment, the financial concerns had been eased and the wolf kept at bay. With prayer, faith, and effort, they would make their way. Strong families do this, something Richie reflected on as he thought of Jooster and how empty his life had been.

After breakfast, Richie visited the garage and was surprised to see several of his school mates there. Among them was Steve. He was attending the county college, so he and Richie had an informal battle as to whose educational achievements had more merit. They so loved to rub it in and had a great deal of fun doing it.

"Hey, Rich," he remarked, after the usual hijinks were dispensed with, "that was a great thing you did for your family."

"Huh?"

"The car thing, you know."

"Where did you get all this?"

"Jenn called my cousin Amy last night and blabbed all the details. And if I know anything about communications in this town, it'll make the rounds pretty fast."

"Gee, I wish she hadn't done that. It's a family thing, ya know?"

"Drink it in, man, all you're goin' ta get is a lot of 'Oh, what a good boy he is,' and that sort of stuff." Steve chuckled as he tenderly punched his friend in the arm.

True to his predictions, Richie would be inundated by many friends and even some strangers with a show of appreciation for his sacrifice.

"Hey, money bags, glad to see you!" Pete shouted as he emerged from the paint shop.

"Is Gordy around? And thanks."

"Back of the shop." Gordy was removing a part from the soon-to-be resurrected glop of a car. Looking at it, Richie envisioned a long haul, his previous expectations being tempered by reality. Money? Not at this time. This was allayed somewhat by the helping hands willing to contribute in any way possible, their means allowing it. Steve had brought some friends with him who were taking automotive courses at the college and whose skills could be useful. They were eager to flout their expertise, and Richie welcomed that. He made a point of getting to know any and all who'd be a part of the restoration, even going so far as to list all the names of his benefactors.

Gordy informed him that he was going to strip down, clean, and have the carburetor in tiptop condition. The engine had been drained of any fluids and checked for any defects. So far, things looked promising. The day was spent on the car with what skills he could contribute. It was difficult at times, but he shared this with those who likewise confronted the challenge with energy and spirit. The future of this dream car and how it'd look when finished propelled his efforts just like a youngster putting together a favorite model. The world was full of trials and disasters, death and destruction. In this little corner of the universe nestled a rebuttal to that discord, only because the participants made it so. If only it could be made contagious, to be replicated elsewhere.

Reaching a point of satisfaction and noticing the time, he gave a "Well done" to his friends before leaving.

"Nice work, Rich, only another one hundred years before completion," Harve bellowed above the noise of the belt sander, a friendly snicker on his face. Throwing a shop towel at the ducking agitator, Richie stepped outside, watching the sun hiding behind the trees. Time to get home, shower, and pick up Vicky for dinner and a movie. If Steve's prediction was true, she'd be all over him with questions, probably anointing him as a knight in shining armor and slobbering all over him—hey, not a bad come-on. *A little modesty, Rich, a little modesty.*

He needn't worry about projecting any modesty, as Vicky's reaction was mildly inquisitive but mostly supportive as to be expected. It was this lack of fawning that she imparted to him, sincere and to the point and comforting, which impressed him.

"Oh, Rich, it must have hurt, but I'm sure that in the end, nothing could have been more satisfying." In this he realized that the buzz agitating his subconscious was indeed a sense of satisfaction, only he hadn't been able to rise above the disappointment to discover it. Her presence and words left little to the imagination that, without her, his existence would be incomplete. Oh, he would survive and plod about as before, but when compared to her becoming a fabric of his life, there would be a void, never knowing what was missing. We can appreciate the measure of what we dearly have only when losing it. Richie had yet to make this conscious conclusion, but he needn't have to. What he had didn't need to be defined; it was woven into his heart.

The romantic dinner atmosphere was in conflict to the ambience at Marco's, which was austere. But none of this could dull the optimism and mutual enjoyment shared quietly, their little open secret there for all to see. They were both evolving from starstruck lovers to a plane of maturity to be admired. Hand in hand they reinforced each other's persona, reinforcing strengths and dealing with any weaknesses, not by design, but instinctively.

Just before leaving, a little figure scooted up to their table, a radiant face framing an irresistible smile. "Hi, man," a loveable greeting so fond to Richie.

"Hey, little guy, how are you?" The squirt unabashedly climbed onto a willing lap, his arms draped around his friend's neck. Vicky was taken with the familiarity and delighted in the warmth of the two.

"Pip, you know better than that," a parental admonishment in the offing. His mother, unable to halt her son's impulsive dash, excused his intrusion.

"Donna, it's okay, he's no bother at all, are you, buddy. Vicky, ah, this is Ms. Donna Glass." The slight hesitation in Richie's voice was all Vicky needed to unveil the source of his past anguish. There was no contempt or resentment, all that was past, only an appreciation for a fine-looking woman and her son. They had been and still were a part of Richie's life, and she would not intrude on that.

"I'm glad to meet you. Would you care to join us?"

"I'd love to, but we have to run. Nice to have met you, and please accept my apologies."

"Same here."

"Wait, I'll walk you to the door," Richie offered.

"C'mon, squirt, give me your hand."

As they neared the entrance, Donna halted and turned to Richie, urgency in her tone as she spoke to him. "I have to speak to you when you have a chance. Here's my number. Please, Rich, it's important."

"Sure, Donna, I'll call you tomorrow after work, okay?"

"I could always depend on you, thanks."

He felt unsettled. What was so dire that she seemed almost desperate? Returning to the table, Vicky sensed his concern but made no effort to pry it from him. "She's a lovely woman, Rich, and her child is adorable."

"She's had a hard time of it, losing her husband and being alone."

"Really, I feel for the woman. At least you are here for her." This admission removed all doubt from Richie's mind about Vicky's attitude toward Donna. The "other woman" was a person in need of support, and she cherished his role in supplying it. "The little fella seems quite taken with you."

"Yeah, he's a joy, that's for sure. It pumps me up when he grabs me like that."

She looked into his eyes, placed a hand alongside of his face, and quietly said, "You'll make a great dad one day." Her words mirrored the inevitable they both envisioned. A gentle kiss and off to the movies.

Somehow, he couldn't shake the foreboding of Donna's words, which in turn colored the rest of the evening. Even the good-night ritual with Vicky provided little relief as his concern lingered, and that'd last until he saw her the next day.

He tried his best to lay aside his uneasiness, but it was difficult to do. What was it that was so upsetting to Donna? Whatever it was, he was glad she came to him. Her only other choice were the few others she knew who lacked the intimacy necessary to ease her dilemma. Thankfully he finally finished his rounds and called.

"I'll be over in a few minutes. You okay?"

A soft voice, slightly trembling, replied, "I'm okay, just trying to get things together. I'm glad you're coming, thanks, Rich."

Okay, I don't know what's going on, but if anybody or anything is threatening her, by heavens, they'll pay for it. His protective nature took full bloom as he imagined the worst. This gentle woman had suffered enough, and woe be to whatever it was that was causing this grief. The Buick never traveled as fast as it did that day and in moments he was there.

Leaping from the car, he rushed to the door, repeatedly knocking as if to summon a quicker response, not knowing what to expect, but primed for retribution if needed. Donna responded to the incessant rapping, momentarily startled but reassured when she saw it was Richie.

"What on earth—"

"Sorry, I had to make sure you were okay, that nobody was giving you a hard time."

She took both his hands in hers and, looking at his grim face, appreciative of his protectiveness, replied, "Rich, no one's bothering me. It's a little more complicated than that."

"Please, what's going on?"

"First, come in, take a seat and unwind. What I have to say is unavoidable, and your friendship means more to me than you know."

Oh no, she's sick, that's it. She's really sick, his troubled mind conjured. *No, not now, she's too young.*

The thought had barely imprinted his consciousness when she uttered, "I'm leaving Pineview!"

"You're not sick or anything?"

"Where did you get that idea?"

"Well, gee, you were down in the dumps and acting weird and I…You sure you're not sick?"

"Absolutely, where did you get such a notion?"

"Well, you've been acting worried, and now when you sat me down, I thought the worst."

"That's awfully sweet of you, but my health is not the problem. And that's what I wanted to talk to you about. My mother is all alone, as you know, and has been waiting for my answer about coming to live with her. Shortly after Jerry and I were married, my dad passed away. Before we moved here, we were able to keep her company, visiting often and celebrating the holidays. I was worried when Jerry's work took him here, but Mom was fairly independent, not wanting us to worry about her being alone. After Jerry passed, she offered her home to me and Pip, but I wasn't ready for the move. Now, I'm ready to do this. You understand, don't you?"

"Gee, Donna, that's family. Who can argue with that? It's your mom, and no one can fault you for that. I was relieved that you're not sick or anything, but now I'm down in the dumps. You and the little guy have been part of my life." He reached over and embraced her, a feeling of impending loss glossing over his attempt to remain passive.

"Hey, man." The sound of a youthful greeting spurred a thankful respite to what was becoming a shroud of gloom.

"Hey, little guy, c'mere." The trusting nature and joyous appeal of the tyke dispelled for the moment the empty future that lay in store for Richie. The ritual they shared, the openness of anticipated companionship, these and other elements of their friendship, soon to be history. Here and now was to be their focus, however, and what came later would take care of itself.

"Does he know?"

"Not yet, I'm trying to find a way to tell him so that's he'll understand, especially about you. Right now, his young mind might be able to handle the separation, but I don't know. He loves you so much." Tears were beginning to well in her eyes.

"Mommy hurt? You cry."

"No, dear, Mommy not hurt." At least not that the boy would know or understand now. Maybe in the near future. Cradling Pip's head in her lap and stroking his hair, Donna continued. "After Jerry passed, life was empty as I made only a few friends. They in turn offered their kindly solace, for which I will always be grateful, but the real turning point came after your return from college and meeting Pip. He was so full of your presence that all he could talk about that day was 'the man.'

"His happiness was contagious, and I began to think of you. No"—she chuckled—"I wasn't out to hustle you. You seemed so fresh and unpretentious, something that contrasted with the polite but uninvolved contacts I encountered.

"Secretly, I also wished to see you again, to relieve the sameness and dull routine. After all, we're talking about this thriving metropolis Pineview." Again chuckling at her satire. "You have a gift, a gift not bestowed on all people."

"And what would that be?" A slight self-consciousness responding to the sincere accolade.

"You are what you are, no window dressing, no posture other than your own. Pip knew this right from the beginning even if the philosophy was beyond his understanding. Kids are always the best judges."

Oh, boy, now she's going to kiss my ring or somethin'. The private mirth was quickly subdued by a cold reality. An important part of his life had a half-life of only so many days, weeks, or hopefully months.

"It will still be a while before I finalize the move. I dread it with all my heart. Please be there for me."

"Always." He then clutched both of them with as much reach as his arms provided, the stillness magnified by the soft breathing.

The following day found him laboring under the soon-to-be heartfelt loss of his friends. Of course, he realized the impact her decision had created, but family came first. In a way, they were also family to him, and he was sure the feeling was mutual. The deliveries were sparse, the in between time giving him too much to think about. In this he was practically alone, having shared very little about his friendship with Donna to his family. Vicky was out of the question, though he suspected she might give him some moral support. No, this affected him alone and no need to involve others. Richie was maturing fast, but in this instance, he forwent the comfort and insight that may have eased his concerns.

A stop at Pete's Garage found a growing number of wannabe restorers plying their trade on his car. Pete had an eye on them, and with Gordy hanging around, no substantial harm was done. To their credit, their help was fairly consistent with the goals in mind. More often it was just cleaning the various parts removed or making some minor mechanical adjustments. Harve informed him that the grime covered what turned out to be a surprisingly intact paint finish. What had to be treated was minor and could be accomplished without adversely compromising the restoration value. Gordy was set to reassemble all the components of the engine, and in a few days, fingers crossed and a prayer offered, the rebirth of its main mission in life would be attempted. The energy was really flowing and helped to dilute the dour revelation of the night before.

"Gotta go, guys. Thanks for doin' a good job. Gordy, I want to be here when you fire 'er up."

"You bet, pal, I'll see to it."

The distraction gave him a little solace as he tried to put things in perspective. He had to learn that not every problem had a positive solution. One can only do so much, and trying to tackle every misfortune usually ended with a formidable burden. Oh, so young and slowly coming to grips with the realities of life. In a way, he slowly edged his way toward that goal, though it would take time to blossom. Given his burden, he nonetheless refused to let it color his association with friends and customers. The rest of the day passed without a hitch, and dinner that night was the usual fare of the Pharaohs.

The next day found him at the Perkins farm, upholding his part of the deal that gave him his Mustang. Mr. Perkins was up to his usual inventiveness with the odd machine part here and there, much to the admiration of Richie. The man was a genius who shunned publicity for his endeavors and was that much the happier for it. Plenty of time after he passed to that workshop in the sky for the anticipated drooling of art critics extolling his works of art. The work had a soothing effect on the young man, and the coffee break was most anticipated. With a lull in the chores and sipping the exotic brew with Mr. Perkins, the small talk centered on the gift Mustang.

"Well, son, how is the bucket of bolts comin' along?" The smile on his face betrayed a sincere interest in the project.

"Well, sir, it looks pretty good at the present. My good friends are lending me a hand, and it takes a load off my mind."

"Glad to hear that. Look, I'm not in the dark about what this thing may cost you to complete. If you're willing, I'd like to sponsor you."

"Really? I don't know what to say, you've done so much for me already."

"It's not like I'm goin' to ask you to plaster that crate with my logo or whatever, just like those fanatics do at NASCAR. You can't even tell what kind of machine they have with all that junk on it."

Laughing, Richie replied, "I know what you mean. Any ideas?"

"Well, if Pete agrees to it, how 'bout I have some placards plastered on his walls?"

"Gee, I think that'll work, and knowing Peter, I don't think it'll be a problem."

The farmer's response was to gulp down his coffee and slap Richie on the back. "Okay, it's a deal." The amount didn't matter, as the offer was beyond anything he anticipated. *As long as I live,* thought Richie, *these and the other acts of kindness will be repaid as best as I can do it.* Young oaths of restitution often fall by the wayside during the tumult of life and its distractions. In this case, Richie will more than uphold his oath in the future.

To Richie, the farmer's lot seemed secure, attested to by his easygoing manner and unconcealed confidence. *Does anything bother him?* he thought. How he wished that was the case with his family, especially his dad. No shrinking violet, Brian nonetheless showed some signs of the pressure he now faced. His outward demeanor concealed any reservations he had, but that was for the benefit of his family. But Richie was cut from the same cloth and assumed, rightly, what his dad was going through. His gesture with the car money helped alleviate any immediate crisis, but what the future had in store was something he dwelled upon, but with no real resources to address them. If and when crunch time came, he told himself, they'd muddle through.

The sweat of a hard day's work boosted his outlook. Nothing like wrenching a muscle or two to appreciate the downtime later, after a soothing bath. He liked the outdoors because they revealed a crispness absent from the town, the quiet springing mental visions of his past, present, and possible future. It's a wonder his musings didn't distract him to the point of dropping a load on his foot or running the tractor into a ditch. If he had any children, this is what he would have them do. To be reliant upon their own energies and efforts. He'd seen some of the younger kids with electronic gadgets. That, while miraculous, tended to replace the instinctive reactions and imaginations so taken for granted in the younger set. When the time came, he assured himself, that'd be something he'd address.

The day ended with Mrs. Perkins bringing him a basket of goodies. Oh, how he loved the various treats, so tempting that his resistance to quickly gulp some down was reinforced by the consideration for his family, not to mention the anticipated stern tongue lashing from his mother. Filling his lungs with the sweet air wafting in from the fields, he bade goodbye with a handshake and a hug.

Part Three

Would he miss not going back to college? The thought had challenged him more than once but resolved itself in the practical view of things. No money, no college. Simple. But again, would he miss it? Truth be told, he couldn't say. His courses were varied with no clear idea of where he wanted to go; that would have been addressed during his second year. In a sense, with his goals in a flux, to pursue an education now was out of the question, not to mention unaffordable. In this respect, he was no different than hundreds of other college-inclined youths. Another contention was his growing involvement with Vicky. As far as he was concerned, it was the real thing, and only the future would reveal the outcome. There was no doubt as to what that'd be. But for now, he had to deal with the current offerings of life.

The diversity of his everyday challenges gave impetus to his need to deal with them in as honest and effective way to be able to chart the best course. His guardian angel most likely was submitting resignation papers, or consulting with Solomon. To sum up a small portion of his dilemmas, there was Donna and Pip leaving, Dad out of work, college off the boards, and cashing in the car won in the raffle. On the other side of the ledger, the 'stang was making progress, a sponsorship by Mr. Perkins a blessing, Vicky was very much in his life, and a part-time job. What was to be a period of rest and contemplation became a trial and triumph on many fronts. He would address each in order of importance or when they surged to the forefront.

The week passed with the routine of deliveries, visiting the garage, and enjoying the company of his girl. The sameness was almost numbing, something that he quickly became accustomed to. The human psyche is not equipped for daily splurges of excitement or radical change. If so, boredom would be intolerable. Finishing his work for the day and returning home, he was surprised to see a sleek black limo parked in front of the house. As he parked in the driveway, several well-dressed men exited the home from the front door. They turned and waved to the occupant, entered their vehicle, and drove off. *What was that all about?* he thought. Quickly entering the kitchen door, Mom was clearing the table of several cups and plates. Looking up, she smiled, humming a song she always invoked when something special occurred.

"What's up, Mom? Why the glad face?"

"I'll let your father tell you."

"Tell him what?" his father retorted, entering the kitchen.

"Stop being coy, you know very well that you were dying to tell Richie, in fact anybody you'd corral, into listening to the good news."

"Yeah, Dad, what's goin' on?"

"Sit down, my fine first and only son." Taking a seat and fully alert to some news of great import or so it seemed, Richie could only wait while his father set the stage in his own, agonizingly slow, dramatically drawn-out process to garner full impact. "Those fellows that just left. Ya see them?"

"Yeah, Dad. Who're they?"

"Getting to it, getting to it." Taking a seat and savoring a mental rush for several moments, he finally got down to business. "Those men, son, are your future."

"Huh?"

"Let me explain, my boy. Those men are the sons of the late Mr. Garrison. Remember how I railed about their policies at the factory and what it would do? That was several weeks ago, and what I said would happen, happened.

"In this business, it doesn't take long for the bottom line to show the results of any corporate action, good or bad. Well, it started to come in, and it wasn't good." Pausing, he took a gulp from the ever-present cup of coffee that Lynne managed to keep filled. Sated, he continued. "They called and asked if I'd consent to talk with them. 'About what?' I asked. 'About the factory,' they said. 'How'd that concern me,' I replied. To that they said it would be better discussed face-to-face. 'Okay,' I said, 'come on down.'"

"Gee, Dad, what went on?" His mother placed a glass of tomato juice in front of him, bringing a welcome respite to the day's work and heightening the anticipation of his father's unfinished story.

"The sad results they were experiencing caused them to relive my warnings. Remember, these suits are only interested in the boardroom, not the workroom.

"They may have some expertise in what they do, but sometimes they're over their heads."

"What'd they want, Dad?"

"They wanted my input on what corrective measures that needed to be taken in order to reverse the 'negative trend,' that was their word for it. Negative trend my eye. Outright disaster, I told them. I had nothing to lose being frank with them. They had to be shaken, and by golly, I was goin' to do it royally." Richie felt a surge of pride hearing his dad and how he stood his ground. The man was genuine, no fluff but downright real. "Well, son, I told them I wasn't a magician and could only tell them what I thought would fit. Before that happened, I said that Paul and some of the guys that were out had to be rehired. They said that if things worked out, they'd see to it, but only if improvements were seen in the bottom line. In our business, it doesn't take long to see any results whatsoever, so I gave it a shot."

"What didja say, Dad?"

"To begin with, their father was a great guy. In trying to foster a business climate, he offered too many loss leaders. Sure, they were snapped up but failed to generate the return revenue he hoped for, but it was a trend he failed to fully realize, the success in other areas obscuring its failure. They had to go. Second, I told them flat-out that a lot of the machinery had to be updated or replaced. They were inefficient and costing profits that could've realized with better equipment.

"Their eyes bulged from their heads when I told 'em that. Shows how much in the loop they were. All those good years kept them from seeing the inevitable. The workers would have to be trained constantly as the markets changed a lot. In-house was good as long as it was top notch or, if necessary, outsourced." Richie's dad glowed as related the discussion, rightfully proud of his observations that the owners seemed impressed with. "Finally, I said that what good were our products if no one knew about them?" Here, he exaggerated a little but not by much. "We need to push our products, advertise nationally." This had been a hallmark of the company but unexplainably had slowed to a trickle, which may have contributed to the slowdown in profitability.

"All in all, Dad, how'd they react to all this?"

"They want me to head up the rebound and gave me a lot of leeway. If it works out, we can save the factory and maybe even add jobs." His elation brightened the kitchen, not so much as light, but the lightheartedness and outright joy that emanated from his pure delight in the prospects and challenges that awaited. It was a wise choice. While not steeped in the intricacies of corporate mayhem, he was grounded in the pragmatic understanding of his profession. He needed no doctorate or diploma to know how to assess and correct what he saw as the root causes of a business decline. He may be wrong, but the alternative was a glaring possibility that needed no further encouragement.

"And with that, my number one and only son, perhaps we can start talking about college again."

"Dad, we still don't know what's goin' to happen," Richie offered, trying to conceal his hesitancy and most certainly his doubts about returning. It was now that he suddenly realized that his higher education seemed distant and not as consuming as it had when he first left home for that far distant campus. It was difficult to reconcile this turn of events, happening so fast as it did. Trying to put off a conflict with his dad, the subject was mercifully changed when his mother exclaimed, "I'm so proud of you, honey. You'll change things, I know you will."

"With you as my fan club, how can I fail?" His mirth coupled with an endearing embrace of his soul mate. Using that as a ruse, Richie excused himself, slapping his dad on the shoulder and winking at his mom as he left the kitchen.

He'd need some time to sort things out. The last thing he'd want would be to hurt his dad after the sacrifices he'd made to see that his education was assured. List another chink in the chain of gloom. Now he really needed to talk to someone and to get a read on what to do next. He called Vicky and asked if she was free.

"Well, there's that handsome quarterback from community college or the handsome drugstore clerk, and I'm finding it difficult to choose."

Okay, two can play that game.

"I only wanted to show some courtesy as Gloria called and felt alone."

Click! He waited for several minutes, and the phone rang.

"Hello."

A boisterous laughter followed. "Okay, tiger, I'll save you from torture and agony. What time?"

"Pick you up at seven." Her humor was a tonic, something he was going to need in abundance.

Seated beside him, he felt a security by her mere presence, hoping it would transform into the answers he needed. She felt his tension but didn't push the issue. He was silent, but not in a dismissive way, as if trying to formulate the questions he had to ask, an attempt to justify his lack of interest in returning to college. He drove to the park and pulled to the side of the road.

"Okay, tiger, what's up, if not for my charms?" Her jest took the edge off his outlook, and he took a deep breath, turning toward her with his arm around her neck and pulling her a little closer.

"I'm in a bind."

"How so?"

"Well, there's a good chance Dad will be working again, and he wants me to go back to college."

"That's great, I mean, him working again and college back in play."

"That's just it. I don't think I want to go back. It's a feeling that climbed into my brain, and Dad jiggled it loose. Vick, I love my dad, and this is going to hurt him, but I don't know what to do. If I go back, I'll be miserable. If I don't, I'll be miserable. What can I do?"

With both her hands tenderly cradling his face, she pulled him closer and kissed him tenderly. "That's what I like about you, tiger, you give a lot and take very little. Listen, you're no different than a lot of other kids who have to square themselves with their parents. But that's why they're there, to love, nurture, and guide you. If they've raised you right, whatever dilemma you face, you do so together. Their interest in it is not what they want, but that which you strive for. Sure all parents want the best and maybe infuse themselves in the process, but when the hammer comes down, it's your nail that's being driven, and a good set of parents will realize that."

Wow, not only pretty, but a good thinker. He sat for a while, digesting her words and their impact. Now he understood that whatever course he takes, he needn't be afraid, maybe a little concerned, but trusting his parents' response.

"Vick, if I haven't said it often enough, I love ya, girl. You gave me a breather. It won't be easy, but better than if I went into this alone. Thanks, hon." His embrace was one of gratitude and hers gratification for easing his concerns. The rest of the evening was not wasted on trivialities, and a revitalized young man later entered his home with a renewed sense of purpose. The night was fairly gone, so he plopped onto the porch to watch what was left of a meaningless game after greeting his parents. Dad with his paper and Mom knitting or whatever she does with those pig stickers.

After a few deliveries, Richie was going to have lunch at home, and he expected his father to do likewise since his new duties allowed him a little more leeway. He rehearsed a few lines in preparation for his declaration of independence and quickly shelved the idea. What he had to say had to be from the heart and not scripted. His father's nose for sincerity was too keen for that. The door opened, and the moment was at hand as his dad greeted Mom with a kiss and mussed

Richie's hair with a flourish, a sign of "Everything's right with the world" attitude.

"Man, I'm starved," he quipped.

"Dad, I have to talk to you." A slight lump was rising in the boy's throat.

"Now?"

"Yeah, Dad, it's kinda important."

"You're eloping with Vicky."

"Maybe that would be easier to say."

Sensing the imploring tone in his son's voice, Brian became serious as he focused his eyes on the boy's evident discomfort. Placing his hand on Richie's shoulder as a sign of fatherly interest and support, he invited his comments.

"Okay, Rich, I'm all ears."

"Dad, Mom, you've done so much for me in my life. I've always had your support and the discipline I needed when I went off the chart. At times I wondered how you could put up with all my nonsense, and it was because of your love for me and Jenn, something I never fully appreciated, because I was a kid, and kids don't really know these things, at least not then."

His mother wiped her hands on the white-and-blue apron that snugly fit her petite form and sat alongside her son. This was not some idle banter but a coming-of-age type of moment, something set apart from the usual trials associated with a growing youngster and the normal conflicts encountered along the way.

Their son had evolved, just like a moth struggling to free itself from its cocoon and becoming somewhat different from before. Not many parents get to see this transformation as they were seeing it, and the revelation was both heartwarming and suspenseful. They were quiet as he continued, hoping that no dire circumstances were besetting him. He had demonstrated a youthful maturity when he had sacrificed his car for his family, but this was different.

"What I'm trying to say is that I don't want you to think that what you've given me was in vain, it's just that…er, gee, Dad, Mom, I'm floundering here." Taking a deep breath, he continued. "Someone told me that any problems were faced together as a family, that as I was nurtured by your guidance, you would want the best for me, but it was what I wanted that meant the most. If that made me happy, you'd be too, does that make sense?"

"As far as it goes, son, but what are you trying to tell us?"

Looking into his father's eyes and prying the last bit of restraint from his hesitation, he replied, "Dad, I've decided against returning to college, I've lost the feel for it. I wouldn't be happy going back, and I feel terrible after all you and Mom have done for me."

There was a slightly painful look in his dad's eyes, and his mother held both hands against her chest as if offering a prayer. There's no doubt that they were caught off guard by their son's admission. That was natural but revealed little in how they'd address this latest issue. Brian clasped his hands together on the table and stared at them as he wrestled with an answer to his son's apparent distress.

"Your friend is right, son. Sure, we want what's best for you, but in the end, it's up to you to determine what that is. All parents want their children to have a future and believe college is the first step toward that goal. In many cases, that's true, but not the sole gauge for planning one's future. If you had told me this when you first came home, I would've argued with you. But you've shown me a different boy than the one we sent off to college. I can't say that this is the right decision, only that you're the one who has to make it, and the right or wrong doesn't matter if that's what you believe. Only time will tell."

The weight on Richie's shoulder began to lighten as the vindication of Vicky's counseling became clearer. Reaching over and taking his dad's hands in his own and looking at his mother with a sign of relief, the young man felt release from his torment.

"What are your plans now, son?"

"Well, Dad, I haven't given it much thought, but you know, I can't have a better example of what to do than the person who's sitting beside me."

"You can't mean your mother, do you?"

The tension was cut as the laughter that followed filled the kitchen.

"Yeah, Dad, I'm dying to be a house son, or maybe, if things work out at the factory, I'd like to work there, starting from the bottom like you did." A quick trip down memory lane briefly flitted across Brian's thoughts as he recalled his first experiences at the plant.

The years were informative and rewarding as he mastered his trade to the point of being the go-to guy. Looking at his son, he envisioned the same results, something he'd have concluded even if it wasn't his son. If he was fortunate to have him at his side, oh, the things he'd teach him.

"No guarantees, but it'll be top on my list."

"Thanks, Dad, I appreciate it."

"Oops, time to go, see you guys tonight."

"Bye, hon. See ya, Rich."

With that, Brian left a very happy kitchen in his wake.

"Gee, Mom, God was good to us today." He embraced his mom with a lingering hug that almost concealed her diminutive form.

Wiping her eyes, she brought her son's head down to her level and kissed his forehead, cheeks, and lips. One thing about love, it can never be said too often or exhausted as it is the eternal expression that dispels sorrow and elevates selfless ambitions for the good of others.

With his problem resolved, Richie finished his rounds with a clear head. He stopped off at Pete's to check up on his dream car. The attraction was still evident as three or four of the guys were climbing over, under, and into the frame of his beauty.

"Hey, Gordy, looks like it's starting to come together."

"Well, Mr. Perkins stopped by and dropped off some posters he'd made years ago, and Pete was only too glad to put them up where they'd be visible. Also, that kind gentleman handed over some dinero to Pete to defray some of the costs, and that really came in handy."

"Listen, Gordy, I don't want to push Pete too far with the expenses, but if it comes down to a problem, just shelve the project until I can muster some cash elsewhere."

"Rich, what Mr. Perkins brought in will hold us for a while, but if push comes to shove, I'll give you a heads-up."

"Thanks, Gordy, you guys have been the greatest." Turning to leave, he shot a quick glance at the somewhat unrecognizable jumble of metal that was slowly coming together. His mind envisioned a sleek, polished beauty, causing him to hesitate, standing there like a kid gaping at a window candy display. It didn't seem real, but it was.

"Like it?"

He turned to Pete's inquiry and was all smiles. "You guys are magicians. Can't wait, Pete."

"I like it myself, I mean, the way the guys have been helpin' out, not to mention the work they bring me. It's a win-win deal."

Several days later, as Richie passed through the kitchen, he heard his dad on the phone. He inadvertently heard his dad speaking, making out a partial statement, "Do what you can, and it has to be when I asked…er, hold on. Oh, hi, Rich, be with you in a minute." His actions almost seemed furtive, but what the hey, my dad the spy?

"No need, Dad, goin' to take a shower and a quick nap." Brian held this hand over the mouthpiece and waited until Richie left the room before resuming the conversation.

Supper was the usual satisfying offering of his mom, and his dad seemed buoyant about the factory's outlook, but he wasn't waving the victory flag yet. Several men were rehired, and some new equipment was brought in. The young owners had contacts in the advertising field and were mounting an aggressive campaign to highlight the company's products. Richie could only hope it led to his being hired.

"Ben called while you were asleep, dear, and asked if you'd see him. He'll be over after supper."

"Know what he wanted?"

"Not really, but he sounded excited, so I knew you'd be interested." Mom was right about that. It looked like some of the good things that happen to other people would also be happening to Ben; at least he hoped so.

He sat on the front steps, the night being balmy, and waited for his dear friend to arrive. Not being able to drive was no deterrent to the young soldier, who chose to troop over on foot rather than hitch a ride.

"Hup, two, three four, hup, two, three four," Richie chanted as he caught sight of Ben approaching. He rose and grabbed his buddy in a bear hug. "What gives, pal, Mom said you were wetting your pants?" A rub Richie couldn't resist laying on his friend.

"Hey, rube, a little more respect, you're talking to a hero."

"It's okay, that's all I'm giving you, a little respect."

The wrestling match that followed found the soldier completely in command and Richie prostrate with a look of faux fear on his face.

"Oh please, sir, spare me."

"I have to, rube, I can't afford the flowers." Offering his hand, he pulled his laughing comrade to his feet, another embrace ensuing.

"Everything okay?"

"Sure, I just wanted to let you in on some good news."

Awright, good news rather than bad. "You hit the lottery."

"Better than that. I received word from the Army that they're taking me back. I'm eligible for retraining after being fitted with a new arm. I'll leave next month."

"Gee, that's great news, Ben."

"But that's not the best part. Are you ready?" What could be better than being taken back into the fold? Ben was cut out to be a soldier and was far superior with one arm than those with two. "Well, buddy, I asked Gloria to marry me." The shock was like a thunderstorm, hurricane, and tornado rolled into one.

"What?" The exclamation was more celebratory than derisive. "You dog you. When, where? Wait, did she say yes?"

"Practically knocked me to the ground as she leapt into my arm. Boy, she's heavy."

They both let out with a yowl, the noise bringing the rest of the family to the door.

"Who hit who first?" chimed Brian, recognizing a moment of jocularity between the two.

"Heavens, when will you two ever grow up?" Mom chipped in.

"Mom, Dad, Ben's getting married. He asked Gloria, and she said yes."

"I wanna be a bridesmaid," chirped Jenn. Lynne flew down the steps and wrapped her arms around the jubilant prospective groom. "Uncle Ben, can I? Can I?" shouted Jenn as she tugged on his jacket. Placing his hand on her head in a fatherly manner and giving her a smile, he nodded an okay. "Ooooh, wonderfully awesomey," she blurted.

"Awesomey? What planet did that come from?" interjected Richie. Brian joined Lynne and gave Ben a robust handshake and gentle head butt of approval.

"To the kitchen. A proper celebration is at hand," the elder Murphy commanded. Soda for Jenn and wine for Brian and Lynne with the guys downing cider.

"Father Al at St. Rose will marry us, and we'll have a few days before I have to leave. Unfortunately, Gloria will have to stay behind while I rehabilitate, and after that, I'll be assigned somewhere with Gloria joining me at that point. Rich, you'll look after her for me, won't you?"

"We all will," said Lynne. "This house will always be open to her." Richie now felt a brotherly responsibility to maintain that promise, and the solemnity of the moment brought on an impromptu prayer to affirm that promise. All sorts of questions and offerings bombarded the affable young man to the point where Richie had to tear him away.

"C'mon, guy, let's move."

"Thanks, Mr. Murphy and Mrs. Murphy, and of course our bridesmaid, Jenn."

Richie grabbed his hand and whisked him out of the kitchen door.

Man, what a night. They both walked to Ben's home and talked well into the morning.

"Rich, I didn't say what I really wanted to with all the excitement."

"And what would that be, pal?"

"I'd like you to be my best man, although that's only partially true." Snickering on top of a solemn request. That's Ben all right. "I'd a slugged ya if you didn't, of course." Rich had been honored. The hero status had faded only to the point where their friendship predominated as this gesture demonstrated. Saying good night, the walk home gave Richie a chance to think about his future with Vicky and hoped it would produce the same euphoria visited upon his friend.

Richie had a light schedule, and Mr. Rosen excused him for the rest of the day. It was nearly noon, and he relished the thought of having a hot lunch. Entering the kitchen, he heard his dad, also home for lunch, on the phone. Not being inquisitive, he couldn't help but notice the urgency in the conversation. Upon seeing his son, Brian abruptly asked the other party if he could call him back, quickly ending the call.

"Uh, hi, Rich, you're home early." His effort to act nonchalant was weak and unconvincing, which troubled Richie.

What was Dad hiding?

"Oh, Rich, I didn't know you'd be home for lunch," his mother countered as she came into the kitchen. This distracted him from his concern for his dad. "Yeah, Mom, there wasn't much to do, so Mr. Rosen gave me the rest of the day off—with pay."

"Okay, you two, what do you guys want?"

The meal was fulfilling, but Richie still had a lingering discomfort and hoped it was something silly. Yet he didn't want to open a can of, whatever would be in it, and possibly offend his father. After Brian left for work, Richie asked his mother in a very casual manner if everything was okay with dad, if everything at the factory was okay, using that pretext as a way of discovering if indeed anything was out of sorts.

"Oh, the usual gripes, but nothing he can't handle."

Somewhat mollified, but not completely, the boy tried to put the incident to bed, hoping he was worrying for nothing. During the end of the week, with a free day, he drove to Pete's Garage to check up on the rebuilding progress. Stopping in the office, he found Pete going over a stack of bills and orders.

"When're you goin' to hire a secretary?" he needled Pete.

"Don't need one, I'm a human computer. Hi, Rich, what can I do for you?"

"Just came to see my dream girl."

"Oh, yeah. Listen, Rich, things are comin' to a crawl on that. We used up the funds Perkins gave us, and right now, we're at a standstill. The fine-tunin' has all been done, but we're at a stage where the rest of what we have to do is goin' to need more cash."

Richie was not completely surprised. This was not a project he anticipated being done on the cheap anyway. "Hey, Pete, no problem. You and the guys have been more than fair to me, what with all you've done so far. If you want, I can move it out somewhere so you can use the space."

"Are you kidding, it's a magnet for all kinds of work I'm gettin', so don't worry your head about that."

A last look at his baby covered with a tarp, and with a sigh, he thanked Pete again and left. Pete rose from his desk and walked to the door, watching his young friend drive away. He glanced at the tarp and smiled.

Having nothing else to do, Richie drove to the factory to see if there were any discernable improvements. The plant looked the same on the outside, but many improvements were evident on the inside. The manufacturing section had new equipment, the packaging and delivery sections were updated with a new layout and computerized tracking, and the whole interior was brightened by improved lighting fixtures, which dispelled the semigloom he had witnessed on previous visits. New trucks were in evidence, indicating that the current owners were committed to turning things around.

"Hey, guy, like what you see?"

"Gee, Dad, it looks great. You guys really did a great job, and so fast too."

"Have to hand it to the Mr. Garrison's sons. They took to heart what Paul and I told them what was needed and they wasted no time. Within a couple weeks, three at the most, look what's happening. I think we've kept the wolf from the door. Now we have to see if we can keep him away."

Man, can I live up to that? Richie knew that his dad would be a tough act to follow, but if he were to be put on the payroll, he'd make him proud of his son.

Dinner was devoid of the apprehension that had fueled Richie's earlier concern about his father, believing that what he observed was probably overblown. After all, how many times had he acted like he was hiding the crown jewels or something similar? No, everything was nearly right with the world. Ben getting married, Vicky on his arm, a possible job at the plant. The real fly in the ointment was Donna and Pip. The poor woman had gone through quite a bit, and soon they'd be leaving. She was strong but needed some happiness in her life, much of which was in the person of her son, Pip. The little guy was a candle in the dark, his sweetness and energy a source of comfort to his mom. His mark on Richie had been etched deeply, almost as if he were his little brother.

Still no word on when she'd be leaving and he secretly hoped it'd never happen. Thinking back on all that had occurred since he came home from college, the highs and lows were to him monumental. For such a young person, he somehow had managed to survive the pitfalls and even benefit from them. Without consciously acknowledging it, he had become hardened to the effects, not in a dispassionate way, but hardened to the negative influences so that his basic nature remained untouched. For that he had his friends and family to thank.

The following day loomed with promise, the weather delightful, a shining sun relinquishing the chill from the bones, especially in the older people. Since Richie's deliveries were in the area, he decided to stop by and see if Donna was home. She answered the door, pleasantly surprised, and stepped out holding her index finger across her lips. Pip was napping.

"Pip didn't feel too good last night, and I want him to get some extra rest."

"I hope it's nothing to worry about," he asked, with concern in his voice.

"He'll be okay. What's up?"

"I guess I'm actin' like an old biddy, any news?"

"I'm still waiting on my mother. She pleaded for me to come, and it won't be long before…" Her face lowered and turned from Richie. She was experiencing the same angst he had been subjected to.

He pulled her into his arms, his silence echoing her emotions. What was there to say? What could be said? Her soft sobs continued for as long as he'd allow it. While he may feel being an older brother to Pip, he allotted himself the privilege of being a younger brother to Donna. Knowing how he felt about Vicky, he marveled at the resolve and courage Donna must have summoned to endure the loneliness that was her constant companion. Stepping back, Donna looked at

Rich with a thankful gaze. He had filled some of her emptiness, and for that she'd always remember him, no matter where she'd go.

"Vicky is one lucky girl. You two will make it, I know. Don't lose her." She kissed him on the cheek, her warmth radiating through his body. "I'll call when I get some info, okay?" A parting hug and she reentered her apartment.

Dang, why does life have to be so unfair? an angry Richie thought. He recalled many instances of those less deserving who garnered the benefits and promises that were seemingly denied to Donna. If only. If only. Those are words all of us use to figuratively redress a wrong or unfairness. Shaking his head, he continued her delivery route. The activity lessened his disgust, and he tried to dwell on things a little more cheerful. One was his car. Sure, it'd be ages, but when it was done, oh boy! He visualized cruising down Main Street for all to see his jewel, especially with Vicky by his side. Man oh man.

The next several weeks were as routine as they could be for our stalwart hero. The sameness contrasts with the lack of anything earthshaking or dire, which wasn't all that bad given the alternative.

The factory was gaining momentum, his work at the Perkins farm pleased him, Mr. Rosen has been a great guy to work for, and Vicky has been a jewel. But inevitably, when the sailing is clear, a storm cloud rises to mock complacency. Richie has finished his day's work, looking forward to some downtime before supper. His youthful form hadn't been impervious to the accumulated strain of his manual labors, and he had to content himself with a snooze now and then.

"Before you get comfortable, Donna called. She'd like you to contact her right away," his mom volunteered as he entered the kitchen. A shiver ran down his neck. He sensed that which he had consciously avoided. She was finally leaving. He submitted to the anticipated gloomy news and dialed her number.

"Rich, so glad you called. Mom is all set for me, and I guess…" A strained silence. "I guess this is it, I mean, we're going to be leaving."

"How soon?"

"Tomorrow. Could you take us to the bus station? I'd love for you to come over now, but two goodbyes are something I couldn't handle. I'm trying to come to grips of the reality of leaving, and it's like a bad dream." Richie understood that what she felt would probably play on him also, and as much as he'd wanted to see them now, it'd end up badly.

"You can count on me. Does the little guy know?"

"He's been told we're visiting his grandmother. In time he'll learn the truth." The finality had a sledgehammer effect on his stomach. He swallowed what he thought was his tongue, trying to suppress the knot in his throat. "We'll be traveling light. Our landlord will be forwarding the rest of our belongings at the end of the week. Oh, Rich, I'm so torn. But I have to look out for Pip, and he'll have another person to guide him."

"You didn't do a bad job yourself, but I understand."

If this was what it felt to lose a pair of sweet friends, how on earth would he be able to withstand the loss of his life, Vicky? He shook the thought from his head. Noting the departure time, he assured her he'd be there with ample time to spare. Hanging up, the loss of his friends was already imprinting itself on his fragile nature. He now felt the loss of consolation his family may have provided if only he'd confided in them. There had been a reluctance to do so, especially after his mistaken romantic episode with Donna. He feared disclosing his lack of poise, his lack of discretion, and in some way put them on a different level from all other things he shared with his family. Now he came to realize how wrong he was. Mom and Dad had the stuff to see what'd happened, and their counsel would've been supportive. The learning curve never ends.

That night, after dinner, he elevated his status to manhood by confiding in his parents. His distress was obvious as he recounted not only his missteps but the elation of enjoying this lonely family, especially the little boy. They listened as any loving parents would, reassuring him that what he was experiencing was natural for anyone who'd answered the call from his heart. Brian eased his outlook somewhat with a saying he'd heard.

"'Kindness is a language that the blind can see and the deaf can hear.' You know who said that? Mark Twain." Though late, the solace offered by his parents gave him some relief and hardened him for what tomorrow would bring. So he hoped.

When the time came to counsel his children, he only hoped that he'd measure up to his parents' standards.

"Good night, son, know that we are with you. Let your heart guide you, you can never go wrong there."

"Thanks, Dad, you and Mom have been a rock for me."

As the boy left for bed, Brian turned toward his wife, arm around her shoulder for mutual comfort, and exclaimed, very proudly, "We did good with him."

The morning's drizzle and gray overcast mirrored Richie's mood along with a bittersweet observation. He'd at least see them off, and then the emptiness. If he could wish not catching that ball, to eliminate the dread in his heart, then all this'd be another world. No, hell no, memories dictate why you do what you do. To relive tasting that new ice cream flavor, the camaraderie of friends, that first kiss—these are the essences that drive us to cling to what is dear and in some ways learn from the unfavorable experiences in order not to repeat them. He smiled as he recalled his first encounter with the little squirt. How could such a small bundle squeak into his life without so much as a warning? *Who cares. He did it, and I'd not change it for the world.*

Donna. Another entry into his life who taught him love, a selfless love that inspired him to understand the many forms of this cathartic element of life. He prayed that the mercy of the God be shed upon her and the child so that they need not be alone for long.

His heart jumped as he approached her apartment. She'd been waiting at the door and, upon seeing Richie, grabbed her two small bags, led Pip out, and locked the door by the inside latch. He exited and took her baggage, whispering a hello, not wanting to directly look at her. This was too real.

"Hi, man" broke his reserve, and the little tyke ran into his arms. Oh, how he relished the feel of this munchkin, not wishing to let go. "I go Grammy," he joyfully blurted.

"Hey, that's great. You're goin' to have lots of fun." His smile was as false the beard he wore during Halloween.

"You go too?"

"No. I can't, I have to work, and the boss wouldn't like it if I didn't show up."

Placated with the explanation, Pip was let down and seated in the rear with his mother, the seat belt accommodated by a booster seat.

Donna and Richie tried to carry on as if all was normal to spare the boy the finality that was coming. Although it was possible, in his heart the young man knew he'd probably never see them again. And no, he'd still keep those precious memories, all that'd be left of his encounter and fulfillment with these two irreplaceable beings. Small talk was minimal, enough to avoid the uncomfortable silence, enough to preclude the flood of what surely would be a litany of all they'd shared. Best left for their goodbyes at the station.

The depot was small but surprisingly busy, with those leaving and those arriving, along with the usual retinue of greeters and good-byers. They approached the bus designating their destination and paused, exchanging envelopes containing contact info. There was no flood of memories to recount, no need, as they were part and parcel of each one's memories, forever inscribed in heart and mind.

Richie looked and felt uncomfortable, fidgeting and unsure how to say goodbye, possibly a last goodbye. Donna sensed his unease. She approached, placing both hands around his neck and lowering his face to hers. Her lips deeply merged with his, an inviting kiss, a loving kiss, and a goodbye kiss, not hurried, but serene. He pulled her form closer to him in response, and any who cared to see them would have thought two lovers were parting, but that had already been decided. Reluctantly she separated from his lips and reached up to plant a kiss on his forehead. Stepping back and peering into his sad eyes, she whispered, "I love you."

"I...I do too."

As if on cue, an unmistakable tug of his jacket broke the solemn moment. Turning to the culprit responsible, Richie bent down with both knees, absorbing the wetness of the pavement.

"Hey, buddy, ready to go?"

"Ya."

"You listen to your mom, okay?"

"Okay."

"And don't forget to write me."

"Ya, R-R-Richeee." That did it. What resolve he had mustered now evaporated, a torrent of tears cascading unashamedly down his face. He grabbed Pip and submerged him in his arms so that it seemed he'd disappeared. If he could, he'd never let him go, but that only happened in the movies or pulp fiction.

"Tickets, please." The electronic exhortation broke the revelry. Richie looked up, Donna also in tears, and grabbing Pip, the three draped their arms around each other. Final kisses were exchanged, and as they entered the bus, each in turn waved and weakly smiled.

He walked along the side of the bus as they made their way to reserved seats, absorbing the moment that would soon be gone. His reservoir of tears was in full supply, and he tapped it greedily. Slowly the giant transport pulled away from the depot.

Instinctively he wanted to chase after it, to grab it, to stop it, but faced reality. Ignoring his safety, he stood in the middle of the street, watching a part of his life diminishing in size. Then, his heart jumped. At the rear window, a little figure had climbed upon the seat and was waving wilding at him, mouthing words that if heard would be "Richee, Richee, I love you." And then it was gone. The emptiness in his being was total, even to the point of ignoring a motorist's blast from his horn. Indifferently he made his way back to the Buick. Driving home, the essence of Donna's perfume lingered as the last reminder of her physical presence.

Pulling into the driveway and glancing at the back seat, he spotted a small folded piece of paper the size of a post card. He unfolded it and smiled a smile of lament and joy. In his own hand, Pip had scribbled three stick figures, as only a three-year-old could, and Donna had obliged him with the writing. "Mommy, Me, Richie, I love you. Pip." He'd forever treasure this most purest expressions of love. Entering the kitchen, Lynne saw the anguish her son had experienced and remained mute outside her normal greeting.

"Some breakfast, son?"

"Not right away, Mom, I…I…oh, Mom, they're gone." Cradling his head in his arms upon the kitchen table, he again surrendered to that most human of emotions, a testament to his loss. Lynne held on to him and let him cry.

The following days were difficult for the wounded hero, but life went on. If anything, he reenergized his relationship with Jenn, inspired by the youthful zeal of Pip. Not that he had relegated her to a lower tier but sought to avoid taking her for granted. Her brightness dispelled some of the gloom, and her precocious counsel was welcomed. She was like a little mother to him, and he relished the attention. Mom gave comfort by just being there or trying to answer the rhetorical questions her son would pop from time to time to justify what he had experienced or wondering what would happen next. So many possibilities, so many avenues to explore so that eventually he began to see the pointless end of this exercise. Dad was still a rock, who, upon viewing his inputs, one'd tend to believe he was dispassionate. Far from it. He based much of his advice or contributions in a manner that was devoid of emotions in most cases. This allowed him to see the true nature of any problem or threat but didn't mean he was untouched by the hurt or happiness it generated.

His son was his heart, and sugarcoating any conflict or exaggerating a swell of good tidings could only mislead the boy. Fortunately, Richie had learned much of this from his father's example and prospered from it. Part of his healing was due to this ethic.

Just as the family was taking their seats for dinner, Richie came bounding in, chirping like a cowboy at a rodeo.

"She's okay, the family made it. The little guy spoke to me."

It didn't take any stretch of the imagination to divine his joyous outburst. He had been troubled that Donna hadn't called, but the impatient youth had to reckon with her needs first, which he obviously didn't. The traveling was arduous and lengthy, the greetings at home all-consuming, the unpacking and a myriad slew of other things that tended to delay a prompt notification of arrival. Between gulps of his favorite meat loaf, he related Donna's homecoming and all that went with it. Just the sound of their voices rejuvenated his spirits so that most of his worries had been laid to rest. He could look forward to more artwork from Pip and regular mail with photos.

There was so much exuberance that any familial concerns were easily set aside.

When he next saw Vicky and displayed the same joy, she feigned indignation that her attentions were being pushed aside by "that other woman."

"Honest, Vick, it's not like that, really."

She amused herself with pulling his chain but saw the earnest concern in his face. "Easy, tiger, lighten up. How could I not feel happy for you? Just teasing."

"Yeah, but I was messed up there for a while."

"Don't I know it. What hurt you was hurting me when you told me about her leaving and there wasn't much I could do but be there for you."

"You're always there for me, but sometimes the pain is nontransferable. Still, you kept me from being alone, you and my family."

With nothing but sunshine in the foreseeable future, a contented young man resumed his normal routines, as normal as he could make them. Much had happened that was unforeseen, more than most people could ever expect to encounter in such a short period of time.

To his credit, he weathered the cascade of turmoil and exultation, not consciously ticking off the plus or minuses, but aware that the cumulative effects of his experiences had left their mark. The innocent, wide-eyed lad who returned home from college for the summer had disappeared, replaced by a hybrid, a receding youngster and an emerging man. There were no stark contrasts but a gradual fading of one form as a new one took its place. His family most naturally saw the creeping transformation, accepting and reacting to this as a rite of passage, more so than he did but doing so in the most casual of ways. Those of youth often neglect these visible or emotional milestones that chart their future as they scramble to pursue their goals in life. In some ways, comparable to the beautiful transformation from cocoon to butterfly.

Saturday night, before supper, Brian informed Richie that Sam Masters from the VFW had asked if they would like to attend a small ceremony honoring Ben for his service.

"No kiddin', that's great, Dad. I know he'll get a kick out of it."

"Mom and Jenn would like to come too, so we'll make it a family outing."

"When's it gonna be, Dad?"

"Tomorrow at one. Maybe you can ask Vicky if she'd like to go."

"Planning on that, Dad. She likes Ben, and I guess Gloria will be there too."

"He's a fine boy, son, and I know he'll expect you to be there." Indeed, they had been friends for years, and to honor him was a resolute obligation.

On the following day as the time drew near to leave for the VFW, Richie told his dad that he'd pick up Vicky and meet him at the hall. "I'll meet you in the parking lot, and we can all go in together," Brian announced to the boy. "Your mother's going to pick up a gift beforehand, so wait for us."

"Ya got it, Dad."

The drive to Vicky's home was filled with expectation. How glad he was that his buddy would feel the gratitude of his friends and bathe in their admiration. He'd lost so much, and this little celebratory gathering was a tonic much needed and deserved. Vicky was waiting, dressed in an attractive form-fitting blue dress with white trimming that conveyed an image rivaling those seen in modeling magazines. *Gee, she is beautiful and mine,* he mused. Smiling, she plopped onto the seat, reached over, and planted a kiss on his cheek.

"Ready, Jeeves, onward to Camelot." Her cavalier attitude seemed a little contrived, but he had no time to divine what her motive might be. Just being a woman, he thought.

She peered at him while he looked straight ahead but turned her gaze away whenever he glanced toward her, always with a slight smile on her lips. Women.

Soon he approached the VFW parking lot and found his family waiting. And of course, Clifford tagged along, most likely at the urging of Jenn.

"Ben here yet?" he asked his dad.

"Waiting inside."

The lot was filled, great. He'd be feted royally. He remembered the ovation Ben received at the dance and how flustered he was. Oh, how Richie laughed but was rewarded with the memory of the warm reception Ben received and noted it'd be no different now. Nothing too good for his dear friend. Add to that the coming nuptials. Boy, life is great. What could be better?

Mom held a small box, most likely a gift for Ben. *Wonder what she got him?* he thought. Dad opened the oak door festooned with military insignia, allowing his wife and the kids to enter. Vicky preceded Richie into the hall, allowing him to reach back to pull the door shut. As he swung around, he was bombarded with a loud and very vocal, "Happy birthday!"

"Huh, what…" Stunned for the moment, he stared at a large banner repeating the vocal salutation as a crowd of joyous greeters surrounded him. "Dad, Mom, my birthday isn't till next week."

Brian replied, "Then it wouldn't have been a surprise, would it?"

"Gee, you got me there. Boy, did you get me."

"Hey, pal, happy b-day," uttered Ben as he made his way through the throng.

"You dog, you. You knew all the time, didn't you?"

"Hey, payback for the dance." He chuckled.

"What's not to like?" Glancing at Vicky with a wry smile he queried her. "You knew all along?"

"Tiger, it was all I could do not to give it away in the car. I was bursting with excitement, wondering how you'd react." She then gave him a semi-apologetic kiss on his cheek to atone for her amateurish deception. The well-wishers, one by one, paid their respects. Mr. Rosen, the Perkins, Pete, his very good friend, and of course, noting the selection of pies and cakes, one didn't have to strain too much imagination to know who supplied them. Gloria, prettier than ever, gave him a delicious kiss which Vicky prudently ignored. Other neighbors and friends were on hand, showering him with a bounty of gifts. His mother asked him to hold the small box for a while. He was assuming that he'd be the one to give it to Ben. As the mass settled down and took their seats after loading up at the buffet table, Brian placed his arm around his son's shoulder, clearing his throat as a sign of an impending pronouncement.

"Rich, you've done at lot since coming home, and your family couldn't be more proud of you."

"Thanks, Dad, I appreciate that."

"As a result of certain circumstances, I have to ask you to give up your part-time jobs."

"But, Dad, I can't keep spongin' off you and Mom."

"You won't have to. Starting Monday, you're on my shift at the factory."

"What? No kiddin'? Man oh man." He left no doubt among those gathered as to the effect it had on him. "Yoweee, wow, oh boy. Really, Dad, really?"

"Yeah, really."

He nearly took his father's hand off at the wrist as he pumped it excitedly. Running to his mom, he smothered her with kisses, then grabbed and swung his sister in a wide circle of celebration. Eyeing Clifford, he paused and dismissed any thought of a physical demonstration, much to Clifford's relief. Word spread among the guests attesting to the cause of Richie's wild mirth, and supportive applause rang through the room. "Gee, Dad, this is the best birthday gift, even better than the bicycle you got me that I always wanted when I was a runt."

"You'll do good, kid."

As soon as Richie sat down, Jooster came running in, flailing his arms and excitedly grabbing Richie by the sleeve, pulling him toward the door.

"Hey, what's up, Joos, what's the matter?"

"Rich, somebody drove off with your car. I knew it wasn't you, but before I could do anythin', he headed outta the lot." He rushed with his friend to the door, feeling rage for whoever would trash his special day. Seeing the turmoil being generated, many guests left their seats to follow the pair as they burst through the entrance. True, his car had been taken. It was gone. But that wasn't the heart of the matter. No, it was something more, much more.

It was true, his car was gone, but its absence was overshadowed by an intriguing sight. Glistening in the sun's brilliant glow was a most magnificent article. Metallic blue paint, adorned with pearl-white trim, encased the form of a 1971 Mustang. So caught up in the mesmerizing beauty before him, he failed to comprehend for the moment what it meant. His reasoning was suspended by the sudden impact, and his mind darted back and forth, trying to tie together a cascade of thoughts. He had a car like this; it was in bad shape. No money to fix it. Maybe later. It was there, but in a fairyland sort of way. His subconscious rooted through the mayhem, tugging at his consciousness, urging him to accept the reality of what lay before him.

A hand on his shoulder broke the stalemate, his mother standing beside him. She handed him the box he'd left on the table.

"Open it, son."

Trembling, he untied the ribbon from the container and removed the lid. A small piece of paper greeted his eyes with a simple message, "Happy birthday, son. Look further." Removing the note, beneath it lay a key, with an attached logo. 1971 Ford Mustang. Mouth wide open in disbelief, looking at the car, then at his parents, he really had trouble putting a handle on his reactions. *It can't be, it's a miracle, man oh man.* These and other electrifying emotions poured out as he grabbed his parents in a bear hug, burying his face on their shoulders. The moisture in his eyes had barely begun to coalesce when his dad asked him to look again at his car. Emerging from several parked cars and from around the side of the building came a litany of the many friends who had helped in bringing to life Richie's dream. Gordy and Harve, the guys from the community college, Steve, and others who had contributed their efforts in the restoration.

They had all conspired to make this a birthday to remember and succeeded handsomely. He merged himself within the confines of his friend's embraces and handshakes. Each one was addressed with the solemnity of prayer service, for they had borne a gift beyond any practical expectations. With the last acknowledgement, he bellowed aloud, "Okay, guys, let's eat, drink, and be merry, but only if you're twenty-one." Moving toward the door, he grabbed his father's arm. "Dad, how the heck did this happen?" As he began to answer, he summoned Pete to join him.

"Explain the miracle, Pete."

"Well, Richie, your dad called to ask how the project was coming. I told him that in months you might have a car, considering the lack of funds. Then he said to pull out all the stops, that whatever cash he needed would be available. He stressed the fact that if possible, the work had to be finished before your birthday. Man, that had us hoppin', but we were determined to get it done."

Brian looked at a bewildered boy and continued. "Look, I was back to work, and I felt badly that you had to sacrifice your new car for the welfare of the family. I could do no less.

"The money you'd given the us was partly used to finance the restoration. The several times I called Pete, I almost queered it all when you came in while I was talking to him. I'd only hoped I hadn't tipped it off. Pete went along with the ruse when you'd visited the shop and told you of the shutdown. We wanted it to be a big surprise."

"Gee, Dad, here I thought you were in trouble or somethin', 'cause you never acted like that. What a relief."

"Whatever money that was left has been deposited in the bank in your name."

He was overwhelmed, more so because of his youth and selflessness. What he had sown, he began to reap, doing so with the scythe of love bequeathed to him.

Retiring to the hall, the participants reveled in the celebration. Mom and Dad secure in their son's present happiness, Vicky growing ever more the person in his life, the myriad friends who had also sacrificed a part of their lives to guarantee a dream come true.

Maybe in the movies or a novel or in fairyland, these things happened, where a joyous result survived pitfalls and failures or disappointments. Only this was real life for the Murphy family and of the souls that were touched.

This indeed was a slice of life, a small portion of the existence they and others would share, a small examination of time that held so much for so many. How wonderful that in the scheme of things, these many and varied events could be and would be replicated elsewhere. Now the future was left for them to explore, not a novel or movie, but real life.

BROTHERS

A brisk morning accompanied by a warm glow from the sun awaited a ten-year-old sleepyhead. Scooter, like all other youngsters, especially during a summer break from school, milked the last few minutes of delicious comfort from his bunk bed. What would he do today? The park, the fishing hole, a stickball game? He reveled in the choices that he would be master of; after all, any youngster delights in being able to command his own little world destinies. Anticipating the call from his mother at any moment, his mouth began to water at the expected breakfast feast she always prepared for him. A horse and Scooter have a lot in common: they can eat and eat big.

Her cheerful face greeted his yawning features as he reached up to her rosy cheek and planted his first of many kisses.

"Well, what's on for today, Scoot?"

"I guess I'll meet Jackie, and we can play in the yard."

"Sounds good to me. Besides, Mrs. Jenkins will be here with her poetry club, and I doubt that'll interest you much."

"Yah, ya sure got that right, Mom." Both of them chuckling. He was a bright light in her life, and since his dad passed away, his love was his father's love. The breakfast met his adolescent expectations as always, his uninterrupted but careful slurping attesting to its satisfying taste.

"If you want anything, just yell."

"You bet. I don't want to get anywhere near Mrs. Jenkins. She hugs too tight, and when she pinches my cheek, it hurts." Again, they both indulged in a more pronounced laughter, Scooter pecking her cheek and running out the back door.

Maryann peered through the window as he raced to his assorted items of interest. Her look was intense and had a meaning far beyond the normal concerns that any parent has. She sighed a sigh of acceptance and blew a kiss at him, bringing attention to other matters, such as preparing for the "dreaded" visit by Mrs. Jenkins.

"Hey, Jackie, you made it."

"You bet, pal. What do you want to do today?"

His wavy blond hair was always a mess and awfully blond. "Well, Mom wants me to stay in the yard while what's-her-face visits."

"Don't you like her cheek pinches?" the mischievous Jackie spouted.

"You wouldn't say that if your face was mangled."

"Aw, forget it and let's do somethin' different."

"Like what? You're always comin' up with weird ideas."

"Hey, the weirder, the better. You want to do baby stuff?"

"Nah, I guess not. Hey, let's build a fort."

"Great idea, buddy." The challenge excited Scooter as he looked around the yard for any conglomeration of leftovers, parts, discarded items, and other "treasures" that a young mind could utilize to create a stronghold impregnable.

Whatever the effort, it proved less formidable than a wet paper bag holding weights.

"Well, so much for that idea, Jackie."

"Hey, no sweat, we had fun doin' anyway."

"Yeah, you're right, at least it kept me outta the grips of Mrs. Jenkins."

Eventually, the all clear was sounded—the dreaded cheek pincher had left with her mob, and he was free to enjoy life again. Jackie bade goodbye, and Scooter, his appetite reenergized, trooped into the kitchen.

"Enjoy yourself, honey?"

"Pretty much, Mom. One thing for sure, I'll never be an articheck."

"Architect, dear."

"Whatever. Hey, Mom, do we still have to go to the doctor's next week?"

"Yes, honey, he wants to make sure you can still cause people to suffer your hijinks."

"What's that mean?"

"Oh, when you pull Wendy's pigtails or throw water balloons at Mikey."

"That's not hijinks, that's fun." His enthusiasm was infectious, a source of consolation to a worried mother. Her concerns were duly concealed from the young sprite as she watched his dedicated mission to devour the sandwich offered him.

The summer allowed her to be closer to her son, wanting him to feel secure in the absence of his father. Being a chemical engineer stroked the imagination of Scooter as his father would describe various projects he'd worked on. The mystery of how various components could produce varied results fascinated the tyke. His mother had purchased a starter chemistry set, but the boy felt the connection to his father too great, the presence of the kit engendering melancholy. The bond he had was great, maybe too great to absorb in his dad's absence.

The boy was practical in his aims but still reverted to the unkempt, mischievous, and carefree attitude that most youngers indulged in. Maryann did not let her personal loss fester into a morose posture that would eventually affect not only her pursuit of life but that of her son's. She jealously guarded against any intrusion, physical or emotional, that would disturb the relative normalcy they attained. Then she pondered the treatments that Scooter was undergoing and lamented as only a mother would that he was too young to be burdened with this, the notion causing tears to cascade down her cheek and staining her apron.

After the loss of her husband, her boy seemed morose and sullen. Not waiting for any other vindication, she brought him to her physician. To deal with the issue, he recommended a behavioral doctor, which he was now seeing.

After prayers, Scooter would mentally plan his activities for the morrow and snuggled into his bed. Mom came in for the customary tuck in and kiss, the boy smiling the smile of a contented child knowing his mom was the greatest. With this, he slumbered after only examining two earthshaking missions he would undertake the next day with Jackie.

No need for an alarm clock as the wafting smell of pancakes and bacon teased at the boy's nose. Clothing donned at the speed of light, his mouth watering, he scampered to the kitchen, placing an obligatory kiss on his mother's cheek and jumping onto his chair. For him, the wait to dig into the delectable morsels seemed like an eternity, relieved only after his mom satisfied his craving with a steaming plate.

"What's up for today, honey?"

"Think I'll head over to the ball field for a pickup game, most likely Jackie will meet me on the way."

"How do you know, dear?"

"Aw, he always shows up, especially when I leave the house, like he's got radar or somethin'."

"Well, be careful and don't get hurt."

"Mom, do ya think I'm a kid?"

"Exactly, just don't do anything stupid."

"The story of my life. Okay, Mom, I'll watch it." Wolfing down the last of the pancakes, he bolted for the door, halted, retreated back to his mom standing with a demanding stance, and pecked her cheek. "Bye, Mom."

Sure enough, his pal Jackie was waiting for him.

"Where to, Scoot?"

"The ball field, see if I can get some swings in. You playin'?"

"Nah, I'll just sit it out and root for you—you'll probably need it." There was no end to the back and forth, the give-and-take enjoyable as they trekked toward the field. Running onto the field, the usual commotion injected itself as each boy vied for a certain position or his place in the lineup.

When the dust settled, Scooter was playing shortstop, not his best position, and last in the batting order. This elicited a scrawny yell from Jackie, "Hey, Scoot, don't they know you're famous?"

"Aw, dry up."

Jackie had no mercy on his friend and would have more to dump on him later. Poor Scooter, this was not his day. The effort was there but not the results, making three errors and striking out twice. The exercises in futility was born by several other players as well, the excuses offered and rebuffed by the more talented players and in a small way giving some cover to Scooter. Fortunately, these boyish jousts tended to evaporate upon leaving the field, as they were friends, albeit rivals.

"Boy, Scoot, you played like a girl." The needling ignited a burst of reproach from the offended party.

"Did not."

"Did so."

"Did not." They both began to laugh, a sign that erased any further assault upon Scooter's abilities. He enjoyed his friend, knowing nothing would ever make him stay mad when his chain was pulled. There was a certain expectancy in their relationship that Scooter thrived on, something the other kids couldn't generate. This trait was more or less instinctive rather than deliberate, his young mind not attuned to the realization that would dawn on him as he grew older.

"How 'bout a soda?"

"Nah, you go ahead."

Entering Daley's water ice store and buying his drink, they both took a seat near the window.

"Hey, Scoot, that's Marily Kate, isn't it?"

"Yeah, nice kid."

"Has a sweet spot for you too."

"Does not."

"Does too."

"What're you, writing for 'Dear Abbey'?"

"Lighten up, Romeo. Just sayin'."

The blush was almost gone when she came into the store with her dad.

"Hi Scooter."

"Er, hi, Marily Kate and Mr. Woodson."

"How goes it?"

The boys' response mirrored that time-honored reply of "Great." With that the gentleman smiled and moved on to a table, Marily eyeing him and flashing a sweet smile. It wasn't that he didn't like her; he did, but to admit it to any other guy was terminal. You just didn't mess with girls, or the guys wouldn't give you any peace.

"Let's beat it, I have to be home soon." A flustered look on his face hastening the departure.

"Okay, I probably see ya tomorrow."

"You bet."

Summer was a time of simple pleasures for the kid, but he also owned up to a mature standing for his mom. The proceeds from the life insurance provided some cushion that dealt with the family finances, but there was always the need to supplement that with other sources of income. Fortunately, his mom being a former teacher, she was able to tutor many of the children in town. Her persuasiveness and hands-on treatment endeared her to the students and their families. What revenue she received, while not excessive, sufficed enough to keep a baby wolf from the door. Scooter would run errands or do menial tasks for which he received a nice little sum. When his mom first objected to his offer to contribute to ease the family's expenses, he stood proudly and with all the effort a nine-year-old could muster. He proudly proclaimed he was the man of the house, hoping his facade of courage would win the day.

Maryann, touched by his sacrifice, embraced her son, tears rolling down her cheeks and penetrating her son's collar and shirt.

"Gee, Mom, you don't have to get so mushy," he cried out, knowing he'd hit the right cord. He was now man of the house, ouch. "Hope I don't have to take out the garbage all the time." He mimicked the refrain his dad always uttered, the surest way to needle his wife.

This newly confirmed stature did little to ease the emptiness that vied for his conscious attractions. He envied the other kids, whose father's presence and encouragement on the field, at school events, or playing in the park only served to remind him of his loss. There was no bitterness, only the empty feeling that hung on him like a dark cloud. His mom made huge efforts to ameliorate this burden upon the youngster by injecting herself into much of his routine, unobtrusively of course. Contrary to the "Aw, Mom" attitude displayed by youngsters when feeling their sovereignty endangered, he welcomed, even sought her participation or counsel. The comfort at these times kept at bay the gray clouds.

The following morning found the tyke invoking human fear into the scampering squirrels in the backyard.

"Yo, Scoot." The familiar greeting from his friend Jackie. "What's up?"

"Goin' down to the pond, maybe fish."

"Works for me." Scampering to the kitchen door, and pushing it open a tad, he yelled, "Hey, Mom, goin' down to the pond with Jackie."

Wiping her hands, she opened the door and handed him a snack and drink. "Be careful."

"Yeah, yeah, Mom." The prerequisite kiss and he was on his way. As he strolled down the street, she kept her eye on him, not so much for his safety, as this being a small and friendly town where almost everyone knew each other precluded any thoughts for his well-being. No, it was a deep concern that Scooter's trust in his friend's companionship was as deep as need be to protect him. He wouldn't be able to stand another profound loss.

"Hey, Jackie, do you remember anything about your pop?"

"Nope."

"Gee. I'm sorry. Hope I didn't go where I wasn't supposed to go."

"Nah, no problem. I don't think I ever knew him."

"Really?"

"Yah, I guess it's one of those things. At least you knew your dad, and that makes me glad. In a way it brought us together. But you know, I have a warm feeling about what my mom might have been, even though I can't remember."

These were the exchanges that drew Scooter closer to Jackie in a way that partially subdued the gray emptiness.

At the pond, with the line in the water, lying on the ground chewing on a grass stem, he allowed the sun to bathe his face. A soft voice settled onto his ears, causing him to bolt upright.

"Hi, Scooter." It was Marily Kate, accompanied by her father.

"Hi, MK." His pet name for her, not out of sentimentality, but because it was shorter. "And Mr. Woodson."

"We're headed to the Pavilion. They have a small band playing today."

Music was not his forte, and thankfully they didn't ask him to accompany them, although a forlorn look by Marily Kate begged for him to join them. Not wishing to encourage the moment, he kept eye contact with the ground and resumed his lying posture.

"Boy, that was close, Jackie."

"Hey, you're talkin' to me, bub. I know you have a sweet spot for her."

"And you better keep it to yourself, buster." Buster was a name he often used when Jackie hit his wrong side. What did he know about women?

The fish were also on the wrong side, not a bite to be had.

"Guess I better mosey on home."

"Yah, it's about that time, Scooter."

"Hey, Jack, we get along pretty good, don't we?"

"Sure we do, pal." All kids want to feel that they are in sync with the other kids, and Scooter especially with Jackie. "I hope me talkin' about your dad didn't mess with you."

"Like I said, I don't think I ever knew him."

"Gee, Jack, I hope one day that will come true for you."

"So my heart will break like yours if I lose him?" The sudden hurt in Scooter's eyes prompted Jackie to gloss over his unthinking remark. "Sorry, Scoot, that came out wrong. It's just that I don't need anything right now except what I got. It's one of those things, ya know?" The forgiving nature of a youngster, any youngster, was evident in the smile Scooter flashed at his best friend.

"See ya tomorrow?"

"Yah, I guess so, er, wait. Mom's takin' me to the doctor tomorrow, so it'll have to be later."

"No problem, I'll catch ya then."

Hunger pangs spurred his entry through the kitchen door. "Hi, Mom."

"Hello, dear, any luck?"

"Naw, but that's okay."

"How 'bout a bite?"

"Sure. Mom, do we really have to go to the doc tomorrow?"

"Yes, dear, but it's only a checkup." The boy had a lot of questions about that. He'd seen the doctor quite a few times but never had to take any medicine, and if he was seeing a doctor, wasn't he sick or something? Maryann tried to keep the reasoning for the visits in a simple fashion, not wanting the child to try and comprehend what she herself was finding difficult to accept.

"Right after that we can drop in at Burger Kitchen if you want."

"Really, that's great, I love their stuff." As long as he displayed the carefree attitude most children displayed, some of her concern was allayed but not completely dismissed. As a mother, and she was a good one, her first and only purpose was to ensure her son's welfare, to make sure the light shining in his eyes never faltered in their brightness.

As they waited to enter the doctor's exam room, Maryann made small talk with her son to while away the usual wait that many patients endured. Asked how he liked Dr. Groom, Scooter responded festively, "Gee, Mom, Dr. Doom is pretty cool."

"Scooter, really."

"It's okay, Mom, I already used that on him, and he laughed."

"Well, it's not proper." Before the subject continued any further on, Scooter spied Marily Kate entering the reception area with her father.

Oh my gosh! he mentally screamed. *She's goin' to see me.* His fear was the impression of invincibility he projected, at least in his own childish mind, and the thought of her seeing a damaged hero was devastating. Not to mention his futile efforts to suppress the growing feeling of being attracted to her.

Squeezing into a corner was not an option, so holding on to his mother for moral support, the pair approached.

"Hello, Mrs. Moore, and how are you and Scooter doing?" His manner was pleasant and being a fairly good-looking man made the salutation enjoyable.

"Well, Mr. Woodson, thanks for asking. Dr. Groom will be seeing my son shortly. And how are you?"

"Oh, I'm fine, just brought Marily Kate in for her routine checkup." They chatted for a while until Scooter was paged. "Okay, no funny business," his mom cautioned.

"Scout's honor, Mom." His fingers crossed behind his back, and a sneaky smile ensured that what would happen would happen.

"Mrs. Moore—"

"It's Maryann." Her reply a soft request.

"Okay, and I go by Richard, or Rich. It's funny, missus—er, Maryann, but we haven't been living here very long, and I've seen you at the school meetings. Everyone's been pretty nice, especially for Marily's sake. You seem to be a favorite with many of the people I've talked to."

"Oh, I don't know about that, er, Rich?"

"Yes, Rich."

"But it's a nice compliment."

"Getting settled has been a bit of a chore, what with being transferred from my company to this area, insurance business."

"And how does Mrs. Woodson like it here?"

"She passed away last year and—"

"Oh, I'm terribly sorry."

"We've managed to put a lot of it behind us, and right now Marily's my main concern."

"My son is in her class, and I believe he thinks a lot about her."

"At least my daughter thinks so." A gentle grin creasing his mouth. "My daughter likes him too."

"Mister, er, Rich, and if I can be of any service to you and Marily, don't hesitate to ask."

"That's very generous of you. Scooter mentioned to my daughter that you also suffered a great loss, and may I return the service if ever needed?" They spoke for some time, and it was just not small talk, until his daughter and he were taken to her doctor's office. "Perhaps we'll see each other again, I've enjoyed talking to you." His voice seeming to solicit a favorable response.

"I would enjoy that," she replied.

Soon after they left, Scooter pranced from the doctor's exam room.

"All done, Mom, and he wants to speak with you. I'll wait here."

Every visit, she thought, was one step closer to helping her son manage and one day eliminate the root cause of concern that the doctor sought to treat.

"Mrs. Moore, how are you?" Dr Groom intoned as she stepped into his office.

"Any progress, Doctor?"

His reply brought hope and disappointment. Progress was being made but slowly. There was no telling when a positive result would occur, and that the therapy prescribed be continued.

"Thank you, Doctor." Resignation in her voice.

"Ready, Mom?" chirped her son, his perkiness shaking off some of her gloom. "What'd he say, Mom?"

She could see the puzzlement in his face. He thought he was healthy enough, no pains or tiredness, none of the impairments that a young boy would know immediately. Her reply was comforting but lacked any details that satisfied the child, and being a child, his attention was easily diverted.

"How 'bout a pizza?"

"Gee, that's a great idea, Mom."

Munching hungrily on his peperoni, sausage, cheese, and mushroom slice, his contentment was suddenly sidetracked when his mother asked about Marily. Again he feigned a disinterest to disguise his desire to avoid his mother's scrutiny and the chance she could spill the beans to some nosey people.

"She seems very nice. Do you get along good in school?"

Oh boy, how can I get out of this without looking geeky? he thought. He wished he could be like a politician who says one thing but means another. And to compound his dilemma, who should enter the shop?

"Why, Mr. Woodson, so soon we meet."

"Well, when your child's stomach growls, nature, or should I say, my girl's plea for relief."

"Please sit with us."

Those words sent a shiver down Scooter's neck. Now he'd have to face MK, who was already gawking at him with her beautiful blue eyes. If he had no interest in her, it would be dandy, but to a youngster being bitten for the first time by a natural attraction of which he had no idea how to handle it, the inner tension forced him into a verbal retreat, which didn't last long.

"Scooter, do you think you can help me with some lessons the special summer sessions are going to have? Dad thinks I should ask for help from my classmates because he wants me to learn with them and to become better friends."

Summer sessions? Friends? Yikes, she's leaving me no room to sneak away. "Er, well, I think I may be able to do that after the weekend."

"Scooter," his mother interjected, "your chores are caught up, and the field is too muddy to play on, so why not invite her over?"

Gulp and double gulp. How could he avoid this oncoming train? He couldn't. His resolve diminished. All he was capable of saying was, "Okay, Mom." The smile on Marily's face bore into him like a dentist's drill.

"That's very kind of you, misse—er, Maryann. Are you sure it'd be no trouble?"

"Nonsense, if it can help her in class, I'm sure Scooter would be more than happy to be of assistance." The coffin was nailed shut.

"Mom, why'd you hafta go and do somethin' like that?"

"Like what?" Driving with her eye to the road and listening to her son, she sensed his reticence to having Marily come to the house.

"Her, I mean, she's smart. Doesn't need a guy like me to teach her what she might already know."

Maryann, being a mother and wise to the ways of women, even young ones, quietly laughed to herself. MK had her sights on Scooter, and there was nothing he could about it if the young sweetie played her cards right. The innocence of it all removed any dark harbingers of an unpleasant outcome.

"Yeah, Jackie, she's comin' over Saturday, and I guess I won't be able to see ya."

"No problem, it's just as well. Let me know how it turns out."

"Righto, chum. You'll be okay, what with me not being around?"

"Sure, no problem. See ya after, and you can tell me how goofy you acted and how she swooned at ya."

"Like I'd tell ya anything. Beat it."

Jackie's laugh still echoed in Scooter's ears as he tromped in through the kitchen door.

"Who was that, honey?"

"Oh, Jackie, and he was makin' fun a me."

Instead of laughing, Maryann eyed her son with a sigh of resignation. Although she knew Jackie was part of Scooter's life, she had reservations about the companionship. Still, she had to let things play out for the good of the boy.

The summer sessions were a killer. He hated the drab presentations, but that's because he was still fighting his feelings for the young lass. He muddled through as best he could, being polite but not endearing. Then another fly in the ointment merged with all his other woes. When Mr. Woodson dropped him off after class, his mother, after fixing him a snack, asked him if he would like to go out for dinner. This didn't happen very often, and when it did, he jumped at the chance. Mom's cooking was the best, but he also liked to try the different dishes that appealed to him just by reading the contents of the menu. The descriptions of yet-to-be-gobbled delights watered his palate to no end.

"Hey, just great, Mom. Where to?"

"Luigi's." Just the sound of the name brought his saliva to a boiling point.

"Okay, get cleaned up and try that new pair of slacks with matching pullover."

"Boy, this must be a special event or somethin', what with the new duds. What gives, Mom?"

"Nothing, sweetheart, I just want you to look good when Mr. Woodson picks us up."

Woodson, as in Marily Kate? his mind screamed. He was doomed. It was one thing to help with her lessons, but that was business. This was different. Now he'd have to endure her googly eyes and try not to respond. He was still trying to mask that which every young boy experiences, plus his fears that the other kids would mock him and his "sweetheart." Maybe his dad would have straightened him out and removed the conflicting trend he was in.

The trip to Luigi's was uneventful but a tad uncomfortable to the young lad, being seated alongside Marily. The small talk was limited, something he'd never remembered being one of her shortcomings. Maybe she wasn't feeling well. Welcomed by Luigi, the quartet was seated at a beautifully adorned table with Italian accents. The walls were covered with frescos, introducing an air of the Italian countryside and villages. The menu alone brought a rush of saliva enveloping Scooters palate, a harbinger of food delights to come. The order taken, drinks and breadsticks filled the interim, with the normal chatter merging with the sounds of other diners conversing. Still, something became readily apparent to Scooter. MK was very silent, aloof from even his cursory attention. More so than in the car.

His enjoyment of the meatballs and lasagna was muted to some degree by his table partner's "going through the motions" posture. Even his attempt to chat with her met with indifference. *Whoa, what's going on here?* The dinner, although inviting, left a subdued taste in Scooter's mouth. Something was wrong, but what? The prospect of chocolate pudding for dessert did nothing to wean him from his concern for MK's somberness.

"Hey, guys." Mr. Woodson's voice breaking his spell. "Let's explore the garden."

The lavish and beautiful display of greenery mimicking that of the Italian courts were one of Luigi's famous attractions. Business deals were consummated in the friendly environs, lovebirds swam in the sea of romance encouraged by flowers, and amateur gardeners would take stock of the varied greenery, hoping to replicate some of the fantastic plants in their own gardens. The fresh air complemented the sweet aroma that was ever present.

Pointing to the far side of the courtyard, Mr. Woodson called attention to the small waterfall and began to lead the group in that direction.

"That's okay, Dad. I'll sit here for a while," Marily dryly told her father.

"I'll stay with her," Scooter quipped.

"Okay, we won't be too long."

As they moved off, Scooter began to speak. "Er, MK…I—"

"Let me speak first," she interrupted. "Scooter, I've always liked you and hoped you would like me. I knew you were a little shy."

Shy? No, I was protecting my image with the guys, he mentally replied.

"I wanted you to be good friends and share the fun other kids had. Like Marcy, Peter, and Gwenn." These were classmates, and their bonds were very evident. "I thought that helping me with my lessons, you would get to know me better. It seems the more I tried, it didn't seem to change you at all. I feel very hurt. I wanted so much to have you as a friend, not a boy who looks like he would rather be someplace else."

That stung. She bowed her head and softly sobbed, her hands clenching each other in her lap. If this was a wake-up call to maturity, it worked. He felt like a heel and wanted to redeem himself, but that wouldn't be easy. Taking a chance, he reached over and placed his hand on hers. She responded by unclenching her hands and, with one, placed it over top of his.

"MK, I'm a jerk and didn't know it until now. I was trying so hard to prove that I was one of the guys, that I didn't think of anyone except myself." It was now that he began to garner a sense of self, in that whatever he may choose to do, it will affect something or someone else. Only with a conscious effort can he determine the best direction to take. For a ten-year-old boy, this assessment was more innate than actual awareness, his basic goodness the foundation for all that he attempted to do.

"I was hoping you'd say something like that."

"That I'm a jerk? That's a given."

"No, not the words, the fact that you admitted to something, a fault, so to speak, that most people would not be able to admit."

"Well, if that's a fault, San Andreas has nothin' on me."

"San An—oh, that's clever, Scooter, I like that." Her chuckle dissolving the frowning wrinkles into smiling ones. The whole atmosphere changed from one of gloom to a sunshine brightness, both smiles reflecting the welcome transformation. Then Scooter, in a moment of impulsiveness, reached over and planted a kiss on her cheek. Suddenly taken aback, she quickly composed herself, and straightened up stiffly, showing an apparent disdain for such a bold move, her nose up in the air. Then she burst out laughing, dismissing the frightful look plastered on Scooter's face.

"You're not mad?"

"Of course not, silly. It was a nice thing to do, and I think maybe it means we can be good friends."

Relieved that his relationship had been salvaged, a weight had been lifted from his young shoulders. Just then, his mom and Marily's father approached, their tour of the garden concluded, Maryann's expression and comments doing great justice befitting the lush and varied greenery and florals.

The drive home was not the ordeal for Scooter as it was before. In fact, the whole mood of the car was enhanced by the unfettered conversations that filled the air with a normalcy that replaced the moodiness only a short time before. This release encouraged a lively give-and-take between to two youngsters which didn't go unnoticed by the adults. Maryann was grateful for the positive change in her son.

In the following weeks, Scooter had plenty to tell Jackie, who didn't show up quite as often as he used to.

"Hey, pal, somethin' wrong?"

"Whattaya mean?"

"Well, it's been a few days since you bugged me."

"Aw, you seem to have things on your mind, or should I say a sweetheart?"

"C'mon, Jackie, that's not fair. We're only friends."

"Yeah, that may be so, but I feel like things are changin' between us."

"Hey, that's crazy."

"Listen, you told me how Mr. Woodson has taken your mom to dinner several times and without you."

"What's wrong with that?"

"Don't you see, knucklehead, that they might get together?"

"You nuts or somethin'? Ain't gonna happen."

"Don't be too sure of that, dopey. But if it does, how're you gonna take it?"

Scooter was finally forced to confront this very fact he had hidden from himself, not because he didn't like Marily's father, but because the love of his father would not allow for another person to fill his place.

"Ya know, Jackie, I'll be honest with you, I don't know how'll handle it."

"Hey, we're pals, I'm sure you'll come up with somethin'. And ya know, it may not be that bad, being he seems like a nice guy. Gotta go now."

"See ya tomorrow?"

"Maybe."

As Jackie left, Scooter pondered the "What if" that his friend left him with. Sure, Mr. Woodson was okay and all, and Mom did like him, but this was new to him, and he'd have to find a way to deal with it.

The sessions with Marily were enjoyable, and as he worked with her, he began to see her in a different light. *Holy cow,* he thought, *if Mom and Richard did get together, I mean, really as becoming a family, Marily's going to be my sister!* The jolt caused his partner to notice his focus on her, his eyes frozen to her face, as if seeing something that could be or would be a whole different world. This was going to take some getting used to.

That night at dinner, he had to find an answer to the conflicts plaguing him.

"Mom, can I ask you somethin', and promise me you won't get mad?"

"Hey, man of the house, why so serious?"

"Well, I don't know how to ask ya, it's kinda somethin' that's been buggin' me, and I gotta know."

"Know what?"

"Well, ya've been seein' Mr. Wood…er, Richard for quite a while, and he seems to like you, an' ya seem to like him. Mom, what does it mean?"

"Okay, sport, let's clear the table and we'll talk about it in the den."

Seating themselves, she took Scooter's hand in hers and looked at him with soft eyes and a gentle smile, then paused for a moment, looking at the ceiling as if to collect her thoughts.

The boy was in a quandary, something she wanted to dispel, and the only way to do that was to be as straightforward as could be. She related the few past weeks that had brought about a new relationship that had blossomed for her, and that her only care was for Scooter's approval. Knowing the love he had for his dad, she wondered how it might affect him. Telling Scooter of her concern, he felt a tinge of guilt, a guilt born of his need to hold on to his father's memory. Then he looked into his mother's eyes and saw a hint of yearning, yearning for his acceptance of what she wanted and needed.

"Mom, can I still love Dad if you and Richard, ya know, make it a family?"

"Dear, you will always love your father. But that's what love is all about. It can never be bottled up like soda. Love is a gift that has no boundary, it's like sunshine, it touches everything wherever it's allowed to flourish."

He thought about that for a moment and said, "Ya know, Mom, I'm glad you're my mom."

"And I'm glad I'm your mom." A squeeze of her hand reinforcing her words.

"Mom, as the man of the house, I…er, well, I think there's room for one more, if it comes to that."

She leaned over and planted a tender kiss on his forehead.

In the days that followed, his entire outlook transformed from one spectrum to another. Whenever MK and her father visited or took them to dinner, he found that indeed there was room for another man of the house. This he reconciled with his father's place in his life. His routine became more settled, but oh, how he missed his friend. He hadn't been around lately and was concerned that maybe something had happened to him. And one day while Scooter was shooting some hoops in the backyard, "Hey, Scoot" rang from a familiar voice, catching his attention.

"Jackie? Where've you been?"

"Oh, around. It's not like you lack for company."

"What's that mean, dork?"

"Listen, I can tell that you and MK are goin' good, and you even seem to be in good with her dad."

"What's that got to do with you bein' AWOL and all?"

"Let's talk." Scooter was struck by the way Jackie said that, as if he were in trouble of some sort. "Scoot, you and me have had a blast, somethin' a lot of the other guys don't have."

"Are you in trouble? I don't like the way yer talkin', like somethin's gonna happen."

"Well, yer half right. No, I'm not in trouble, but I don't think I'll be able to see ya as much anymore."

"Are ya movin'?"

"No, nothin' like that. Scoot. Just look at where you're at. Your mom's happy because of MK's father, and you seem to be getting along. I know he really likes you, and you really have changed a lot."

"But what's that got to do with you pullin' a Houdini on me?"

"Not true entirely, but you have to do what's right for you. Get to know Mr. Woodson better and really show MK that she's great. I'll be around, so don't fret."

If Scooter had known what a Dear John letter was, Jackie's words would have applied. He treasured meeting him, especially after his dad died, and Jackie seemed to know how to talk to him. Their friendship carried him through a lot, and now the prospect of him not being there when he needed him was a bummer.

That night at dinner, he confided to his mother his disappointment at what Jackie has said.

"Honey, I think you should listen to his advice."

Her words were more of a salve for her than the gloomy lad. Jackie had always been problematic in her estimation, and although he seemed to bring some comfort to her son, perhaps this was better for all concerned.

True to his word, Jackie failed, except for one instance, to meet up with Scooter. Scooter in turn worried about his friend, remembering all those times they clowned around and did all kinds of goofy stuff. Time heals a lot of wounds, but the scab hadn't really formed on his, and when it did, he'd probably rip it off. He couldn't forget his friend. The frequent visits by MK and her father soon became a welcome treat, as his fondness for them began to grow. Most of his reservations had evaporated in the closeness that was being forged. There was no doubt that in the end, he would be part of a new family.

Then he was hit with a bomb. Jackie appeared one day as Scooter was leaving for the field.

"Hey, sport, hold up." Turning around, Scooter was glad to see his friend.

"Boy, it's great to see you, Jackie, what's up?"

"Nothing you're going to like."

"You're in trouble, aren't you?"

"No, pal, it's not like that. Maybe worse."

"Will ya stop with the mysteries and tell me what the heck's goin' on?"

"I won't be seein' ya anymore."

"No, no, that ain't true, you're my buddy, it can't happen."

"Look, Scoot, ya don't need me anymore, not with what's going to be your new family."

"So what, lots of guys have families and friends. Why is this so different?"

"It just is, and you'll understand after a while."

"Understand what, that you're cutting out on me? Some friend."

"Always have been and always will be, only in a different way. Remember me, this way I'll always be with you."

Choking back an eruption of tears, Scooter looked pleadingly into Jackie's eyes, hoping that this was a bad dream or, worse yet, a nightmare. But reality prevailed, and in silence and a wave of his hand, Jackie turned and walked away, never looking back. Understand? What's to understand? What did he mean? A saddened boy turned back to his home, entering the kitchen where his mom was making some tea.

"That was fast, honey. No one at the field?"

His only answer was to draw up the chair and fold his head into his arms across the table, a sob or two attracting Maryann's attention.

"Scooter, did someone hurt you?"

"It's not like that, Mom." Tears were flowing down his reddened cheeks. Immediately Maryann sat beside him and embraced his quivering body.

"What's wrong, honey, what happened?"

In a tortured manner, he related what Jackie had said. The boy was terribly upset, something she had never seen before. In what may be described as cruel, she was glad, not of his pain so much as for the benefit that could result from it. The issue with Jackie had finally been resolved, or at least she hoped so.

His absence from Scooter's life signaled a new and better future for her son. Now she had to tend to his emotional needs and assure him that everything would be okay. In the following days, MK and her lessons, a drive to the park with Richard, and other activities seemed to lessen his despondency. Maryann would listen to him, and little by little, Jackie, while not completely dismissed, became a smaller part of the conversations.

"Mom, Jackie was a good friend, and I miss him an' all, so is it okay to still think of him, even though he's gone?"

Carefully, not wanting to undo the progress made so far, she reached for an answer that would not only satisfy him but address her concerns. "Honey, remember when you talked about Richard and how you felt about what it would mean to the memory of your father? That it was okay to accept one thing and still hold the other in your heart? No, I believe that since he was a part of your life, it's something you can't easily erase. And I believe he'd want you to go on and live your life without worrying about him. That's what a true friend would want."

"Gee, Mom, I get it, thanks." Hugging her, a happy boy could now shed a burden even an adult would find hard to carry. She held him and closed her eyes, thanking God that maybe his ordeal was over. Scooter headed for the yard, and in what was an instinctive impulse, he glanced long and hard at the sidewalk, where his friend usually appeared, maybe in hopes he'd appear. *No, Mom said it was over, time to go on to other things.* With this mental directive, Jackie was put away, with a thanks for his comradeship that he'd always cherish.

The routine of daily life was pursued with all the vim and vigor a youngster could muster, not a cloud on the horizon. He became the self-appointed protector of MK as the probability of her becoming his sister bore more fruit. Family always came first, and he would see to it. This was equal to his being "man of the house," and he reveled in the role, almost like a knight in shining armor. Dreaded school was around the corner but with a fresher prospective. MK would probably be in his class again, and he looked forward to the new association. Richard revealed himself to be a very considerate man and surprisingly very active. Often he would challenge Scooter on the backyard court, often being trounced by the boy. That didn't matter as the genuine interest showered on Scooter delighted him.

Many times just the two would drive off somewhere, whether to the mall or the diner, for some chow. This mano a mano and what better way to build a relationship than to discover different interests and activities. Richard was a wise man who let the flow of the moment determine itself rather than any input on his part. No pretense, no false promises, just letting things happen. Sometimes, Richard would surprise Scooter when he needed advice to resolve some question concerning his computer or some other matter that required some resolution. The effect made the youngster feel eight feet tall.

Richard was also a sensitive man that courted his affections with the same consideration that he displayed with the boy and his mother. If he had a temper, it never surfaced, although he demonstrated frustration now and then over some miscue or missed opportunity. Any faults only seemed to bring him closer to the ones he cared about, especially Scooter, who at one time thought Richard was unapproachably perfect.

"Okay, Scooter, your mom said it was okay if we hauled off to the concert in the glen. Marily is waiting in the car for us."

"Okay, Richard, be right with you." Placing the obligatory kiss on his mother's cheek, he scampered toward the door. The sun was heading toward the horizon, signaling a night filled with music.

"I'll wait up for you, sweetheart," she called to him from the door.

"Okay, Mom." With that, the car sped down the street and turned onto the country road leading to the glen. It would be a leisurely thirty-minute drive.

"I think you kids'll really enjoy this con—"

"Watch out, Dad!" Marily shrieked as a fawn darted in front of the car. Desperately he tuned the wheel and swerved away from the startled animal. Trying to recover, the car was caught in the softness and mud of the berm, its wheels spinning uncontrollably, unable to manage any degree of traction. Swerving from one side to the other, Richard forgivably oversteered the car, the machine reacting in like manner. He saw the edge of the road approaching rapidly but was helpless to prevent the expectant plunge through the brush and down the slope of a ravine. Hitting a stump, the car rolled over several times while descending to the bottom before resting on its side. Inside, there were soft moans and then silence. A wisp of smoke began to curl from the dislodged hood, generated by a damaged electrical cable flickering erratically. A mass of brush and leaves had collected in the engine compartment, dangerously close to the cable and ominously near the fuel line.

Predictably, the law of physics prevailed, and the mass of debris started to burn, soon to engulf the fuel source. As the flames began to grow, the occupants were unaware of their fatal situation, unconscious and alone.

The glow grew larger, casting grotesque shadows across the trees and bushes, as if awakening dormant creatures held at bay. The interior of the car was still.

Maryann was puttering around the house, straightening the living room and setting the dining room table with paper plates and a variety of snacks, knowing she'd have a hungry mob on her hands. It reminded her of earlier days when she did the same for Scooter and her husband, the pair fighting over the choicest offerings in mock combat. It seemed that perhaps this would be a second beginning. Then the phone rang. *I bet those guys are going to be late or something,* she jokingly chided herself.

"Hello. Yes, this is Mrs. Moore." She abruptly froze as the caller spoke to her, informing her of the accident, her face turning pale as the blood receded from her soft skin. Staring without seeing, her mind and body filled with anxiety. All she could do was reply robotically as she replied to several questions.

The conversation was diplomatic from the inquiring source, and transportation would be provided shortly if needed. Numb, she replied, "Thank you, I have no car." Her voice was starting to tremble and break up, requiring her to repeat herself. Hanging up, she gathered her coat and purse, locked the rear door, and sat on the sofa, waiting. What was it the nurse said? That her son and his companions had been in an accident, and the boy was able to give them her phone number, that he was hurt, but not too badly, although he and the others were admitted. *No, I can't lose him too,* she cried to herself, gripping the arm cover on the sofa and almost shredding it with the sheer force of her emotions.

A knock on the door, and she quickly jumped up, almost tripping over the throw carpet in her haste to answer it.

"Evening, ma'am, I'm Officer Curtiss. The hospital asked me to transport you there."

"Oh, thank you, Officer. Please hurry, my son is hurt."

"Don't you fret, ma'am, I'll have you there in a jiffy." The manner of the officer suggested that he'd performed this service before, and his calmness seemed to settle Maryann somewhat. He spoke that he had a son, and it was par for the course to get banged up now and then. The way he spoke eased her anxiety somewhat, and his son's history filled the trip to the hospital.

Arriving at admissions, she was promptly met by the attending physician and was assured that her son's condition was stable, and after he was settled in his room, she would be permitted to see him. Inquiring about Richard and MK, she was gratified to learn that they too were in stable condition, suffering a few bruises but no broken bones. A silent thankful prayer came to mind, her closed eyes signifying to the doctor a moment of spiritual thanksgiving. He waited with an appreciation for her anxiety and relief, having seen so many of life's twists and turns, not to intrude on this expression of gratitude.

"Oh, I'm sorry, Doctor, as you were saying?"

"Officer Curtiss will escort you to the waiting lounge. When your son is ready, I'll send for you."

"Thank you, Doctor." The calmness of his directions easing her anxiety. Entering the lounge, she turned to the officer, her eyes preceding her vocal and trembling need to learn what happened.

"Well, ma'am, I was on my usual patrol when this young feller waved me down, all excited and everythin'. 'What's the matter?' I asked. He started yellin' about a car that ran off the road and pointed in that direction, asking me to hurry. Good-lookin' boy too, what with that mop of wavy blond hair."

Maryann froze. It can't be, how could it? No, there's some mistake. "Are you sure his hair was blond?"

"That's a funny question to ask me, but yes, ma'am. Any reason why?"

"Did you get his name?"

"No, ma'am, I just hit the gas and headed where he pointed. Good thing too. I could see the light down in the ravine and guessed the car was on fire. Grabbed my squad extinguisher and raced down as fast as I could. Emptied the darn thing but couldn't get it out. I forced open the door with my nightstick, and one by one I pulled them out. That was pretty lucky, I guess. The fire was just about to reach the cab.

"The man was able to stumble up the slope, and I had both kids. I took them as far as I could and laid them down, but I could only carry one at a time uphill. After they were all safe, the fire must have reached the gas tank. Thank God I got them out."

"Please, let's sit, I have to ask you something. You asked why I questioned you about the boy."

"Yes, ma'am."

"Scooter, my son, has gone through a difficult time these last few years."

The officer displayed a sympathetic face, which earned him the gratitude of a shaken woman. How often did he have to hear things like this? Maryann thought. "My husband passed away, and it was devastating to my son, who adored his father. I can't begin to tell you how his sadness just ate at him, and I was helpless to do anything about it. Just when I thought I reached my limit, he came home from school and said he'd met a boy about his age. He said he liked him and that they both hit it off together. Officer Curtiss, you can't imagine the relief I felt. I thanked God for bringing him a friend.

"'What's he like?' I asked. 'He's pretty cool, even if that mop of blond hair covers half his face.' 'I'd like to meet him.' 'Okay, the next time I see him, I'll ask him.' Well, this went on for a few days, and still I hadn't met the boy. You know how mothers can be. I wanted to make sure he didn't associate with someone that I'd have to worry about. Then one day, while in the kitchen, my son was in the yard shooting hoops. Then I heard him voicing a welcome to someone, and I thought perhaps it was his new friend. Wiping my hands, I went to the kitchen door to introduce myself. There was Scooter, talking to someone, but I was unable to see him. Perhaps he was on the side of the house where I couldn't see him.

"Walking down the steps, I was afraid that I'd give the impression that my son was a mommy's boy, but to my surprise, I couldn't find anyone. 'Scooter.' 'Yes, Mom.' 'Who're you talking to?' 'My new friend Jackie, Mom.' 'Where is he hiding?' 'Oh, Mom, stop kiddin', he's over by the swing.' Expecting to see a youngster playing a joke on me by hiding and then jumping up, I saw no one. Was my son teasing me? He continued talking to who knows who, and I started to get nervous. It was scary. Trying to remain calm, I called our family doctor and explained what had happened. He recommended a behavioral physician who might be able to help me.

"I wasted no time in making an appointment, and upon meeting him, he had a manner that made me feel very comfortable, which I needed. My son had to have the best, and this doctor's preliminary questioning of my son removed any doubt. Most of his counseling was just between the two, filling me in after each session. The loss of his father had triggered a desperate need to fill the void, and apparently what filled the bill was an imaginary friend. While no means unusual, in Scooter's case, it was extreme and had to be handled very carefully. I was told what to do and what not to do to keep my son on the road to recovery.

"I learned to deal with this phantom, no easy thing for me, but I muddled through for the sake of my boy. Strangely, aside from his imaginary friend, he was like any other youngster, always hungry, interested in sports, or playing games with the other kids. As long as he didn't change his behavior, I was content that the doctor's treatment, mostly weekly sessions.

"Oh, I'm sorry, I just keep on talking."

"That's quite okay, ma'am, I'm listening to a worried and caring mother, and I never get tired of that."

"You're very kind, just talking to someone gives me some release. I don't know what I'd do if you weren't here, God bless you."

"So how did the sessions go?"

"As well as can be expected, I guess, I mean, it's not like mending a broken arm or stitching a cut."

"I guess not."

"To be frank, I was impatient, wanting it to be all over, but I realized you can't rush something like this. Every day brought hope of a change, and then things started to do that, change I mean."

"How so?"

"Through my son's classmate, a young, lovely girl, I met her father. He became a good friend and then something more. As time went on, my son's dependency, if you can call it that, with his friend grew less and less, until one day, it was over."

"How's that?"

"The young man told my son that he wasn't needed anymore, that he had other people in his life now. Scooter couldn't understand that. Kids always stick around, one way or another. He was heartbroken, and it took time and the kindly attention of his classmate and her father to bridge the gap that he had to cross."

"I guess the boy's been through a lot, ma'am, and I hope things work out for him. It's lucky that kid flagged me down."

"You mention he had a mass of blond hair."

"Yes, ma'am, and I know where you're goin'. Look there are all kinds of kids that look like that or pretty close to it, and let me tell ya, that was no imaginary boy who screamed for me to help. From what you told me, his friends were just the right ticket to set him straight, enough that he didn't need an imaginary friend anymore."

"Are you sure you don't work for Dr. Groom?" she replied in a relieved chuckle, a welcome break from her despair.

"No, ma'am, just tellin' like it is. You don't need any mysteries here, just the good thoughts that your son and the others are goin' to get better."

How fortunate, she thought, that the man in blue was not far off from being an analyst, that his company and words conveyed a depth of understanding rivaling her own doctor's.

"Officer Curtiss, I'd like to share one more thing with you."

"Yes, ma'am?"

"Maybe one of the reasons I'm so protective, besides the fact I'm a mother, starts years ago. You see, when I found out I was pregnant, my husband and I were overjoyed. We didn't want to know whether the baby would be a boy or girl, you know, the usual phrase, 'As long as the baby is healthy.'" Maryann paused and pulled a handkerchief from her purse and dabbed her eyes. "Surprisingly we were blessed with news of twins. Oh, how me and my husband felt, twins! When I went into labor, the pain was overcome by the joy I'd have with two bundles of love. The first child was a boy, and his name had already been picked, James. As he grew, he was so fast that my husband called him a scooter, which became his nickname.

"The second child was a boy also, and I couldn't wait to hold both of them in my arms. Resting and waiting in my room for the babies to be brought to me, my doctor came in, and the expression on his face puzzled me. He sat on the edge of the bed and grasped my hand, and suddenly I sensed unwelcome news. Quietly he explained that James was a beautiful boy and completely free of any problems. Then he paused, and I started to shiver. Squeezing my hand, he said that the other child was doing poorly with some medical impairment I've never heard before, something almost irreversible.

"He asked me if I would like the baby brought to the room. I felt like no one should have to feel, especially after giving birth and discovering only part of my world would survive."

"Look, ma'am, you shouldn't torture yourself like this, just worry about your boy."

"You needn't worry about that, in a way, it's helping me cope. I had to survive that as I have to survive this, for the sake of my son."

"I think I understand, ma'am, you're a brave woman."

Smiling at the comfort his kind words brought, she continued. "They placed my little miracle in my arms. How peaceful he seemed, quietly gurgling and flexing his little hands. I held him long after the Lord welcomed him, trying to fill the loss with the gain of the other child. And now, looking back on the many events that gave me pause, I think I'm beginning to understand the signs revealed to me that in my ignorance, I did not fathom. I was blessed and didn't realize how much. You see, as I was holding my baby for the last time, it was only fitting that he be announced in heaven by his name—Jackson, or if you prefer…Jackie."

Cleared for Takeoff

The elderly gentleman, alert and amused, cantered along the sidewalk, fronted by two impetuous and joyful youngsters. His gait was hastened by the animated pulls and tugs by the two urchins, something he tolerated with patience and a great dose of love.

"C'mon, Poppy, we're going to miss Jet Ace!" one of the tykes shouted.

"Hold on, tiger, I'm not as young as you." *And I can't remember if I really was,* he chuckled to himself. Their animation spurred him on a little more than usual; he didn't want to disappoint them by missing one of their favorite Saturday morning TV shows.

Reaching their home, they detached themselves as quickly as a boxcar separating from a switching rail. Into the house they scooted, leaving their mentor behind. Exhaling a hurried gasp of air, he mounted the steps at a measure pace, the small reserve of energy depleted by his charges. Entering the hallway, he glanced into the family room, where two figures adorned the floor in unpredictable postures, their eyes glued to their favorite show.

"Hi, Dad," his daughter Megan quipped over her shoulder as she prepared some snacks for the boys. "How'd it go?"

"I survived, but boy, they're really becoming a handful."

"Maybe you shouldn't be spending so much time with them if it's causing you a problem," she replied, concern etched on her face.

"Are you kidding? They're the main reason I get out of the bed in the morning."

"I know, Dad, but I worry about you."

"Hey, what's to worry, I can handle them."

"Yeah, I can see that," she replied in a sarcastic laugh. "How 'bout something to eat or drink?"

"What kind of drink?"

"Daaad."

"Okay, okay, iced tea. I'll go sit with the kids and maybe learn something from them." *Yeah, like their hero who probably was 4-f and never served a day in his life,* he growled with an inaudible mouthing. Plopping on the sofa, his presence was barely noticed by the sprawling heap on the floor. He lay his head against the cushion, content with his lot in life and musing about the good fortune he's had, or a blessing, as he often called it. The relaxing figure belied an inner strength that if possible to physically measure would exceed not a few standards.

Born in the Midwest and raised during the Depression, family life was difficult but, being a tight-knit family, endurable. The son of a farmer, he learned the value of what was important, mostly that the hard work in the fields was a godsend in that the good earth could sustain them with its bounty. He was a good son and listened to the advice he gleaned from his father, Craig. Religion was an integral part of their life, and it mattered not that the trek to a distant church, Our Lady of Sorrows, consumed hours.

As any young boy, he was adventurous, and when his chores permitted, he could be found at the creek, fishing for catfish or any other fish that might grace the dinner table. Or maybe he would hike through the woods and wonder at the different animals that inhabited the leafy and brush-filled domain. He was enchanted by cars, since he saw so few of them, and marveled at their operation. This bent was to have an impact on his future.

It was not always work, and his parents knew that some leisure was needed to get through their trials. As such, on rare occasions the family would head to the fair grounds. It was during one of these excursions that the boy was captivated by another motorized object—an airplane! The barnstorming pilot would, for a price, treat anyone to a flight around the field. He pleaded with his father to allow him to inspect this invention of wonder.

"Don't make a pest of yourself," he cautioned.

"Okay, Dad, I'll just look." With that he scooted to the fence where the plane was closest and gazed with wonder that this combination of wood, fabric, and metal could release one from the grip of the earth.

His mother, Sara, was a handsome lady who was a bulwark for the family, as most women are, especially during those trying times. She would squirrel away the few coins she received from her seamstress talents. Clothes were expensive, and her handiwork at restoring damaged fabrics was a boon to those who sought her services. Her customers, like many in those times, were not blessed with a surplus of money outside what they needed to survive on.

In fact, many times she would take produce or canned fruit in payment. This was the atmosphere in which the boy was raised.

She observed her son as he approached the pilot and began an animated conversation of which she could only guess. The man responded with his own gyrations, simulating flight movements and patterns. He placed a hand on the boy's shoulder and gestured at the aircraft, the conversation between the two barely audible but congenial. She flirted with the notion to satisfy his desire to fly but backed off.

This was a luxury they could ill afford. Approaching the pair, still engrossed in an avid conversation, the pilot turned and doffed his aviator's cap toward the boy's parents.

"I hope he wasn't too much of a bother," the father exclaimed.

"On the contrary," he replied, "the boy has a natural appreciation which impressed me. I really enjoyed talking to him."

"Thank you for your time, sir," replied Craig. The boy's eyes were glued to the craft as if mesmerized, and only by shaking the boy's arm did his father get his attention.

"Let's go, son."

As they walked away, the pilot interrupted their departure with an offer to fly the boy.

"I'm sorry, sir, but—"

"Bob Driscoll, ma'am, at your service."

"Mr. Driscoll, we can't afford the cost, but thank you anyway."

"Sir, Ma'am, if I may? I've had a good day, and the keen interest your son has in flying is somethin' I couldn't ignore. Tell you what, if he's willing, and you are too, at the end of the day, I'll be needin' some help puttin' Ole Betsy, that's what I call her, away for the night. I really could use some help in that regard." This wasn't entirely true, but he didn't want to offend what seemed like a proud family with what seemed like charity. "And to top it off, before we put her up for the night, we'll take a spin together, how's that?"

The boy's mouth opened in disbelief, *Me? Flying?*

"Sir, that's too generous," protested the father.

"Shucks, no, it's not, you know what it's like getting decent help?" Again straying from the truth a mite. "What's your name, son?"

"Gee, Dad, can I go, please? Er, it's Charles Albert Madson, sir."

"No need to be formal with me, lad. I'll call you Chuck, okay?" That was the nickname he carried from that day on. "How 'bout it, sir? You can't deny him the thrill of a lifetime."

Scratching his head, indicating a moment of thought, he turned to the boy with a smile on his face. "Okay, son, I guess it'll be okay."

"Gee, thanks, Dad." A look of unfettered glee beaming from his face.

True to his word, the boy got to fly. Liking the area, Bob set up shop at the local dirt airstrip, renting flying lessons for income. When chores were done, Chuck hiked over to the canvas hangar where Ole Betsy was stored and cleaned her canvas and wiped down the engine. Every now and then, Bob would plop Chuck in the front cockpit and explained the dual controls to him. The beginning of a fateful association was being born from the friendship that was developing. On one occasion, Bob hopped into the rear seat and started the engine.

Once aloft, he shouted through the tube speaker for Chuck to take control of the stick. Nervous and hesitant, he did, feeling the plane respond to his up or down input. Bob could easily override any excessive action, but the plane rode contently. This was the beginning of the boy's unspoken quest to actually fly an aircraft. The rest, as they say, is history. Bob and the family became good neighbors, and as Chuck's mentor, the boy could not have had a better one than Bob.

Happy the day that Chuck earned his pilot's license thanks to the tutoring of Bob. That was the perfect graduation gift as he left high school. Being exceptional as a student, he earned a partial scholarship to the local college. His two years were interrupted when WWII erupted, and with his parents' approval, he signed with the Army Air Corp, which in 1941 was designated United States Army Air Force. His training was arduous, and he would not allow himself to neglect any facet that could improve his skill as a pilot. It seemed forever before he would receive the coveted wings badge that declared him a full-fledge pilot.

Known as a team player, he made many friends, some he would sadly lose during the course of combat. Some thought his demeanor was too passive for a combat pilot, but when putting his Mustang through its paces before his peers, he dispelled that notion, that and his impassioned condemnation toward the enemy that had brought sorrow to the world. He hoped his contribution would hasten their end.

Before embarking for England, he returned home on furlough. Friends had gathered to celebrate his new commission, and of course, Bob beamed with delight that his student was now something to behold.

"Now don't get cocky out there, son. Them Jerries are pretty damn good at what they do."

Bob had been a pilot in WWI and a pretty good one. Though planes had changed, the tactics were the same. He enjoined Chuck with the same advice his instructors had imparted—always know where you are, and keep your head on a swivel. Attack out of the sun when possible. Always have the altitude advantage over your foe and bore in close before firing.

Not one to resist pulling Bob's chains as he had done so many times before, he admonished his friend that now he was flying a *real* airplane. In a fit of faux anger, he punched his onetime helper in the arm and tousled his hair. Somberly he said, "Bob, I'll try to remember all you taught me. I'll be okay, I promise." The family took him to his port of embarkation and said their goodbyes. Now, he was in God's hands.

His posting was to the Fifty-Fifth Fighter Group, 343 Squadron at Station 131 Nuthampstead, England, at Hertfordshire. And it was to that fabled group, the mighty Eighth Air Force, Fighter Command, which alone inspired him. He had a lot to learn, and the other members of the squadron made sure he knew what was expected of him. Not because they stuffed shirts, but because the life of one depended on the other. Their infusion of info was formal but amiable, which relaxed his approach to learning the ropes. He initially felt that being a newcomer he wouldn't have the same camaraderie that had been woven among the proven pilots.

But these were birds of a feather, so to speak, and any of their kind could expect the respect and concern of his peers, unless proven otherwise. Taken to the field, they pointed out the plane he would be flying, a brand-new Mustang. He was elated as a child opening his Christmas gift, and being twenty, why not? Seating himself in his new mount, he reveled in the thought of piloting this thoroughbred. Taking his penknife from his pocket, he inscribed the letters *CAM* and the date just below the canopy track. His bird was christened.

The first few weeks were given over to training, familiarity flights, and the other essentials needed by a freshman pilot to prepare for combat. His friendliness and good nature made an immediate impact, and he did not want for friendly conversations, whether indulging in small talk or, more importantly for him, to glean from the combat vets their observations and tactics firsthand.

Finally, nerves animating his need to focus, a combat mission! Flying wing with a proven vet, his first mission was an escort for B-17s on their way to Germany. The Mustang finally satisfied the need for an escort that could provide protection all the way to Berlin and back. Remembering the admonition of his peers and good ole Bob, he swiveled his head around and around like a good wingman to provide warning of any enemy aircraft that may attack them.

Following the mission and on the way back to base, Chuck became separated from his flight and cursed himself for being so negligent in allowing it to happen. He later learned that happened more times than not, even with the proven flyers, but for now he berated himself with some choice words. Flying on a heading leading him back to base, he came across a B-17 Flying Fortress trailing smoke from a damaged engine.

This was like meat on the table for any attacker. Many bombers went down this way, as they had no supporting planes to assist them. As he approached the wounded bird, his keen eyes detected a descending object, approaching from the stern position. It was an ME-109 attacking the damaged aircraft, like a diving falcon sensing an easy kill. This weapon of the air was deadly, especially in the hands of a skilled pilot. Weak defensive fire from the Fort indicated more damage and casualties than could be seen from his position. The German fired his guns, shredding aluminum from the fuselage in a murderous assault.

Chuck had been too far away to intercept the aircraft but now shoved his throttle to the stop, his charge accelerating as he moved to the attack. His extra speed allowed him to catch up and trail after the enemy plane. Perhaps this pilot didn't adhere to the same advice that Chuck had religiously followed, by not checking his six, the position behind his tail. Chuck slowly closed the range until his sight was full of wings and fuselage before triggering his guns. The staccato drum of the .50-caliber slugs echoed through the cockpit as they ripped into the unsuspecting target, great sections of metal disintegrating in the barrage.

This airman had enough as the craft inverted and the canopy separated from the mangled machine, the pilot ejecting from the cockpit. His body twisted and turned before his seat pack released a parachute. For this Chuck was grateful. His reasoning being that this was akin to two knights in a contest of survival, one on one. In fact, when a plane was dispatched, it was the plane that mattered in the conscience of most pilots, not the life of the combatant. In a skewed way, considering killing is a great part of war, it eased the concerns of many pilots.

Returning to the damage craft, he flew off its starboard wing. The Big Friend rocked his wings in a sign of gratitude to the Little Friend, the Mustang responding. Enduring the monotonous drone of the engine, the impact of what he had done finally impressed itself on him, and he shivered a bit. He thought that it's true that when you have to act quickly, it's by instinct, emotion taking a back seat, or else you may have wavered by deliberating rather than acting. For this he was thankful that he performed as he did in saving his comrades. He continued his scan, hoping that they were free of any further attacks. The speed of the larger aircraft was just above stalling, and it took an eternity before the coast of England appeared, and the tired aviator was relieved and grateful that the ordeal was over.

The '17 peeled away to head for its base, the pilot waving with great animation in a show of appreciation. Chuck felt humbled that he was instrumental in saving these brave souls. After landing, some of his flight mates ran up to him, curiosity being the coin of the day.

"Hey, newbie, where were you?" The tone jocular but concealing a great relief for his return.

"I got one" was his first utterance. It was automatic and received hand slaps on his back and a roar of approval.

"Ace, ace, ace!" Now he felt as if he really belonged and returned their jibes with his own.

"If you treat me nice, I might even show you how to do it, nothing to it." This, of course, encouraged a round of nooggies.

Several days later, he was called into the CO's hut.

"You wanted to see me, sir?"

"Yes, sit down. I have something for you." Reaching under his desk, he retrieved a cardboard package. "I'm impressed by the way you handled yourself the other day, and I guess others felt the same way."

"I beg your pardon, sir."

"The CO of the bomb group and the crew of the 'Fort you saved wanted to show their appreciation."

He handed the hefty package to the wide-eyed youngster who received the package hesitantly, as if maybe he wasn't supposed to be rewarded. "Take it, son, it's a sign of gratitude."

Returning to the field, he encountered some of his squadron mates.

"Hey, Chuckie, why the ole man have you on the carpet?"

"Naw, it was nothing like that." He proceeded to explain the circumstances of the package in his possession. Seeing the mounting interest in his friends, he pointed to the rec hall. "Let's go over there and see what kind of loot they gave me." Upon opening the carton, the young man pried an envelope taped to the lid. "Hold on, guys," he muttered as he read the contents. Silently he folded the letter and placed it in his shirt pocket, the look on his face restricting his fellow pilots from asking what it said.

"Okay, let's see what's in here." He retrieved a bottle of brandy, scotch whiskey, bourbon, two jars of caviar, marmalade, six bars of chocolate, and two boxes of cookies and two cartons of Lucky Strikes. "Holy cow, they must've thought I saved the whole group," he responded in an unconscious remark of admiration. "Look, fellas, I don't drink or smoke, so help yourselves." The words no sooner left his lips than the booze disappeared more quickly than an ice cube in a frying pan. "But leave the other goodies for me," he countered, with a unified response of disappointment from those who had been fleet of hand.

The experience taught him that indeed there was a bond between those who inhabited the skies, whether fighter, bomber, or any other warbird. As the missions mounted, so did his toll of enemy aircraft. He soon had four to his credit, the enemy balkankruz, or cross, signifying the kills, painted on his fuselage. His skill also elevated his status to element leader, the leader of a two-plane unit that formed a fight of four aircraft. Enemy aircraft were slowly being depleted, but those that remained were as deadly as ever.

During one escort mission, his flight had been released from close escort to allow the fighters to be more effective.

This policy had been introduced earlier so that free-ranging aircraft might intercept the enemy at a longer range from the bombers. Being too close to their herd, any reaction to incoming aircraft would be too late. Scanning the skies as usual, Chuck spotted a speck in the distance and relayed that info to his flight leader.

"It's all yours, Chuck, if it's a bandit. We'll cover for you."

Even though the leader wanted Chuck to get his fifth kill, thus enabling him to become an ace, he was also in a better position to pursue the craft. "Okay, Jock, let's get 'em," he squawked over his throat-activated radio to his wingman. Winging toward the direction of the sighting, the two aircraft closed on what turned out to be a Folke-Wulf 190, a deadly machine, especially in the hands of a seasoned pilot. As they moved in, Jock keeping an eye on his leader's tail, the enemy began to maneuver in a fashion that indicated he had become the prey. He reacted instantly to evade all their efforts to claw him down, his aircraft nosing over and diving. As he did so, the wings revealed bright-red tips and a white propeller hub.

The Mustang was and is a more maneuverable aircraft, and Chuck kept on his tail but not within range to open fire. The descent ended when the lead plane leveled off and flew along the ravines and valleys of a mountainous area, with Chuck right behind. Flying on the deck was dangerous, any ham-fisted input on the controls at this speed nullifying any corrective effort to avoid ploughing into the hillside. *This guy's way beyond good,* Chuck thought to himself, the sweat seeping out from beneath his leather head covering and then cooling on his neck.

His adversary's moves thwarted any attempt to line him up for a kill, leaving the pursuer no other option but to keep shadowing, waiting for a mistake. He also lost his wingman.

Maybe this pilot knew the area very well, for his moves appeared to be programed and automatic. As such, being careful in his own maneuvers, Chuck began to lose some ground.

This became very evident when rounding a bend, he lost sight of his quarry. *Where are you, where are you,* Chuck repeatedly whispered as he scanned the sky around him, with no luck. Lifting his craft from the valley to get a better overall view of the sky, a small speck dead ahead, growing larger with each second, answered his question. With skillful maneuvering, the rabbit had turned his craft around to confront the hunter.

Flashes from his wings indicated the firing of the four twenty-millimeter cannon embedded there. Wrenching his stick violently to the side, the Mustang bolted from the stream of rounds, with only a split second to spare. The 190 shot past, his attempt to knock down his antagonist an added incentive for Chuck to finish this guy off, or those chocolate bars were going to be orphans. Fortunately, the pursued aircraft failed to revert to the tactics that served him so well and elected to shoot skyward.

Again his tactics were about all that Chuck could handle, the elevation allowing for dives and quick ascents, both pilots twisting and turning. The exhaustion was something not felt before, at least not in this magnitude. At last, a mistake was made, and not by the American. Lining up quickly and acquiring the target, the guns spoke for Chuck's intent. Sparks could be seen sprinkling over the target as the rounds made contact. Soon a dirty gray plume of smoke started to trail from a damaged engine. Just as he was ready to fire another burst, Chuck saw with disbelief the crippled foe disappearing into a cloud bank.

Darn it, he berated himself, *that guy's goin' to use the cover to duck me.* Thought of a fifth kill didn't enter his mind. This was business, not vanity. He too flew through the white mist, and as he broke into the clear, he couldn't expect to see what was before him. Flying straight and level was the 190. Not wanting to look a gift horse in the mouth, he steadily closed and placed his prey into a perfect firing position.

Slowly he began to put pressure on the trigger but stopped just short of firing. It wasn't evading or trying to escape. No increase in speed to elude.

It was then that he experienced a foolish compulsion: curiosity. Curiosity in this business can get one killed. Disregarding nature's tools for preservation, caution, and common sense, he eased out of his stern position and brought his craft abreast of the enemy. Looking over, he saw the head of the pilot lying against the canopy, most likely wounded.

The figure stirred, his head facing his adversarial companion. *This man has to leave that plane or he's going to die,* thought Chuck. Hoping the man could see him, he gestured violently in the manner suggesting he bail out, repeating the motions over and over. Finally the reaction was a head movement from side to side, indicating an inability to do so, the wound probably severe. His raised his hand is if in appreciation for the gesture.

This illustrated the contradiction of war where one tries to take the life of another and then offers advice to preserve it. Damn this war! As if to relieve Chuck of any further anguish, the plane began to descend in a shallow dive, it's eventual destination a broad pasture below. Maybe it will be quick, Chuck thought as he followed the terminal glide to its eventual fate. Perhaps the pilot had some energy left, for as the ground rose up to absorb the collision, the craft's nose lifted enough to allow a bone-crunching belly landing. Metal separated, and dirt flung itself in great clods, the resultant cloud of debris obscuring the intruder for a few moments.

As he circled the wreckage, the victor felt no great elation, other than having done his duty. Compassion is a generous gift and is recognized as such during the expected expression of that most human trait. But sometimes things are done in opposition to what is expected, and in this matter it was exercised. With his senses reeling against what he was contemplating, he overrode that compulsion with another one—he was going to land!

It could cost him a court-martial, but he was driven by a sense of compassion, war's least likely attribute. Gauging the terrain, he plotted a fairly flat section of turf and began to descend, carefully searching for anything that would foil his landing. Slowly, slowly, and a thump signaled a successful mating with the earth. The plane taxied as close as it could to the smoking wreckage. Leaving his engine running, Chuck leaped from the cockpit and beelined toward his fallen foe.

The canopy had been knocked off its rails by the impact, making access to the motionless figure easier. Ascending the wing, he found the pilot slumped against the head rest, moaning and attempting to reach out to Chuck.

"Take it easy, fella, let's see what we can do for you." Tenderly he pulled the shoulder harness free and brought the form closer for him to examine his condition.

Removing his leather head covering revealed a blond-haired youth not much older than his benefactor. A thin trickle of blood ran from the corner of his mouth. "Hold on, pal, let me look you over." He noticed a tear in his uniform surrounded by a crimson stain. *Damn, he's been hit in his chest area,* Chuck thought, shaking his head at the prospect of survival. Looking out over the landscape, he spied a stream, very close to where he landed. *Brrrrr,* he lamented, *I could have cashed in my landing gear if I'd landed any closer.* Not dwelling on his good fortune, he leaped from the wing and hurried to the waterway.

Removing his own headgear, he opened it as wide as possible and scooped up an inviting measure of cool water. Racing back to the wreckage, he placed the edge of the makeshift canteen to the injured man's lips. The flow was hungrily gulped by the parched mouth, so much so that a second trip was made to the stream. "Danke," the grateful pilot uttered, his black eyes teeming with unspoken thanks. Water was also poured over his head to provide some comfort.

What can I do with you? Chuck thought. *I can't take you with me, and I can't stay.*

Though severely wounded, the flyer reached into his tunic. His would-be rescuer, alarmed by the movement, backed away, suspecting a weapon. Withdrawn, the hand held a brown wallet, delivering a sense of relief. Holding it outward to Chuck, he uttered, "Die familie, elternyeil, danke."

"C'mon, let's get you out of here."

The resulting effort proved useless as both his legs had been badly smashed and pinned by the instrument panel and other structural damage. "Nein, nein," he moaned, his face etched in pain and realizing it was hopeless.

"Maybe somebody can help you, pal, I can't, heaven knows I tried." Perhaps he couldn't understand the words, but he felt the tone and knew his foe had tried his best. Just then, a burst of flame erupted from the engine and started to lick its way backward. Fuel from the ruptured tank had saturated the ground under the plane, a harbinger of disaster.

Horrified, Chuck again tried to extricate this broken soul from the cockpit but failed, so magnificent his efforts. The young man, knowing his fate, clasped both hands around Chuck's arm and pulled him close. "Danke, friend, see, I know some English," he said with a weak smile then said, "Go." With that, his body went limp and a small escape of breath from his mouth heralded his release from this earth. His eyes still peered ahead but could not see the American or anything else. Chuck lowered his eyelids and leaped from the craft, the fire approaching the cockpit.

Heading for his plane, he turned and raised his hand to salute a fallen warrior. This closeness erased the anonymity of war, and for that he was grateful, for it reminded him of the humanity infused in his being. He had been afraid that in the heat of combat or when boasting of his victories, this would have been forgotten. Enemy or not, they were real souls.

As he took off, the fire began to consume the plane in a huge pyre, bringing to mind the tradition of the Norsemen so long ago. A longboat, with the body of one of their own aboard, was guided into the waters and set afire. This was an honor to all those who were going to Valhalla. He circled several times and hoped his entry into Valhalla would be welcomed.

As he winged home, he knew he couldn't claim a victory by what he had done, which of course would end his service. Instead, relying on gun camera footage and verbal testimony that he had seen the plane crash, the claim could be verified. This was one kill he would always remember for more than one reason; most of which was the impact it had on him tending to a wounded foe.

The debriefing after landing was the usual, and he was congratulated for making ace. Ace, what a singular honor. His plane captain joyfully added the new cross to the other four.

Alone in his billet, he removed the wallet, some crimson still on the edges, and opened it, removing a photo, perhaps when the flyer was a boy in his teens. What may have been his parents flanked a tall boy, who had his arm around a smaller one, possibly his brother. Another photo, of a later date, showed the parents beaming with pride at a youthful son, dressed in a smart Luftwaffe uniform. Next an identification card. His name was Otto Bruner, twenty years old. Lord, only twenty.

A visiting Red Cross unit the next day provided Chuck with the only chance he saw for getting this back to the family, a longshot, but the only one he had. Approaching a worker, he explained his dilemma, minus the gruesome details. The woman took the wallet, smiling at Chuck.

"This is very considerate of you. We will be meeting with a Swiss delegation soon, and I am sure they will make an attempt to, er, excuse me, your name?"

"Ah, Lieutenant Charles Madson, ma'am."

Scribbling his name on a pad, she looked up and continued. "All efforts will be made by the delegation to forward the wallet, I'm sure."

"Thank you, ma'am."

The burden removed, he returned to the rec hall and reminisced about his encounter and only hoped it wouldn't repeat itself for obvious reasons. Soon, the war ended, and he returned home to be posted at Maguire Air Force base. While on furlough, he met a very enchanting young woman and, just as he did with flying, approached her with a dedicated zeal. The result was as certain as his victories in the air. Carol and he soon tied the knot, and the product of this union was his daughter, Jennifer. Completing his military obligation, they both settled in a beautiful suburb, Haddon Heights, New Jersey. A part-time job kept him active along with other pursuits.

Unexpectedly, he received a letter from the State Department, puzzling the retiree and his wife. The first page was a cover letter describing the following contents.

> Mr. Madson,
>
> The State Department received an inquiry by the Swiss embassy representing an interested party in locating you, the purpose of which is to facilitate the rendering of a communication. Having read the request, and approving it, I submitted any further steps to be taken up by the

Defense Department, as the request concerned your past military service and actions, as all records pertaining to you during that service are in their possession.

Holy cow, thought Chuck, *what the hey did I do?* Continuing reading the correspondence, he was informed that the second envelope contained the communication that was meant for him, the data provided by the Defense Department expediting the process.

Puzzled, he withdrew the envelope and withdrew the content. Opening the folded missive, he scanned the words that had been in the making for years.

> Herr Madson,
>
> I apologize that what you needed to know was late in coming. Let me explain. During the war, my brother Otto served in the Luftwaffe. I was younger than he but remembered him well enough to miss him when he was away. My parents were loving and doted on both of us. We received a notice from the air ministry stating that my brother was missing. My parents were inconsolable and grieved at the news that their son could not be accounted for. Their only hope was in the notification indicating a missing status, which gave them some semblance of hope. With the war over and no further word, their hearts were shattered with the almost certain knowledge that he was dead. Several years later, with a normalcy slowly being built in our nation, we received a notice from the Swiss consulate, that they wished to have my parents present themselves to their offices. It was there that they returned to them the wallet and photos of my brother. Their sadness was tempered by the knowledge of finally knowing his fate. Another

thing that brought some solace to them was the return of his last possessions.

Not so much in receiving them, than in the fact that you took pains to see that they were returned. We had many questions then, but now they seem unnecessary now to pursue them. Only know that your kindness brought a form of closure to my parents. While grieving his loss, we know that he was not alone at the end, and I think that is a measure of solace that can never be repaid except in our hearts.

Those years were turbulent in trying to rebuild our lives, and the wallet was put aside along with the accompanying correspondence providing your name and other identifiers. As time went by, other urgencies took precedent and, while inexcusable, resulted in the misplacement of your identity. Recently, my father passed away, and while gathering the necessary paperwork to settle his affairs, we discovered the information that had laid dormant for so long. My mother insisted that we return the overdue thanks deserved by your kindness. The Swiss were able to help us by getting in touch with your government. Explaining our plight, they seemed to move heaven and earth to obtain what we needed. As a result, we forwarded this letter to your government with the assurance you would receive it.

Again thank you for what you have done for our family,

Your servant, Hans Bruner

Chuck would keep that letter as a reminder of the two faces of war: conflict and mercy.

He and his wife built a wonderful life filled with friends and, of course, their daughter, Jennifer. He was a spiritual person and became an usher at church, and Carol always fussed over what he would wear that Sunday so he could look good. This was a form of jousting that both enjoyed by needling each other.

After forty-two years together, she sadly passed away. At the urging of his daughter, he reluctantly sold his home and moved in with her husband, Bernie. The clincher was the two grandsons that adored him. Their Poppy could do anything, as he recalled them bragging to anyone who would listen.

"Poppy, Poppy, wake up, are we goin' to the museum?"

He'd dropped off in one of those naps reserved for the men of his age, although he'd bristle if called *old*. "Older," he'd reply, "not old." Through a lazy yawn he out, "Okay, munchkins, kiss Mom goodbye and we're on our way."

Squealing with delight, they scrambled out the door and waited impatiently for the "older" man to open the car door. Ryan, the older of the two boys, was excited because it was a museum with airplanes. "Can we sit in them, Poppy?"

"I'm sure they'll allow it," he said with a knowing smile. CJ, the younger boy, usually followed his brother's lead—if he liked anything, so would he.

The Victory Air Museum, located on the site of a small airport, was a product of aviation enthusiasts who had pooled their resources to provide a very inclusive array of aircraft, from vintage to modern. Pete McAllister was the manager who was a friend of Chuck's. Whenever a new craft came in, he'd always call him so that he could examine and critique the new addition. It was a courtesy, and both enjoyed the give-and-take that eventually developed. To say the boys were captivated would be putting it mildly. Their eyes were as big as saucers as the dormant machines still exerted an influence just by being there.

"Hey, Paul," called Pete, "keep an eye on the kids for a few minutes."

"What's up, Pete?"

"Got somethin' to show ya." They walked to the rear of the building when his friend nudged him. "Like it?"

Chuck's face brightened up with a smile and an "Oh, wow, where'd this come from?" Before him lay a very familiar form that he'd never forgotten, an old friend from the past. His initial joy was tempered by the sad condition of what once was a stately and inspiring sight to most who saw it. In dreadful condition, as if wounded by a hunter, rested a P-51 Mustang, a plane he loved. "Where'd you get it, Pete?"

"Josh Butler. Does restoration work and wanted to unload it. Said that he has too many projects, and it was taking up space. He wanted to scrap it, figuring the parts were worth more than the plane. I'd been toying with the idea of adding to the collection and figured I could work with it, so I made a deal with him, reasonable too. But ya know, I bit off a little more than I could chew. I'm thinkin' of recoupin' my investment by selling it, but I haven't made a decision yet."

Chuck stared at this past beauty and mentally wept. To see an icon of air superiority degraded into a lump of lifeless metal.

"Hey, buddy, I've got a few things to do, and I know you'll want to have a closer look. Take your time." As Pete left, the former pilot felt the pull of years earlier with his first Mustang. He approached slowly, as if attending a wake, the sight stirring long-dormant memories. The painted emblems had faded, the nose art was covered with soot, and the gleam of the aluminum wings and fuselage tarnished by layers of grime. To add to the dismal sight was the odd tilt of the aircraft, rendered so with the left landing gear folded under the wing.

What a sad ending and for a moment he wished he hadn't been shown the plane. He leaped onto the wing and accessed the cockpit. The interior mirrored the same disarray; this was his office so long ago. An impulse motivated him to climb in, and he seated himself, half expecting his plane captain to strap him in.

He closed his eyes and tried to remember the sweet sound of his Merlin engine coming to life. He tried to remember his release from the earth as he soared into the sky, an elation that never diminished. He peered over what would have been the gun sight, to view the sleek lines of the engine cowling. Glancing to the side, something caught his eye. He pulled out his hanky, spitting on the cloth, and rubbed the area in question. As the grime was removed bit by bit, what started to appear electrified Chuck.

"Holy cow, I don't believe it. It can't be real." But it was real. Staring in disbelief, his eyes welded themselves to the long-ago etched initials *CAM* and the date.

This was *his* plane! His partner for all those missions. He sat stunned, not wanting to know how it became a derelict, not wanting to feel the sorrow that the machine would have if it were alive. He patted the coaming as if to provide solace.

"Hey, Chuck, what do you think?" yelled Pete, returning from his errand and interrupting a sober reverie. Alighting from the plane, Chuck told Pete about what he found. "No kiddin', what are the odds on the—?" He could see that the former flyer was down, so he dropped the subject. "Gee, those kids of yours are great fun," he spouted, hoping that would do the trick. Perking a little, visualizing their predictable antics, he asked if they'd been any problem. "Not at all."

"Hey, Poppy, we had some cool things to look at and do. We both even sat in one of the planes," Ryan delightfully chirped as he grabbed his grandfather in an energetic hug.

"Okay, mites. Let's hit the road."

The little voices oohing and ahhing all the way home lightened his mood somewhat, but he couldn't shake a nagging feeling from the past. At home the two cherubs scooted in the house as always, corralling their mother with vivid expressions of their adventure.

"Hi, Dad, I guess the boys really...what's the matter, Dad? You don't look right." Concern written on her face. He was an old man, and any change that indicated a problem worried her.

"Naw, I'm okay, just tired. Gonna take a short nap. I'll be in for supper."

"You sure, Dad?"

"Yah, I'm fine," he whispered as he kissed her on the forehead. Closing the door to his room, he slumped into his sofa and tried to put in order the events of the day. It wasn't just knowing that this was his plane. It was deeper than that. Something he had submerged in his consciousness, something that he knew happened but wasn't really sure if it did. It was one of those mysteries that defied a definition much less a solution.

Reluctantly, but with a knowing resignation, he reeled his memory back to that fateful day. Flying homeward, his flight became a flak target. A loud crash on his fuselage indicated a strike which violently tossed his plane from its line of flight. In doing so, Chuck's head was slammed into the canopy, dazing him. At the same time the aircraft began a dive which, for the moment, he was unable to prevent. With such a clean design, the speed mounted phenomenally, and certain destruction was imminent. Gradually, his head began to clear, and he responded to his predicament by hauling back on the stick, horror etched on his face.

The effort seemed to be mired in concrete as the movement was minuscule. The earth reached for him like a long-lost lover, the looming disintegration doubling his resolve and strength to avoid it. Gradually the nose began to hint at success, the horizon lowering to almost touching it, but was it too late? *It's not enough,* he frantically thought, as the pressure forced his tired body into the recesses of his seat. With that, a gray haze enveloped his consciousness, perhaps a blessing to what would be a violent end.

As the fighter continued its descent, a shining mist appeared in its path, as if inviting it to enter. Gradually, Chuck's head began to clear, trying to put things together and quizzically wondering why his plane was still flying, knowing it had to crash. Where was he? What was shrouding his plane? A streak of blinding light pierced the fleece-like covering, causing him to shield his wincing eyes. Emerging into a clear blue and inviting sky, he marveled at being alive, the first miracle.

The second miracle was spotting a landing strip below, but whose? It didn't matter, he had to land his damaged plane before it fell apart. Approaching the end of the runway, he lowered his landing gear and glided onto the runway. He can't be faulted for ignoring an anomaly that his intensity for self-preservation prevented him from observing. He taxied down the runway when he observed a vehicle heading his way. He fingered his shoulder holster, ready to extract his .45-caliber automatic in case it was an unfriendly visit.

Breathing a sigh of relief, he recognized the undeniable form of a jeep. He braked the plane as the driver waved to him and then turned the jeep around, displaying Follow Me imprinted on a placard. With his eyes intensely glued to his guide, again the anomaly eluded him. Finally an empty space appeared into which the jeep led the craft. Happy to have landed in one piece and on a friendly base, he leaped from the plane and approached, no, he excitedly ran to greet the driver. He stepped from the vehicle and presented a crisp salute. Chuck was almost tempted to hug him, so relieved as he was, when he was addressed by the sergeant.

"Welcome, Lieutenant Madson. We're glad you made it."

"Wha…how do you know my name? Oh, yeah, my guys probably reported me missing and called it in."

"Not exactly so, sir, but all this will be explained to you. Please, let me drive you to headquarters and you'll be briefed."

Jumping into the jeep and turning onto the runway, the anomaly now became evident. "Sergeant, why are there so many different aircraft types lined up? Are they shooting a documentary or somethin'?"

"No, sir."

"But this is unbelievable, and there, that's a biplane."

"Yes, sir, it belongs to Frank Luke."

"Oh, it's like a museum, right, a collection of various aircraft?"

"Not exactly, sir."

Confused, he witnessed many aircrafts that didn't belong in this theatre of war. "How about that P-38? Most are operating in the Pacific, right?"

"Yes, sir. That machine belongs to Tommy Maguire. Oh, there he is now, inspecting it like he does every day."

"What? That's impossible because he's…"

"Yes, sir."

"Are you telling me that I'm…"

"You got it, sir." Stunned, he tried to speak, but the words just backed up into his throat, finally bursting out with an uncontrollable flurry. "Whoa, Lieutenant, calm down. Everyone who comes in acts the same way, but it's not anything to worry about."

Nothing to worry about? Chuck screamed to himself. *I'm supposed to be dead, and he says nothing to worry about?*

Gaining some composure and influenced by an intense curiosity about the different planes, he prodded the sergeant, asking why there were some planes attended to and others sat alone.

"That's the interesting part. Those pilots, like you, are with the planes they arrived in. Orders from the Boss."

"What about the others?"

"Those planes are prepped and ready to receive the pilots who flew them but whose time hasn't arrived." He pointed to some examples, such as Dick Bong's P-38, Frank "Gabby" Gabreski, his powerful P-47 ready and waiting. Other names he recognized, while others eluded him, some already present, others to arrive at their time.

"But what about those other planes? They don't even have propellers. How do they fly?"

"All that will be explained too, sir. We have a great ready room, and I'm sure you'll enjoy the camaraderie."

Line after line of aircraft flowed past his eyes, his bewilderment uncontainable. Finally, they approached what appeared to be control tower, administration center, and base ops all rolled into one. It was military all right, but inviting and warm. He paused by the jeep, gazing over a huge complex. They entered, the sentinels sharply saluting and presenting arms.

"If I'm…ya know, why do the guards have rifles?"

"Ceremonial, sir. We have nothing to fear, but like to make the new arrivals feel welcomed with procedures they were used to."

Hell, he thought, *I didn't get too many impression like that when I was…oh well, that's in the past.* They proceeded past the welcoming desk, where a corporal checked off his name. Chuck was very impressed that he hadn't even asked for it. They strode down an immaculate hall, their footsteps bounding off the tiled floors and preceding their progress. The walls were festooned with hundreds of photos, pilots past and present. The layout was spartan, befitting a fighting organization, although not drab. They passed several offices, administrative and otherwise, to service the function of…what was the function? Chuck thought, as he followed the sergeant. At the end of the hall appeared an ornate double door, adorned with aviator wings.

"This is it, sir," the sergeant quipped. "Please follow me." They entered a large anteroom with a WAC receptionist seated at a large desk.

"Welcome, gentlemen. New arrival, Sergeant?"

"Just came in, ma'am."

"The adjutant will see you immediately," she responded, pointing to a door and motioning both men to enter. Inside, a gentle-looking old man, dressed in a uniform of the past, looked up from a mound of paperwork and addressed the duo.

"What do you have for me, son?" The sergeant handed him a sheet of paper. "This is our new arrival?"

"Yes, sir, just came in."

"As if I don't have enough work to do. Oh well, let's see what's what," the harried administrator groaned. "Hmmm," he sounded as he leafed through a pile of papers and then another stack. Back and forth he searched for something, while a nervous lieutenant stood at ease, of which he was not. "You sure this is correct?" he questioned the sergeant.

"Yes, sir, as far as I know. This was the information given me."

The old man was kindly and glanced apologetically at the lieutenant for the delay.

"Oh my dear, this is embarrassing," he muttered. Pulling a file from the heap of papers, he lamented, "I didn't see this before. It seems, Sergeant, an error has been made."

"Error, sir?"

"Yes, this young man has not been slated for arrival, it's a mistake."

"Mistake, sir?"

"Yes, you're going to have to send him back."

What? Send me back? I'm dead and they want to send me back? To where? How? Why? Chuck recoiled in a mental frenzy.

"I'm sorry, young man," the adjutant said, a sad look in his eyes and unspoken understanding as to what Chuck must be going through.

The sergeant saluted and nudged Chuck, who followed him out the door.

"This doesn't happen too often, sir."

"Now what?"

"I'm taking you back to your plane."

They walked down the corridor, a thousand thoughts running through a thoroughly shaken airman.

"Look, I was the star attraction of the day, and now I'm chicken liver. You don't run a very effective outfit here."

"Sorry about that, sir, but even here we're not perfect. Things will work out."

"What's that supposed to mean?"

"You'll be flying out, sir."

"But the damage."

"Out here it really doesn't matter. You came in just fine, and you'll leave the same way."

I'll wake up, I'll wake up, he muttered to himself, hoping it was a dream on the verge of ending. No such luck. Reaching his plane, the sergeant helped Chuck with his flight gear, assisted his climb to the cockpit, and adjusted his harness as he settled into his seat.

"Don't think too badly of us, sir, maybe we'll meet again if I'm still here."

Surrendering to the inevitable, Chuck offered his hand to the amiable sergeant, smiled, and taxied to the runway. Pulling his goggles down, he glanced once more at the display of aeronautical genius parked along the perimeter.

Looking at the fluttering windsock to gauge wind direction, he guided the Mustang to the correct airstrip. Running up the revs on his Merlin, he began his takeoff run. The abrupt lightness of the plane indicated the separation from earth, the elation of flight a tonic to his sorely abused nerves. His final instruction was to fly at a certain altitude, on any course he chose. Moments later, a billowing cloud appeared in his flight path. As he approached, a gray haze overcame his consciousness as his plane plunged into the yielding vapor.

Emerging from the mist, the Mustang was in the same diving predicament that Chuck was trying to manage when they first disappeared. *What the heck, didn't I just go through this before?*

The emergency of the moment forestalled any attempt to make sense of anything. Again he strained and strained until the wounded bird began to lift its head toward the sky. In what seemed like an eternity, which was what he faced, the fighter cleared a stand of trees with not too much to spare. His heart pounding and the sweat beginning to ooze from every pore on his body, he turned on a course which would take him home. Too much time to think, too much time to wonder if it was real or a dream. When he sided with one notion, another would replace it, the uncertainty taking a toll on his now fragile nature.

Several aircraft joined up with him, the company most welcome. His flight most likely had returned to base and no doubt had reported his plane as probably lost. As he lined up for a touchdown, he saw a group of men near his unit's placement stands. Each position contained an aircraft, except one, his. He barely cut his engine after parking when a throng of guys jumped onto the wing and overwhelmed him with expressions of relief and of course the questions. The questions. Sticking to what he only knew as factual, he described the flak burst and losing control of his aircraft; how he struggled, and managing to avoid a near-fatal dive.

Even if he wanted to tell them the other side of the story, the fantasy of it all would be impossible to explain. No, he'd keep this to himself, and even then, he wanted to forget it altogether. With the passing of time, it faded, slowly, until he forced the entire episode into the furthest corner of his mind. It was there, but like an unwelcome neighbor, he refused to visit. Until today.

He really couldn't answer as to why he had an aversion to this experience. He wasn't a coward, that was proven in combat. Perhaps if it was real, would he still be accepted after being rejected? If it wasn't real, the only thing he lost was sleep. It was not being able to reconcile these two different possibilities that plagued him.

With the help of the boys, he turned to other grandfatherly pursuits that helped him cope. Their mirth and merriment could banish any cloud, and he eagerly indulged with them. Maybe one day, finally he'd come to terms with his past. Not too long afterward, he received a call from Pete. He had called an airplane parts distributor after deciding he couldn't take on the Mustang project. As a courtesy, he wanted to know if Chuck would like to come down and maybe salvage some souvenirs from the hulk before he sold it.

He felt a sharp twinge. This was an old friend, and now its days were numbered.

"When's he comin' over?"

"Day after tomorrow."

"Okay, I'll be there in the morning. Thanks for the heads-up, Pete."

"Least I could do, buddy, see ya tomorrow."

The next morning, he told his daughter where he'd be heading, regretting having to see the final days of his aluminum warrior. Entering the shop, Pete was overseeing a shipment at the loading dock.

"Hi, Chuck. As soon as I finish here, we can go and take a look."

"Take your time." Spotting the lounge chair, he decided to plop and maybe read a magazine or two.

For a short time, he skimmed through parts of outdated issues and then decided to go over to the plane and see what he'd like to strip. He approached slowly, a somber feeling starting to creep up on him. This was it, the end! He visualized the beauty that once graced this magnificent aircraft and how the hand of fate decreed its demise. Stepping upon the downed wing, he inched his way to the cockpit, his office so many years ago.

Unable to resist the urge, he slipped into the seat, pulled the canopy past his head, and took a glance at the initials he had baptized the plane with. That rendering made a bond that rivaled many a friendships he'd forged. Alongside the seat was a weather-beaten leather head covering, the goggles seeing better days. Chuckling, he donned the gear to relive the old days.

He leaned back against the headrest, reminiscing about the adventures he was part of and proud of his service.

Imperceptibly, a change started to manifest itself then became more evident. "Now what?" he whispered, unsure of what was occurring. As he watched, the yellow tinge and soot that had marred the canopy's sleek lines began to dissolve and retreat, melting away to reveal a pristine surface.

Transfixed, he was aware of a similar process occurring on the wings. The grime and dirt, the stains of unknown contributors, also began to relinquish their hold, showcasing a gleaming aura. Adding to that, the left wing began to ascend to its proper position, the ugly tilt removed. A damaged propeller stiffened its bent blades to align perfectly on the hub. Not to be outdone, the glare panel on the nose cowling regained its former glory, the charcoal coloring accenting the polished aluminum. Accompanying this transformation was the resplendent colors of the various markings that identified the nationality and unit.

Another dream! No, not again. This can't be happening. His mental protestations failed to abort the change in progress. Now the instrument panel shone as brightly as the day it was installed, and the gun sight now adorned its proper position. He felt a shift in his clothing and looked down to see the uniform he'd worn in battle, clean and creased. It was then that he surrendered to whatever force had bedeviled him. *Whatever comes will come,* he thought, finally feeling the peace of release.

As if responding to his will, the propeller started to rotate, slowly at first then faster and faster, accompanying the sweet roar of his Merlin engine. Gradually some sense of purpose and understanding began to dawn on him. Fully engaged in the reanimation of his plane, he began to smile. It was over. No, it was beginning. And so it was, for over his intercom came the order, "You are cleared for takeoff. You are cleared for takeoff."

The Mustang lurched forward and gained speed as he pulled back on the stick to haul it into the air. Ahead was a billowing cloud, and as before, it swallowed the resurrected man of war. Chuck had a parting thought: *Sergeant, I do hope you'll remember me.* And then he was gone.

"Hey, Paul, is Chuck still here?"

"Yeah, boss, he's sitting in the lounge chair up front."

Pete was a good friend and wanted to make sure that Chuck got what he wanted. "Sorry to hold you up, buddy, but I'm ready now to…er…Chuck, Chuck, hey, Chuck, wake up." He looked asleep, a peaceful sleep that was in reality a release from his earthly presence. Pete stood and looked with sadness, realizing his friend was gone, a great guy.

His mood was somber and hesitant when the distributor arrived the next day to assess the Mustang. They both walked to the plane, the agent circling the downed bird and commenting that the "heap" might bring some value to his company. The reference stung Pete, but it reinforced what he had decided to do.

"I'm sorry, but I've changed my mind. It belonged to a good friend of mine. It wouldn't be right sellin' it."

"Okay, if you change your mind, call."

Don't worry, buddy, I'll keep her safe, he vowed. *I hope, ole man, that you'll find a peace uniting you and your other squadron mates,* he quietly prayed.

Yes, Pete, another patriot was reporting for heavenly duty.

The Little Ones

The MacKenzie Tree Farm transformed magically as the MacKenzie Christmas Tree Farm when that joyous holiday approached. The white pines, Douglas firs, blue spruces, and other species were grown and groomed, waiting for the flood of families seeking to pick the perfect tree. For years, the family had been touted as the best place to harvest a symbol of Christmas, and very few passed up the opportunity to test that label.

Each spring, the planters would cull the dying or undeveloped stands and plant new ones. Growth would take a few years, but a rotating system guaranteed that full-size specimens would always be available. This was a business, and as such, care was taken to ensure a product in ready supply but also attractive. During the growing season and even up till the special day of celebration, the trimmers would correct any malformed tree into a respectful, if not a handsome addition to the living room for display.

There was also a sentiment, some would say fanciful, in that the owners and workers felt a certain attachment to the creations they tended to, seeing each tree as a source of happiness and inspiration to the customers. The smiles of the buyers with their children were a tribute to their product and the brightness it was sure to create.

Not all planting went smoothly or produced the desired effect, but that was the gamble any business was exposed to. But the successes overwhelmed the drawbacks and with it the pursuit of filling any void, lest there be fewer trees for the animated tree searchers.

This was the atmosphere that prevailed all year long, as the off holiday season was also quite busy with lengthy orders by landscapers and the green thumb of the homeowners who sought to beautify their grounds.

Tom MacKenzie, the eldest of four sons, managed the farm for his father, who was semiretired but still contributed his input when asked or volunteered. They shared a similar view of the farm, what it meant to them financially, and all endeavors were made to ensure that end.

Of the various plots that were selected for planting, one would contain Douglas firs, a hardy evergreen. Many dozens were planted, and the start-up for their growth began. It was in this gathering of saplings that the certain aura of companionship would develop. After two seasons of growth, the field looked pretty good. Tom and his father inspected each and every tree to weed out the nonperformers or to trim those in need of shaping. The sameness of the work ensured perfection, a master's touch with the shearing tools a work of art.

"Son," Tom's father called, "I don't like the looks of this one." He was pointing to a small evergreen. Compared to the others, it was smaller, smaller than normal.

"Let me see, Dad," he responded, carefully sizing up the small evergreen. "Hmm," he mused to himself as he circled its form, looking at every branch and the trunk itself. "Pop, I think you're concerned about its size, but to tell you the truth, it's a pretty little thing."

"Ya, I know, but if it's a dud, we lose the space it's in. That's not good business."

His father was not a hard man but from the old school, growing up and poor, where sentiment had no place in putting food on the table. This had been ingrained into his work ethic, thus the prosperous business he had built. It was difficult for him to reverse that attitude, but when kindly persuasion was used, he would give in.

"Look, Pop, it's only one tree. I'd like to see if we can make it flourish. Think of it as a challenge."

"Okay, but it's on you," looking at the tree over his shoulder as he walked away. Tom called one of the workers over and directed him to work the soil around the tree and add what nutrients that might help. For the rest of the season, up until the Christmas feast, due care was given.

As the third growing season for the plot began, Tom inspected his project and was a little disappointed. No measurable growth was evident; however, its form was ideal.

"Any luck with the outcast?" His father chuckled.

"Could it be that piece of ground has a deficiency and can't provide what the tree needs?" Tom murmured to himself.

"If that's the case," his father replied, "that's one unlucky fella, considering all the acreage we have and it landed on the worst part."

"Are you ready, Chip?" inquired a father as his son donned his coat.

"Almost, Daddy" was the cheerful reply. Terry Hartford beamed at his five-year-old son, a sign that today would be filled with all kinds of adventures.

"Are you sure he can do this?" his wife, Maddy, asked with a wistful look at the bundle of excitement raring to go. "The doctor said to keep him from getting becoming too excited or exhausting himself and he should be fine." The little guy held on to his daddy's hand with both of his, peering upward, returning his father's gaze.

"Okay, sport, let's go." The urging was not needed as the tyke moved as fast as his condition allowed.

"Beat ya, Daddy." He laughed as the father took him up in his arms and gave a gentle squeeze along with a kiss on his forehead. "Yuk, Dad, that's what you an' Mom do, not me!" he shrieked a delicious comeback. All tucked in, they headed for the land of enchantment, for that was what it meant to the boy. Terry looked at his son with deep affection and a silent prayer always on his mind if not his lips.

It hurt that all he could do was to follow the doctor's advice and medication when needed. The affliction was fairly rare but could be fatal if care was not taken. With this in mind, he resolved that nothing would harm his son, praying to God that this was one angel he'd not need for quite some time.

Arriving at the farm, Tom's father, Mike, met the pair as they approached the grove of greenery stretching from one field to another. Chip jumped excitedly at the prospect of running into this man-made forest to find the perfect tree.

"C'mon, Dad," he quipped, pulling on his hand in an exaggerated tug, his father allowing himself to be herded into the maze of growth. He bathed in the exuberance of his son's eagerness, hoping that this expression of unresisting glee would be as effective as any medicine might be.

Tree after tree did not surrender to the scrutiny of the tiny purveyor, as he leaped from one to another. Mike reacted to the antics with a small chuckle as he approached Terry.

"Looks pretty intense, doesn't he?"

"Mike, it's almost, just almost as good as medicine," the elder man said, knowing of the boy's condition. The families had known each other for years. In fact, Terry worked on the farm as a teenager. The friendship was further strengthened when the MacKenzies held a benefit barbecue to raise money for the boy's treatment.

"Well, whatever he picks will probably be the best one I got. Can I hire him as a tree greeter?"

"Ya know, Mike, he'd probably fill the bill."

"I believe you're right."

Chip's bounding inspections came to a sudden halt. He now stood before the orphan of the grove, his eyes roving over every branch and needle. It was almost a reverent posture.

"Terry, look at your son. He seems frozen."

"Whatever it is, it sure seems to have a lock on him." Approaching the boy, his father laid a soft hand on his shoulder. "What's up, Chip."

His lips had been moving in sync with visions plowing through his nimble mind, all generated by this lonesome pine. "Gee, Daddy, I like this tree, but it seems so alone."

"What do you mean, son?"

"It's smaller than the others, and I think it might be scared."

"Oh, you mean intim…er." He paused to find the right words, something a five-year-old could grasp. After all, this is a tree for Pete's sake, he chided himself. "Well, Chip, if it were alive like you and me, yes, I guess he'd feel unprotected, but just like our family, these other trees are his family, and I think they'd take good care of him."

The boy smiled, and his dad could see the beaming glow in his eyes, reassured that the little fir was in good company. It also filled Terry with this gift of happiness that a few words inspired. It strengthened his belief in the healing nature so evident in the joy embracing his ailing son. A field hand sauntered by and, seeing the pair invested in the diminutive sprig, remarked, "You're better off getting a bigger one, that there will be mulch tomorrow." Although the boy didn't know the meaning of what mulch meant, the tone and suggestion struck him with horror. He instinctively knew a cruel fate awaited this orphan. Looking up at his dad, his eyes began to water.

"Daddy, they can't take my tree, please, please."

The word *my* conveyed a bonding that removed all doubt as to the pending fate of his son's concern. He arranged with Mike to prepare the tree for the journey home.

"Sure, Terry, I'll have it cut down."

"No, Mr. Mike, please," Chip said, startling the man with this sudden outburst. "I don't want you to hurt it."

"That's a good idea, Mike," said Terry. "If it makes him happy, I'm happy too."

"No problem, Terry."

Digging the pine from the ground, he wrapped the balled dirt and roots with burlap and carried it to the car. Chip dogged his every step, watching and guiding the man with his youthful zest.

"Watch out for that hole, Mr. Mike" or "There's a person in your way."

Mike smiled and voiced his appreciation for the help the little guy was sincerely providing. Securing the netted bundle to the roof of the car, Mike bade Terry farewell, wishing him the best for Christmas and thanking Chip for his "invaluable" help.

"Anytime, Mr. Mike, and when I'm older, maybe I can help with trees, since I know a lot more now."

"You bet, son. I'm goin' to put you down on the payroll in a few years."

His mouth agape, he turned and looked up at his father, who returned a very comforting comeback. "See, you showed them your stuff." He said that with some reservation in his mind, hoping the boy's condition would improve to the point where this magic could truly happen. Jumping into the car, Chip urged his father to hurry so that he could tell Mom all the good news. The drive home was peppered with the boy's questions and scenarios he laid out for the decoration of the tree.

His mind had conceived a grand display, and Dad would have to make it happen, but of course, he'd provide advice and direction. After a short while, the excitement of the day took its toll, the boy speaking very slowly then not at all. His peaceful face displayed contentment and a well-deserved rest. So sound was his sleep that his father carried him into the house and up to his bedroom. Removing his clothes, he nestled his firebrand under the covers, placing a tender kiss on his forehead.

"Night, Daddy," the drowsy son intoned very wearily and turned on his side, now completely divorced from the world.

"How'd he do?" Maddy asked when he entered the family room.

"I wish you'd seen him. He was a firecracker and made an impression on Mike."

"I saw the tree, was that the best you could find?"

"For Chip, it is. You should have seen the way he looked at it and how he reacted when he thought they were going to cut it up. Maddy, that tree was more of a tonic than that medicine he's been gulping."

"He didn't overdo it, did he?"

"A tad, but the kind that can only light up his zest for new challenges, after all, he's a kid."

Snuggling against her husband's broad shoulders, she sniffed very lightly, a sign of tears to follow.

"Hey, don't go south on me. He did great, nothing to worry about."

"I know, sweetheart, it just seems so unfair. He's only a child."

"Yeah, but a spunky one. You know what I really love about him is that he knows he's sick but doesn't milk it or show any sign of self-pity. Maddy, our son will be okay." That last part was only a fervent hope, something he had no control over except to pray hard.

The following morning, the little sprite jumped into bed with his father, shaking him awake. "Hey, what's up, sport?" No sign of displeasure at the rude awakening.

"The tree, Daddy, the tree."

"Plenty of time for that later. Here, slide in beside me and your mother."

"Hmm, it's nice and warm, Daddy." Placing each of his outstretched arms under the necks of his parents, his dewy eyes closed with contentment and a soft snort.

"Hey, you guys, breakfast," Maddy called from the kitchen. Again the race to the breakfast table was won by Chip, who playfully gloated to his father.

"No fair, I was shaving." He grabbed the boy and tickled him silly, the shrieks, if heard by an outsider, who have indicated mayhem. This was followed by a hug and kiss, which again aroused the boy's sense of yuckiness. "Wait till you're older and you meet a girl. You'll change your tune."

"Uh-uh," he spouted back.

"We'll see," his father laughingly responded, tousling the child's hair into a disheveled mess.

After breakfast, Chip's mood changed. He put his arms around his mother's thighs and lightly groaned. Disturbed, Maddy knelt down and held him close.

"What's the matter, sweetheart?"

"I don't feel too good, Mommy." This was not unusual, given his condition, but was of great concern because it was the comfort of their son that mattered the most.

"C'mere, sport," his father quipped, picking up the little bundle tenderly and walking to the family room.

He placed the boy in the sofa chair close to a warming blaze in the fireplace. Draping a throw across his body, Terry brushed his hair back and caressed his tiny face with a soft brush of his hand. "Guess what, squirt?"

With a subdued response, the boy answered back, "What, Daddy?"

"You sit here and rest. I'll be right back." Passing through the kitchen and reassuring Maddy that the boy was resting, he went outside to the car. Unlimbering the netted package on the roof, he reentered the house and proceeded to the family room. The boy was semidozing, unaware of his father's presence.

Cutting the netting from the tree, he placed the ball root into a large ceramic pot and straightened the figure so that it was perfectly erect. Chip's eyes opened, and what was an indifferent posture now became rigid with excitement. "Daddy, Daddy, the tree." Before his father could do anything, the boy escaped the warmth of the throw and scampered up to the green fir, standing transfixed before its diminutive form. Terry noticed the fire in his son's eyes that contrasted sharply from what it had been before.

The little fella's body seemed to be invigorated, no sign of a tired pup just moments before.

"Maddy, come here," Terry called. Hurrying into the room, hoping nothing extreme had happened to her boy, Terry pointed to their son and his apparent resurgence. The tot moved from side to side, eyeing every branch and, if possible, every needle. He turned toward his parents and let out a gleeful squeal.

"Daddy, Mommy, look! My tree!" With both of them relieved, they placed their boy between them, each holding a hand.

"You bet it's your tree, Chip, and tomorrow, we'll put all the trimmin's on it."

"I can help, Daddy?"

"Of course, squirt, it's your tree." Whatever magic or power or whatever you'd call it, the small needled form had wrought a remarkable change, its effect galvanizing an elusive hope for normalcy in the lad's condition. "Okay, my man, you get some rest now, because I'm goin' to work you hard tomorrow."

Picking the little fella from the floor into his arms, he strode to the sofa chair and, with a sigh of relief, sat down, cradling the still-animated bundle. Nestling his head against his father's chest, the tyke slowly unwound and soon fell asleep.

The spike in the emotions that Terry felt slowly subsided. Was it too much to believe that a turn for the better was in sight?

While encouraging, he knew that this one offshoot of hope had to be taken with caution, not wanting to invest too much into something that may evaporate as suddenly as it appeared. The following morning found the family gathered around the tree, decorations being festooned on every branch. The few that fell to the floor and broke were cause for laughter and ribbing, especially for Chip, who, with his small hands, contributed his share of demolition.

The trimming was pleasant and eventually finished.

"Daddy, I feel a little tired."

"Well, you did quite a bit. Let's take a rest." Picking up his boy, Terry laid him on the sofa and covered him. The look on his son's face showed that it was a good tiredness, not brought on by his condition. For this he was grateful.

The next day, Chip was taken to his doctor for a follow-up exam. Afterward, the doctor informed the parents that he was pleased with the results of his examination of the child. He cautioned however that it remained to be seen if this was a maintainable progression. As a doctor, he marveled at the improvement, as he had seen other cases that lingered for some time before improving, if at that.

Driving home, a sense of relief enveloped Terry and Maddy, tempered by the doctor's warning. But even so, they couldn't suppress their growing hope of better things to come. And indeed they deserved it.

Whenever the boy stood near the tree, one could only imagine the attraction each brought to the other, especially if a tree could react at all. Whatever the reason, the benefits to the boy and especially his parents were an early Christmas present. Still, the boy still had a life away from the tree, not just a preoccupation.

Well, maybe a little bit of one.

Christmas was celebrated with all the solemnity and joy it occasioned. After the New Year, Terry took the balled plant behind the house and placed it into a predug hole. Carefully spreading the burlap from the soil and roots, he placed rich soil around the base and packed it firmly but not too tight. A generous layer of black root mulch protected it to some degree. The telling would be in the spring if the tree had taken root.

Chip would gaze out from the kitchen window, asking his father if the tree would be okay. He was honest with his son, laying out all the pros and cons, so that if things didn't work out, the boy wouldn't be caught by surprise.

"Well, Chip, these plants do okay in all kinds of weather, but first they have to be in the ground long enough to let their roots take hold."

"You mean if the tree likes the dirt, it will be okay?" His simple observation was close enough to the truth.

"I think so, buddy, but I don't want you to worry so much."

"But, Daddy, it's all alone out there."

"Well, he has you for a friend, so I don't think he will be alone."

"I'm going to visit him every day to make sure he's okay." The intensity of the boy's vow encouraged Terry that perhaps this was the motivational asset needed for his recovery. It was a longshot, but there were definite signs for the better. Now, time would tell if they proved correct.

The joyous season of spring arrived, still a little chilly, but bracing. The winter had kept the youngster inside most of the time, and now he spread his wings, so to speak. He ran up to the fir, eyeing it with studious intensity, every branch and needle, so it seemed, at the mercy of his scrutiny. Circling it several times, he yelled out to his father.

"Daddy, Daddy, look. The ends of the branches are different colors!"

"That's because the tree is growing. The different colors show that the roots did 'like' the dirt."

The little guy beamed at his friend, as he would with one of his pals. Before the fall had arrived, a foot of new growth adorned the tree. "Gee, Daddy, it's getting bigger than me." His boyhood delight was infectious and carried over into dinner. "Mommy, you should see how big it got, and Daddy says it will get bigger." Her spoken reply was mentally assisted by a prayer that her son might be whole again.

The following trip to the doctor's office might seem that the prayer was answered, at least in part. The doctor, usually a very conservative physician in his diagnosis, appeared very optimistic. Kiddingly, he retorted, "I don't know what you're feeding him, but keep it up." This jovial banter swelled the hopes of the Hartfords, bringing some tears to Maddy's grateful eyes.

Every day, Chip would stand in front of the growing fir as if he were talking to someone or something embedded in its branches. Whatever one may have thought, there could be no denying that somehow, this plant of nature had, in some unknown way, became part of a little boy's imagination. And any child's imagination is beyond any scriptwriter's ability to replicate.

Every year saw added growth to the once ignored and threatened tree, its greenery flourishing in soil that was mixed not only with soil and mulch but a fervent hope that what succeeded for the tree would be the same for a young boy. And as if to prove the fulfilling of that hope, the boy standing before the looming growth was now a young man. And with him was his five-year-old son. When he was old enough to understand, Chip related his relationship with the once overlooked fir on a path to extinction.

"Gee, Daddy, it's bigger than you."

"Yes, it is, Chipper, but once it was only a little bigger than you."

"Really?"

"Really."

If one were to fathom the almost mystical bonding of two imperfect specimens, what would their conclusions be? That the tree healed the boy, or that the boy saved the tree? Whatever their findings, suffice it to say that something did happen that ensured the survival of these two creations of God.

Forever

Michael "Mickey" Harris is one of those irrepressible young men who can turn a gloomy rainy Monday morning into just a distraction by his sunny disposition. His gaiety is matched by his jubilant energy, as he trolls the city streets in his delivery van. Having started a floral business a few months earlier, he has dominated the art of not only creating beautiful displays but of also selling them.

Word of mouth is the best advertisement to ensure a flock of customers and in his case, the results were great. Having attended a college near home, he became fascinated with plants and flowers in the horticultural department. Taking the course, he became quite proficient in growing and artfully displaying the colorful and aroma-drenched blossoms. The next step, urged on by his mother, was to start his own shop after graduating.

His student counselor was of immense help in sketching a plan to obtain the necessary funding and sources of supply. It was a heady experience but one the young man was eager to tackle. His immense popularity was a magnate that drew suggestions and offers of help from his classmates. This alone was a source of encouragement that dispelled any doubts he may have had.

Prior to graduating, he scouted the area for a suitable location and was pleased to find an empty shop that had been closed for so long, which the leaser was only too glad to offer a very reasonable rental agreement. Not yet ready to start, it was a risky move, but the deal was too solid to pass up.

Mickey recalled his younger days when his father was rooted in the family garden, all kinds of vegetable plants receiving tender care by his father. Maybe this was how he got the itch to pursue his goal. Smell 'em or eat 'em, it was all the same. Mom would laugh when he bit into a pepper with the unusual biting taste that had him scouting for the water hose. He had fun poking around the different plants and listened with interest as his father described each vegetable, adding some questionable attribute to a particular specimen, such as the carrot.

"You see, son, if you eat carrots, they're good for your eyes."

"You sure, Daddy?" the boy hooked on the legend.

"Why, sure, son, you don't see rabbits running around with spectacles, do ya?" His father roaring with delight.

Those days were filled with familial love that bonded the family as it should be. Later, his sister, Julie, was added to the family. Mickey became self-appointed protector of his little sister, something he would lament at times when he began dating. She became very attached to him and, like some females, would feel a tinge of jealousy at sharing him with someone else. Still, they were a compatible pair, sharing many confidences and viewpoints. This would play out in later years, when he established his floral business. Needing help, Julie was the perfect person to work the shop with him and tending to the phone orders, provided he got them.

He tutored her on arrangements, knowing he couldn't do that and deliver at the same time. When not making the rounds, she paid strict attention to his directions and began to develop her own style of groupings and arrays.

"Boy, you learn fast, Jule."

"Well, I have to save my big brother from disaster," she would poke at him.

Mom was also a big help, filling in from time to time to spell Julie and also bringing her sought-after baked ham and potatoes to the starving pair. Her pleasant voice made her a natural in taking orders and the assurances that they'd be delivered on time. She tried her hand at arrangements but was better with vegetables, Julie and Mickey teasing at her futile efforts. This was truly a family affair. Some semblance of sorrow hovered over the family because the patriarch of the family, Jonathan, had passed away while Mickey was at college. He almost gave up his studies, so crushed was he by his dad's loss. His mom took him to task, saying that this was not the way he was raised. You start something, you finish it. This rebuke sent a message he would live by: you start something, you finish it.

So it was with that he launched his venture. Part of the outlay came from his father's insurance, which Mickey heatedly tried to refuse. Martha, his mom, was more resolute, and in the end he acceded to the funding only on the proviso that he'd repay it, provided he was successful. The rest was a loan from the bank, with reasonable interest rates. With that part of the table set, he placed ads in the paper and also hand bills which Julie passed out at very location, person, or storefront she encountered. Now the wait. At first, the phone elicited a wrong number, the only action for several days.

Finally, an order was placed only because the customer was on short notice and had to have it immediately. A bee would have admired the busy endeavor associated with his species. The order was filled, delivered, and a grateful buyer included a handsome tip. Of course, the first bill was encased in a frame and proudly displayed on the wall, but only the one dollar note, the rest more valuable than on a wall.

Slowly, surely, and predictably, one order led to another, and in a few weeks, the flow was fairly good. Julie became more proficient, and Mom was a great asset on the phone and in the food department. For transportation, his high school buddy sold him a panel truck that had seen better days but still functioned, even though it had a tendency to overheat. Hence, the five-gallon container of water snuggle in the rear. It was grueling and tough, but he always remembered what his mother ingrained in him.

Okay, the boy was on his way. Eventually, he'd replace "old faithful" with a newer truck, but that'd have to wait until he made enough money or it gave up the ghost. The town was pleasant, being a partial suburb and country town. The Main Street had all the amenities, post office, municipal building, etc. A junior college added some apartment units for students, and the weekly dances were a source of revenue, flowers, and corsages being purchased to enhance favor from the recipients. Life was good. Finishing his deliveries for the day and the swine cell phone silent, it was time to pack up and head for the barn. Passing through the college campus brought back memories of his time in high education. Reminiscing, his nostalgia holding sway, his musing was suddenly interrupted by a shrill scream. He jolted back to reality and swung his head around to find the source of this desperation. Passing one of the dormitories, he saw heavy smoke billowing from a second-floor window.

Immediately he rammed the truck over the curb onto a patch of grass and jumped out, heading for the entrance. Wrapping his handkerchief across his face, he knew it would do little to prevent inhalation but ignored the consequences. The hallway was clear, but students were rushing down the stairway, and above the clamor, he heard a voice screaming for help.

Barging past the downflow, he emerged at the top landing, dense black clouds of sooty smoke engulfing the space above his head and soon would fill the whole area. Yelling to alert the panicked voice that he was near, a subdued moaning emanated from inside a room down the hall. Knowing he had little time to waste, he plunged through the black coils of smoke and halted at the opened door. At his feet was a body coughing and gasping. Grabbing a woman in his strong arms, he headed for the stairway and safety. It was not to be. As he approached the landing, a portion of the ceiling crashed down upon him, causing both parties to tumble down the stairs. He felt the impact across his back and arm but instinctively held tightly to his bundle. Reaching the bottom of the staircase, Mickey's consciousness began to fade. Glimpsing at the limp form, he was gratified that she was still in his arms, then all went dark.

Time lost definition in the embrace of unconsciousness, which slowly returned to Mickey, but barely. He heard voices shouting instructions, "One, two, three," and a sudden jolt to his body as he was pulled from a gurney to an exam table. Mumbled voices floated over his attempt to comprehend what was going on. Patches of light and moving bodies flash across what little vision he had. He picked up bits of conversations. "Great deal of smoke inhalation," and something fastened across his face, a hissing sound and cool air. "May have a broken arm, get him ready," and the darkness again.

Mickey could always grasp any situation and pretty much knew how to deal with it. But now, something different was going on. He was standing beside a bed, a figure's head bandaged, the scarlet oozing beginning to penetrate one side. *Hey, what's going on?* he thought to himself, shaken considerably. *Where's the girl? Where am I?* Several people attending to the prone figure ignored him completely. *Hey, where am I?* They continued working to assure the patient was secure and turned to leave. As they did, he stiffened as he saw the face of the person they were ministering to—his face!

Wait a minute, I'm right here, who's that in the bed? He reached out to shake the form, but his hands passed through the unconscious man. Not understanding what was going on, he tried to convince himself he was dreaming and he had to wake up from this nightmare. Just then, a nurse entered the room, and as he tried to speak to her, she passed right through his ethereal form. His mind was just about ready to snap when he heard a voice.

"Mickey, son, over here." Turning, he again stiffened with disbelief—his father!

"Dad, is that you, really you?" What cruel twist of fate was toying with his mind. *Please, let me wake up.*

"Mickey, come with me." His shaken form did not resist, and he could only guess as to what would happen next. Leaving the room, the pair entered a featureless plane, bright with a glowing pall. The man before him smiled and tried to comfort his bewildered son.

"Mickey, listen to me. I'll try to explain what's happening."

"Dad, is that really...but you died, how can you be here?"

"Be patient, son, I know this is a great shock to you, just as it was for me when my father came to me when I passed."

"Dad, please, I don't know what's happening to me, am I going crazy?"

His father looked at his shaken son, regretting not having the solidity to put his arms around him. "No, you're not crazy, but you're going to have to get a hold of yourself if you want to know what's happening, can you do it?" The words were not conciliatory, but sharp, intended to snap his boy back into the situation.

"Okay, Dad, I'll try, honest, but please help me."

"First, why I'm here. You were severely injured and—"

"I can't remember what happened to me—"

"That's what I'm getting at, now listen carefully. I was sent to bring you back with me—"

"I don't understand, take me back where?"

"Let me finish, son, and you'll understand."

"Sorry, Dad," replied the chastened and frightened young man.

"Souls, such as yours as well as mine was—are destined for one of two worlds. The life I shared with your mother, who blessed me with my children, could not have been possible without thanking God and doing his will.

"No, I'm no angel but rather a guardian for those of my family when their time arrives."

"Arrives, what's that mean, Dad, that we're dead?"

"In most cases, yes, but that's not the whole story. You see, there are times when I can only advise, since my subject is in limbo, so to speak."

"In limbo? What's that supposed to mean? Am I in limbo now?" An exasperated and scared son was reaching his limit of composure.

"Again, settle down, boy, you're making it harder than it has to be. I can't fault your emotions. Finding yourself in this strange position would rattle anyone, but please, hear me out." The father's voice was more urgent and reaching his limit of composure.

"Why you're in this situation is complicated. You're not dead, but in another phase."

Mickey felt a strange relief knowing he was not dead, but what was he?

"This may occur, but I don't know for sure, that's why I was sent. Roaming around with no clue as to what's happening to you wouldn't be fair, an explanation was in order, hence, here I am."

"But, Dad, doesn't God decide if I live or die?"

"Overall, yes, but not in the way you and I know. He allows all things to happen in their own way, assisted by prayers and hopes of others and by the medical help being given.

"And the reason you can't remember anything about your injuries would be a detriment to the joy that is waiting. No sorrow is allowed, as his domain is free from the cares of this earth."

"Then I'm dead?"

"No, let's just say you're in a holding pattern. If it comes to that, I'll return for you. In the meantime, you will be confined to the hospital, free to move about. Don't worry, no one will see you. It's an experience you may find interesting." As he began to fade, Mickey lunged at his father, to hold him back, to give him courage, but his effort was futile. Truly alone and shaken, he pondered what he would do next, if only to keep him from breaking down completely. But what would he do or could he do? He had no substance. *Okay,* he said to himself, *I have no other choice but to wait it out, but how?* He began to idly walk down a hall with patient rooms on either side. He dared not go back to his location for fear of succumbing to the unnerving sight of his body lying bandaged and inert, who wouldn't?

Walking past and through various hallway appliances and medical equipment, he paused at a door and peered inside. There were two beds, one on which lay an adult female. On the one nearest him was a little boy, perhaps no more than fours years of age. An impulse urged him to enter, and at the foot of the bed, he glanced at a chart. Sure enough, the boy was a half year older, and his condition was such an adult was allowed to cohabit the room. *Poor little guy,* he thought to himself.

The child had been very still, his breathing faint, but something aroused him, and as he opened his eyes, he looked directly at Mickey and smiled. *Huh? No, he can't see me* was his incredulous thought. To put that analysis into the trash bin, the lad waved to him.

"Heyo, mister."

Whoa, this can't be happening, how can he see me? The woman, startled by the boy's movement, rushed to his side.

"Tommy, what's wrong?" She felt his forehead, an instinctive reaction to his apparent unusual behavior, her feverish actions spurred by an unanticipated change in his previous dormant condition.

"Mommy, nice man," he weakly spoke, pointing in the direction of Mickey. She turned, and he could feel her eyes passing through him.

"What man, sweetheart?" she said in a worried reply. The boy cupped both hands over his mouth and smirked. This was like playing a game. She pressed the call button, and shortly a nurse appeared. "Nurse, he awakened and spoke."

"I'll call Dr. Herman immediately." Not reading beyond the boy's age on the chart, Mickey had no understanding of his condition. Now his unseen presence allowed him to sit in on the following events.

The doctor came through the door in an urgent fashion, fostered by the nurse's description of the boy's unexpected consciousness. He had attended the youngster when he first entered the emergency room, his mother in tears at the condition of her son. Mickey watched with great interest at what seemed to be a minor miracle at work. The doctor thoroughly examined the boy, ignoring his giddy laughter as he pointed to Mickey.

"He did that when I awoke," exclaimed his mother, sensing something beyond her comprehension but dismissing it as a state of anxiety.

Turning to the anxious mother, the doctor was quite positive in what he discovered, a sigh of relief reflecting from her face. The invisible presence in the room could only feel a great sense of appreciation from what the doctor had said. His whole mood started to change, from a self-absorbed, troubled soul seeking an answer that seemed elusive to a more settled attitude. He envisioned that maybe he did have another path to follow other than being morose.

Everything was unimaginable, as it would be for anyone, but still he conjured that perhaps he had a hand in the boy's improvement. *Nah,* he said to himself, *how could I have been of any help in bringing the boy around?* This will never be known, no evidence or proof that he indeed had any effect on the outcome. Still, the mysteries of life create certain moments where the accepted is suspended to allow an indulgence of what we want to believe.

Even so, Mickey felt elated, if not the instrument of improvement, then at least a witness to a heart-touching moment. Instructions were given to the nurse, and before he left, the boy's mother embraced the doctor, her tears staining his shoulder. With that, Mickey began to leave and turned around upon hearing, "Nice man, see me again?" The tyke was soothed by his mother into a reclining position, which failed to prevent a wave of his little hand at Mickey.

"You bet, squirt," he replied, signaling with his hand in a high-five motion.

His moodiness somewhat subdued, Mickey wondered what other surprises were in store. Another child caught his presence as he continued his exploration of the various levels. Again, there was the notion of recognition, of eye contact. He started to revel in his Invisible Man identity, as interchanges between he and the children became more frequent. Needless to say, their parents or guardians seemed confused, greetings from their chargers directed at nothing.

The saving grace was that children do these things all the time, which explained their juvenile behavior and were taken as the norm. He began to ponder why no one else save the little ones could see or hear him. Somewhere he had acquired the subconscious belief which assumed that children were the purest and most innocent of lives and could see things that adults could not. That belief existed because he as a child saw many visions denied to older people.

And as a child, his expressive nature at what he saw was never ridiculed by his family, for they believed the essence of his descriptions as a spiritual sign. This quality fades as a youngster grows older, as it did with Mickey, and is forgotten, but not entirely. He stopped suddenly, the entire series of events coursing through his mind. Now he sought a venue in which to examine and reconcile what had profoundly affected him. He found what he needed from a wall directory and headed there—the chapel. The serenity dispelled some of his uncertainties, dried up any residual anxiety, and installed a soothing calm.

He prayed for acceptance of any adversity that awaited, asked for forgiveness of past misdeeds, and asked for a benevolent outcome. He meditated for some time, a silent admission of a greater power at work.

"Hello."

Startled, Mickey turned to address whoever it was. She was stunning, an angelic face, brown eyes, unadorned lips so perfectly matched to her face and streaming locks of auburn hair.

"Are you my angel?" he blurted unexpectedly.

"I beg your pardon, angel?"

"Forgive me, I thoug—wait, you can see me?"

"Yes, and apparently, you can see me? No one else can."

"It comes with the territory."

"What a strange experience, people walking by and through you, as if you didn't exist."

"Well, technically you don't exist, at least not in their world." Mickey was taken with her beauty, but to what end. He dismissed the thought, intrigued that another spirit had joined him. "I'll guess you're waiting for clearance?"

"Clearance?"

"What I mean is, are you waiting to find out what's going to happen to you?"

"Yes, it's so unreal. I can't remember anything about how I got here, and then my grandfather appeared. He said that a final decision hadn't been rendered yet on where I'm to end up, and until then, I was a 'free spirit.' He laughed when he said that, which kind of made me feel better, joking and all."

"My dad was a little bit harder, but I can't blame him, I was out in orbit."

"By the way, I'm called Squeaky."

"Squeaky?"

"Yeah, when I was smaller, my voice sounded like it needed three-in-one oil." Her shy laughter brightened the moment.

"Well, Squeaky, I'm Mickey, but not the mouse." And he too let out with a ripple.

"Well, Mickey, I guess we're marooned in this place, how dreary."

"Whoa, wait a minute, Sqeak, that can be changed."

"How?"

"Well, did you notice that the kids seemed to see you?"

"Yeah, that's right, but I was too nervous to notice."

"I think one of the bright spots in our predicament concerns the kids."

"How so?" she spoke, her eyes widening as if a life preserver had been tossed to her. He told her about his encounter with Tommy, a boy whose illness he could not define but was a serious concern to his mother and with his doctor.

"So you played Dr. Kildare."

"No, actually, I did nothing at all. The boy did it. He saw me and was amused no one else could. It'd be great taking credit, but for what, being there?"

The girl looked at him and saw the effort at modesty but also recognized something else. Mickey was no showboater, no grand stander, and perhaps that quality was evident, even to a child. They say children are the best evaluators of people, and Tommy, even for that brief presence, knew the character of Mickey.

"Well, until we know better, we can stroll around and see if we can do something for the kids."

"If what you told me about how Tommy reacted," Squeaky injected, "it'd be terrific. These kids don't deserve this."

"That's pretty cool of you, Squeak, and maybe we're here for that very reason."

The young girl smiled and presented a different picture than when they first met. She seemed to shake off the fears that saddled her, enthusiastic for the new role she'd share with Mickey. In the short space of time that elapsed from their first encounter, both spirits had evolved from uncertainty and penance to a force on a mission.

"Here's Tommy's room. Let's see how he's doing."

They entered and immediately were greeted with a perky "Heyo." The youngster had been reading a children's booklet and, upon seeing the pair, was ecstatic. His mother turned around from the dresser and questioned her son.

"What is it, Tommy?"

"Nice man and lady," he responded, pointing to them. She didn't bother to correct him. If whatever he imagined could spark his vitality as it seemed, she showed a willingness to welcome it without question.

"Thank them for the visit. Now you need your rest."

"Okay, Mommy. Bye, nice man and lady." As he slid under the covers, his mother yielded to her curiosity and looked at where her son pointed. With an uncertain smile, perhaps feeling a little foolish, she thanked them.

"Wow, that was great, Mick."

"I knew you'd enjoy it."

Their trek around the hospital yielded similar results. Children don't always scare as adults may, the children appraising the pair with youthful vibrancy and laughter, the latter at the expense of the nurses' annoyances. Mickey could not stop an attraction that was slowly creeping into his thoughts. Squeaky began to grow on him, and even then, he tried to resist. To what end?

No, it was something that could not be dismissed. His dilemma was how to conceal this growing admiration; after all, they just met. Mickey had a few romantic interests, but they never panned out. This was something different, her face, her attitude, but whatever its hold on him, it was like a viselike grip. Not getting tired or hungry was a new experience for both of them, allowing unbelievable opportunities to investigate new avenues of contact and exploration. This helped to temper his problem.

For several days, they became quite adroit at encountering the youngster without too many problems.

Then Mickey began to notice a subtle but definite change in Squeaky's moods. Her eyes spoke what words failed to say. He started to let in a little of what he had tried to suppress, knowing it was futile, and again, to what end? They paused on their rounds, initiating small talk, and he looked into her eyes, not listening to a word. She had stolen his heart. He began to say something, to profess some sort of acknowledgement as to how he felt. A figure appeared, walking toward them, and she stiffened noticeably.

Sensing her discomfort, he asked what was wrong.

"It's my grandfather, Mick. I'm afraid." He wished he could hold and comfort her, knowing that a decision had been made. "Let me talk to him, Mick." He watched as she hesitantly marched toward the elderly man. For some time, they spoke, with the man controlling the conversation. He appeared to comfort her, and then she cupped both hands to her mouth, letting out a suppressed moan. Mickey was alarmed, wanting desperately to know what happened.

Finally, she turned, her head down, and approached a now shaken young man. Tears were flowing down her cheeks, her mouth quivering.

"Squeak, what's wrong, what did he say?" he asked, looking at the older man with contempt. She did not deserve this, whatever it was that brought on her distress. Then he remembered what his father had said, that when the time came, he would come for Mickey. No, no, please don't take her from me, please. She came up to him, his heart racing, if that was what spirits still possessed, and knew what was to come.

"Oh, Mick, my grandfather said he's come for me. I said I didn't want to go, but it was out of his hands. He tried to make me feel better, telling me it was a new life of light and calm."

"Believe him, Squeak."

"But, Mick, I…"

"I know, I felt it too. Look, wherever you go, remember, in my heart is a place for you, and that will never change." They approached each other closely, as if in an earthly life, they would embrace. As they faced each other, a light shone from above, revealing a sudden transformation. Spirit gave way to flesh and blood, the tone of their skin and hair and eyes in full color, the majesty of touching and holding now a reality. With no hesitation, their bodies merged for a first and final embrace, his cheek upon hers, whispering how he felt. Her reply, interspersed with sobs, were as heartfelt. How long they clung to each other didn't matter, only that they did. And a knowing grandfather was in no hurry to interfere.

Slowly the light retreated, signaling the departure of a reluctant young girl. Mouthing an endearing expression, she turned and joined her grandfather. They walked slowly, and she turned for one last glance, Mickey wanting to run after and prevent her from leaving and knowing he couldn't. He watched as they slowly faded away. Alone, he suddenly realized that what he was experiencing was sadness, but how could that be? Didn't his father say that sorrow was not permitted here in heaven? Why did he have this feel—

A darkness closed over him as stealthily as a thief, a sensation of drifting in a void, spiraling downward and downward, then nothing.

Time has no meaning if it cannot be measured. Hushed voices started to penetrate the wispy grayness that had appointed itself upon a reviving young man. The voices become more excited as a small glow of light pierced the veil.

"His eyes are reacting to the light. I believe he's coming around." The doctor finished the last of his examination and turned to a woman and her daughter. "He's been through a lot, but I'm convinced he'll beat this thing."

"Oh, thank you, Doctor. Can we stay with him awhile?"

"Yes, but try not to rouse or excite him. He's not ready for that right now."

The pair hovered over the prone figure, the older woman holding her daughter close, silently crying. "Oh, Mom, he's going to be okay, thank God. I've prayed and prayed. What would we do without him."

His eyes opened, a momentary start to the only family he had. They didn't utter a sound but clung to each other, expressions of surprise and relief etched on their faces. Softly his mother thanked God and caressed his face. He smiled and, comforted with their presence, slipped into a deep sleep.

That evening, when he awoke, with only the monitor's sound to keep him company, he tried to make sense of his ordeal. Was it real or a dream? Over and over he played the same scenario, frustrated at his conclusions. No, it couldn't be real, then again, it's possible. These rival thoughts mentally exhausted his fragile state of mind. If it was real, he experienced the pinnacle of every lover's desire. If not, it was a cruel illusion. His efforts proved fruitless, and to keep some sanity, he deferred any further attempts.

A week had passed, his family constantly on hand, bringing him, albeit under the table, Mom's cooking. He lightened up a little, not wanting to risk another bout of memory chairs, as he called it. During one afternoon, being alone for a few hours, his nurse made a visit.

"Mr. Harris, a couple is waiting to see you. If you rather not, I'll inform them."

"No, no, it's okay, I could use a few new faces."

A well-groomed middle-aged man and an equally attired woman, also middle-aged, entered the room, the woman holding a bouquet of flowers.

Mickey motioned them to be seated, but instead, they approached his bed, the woman offering the flowers while grabbing his hand tenderly.

"Mister Harris."

"Please, sir, Mickey."

"Er, well, Mickey, my name is Marsh, Patrick Marsh, and this is my wife, Samantha. You don't know us, obviously, but we know quite a bit about you, not personally, of course, but for what you've done."

"You have me there, Mr. Marsh."

"Patrick."

"I mean, what've I done that brings you here?"

"To pay you our deepest respects. Our daughter, Melanie, had been a student at Mercer Community College. She was excited at embarking on a richer life and wanting the education to ensure it."

For some reason, Mickey began to be uncomfortable, why, he didn't know.

"She was a pretty and intelligent girl, full of life. As all parents, we were and are proud to have had her."

A strange sensation began to grow inside Mickey as he listened to an outpouring which parents usually lavish on a loved one.

"That's why we're here, mist—er, Mickey. We want to thank you for the heroic efforts you made to save our daughter."

Now the pieces started to fall in place. The fire! "We've heard many accounts about your selfless attempts to save her, injuring in the process. Many students praised your actions. We wanted to meet our hero and thank him for his efforts and to aid him in any way we can."

Mickey was at a loss for words. This was so unexpected. How do you respond to loving people, while mourning, still take the time from the grief, to honor you? He tried reverse praise.

"Pat, you and your wife duly deserve the credit for what your daughter was and wanted to become. I too have a loving family, and it's because of them that I am what I am. Parents are everything, and your gracious praise befits you as well."

The man grabbed his hand with both of his, his eyes welling with tears. His wife leaned over, and her lips caressed his forehead.

"Son, please come to see us when you are well. We'd like to know everything about our daughter's final moments and are comforted that you were with her." With that, they bid goodbye and walked toward the door. Samantha turned toward Mickey and said, "You know, son, Squeaky would have loved you. She always told everybody that her voice needed to be oiled, it squeaked so much."

"Squeaky?" His exclamation being mistaken for clarification rather than shock.

"Yes, it was a funny nickname, and that's one of the things we'll remember fondly. Don't forget, please visit us."

With that they left a stunned young man. He grappled with the impact of this revelation, trying desperately not to submit to a total acceptance to what he'd heard. It was too much of a coincidence, he told himself, that his dream and the girl were connected. No, he'd endured too much, his mind racing, only because if it was true, he'd suffered a loss that would haunt him every day.

His faced buried in his hands, he cried, knowing in his heart that what he hoped for had been taken from him, gone from an existence that granted him his greatest joy.

Time would be needed to ease his mind, to be kind to him, to allow him to immerse himself in the belief that one day, maybe, he'd see her again. That thought he kept in his aching heart for the rest of his life. No, he didn't even consider another love, for what love he possessed had been foreclosed on that day long ago.

Time passed, and eventually, his time did come, with certainty. He found himself in a surrounding that he began to recognize. It was featureless with a glowing pall, the same as when he was with his father.

Well, if it's the right place and I've earned my wings, will Dad show up? he nervously mused.

A figure approached, long auburn hair, brown eyes, and a mouth that matched her face perfectly. If there were to be a crash of lightning, it would go unnoticed.

"Melanie?"

"Squeaky."

Oh, how he wished he could hold her, but that paled as his desire to be united had been granted. At least he hoped so.

"My poor lost soul, now we're together," she spoke, fulfilling that wish. They strode together from the pale glow into a wondrous light that revealed an undreamed-of beauty before them. And this would last forever.

FRATERNITY

The sun's rays bathed the resting body of Gil Madden as he dozed contently on his recliner. Nearby, his wife, Jennifer, attended to their two children, Mason and Maryn. The two played blissfully but were aware of their father's need for rest and, therefore, belying their young years, were careful not to disturb him. Mason was a free spirit of seven and looked every bit like his father, a strong chin, graceful mouth, and sparkling blue eyes. Maryn favored her mother and, by any standard of a five-year-old, was pixyish and engaging. Relying on their self-restraint, Jennifer absorbed their antics, ready to intervene if needed. Her eyes drank in the two, and she marveled at such a gift God had given her and Gil.

Things had changed quite a bit from what they were two years ago. Her mind flitted over the intervening months and touched on the many salient points that had become indelible in her mind. This was a loving family, and that love would be needed along with great fortitude to brave the hurdles placed before them. Her lot was similar to many others, for she was a military wife and all that entailed. Being part of this community afforded a certain amount of camaraderie and support, much of which was always given freely, for this life in the services always revealed the best of all who served.

She eyed her husband, trying to anticipate any need that should arise. A small bird, possibly a wren, alighted onto her husband's arm. Instinctively she was about to shoo the feathered mite away but held back when she saw her husband's eyes open, gazing on the small creature. He smiled, a sign of acceptance, as the small creature, as if in knowing response, animated its head up and down and in a small circle, hopping closer to the prone man's face.

"Hey, little fella, how are you?" Gil muttered. Jennifer relaxed, confident that the encounter was a welcome tonic, her eyes gazing upon a mutual acceptance of nature's gift. The stay was brief, but the encounter lasting in its effect. Gil had shown a sign of awareness, a sign of progress.

But these had happened before and had quickly evaporated.

Would this be different? She resigned herself to whatever may happen, as she had done for the past two years. Her initial shock and heartbreak had receded to the back corners of her mind as she strove to open her heart to nothing else but her husband's needs. These were hard times, but her strength of resolve plus her children were motivating factors that sustained her. She gazed upon his relaxed form and, as she had done many times before, rewound the beginnings of her association with this wonderful person.

They had been neighbors, his home across the street almost hidden by a great weeping willow. They were both very young, and the shyness of their first meeting was very apparent. Of course, curiosity proved to be the best cure for uncertainty, and it wasn't long before they sought each other out when the opportunity presented itself.

Their parents were friends, so any intrigues or conflicts between the two were accepted as the norm for nurturing friendships. One characteristic that always rankled Jennifer was Gil's penchant for teasing her. This was handled with a measure of maturity in that she often dwelled on his many good attributes, which seemed to outweigh his irksome manners. Of course, this didn't refrain her from a just retaliation when the occasion presented itself.

"Wow, that was a neat hit back, Jen," he would exclaim, most charitably, when she did get the better of him. But this was a brick-by-brick building of something that would prove to be as solid. Sadly for both, they each attended separate elementary schools, which no doubt fostered a yearning for companionship lost. This tended to be a positive aspect, for it strengthened their friendship by dint of the absences. After school found the two pairing up to resume what young people tend to do. Their youth insulated them from any notion of romance, which didn't mean that what they developed for each other wasn't real, only that they didn't recognize it as such, at least not then.

Youth has a way of setting priorities that befuddles adults, who most certainly know better, so it would seem, but not always. Things started to change somewhat when they entered junior high school together. Their closeness continued in the same way as before, although inklings of romantic notions sometimes intruded, especially with Jennifer. Gil was still surfing the "guy" stuff, but Jen started to blossom into a new world that seemed in conflict with her "platonic" take with Gil. After years together, it was difficult to shed the conformity that had developed. Even Gill began to experience things counter to his accepted view of things. Overtures by pretty girls had the effect of causing him to stutter or stumble for an appropriate response. It was a different world.

This of course was not devastating; in fact, it opened up a new sense of appreciation for both of them. They began to realize that their juvenile past had receded into history, and a pre adult experience awaited them. Loyalty, bred from years of closeness, soon morphed to its inevitable conclusion. A sweet kiss sealed their unique union; there could not be, nor would there ever be, anyone but each other. Through high school they continued, a known pair to all the other fellow students. In fact, they were the gold standard by which other couples tried to emulate.

Graduation signaled a new venture, for now they were cast to the wind, so to speak. Having spoken to Jen many times about his interest in the military, it was no surprise, although not entirely acceptable to her, that he enlisted in the US Army. She had forsaken college to work in her family's flower shop and wouldn't have gone to college anyway, fearing a more acute separation from her love. She counted the days until he would come home on leave, while fearing his eventual posting to some far-off duty.

Receiving a furlough before being posted on assignment, he surprised her with a marriage proposal, which of course was accepted. Their honeymoon was brief but fulfilling, but the future was not too certain. What would come next, for he received orders to his next posting? Following him to his new billet, she lived in a rented unit for a while before he was able to secure living quarters on base. This new life for both of them presented the usual challenges all young couples face, but they made it work. Gil loved the military, and Jen made every effort to share in his efforts to excel, while he was mindful of the extreme transition she had made and went to great lengths to provide her with what comfort and care that he could.

His work ethic was rewarded with several promotions, and he had thought that one day he might become an officer, but one thing at a time. Jen made many friends with the other families living among them, and it started to become old hat in her and Gil's routine. Military families share a unique association, for it's only with each other that they can seek support, whether it be consolation for a loss or jubilation when celebrating a joyous occasion. It was during this time that Jen started to explore writing, to fill the downtimes when Gil was away.

She began with a daily journal and enjoyed it so much that she expanded it to fictional plots, based on her past experiences and the various insights that the military life had provided. Many times they would laugh at some of her plots as she would bounce them off Gil to assess the accuracy of a military theme or technical term. During his absences for maneuvers or other military requirements, this helped lessen the loneliness, and her adroit writing began to reach a level where she felt confident in submitting them for publication. To her surprise, several short stories were accepted for publication. The monetary gain was secondary to the thrill of being published, and Gil boasted to all his friends that he married a soon-to-be famous author. The financial aspect was a boon to the struggling couple, but they were careful not to rest their plans on any future submissions.

Not too long afterward, Mason came along, filling the empty moments of Jen's life with unbounded joy. Gil couldn't brag enough about his son, almost wearing his fatigue pocket out, pulling his wallet photos for display at the drop of a hat or, in this case, a helmet. These and other antics by the proud parents singled them out to the "established" families, who supported this pride with their own accolades. When Mason was three, his sister, Maryn, joined the club. Gil's displays were not as flamboyant but still revealed his bursting pride for his new arrival. It wasn't too long before Mason was crawling over, in, under, or between any piece of military hardware. Under his dad's watchful eye, he seemed mesmerized by the sheer bulk or size of things like the "urmor vickles," as Mason was fond to utter. He was a good little fella and rarely caused trouble on his outings, but every now and then something he spied caused him to flit away at supersonic speeds to investigate.

Being close-knit, the community of billets bred a sense of comradeship and closeness that was singular in its effect as compared to civilian acquaintances. Not that they were snobbish, it was an ingrained association borne out of the similarities generated by danger, loneliness, uncertainty, and possible death. Even newcomers were steeped in this unwritten code, for the uniform was the catalyst that bound them together.

Gil's work ethic and diligence resulted in earning the rank of sergeant. Jen was thrilled, as the new rank came with an increase in pay but also because she was terribly proud of her husband. His company was part of a mechanized unit, and his squad was designated as a point group. In action, they would proceed before the main force to gain intelligence or to ferret out any ambush. To this end, Gil would brook no mistakes, his careful eye finding any flaw in his men's disposition during training. He impressed upon them the magnitude of their responsibility time and again until it became second nature. Training honed the quick and automatic response that spelled the difference between success and disaster.

During times when the families hosted get-togethers, part of his squad would attend, Mason invariably dogging each one about what he did in the unit and if he liked his dad. The men were thoughtful and enjoyed the little tyke. Sam Gross was a bear of a man, which belied his gentle nature. When Mason confronted him, he was a little scared of this giant, but curiosity and inquisitiveness overruled that impediment. Before long, Sam had him on his lap, regaling his specialties and filling the lad with all kinds of stories, careful to avoid any gory incidents. It was then that Mason adopted him.

Benny Richards was slightly built but solid. He could bench press with the best of them. His keen eye and appreciation of the lay of the land worked immeasurably in determining how the unit would advance, able to detect something awry or threatening, almost as if he had built-in radar. He was the true point man of the group.

Ken Murcer was a dependable man in any army, and his rear guard role was critical and handled with an ability that infused the men with confidence in their safety. This was why the training was so intense, something the men did not gripe about, for they knew the consequence of a broken link in the chain that knit them together.

Gil not only had a good working relationship with his squad but was genuinely friendly with them, especially Sam, Benny, and Ken. They would often pal around off duty, or Jen would invite them to dinner. This measure of friendship increased their desire to eliminate any flaws in their performance, and on many training exercises, the brass would often comment to the squad's immediate superiors the satisfaction of witnessing the performance of a well-oiled machine. It soon became apparent that Gil's unit had reached a level desired but not often attained. Self-satisfaction aside, this confirmed to the men their worth, purchased with untold hours of sweat, grime, and exhaustion.

As with many instances in life, what Jen feared came to be. Gil's unit had been called up and would be sent to the Middle East. They were to relieve a similar unit, and the need was urgent. Within two days they would be gone. The flurry of activity could not go unnoticed on base, and it became evident the unit was moving.

Those families unaffected displayed their compassionate bent by scooting over to the various billets, professing support and consolation. With many of the men and women gone, those left behind would need this comradeship, if only to lessen the loneliness. The organizational value of the military contributed to this nonmilitary structure of support. In this, Gil was secure in his appreciation on how Jen and the kids would fare.

This didn't make it any easier when the time came to leave. Maryn thought the gatherings were a party and therefore didn't endure the pangs of what would be a long separation. Mason, a little confused by all the activity, was quietly taken aside and held in his father's arms.

"Hey, little buddy, Daddy has to go away for a little while."

"Why, Daddy?" A tear was beginning to appear in his eye.

"Well, you know there are bad people hurting other people, and we have to stop that."

"But why you, Daddy?"

"Mase, it's what Daddy joined the army for, to help other people. Remember when your friend Jackie was being hit by that bully John?"

"Yeah?"

"Well, what did you do?"

"I went over and pushed him away and told him not to hurt my friend."

"Well, Daddy is going to do something like that, push the bully away."

"Gee, Daddy, that's cool. But make sure they don't hurt you." The tear was slowly running down his cheek. He wiped it away and, trying to be a little man, stifled a sob or two, hugging his dad with all his might. Jen embraced the both of them and with well-wishers standing by, he jumped into a Humvee, waving goodbye until he was out of sight. Jen stood there, trying to freeze the sight of her husband in her mind, wanting to keep his image forever present, something only the shock of the moment could impose on a reeling mind. She grasped her children tightly and stifled a tear or two then led them back into their quarters.

Letters helped relieve the loneliness, and with the miracle of Skype, she was able to see and talk to her love. Maryn was giddy as she thought her daddy was in a TV show, not understanding the process, but Mason had a good grasp of the innovation and had a ball with his dad. Question upon question which the sergeant unflinchingly answered, his son's eyes wide with wonder at some of the answers. Then there were the private moments between the two separated hearts that relieved some of the void they both felt. Especially endearing to Jen were the letters. Where spoken words evaporated as soon as they were uttered, she would pour over every written word time and again to renew herself and envision the moment they would be together again.

Her daily routine and friends enabled her to live each day with hope and prayed for the safety of her husband and the men he served with. She looked forward to the face-to-face chats, the children enjoying it immensely. On one occasion, she was unable to make contact but thought nothing of it; after all, he was a workingman and couldn't expect him to be at her beck and call whenever she wished. The following day was the same and the day after. She began to experience a haunting feeling. Where was he, why didn't he contact her?

A knock on the door would soon confirm her fears. As she opened the door, her body stiffened. Lieutenant Kyle Johnson, an aide to the base commander, stood passively before her, his facial expression somber. Unable to contain herself, she flung her slight form upon the lieutenant, flailing away with both forearms and clenched fists against his chest, shouting, "No! No! No! I don't want to hear it!"

The young officer, tasked with this type of duty, stood his ground admirably and allowed her to expel her anguish. She threw her arms around his shoulders and buried her face on his chest, her tears staining his blouse coat lapels and pockets. To him, this was a badge of honor. He had been wounded twice and knew what his wife had gone through, and his empathy was in large supply.

Allowing her to set the pace, the lieutenant was soon released from her grasp, an embarrassed look on her face. "I'm terribly sorry, Lieutenant, I lost it, forgive me."

"Ma'am, there's nothing to forgive. The news I have is hopeful, but please, be seated on the sofa and I'll fill you in." The word *hopeful* dismissed the thought of death, and a relieved sigh escaped her lips. She listened intently as the story unfolded.

Gil and his unit were on a scouting mission when they came under fire. He and three of his men were wounded, one fatally. He proceeded to describe in general terms Gil's injuries, and with each telling, she moaned or would utter "Oh, no." He continued, "They were extracted and taken by 'copter to their base hospital."

"Oh my heavens," Jen responded. "Do you know who they were?"

"Yes, ma'am, but I'm not at liberty to reveal their names. I have to contact their families also."

The hurt increased, for surely she'd know the men who'd been hit. Her thoughts and prayers now went out to those families.

"Ma'am, I'll keep in contact with you. He'll be flown to our medical facility near the base as Walter Reed is shutting down. At least he'll be close to you and the family."

Thanking the lieutenant, she saw him to the door, where he gave her a handshake and salute.

Her mind was racing with conflicting contingencies—the children, his parents, her parents, and heaven knows what else. After who knows how long, the children, arising from their nap, came bouncing in.

"Mommy, why are you crying?" piped Mason. Maryn just looked, not really comprehending her mother's emotional state. Wrapping her arm around the youngest, more for moral support than anything else, she asked the boy to sit beside her.

"Mason, I have received some news that is sad, and I want you to listen to me carefully, understand?"

The boy's face, even for five years, took on a resigned facial expression, something he would do when he had been scolded or chastised for something. But this was different, his mother's tone not challenging or confrontational but pleading, and his manner was unresisting to whatever she was going to say.

Jen recalled trying to explain in a gentle and sensitive way that Mason's daddy had been hurt. It was difficult to impress upon the young boy the harm that had come to his father. Being hurt to his young mind was scraping your knee on the playground or bumping your head on the ground, requiring but a mother's kiss to soothe the pain. Try as he may, the boy tried hard to understand his mother's faltering attempts to be as gentle as she could. Finally, to her surprise, he said, "Mommy, if Daddy is hurt, that's okay, because you and I will take care of him, and he will be better." Grabbing her son, tears rolling down her cheeks, she blessed God for giving her such a son.

After several days, Lieutenant Johnson, after phoning Jen, arrived at the billet to escort her to the hospital, a female sergeant staying behind to look after the children. The drive was short, but her nerves began to fray on her composure. How would she react, would she embarrass him, and many other conflicting thoughts pressed upon her mind. Upon entering his room, all this vanished as she saw her husband and knew only her love for him was all that was needed. She approached his side, and he was sleeping, a peaceful sleep, thank God.

The lieutenant informed her that he would wait for her in the lobby and to take all the time she wanted. He pulled a chair to the side of the bed and seated her, a thankful smile rewarding his effort. Turning to her love, she only now focused on his condition. The upper portion of his head had been wrapped in a thick winding of gauze, his right arm was in a cast, and his right leg elevated in a sling.

"Oh, my poor darling, what did they do to you?" she silently lamented. Taking his hand in hers, she gently ran her fingers over his. This stimulus caused the wounded warrior to stir, startling Jen as she didn't want to disturb his rest. He turned his head toward his wife and opened his eyes.

"I must be in heaven. There's a beautiful angel beside me."

As carefully as she could, she joyously placed her head on his chest, citing her love for him. He placed his left arm around her warm form and clung as tightly as his strength allowed. The long pent-up absence was released as both souls united with each other again. How glorious, how sweet, how sad. The time fled without concern for the couple, as time has a way of doing. Her stay was all too soon over. Leaving a parting kiss on his lips, Jen reluctantly left her husband and, at the door, turned and blew him a kiss, mouthing "I love you." Down in the lobby, Jen greeted the lieutenant with a smile mingled with tears of appreciation.

On the drive home, her mood was pensive. How would the children react? But that was some months away, giving her time to find a way to insulate them from the shock of seeing their father so incapacitated. Perhaps a visit or two when he is able to move in a wheelchair. These and other thoughts fought for primacy, her strong will being the determinant as to what she would eventually do. Being the wife of a soldier had bred into her this attribute, and she would tread lightly, careful at every turn to resolve any concerns.

Eventually she decided against sticker shock and would bring the children for brief visits, hoping that by seeing their father for short periods, they would gradually get used to his condition. On the day she brought them, all reservations vanished like a mist exposed to sunshine. Upon entering the visitor's lounge and seeing their father in a wheelchair, Maryn outran her brother into her daddy's arm, notwithstanding the bandages and casts. They had a sense of tenderness and did not overbear on their dad, clinging like magnets to metal. Gil looked at the children, soaking up their sweet presence after so long apart.

Jen kissed his cheek and took a seat next to him, allowing him to release his pent-up love for his children. As she watched, she was awed by what her husband was doing, especially after consultation with the doctors. She was told of his injuries in detail and what to expect. His head wound caused the loss of vision in his right eye, while the muscles and tendons in his right arm were useless. He could barely move it, if he exerted enough effort, but for intents and purposes, it was gone. The wound to his left leg severed a nerve and caused other damage which would severely impair its movement, if at all. But most of all, and the thing that concerned her the most, was that his head wound had brought on an unstable condition.

She listened intently as the doctor described the nature of this condition. He would have moments of lucidity for a length of time and suddenly would lapse into a morose state, these occurrences alternating with each other.

"When he's in that state, it's another world," the doctor volunteered. Therapy had shown that in time this could be reversed, but it would be a long haul. After another month, he would be free to return home, provided he has in-house care, and periodical return to the hospital for therapy would continue.

That he was lucid now was proven by his attention to his fawning children trying to outdo each other for the attention of their dad. Now she had to wrestle with home care and was relieved to know that arrangements had been made to supply support personnel during certain hours of the day. She would later be gratified by the additional help provided by many in the military community. Truly this was a bond of friendship borne of the many tribulations that others had experienced.

Now she had to contend with the thought of telling her husband that he had lost many of his friends. The doctors had advised withholding any details of his combat unit until he was more stable. Too soon and he may have an adverse physiological reaction. Somehow she would know when the time was ripe. They were his men and her friends. As with any situation concerning casualties, she soon learned the identities of the fallen and injured through the time-honored system of the grapevine. She felt the loss almost as much as those affected and lent her support to their needs. They responded in true fashion by offering their own solace. In this heart-wounding setting, many rose to the occasion.

Sam Gross, Mason's adopted friend, would not be coming home. Married for eleven years, his wife had just delivered a baby boy, Sam Jr., who would never know his dad. Some would rail at the injustice of it all, but those in the military were stoic when subjected to the unthinkable. His wife, Anne, was cut from the same cloth of fraternity.

Benny Richards, how Jen laughed at his corny jokes, the same ones that kept the unit loose. He was a sweetheart, occasionally bringing her flowers, lightening up her day, and to the sham dismay of his sergeant, who quickly gave him a head noogie. The two were real buddies. He too left a wife and a pair of teenage boys, both wanting to be just like their dad.

Ken Murcer, a dedicated rear guard guy, one that Gil would put his life on the line for. He was an avid hunter and as such knew what to look for when hunting prey or scanning for surprise attacks. He'd just been married to a sweet girl named Ellen, and they hoped to raise a family.

The latter two had been severely wounded and would not survive their injuries. This was cruel as it been hoped, and indications were, they would survive. True to their comradeship, through their pain, they asked if Gil was okay and were glad to know he was still alive. Especially after what he had done for them. Jen learned that the wounds Gil incurred were as a result of his actions toward his men when they had been attacked. Her pride in him was tempered by the very incident that evoked that sentiment.

That was almost two years ago. Gil was told that his buddies were lost, and he was moved to the point of tears. In a sense, this was good. He was reacting normally, and it could signal an increased recovery, although his relapses, occurring more rarely, still plagued him. She eyed his resting form and the kids playing softly. They had been a tonic to him and showed no reluctance to engage him despite his impaired form and lack of mobility. The casts had been removed, serving their purposes, although it didn't promote any activity. Once in a while he would strain his right arm in an attempt to lift it, smiling at an effort that produced inches of movement. His left leg was without sensation, and any effort there was wasted. Still, when he was with the world, he was alive and talkative, teasing the children and trying to crack jokes like Benny did.

Jen was grateful for every step made, but in the end, he would never be whole again. She was resigned to this and submitted to her vows of "for better or worse." Maybe in the future, some medical advancement may happen upon the scene to restore him to some semblance of normalcy.

Then she was left to ponder a bombshell totally unexpected. Lieutenant Johnson had called, wanting to visit with some exciting news. He strode into the rear yard and seated himself in a lawn chair. Gil was still napping, and the young officer leaned over to her and quietly asked her if she had some glad rags.

"Why, are you going to take me dancing?" she chortled.

"Well, maybe not that flashy, but I do think you're going to love what's going to happen."

"And what may that be?"

"Mrs. Jennifer Madden," the lieutenant pompously strutted, "you are hereby ordered to bring your husband to the White House on the date so entered."

"What? What date, what for?" Jen was getting so excited she almost woke Gil with her outburst.

"Ma'am, I'm so happy to be the one to bring you this great news. The president of the United States has requested your husband to attend a White House ceremony where he will be awarded the Medal of Honor."

Stunned, Jen was speechless for several long moments, looking at the young officer as if he had told her she'd won the million-dollar lottery. As far as she was concerned, it was better than the lottery.

"Sometimes these things take a while to work up through the chain, but it made it, and I can't think of anyone more deserving." Jen started to sniffle, Kyle putting his hand on hers. "I'll make all the arrangements, so don't worry, everything will be copasetic." Jen always got a kick out of phrases like that, as if "Everything will be okay" would not have sufficed. As he bid farewell, he turned, delivering a crisp salute toward the main object of his visit, an honored warrior.

Still excited, Jen took the embossed missive in her hands, and her eyes greedily scanned over the words of invitation. The date listed gave her ample time to make the personal arrangements necessary for the trip. She'd dig out one of his uniforms which hadn't had much use and would be ideal. She'd make his boots shine like diamonds, and his decorations would be pinned perfectly. Now all she had to do is regale her husband with the great honor awaiting him.

"Please God," she intoned to herself, "let him be right with the world."

As if in answer to this missive, Gil opened his eyes. "Lunch yet?"

Oh good, she thought, *he's ready to hear the news, such wonderful news.*

She sat on the edge of the recliner, stroking his hair, an air of exhilaration oozing from her joyous face.

"Honey, what say you, I and the kids get away for a while?"

"You bored with me already after eight years?" He laughed.

"No, silly, I thought a change in our routine would be great."

"What do you have in mind, my love?" His playfulness mirrored as his left arm reached around her waist, pulling her closer.

Grabbing his hand with hers in a gentle squeeze, she tried to think of the best way to tell him the great news. There was no specific way than to just let it out.

"Honey, I've great news."

"You love me."

"No."

"No, you don't love me?"

"No, er, yes, I love you, will you be still for a moment?"

"I can't be any stiller than I am now."

"Oh, why do you torture me so?"

"Because it's so easy." He laughed.

"No, be serious for a moment and listen to me."

"Yes, sir," he snapped.

Gripping his hand tighter and taking a deep breath, the words flew from her mouth. "You're going to be awarded the Medal of Honor."

"Okay, what's the punchline?"

"Gil, I'm serious. Here, look at the invitation."

The smile left his face in reaction to her serious tone and gazed at the folder in her hands, his lips moving in unison with his eyes as each word was consumed.

"Holy cow, you sure?"

"Of course, that nice lieutenant Johnson delivered it and will make all the arrangements for us. Oh, honey, this is going to be great."

News like this could not be contained, and the Madden family was plagued with well-wishers, calls, cards, and the base commander's visit. Gil was embarrassed to a certain degree but was gracious with his acknowledgements. He wanted to say that there were others more deserving of the award but refrained, not wanting to appear ungrateful. In the evening, in a lucid moment, he recalled the horror and carnage he lived through, the injuries received while trying to defend his men. He failed to shed the guilt that he felt, the natural feeling that any true leader absorbs who commits to his charges as he did. The nightmares were not as frequent, and with Jen's patience and soothing comfort when he'd scream himself awake, they were more bearable.

The night before leaving for Washington, Gil asked his wife to do him a special favor.

"Honey, of course, what do you need?"

"First, I want to thank you for finding the locations of the guys." Gil had learned that a new section of the Arlington National Cemetery had been opened for new burials. As such, his comrade's resting places, if in that section, would be fairly close to each other. They were. "Honey, before going to the White House, I want to visit my friends. But promise me, even if I'm out of it, promise me you will still bring me to them." His pleading eyes bore into her with his resolve, that no matter what, he would share his presence with their remains. He could do this; they could not.

"Gil, I'll make sure of it." And she would.

The trip to DC was enjoyable, the sights so wonderful to be hold. And then came the moment that was more special to Gil than the award he would shortly receive. They arrived at the burial place of heroes, their mission to pay homage. Then came the moment Jen feared as she watched the light recede from her husband's eyes. He was now in that other unfathomable world. Would he be able to join with his friends as he wished? Undaunted, and with the assistance of Lieutenant Johnson, they made their way through several rows of newly interred warriors and worked from the chart that displayed the locations they were seeking.

A name leaped from the glistening marker: Benjamin Richards. Jen paused, silently laughing at his corny jokes, a wistful smile creasing her lips. He was dear to her, as all of them were. She prayed for his soul and then wheeled Gil beside the plot and stepped back with her escort. Whatever the call that penetrated Gil's veil from reality, it reached in and opened a corridor that settled on his friend's grave. He reached out and embraced the white marble. The scene in his mind then changed as he was transported back to that day of combat.

Benny Richards was leading the squad along a dusty street, the wind churning the loose debris into a cloud and making it difficult to breathe. He was perhaps twenty meters in front of the unit with flankers on either side. He moved forward slowly, his head moving from side to side and up and down. He was looking for something out of the ordinary. In an ambush, nothing is out of the ordinary, requiring a keen sense of awareness and an innate sense of experience to find any loophole that exists. The men kept cadence with him while also scanning the environment for trouble. His steps slowed down and his body movement likewise, and then he stopped, raising his arm with the palm of his right hand waving in a backward motion. The men froze as one.

He repeated his head movements almost as if he was sniffing the fragrance of a flower wafting in the dirty breeze. The concern on his face was unmistakable as he stepped back. At that moment, a tremendous blast erupted from an IED (improvised explosive device), disguised in the form of concrete curbing. Not being fully abreast of the explosion, he was saved from being torn apart, but nonetheless, the shock wave catapulted his limp body into the air like an acrobat somersaulting. Crashing to the ground, his many wounds stained the ground with a bright crimson fluid. Telling his men to hold their positions, Gil threw his rifle to Ken and darted toward his fallen buddy. Just barely reaching him, another, smaller ball of fire shot out from the opposite side of the street, inflicting a searing pain across the right side of his head, his helmet mirroring the same type of damage. Momentarily stunned, and barely conscious, again he ordered his men to stay in place. Reaching down, he grabbed Benny's shoulder harness and pulled him to an alleyway and called for a medic.

"Gee, Sarge, you're hurt bad," Benny snorted, Gil's head wound dripping blood on his friend's chest.

"So are you, pal. Take it easy." He moved aside to let the medic take over, refusing treatment himself until his point man was treated. "Be alert, guys, that could be the start of somethin'," the Sergeant barked. It was then that he noticed he couldn't see out of his right eye, the full impact of pain making itself felt. To confirm his fears, small arms fire raked the ground around them, the men seeking shelter where they could. As this scenario played out, a fog-like haze began to cloud his vision until the bright gleaming marker he was clinging to reminded him of where he was. Jen sensed that he had made his communion with Benny and turned the wheelchair in another direction.

"You okay, hon?" she murmured, unsure of his lucidity and was surprised at a slight nod of his head. As they moved on, Gil began to see a slight glimmer in his right eye. More and more, the dark mantle that had shrouded his eye's vision was slowly melting away.

What's this? he thought as his vision slowly began to reassert itself. *It can't be, but I can see, holy cow,* he thought. *I can see!*

How glorious, a miracle, he could see again.

The walk was short, and the group soon came to the next point of honor. Sam Gross. Again Jen wheeled her husband next to the marker and stepped back with her escort. She remembered how her son cried when told of his passing.

"Is he in heaven?" he intoned in the innocence of his age.

"You bet he is, honey, and I know he is looking to take care of you and Daddy."

"I miss him, Mom."

Gil was stirred again by a benevolent force that alerted him to this second resting place, and he placed his hand upon the gleaming sentinel guarding his friend. Faint images vied for prominence in his mind as he drifted back to the fateful day.

Several figures were seen running across the rooftops, and Sam angled to get a better read on them. As he fired, taking them down, he was flung to the ground by the impact of a bullet fired from behind him. Rolling over to face his assailant, he poured a withering fire into the gunman, who was decimated.

Gil had just emerged from the alley, as Sam went down and screamed, "No, not you, Sam! No, damn it!" Instinctively he raced to his down colleague, hoping that he was just wounded. Blood was oozing from the side of his mouth, and he was gasping. Kneeling to the side of the injured man, Gil felt two sharp jolts to his right arm, which knocked him on top of Sam. The small arms fire was continuing, and no one could expose themselves without being hit. Gil, in immense pain, struggled to raise himself up. As with Benny, he grabbed Sam's harness and pulled him as far as he could before helping hands reached out to aid him. In a relatively safe position,

Gil looked at the glazed eyes of his son's pal and knew he was gone. Anger raged in his heart, and he screamed insults and epithets, raging like an injured animal, something counter to his basic character.

The pain in his arm muted some of his outburst, but not by much. The medic was tearing his sleeve apart, trying to tend to the wounds, but Gil's animation in directing his guys made it difficult. A haphazard patch was applied with the hope it would hold. Gil knew he couldn't dwell on his friend's death and tore himself away to resume visual and verbal command.

"Okay, guys, we're wrapping it up, there's too much incoming and more of 'em seem to be popping up." As the men made a cautious withdrawal, Gil made sure that his two friends were taken with them. As before, the images started to fade, and his next inward recollection was the hallowed ground beneath which his buddy lay.

His stay was long enough for Jen to assume he had made his peace with Sam and directed the wheelchair to the final destination. As they dutifully strode their way forward, Gil began to feel a sensation in his right arm. *Feeling, true feeling, oh my gosh, my arm is alive,* he blurted to himself. *I can't believe it. Man oh man, how'd this happen.* His joy was almost uncontainable, but he wanted to make sure it was real, so he maintained a wait-and-see attitude.

The somber trek ended at the final grave, Ken Murcer. The same routine unfolded with solemnity with Gil laying his head on the perturbing member of the marble marker. His world then retreated back to his day of trial, and he found himself enmeshed in turmoil and the cacophony of entangled sounds of gunfire and shouting.

He became aware of his own voice urging his squad to safety, trying to fire his weapon with one arm. The hail of bullets was daunting, and it was going to be a close call for the unit to extract itself. Out of this mind-boggling commotion stepped Ken Murcer. Cradling his SAW (squad automatic weapon), he purposely exposed himself, spraying likely targets with the full lethality of his weapon. Wherever he pointed his weapon, the targets stood no chance. He darted from one position to another, crying out to hunkering men to move out while he covered them. It was insane, the man knew no fear, but he was being too gallant, something he would scoff at if confronted with that analysis.

One by one the squad slipped away to relative safety. Ken's act was consistent with all brave men who put the welfare of others before their own safety. With Gil urging him to withdraw, Ken grunted an "okay," spraying the last of his ammo into what targets he could make out. As he turned toward Gil, he bolted forward, the force of a bullet propelling him to the ground. The torture of another one of his men down moved him to again risk his own safety for the fallen soldier. The pain of his arm notwithstanding, he leaped from his position and scurried to Ken's side. With one arm he dragged the moaning man backward, bullets kicking up debris around him.

Within feet of safety, Gil felt a painful and searing impact on his left leg. The blood oozed out indifferently as he clenched his teeth and continued dragging not only Ken but himself toward cover. Several men provided covering fire until they were out of harm's way.

"Ken! Ken!" he shouted, trying to get a response.

"I'll be oka—"

Thankfully, he passed out. Tears began to well in Gil's eyes until this image blurred and began to drift away, until the hardness of the stone jarred him back to his reality.

Even in that involuntary enclosure from the real world, he was able to surmount its hold upon him, the memories of his friends too strong to deny him their place in his mind.

As Jen and the lieutenant headed back to the limo, wheeling a fulfilled veteran, Gil experienced tingling in his left leg. It continued slowly then came on so strong that his leg felt alive! Could this be another miracle? He flinched his leg, feeling movement and the sense that it was part of him again. His inner joy was unimaginable. He could not only see but move his arm and now perhaps his leg. *Oh, God, you are so wonderful.*

The trip to the White House caused Jen to become highly nervous, as to be expected, while Gil bathed in the luxury of his new condition. They arrived at the gate, and after the inspection of credentials, proceeded to a warm greeting at the entrance to the stately building. Gil was moved by the attention lavished upon him and his small group, including the children. Jen was grateful of this opportunity for them to see something they will always remember, as she watched their heads swiveling in awe at the grand majesty of the interior.

An aide led them to the entrance that led to the presentation room, where the chair-bound Gil was ushered in. No sooner did the party enter through the impressive portal than sound of people rising echoed off the walls, followed by an immense ovation and the clapping of hands. Those of the military persuasion maintained an extreme military posture of deference, their salutes mimicking one another in absolute perfection. Gil luxuriated in the show of admiration, as did Jen, while Mason was dumbfounded at such a commotion.

Gee, he thought to himself, *they don't even know my dad, and he's getting all these claps and hollers.* The boy did not really comprehend the magnitude of the honor that'd be bestowed on his father but relished the attention.

Gil was wheeled to the front of the audience, where he was greeted by the president, who patted him on the shoulder, shook his hand, and whispered in his ear. He was ecstatic, smiling broadly at his wife and the two children who were waving madly at him. The ovation continued with the president graciously waiting for it to subside. When the room became quiet, he walked to the microphone and, following the usual pattern of ceremonies, cited the name of the honoree. He followed up by reciting inspirational incidents and actions that made our country proud of its warriors. All this intended to focus on the man to be honored.

Then he began reading the citation describing his heroic actions that resulted achieving the highest military award possible. Many of his counterparts in the audience shook their heads in admiral acknowledgement of his efforts and sacrifice. Gil heard the words and stiffened with sadness as he relived each accounting of the men he rescued while accumulating his wounds. When finished, the president stepped over to Gil with the ribbon decoration in hand. With a movement that even surprised him, Gil rose from his chair and stood at attention, while the chief executive strode behind him to place the ribbon around his neck. That done, he turned to face Gil, who reached out and shook his hand. Then ceremoniously, the veteran presented a sharp salute, his face a portrait of the dutiful soldier. The president nodded and, side by side, wrapped his arm around Gil's shoulder, citing to the onlookers, "This is a true hero."

The applause vindicated the verbal honor, and Jen wept with joy as she held her children to her side, with Mason shouting, "That's my daddy!"

The president again waited until the room was quiet, and after several other routine announcements, the ceremony concluded. The gathering began making its way to the exits, but more than one officer, soldier, lawmaker, or ordinary citizen made their way to the crowd, congratulating the man honored.

As the throng thinned, Lieutenant Johnson began to wheel Gil away, Jen and the kids in tow.

"Mrs. Madden?"

She turned and was greeted by the president. "Yes?"

"Let me say how proud you and your family must be."

"Thank you, sir."

"When I read the citation, I was deeply impressed by the actions of this brave young man. His sacrifice prompted me to inquire further about his care and treatment. What I learned saddened me greatly and only hope that one day he'll be whole again."

"Thank you, Mr. President, your concern is moving."

"After I placed the ribbon around his neck, and standing before him, I observed an effort to rise from his wheelchair, an effort reflected in his face as he grimaced slightly. Then the motion of his right arm, rising several inches from the armrest. I took his hand in mine and shook it, after which his body straightened significantly and again the effort to raise his arm. Tell me, do you think he was aware of what was happening?"

"I'm not sure, sir. Perhaps. It would have been a crowning achievement to have met you. I think that would have meant as much as receiving the medal. Thank you, sir, for your interest."

Shaking his hand, Jen took the children by hand and followed after her husband.

Bonds of friendship transcend the usual routine of everyday life and its impacts. Into this man, the spiritual essence of his fallen comrades flowed most generously and divinely into his being so that for this moment in his life, he would enjoy the gratitude of his nation.

Passing Tribute

Under a blue sky, bathed in the bright rays of the morning sun, the navy launch plied its way through the choppy green waters of the bay. The constant spray, kicked up by the speeding craft, cooled the face of Gil Duncan Jr, a man on a mission. He's editor of Navy News, a publication dedicated to the history of the US Navy, past and present. Articles run the gamut from ships, battles, personnel and other associated activities. Today his task is twofold and personal. A final chapter is to be written of a ship belonging to a legendary, but controversial class of ships, the Clemson destroyers. Built too late to see service in WW I, all 156 were laid up, apparently to rust away, as the Navy had no use for them. As were the Wickes class, all 111 of them. They were sturdy but wet ships, distinguished by their flush decks and four stacks. Their speed was an impressive 35 knots or so and were armed with 4 inch <u>main</u> guns and torpedoes.

Eventually some ships were activated and many served in the Pacific region, where at a later date, they would suffer severe losses in combat.

WW II sprang up, and in exchange for base leasing, 50 ships were transferred to the British Navy, sorely in need of escort craft, a precursor of the famous Lend-Lease Agreement. Even though obsolescent, they still had plenty of fight in them, but of course, you had to make do with what you had.

Now, two years after the end of the conflict, unneeded or obsolete equipment were being jettisoned or transferred to other nations. In the case of the four stackers, there was no question of their fate. Most were destined to be scrapped, and since ecological concerns had not risen to prominence, some were tagged for target use, complete with corrosive or caustic contaminants, still aboard.

As the launch approached the destroyer, she rode easily among the swells with a proud look but also a sadness if a ship could conjure such an emotion. Gil's memory sprung into action as they approached the grey steel steed. He had the pleasure of speaking and meeting with some of his dad's shipmates, and the dialogue swelled his chest with pride, not that it was absent before hand, but intensified with the stories he heard.

Gil hand known that his father attended culinary school part time in the mid twenties, hoping to establish a career in the art, but was forced to drop out due to expenses. Prior to that, with what experience he gathered, he would try his different take on food creation at home, but his wife Jean would have none of it, gently serving notice that the kitchen was her domain. Jobs were getting scarce, and after talking it over with his wife, he enlisted in the Navy, Junior was only 10 at the time, but was excited that his dad joined what he thought was an adventurous branch of the military.

After boot camp or basic training was completed, he signed on for mess duty and took another shot at learning the food preparation courses offered by the service. Something clicked in him and he took to the training with vigor. Completing the program, he now had to be assigned to a venue to practice his new found skills.

Jean rented the house to some friends and moved to the home port Gil was posted to, his absence a source of loneliness, while young Gil was thrilled to be with his dad again, hoping to see and board the ships that crowded the port. The fact that he was not primarily assigned to a fighting position or one more representative of a manly stature, as the boy saw it, Gil gently chided to boy, telling him every position meant something, not the glamour, but the responsibility.

Looking at the man, you would've thought he was in the engineering section or some other position requiring brawn. His six, five inch height plus a robust 225 body built like a tractor, belied his finesse with shipboard cooking.

His shipmates remarked that Phil Duncan was a bear of a man, but as gentle as a teddy bear, unless of course someone stupid enough to challenge him made the mistake of doing so. Even then, his response was not as extreme as one would suppose. In the end, the unfortunate sailor became his friend as most of his shipmates did.

Finally a ship posting, an old four stacker. The only thing that concerned Gil was if the galley would serve his needs. Bring new to the crew, he made it appoint to meet as many of them as he could, to know them, their histories and so on. The true test of his talents came when the first mess was served. He needn't have worried, as the garbage containers were almost empty.

Several years and a few more ships to serve aboard, culminated in achieving a rank he coveted, Mess Specialist Chief, (MSC) By word of mouth, his ability to satisfy any hungry stomach was legendary. This was no little accomplishment, as Navy food was considered the best, especially for ships at sea for long durations. His devotion to altering a menu with little added enticements turned a good meal into a great meal.

The rumor spread, whether true or not, that he could transform Spam into a New York steak.

Those that served under him knew that he would brook no n less a service than the best. His joviality. Calmness and overall demeanor melted away any reticence to converse with him and many are the times a crowd of them would shoot the breeze on the fan tail, each one trying to out do the other. When on shore leave and in company with his mates, he made sure they took no untoward liberty with their liberty—in other words, 'don't do anything to embarrass the ship or the captain.' That didn't preclude having some drinks and letting loose a little after weeks at sea, but it was moderately contained.

Welcomed shore leave saw him dote on his son and relieve the loneliness of his wife with tender affection. The young lad jumped with joy when allowed to visit his dad's ship. He ignored the comments of his peers when they bad mouthed the 'ancient' destroyer his was posted on, pointing out the sleekness of the newer types. Remarkably, his recital of what his father had said to him about responsibility, stifled any recurring putdowns and even made him a sort of junior philosopher with the kids. After all, what do we know, they were kids.

Frequent postings to other venues were part of the package the family endured. For Junior, it was an exciting prospect of different ships and surroundings. For Jean it was the expected part of what all military families experience. Even so, a change of scenery was always welcomed unless it was in the northern reaches of Alaska she would joke. "I don't think we have any bases up there," He would jokingly reply.

Then the jubilant day arrived signaling the boy's 17th birthday. It was more than the passing of a numerical milestone, it was, to young Gil, his ticket into the Navy. While his mother harbored a reluctance to see her only child prancing around the world or something like that, she was proud that he'd want to follow in his father's footsteps. He'd wanted to be just like his father, except food handling was not his forte. He craved adventure and derring do, sword in hand and a dagger in his mouth. Of course his dad would bring him down to earth with the realities of what he'd face.

Even so, the boy was fired up and off to the recruiting station they went. Papers were filled out and a preliminary exam followed. What was to be routine exercise turned out to be devastating. Young Gil had a mild respiratory condition which was sufficient enough to disqualify his admittance into the service. One of the reasoning factors had to do with a possible posting to a unit which required a one hundred percent physical qualification. This was a period when only the most fit recruit would be allowed to serve. Years later, when every able bodied men were needed, he'd have passed.

Gil tried to ease his son's dejection as well as he could, but the thought of a possible father-son team up on the same ship washed away with the tears rolling down son's cheeks. His mother, slightly relieved at the rejection, shared his emotions as any loving mother would and the boy unashamedly collapsed into her arms, her comforting embrace soothing his pain as it did the many times he was a child.

During the ensuing days, school, part time work and the companionship of his dad did much to help the boy overcome his doldrums. He was encouraged to finish school and possible college, which in itself posed a financial hurdle, but there was time to consider the options.

Gil had the chance to serve on a newer class destroyer, a sleeker type than the old four stacker. As long as the galley was up to his standards, that meant very little, for you don't live by the glamour of a ship. It's the punch in can deliver. Still it was attractive and his new shipmates, as with most sailors, would defend the honor of their ship if she were, maligned, and that could lead to dire consequences.

As the years passed many changes were developed. Young Gil had married and was working as an intern for a publishing company. The department he was assigned to involved naval projects which pleased him to no end, especially when he got around to bragging about his dad.

Gil was back aboard an old four stacker, reviving a feeling of being reunited with an old friend. Subconsciously he had always carried a fond attachment for the gray smoker as he called her, the plumes of smoke belching from her stacks an unmistakable sign of her presence.

His rating had made him eligible to assume direction of both the wardroom and the galley. After requesting permission to come aboard, he checked in with those designated personnel that he was responsible to.

Afterwards, after stowing his gear, he inspected the galley and was satisfied. Later that day, he was summoned to the bridge, where the OOD led him to the CO. a Commander named Chris Nardussi and it was a slight surprise to learn he hailed from the same home town of Orangeburg where Gil was born.

He was a young fellow, but displayed the impression of a good CO. They spoke for a short while, comparing recollections of their home town and Gil was impressed with the young officers bearing.

SLICED FROM LIFE

"Chief, I'm in a bind which I hope you can help me out with." "Certainly sir, how can I be of assistance?" "First let me say that your talents have been sung to high heaven by many officers that I've served with." "Pardon, sir?" "Okay, I didn't say that right, but what I mean to say is that you have become sort of a celebrity." "Blushing just a trifle, something foreign to Gil, he replied, "How's that sir?" "Your messes man, your messes." The eyes of the CO flashed wide as if he was attending to a celebrity and in his mind Gil was a celebrity.

Look, you just been assigned and I'm sure you have lots of things to do. This communique I received puts me in a hole. "How's that sir?" The Admiral is hosting a delegation of bigwigs tomorrow night and wants to hold the festivities on board. It's short notice, I know, but can you put something together that will at least pass as a decent meal?"

The gauntlet had been dropped. Gil could never resist a challenge and an opportunity to display his culinary skills. "Count on it sir. Let me know the particulars, time, number of guests and so on." The CO let loose a concealed sigh of relief as Gil left the bridge.

Returning to the galley, he summoned the mess chief and ran the dilemma the CO faced by his counterpart. Together they cobble together a basic outlay of what was needed. Building on that, Gil worked his magic and impressed his assistant with the embellishments that would turned a good meal into a great one. The supplies were garnered in sufficient quantities to meet the gathering and all other amenities were attended to.

Needless to say, the evening was a success as far as the meal went. The next day, the CO confided in Gil that an Admiral had hinted at stealing the Chief away in a complimentary joke while others commended the CO for being a gracious host. "Chief that was a great feat you pulled off." "Thank you sir. By the way, will you sample this for me?" He handed the young officer a plate with a sumptuous mounded of chocolate pastry.

Taking a spoonful, the CO closed his eyes, while raising his head and moaning a sound signaling the desired effect that Gil hoped for. "Chief, for sure you'd better not let the Admiral taste that or you're gone," he quipped, still reveling in the delicious treat. "I'll be very careful sir," both of them chuckling.

From that day onward, Gil took the CO under his wing, of course without being obvious about it. In a way, a certain bond had been cemented between the two, that while not dismissing the formality demanded of both, bent the rules ever so slightly. This was the beginning of a 'happy ship.'

Clouds of war loomed on the horizon, and when Gil brought the CO coffee, they would discuss the situation and both felt that the Us would be in it up to its neck. Germany soon invaded Poland and WW II was off to a flying start. There was a degree of concern over the Japanese aggression in China and both felt a conflict with the 'Rising Sun' was not too far off.

As this anticipation was bearing fruit, Gil's ship was ordered to the Far East to join the Astatic Fleet under Admiral Thomas C. hart. Jean was heartbroken but bore the move as bravely as she could. Young Gil was concerned that his dad's new destination could conceivably meet with unexpected consequences, since there had been rumblings between Japan and the US.

Both were at the port to see him off, the ever-present plumes of smoke and ashes trailing the ship as it headed out. After a stop at Hawaii, the ship continued on to Cavite Naval Base in the Philippines. From there it received orders to join with several other destroyers in patrol activities. The CO ensured that the crew was informed of the tensions that had resulted in the ship being deployed to the Pacific and to be alert for anything suspicious they may encounter.

The crew had good response times during drills, the CO confident of the performance of his sailors. Now was the time to iron out any glitches and the repeated drills eliminated those that arose. Short of combat, they would be ready and as young as they were, itching to show what they could do if pushed. They were ready.

Then it happened. Pearl Harbor had been attacked and all ships were put on alert. They didn't have long to wait. The Philippines were assaulted on December 12 and because air support had been devastated by an air attacks on all the airfields the Asiatic Fleet was ordered to Java. It was here that Gil's ship was detached to escort a

SLICED FROM LIFE

transport loaded with American civilians and a potpourri of other nationals The sortie was thought to be reasonably safe, though not without danger, as the Japanese Imperial Navy was occupied with supporting the invasion of the Islands.

Fortunately the ship had replenished its food stores the previous month and had refueled in Surabaya, Java. Late that night, the darkened destroyer followed the transport Wyoming in the direction of Australia. All hands were alert and nervous as what might be hidden in the darkness. For two days they eluded Japanese patrol plane by sheer luck and had made good headway.

It was early morning and a slight fog mass lay ahead of the two ships. Gil sensed some protection in that and proceeded to the bridge with a steaming pot of coffee and some pastry desserts for the CO and others of the bridge contingent. It was shortly after 0830, the usual time he frequently attended the bridge. "Ah, Chief, just in time, hot coffee." "And some pastry sir."

"Ship dead ahead, coming out of the fog," the lookout blared over the speaker. The CO and OOD peered through the mist to get a view when a distant report was heard. A flash of flame and billowing smoke resided over what was once the forward gun mount. Seconds later, a hellish crash rendered the port side of the bridge, knocking everyone to the deck.

Gil had fallen alongside the CO and as he struggled to his feet, the red stains across the skipper's chest spoke for themselves. He attempted to lift the injured officer, but was pushed away. "Chief, man your post," the groaning voice ordered. "But sir, you nee——," "Go," the stricken Commander ordered again. Gil hesitated, feeling anger and a need to help his CO, but realized the ship had to come first, it couldn't be otherwise.

After he sprinted out the hatchway, the injured man, coughed several times, rolled onto his side, and his eyes closed, for the last time. Orders were barked to the helmsman and others that were still able to function. The OOD ordered full rt rudder and flank speed, to move as quickly as possible away from another salvo. Too late, for another round struck the aft part of the ship, piercing its plates and detonating in the fire room. Wing fuel tanks, above the water line, were also punctured, creating a blaze in the fire room.

The blast also disabled one of the geared steam turbines which hindered maneuverability as well as speed. Apparently satisfied that the damaged ship posted no further threat, the enemy ship turned its attention to the transport. In short order, it rammed two Long Lance torpedoes into the helpless vessel. In less than ten minutes, she went under, the screams and pleas of the helpless human cargo, wafting across the wave tops.

That done, the enemy destroyer turned to finish off its counterpart. Four inch return fire was not as effective as the five inch rounds that had devastated her. Confidently, the enemy moved closer for the kill and at that moment, a Dutch B-10 bomber approached the carnage and released two bombs. While not making any hits, it was sufficient for the fortunate ship to turn tail and head back into the mist.

Back on board the stricken warship, surviving bridge officers and personnel barked orders to contain the effects of the damage received. The fireroom hit was especially a concern, the wing tank's fuel gushing into the compartment and catching fire. Gil's repair crew were dispatched to contain the damage and to rescue survivors. That order need not have been given; these were their shipmates.

A fire hose was quickly connected to a standpipe and the stream of water played on the entrance to the fireroom. While not dousing the flames, the force of the stream forced the burning oil back somewhat, allowing the party to enter. Even with fire retardant coverings, the danger was only minimized. But that small opportunity allowed them to scan for survivors through the thick smoke.

Laying on the deck where the smoke was thinnest, Gil could see a heap of bodies, and some moving desperately to escape the flames. He ordered the hose to play on him as he crawled forward to effect a rescue. The force of the water was dampened a bit by his fire resistant gear and he managed to reach a group of semi conscious shipmates and managed to pull seven of them to safety, one by one. Four others had died. Crawling back after determining there were no others he could not see damaged overhead beam came crashing down, pinning this body to the deck. It was too much and the culinary celebrity, a great friend to his shipmates, died a heroes' death.

The skill of the repair party contained and eliminated the fire, sorting through the debris for their comrades.

Topside, the ship made way to the area where the transport went down and rescue any survivors they could find. Of the 600 plus passengers and crew that debarked, only a hundred and twenty were still alive to be hauled aboard.

The next day was a somber occasion. Seventeen of the ship's company had made the supreme sacrifice. With a solemnity broken only by the waves of the water being pierced by the bow racing through the sea, and the sobs of the female survivors, not many eyes were devoid of tears as one by one, flag draped forms were cast gently into the deep.

The last laid to eternal rest was Chief Gil Duncan, a chef's cap tucked along side his form. Many in the crew apologized to the survivors for not being able to prevent the attack. This was nonsense of course, but this was a proud ship and to have something like this happen, was a blot on their collective consciences.

Young Gil's mission was to photograph varies areas of the ship for his publication, but the most important thing for him hung on a bulkhead in the galley. A plaque had been attached with a short recital of the battle action which read as follow:

While escorting the transport Wyoming, this ship was engaged and damaged by a Japanese destroyer, preventing any retaliatory action that would have saved her from destruction. The aborted effort also claimed the lives of seventeen shipmates. (The names of those lost were listed, with Duncan, Gilbert MSC emblazoned at the bottom.) We will always honor our fellow crewmates for giving their all.

Engulfed by the emotion flowing through his being, he said a silent prayer, and would return to retrieve the plaque after filling his photographic requirements. As he photographed the galley, visions appeared in his mind of the cooks preparing a meal for the crew and his dad hovering over them to make sure everything was to his liking.

On the bridge, he saw what his father had seen and regretted, having to leave his wounded captain, The pictures were getting emotionally harder to snap, Other sections of the ship received the same process, but it was in the fireroom, the quiet and empty section, was when the full impact of what his father had done, was felt. The lives he saved, the effort he expended to save his comrades; how proud to have been his son.

He returned to the galley and again read the inscription, his pride growing ever stronger.

His reverie was broken by one of the sailors who escorted him. "Mister Duncan, we'll wait on the fantail 'till you're finished. But if you need anything, give a holler." With that he paused a while longer, staring at a piece of history and visualizing the actions of his father. Turning abruptly, his head struck the edge of the hatch. Dazed, he slumped to the deck a gray mist enveloping his eyes until he drifted into unconsciousness. It wasn't until his body felt the pulse of a rolling movement, that he began to revive. His senses reeled at the sight of a foaming sea and movement!

What's this, we're under way, how's that possible? What the hell is goin' on? "Hey Chief, snap out of it, the CO's waitin' for his java." "Huh? What?" What's he talking about?. He looks down and observes the tray he's carrying with coffee and pastries. "Ah, er, yeah Art, guess I better get movin" Wait, I don't even know that sailor and called him by name. "Ya better hurry, its 0830." His head spinning, Gil frantically searches for an answer to this nightmare. Yes, that's it, it's a nightmare.

A spray of sea water from a rogue wave douse him to the realization that he's not dreaming, but he has to be, and wiping his eyes he Not knowing why, he drops the tray and charges for the bridge. Again why? He catches sight of a transport off the port beam. Instantly a shock envelopes his body, but why? And why did that sailor call me Chief. Then another alarm strikes his fragile senses, 0830! Why is that important? The time, the time, that's it! He bolts toward the bridge, almost knocking down several crew members in the process.

Even with this unexplainable haste, he experiences an urgency that perplexes an already confused mind. Why? Why?. Without hesitation he bursts onto the bridge just in time to hear the squawk box informing the bridge of a ship dead ahead. Startling the CO and

SLICED FROM LIFE

other personnel, he rushes toward the helmsman, brushing him aside and turn the wheel hard left. In spite of this move, astounding the bridge crew, a shell already in flight, demolishes the number one gun into oblivion.

So quick were his movements that evaded any interference Turning, he tackled the captain to the deck just as a second shell struck outside the rear portion of the bridge. Shards of shrapnel penetrated the enclosure, wounding several men. "What the hell are you doing Chief? the flustered CO thundered. As Gil helped the stunned officer to his feet, General Quarters are sounded, activating all personnel to their combat posts.

Occupied with fighting the ship, he yelled, "we'll talk about this later Chief, right now get to your post." "Aye, sir," Gil responded and left the bridge hurrying to his assigned unit, a damage control party. Wasring no time the skipper ordered, "left full rudder," the helmsman repeating the order. "Okay, Nip, lets see how hungry you are, do you like fish?" The 4 inch guns all came into play, the ship broadside to the enemy, thus unmasking all the weapons. The CO ordered the torpedo section to swing the tubes out, a, get a bearing and when ready fire. Momentarily, four silver projectiles plunged into the water racing toward the enemy ship.

Meanwhile, as Gil raced to his party, he asked himself, 'how the hell do I know where I'm going, I've never been on this ship?' Whatever it was, he knew exactly where to go and the men that he joined. "Chief, what kind of action are we in,?" one of the men asked. "Jap destroyer Ken, knocked out number one gun and scratched the bridge." Again he thought, I've never met this guy and yet I know his name.

Topside, the enemy ship was consumed with returning gun fire and tried to evade the torpedoes, combing the first two, but unable to avoid the second pair. A geyser of smoke and flame lit up the gray overcast, the ship breaking in two. Fragments of steel peppered the ocean's surface after being propelled skyward by the tremendous force of the twin explosions. The cheering of the crew resounded throughout the ship, but quickly abated. S A shell fired before the explosion struck the starboard wing tanks and penetrated the fireroom. Ordered to the damaged compartment, a hose was coupled to a standpipe. They played the stream to prevent the flaming oil from spreading. Gil lay on the deck to get a better view of any possible survivors. Spotting a number of semi conscious crewmen, he struggle forth and retrieve them one by one, at least those still alive. Subconsciously, he knew how this had to end. It jived with all he'd done without knowing how or why.

In this manner, he exhibited a bravery symbolic of his father which enabled him to face the inevitable. It wasn't long in coming, As it struck, his consciousness yielded to the impact, the pain muted.

"Hey, mister Duncan, are you okay," one of the launch sailors exclaimed, as he roused Gil. "Huh, awh, I feel dizzy." "You have a small gash on your forehead, what happened?" I must have bumped into something. How long was I out?" "After we left you we waited over an hour and not seeing you, I went back and found you on the deck."

Thanking the sailor, Gil asked him for a little more time, which the sailors obliged, He intended to retrieve the plaque, only this time he experienced a connection to what his dad had done and the mysterious hallucinatory dream he lived. It was a dream, no a nightmare, wasn't it? Looking at the wording on the plaque griped him and stoked a fantasy only a fiction writer could dream up.

While escorting the transport Wyoming, this ship was engaged and damaged by a Japanese destroyer. Undaunted the Commanding Officer responded in the grand tradition of the US Navy, by attacking the enemy warship. Outclassed by the enemy repower, he nevertheless executed a successful torpedo attack which destroyed the enemy. The transport Wyoming, which they had been escorting, was untouched and its cargo of personnel unharmed. The action also claimed the lives of sixteen shipmates. We will always honor our fellow crewmates for giving their all. The crew of this fighting ship salute them. Here are the names of our friends and heroes.

Gil read them, one by one, and at the very end, Duncan, Gilbert MSC. He closed his yes and wondered what fate had prescribed for him. Was it real? How could it be? And et, he couldn't deny the inscription. Only he knew of this second chance at redemption, something no one would never believe, something he almost couldn't believe himself, except he had lived it.

And if he had lived it, he would honor his father and those who died with him. The plaque would remain with the ship. It would surrender itself to the courage that had created it and rest with those souls, a sentinel always on guard.

A week later, as an honor and courtesy to the men who had served on the slender greyhound, former crew members were afforded the opportunity to attend the final moments that would send the ship to the bottom.

A command shop directing the exercise was crowded with personnel lining the rails, foremost, the former crew. Gil had mixed emotions as he looked out at what seemed to be a ship, knowing its fate, proudly holding its place, riding easily among the swells that caressed her flanks as if to sooth her.

The loud speaker announced that a submarine would dispatch the target with a torpedo. Every head, eye, stomach and muscle, tensed awaiting the strike. Then an explosion amid ship tossed a plume of seawater into the sky. The ship shuddered, but refuse to die. A second explosion soon followed, rendering the reluctance to sink useless.

Slowly, the entering water made evident its effect, as she settled by the bow and in doing so, whether by currents or some other factor, turned toward the command ship as if to say goodbye.

The stood erect, raising hands to their foreheads in salute of their former home. Slow it was and painful for many as the waters closed over her for the final time. Gil knew that the spirits of those men lost, were manning the watch, swabbing the decks, or serving the mess, if only in his fantasizing mind. A lesser tribute would not suffice. Rest easy dad.

The Visitors

The dark rain-swollen clouds mirrored the saddened hearts of the citizens filing by in long lines leading to the cathedral. Their beloved king had passed away, its loss felt as keenly as that of a relative. For over forty years, the head of this principality had ruled with a benevolence unsurpassed when compared to other ruling families. But it wasn't an unlimited benevolence; it was balanced by a thoughtful and insightful understanding of his subject's needs and the best way to fulfill them. Charity had its place, but so did self-reliance and productivity. The realm had at one time seen dire days that begged for relief, and upon assuming the throne, the new sovereign set about the long and tedious transformation needed.

What set him apart from the usual appointments of royalty was his regal calmness and unspectacular garb. Together with his kind face and calming voice, he relished receiving his subjects at court and put to rest any apprehension that many feared they would have in approaching their monarch. No, he didn't relinquish all the trappings of royalty but only used them sparingly, when necessary. This did not escape the attention of the populace, and in time, their pride in their king knew no bounds. No one was indentured or bound by any note of servitude unless it was voluntary. Merchants were divested of any inclination to cheat on their goods or taxes, for by doing so would eventually diminish their trade and tarnish their reputations.

Almost unthinkable at the time, he would have the people select a few of their company to serve on a citizens' council that would address the needs of the commoner. They would hear any complaints brought forth and debate among themselves what they believed to be the best remedy and then to present it to His Majesty. This forum alone is believed by many to be the capstone that connected one end of the royal bridge to that of the subjects of the realm.

Lest one think that all problems were solved, he would be greatly mistaken. But this far surpassed other societies that abutted this land of innovation and promise. The failures accented the successes, but the people were realists, and this only because of the protocols installed by their leader. Through the years, a bond grew between the governed and he who governed.

It was against this history that the loyal subjects of the king paid their last respects. True to his bearing as a man for the people, his bier was plain and the clothing unadorned but moderately fashionable. The wailing of the women and even some men was testimony of what they had lost. Among those seeking a last audience with their king was a farmer named Stefan. He had traveled a fair distance but would have climbed the most daunting mountain if need be to pay his last respects. In his company was his wife, Magda, a handsome woman who, like most of the women in the land, was a strong and uniting presence in the family. She appreciated the status of equality that had been earned grudgingly over the years, due mostly to the reforms made possible by the one they honored today.

Eleven-year-old Josef, their only child, paid a sober and compliant respect to a man he had never met but heard so much about. In the evenings after supper, when Mama would sit by the candle sewing and Papa would sit in his favorite chair, puffing on a pipe older than the boy, he would hear stories about this fabled person that made him seem more personable than royal. If only he had had a chance to meet him in person. Would there ever be another one of the royal blood to carry on like he did? One could only hope.

The king's son, of whom the people knew little about, would assume the throne in the coming weeks. Although not a stranger to the public, his presence had been overshadowed by the dynamic energy of his father. Therefore his quality was unknown, and a prayer was said for him by many of the families that he would walk in his father's steps. The late king's advisors and aides gave hope that any failings the younger may have would be tempered by their sage instructions.

Leaving the cathedral, the family headed home with the moistened skies adding to their physical and emotional discomfort. The countryside itself seemed to be in mourning as not one iota of color, lest it be gray or black, could be seen. All the gloom was not entirely confined to the loss of their sovereign. Being a farmer is an occupational chess game at times, and in this season, Stefan had faced a check, if not a checkmate. Crops were a major source of his and any farmer's income. This had been a mixed year, with certain crops doing well, while some withered or didn't fully develop.

He had lived on hard times before and was confident it could be done again. Thank God for the support of his wife and son, who had been denied many of the comforts and necessities of life. But this was their chosen life, and they would make do.

The province was a mixture of success and failure, and no different from other governed areas. What set it apart was the acknowledged need of some and the apparent well-being of others and how they were addressed. It was heartwarming to see hands-on efforts by small groups who combined their assets to be distributed where needed. In times to come, those who had been aided returned the largesse and, in many cases, to those who were benevolent to them when they were down.

While a cheery display to be envied, it still left whole swathes of the principality in dire straits. This had been a very trying year, and while basically sound, the country did not have much breathing room. It was mainly through the many reforms that it was able to weather the shortfalls. Now to await the new rule and what it could portend for their future.

The crowning of the new sovereign was austere at best, in keeping with the current situation. As a result of the late king's foresight, a small financial reserve had been amassed, mainly to address situations that would one day require their use. There had been times when the temptation to exhaust this reserve was so overwhelming that it was with great sacrifice and fortitude that the option was rejected. And in the main, the decisions proved correct, therefore maintaining the integrity of the funds for the future.

This was the case besieging the new monarch. How he viewed the status of the land would dictate his remedy, and it would be no easy task.

Stefan had farmed for many years and in doing so had learned the lessons of life that came from the toil and grind demanded of his profession. He was a stoutly built fellow with a shock of premature white hair that suggested an age entirely beyond his forty years. His arms were like tree limbs, sturdy and powerful, his legs likewise. His face was kind-looking with eyes that could fix a person's attention just by a casual glance. His temperament was that of one who had known many adversities, so any offense or insult was taken stoically. Vengeance was not his thing, as it solved nothing and only intruded on the time he needed to perform his chores. Nothing could be wasted, most of all time.

Outwardly, he seemed unperturbed, but he was a man of passion, moved when the moment demanded it, and not frittered away on nonsense. He was frugal with his time but lavished it on his family and considered himself blessed.

Several weeks had passed since the beloved king had been interred at the cathedral vaults. Expectations grew as to the course the new monarch would chart, hoping that his foresight would be on a par with his father's. Even so, life continued, and so did the ills or good fortune.

After a hard day in the fields, Stefan and his son relaxed for a short time before returning home. While Joseph fed the horse with some wild grass and petted its flanks, he looked to his father and asked if things would get better.

"My son, we get what we earn. If things are favorable, we get more. If not, we get less. The important thing is to work so that we can be secure in our lives, be it with food or shelter or even with money." The last part evoked a wry bit of laughter; money, ha, who had any?

Josef looked to his father with a great faith instilled by his short years of life that had been strengthened by his father's guidance.

"Father, we have our farm and Mama to take care of us. I am happy." Stefan's pride in his son was not just a birthright, it was the manner in which the boy viewed life and the respect he displayed at all times. He could not imagine life without him. Would that he could provide more.

The house reeked with the delightful pungent odors of a dinner being prepared for the hungry men who labored so hard. But the fragrance could not conceal the paucity of the meal, even though Magda had labored so hard to stretch what was available. Grace was recited, and before the portions were meted out, a knock on the door interrupted the tranquil gathering. Wonderment crossed Stefan's mind as he rose from his chair and approached the door. Neighbors were far and few out here in the countryside, and most would not intrude upon a family during dinnertime.

As he opened the door, his first inclination was to shut it quickly as he viewed the person before him. However, curiosity squelched that idea, and he stepped beyond the doorway to face this stranger.

"What can I do for you, my friend?" was his initial and automatic response. The man before him was pathetically clothed, his tunic a ragged assembly of patterns that defied description and was in dire need of washing. "My dear sir, I mean no offense to you and ask forgiveness if I have disturbed your evening. All I ask for is some water to sate my thirst as I have traveled far."

Stefan looked at the bedraggled fellow and could not in all good conscience turn him away.

"Come, enter my home and I will see to your thirst."

Doing so invited a fair chance of danger, for it was known that at times desperate people had committed acts of theft, robbery, or worse. Still, the farmer sensed an urgency that could not be denied. He escorted the man into his home, as Magda, who had risen to see what was happening, almost collided with the invited guest.

"Oh my heavens, are you all right?" she blurted out upon seeing this disheveled stranger, more affected by his clothing than his obvious need for a bath.

Defying his apparent destitute appearance, his reply was appreciative of the woman's concern. "Oh my, I am quite all right, my lady, and I beg your forgiveness in causing such distress. I've had a difficult time which I pray not to lay at your feet."

"Nonsense, I'm not made of jelly, but thank you for your interest. Now, before you collapse completely, have a seat." Her arm guided him to the table. Hospitality had been a second trait ingrained in this family, as indeed it had been in many others. The loneliness and the need to depend on others at various times kindled this act of humanity so much so that to ignore it was a stain upon family honor.

"Let me rest for a short while, and I will be on my way," he uttered as Stefan handed him a glass of water.

"Rest you shall and not for a moment," Magda replied maternally, "and not on an empty stomach."

"But, my dear woman, I have no money and do not wish to impose on you."

"Your words are better placed than your manners. If we sought money, you would not be sitting at our table but beating the dust in the road. Now shush and tell us about yourself while I tend to things. Magda had put herself in a precarious position. The food had just about been enough for the three of them, but with another mouth at the table, the portions would tend to be meager. She looked at Stefan and knew that he approved of her thoughtfulness to the stranger. A smile and slight nod to her was all that was needed. Their years together had solidified an understanding that precluded the use of words. Josef looked at the new member at the table and didn't quite know what to say or do. Visitors had been too far and few to imprint on him certain courtesies or actions. He needn't have worried.

"What a fine-looking boy you have, I would say about ten?"

"Oh, no, sir, I'm eleven—oh, excuse me, I didn't mean to interrupt you."

"Don't worry, lad, no offense taken. I would guess you are the man of the house?"

Josef's face turned a slight shade of red as he lowered his head, gulped, then getting his wits about him, quickly rejoined with "Oh no, sir, my father is the boss, er, I mean the man of the house. I'm too young to be a man." The adults broke out into a burst of laughter as Josef looked on wild-eyed. Had he said something funny?

"He is a man, a little one, but he is a man," intoned his father. "He is my right hand man in all that I do." The boy's chest puffed a little, and he felt as tall as any man.

While the men chatted, Magda tried to assemble what food there was that could garner some satisfaction. She deliberately withheld a small portion from her plate, adding it to the fourth setting. Taking the next day's portion of bread and adding some dried fruit that usually managed to keep from rotting, a fine-looking although not filling meal was brought to the table. Before sitting, she quickly went to the cupboard and remembered a bag of mixed nuts that a friend had given her the week before. At least this would satisfy the urge to chew, a self-indulgent smile creasing her face.

The informal setting elicited a banter that ignored the state of the man's attire or origins. The latter was soon addressed when he spoke casually about his present situation.

"My name is Paul, having traveled from the northern provinces. I have been away for some time, and then word reached me that a dear relative had died."

"Oh my soul," declared Magda. Even Stefan reacted with a slight jolt.

"My journey will take me to the homestead so that I may pay my final respects. And because of your kindness, the path has become easier."

As he spoke, Josef eyed the unfinished portions on his guest's plate, his eyes glancing at the morsels, then darting to Paul's face as he spoke and down again at the plate, his lips pursing. This had not gone unnoticed by the guest, and he waved the plate toward Josef, saying, "I have had my fill, and if you wish, my young man, can you relieve me of my excess lest it go to waste?" A diplomatic exercise that brought joy to the boy and a silent thank you from his parents. Disheveled he was, but not his honor.

"Tonight, you will stay here and gather some rest for your journey tomorrow. Magda will bring some bedding, but all we can offer is the floor."

"Tis better than the cold ground, bless you."

"I have some wine which I think you will like and could help you sleep, ha, ha."

"I need no wine for that but will enjoy the vintage with you, my good host."

They emptied the last of the bottle which provided as fair glass for each. Paul related to Stefan that his circumstances had come about by unforeseen events that he was powerless to overcome. Much of what he had was lost, and he was reduced to his present state. He said this without rancor and impressed his host with his lack of hostility. With that, all retired for the night, Josef bidding his new friend good night.

Stefan and his son would be gone to the fields before their guest awoke, and he took Magda aside instructing her to give him the tunic kept in the closet. She was to relieve Paul of his polyglot coat, refusing any resistance on his part to refuse the gift. No man should be forced to honor his dead in clothes that would be better burned. And indeed, Paul did refuse the offering, but Magda was steadfast, and her blunt threat of mayhem was enough to convince him otherwise.

"Your kindness has eased my trials. I wish you and your family the best of fortunes." With that, he strolled away, adorned in his better tunic and looking less sinister.

Out in the fields, father and son toiled to reap a future harvest, both addressing their chores in silence until Josef paused, leaned against his rake, and staring at the sky, said, "Father, that Paul seemed like a nice man. What do you think happened to him? He seemed sad."

"Misery, my son, comes in many forms. It is well to let it lie unless the one afflicted decides to share it. Sharing is a form of healing, especially when you are in sympathy with that person. I believe he is a noble person, not asking any more than what we could provide. But our attention to his troubles seemed to ease his pain."

Josef was a thoughtful son, but his life was lonely except on Sundays, when the family journeyed to the city to attend Mass. Afterward, a pleasant day was spent at the park near the river, where many of the young people gathered. It was here that Josef truly enjoyed himself, like any youngster would, playing with his friends and sharing all kinds of stories. Stefan lamented the bare existence at the farm, where the boy was obedient to his duties but also alone. How he wished for closer neighbors. Josef never really complained, and although outwardly content, he too felt the absence of his peers. Nevertheless, his father was proud of his youthful exuberance whenever he undertook and completed any task his father gave him.

In the days that followed, thoughts were voiced as to the outcome of Paul's journey to his relative's funeral. "Father, do you think we will see him again, I mean, will he return your tunic?"

"Son, a gift given is just that, a gift. There is no tasking that it be returned, for then it would not be a gift. If it is returned, fine, but do not look for that, and you will be satisfied." Josef thought his father to be the wisest person he knew. His counsel always filled his desire to learn and he never shied away from asking any question.

After another day in the fields, the tired pair settled near the fireplace after supper. Magda occupied herself with some knitting, and Stefan started to doze. Josef lay on the floor, staring at the ceiling and imagining all sorts of things that young people fill their minds with. A sharp rap on the door startled everyone, and raising himself from his chair, Stefan, looking quizzically at his wife as if she might have any idea who it could be, proceeded to the solid oak portal.

As he approached the door, he could hear a somber wailing and presumed that some unfortunate person may have been injured. Flinging the door open wildly, he saw a limp form crouched at the base of the threshold, head pressed against his forearm and crying uncontrollably. Fearing that he was physically hurt, Stefan knelt at his side and tried to calm him not only to ease his noticeable pain but to discover the source of his torment.

"My son, are you hurt, is there anything I can do for you?"

"Yes, I am hurt, but not in the way you think. Oh, that I would be dead and rid of this misery."

What, thought Stefan, could induce such a plea for death?

Placing his arms around the waist of the poor wretch, he lifted him up, and led him into the house. "Please, the sack, you must find the sack." Looking to the ground, Stefan saw a gray leather bag not too far from where the distressed person had fallen.

"Josef, come to the door."

"Yes, Father."

He then directed his son to retrieve the bag and in doing so led the man to the dining table chair.

"Magda, do we have any spirits left?" His wife had been startled by the loud knock and the commotion she heard between her husband and the stranger. Upon seeing the helpless man being ushered in, she attended to her husband's command and searched the cabinet, obtaining a small flask of brandy.

"My husband. It is all that I could find."

"Here, young man, sip this slowly and regain some calmness." The brandy was gulped rather than sipped and gradually the haggard guest began to become more settled. "Now, sir, what is this nonsense about wanting to die. No one wants to die, at least not willingly." Just then, Josef, strode to his father's side and handed him the leather bag he had retrieved.

"Father, it is very heavy, but I took care to handle it gently."

"Very good, my son, now fetch me a basin of water for your mother. Magda, get the cleaning towel and wipe his face so that we can get a better look at our young friend."

Having cleaned the soil residue streaked with tears, the face that appeared looked fairly handsome but a little haggard. The brandy was now taking effect, and the poor person's manner seemed subdued and compliant. Stefan's fatherly manner had a soothing effect on the man, responding in a more coherent manner to further questions.

"Now, tell us, what could be so terrible that you would be willing to throw your life away? Nothing is that dire."

"Oh, kind sir, you are wrong, so terribly wrong." His eyes started to well up, and Stefan had to do something to prevent another breakdown before he could find the source of this poor soul's suffering.

"If you tell me the story, the whole story, perhaps it will ease whatever it is that's so bedeviling your conscience. We will listen without judgment or condemnation. All we want are the answers that will put you at ease. Can you do that?"

The eyes still were welling, but there seemed to be an acceptance of the assurance promised by Stefan that his tale could bring some relief. Josef, seeing the pain on his face, placed his hand on the man's shoulder, a feebly but appreciated effort to bring him consolation. He smiled at the boy's gesture and turned toward Magda and Stefan, more composed than before.

"I am not what I appear to be, a derelict, a discarded piece of humanity, but in some ways I feel that way. You would be surprised to know that I am somewhat landed, a fully employed individual, or at least that's what I used to be. Let me explain." He paused to gulp a glass of water, wiping his mouth by running his sleeve across his face and then refocusing his attention to his hosts. "I am Johan, from the House of Rupert in the province to the south. My position was as first valet to my lord and was entrusted with many duties, as you can guess.

"For nearly a decade, my services were impeccable, but as it is with human nature, I succumbed to gambling. At first it was minor and entailed very little money, but the lure of the challenge, to be able to best another in games of chance, began to grow as an infected wound. Little by little, my debt grew, and only by deceit was I able to keep this from my lord, for if he discovered this fault in me, it would end my employment. He did not approve of any failings to those in his employ. It came to a head when several of my creditors threatened to reveal my dilemma if payment was not forthcoming.

"Where, oh where, would I secure such a princely sum?" He had been looking at the floor while reciting his pain, as if the shame of it had to be concealed from his benefactors. Stefan looked on quietly, allowing the discourse to soak in as he could imagine the threat of discovery ending a man's position in life but also wondering as to how this seemingly intelligent person could fall prey to his fate.

Josef listened intently, but could he really know what he was hearing? This was alien to him, as he had been brought up to revere honesty and trust. Whatever his personal conflict, he was drawn with sympathy to the man's predicament, not so much for his weaknesses, but because he had some of his own, and this he could relate to.

"I knew that the noose was tightening and had to move quickly. The treasure room was in my care, and I therefore had access to anything it contained. Many of the valuables were rarely used, except on special occasions, and I felt that if I was able to secure a piece of great worth, it would solve my problems in the short term. But even then I knew I could not win. Even if successful, the theft would eventually be discovered, and as prime protector of the room, my scheme would point directly to me, and I would be undone."

Stefan followed the tale and the anguish enveloping the narrator. He glanced at Magda and squeezed her hand, a silent admission of his sympathy. That and only that, for he could not countenance any crime, no matter the root cause. The man then became quiet, closing his eyes, his face contorting, and one could only imagine the demons he must be wrestling with. Abruptly, he sprang to his feet, shouting, "I am a coward, I am lost. Oh, what have I done?" With that he knocked over the chair, almost sending Josef to the floor, and raced toward the door. Stefan was caught by surprise and could only watch helplessly as the tortured soul bolted into the night.

Stepping outside, he peered into the darkness but failed to see anything of movement, as if the man never existed. With bewilderment, Stefan returned to the living room and explained to Magda that their guest had disappeared, giving a gentle hug to Josef.

"Father, what was he talking about? Why did he run like that?"

"The ghosts of conscience have a way of making you do things you thought you were incapable of. His ghosts were very real to him."

"I will pray for him, Father. He seemed like a nice person, and I felt sorry for him."

"So did I, but that did not seem to help him. Here, give me the bag he left behind."

Seating themselves at the table, the patriarch untied the tassels and reached into the damp opening, retrieving a most beautiful tiara. Magda held her breath as this was beyond anything she had ever seen. The stones were dazzling in their color and brightness, embedded into a gold and silver frame that enhanced their beauty even more. Whoever wore this would indeed be the belle of the ball, so to speak.

Stefan, although impressed by its mere presence and value, was not one easily moved by wealth. It may be a measure of one's financial worth, but all too often it dictated how people responded to each other, and not always in a complimentary way. No, wealth was only a means to an end, not an end in itself, and he would have no part of that.

"Father, what we do?" The thought had begun to rise in his mind that somehow the valued item must be returned, but it would mean traveling a fair length and in doing so keep him from the fields.

"Magda, in the early hours, I will set out to the House of Rupert and hopefully return before the day is gone. Josef, you will tend the fields where you can, but don't overwork yourself. Now let us all go to sleep and pray all will go well, especially for our friend."

In the dawn darkness, Stefan prepared the wagon for the journey, having grabbed some cheese and fragments of bread. He begged Esmeralda's pardon, his trusty horse, for taking several handfuls of oats and proceeded down the road, Magda waving him on and worrying for his safety. The trip was slow and plodding, providing ample time to absorb and examine what had happened the previous night. He shook his head and lamented for the young man's future. He prayed that no situation would ever arise that could do to him what he had witnessed.

The sun had been up a short while as he drove down the path to the brilliantly white mansion that screamed wealth. Knocking on the door, he waited until a valet opened the door. Believing him to be a merchant, he was ordered to the rear entrance. No, he desired to see the lord of the house. Being rebuffed as just a commoner, he withdrew the tiara from the bag and waved under the nose of the startled valet.

"Will this buy me an audience?" he barked at the confused servant.

"Wait one moment, sir." The door was slammed shut, and for several long moments, Stefan was left to cool his heels.

Suddenly, a growling, contemptuous voice of authority was being laid upon an unfortunate underling for failing to allow Stefan entrance to the house. Apparently wealth did open some doors.

"My good man, Menos tells me that you have a tiara that belongs to me. If that is true, I am sorry that you have been put through this disservice."

"My Lord, I seek only to return what belongs to you, and then I am off."

"Let us go into the library, and you can tell me all about it." The wealth of this man did not interfere with his sense of hospitality, and Stefan felt as an equal, man to man, as it should be.

"Please be seated. Menos, a glass, no, two glasses of wine. I hope the early hour has not dulled your taste for such a fine vintage."

"My lord, you honor me, but I believe this is what you want to see." Extracting the tiara from its confines, he handed it to the now-perplexed master.

"My heavens. Where did you get this? We were going to present this to my daughter on her eighteenth birthday. I had no idea it was gone." Stefan reluctantly recounted the details of what occurred the night before, only in that he did not wish undue punishment to be meted out.

"My lord, he was extremely penitent, and I believe he was on the verge of doing himself grievous bodily harm. I plead on his behalf that you be lenient with him."

"Hrummph, maybe I will, I don't know until we find him, that is, if we do. Now, what can I pay you?"

"Will you spare me some bread, cheese, and jerky for my return trip, and maybe a little wine?"

"What? Is that all? Come, my good man, it is not every day that I can repay a grand gesture."

"Sir, if it will enlighten you, pray that whatever you feel the worth of what I have done be given to the needy."

Moved by this generosity and adhering to Stefan's wishes, the lord did more than just a paltry handout, matching in kind with items from his larder. He parted with a warm handshake and a very special bottle of wine, winking that it shouldn't be drunk too quickly, lest the full flavor be lost. This was a man that, devoid of his title, would always be welcome in Stefan's company.

The trip home consumed valuable farming time, and it was near dusk that Stefan returned home, loaded with several baskets of food and delicacies that he had only heard about, much less experienced.

Magda was overjoyed but was a little stern with him. "Do you know where your son is?" she ranted. "He is still in the fields. That boy hardly had any food. He was trying so hard to please you."

"My loveplum." It was a term Stefan trotted out when he was assailed by his beautiful wife for one misgiving or another. "He will survive. I am so proud that he feels that way. Would you have him shirking?"

Mollified somewhat, she kissed him on the cheek and slapped his rear end. "Call that boy in, or the devil will be at your side." She laughed. Supper that night eclipsed any that they had had for ages. He remembered the lord's word and drank slowly, the temptation always present to gulp it down. The sleep was especially restful, no doubt ensured by the quality victuals.

The next day saw a repeat of hard work and exhaustion, the latter a receipt for the labor expended, paid in full. As a farmer, crops were the mainstay of Stefan's income, and aside from the side work of carpentry and smithing, he was able to provide a sufficient, although lean, standard of living. The season had been rough but endurable, and a promise of renewal was in the offing.

Finishing for the day, the man and his son returned to the welcome warmth of their home. After washing up at the trough, Josef observed a man walking in a strange manner along the roadway that skirted their farm.

"Father, that man seems different and in a way funny."

"What do you mean 'funny'?"

"Look at how he is walking. He has a stick and is waving it from side to side. Is he swatting flies or something?" Stefan had seen this before and knew what had befallen the man.

"My son, I think he is blind. Why is he alone?" he mused. Overcome with curiosity, the pair hailed the gentleman, who stopped as a result their overture. "Hello there, kind sir. What are you doing out here alone? Surely you may come to harm by yourself."

"Oh, and who is addressing me?"

"I own the farm by the path you are walking on and was concerned by your apparent condition."

"Oh, is it that obvious?" the fellow replied with a small laugh.

"I mean no disrespect."

"Of course not, my son, I was only teasing. It's not something you can hide very well." His jovial response eased the slight tension and allowed Stefan to offer the traveler a refreshment of water.

"Please, let me guide you under the shade of my tree and provide you with a cool cup." Stefan, taking the man's shoulder pack, led him to a cushioned bench, the gentlemen slowly lowering himself and letting out a sigh of gentle relief as his body settled upon the soft matting.

"Oh, that feels good." And drinking the cup of water placed in his hand, he retorted with a long, "Ahhhhhhhh, that is most refreshing, thank you. Now tell me again who you are, for I thank you for your kindness."

"My name is Stefan, and I have a son, Josef, he who placed the cup in your hands."

Magda, hearing the voice through the kitchen window, investigated the gathering, wiping her hands that had been slicing an onion.

"Hmmm, I smell the fragrance of an onion, is it not? Yellow or white?"

"Why, yellow, my good man, you are very observant. And pray, who may you be?"

"My name is Victor, and because of my less-than-complete faculties, I do indeed have to be observant." Stefan pointed at his own eyes with his finger to alert Magda to the man's blindness.

"Oh, I am so sorry, sir."

"Nonsense, it is what it is, but I appreciate your concern. I am formerly of the southern province. To satisfy your curiosity about my impediment, it came about very gradually and was something I've learned to live with. I'm not totally devoid of sight, but what I see is very limited and obscure."

"How do you live? I mean, it must be very hard." Josef's remark was impulsive but instinctive, catching his tongue quickly to limit his embarrassment.

"My son is not always this rude, sir," spoke the matriarch of the family. "Please forgive his bad manners."

"My dear," he spoke with a light air in his voice and not a trace of annoyance, "leave the child be. His curiosity is what makes a child tick. But to answer your question, lad, I had been a worker at the state saw mill and could plan most of my routine with great exactness.

"Care must be taken when dealing with those dreadful blades, for if you make one mistake—*swoosh*." Josef's eyes winced at the description of bloody mayhem. "And off with an arm or leg. This habit was later helpful in my daily activities, for I had to know what was around me and how to deal with it. But oh, forgive me, I tend to be too informative."

Gulping down a freshened cup of water and gaining the abject attention of his hosts, he continued. "When I learned that my sight would be failing, I put away a small sum of money and sold some of my possessions to see me through the coming lean times. It was then I received an invitation from my sister, that her daughter was to be wed and beseeched me to attend. She had always been the apple of my eye, the one I could see out the most."

His little joke brought a maternal smile to Magda.

"And I consented. By this time, my funds were nearly exhausted, save for the wedding gift that I carry in my pack and having no funds for transportation, I determined to travel by foot. I dared not inform them of my shortfall, as their financial situation was strained as it were. They would have sacrificed to fund my travels, something I could not allow." The joviality disappeared replaced by a melancholy posture, privately wishing he could be more than what he was at this point in his life, not for himself, but for his sister and loving niece. For several moments he remained mute, staring into the distance, thinking his thoughts, and then quickly, he reverted back to his engaging character and begged their pardon for dampening their spirits.

"No apologies needed, Victor. When it comes to family, there is no greater bond nor feeling that has to be explained or excused."

"Well, I have wearied you enough with my concerns, so off I will be."

"We wish you well, Victor, and that of your niece. Here, let me at least point you the way."

"Thank you for your kindness and attentive ears." With that the stranger strode down the road, again whipping his rod from side to side. Josef looked at his father with saddened eyes as if a silent plea were streaming from them. Magda had tears in hers as she turned to enter the cottage. Stefan stared hard and long at the retreating figure and shook his head, uttering a silent prayer.

The sparse dinner was less than that as the room filled with a force of unfulfilled expectations. Not a word was spoken, and the chill was unnerving, not because of what was done, but because of what wasn't done. Finally Magda looked up from her plate, looked at Stefan, and quietly spoke. She had been his wife for over twenty years and before that a young girl in the village where they both lived. He always had an eye for her, and she did not shy away from his innocent small talks, knowing he was a little withdrawn, and this endeared him to her. There was no pretense at being something other than what he was. They grew closer as the years went by, knowing each would one day live together.

Her strong will and lack of airs marked her as a woman who could wield great influence and not be dissuaded by the difficulties that deterred others. She as well as her husband had founded a home not just to live in but to live for. More often than not, it was her will, benevolently in most cases and stern in others, that had molded a family of stern stuff. She now exercised that will, by gripping Stefan's hands in hers and said, "You know what you must do." He thought he had but was hesitant, knowing that again he would be placed in a position to expend scare resources. Rising from his chair, he told Josef to harness Esmeralda, walked over to his wife, and placed his arms around her waist, kissing her on the neck.

She swung her head gently back to engage his forehead and squeezed her hands around his.

"I love you, loveplum."

"I know you do or you would not be living in my house."

"Your house?"

"You know what I mean, my handsome man." With that she turned around and hung her arms on his neck, drawing his face against her lips. "Now get going, lest the poor man faint from his trials."

Josef had the horse and wagon ready and begged to go with his father.

"Son, I need you to be the man of the house while I'm gone." With that he hugged him and jumped onto the seat, yelling a command to the horse and lightly flicking the whip. Off they went, with Josef trotting behind for a short distance before returning to the cottage.

"Don't worry, Mother. Father will be fine, and I will take care of you."

She mussed his hair, smiled, and said that she knew he would. Both watched as the wagon disappeared into the darkness then closed the door and retired to the living room. It would be a lonely night.

Were it not for the full moon, Stefan might easily have trampled the dark figure plodding along the road. "Victor, it is I, Stefan, hold up."

"Well, my friend, what can I do for you?"

"It's what I can do for you. Feel your way along the horse's flank toward me and grab my hand. There, now swing to the side and grab the guard and lift yourself onto the seat. Now doesn't that feel better?"

"The seat is hard, but my feet feels better, thank you." A broad smile betraying gratitude.

"Where to, my friend?"

"Beyond the next village is the home of my sister. It is not too far away."

"We can forget getting there tonight. By the time we reach the village, it will be way too late to continue on. We will rest up and leave in the morning."

"I do not believe sleeping in the wagon will improve my rest, Stefan."

"Do not worry, something will turn up."

"I do believe your optimism exceeds your grasp of reality, but I submit to your wisdom."

Upon reaching the settlement, Stefan wheeled to an inn on the outskirts called the Jackal. He instructed his half-asleep passenger to be patient, remain where he was, and he would return shortly.

Knocking on the door several times, an irritated and yawning individual swung the portal open and demanded to know who forced him from his sleep. "It's the middle of the night, you knave."

"Emil, it's me, Stefan."

"Stefan? What are you doing here?"

After a decent explanation concerning his passenger, Stefan pleaded for a room only until morning. He himself would sleep in the wagon and at a later date reimburse the owner for his trouble.

"Nonsense, Stefan. You have aided me many times without asking for any payment, I could do no less. And, my friend, I have ample room for you also."

The morning quickly arrived, and being a farmer, he was used to the limited time of rest. "Where is my friend?" he inquired on the innkeeper.

"He woke me up as he was about to leave and told me not to bother you and that where he was going was very close and he did not want to burden you further."

"He was blind, Emil, and who knows if he can find his way."

"He said he was perfectly fine and insisted that he go on his way without any fuss from me. I tell you, Stefan, that man is beyond belief. I admire him."

Returning home, Magda and his son greeted him in the late morning sun. After relating the night's adventure and the man's quick departure, and following a small breakfast, it was off to the fields. All day, the farmer's thoughts were on the sightless man and the energy and optimism he displayed. Could he do the same if misfortune fell upon him? Several weeks passed, and not a day passed that Stefan did not think about the unfortunate people he had met. What about the rest of the principality, there surely had to be more like them. He was one man, and what could he do other than what he had already done.

The family had just returned from Mass when an elegant carriage appeared along the roadstead. A coachman hailed the family and inquired as to their name. Stefan rebuked the fellow and inquired why he should give his name to a stranger.

"If you are the man named Stefan, I must speak with you. I have been sent to give you a message." After affirming that he was, the coachman reached into his pouch and withdrew a cylindrical object. "Please, sir, I mean no harm, but I have been instructed to hand you this scroll."

As he unrolled it and read the contents, Magda noticed that her husband seemed taken aback and stunned. This would not do, and she yelled at the emissary, "What have you done to my husband?"

"Madam, I only bring tidings and know nothing of its intents or purposes."

Calming his wife, Stefan handed her the scroll. Her eyes widened as she scanned the words. No wonder the reaction of her husband. The new king had ordered the family to an audience at the castle within the hour if the coachman had found them at home. But why? What have they done to draw the ire of the king? The coachman stood patiently and waited as the family reluctantly entered the coach. Off they went, concern not easily disguised, but each in support of the other, not knowing what awaited them.

As they passed through the castle gates, they saw what very few had seen, especially among the commoners. The courtyard was huge, the walls tall, guarded, and forbidding. The massive doors were resplendent with lavish carvings and gold leaf, highlighted with a deep-red color overall. Two sentries manned either side, their halberds gleaming in the sun, their brightness conveying a look of consuming fire. As the coach doors opened, they were motioned toward the entrance, where a handsomely dressed figure bade them to follow.

They passed through several rooms, many of which had suits of armor, weapons, and banners displayed in all their royalty. The wonderment of what they were seeing overcame their initial fears, as two emotions such as these could not exist at the same time. It was a welcome experience soon culminating upon entering a most grand and large hall. Adorned on either side was a repeat of the various armors, banners, and other displays of royalty, accented by the clacking footsteps of their guide. The echo seemed to amuse Josef, immersed as he was in the splendor around him.

Magda almost collided with the guide as her head swiveled from side to side, while Stefan composed himself enough to feel a certain degree of apprehension, which was soon validated by the sight at the end of the hall. There, seated in a large and ornate throne, was a regal figure whose identity could not be denied. The king! As they approached, the guide bowed deeply and in a stately voice announced the presence of the family and, in a subtle motion, urged them to bow.

Walking away, he left the family in the presence of their monarch, and at this moment, they felt very alone. A few attendees were at the side of the king, ready to do his bidding and eyeing those before them, a formal but necessary precaution.

"Welcome," said the seated figure. "I take it you are Stefan?" With mouth agape, the farmer could only nod his head to acknowledge the question. "Then that lovely lady must be Magda."

The reference startled the woman, causing a red blush to brighten her face. With eyes downward, she replied, "Yes, sire."

"And the small gentleman with you must be Josef?"

Again, his impulse leaped to the fore, and he blurted out, "Yes, King."

Delighted and amuse, the king rose and pronounced in a very casual way, "Let us leave this man-made cavern and reside to a more suitable venue." Led by the attendees, and some notables, the group entered a smaller room that belied the royalty that used it.

The furnishings were handsome enough but not overpowering and seemed to invite a welcoming atmosphere. When all had been seated, the king asked if the family had any idea as to why they were summoned. It was a rhetorical question, for indeed they had no such knowledge and would be hard-pressed to provide a reply.

"Allow me. When I was growing up, my father spared no expense to educate me, but the greatest enlightenment I absorbed was to bathe in the example that he displayed in all things related to his subjects. My formal education could only teach me the established rules of science, literature, math, and so on. These things you learned by rote, intelligence, and other intangibles that allowed you to function in a predictable manner."

Rising, he motioned with his hand to forestall a likewise effort by the assemblage. Pacing very slowly, his words were measured, as he pondered each sentence to ensure a full understanding.

"But you cannot glean from books or other stated materials the deep-rooted concerns and cares that are only formulated by a heart open to compassion and understanding. Being a king does not make you wise, for a peasant can be wiser than a king. When I assumed the throne, I knew what was in my heart, but it was not enough. It had to be paired with the desires of my subjects. My father once told me that you must know what your people think, what they need, and what they will do without to remain content."

Comparisons to Solomon would have been easily dismissed, but the king's words showed a vision comparable to the biblical figure. He then turned to Stefan, still struggling to find his place in this drama. "To honor my father's sage advice, I embarked on a scheme to learn what I needed to know. You, sir, may feel a certain deception, but as you will find out, it is not entirely true."

Deception? What is he referring to? I know of no deception. These thoughts now competed with a heightened emotion of suspense.

"To learn what I needed, I sent several envoys into the populace to gauge their reactions to certain scenarios. The results were mixed, but not altogether unpredictable. Fortunately, one encounter showed great promise, so much so that I tended to challenge the odds of it being repeated."

The king beckoned with his hand, and in obedience to the overture, a figure strode to the sire's side. Over his arm was draped a familiar article of clothing.

My tunic! shouted Stefan's mind. *My tunic. And is that Paul?*

"My friends, this is my son, Paul. Many may not recognize him, as for many years he had studied abroad, served in the military, and of late was my diplomatic envoy abroad. Returning to honor his grandfather, I related to him my desire to provide for our people and how best to reach that goal."

The dress of the young man differed so greatly from what he wore when Stefan first brought him into the cottage, thought Magda. He was more handsome and evidently smelled a lot better also, she silently chuckled to herself. Josef's mind raced to the meal which Paul had graciously shared with him. His boyish mind had elevated this man to that of a mythical hero, the knight in shining armor. Paul stared and smiled at the boy, convincing Josef that he had read his mind.

"I volunteered to walk the provinces, and it was by sheer chance that I chose the cottage that provided me with relief. The kindness was enough, but it was the firm acceptance of what I appeared to be that disclosed a man of honor and an understanding of the plight of others. These are traits beyond the level of charity."

As he spoke, Stefan felt as if an intense beam of light was bathing his being. Every head had turned in his direction.

The king had said that there was no real deception, and in this instance, what little there was hinged on the fact that Paul's clothing had been lost in transit. It was thin but supported the contention of honesty. This to the exclusion that he had also returned to pay respects to his grandfather.

"And with that, Stefan, may I tend to you this fine garment?" Walking over to a flustered and overwhelmed simple farmer, the two embraced amid a smattering of polite applause.

As Paul took a seat beside his father, another guest entered the room and made way to the king.

Could that be Johan? recited a startled Magda to herself. *It is. He looks so different, so calm.* Stefan could not believe the serene posture and gentlemanly manner that contrasted with his berserk-like conduct not too long ago.

"Let me present my nephew Johan, who resides in the House of Rupert, my brother's residence in the southern province. His story is most interesting."

"Paul had told me of his good fortune, and I was fascinated to duplicate his experiences. I love theatre and drama and decided to indulge my fantasy of being a man lost to the world. I truly felt remorse in duping Stefan, as his pain for my condition was evident.

At no time did this family look down upon me, intent only in hearing my tale and providing me with succor. And, Stefan, I do have a gambling problem.

"My father consistently brings me up short in any area of gaming we engage in, and I've lost count as to my losses. And my sister did receive her tiara for her eighteenth birthday, intrigued by her brother's thespian exploits." Walking over to the still-overwhelmed Stefan, he repeated the cordial embrace of his predecessor and retired to the side of the king.

Another summons and yet another story began to unfold. It was now Victor's turn to enthrall the now captivated audience with the faux trials of a wayward blind man. Gone was the walking stick and present was a man of great dexterity and mirth as he strode to the side of his king.

"May I introduce you to my keeper of the books," spoke the lord of the castle. "He is responsible for much of my learning, heaping upon me the classics, languages, and all sort of dull things." The last part eliciting a relieving laughter. "I owe much more than I could ever repay. His guidance and wisdom shaped many of my father's and my own ideas on rule."

"My liege is much too kind. His request to test the young man was an elixir for me, as I was under no constraints or limitations in my task. At no time did I even know what I would say or do, save to be a challenge to his subject. Where do we find souls like this? And will we ever have enough of them? Stefan, I do have a vision deficiency, one that can only be alleviated with the spectacles I am wearing, for without them, I am indeed blind as a bat. But you were not blind to the needs of a destitute wayfarer, seeing with your heart and not just your eyes." Nodding to Stefan, he also retired to the king's side.

Again motioning those seated to remain so, the king stood erect and beckoned Stefan to come forward. He complied and bowed before his sire, who then placed his hand on the honored man's shoulder. "My loyal follower, in these three instances you have displayed a quality that if only one was fulfilled, no more could have been asked of you. In the first instance, charity was displayed to its fullest, in the second, trust, and in the third, compassion. I need someone who will roam the provinces, seeking audiences with those who have complaints or seek redress, someone who is from the earth and can separate trickery from sincerity, someone who has lived the life of sweat and toil and knows the cost.

"Together, with my advisors, I will have a true base from which to make those decisions necessary to improve the lot of my people. Can I convince you to accept the task?"

His mind reeling at the importance being thrust upon him, and not wishing to offend the king's request, he nevertheless regained some composure and replied, "Sire, what of my fields, how will I be able to tend to them if I am not there?"

"If you accept my warrant, in your absence I will appoint field hands to tend to needs of your farm according to your instructions. I do not command you to do this but humbly ask this of you. What say you?"

Again the innate character of this man came to the fore, compelling a decision that seemed so right. "My liege, if the service you require of me will aid our land, I accept." He need not have bothered to seek approval from Magda or Josef, their pride jubilantly evident as they swept aside decorum and rushed to his embracing arms, the king relinquishing the floor with grace and subtlety.

The years that followed proved the wisdom of the sovereign's choice as a wise ruler had made a wise decision.

Mustang

The soft breeze wafting down from the verdant hills brought welcome relief from the morning heat. The workers felt the pleasant coolness and continued their chores with a little relief. Life on a horse-breeding farm can at times enact a diversity of small inconveniences, much of them shrugged off with nary a complaint. A breeding farm requires consummate knowledge of the animals tended to, and Matty Collins, an eleven-year-old son of the owner, Chad, has impressed many a customer with his knowledge, abetted by his perky mannerisms.

His love for animals, horses in particular, stems from an innate appreciation inspired by contact with the various forms of life that make their way into his world. No animal is resented, but the more dangerous ones are respected due to their defensive nature when aroused. All this he learned from his mother, who coached him as soon as he understood the lessons she instilled in him. A quick learner, he impressed anyone fortunate to hear him flaunt his knowledge, concealed smiles reflecting their enjoyment.

Of course most of those subjected to the "font of wisdom" were the loyal employees who catered to his dreams, but only in a responsible way, so as to lessen the possibility of spoiling him. They need not have worried on that score. All this came crashing down and may have disappeared forever if not for the comfort of his father and his workers. He lost his mom when he was six, the hurt devastating to the youngster as it would be for any boy.

Slowly, with chores that helped to occupy his mind from succumbing to the inertia of idleness, and the debilitating emptiness that had once been filled by his mom, he began to resume his daily life. His dad instilled a strong guideline to deal with disappointments, not so much in words, but in how he handled everyday life. The example displayed from solving work problems, the loss of business, or any myriad of challenges steeled the boy in an unconscious way. By observing and even assisting where necessary, he stored up every iota of how things could be done and utilized them when needed.

Still a boy, sometimes at night he'd steal into his dad's bedroom and slip under the covers, his father drawing him closer with his arm. Sobs escaping from his face buried into the chest of his comforter, were relieved by the gentle stroking of his curly hair, and soft words of love. He began to grow beyond his years and yet was still a boy.

As any youth, especially one immersed in the sea of outdoor adventures, he reveled as each day brought new challenges. He wasn't alone as each and every hand thought highly of the angular-framed sprite. He too was greatly attached to them, and why not? If truth be told, this operation was more a family endeavor than just a business venture.

The wide-open space, occupied by patchy green fields, studded with copses, drought-resistant bushes, boulders and ravines. This mixture of diversity co-opted the sameness of desert-like scenery and invited the inquisitive youth to examine every nook and cranny, adding to his inventory of knowledge. Barring any predators he may encounter, the plucky youth carried a carbine and knew how to use it.

In friendly matches at the ranch, he constantly outdid the field of aspirants for the one and only trophy, a worn-out old boot! An older hand who had retired volunteered his footwear as a symbol of his years of work at the ranch. It was a novel idea, and all agreed that this was to be the Holy Grail to aim for. This did not deter the ever-present penchant for wagering. This was done as if Chad was not in the event, that's how good he was. The winner, though second to Chad, reveled in his newfound wealth, usually fifteen or twenty bucks.

Despite the hard work and monotonous routines, spirits were usually on the high side, although a discouraging word was uttered now and then, more out of frustration than mean intent. And that poor soul brought on the laughter of his compatriots when doing so. The operation itself was modest and fairly profitable. When Chad's grandfather, Mike, first set up shop, it was to help the area ranchers, who were still recovering from the after-effects of a series of droughts, reminiscent of the Dust Bowls, but still needed horses for various tasks, unable to afford more expensive alternatives. Although not blessed with an abundance of capital, the sincerity and low costs won many of his customers over to him.

Although the age of mechanization had bloomed, there was still this need for horses. This was in the late forties, when the muscle needed was true horsepower. Later on, many breeding farms capitalized on siring champion racehorses, and the fee of thousands of dollars were routine. In this case, the need was for work, not show horses. With an eye for selecting brooding mares, his concerns were that they be treated in a loving and humane manner, gaining the trust of their handler.

Any domestic animal will render more service than one treated as just an object of production. The name Collins rang with the assurance of reliable service. Mind you, this was no fast-food-type operation. Mares carried their foals for about eleven months and after birth required a substantial amount of time before they could be ridden or tasked with any strenuous work required. Therefore, a customer had to be assured that what he received would be well worth the cost and wait. While the foal can be weaned in approximately three months, the customer may wish to transport the animal back to his ranch. From there he can best care for the foal, getting it familiar with its surroundings and its handlers.

The quality of his services were such that there never was a complaint about any horses when reaching maturity. All were sound and performed as desired. All this would one day be Chad's. The Collins family had a charm of each generation following the other in determination, ability, and humanity. That was an age where the majority of families lived a life dependent on honesty and the will of God.

SLICED FROM LIFE

The success of any breeding ranch is the quality of its stock. In this area, the Collins succeeded handsomely, as demanded by the founder. Each brooding mare was carefully screened for the qualities needed to succeed. Stamina, reproduction, and temperament, among others. As a result, the ranch thrived, and its brand acquired a well-earned notoriety. Matty, of course, loved being around the mares and foals, resulting in a bond between himself and a sweet mare named Honey.

Although he doted on all the mares, as any young boy would be wont to do, a special attraction developed between himself and Honey. He would visit her stall, offering carrots or some other snack, gobbled up with zest. When exercising, she would nuzzle Matty when he approached and shake her ahead up and down while letting out a stream of whinnies. Snorting also, this was her demonstration of her fondness for the lad. He would always reply with his arms almost wrapped around her neck but also because he wasn't tall enough.

When in foal, he made sure that she was taken care of, all her needs provided for, but truth be told, this concern was meted out to all the mares in foal.

Matty was a great help, as well he should be, for one day he'd be in charge and with his ability to accomplish the many tasks needed, the resultant quality of service was ensured.

All work and no play was alien to the boy. He'd saddle up when not needed and headed out into the fields and ravines to explore. Here he would find numerous examples of life ordinarily unseen. One would be the rattlesnake, and this alone was cause for extreme caution. Wise enough, he'd just observe and avoided any potential threat. Discovering a gopher hole, he would be fascinated if he could actually observe the various tunnels dug beneath the soft earth. These could contain thousands but seemed unlikely when viewing near-empty vastness. Far on, in another direction, tall trees may contain the thatched material of an aerie, a nest for hawks or bald eagles.

One could imagine his compulsion to actually peer into these nests to observe the chicks waiting to be fed. But of course he couldn't fly and surely couldn't climb the tree. These and other marvels of nature attracted his thirst to know and understand what lived around and among the land shared with humans. His father had no objection other than to caution the boy not to be reckless, and being aware of the consequences for not doing so, he abided by this advice. Still, his innate sense of responsibility was all he really needed.

On many a cool evening, a group would form around an inviting bonfire, the main topic, relaxation. When still a sprite, Matty heard many stories that sparked his imagination. Among the men who contributed their memories was a gentle giant named Miguel. He took Matty under his wing and regaled him with embellished stories of the Old West. Wide-eyed, Matty waited drank in every word, visions only a dreamer could create. One of the stories that really sparked his imagination was the introduction of horses that later were labeled as mustangs. These were free-roaming steeds of the American West and were descended by horses brought to the Americas by the Spanish. They were recognized as living symbols of the historic and pioneer spirit of the West. They are considered as surefooted and having good endurance, and the colors vary.

Ever since, Matty would always be on the lookout for these iconic animals, bathing in a realm of assorted attributes usually reserved for famous personalities. Every now and then during his forays into the wilderness, he'd glimpse galloping small packs as they sped across the landscape. Oh, but to be among them, or at least near enough to fully appreciate their charging forms, muscles flexing, breathing accelerated as they chased the wind. Not much chance of that as they're considered feral, and only immense efforts would be needed to tame them.

The magic concept of a mustang never left Matty's mind, the hope being that one day he'd finally get to see this marvelous creature up close, perhaps even touching it. Although forefront in his list of desires and goals, it didn't detract from his present and continuous responsibilities. Being homeschooled, he would research anything of great interest to him. Never bored, he was a moving force to his father, and many times they would explore any topic that grabbed his fancy. Now and then he rebelled on certain issues or demands, for which he paid the price. His father was tolerant but did not allow for these lapses, the resultant loss of a privilege or two sufficing.

The loss of mom and wife never really subsided, which was a testament to the love she generated. But both realized that while they kept her in their hearts, it could dull the pain.

Each day would test that resolve.

While seeming idyllic, life at the ranch was far from it. As in any enterprise, setbacks were the norm. Two of the hands were injured, one seriously, when a pulley, lifting horse meal for storage atop the paddock, snapped. The serious injury may involve the loss of a limb. Driving the pickup to purchase some gear ended with the front axle snapping, resulting in loss of control and redecorating a tree trunk. Of course, to add to the misery, the gearing on the windmill pumping water to a holding tank jammed. Stoically, the damage could be repaired and the injured men hospitalized. Then, as fate was not done with its torture, Honey, who was in foal, suffered a crisis in her stall, lasting for hours, the result being the loss of her unborn charge.

Matty was devastated that his favorite mare had suffered pain and more in her ordeal. He stayed with her as she lay on her side, stroking her mane and whispering to her. A stifled snort seemed to indicate her approval. She would need care for some time, and Matty would see to it. His daily ritual, along with medication, appeared to be bringing the mare around, and within a short span, she had gained strength and was able to exercise. While donating much of his time to the care of Honey and his obligatory chores, he found time to explore the wilderness beyond the ranch.

The respite was needed and welcomed. Too much had been shouldered by the young lad, who'd done so willingly. Riding into the vast spaces keyed his anticipation of any new discovery. How many times had he brought home to his dad a thing or two that either caused elation or avoidance, the latter eliciting howls of laughter. His selection became more discerning, if only to avoid his dad putting the rub on him. Still he enjoyed the ribbing.

After an hour or so, he thought he heard some thrashing sound coming from a wooded ravine. Alighting from his mount and tying the reins to a bush. Taking his carbine, he slowly descended the side of the small gully, weapon at the ready. The sound came from behind a growth of bushes, and as he carefully circled around to get a view of what was causing the ruckus, he stopped short, gulping down a hard swallow. On the ground lay a mustang, unmoving and apparently lifeless. Next to the motionless animal was a slip of a foal, no more than a couple of months old. It kept nudging the still form repeatedly, as if to awaken it, which obviously had been its mother. Stressed out, it tried from different angle, causing it to rustle the bushes, which had alerted Matty.

Attempting to corner the foal proved futile. Taking his canteen in hand, he poured some water into the hollow of a rock and stepped back. The foal raced to the water and eagerly drained the rock's content. Not knowing what to do next, Matty poured some in the cup of his hand and stretched it out. The little guy let out a shrill whinny and cautiously approached the thirst quencher. *Gee,* Matty thought, *it's not afraid of me.* Now what to do. He avoided grabbing the little thing for fear of injuring it. Maybe if he lassoed it, then he could bring it home.

Tracing his steps back to his mount, he grabbed the lasso and, turning around, found the foal standing in front of him. Perhaps the water and gentleness convinced the little guy that Matty was friendly. Not sure what to do, Matty knelt down and placed his hand on the neck of the orphaned animal, stroking it gently. Considering that he was dealing with a wild or feral foal, it was amazing that it didn't race off, instead standing placidly. Matty placed the lasso around its neck and spoke gently, trying to impart a soothing assurance. Mounting his horse, Matty kept the lasso limp so as not to cause choking or injury.

Knowing that the water he'd given wasn't enough, he headed for a small pool fed by an unground spring. It was here that he had observed many species of animals slaking their thirst. Approaching, flying fowl took off, and any ground critters scattered at the intruder. His horse, Tom, started gulping the clear liquid, and Matty had no problem getting his little friend to drink.

"Whoa, pal, slow down," in which the little Mustang looked at him as if to say, "Hey, I'm drinkin', buzz off."

Fully refreshed, the trio continued their trip back to the ranch. The foal seemed invigorated by the water and was very animated, tugging here and tugging there, but not with any intent to escape. It was feeling its oats. Passing through the gate on the way to the corral, Miguel took his Stetson off and scratched his head at the sight of Matty and his captive.

"Did he fight you off and nearly trample you?" he thundered along with his booming laughter. Matty stuck his nose in the air as if to ignore him, laughing quietly at the absurd comment. A few other hands stopped and gave him a high-five salute to celebrate his conquest. This too he ignored as he neared the corral gate.

It was a fairly large enclosure to allow for exercise and grazing. As he approached the gate, Honey trotted over to exam the new arrival. She eyed the little guy with great interest. Until he talked to his dad and figured out what they were going to do, he placed the foal in the corral. He was about to leave when Honey moved to the side of the foal. Almost immediately he began to suckle, without any resistance from the mare. Having lost her own, she was still capable of providing nourishment to the eagerly satisfied customer. Matty stared, taken aback a little, then realized that Honey was as maternal as any mother, human or otherwise. She realized the dependency manifested by the foal's continual suckling and would not do anything otherwise.

Talking to his father, they decided to see what outcome would develop. If compatible with the ranch's operation and not disruptive, perhaps the orphan could be accommodated. Since it was a male, Matty decided to name him Spark, because of the vitality he displayed. Honey became his surrogate mom and, as he grew, became more handsome, and his reddish color gave him a regal appearance.

The months rolled by, and now he became a yearling. It was then that he acted in an unusual manner. Instead of following Honey into the paddock at day's end, he scampered out into the wilderness. There was no explanation for it except perhaps they thought he was tired of the domestic life and wanted to roam free. Surprisingly, in the morning, he appeared at the corral gate and was ushered in, where he joined Honey.

No one could explain this behavior, and if that was mystifying, so were the continual replays of this behavior. It soon became an accepted ritual, since Spark had been feral at one point and it was reasonable to think he still maintained some form of this trait. No one ever discovered why and where he went, a curiosity that would spawn dozens of suggestions from the crew.

Still, Spark was approachable, and Matty would spend some time brushing him down, which the yearling seemed to enjoy. A tasty piece of fruit or vegetable was never refused. Matty decided he would never attempt to ride Spark, not because he didn't think the animal would rebel or resist, but because he cherished the free nature into which he was born and refused to compromise that spirit.

Soon, Honey would be in foal again, but that didn't lessen her companionship with the fast-maturing yearling who would soon enter a second year of life. One day he would assume the mantle as a sturdy and imposing horse. His nightly odysseys still prevailed but had become an accepted ritual. What ignited this behavior? The innate wildness had never been completely purged from his instincts, and the freedom of the open spaces mollified what restraints he felt when in the domestic venue. Almost, but not quite like the Chinese philosophy of ying-yang, but close enough. Also, he had bonded greatly with his rescuer and Honey. This was as close to domestication that could be hoped for without eradicating his basic nature.

Where did he go on his sojourn? Was he keeping company with a pretty filly? Whatever the reason, save for curiosity, it didn't matter. He had two homes, the ranch and the wilderness.

After a long day, the tired hands along with Matty and his dad retired for the night. Music wafting in from the bunkhouse where the more energetic ones still had some powder to burn. A cool brew, a cigar or cigarette, and the luxury of doing nothing. Soon, the sandman had an overload of work to comply with, which he did efficiently, the tired souls whose slow breathing signaled a departure to the dream world.

Lightning had no effect on the slumbering crew, but it did on the paddock. A bolt of lightning struck the building, and sparks of fire began to lick at the unresisting combustible materials of wood and hay. As the flames gathered momentum, the livestock began to churn restively and with fear as the flames began to migrate within the paddock. The smoke soon became an issue, and the churning became frantic. Most of the stalls were gated, but some stock had free rein within the enclosure. They at least escaped through the unbarred entrance, but so few.

The flames were so rapid that anything that anyone could do to save the animals was problematic. Still, the crew was unaware of the horrible fate awaiting the trapped animals, as the paddock was some distance from the bunkhouse and homestead, and any sounds of distress were unheard.

In what would seem to be an inevitable disaster, a reddish-brown form appeared. Without hesitation, Spark dashed into the paddock and, responding to the sounds of distress and without ever being shod, used his hind legs to batter in any stall that had been gated. The heat of the flames seemed to have no impact on him as he raced down from one to another. Eventually he came to Honey's stall, and her whinny alerted him to her presence. Like a demon possessed, he raged at the gate with unrestrained energy and smashed it to bits. His adopted mother darted to the entrance, paused outside, and glanced backward to see if he would soon emerge.

The paddock was cleared, the animals saved from burning to death. By now the commotion of neighing animals and the crashing of rafters into the bowels of the paddock awakened the slumping ranchers, who scurried outside, immodestly clad, to witness the throng of horses, yearlings, and foals being led away by Spark. The devastation, compounded by the sight of all livestock racing into the darkness, was incomprehensible. One moment all was serene and in another all was lost. Chad and Matty had arrived just as Spark and the herd raced into the night. As can be expected, the scene, while devastating, cast another wound to contend with. Chad had lost his means of existence for the ranch. While temporary enclosures and facilities could be jury rigged, without the horses they were useless, comparable to a train without an engine.

"Josh," a disheartened man intoned to a ranch hand, "keep an eye on the embers. The rest of us, get some sleep. No sense in going after the horses in the dark. At first light, we'll head out."

In the wide-open spaces, who knows how far a frightened herd will race from what had been a terrible experience. Fear would keep them on the run, not realizing they were safe now. Chad slept fitfully, if at all, while Matty didn't close his eyes at all. He knew how hard his dad had worked to make the operation successful, and now all seemed lost. Of course, they had no way of knowing that the majority of the stock was saved by the actions of Spark, only that he had spirited them away. A bittersweet proposition, saving and then luring the horses away.

At daylight, the men set out and could only hope that they could pick up their tracks. Miguel had some experience in this matter, and occasionally he'd alight from his mount and examine the marred turf, indicating a mass of hoof prints and a possible direction of travel. As long as they followed the markings, there was hope of regaining some of the stock, but with the wide-open spaces, they could be anywhere, scattered to the four winds.

Approaching a wooded ravine, Matty realized he had seen this before. With heart pulsing, he yelled to his father, "Dad, this is where I found Spark, down below! Maybe this is where he comes at night." With this slenderest of hope, he raced down the slope, brushing by the thickets until he came to an open area. He stopped and froze. There in front of him were the scared stock that had escaped death, and Honey a source of calmness for all the others. Her and the other mares provided confidence for the younger animals and, while still shaken, panic had been averted.

Joined by the party, Matty leaped from his saddle and raced to Honey, hugging her tightly, now that he had assumed a greater height. But where was Spark? He had to have been the one who brought them here. While the men gathered the animals together, he scoured the thickets and then—his heart almost stopped. Spark was lying on the ground and, upon seeing Matty, attempted to rise to greet his friend but exhibited pain while doing so and fell back to the ground. His leg was broken!

Rushing to his loved horse, Matty tried to calm and comfort him, telling him that he was going to be all right and that he'd be fixed up. The tears started to flow as he caressed the trusting animal, knowing that his broken leg meant a drastic outcome. This was a time when an injury like this had resulted in an animal being put out of its misery. That was the practice, to prevent continued suffering. Chad came up and saw the heartbreaking scene.

"C'mon, son, there's nothing more you can do."

"But, Dad"—his face awash in tears and a pleading look in his eyes—"if Spark saved all our horse, why can't we save him?"

His father also began to choke back his emotions, fathered by the memories of Spark and his antics, his friendliness and how he became a part of their lives.

"Go back with the others, son. I'll handle this."

"No, Dad, if it has to be done, I'll do it." The steely look in his eyes convinced his father not to stand in the way. Retrieving his carbine from the saddle holster, he walked up to Spark and embraced him one last time, the horse's eyes looking at him, as he'd always done, with some sort of expectation, perhaps getting back to the ranch and paling around with Honey.

Matty couldn't look at him anymore, couldn't betray the trusting eyes seeking his solace. Stepping back, he raised the carbine, pushed down on the cocking lever, snapping it back into place, inserting a cartridge into the receiver. Placing the stock against his shoulder, the tears blurring his vision, he pointed the weapon at his friend. His finger wrapped itself around the trigger, and he stood there for an eternity, gathering the courage to fire. Young boys are not meant to suffer this emotional trauma, but many do, heaven forbid. He closed his eyes, ready for the last act of Spark's life, but felt a presence near him. Opening his eyes, he saw standing between him and Spark was Honey.

He dropped the carbine and embraced the mare, crying, "Thank you, thank you." He now knew he couldn't or, better yet, wouldn't have fired at Spark. Honey's intervention aroused conjecture of animals responding to situations like this, almost as humans do. Perhaps the weeks of suckling him, the companionship they shared. Do not animals also have relationships that correspond to ours? Whatever the motivation, it saved Matty from scarring his life with guilt and betrayal.

"Dad, we can save him, can't we, we have to. He saved us, didn't he?"

"He sure did, son, he sure did. We'll work something out."

And working something out was what they did.

To soften his material losses, an age-old custom was revisited. Neighbors, clients, and even strangers participated in a barn, or in this case, a paddock raising. Without knowing the underlying reasons for the event, one would believe it was an old-fashioned get-together and BBQ. The spirit of helping a fellow man off the floor was in full bloom. There were still some financial difficulties, but that paled against what could have been a complete disaster. Yes, Spark, through an ingenious suspension rig, was able to heal and eventually return to his usual antics. Honey was never so treasured by Matty for her maternal intervention. Chad was proud of his son and of the ranch hands who supported them.

The soft breeze wafted from the verdant hills again, bringing relief and a new beginning.

Cycle

It's a cool evening as you look over this teeming city of millions. You gaze into the sky and watch the sun fading behind the towering scrapers of beauty and the drifting of the dark clouds. The noise twenty stories below, the unceasing noise of those who keep this nocturnal vigil, snaps you out of your reverie, and it falls as music upon your ears. Perhaps you are hearing it for the last time. The annoying but oh-so-wonderful sounds of life. The sun is sinking rapidly; the clouds growing darker; the noise growing infinitely louder. You look into the distance. There, some miles away, stands a gleaming, towering instrument of flight. Within several days, you will be traveling through the vast void of outer space.

The sun has disappeared now and the sky darker. The noise below is as steady as the breeze that brings the clouds. Now, as always, the metropolis transforms into a gigantic specter of light. You move closer to the balcony and look upward. In that infinite hoard of space lies a planet, your objective. Thoughts begin to plague you again, as they have so many times, uneasy thoughts such as, what sights will greet you? What unknown fate lies in wait for you on that strange world where no man has dared to go? Will there be life? Any living creatures, humanoid or otherwise? Perhaps only the barren red landscape that scientists believe predominates the exterior. Excitedly you wonder how this could have happened, how you got to be involved in man's insatiable desire to conquer space. From early childhood, the lure of science fiction honed your desire to experience the reality of it all. You allow your six-foot frame to relax against the rail, as your blue eyes stare upward, trying to pierce the mystery of that other blue so far above, so very far.

As you stand there, the breeze tugs at your brown hair as though to clear your mind for thought.

Your life has been one of chance, being a test pilot for one of the biggest aircraft companies in the nation, and a good pilot too, as your record attests to that. In this business, word travels when a pilot goofs up or becomes extraordinary. You think that you fell in between those assessments. Still, it was a mild surprise to receive an invitation to the nation's capitol and interviewed for a special project—space exploration! But yours was not the only invitation. You discovered that there were many other applicants vying for the one and only slot available. It has been said that our fate is predetermined, and it must be so, how else could you have left your competition so easily?

Your drive to be first in space outstripped all other considerations, and it was this obsession that allowed you to surpass your fellow competitors. The confidence in your abilities was rewarded by your assignment to the prime training position, although several alternates were chosen in case you faltered. It was something you wouldn't permit to happen, or so you thought. The subsequent training regimen, both physical and cerebral, was so exhausting and intensive that it seemed almost impossible for a mere human to pass. But what kept you on track was that hope and dream to uncover undreamed of knowledge. To benefit whom?

Those countless millions who would never know the how and why of it? No. To you it was the ultimate challenge, something that would never be replicated again, for you would be the first. As your thoughts comb the recent past, you realize time, precious time, is slipping away, time in which you may be seeing this green Earth for the last time. You again peer into the sky. The moon is uncovering itself now as majestically as it always has, and there is the sapphire gleam of the stars. They too seem to be endowed with the breathtaking beauty that has enhanced everything you have seen on this fateful night. And such is the essence of time. Time, such a fleeting thing; it can't be held back, not even for a second. You glance at your watch and realize that you must make ready to leave. Soon, your driver will be here to transport you to the launch center.

You almost hate to leave the comfort that has been afforded you these past few days. To ease attendant pressures, a two-week furlough prior to liftoff was a prescribed benefit, as was the inclusion of this well-appointed apartment, although care was taken to conceal your identity and mission. Gathering your flight bag, you glance about the room, appreciating the quiet moments spent while preparing for your grasp at immortality. Closing the door, you lock it, a strange feeling of finality engulfing you. As you enter the elevator and descend to the main floor, your thoughts are somewhat subdued as you try to hold at bay any misgivings. Reaching the ground level, you quickly exit and walk toward the lobby, spying Sergeant Sal Nicosi, for all intents and purposes, your nursemaid and driver. This man is to you like a master caddie is to a golfer.

"Hi, chief!" he shouts, not letting his sergeant's rank intimidate him. "Ready to go?"

"Yep," you reply. Sal is one of those indispensable people who really run any operation, despite the fact they're almost invisible. He was assigned to you shortly after you arrived at the center, and you recall how he made you feel important without slobbering over you. His informal approach without violating protocol was a natural part of his persona that endeared himself to you. He guides you to the vehicle assigned by the motor pool—a jeep! This was in keeping with maintaining a low profile and, quite honestly, desired by both men because it was and still is a fun vehicle, although the motor pool macs deplore having to find parts to keep it running.

But it is fun to bounce around in this antique. Off you speed to the center, and Sal is not shy in letting other drivers know who rules the road. He's fast but safe, and shortly thereafter you pass through the front gate. After checking in, you're informed of a briefing which would outline your routine for the next few days. Every detail is scrutinized to everyone's satisfaction and tailor-made to allow for all contingencies, no small matter. A first of this magnitude cannot abide any mistakes or omissions and takes several hours with more to come. Of prime concern is fuel management.

As of now, the distance between Earth and your destination is optimum, and the trip to and from this beckoning world is within the fuel capacity of the ship. Upon landing, exploration and testing would be severely limited as separation of the two worlds would begin to widen. A margin of safety is built into the time that would be allocated for these functions and failure to adhere to this schedule could prove fatal.

The next few days see you at orientation and procedural conclaves. Space navigation, fuel conservation, and a myriad of other courses are crammed into your pulsing brain, with very little time to rest or complain. One task you thoroughly enjoy is the proficiency flights to keep your reflexes sharp. You had asked, no, demanded, that a T-38 Talon trainer from NASA be assigned for your use. Over sixty years old or more, you revel in its acceleration and maneuverability. It's a perk lavishly embraced. It was this or any other generation's hot rod.

Was it the age of the craft or a poorly executed control input on your part that saw your right aileron jam into an open position while its opposite remained neutral? The result is a violent continuous roll to the right that threatens to rip the plane apart. Being pressed against the side of the cockpit by centrifugal forces, you struggle to reach the ejection handle, which eludes your grasp several times before you manage to desperately yank it into operation. A blast of ice-cold air slams into your shielded face as the explosive bolts blow the canopy into the sky a split second before the explosive charge beneath your seat propels you upward. Tumbling through air, you feel a sharp jolt as your 'chute deploys, slowing your descent mere moments before you crash into an unyielding patch of desert. Your altitude has only been hundreds of feet over the field. Any lower and the probability of survival would have been negligible. Rescue vehicles race to the scene, and the first one to reach you is Sal.

"What happened, Chief?" he blurts out, an ashen face betraying his deep concern.

Returning to the base, the doctors clear you after a thorough exam. Sal rides hard on you the rest of the day, refusing to let you out of his sight. If he were married, he'd be a wonderful father. The following day, you decide to take the jeep and run over to the commissary and pick up a few items.

As you turn to negotiate the roadway, the left front wheel suddenly flies from its axel, causing that side of the jeep to dig into the ground and upending the whole thing. Your speed is moderate, and you are flung to the ground, rolling as you had been trained to do when completing a parachute drop.

The only casualty is a broken fingernail and some minor bruises. *What is going on?* you think, now the center of attention to half a dozen Samaritans. As to be expected, Sal drives up to pluck you from your fall from grace.

"Gee, Chief," he exclaims, more so to relieve his own fears as much as any consideration for my predicament, "I can't let you out of my sight." You begin to think you're jinxed but quickly nix the idea. Superstitions are verboten; it can get a guy screwed up, and that is the last thing you need and the first thing to avoid.

There are no further disruptions, and the training proceeds smoothly in the days ahead, although you feel a nagging undertow that cannot be dispelled. You manage to shovel it under all the other concerns you shoulder, but it never truly leaves you. You welcome end of training, reflecting on the sweat, anxiety, and anticipation all wrapped up in your own Gordian knot. The next day would be it! Sleep is fitful, if you sleep at all. You rise in the early AM, courtesy of Sal, who comes bearing gifts—a great hot cup of coffee, toast, and some eggs and bacon. He drives you past your ship, a towering Goliath of gleaming metal and mystery, for we can only guess at her capabilities. Her nose points proudly skyward, as if to say, "I am the first, and I will succeed." After getting suited up and led to the shaft elevator, which will take you to the hatch, there is an absence of fanfare.

Just the sincere handclasps of the men and scientists who created this wonder. They had become more than friends, more like family, and suddenly it dawns on you why you accepted this challenge. It is for the dreams that you see reflected in their eyes as they give them to you to make into reality. Rushing up to you and fairly out of breath is ever-faithful Sal. He looks you square in the eye, devoid of his usual levity, and delivers the most perfect salute you have ever received.

"You come back safe, sir, ya hear?"

This is the only time Sal has ever addressed you other than Chief. Whatever selfish motives you may have harbored are now smoke in the wind. These men and women have selflessly labored so that the glory to come would be only second to the honor you could bring to their efforts. And Sal wants you back.

Entering the lift, you feel a sense of complete commitment to justify all the sweat and tears that were shed. Higher and higher you rise, the people below receding from sight, like a memory you can't retain no matter how hard you try. The hatch appears rather suddenly, causing you to flinch a little.

Your nerves, to say the least, are really getting a workout, so no surprises there. What mildly surprises you is the total abandonment of panic, for what sane person would leave a perfectly good planet? Your attempt at humor fails, and with one last gesture, you wave to those below.

You think you can hear someone yelling some encouraging words and the name "Chief," which reassures you that Sal has reverted to type. You cross over the threshold and activate the hatch switch. Slowly, the hatch swings back toward its recess, and a cold sweat creases your brow as you realize the finality of this moment.

With an imperceptible click, the hatch is seated and secured. You clamber up a very short ladder to your command seat that is heavily padded. Once airborne, the immense pressure of the g-forces will do their best to flatten your body and would do so without this protection. Lifting your still heavily clad form upon the seat, you scan the display screens, panel lights, numerous toggles and modules that leave you with the impression of being inside a Swiss watch. Preflight checks are monotonous and time consuming, and the process is rewarding in that no glitches have surfaced. You bring two straps across your chest and buckle them securely. You swing the auxiliary extension panel so that it almost rests on your chest.

Switches 1 and 2 activate the televiews fore and aft.

"Chief, how goes it?" a voice echoes in your headset.

Apparently, Sal's popular nickname has made the rounds. Smiling and feeling a little special, you reply, "Great." The following conversations are more cosmetic than official, as this bird, with some exceptions, is totally automated.

"Minus one minute," breaks the tranquility you were finally enjoying and brings you up sharply. Last of the ninth, bases loaded. One more strike for 300. Touchdown in the final seconds. These are the analogies that flash through your mind and maybe more, but you shake your head to concentrate. You will drink in every second so that one day you will pass all this down to your children. What a great legacy to leave.

"Chief, thirty seconds to go."

You acknowledge with a grunt. Your body involuntary tightens, your hands grip the seat coamings with white-knuckle desperation, and you feel your pulse racing. This is it! This is it!

Five…four…three…two…one…zero. A tremendous vibration ripples through the ship accompanied by a dull roar, which increases in volume by each passing tortuous second. Your grip gets even tighter, if that's possible. In an instant this mass of venture slowly rises from its cradle, flames angrily escaping from its tubes. Machinery hums in protest, metal begins to strain, the intensity increases as full power is brought to bear, while the ship continues to shudder, as if trying to decide if it will fly. Your mind must focus on what tasks you must attend to; pain and distortion written on your face as it reflects the tremendous unseen force. Upward, higher and higher, faster and faster; power, such unthinkable power. They say the human body is stronger than we think and can take unimaginable punishment, though you feel as if you are being torn apart.

You scream to reduce the force upon your body, but more and more you feel a downward squeeze.

How long? How long must you be pulverized like this? When gradually you start to sink into sea of darkness, swirling and swimming into welcome oblivion.

You don't recall how long you embrace that stupor, it must have been several eternities, but as your eyes slowly open, there is the Earth, your Earth, falling away, being helplessly pulled from you. For a moment you reach to grab her but then laugh at your sentimentality. How beautiful. How divine. How can you or anyone tire at this sight, as you hold your trance like that of a loved one?

You then notice a gradual lessening of the g-forces, and eventually normalcy, relatively speaking, returns. The sweat draining from your pores pools at the base of your helmet, providing a slight cooling but sticky relief. The gentle hum of the modules and the whirling of small electrical motors, coupled with clicking circuits, replace the now diminished roar of the engines. You sit for a few moments to fully comprehend what has happened and what it may lead to. You let out a scream betraying a touch of vanity. You did it! Man, just wait. All the things you're going to do and its going… You pause.

Whoa! It takes a few seconds before you dismiss this backslapping and to remember that you're only one part of the equation here. Those left behind should be the ones extolling their achievement, not you. You're only executing what they have forged with foresight and labor, probably wishing they were in your seat.

Beginning to settle in for the long journey, you retreat to the second deck, which will serve as a communications and lounge area. Slightly cramped, it still affords you some walking and working room.

The removal of your bulky space suit brings instant gratification and renewed energy. Automation has its limits, and there are many chores to be done to satisfy your many concerns. Among these are food rations, communications, and the power supply, both for interior use and flight propulsion. As you run through the post-flight checklist, you marvel at the exquisite nature and functions that engines elicit in your analytical mind. Though not as versed in the scientific acumen possessed by the exceedingly creative engineers who created these marvels of propulsion, here in a nutshell, and simply put, is what you understand of these power plants. The liftoff engines provide the brute power to hoist this behemoth into the ever-reaching sky and beyond. That has been the case for decades with little if any change. What really becomes the most dramatic advance are the cruising engines, the ion engines. The core energy source is Xenon, a heavy, colorless, and noble gas found in trace elements in Earth's atmosphere.

Generally unreactive, with a few chemical reactions it can be converted to xenon hexafluoroplatinate, the first noble compound to be synthesized. It is considered as a propellant for ion-thrusted space craft, such as the seventies' satellites and NASA's Dawn spacecraft. Xenon also doubles as a neutron absorber, which can slow or stop the chain reaction in nuclear fission reactors. With a low ionization potential per atomic weight, it can be reduced to liquid at room temperature but easily converted to gas. Its inert nature is also less corrosive to engine parts. These and other properties explored resulted in a breakthrough of unimaginable proportions. The old-style engine emits a steady pulse that remains constant, and in space, this continual pulsing would, over a period of time, result in high velocities. The drawback is the lack of instantaneous power that can be throttled up or down. It is all or nothing. But with this new concept, an instant acceleration can be instantly demanded and controlled, a milestone in space travel. What would have taken months will now be reduced to weeks and the boredom along with it. As you ponder this technological revelation, it reminds you how far mankind has advanced since the Gemini missions, how the disappointment of curtailed space exploration soured a once-thriving industry. Only through the intervention of farsighted individuals and a scientifically awakening segment of NASA and government did our trip to the stars resume.

In the hours that follow, you study the mission profile. Among these, you run through your routine of approach and landing, which you already know second by second. Every aspect has been scrutinized to the point of becoming second nature, and it has to be, for there may be no second chances. The thing about being alone tends to sharpen your senses, and you absorb all the salient points with relative ease. Since maneuver override from Earth is not possible due to certain protocols not being available, the responsibility of bringing the ship in safely falls to you.

This means an ever-vigilant eye to all the controls and their instrument readings to avert any failures. Your computer will be your go-to source for the letdown, so you're not completely on the hook—thank heavens. The ship's velocity is beyond what was anticipated. The power plant, although tested for eight years, had never really shown its true potential, tantalizing its designers with its high performance but for some reason never seeming to peg its upper limits. Oh, it had the speed you desired, but at times during testing, it would surpass itself. As long as the base speed was acceptable, anything else was gravy. It was in your power to utilize this surplus as you saw fit, and the trip to your destined planet will see every drop squeezed out.

At your final briefing, it was decided that after liftoff the usual communications concerning the flight status would be cursory as most functions were being sent back by telemetry. No need to distract you unless absolutely necessary. Once safely on your way, and removed to the second deck, contact would be initiated to give a personal report on everything that needed to be conveyed. Before you see it, you sense something wrong and instinctively turn toward the communications suite. You stare in horror at the thin wisps of smoke leaking from the transmitting panel. Frantically you grab the fire-suppressant bottle but realize that the covering plate must be removed from the panel before you can do anything. Pressing the quick release studs, you quickly gain access to the maze of wiring and miscellaneous connections. Deep inside, you see a flickering light, something on the order of a short circuit, but much worse. The light gains in intensity and begins to engulf its surroundings, the wisp now becoming a blanket of smoke. In a frenzy, you spray the contents of the bottle, hoping against hope that you are in time to prevent disaster. In what seems like a glacial age passing of time, the fire is extinguished, the smoke lingering longer, causing your lungs to burn a little and your eyes to smart. Now, with great dread, you must determine the extent of damage and proceed with repairs if possible.

You're numb, completely dumbstruck. What happened? How bad is it? With a trembling hand and a silent prayer, you grab what tools you need and stare at the blackened forest before you. Test after test indicates that not only is the main unit fried but that all the redundant systems as well. Now you are alone, truly alone, alone with your thoughts, your fears, and your regrets. Yes, regrets. You're regretting what fate has led you to, fearful that this could be a harbinger of failure. You've never really had a doubt as huge as this, and it hangs on to you like a bad cold, only this cold could prove fatal.

You stare at the com unit, and in an attempt at bravado, you spit at the charred remains.

You're not a vain person, but for the most part, you were able to confront things like this, and now you feel vulnerable, something foreign to you. Somewhat subdued and feeling very ordinary, you pause, and in a moment of calmness, you turn toward the view port. You lean forward, bracing your outstretched arms against the bulkhead, slowly lifting your head until your eyes embrace a scene only dreamt of. You gaze, astounded, at the wonderful and intriguing sights displayed; millions of heavenly bodies entombed in a deathlike darkness. You are part of it now, streaming toward the fulfillment of man's dreams. It is then that a strange feeling of power engulfs you, a power that Alexander, Napoleon, Caesar, and Quenton must have experienced. You are the deciding factor in man's quest to wrest secrets from the stars. What comfort you gain from this brings a little solace to your predicament, but you still feel an edginess that does not sit well with you.

Whatever boost you receive gradually diminishes as you think about your isolation. It grows and grows, unseemly so, and you can't shake it. What the hell is wrong? Is this really you? Oh, if only another crewman had been assigned, another person to share the woes inflicted on you. You turn from the port and attempt some type of routine to shake you from your doldrums. With so much automation, there is little except make work or reading several ship manuals and the few nontechnical magazines you ship aboard. As the days go by, the silence is broken only by the monotonous drone of the engines, occasionally accompanied by the sharp clicking of obscure valves and the drone of miscellaneous units. You try to sleep some of it away, but dreams of death, being stranded in space, or having the ship break up around you conspire to often wake you in a sweat.

Day after day, the same routine evolves with deadly regularity, until you approach the edge of apathy. A narrow escape from being pummeled by a hurtling meteor leaves you with only a faint feeling of relief, which startles you into the realization that unless you reverse this demonic tide, all could be lost, damn it. Having fallen prey to a condition so alien to you, it's a wonder that you were not completely overtaken by its hypnotic hold. Ironically, this also reawakens that deep sense of survival all mankind is born with. It also points out to you one of man's greatest weaknesses—his sanity. Much to meditate on.

Coming to terms with this newfound revelation, you know that it can't occur again if you are to succeed in the mission. Forewarned is forearmed, and with this acknowledgment you seem to gain a better prospective of your situation and ways to avert any reoccurrence. You hope.

With a gross luxury of time on your hands and enjoying a snack, you lean back, close your eyes, and mentally drift back to earlier days. Oh boy, the farm. The farm and the fields. Those were the days, coming home from school and walking the whole way, throwing an odd stone or two at the blackbirds and mimicking the moos of the cows in the pasture. After chores were done, you couldn't wait to grab your fishing pole and head to the pond where you could usually get a good fight out of whatever was in there. It was the fight, not the eating. Pop was a hard worker and, after Mom passed on, tried to raise you to be independent and to work hard for whatever you wanted. You were fairly good in school and even wrangled a scholarship to the university. Having worked with all the farm implements, you gained a fair amount of mechanical expertise, which allowed you to pursue engineering.

You met a young girl and thought things might work out between you two but never did. You dated, but nothing came of it. Perhaps in the back of your mind there were too many competing goals, and they just seemed to take precedence. Having a legislative backer, you were able to enter the Air Force academy, graduating with high honors and a hunger to fly the skies. There was no plane you couldn't fly, and rank was achieved fairly rapidly. In furthering your education, it was somewhat odd that you chose to study languages: reading and translating. And currently reflecting on that, it became one of the main qualifications that allowed you to secure the number one slot for this venture. Being six feet one inch, one hundred ninety five pounds on a lean frame, your muscles tended to be slightly pronounced from the gym sessions that you attended regularly. You have a good grip, steady nerves, at least for now, keen eyesight, and a yen to accomplish this mission. But that is one thing you can't hurry.

Time wears a snail's disguise, but eventually you observe a speck out in the ether which could be your goal, the mysterious canal-marked planet that has beguiled men from all ages past. Your eyes are locked onto the screen, and you take no leave for hours, as if waiting for your lover to come to your side. As it looms larger, the knowledge bursts upon you—you've made it! You've done it! As you gaze upon this sphere of controversy, you think of the awaiting glory, if you live to have the telling. Just think, the first human who will set foot on an alien planet! The thrill is in sharp contrast to those earlier days of despair.

In the time remaining before landfall, you inspect the supply chamber, a farther deck below. You do this with the obsession of a bean counter, those same people you had mildly scorned for their intensity to account for every iota. The logic of it all now seems to impress you for its practicality and necessity.

Fully satisfied that you have checked all that you could, you ready the pressure suit and check out the gyro-copter, an amazing piece of equipment. This will be your main means of exploration as ground travel would be too slow. Your schedule accounts for a certain amount of exploration, but everything is timed to a strict schedule.

At launch, this planet and Earth are at their closest position to each other and would remain relatively close for some days, but fuel limitations will require a very spartan excursion. If you linger beyond a certain time, the distance back will be too great for the fuel remaining.

If conditions permit, testing and analyzing equipment, along with a collapsible shelter, will be lowered to the surface. That taken care of, you return to the flight deck, donning that cumbersome suit and hoisting yourself onto the command seat. You swing the control panel to your chest and check the telemetry of the ship.

The atmospheric, pressure, and radioactivity analyzers are brought online, to indicate the nature of the atmosphere. As the ship closes the planet, you scan the viewer for anything of interest or to avoid any unforeseen obstructions. Closer and closer and the void retreats before the advancement of the shadowy globe.

As the ship descends, you're transfixed by the ever-growing image. Your eyes pierce every rut or mark that shows, trying to endow them with the life you hope to find. Anticipation augments your desire for speed, not one delay. You now truly believe that nothing short of death can abort this attempt to affirm your destiny.

Soon you will learn not only the origins of the canals but of other undreamed-of wonders. An alarm signals activation of the computer assist mode, meaning that you will maintain a manual override in the event of an emergency. Gradually the ship veers slightly parallel to the surface and begins to shudder as it slowly points its nose upward aided by the reversal of the ion engines and the maneuvering thrusters. Then in a vertical position, she begins to glide downward, the vibrating engines seemingly protesting the strain put upon them. The deceleration is profound and has an inverse effect upon your body.

The altimeter reading, superimposed on the view screen, ticks off the meters indifferently, and you silently mouth the numbers. Twenty thousand, nineteen, slower and slower. The ground looms menacingly as you make out its rough terrain. Ten thousand, nine… your hands grip the edges of your seat, and your muscles freeze. Nearer and nearer. Five thousand, four, three…you're suddenly weak with a sudden burst of anxiety and the ultimate excitement! Involuntarily, your eyes shut ever so tightly, and your breathing stops. To take off is one thing, but to land…

You're like a child in bed at night, afraid to open his eyes lest he sees the boogeyman. But you are no child, and there is no boogeyman. You dispel the notion of this childhood antic and open one then both eyes. They lock onto the screen and the altimeter reading, the numbers slowing every second, as if tired from an exhausting race. They decrease until a thud echoes throughout the ship! A landing! With unrestrained emotions, you unstrap yourself and race to the port. You scan the landscape and horizon, knowing in advance that the lay of the land would be rugged, hilly, and flat, with distant mountains framing the skyline, but nevertheless, a slight chill runs down your spine. Is it all like this—desolate and colorless, lifeless, and maybe hostile? Well, you won't know for sure, not until you get down there. The instruments have a reading of thirteen pounds per square inch. Good. The atmosphere contains enough oxygen, though thin, to support your lungs, provided the one-hundred-meter dash is ruled out. Additionally, there are no signs of dangerous elements in the atmosphere, which provokes a sigh of relief. The suit will not be needed. Returning to the storage deck, you send the 'copter to the ground automatically. You could ride down with it, but you have a yen to go old-fashioned. Back to the flight deck, pausing slightly before opening the hatch.

What awaits you? Countless jumbled thoughts crowd your mind as you depress the hatch control.

It swings out with an agonizing slowness, while you almost bite your lip in anticipation. You step to the opening and inhale a deep breath of alien air. You cough slightly and waver for a moment, feeling a little lightheaded, a condition that can only be rectified by time. You look down at the surface to ensure no obstructions to your descent. With that, you activate the ladder array and watch as peg-like objects start protruding from the skin of the ship, rungs which will allow you to descend to the ground.

Hand over hand, you make your way down, feeling the natural pull of gravity on your wiry frame for the first time in weeks, a welcome sensation. You pause at the last rung, trying to think of some historic phrase that school kids will one day mimic. Aw, what the hell, just jump!

So with an unceremonious plop to the ground, history is made. For a moment and just a moment, you do not move, trying to comprehend what you have just done. Incredible! Snapping back to the moment, you look around to observe this world of many mysteries. First, the sky. It's a slate blue with nary a cloud to be seen. The sun is so much smaller when compared to how you saw it from Earth. The temperature is a bit more chilling, considering the farther distance, but endurable. The landscape doesn't lend itself to *Home and Gardens*, so bleak it appears. Color fluctuates between gray, brown, and a mixture of both. The topography reveals rolling hills, deeply scarred from what you can see. Would this indicate rainwater washing the surfaces so long ago? The level land predominates and is consistent in its features for as far as you can see—how dull. What really strikes you is the total absence of vegetation, the starkness unabridged by the lack of the color green.

This observation disappoints you, for your private goal was to encounter life, any form of life. Your accomplishment so far is tempered by this sole exemption. Another observation is the lack of wind, a weird sensation or the lack of one. A turn of 360 degrees reveals the same sight for as far as you can make out. Having reflected on the moment and eager to start your mission, the 'copter is off loader and adjustments made to the engine to compensate for the different atmospheric content. Small but not restrictive, you marvel at the genius of its design. It has an automatic hands-off liftoff feature, a protective shell, radar, sensor display screens, and on-demand set-down controls. If it could talk, it would probably say it didn't need a pilot, and on many counts it would be true, but hey, you're the boss, and that's what counts. You snicker a little at this assertion of dominance, absent anyone to impress it with. You also set up a table and research instruments under the collapsible shelter, although sleeping will be within the ship; not knowing what is out there is an incentive to play it safe. With the sun fading, there's not much to do other than to plan for tomorrow's field testing and possibly a small jaunt in the air. You're excited to see what the little craft can do in spite of your career in large fixed wing aircraft. Your first day ends with a contented slumber, which is surprising after your harrowing trip to this un-alluring world.

The next day finds you up early, ready to uncover what secrets this world may surrender. A fairly decent breakfast, if you can call MREs a real breakfast, and down to your shelter you go. Instruments that had been preset the night before yield a volume of information that is recorded and logged. You find nothing out of the ordinary, but you do find info useful as a measuring stick against other data. A little disappointing, but maybe something else will turn up. As you putter, you satisfy a sudden hunger pang with a bite from a power bar, and in doing so, a chunk of it falls to the ground. Not to worry, the maid will be here this afternoon. That sums up your concern about littering the confines of your enclosure. Stepping out for a short while to take photos in the brighter light, you see that the coloration of the surrounding area has markedly improved. But a surprise awaits when you renter your shelter. Kneeling down to gather the remnants of the food bar, there's no trace of it at all! A chill runs down your neck. Is there something or someone lurking somewhere?

You pull out your automatic and step outside, scanning the area in a wide sweep. You turn your attention to the grainy soil in hopes that if an intruder did enter, it would have left some sign. You can't find a thing and try to think of anything that could explain the missing food. Warily and on a hunch, you gather some soil and examine it under the miniature electron microscope. The results are electrifying. Microbes are present in an astounding number, but more significant is their behavior. Trace amounts of the power bar are being ravaged by these creatures. Their appetite seems insatiable as they devour the remnants in what can only be described as a food frenzy. Another experiment reveals that only organic material is affected by these strange creatures. At last, a garbage disposal system not only efficient but quiet and energy efficient. Wow.

Sitting back on your chair, you wonder how many other discoveries like this will you find. Almost lost among your discoveries is the awareness of a deafening silence. Strange, but the very absence of ambient sound, in an odd way, creates a sound of its own, sort of. Imagine listening to vehicles passing by at night in a continuous stream and then abruptly stopping. The silence is so pronounced it almost mimics sound. No birds, no animals rummaging around, no insects with mating calls or whatever other noises they make. Can anyone endure this naturally imposed silence and still function? What other strange things will happen next, you wonder. If not lethal, then perhaps a wondrous slew of encounters and findings that invigorate the imagination. Yes, what else is there? What will you find?

One way to find out is go and look for it, whatever it might be. The 'copter looks inviting as you approach it. Hopping on the seat, the straps are buckled with the eagerness of a child playing with a newfound toy. The controls live up the hype, and before you know it, the craft is airborne and hovering. You glance at the mother ship and dismiss any safety precautions. She's safe enough as is; besides, what could you really do if there is a threat? Don't even think it. A westerly course is randomly punched into the autopilot, and off you go. Relaxing is an almost forgotten privilege as you take in the sights, just as a tourist might do, except there are no guides. The hunt is on.

After two days of fruitless searching, your anticipation diminishes, as you cover a monotonous sameness, over and over again. Your food doesn't taste as good, if it ever did, and your expectations are dimming. There are strange minerals with an unbelievably high ore content and quartz formations of dazzling beauty. But these are furthest from your mind. If only one hint of life could be found, any life save for the microbes. If not, within the next few days, you must leave for home, keeping in mind that the Earth is speeding father and farther away from you.

The next morning is a carbon copy of the others—nothing. You decide to land on a small hill and just stare at the wilderness. You can't describe the hollow feeling that has now turned to bitterness. Where is the life, or a sign of what was life? Again nothing. The desire to succeed is partially tinged with a grab for glory and pride. What man is immune to fame or likes to admit defeat? The serenity and quiet arouse your senses, causing you to become fully and actually aware of what you're seeing. With nothing to hinder your view, the flat smooth plains beyond seem to reflect the sun's rays with their glassy look of smoothness.

The soil appears fertile, though more often than not it chokes on its initial layer of aridness. The so-called canals are nothing more than super ravines and not the embodiment of past rivers, as the topography indicates. The distant mountains are the only tangible signs of normalcy, similar to those on Earth. You feel you may have reached bottom. It's true that your 'copter has great range and speed, but the area covered is only a fraction of the planet's surface. Given that, you feel it represents the rest of this drab world, and with that conclusion, the stark reality is that there is no need to prolong the agony. With several days left, it's best to get a jump on the schedule and head back to Earth. Whimsically, you board your craft and lift off but this time deciding to fly it hands-on.

Just a joy ride and fully enjoying it. It's the least this planet owes you. You take a different route, surprisingly one not used before. As you drink in the sights, a small mountain, or to be precise, a large hill looms into view. Okay, what the hell, let's see what it has to offer, and you let down on a small patch of ground near the crest. Taking a deep swig of water from your canteen and leaping from your seat, you advance toward the slope as a carefree sightseer. Who knows, you might find some cave loaded with relics or some signs of some past civilization. Stumbling, you near the peak, nursing some bruised shins and scraped hands and beginning to think twice about this impromptu excursion. Reaching the top on all fours and head down, you pause to catch your breath.

Several minutes pass before you stand up to look—good lord! Electricity runs through your body and can't help but feel frozen to the ground. Why now? Why so late? You're overwhelmed with competing emotions; amazement merging with sheer gladness. There's no containing yourself as you shriek, "Remains! Remains of a city!" Reacting madly, you dash downward, with utter disregard for bodily safety, tumbling, tripping, smashing into boulders or skinning your flesh with each fall. You emerge at the base of the slope, happily falling flat on your face, which doesn't bother you a bit. What pains you incur cannot dim the exaltation you're reveling in as you pick yourself up and dash among the ruins.

Laughter of sheer joy rings among the debris as the realization comes that there was, and still may be, life somewhere in this world of desolation. Among this rubble may lie clues that you have searched for, and your hope rebounds with renewed vigor, but not for long. You halt and stare at this total destruction and its dire implication. At last, proof of what was once a metropolis. Did they also live their lives as ours did?

Did they have dreams, goals, love, family, and all those cherished things that make up a society? But now, this heap of shattered rock and mangled metal points to one meaning and one meaning alone—annihilation. A sudden air of dire certainty shrouds your heart with a stinging depression. Truly, you have landed on a dead planet. There is no solace to relieve the impact of this setback, and you feel worn and tired. Can all this have been for nothing? The toil, labor, and hopes? You shrug your shoulders and accept what is here. That's all you can do. As dispirited as you are, you're determined to salvage something, if only to balance the scales.

It will be a tribute to those back home who labored and gave so much so that this venture was possible. A little bit of the sting is lessened but also the realization that you were too obsessed and maybe too selfish in your drive to succeed.

For several hours, you examine the skeletons of what were once buildings. An odd relic or two takes your fancy; a strange design eludes you, or the pattern of construction impresses. What once stood proud now lies humbled. Was it self-destruction, as Earth almost suffered years ago, or a natural catastrophe? No way to tell, one way or the other, just the remains holding their secret silently within.

Scanning the area with the video cam, a vision suddenly fills its lens that brings you up short. Your eyes widen as you see an impossible sight. A building! Here amongst the rubble, a building! Hoping it's not a mirage, you run toward it as fast as you can pick your way through the rubble. Again you incur the pain of impatience, banging your shins or skinning your hands as you thread your way through mounds of debris.

Finally and breathlessly, you reach the foundation and stop, the pain of no consequence. Your eyes can't take in enough of what's before you, so incredible is its presence. You examine the walls thoroughly, their whiteness reflecting the brilliance of the sun. The designs impressed on its surface leave you awed as does its seven-sided walls impaled with blending buttresses. The roof rises in a pyramidal shape and is also gleaming white. There appears to be a portal or entranceway, shaped as an abstract sunburst; no doors, just an opening to the interior. Strangely, there are no windows. You scratch your head in wonder as you eye the mystery building. What is it supposed to be? A challenge like this generates the enjoyment and glory of uncovering seemingly impossible secrets, challenges which lend more to man's curiosity and eventual success.

In a short while, the sun will be gone, leaving you with little choice but to spend a night here among the ghosts of a dead civilization. Knowing your avid curiosity and the shortness of time, you doubt that you will sleep at all.

You enter the portal and proceed down a small corridor, which is adorned with the same beauty displayed on the exterior. There's internal lighting, the source a mystery, as no fixtures are to be seen.

Continuing cautiously, your mind whirls with revelation after revelation. Such beauty, oh, such beauty, and all of it hidden, at least until now. You vid cam every square inch; you can only imagine the critical response from the archeological community. And you think, could a race this gifted have been so devoid of common purpose to have allowed themselves to cease to exist?

Musing to yourself, you proceed farther down the hall, approaching a second sunburst, shrouded in darkness and, frankly, foreboding. Half a step through the portal and a soft light envelopes what turns out to be a large chamber, the light growing in intensity, banishing all traces of darkness. The beauty of the facade and corridor pale in comparison to what your eyes behold. A tremendous enclosure, the walls covered with the finest art beyond even the imagination of the greatest artists and craftsmen that Earth ever sired. Further regaling your sweetened senses, the multispectrumed ceiling vaults display hues that put the rainbow to shame. Here encased in a lavish display, enhanced by determined sculptures and upheld by decisive furnishings, is a display as breathtaking as you have ever witnessed. But there is also a strange feeling of sadness; isn't there always sadness whenever there is death? Here too was death, for a way of life was dead. Still dazed, you make way to the center of the room, feeling as if you are the only living substance in eternity; it has that effect on you. Such grandeur, beyond expectation. Could it hold the key that unlocks the riddle of this city?

But what of the source of illumination? It fascinates your intellectual and technical mind, and foolishly, you toy with the idea of an unknown entity lurking about. You shout aloud, hoping for a response, which rebounding echoes oblige. As past experience has taught you, it's not what you can see, but that which you can't see that should be a source of concern. You search about, to no avail.

Moving backward toward the room's entrance, the lighting slowly, with each step, retreats into darkness. On a sudden impulse, you leap quickly forward, again allowing the illumination to reign supreme. You realize your hunch was correct, and why not? This building that contains so many wonderful, if not miraculous things, why not a sophisticated construct mimicking a slightly diminished form of sunlight? A search for the mechanism that controls this phenomenon is not to be found.

The perfection of construction fails to yield a clue as to its location. Such a quantum advance that you wonder how mankind was able to adjust to the quaint and long-forgotten candles. Knowing sleep, however desired, is out of the question, you inspect the myriad objects of palatial designs.

The technique is delicate weaving this same attribute amongst all you survey—the floors, dome, and…wait, transparent cabinets! They are above you on a ledge type second tier.

You scan your surroundings, seeking a means of reaching them. A vertical depression in the far wall with a transparent facing draws your attention. Eagerly you race over, and warily you slide the facing and step onto a platform, and almost without noticeable motion, you are at the second level, all without engaging any mechanism at all, if in fact there is any to activate. What technology. Stepping out of the lift, you scan the many cabinets and determine that their only function is to contain odd, cylindrical containers. Opening the nearest cabinet, you remove one of the cylinders and carefully examine it, noting that it bears no resemblance to anything you have seen before. Inspecting several more cabinets and their and contents, you still can't fathom their purpose. While musing over many possibilities, and glancing about as if to shake a coherent solution from your mind, your eyes are drawn across the way to the other side of the level and catch sight of another cylinder, this one different in size and coloring from the rest. Where the prevailing color was a plain beige, this container is gleaming white and mounting a crest that is absent on the others. A rising spark of curiosity involuntarily rouses a challenge for discovery and solution, a driving force that has now taken hold of you. Snapping up the container in a manner suggesting that it may fly away from you and deprive you of a conquest, you return to the first level to contemplate your next move. Looking about, you look for some type of furnishing so that you may examine your trophy more closely. At the rear end of the room, you see an assemblage that could, with a little imagination, pass for a desk and chair, although the configuration would suit a contortionist more than your frame. What must these beings have looked like? Besides nondescript sculptures and artwork, which was strange, your guess would be just that, a guess. You adjust your body to as comfortable a position as possible. Laying the cylinder upon the surface of the ersatz desktop, you methodically eye its symmetry and try to guess its purpose.

Taking the object in your hands, you rotate it slowly, searching for a means to open it, noticing how devoid it is of any external protuberance, latch, stud, or any other means by which to facilitate its opening. More by instinct than by sight, your probing fingers glide upon the entrancing surface, and after a period lasting no more than seconds, your forefinger abruptly stops at the midsection, where, centering upon the crest, it depresses what seems to be a small stud, almost invisible because it merges with the surface, no outline of its shape to betray its presence. Slowly, with the hint of a subtle vibration, the cylinder begins to part, surprising because the seam separating the two halves is almost invisible. Watching in strained anticipation, the separation completes itself, and within the interior are sheaves of transparent material. Upon closer examination, you find that the sheaves, maybe 143 in number, are decorated with symbols and markings that convey…what?

Gazing upon this tantalizing find and what it may portend, you sift through the sheaves that signal the beginning of another challenge. What does seem to pique your interest is the indication that this may be a language, and if all the other containers hold like entities, then you can surmise that what you have stumbled upon could be—let it be so—an archive or a library! You freeze for the moment, your body tensing at the thought. Will it describe this race and explain all that you have encountered? Since the object before you is different from all the others, it may hold some special knowledge or record, perhaps a key to the past that holds a clue as to what happened here on this planet. And why this building alone remains intact or what had befallen the inhabitants.

As you dwell upon these questions, you think of the many languages that you eagerly absorbed toward a goal of self-enlightenment and are proud of the fact that you were able to be fluent in seventeen languages, both speaking and reading. As a former air force pilot and astronaut, your skills are highly rated, and being thirty-five years old, any vestige of youthful brashness is relegated to the past. What was needed and what was received was a thorough professional, one who could weigh the risks and balance the odds with a great degree of assurance. As a test pilot, you could discover the strength and weaknesses of whatever craft you flew, enabling you to avoid any situation that could prove disastrous. Beyond these mandatory requirements, you were caught off guard when your handlers introduced a new syllabus in your training which went far beyond the norm. Basically, it was a program engineered by far-seeing men who worked unceasingly to perfect a system of crypto-analysis. It was intended as a basic Rosetta Stone, if you will, to unlock the myriad roads and highways of communications. It's based on mathematics, for most things are based on that. You remember how you burned the midnight oil, going hours without sleep. At times it seemed fruitless, but in the back of your mind a small voice urged you on, allowing you to dwell on the prospect that one day you would experience what you are experiencing now.

To give the training more meat on the bones, translations of hieroglyphics and cuneiform or some other ancient form of writing were thrown into the pot. With each success your confidence soared, for this was the part of training that had been the hardest for you and, because of the time it consumed, caused a delay in the launching schedule. But that showed how important you were to the mission. The thought was humbling in that so much faith was being invested in you. Now you vow you will deliver.

You examine the sheaves and markings and arrange them into some sort of order. Your brows rise, eyes partially frowning and, with a slight gusto, exhale a breath of air. You grab your pack and fumble through the assorted gear until you withdraw a writing pad, calculator, and many pencils, and you wearily contemplate a long road to hoe. For hours you dig into the reservoir of knowledge and begin chipping away at what seems a daunting wall. One pattern after another is formed and rejected. Sheet after sheet of crumpled paper falls to the floor as forlorn witnesses to your failures. You lean back, mentally exhausted, eyelids so heavy they feel as if weights are attached to them. There was a time that the floor would have been littered with the carcasses of cigarette butts, but those days are long gone, and you feel the better for it.

Pausing for a moment to collect yourself, you eye the cylinder with a somewhat jaundice view, thinking perhaps it knows what you are trying to do and is purposely thwarting your efforts.

Yeah, that must be it. It—you catch hold of yourself and let slip a small laugh at how you are bamboozling yourself. Lack of success and sleep will do it every time. The work seems futile, perhaps even beyond your comprehension. Still there is a key to be found somewhere, and with that slight bit of encouragement, you resume a task that challenges your ingenuity.

Rousing your resolve against this linguistic adversary is easier said than done, and although the will is there, the pull of nature is even greater, and you succumb to sleep, blessed sleep, unresistingly and unknowingly. For some time you dwell in a domain that is murky and soothing, and when you awaken, you feel refreshed and feeling quite good. A glance at the floor reminds you of a fruitless night, or was it day? Who can tell cooped up inside this fantastic creation. The pangs of hunger also remind you that it has been some time since you've eaten a decent meal. After a small breakfast of dried rations, brought to life with the addition of water and some energy pills, you resume your task.

Throughout the morning (is it morning?) and into part of the afternoon, the failures increase. Your temper flares out at will, and words of dubious etiquette rebound from wall to wall, a needed release from the mounting tension. Aware of the enormity of the challenge and consequences of failure, you put aside a ruffled ego and delve again into work at hand. By early evening, you score your first success by matching a symbol that has appeared quite frequently. Simplistically, it parallels the oft-used letter *E* as a marker to zero in on.

After all the exhausting efforts, at last a light, dim as it may be, can be seen at the end of a long tunnel. You begin to work with the other symbols, and in conjunction with a mathematical formula, you embark on several paths to construct a framework. One step forward and two backward seems to be the order of the moment. As complicated as the task seems, your mind coolly accepts or rejects the findings as soon as they present themselves. A bit here and a bit there. Rome wasn't built in a day. Hour after hour passes, with few breaks, for little time can be lost. To elevate your system to mirror the alphabet is an aspect you hope all your training and intuition will accomplish.

Encouragement attaches itself to each small success, like building a wall, one brick at a time. If you succeed, you can only mouth their words in your own tongue, as you have no way of knowing their vocal characteristics. How strange, provided you get that far. To understand this language, you must commit to memory the basic symbols and markings that are the most promising. An arduous task, but you have no choice. This, like any great reward, demands sacrifice. Sleep, strength, and peace of mind is the cost as demonstrated by your tenacity. Eventually, your broad shoulders fall back against the wall, and a tired mind now recounts over and over, with perfect recollection, every vital symbol, etching, and mark. You resist the temptation to take a breather, anxious to attack the mystery, hoping that this will finally shed light on this planet, its people, and their fate. Grasping a sheaf and taking a deep breath, your eyes focus like a laser beam across the first row of markings.

The tension mounts, your heart races, sweat begins to stream down your face, and then, then you realize your lips moving with a rhythm tied to the movement of your eyes. But more importantly, the symbols begin to speak in soundless words that echo in your head, symbols your mind comprehends!

Not yet ready to yield to success, and suspicious of this windfall, you cautiously retrace the line. Again and again the results are the same, and taking a deep breath, your eyes focus like a laser beam across the first row of markings.

A splash of water across the face is more symbolic than effective, and once again your eyes peer over the first line again, hoping against hope it's not a cruel joke. Too many things had happened, unexplained things that seem to portend that a jinx or hex has been cast over you. Satisfied that your thrice readings were correct, the road test is over, and now you will hit the highway.

Haltingly, you now survey the markings with a dedicated deliberation, drinking in each symbol so as not to miss a, you guess you would call it a word, their word. As you proceed, it appears that what you are reading is not some formal rending, like our Constitution or the Bill of Rights, but some type of narrative. Slowly it unfolds and you drink in each word ravenously.

> I, Zorrel Tau, a leader and member of the Emporium, have been compelled to record a tragic moment in our history, and I am not certain as to the outcome. What will occur must not be forgotten, and this chronicle will enlighten any who finds and reads this, a document of finality, for a disaster is in the offing. To receive the fullest understanding of what I offer, I must take you back through the veil of time and picture for you the fabric of our society. Emerging from a backward and superstitious age, bereft of societal moral values, it was a slow climb from what we once were to what we were to become.
>
> To compare the accomplishments that culminated into today's society from that which we left behind shows the tremendous strides that were achieved. With pride we could claim to have achieved the greatest harmony, without want, fear, or contentiousness. The ultimate in

propriety and ingenuity prevailed. It was a loving world, full of the warmth that love engenders, free from corruption. Our knowledge had defeated time and space, and our first ventures had been planned to reach other worlds.

Our goal was exploration and to share our benevolence, for our needs were already met, and it was a desire to share our bounty. We had triumphed over many of the causes of disease and had defeated the greatest disease of all—war! No longer was there a need to harm each other or to submit to avarice, a scourge of the soul. Our education had reached a pinnacle that ensured many, if not all, contributed to society. Indeed, there were different strata of wealth, but most were contented, not envying the other for each was the other. A world that must have been ordained for us to have.

I am now old, but not too old to remember when the sheen of near perfection began to tarnish. Hatred and discontent began as an irritation, then festered like a small boil that in time erupted and spewed forth its deadly poison. I had just concluded my studies as a prelude to being appointed to the Emporium. As a lifelong service, care was taken to select only those thought to hold the highest values and interest for those he governed. Elevation was achieved by merit and duty to the populace. All that remained was a final examination of my credentials by members of the Emporium.

It was at this time that the seeds of discontent found fertile soil in words that should have adhered to established civility but instead were used to defy the established precedent. The source of this voice was Brek Rel, a rather innocuous man, devoid of humor and with a quick analytical mind. His appearance was consistent with the general population, nothing to indicate the scourge he was to become. To those who listened to him speak, his charisma was not easily dismissed, although most did not really believe what he said.

Slowly, however, like the erosion of land over time, which never seems to have occurred unless one were to see it as it previously appeared, the irritation had begun, and soon a small cadre was born under his direction. Still, it was never really noticed, for how can an upstart impose his will on others when all he had to offer were words. And that was our mistake—words. So started the inkling of distrust assailing our way of governance. When he spoke, his words were sharp and cut as though they might have been knives with the keenest blades. It was new and different to hear of dissatisfaction even if the majority of the people did not really know the true meaning of the word.

It was akin to giving a measuring device to a baby and expecting it to know what to do with it.

Never being challenged before, some sought to explore this new realm, not knowing the pit they would be falling into. Truly, it stirred the young blood into excitement, ignorant of the sorrow they would endure. They had been raised in a garden which grew only flowers of content, and now they were so blinded that soon it would be impossible to reverse the trend.

What preceded all this came about when Rel was refused appointment to the Emporium. Granted, he did not lack for intelligence, but his undoing was his vocal opposition to the body of leaders and how they ruled. Up to this time, his views were moderate and even considered novel. Being rejected unleashed a course of revenge that would be shaped not by ranting but a measured stroke of genius. He would attempt to make himself acceptable to the people by championing causes he had no intent of honoring. By shrewdly honing his image, he hoped that the support he generated would convince the Emporium of their error in not admitting him. To no avail. A small following soon increased in numbers, and his words only became more emboldened. Now they were more accusatory and confrontational, roiling the senses of those who disagreed and promoting that which we had not known for centuries—hatred. It should have been stopped then, but our laws permitted it, even though it bordered on criminality. If we could have foreseen the coming storm, we would have had no choice.

His speeches contained warped truths, just enough to keep him within the boundaries of established law. The majority of the populace refused to accept his ideology, but as I stated earlier, the few that could not or would not think fell before his oratory. Soon the rallies gathered momentum. "Rel speaks tonight" or "He promises a new world" energized the few who soon became many. They listened and believed. The unthinkable became the norm rather than the exception as demonstrations and riots protesting the Emporium's refusal to seat him were used as excuses for the violence. How well I recall the futility in trying to stop him. Our pleas went unheard or unheeded. Because of the centuries of peace and tranquility, there was little need of armed forces, only a nominal contingent of negotiators that policed our people. With nothing but our pleading to stop him, his followers transformed into the very thing we had eliminated eons ago.

What was once a green shoot now became a strangling vine. With mounting pressure, the Emporium was faced with its greatest crisis in eons. Convening for an emergency session, the Initiator, our leader, rose to address those assembled in the silent chamber. His words were soft, and if you did not listen closely, you would not hear. He had given great thought to what he would present to the gathering, revealed by the strain of his voice and the pained look on his face. Assailed by the all-consuming threat that seemed to materialize everywhere one looked and choking back tears that welled in his eyes, he stunned us all by announcing his ruling. By necessity it would be one of appeasement. He did not call it that, but that was the sum effect of his words.

And so the first great battle was met with defeat and shame. No one moved or spoke for some time, transfixed in their seats by this abject surrender. What could they say, so startled by this horrendous decision? By law our Initiator had absolute power in his decisions, unless a majority of the sub-Initiators overruled him. They too were awestruck and could not summon the resolve to do so, partly because they too saw no other alternative. Thus the first of many walls was breeched.

You could feel the hair tingle on the back of your neck. Not because it was disturbing, but because it seemed to parallel the political history of twenty-first-century Earth.

Think of it. A universe apart and yet a mirror image of your own world. What other surprises lie in store? You gulp down some water, realizing that you hadn't had any for quite a while, the freshness feeling so good. Readjusting yourself into a more comfortable position, you tilt your head against your left hand and raise the sheaves with the other. Before continuing, your mind's eye tries to capture the tumult that must have seemed so alien to these unfortunate people. You look down and your eyes pick up where you left off.

> Having committed themselves to a course of compromise, the ruling body summoned Rel, and following the rites of entry, he was installed, smug in the knowledge that the false promises made would lie fallow. Those of his followers who were naive, as most were, had been duped into supporting a suppressed champion. As long as they continued to believe that, he was secure. His secret motive was to eventually supplant the Initiator, but to declare it openly would jeopardize his position and possibly lose all support. It would vindicate the Emporium's initial denial of a seat and open the eyes of his supporters to his true character and purpose. Even in their somewhat political innocence, they would rebel at having been not only so wrong but used. Rel worked very slowly and planned well, his power growing as well as his position on the Emporium. Many works, however self-serving, but seen to be of benefit for the people, enabled him to rise in the hierarchy of the members. The more powerful he became, so did the numbers of his adherents who supported him in any action he proposed. The older and wiser legislators held dimly to the hope that someday the Emporium would find a way to dismiss him. The only consolation bequeathed to them was the irony that the majority of his fol-

lowers resided on the far side of the planet. They took heart that loyalty remained here, where the new age had begun.

Nevertheless, Rel was well abreast of the situation and wasted not a moment going among his supporters and not hesitating to promise whatever he needed to, thus shoring up his base. This included a concerted effort to convert the loyalists to his side, without much success.

Nevertheless in due time, he felt that the right moment had arrived, that he had accumulated the power he coveted and needed to bare his fangs. When the body of the Emporium met to deliberate legislative issues, Rel astounded the forum, and not the least the Initiator, when he rose from his station and demanded, not ask, but demanded parity with the leader. He believed his tenure had achieved so much and that to deny him his claim of recognition was to be short-sighted and blind. As a body, the members rose, and within the memory of the oldest legislator, nothing had ever so shattered the decorum of this august body as the impertinence of Rel. How dare he! But he did not flinch from his demand, ranting on that the fate of this government was in his hands. Stung by the intensifying outcries, he raised his arms for silence, waiting until the uproar subsided. Here I will set down word for word what was recorded on that pivotal day.

"On this day you have rebuked me, a mistake that will ensure a severe penalty. I have not embarked on this course without considering all my options. Your denial of my request leaves me with no choice but to resign from the Emporium, but do not think you are rid of me so easily. I intend to gather my supporters and retire to the

West, where, in that unchartered and unsettled land, I will constitute my own government, and any attempt to stop me will be met with resistance. I take my leave."

As he left the dais, he continued to rage, his anger unchecked as he hurled curses and promises of revenge. His face appeared to be a hideous mask of insanity. This time Rel had overplayed his hand, ironically so. As knowledgeable as he was about the legislative functions, one area that eluded him was the transition of power protocol. The Initiator had been in failing health and only a determined resolve on his part kept it hidden from the others so that it would not impede the daily functions of the body. However, he had confided in me, and against my vehement opposition, to allow Rel to succeed him to the chair. Why? Because Rel had accumulated an admirable legislative record, although much of it centered on his own ambitions, but appeared to serve the masses. Cunning and effective.

As he left the forum, we now well knew that his boast was no idle threat. We refrained from placing him under arrest, lest it create an upheaval that would surely tear us apart. That was the last time I ever saw him. After all non-governmental individuals were cleared from the chamber and the doors secured, the members returned to their seats and were addressed by the Initiator. His face was drawn, and he appeared to be in physical agony. Nevertheless, spurred on by this unprecedented assault upon authority, he calmly and firmly laid forth a foundation upon which to address the coming storm. It was simple and effective, because it was the only solution at this time until other avenues could be explored. First, the populace were to be informed of what had transpired and for all loyal citizens to report any rebellious activity. Although there was little that could be done to prevent hostile action, perhaps a visible show of loyalty from an aroused citizenry would cow those bent on causing trouble. Second, we would enlist loyal supporters to infiltrate their ranks and provide intelligence about his network and how it operated. Third, in total secrecy, select members who had even a modicum of military knowledge or training were to visit all museums that contained the ancient weapons that so excited the younger children. These weapons were to be confiscated and brought to designated locations in hopes that our scientists could examine and possibly reproduce working examples. All staff were first weeded of any collaborators and sworn to total secrecy, punishable—and this showed how desperate we were—by death! The shock was wearing off, but that did not alleviate the stark reality of civil war. For the moment this seemed adequate in forming a coherent plan to address the danger and the members formed into various committees, outlining in detail the steps to be taken.

The night passed slowly and quietly. Anticipating violence, only silence prevailed. Looking back on this day, I am convinced the Rel had established a chain of command that would react to whatever steps we immediately ordered. I had expected a forceful reaction but was mystified that none materialized. Could it be that he had no stomach for bloodshed despite his bravado? I should have known the answer then and there but was preoccupied with the crisis. Through other sources, the answer was as simple as it was stark—Rel had no means either with which to forcefully topple our government. Stalemate. It would not have made a difference except maybe to allay our fears and to feel safe for the time being.

As time passed, reports trickled in from cities and outlying districts alerting us to the drain on these population centers. Once-thriving locals were stripped of a good deal of their citizens, both male and female. It was inconceivable that one individual could commandeer the loyalty of so many. Their ranks would swell the army we knew would be coming. He had done his work well, indoctrinating them with false hopes and promises, and for this he should be damned. How? These were once clear-thinking and sincere souls, and their allegiance to Rel was fostered by his lies that he had been wronged, that he had fought for them against great odds without benefit to himself, which of course was foolishness, but they could not see beyond the false hope he offered. In one respect I admired their loyalty, loyalty that Rel would use against them without their realizing it.

We received reports that Rel had indeed made his way to the western territories, mostly under populated but containing vast mineral resources. The many artisans who joined him would undoubtedly provide the skill to transform these riches into whatever he deemed necessary to accomplish his goals, whatever they may be. Realizing that we still had a margin of time to work with, the Initiator discreetly called together a select group of scientists. To conceal his plans, only myself and two others were alerted to attend this conclave.

One was the chief of security and the other was the financial head. I had no idea as to what he would propose, but noting the secrecy, I suspected something of grave importance, beyond what we were already experiencing. No notes were taken, and each swore an oath of secrecy.

The Initiator's plan was to develop weapons that could easily be brought online and quickly. Time was not on our side, and knowing the ambitions of Rel, he would not waste any of it himself. What few missives that could be found pertaining to weapons were found in military technical manuals that had become almost nonexistent owing to the banishment of war. Weapons taken from the museums were so far gone that they were worse than useless; their material makeup had deteriorated to such an extent that replication was not an option. As all of this was already known from the Initiator's three-part directive.

I had wondered why the additional secrecy. He beckoned toward the anteroom and an individual strode into the chamber.

"Patriots," the Initiator intoned, "may I introduce someone who may have a solution to our problem." He declined to identify this proposed savior, stating that his identity, if revealed, would invite peril. Anonymity assured, he began speaking with a strong voice, contradicting his benign looks and sparse stature. He proceeded to outline a project he was pursuing. Actually, he had stumbled upon it while researching another line of scientific exploration. Intrigued by the reaction of certain applications, none of which he would divulge for fear of disclosure, he pursued this line of experimentation eagerly.

His discourse was mostly in the realm of science speak, and it took a great deal of concentration to keep abreast of his outline. What came through was as imposing and radical a proposal that I would have thought impossible. If my understanding was correct, the power balance would irrevocably shift to our side. I was stunned. Could providence be persuaded to bestow its benevolence upon us? Would this be the bulwark we needed to thwart Rel? Then reality set in. Having soared so high emotionally with a renewed hope of fending off disaster, we plummeted just as low and faster when it was revealed that the prospect of converting his discovery into a practical model was not easily at hand. Yes, the potential was there, but potential means you haven't achieved it yet. The estimated time for the development cycle was ambiguous and not only time but vast amount of treasure would have to be provided. This allocation of funding would have to be merged into other programs to disguise its nature. We were now thinking like Rel in trying to save our people. We were learning deceit. What would it eventually cost us?

Leaving the great hall, we avoided each other lest we become tempted to plumb each other's thoughts and observations as to what we just experienced. Our oath of secrecy helped prevent this. I retired to my residence to ponder the sequence of events leading to this very moment. Not being a strong adherent to our deity, I now realized how much I may have lost by being tentative in my beliefs.

Not that I did not believe, but believed there were other matters that took precedence. At this moment a profound regret engulfed my being. No matter how much I wished to deny it, I knew now what I must do. Moved by a fervor not known since I was a child, I quickly walked to my dwelling. Entering, I proceeded to a small cubicle central to my home. I gazed upon the icon that was central to our belief—the Giver of Deliverance. Never before did I look upon it as I did now. It was a tacit admission of my need, no, all our needs, for a spiritual intervention. Although I could recline, I chose to stand as if this slight discomfort would afford me penance. How long I stood there asking for guidance and rescue I could not tell you, only awaiting the hoped for answer if indeed the request was heeded.

Wow! you mentally exclaim. Of the many worlds in creation, you have found one with an established faith. It's mind-boggling, but upon further reflection, why should it be. Why should the faiths of Earth be seen as only occurring there? You reread the passage again, sensing something that eluded you.

You pour over the symbols until you—yes, there it is! Giver of Deliverance! You stretch credulity when you then underline the first letter of each word. GOD! Call it coincidence, call it a revelation. Call it whatever you will, but personally you prefer that indeed this must be your God too.

How long have you been at this? Sleep begins to beckon again, but you force yourself to continue, so engrossed by the similarities you have discovered. One thing you can be sure of, it does not appear that Tau's prayers were answered.

Society returned to a normal if somewhat subdued existence. Word of Rel's defection soon had no more of an impact than the struggles of inhabitants going about their daily activities. Part of this could be blamed on the absence of any further friction between the two ideologies. To be sure, we were still stunned by the tumult that saw the loss of a great portion of our citizens. Our inner nature responded that perhaps all contention was over. This was supported by a message delivered to the Emporium by an emissary of Rel's. Being a diplomatic message, it spoke of his regret that the world had been fractured but that it was necessary to allow the growth of his followers. They too were suffering as the territories they occupied had a scant infrastructure to support the masses.

One trait ingrained in our society was a drive for self-sustainment, and I felt certain that that would be a driving force in the establishment of a coherent population.

The immediate danger seemed over, but I suspected otherwise. Rel was helpless now, but for how long? Several seasons passed without any further incidents, but the agents we planted during their exodus provided the Emporium with a wealth of intelligence. The trait of our people that I mentioned manifested itself in a spurt of industry which defied the norms. Amazingly, settlements were erected to house the throng of followers. Among the new construction were installations that bore no resemblance to that which would comprise living units. Somehow, his scientists had developed a rudimentary arms development program.

All this was done openly to convince the population that defensive measures were needed. Mind you, this segment of our former society still operated under the illusion that Rel had been wronged. Their manipulation was masterfully crafted so that he was able to steer them in the direction he wanted. Our security head was taken aback by the speed in which the settlements progressed regarding the arms research. When weighed against our own efforts, we were found to be wanting. All the while, diplomatic emissaries periodically visited the Emporium with conciliatory messages and a need to exchange representatives. I bid the Initiator to resist the latter as a strong distrust of Rel's motives prevailed. He denied my suggestion, stating that the citizens had accepted many of the acts of goodwill favorably, and to reject them would seem contrary to the betterment of relations. All Rel's seemingly benign approaches gnawed at me. He could not and would not change. Why the charade?

Another element I had not considered was the reaction of our own. When knowledge of the covert weapons centers became public knowledge, a backlash ensued. Irate citizens marched in protest. They felt it was a betrayal of good faith toward the West. Had they not sought to improve relations? Were there any signs of hostilities? Of course they could not know what we did. We could not justify our programs without convincing them that Rel had them also. The stumbling block here was an inability to prove it.

Adhering to the protesters' wishes, all research was suspended or canceled. I felt that a turning point had been reached, but not in our favor. The Initiator assembled the members of our covert group to evaluate our alternatives. There were few in light of the popular opposition. Assuring that security was tight, the Initiator proposed that while our current research was ended, he now believed he had succumbed to appeasement in failing to challenge Rel. What he had hoped for was tranquility.

But this was the price to be paid for tranquility. I wonder what price we would we really end up paying. He remained silent, as if battling a conflict within himself and then assumed the posture that his position demanded of him, both physically and regally. Although no record exists of what he said next, I can recall that a renewed sense of hope welled up inside of me. He reminded us of the clandestine meeting we once had where we were told of a system that could solve our defensive needs. Though still in an infant stage of progress, it was all that we had. Therefore, the project would continue. Its promise outweighed the objections. Secrecy would increase, which so far had proved excellent, for no one outside of our circle was aware of its existence. Communications would be sparse to maintain its safety. Only when substantial headway was achieved would contact be initiated. If uncovered, our regime would be at an end, and Rel would easily claim victory.

Several more seasons became history and concerns about the West diminished further. True to the Initiator's edict, contact with the secret lair was minimal, but gains were being made. Its location in the southern mountain range provided excellent coverage. This safety factor fostered a boost in morale which enabled our researches to work unhindered and increased the pace of development.

Progress was similar to the expectant birth of new life; you could never depend on the exact moment of deliverance. Although not an outright birth, signs pointed to labor pains. Then a communiqué was received that electrified us. The project was almost finalized, but for a few unforeseen flaws that thwarted completion. With that one exception, what seemingly appeared to be our grand solution was instead disaster lurking in the shadows. This would manifest itself shortly as events unfolded.

The Initiator was growing older. His wish before the Giver would take him was that true peace and reconciliation be a precursor to his demise. Age, however, did not diminish his capacity to see to the welfare of those he governed. At no time did he dismiss his suspicions about the West, nor did he reject any diplomatic entreaty. Reports from our agents outlined a robust and expanding economy that signified a cohesive policy justifying the trait of self-sufficiency. What alarmed us was the development of implements of war, which contradicted their peacefully stated intentions and overtures. No matter how we reported this to our subjects, Rel would distort it and use it against us.

Our borders, surprisingly, were not fortified in any way. Our intent was not to promote distrust, and ostensibly that was their goal also. It was also another ruse to convince us that we had no need to fear their intentions. Reciprocal travel was allowed but seldom exercised. The painful separation of our world sliced across family and fraternal lines. Extreme sadness colored much of our daily activity, and the forlorn effect of those most affected could not be ignored. Our worship centers groaned under the press of the faithful who renewed or maintained their devotion to the Giver.

What happened next could only have occurred in a nightmare. It struck with the force of a blow delivered to one's person from behind, no warning, no expectation. Emanating from the West, a deep-throated sound accompanied by a tremendous shock wave inundated our senses, unleashing searing pain and bone-chilling fear. Those who were able scanned the skies in every direction, hoping to discern the cause of this electrifying phenomena. Families huddled together, strangers queried each other, and all immediate activity ceased. In due time the Initiator appeared on the universal viewers to calm his subjects and vowing to use all resources in determining what had occurred. He had immediately dispatched members of the security forces to the border and attempted to contact Rel's capitol. In the meantime, all should remain calm but cautious and return to their dwellings. Remain calm! It rang hollow. What seemed like the end of our world permeated to our very souls, and well-meaning directives had no currency.

We were in disarray and confusion. What had happened? It was shortly afterward that the Initiator, appearing nervous and frightened, something that did not inspire confidence, spoke to the whole nation.

Through diplomatic channels, it was learned that several enclaves in the west suffered massive explosions.

Casualties were enormous and destruction widespread. The cause was unknown. Efforts were being made to effect rescue and recovery operations. The country was being rallied to provide aid. The Initiator's next statement caused an involuntary shudder to my already assaulted senses.

Rel had refused any assistance from our government. His response was terse and accusatory. Relatives having members of their clan in the West were denied contact and would be refused entry to the enclaves. Something was festering, apart from the disaster, that I could not fathom. What was unfolding? Having known Rel, it would not be good.

Repeated attempts by tele-audio to understand the scope of the disaster were brushed aside with indifference or rudeness by ministry personnel. Privately I could not resist the temptation to blame any and all things upon Rel's shoulders but refrained from doing so publicly. What if I was wrong? I would gladly have suffered that personal indignation if it contradicted my ingrained distrust. Having almost convinced myself of this fable, following events vindicated my original premise. I was summoned to the Emporium. The full body also assembled. Consternation and uncertainty gripped the emotions of the lawmakers. Droning voices and heated exchanges revealed their intensity. When the hall was full, the Initiator entered from the anteroom, nodded to an aide, and made his way to the oratory circle, a place centered in the chamber from which any lawmaker could speak. The viewers displayed his image on strategically located screens as eerie silence descended upon the floor.

The oratory circle rotated, as was the custom to show deference to the various casts of lawmakers. The Initiator felt the assembly's anticipation, and the lowered lighting heightened a sense of urgency. His silence was unnerving, as if he were striving to find the least hurtful words to speak. You could see that his heart was breaking, perhaps because he believed he failed his beloved subjects. Trembling and holding his limbs outward as if asking forgiveness, the terrible truth emerged. Word for word this is what he said:

"War is upon us. Despite our denials, we have been accused of treachery by the West. Rel himself spoke to me from his headquarters and berated me for allowing an antiseparation group to infiltrate his domain bent on causing destruction. On this point they succeeded. Having secured explosives of tremendous power, key areas of the enclaves were targeted to ensure massive damage to the infrastructures while killing and maiming scores of dwellers and workers. Several of the activists were captured and interrogated.

"Rel claimed that they confessed that their training and orders were directed by our Chief of Security. 'This wanton act of savagery will not go unpunished. Our society will demand swift retribution and I will see that it is meted out. As of today, we are at war, and pray to the Giver that he will show you more mercy than you deserve.' I have alerted all defensive units to prepare to engage their brothers when the onslaught comes. Many will face their own blood, those who chose to leave with Rel. I fear the worst. I fear for my land. I fear for our lost future."

He instructed us to organize what resistance we could muster within our respective districts and to appoint liaisons to coordinate with our belatedly organized military staffs.

The only factor that gave us some degree of confidence was due to the organizational framework of our society. While not totally regimented, it nevertheless had a built-in cohesion from which many of our groups could draw from. This avoided chaos and brought many units online reasonably soon.

While we grappled with that, the question still remained as to what really happened. Since the separation, many activist groups had sprung up, but overall there was no real leadership, and their expertise in weapons manufacture was so limited as to be meaningless. Our interior intelligence units could and did confirm this. Receiving frantic messages from our agents embedded in the West, we were able to rule out a cross border assault by rogue units. Our agents were excellent and motivated by a deep desire to protect their homeland. Their reports, when cross-checked with others, eliminated many assumptions and in doing so narrowed the field of possibilities. This process consumed precious time, a commodity in short supply. Regardless of how much we sorted through the evidence, it meant nothing unless we could pinpoint what occurred, how it occurred, and why it occurred. Nothing could prepare us for what we eventually learned. One of our agents had managed to infiltrate the ministry designated as the research arm responsible for technological development. The department of weapons was one component, which included a unit tasked with the creation of explosives. He informed us that the personnel assigned to this effort were top-notch. His technical background allowed him to be included in the teams formed to explore ways of bringing online a finished product. Their instructions stressed the point that the destructive power they were being asked to create was necessary in clearing land, reducing mountains, or for any other imaginable use that furthered the building of their new state. The more potent, the better.

During many trials, failure did not lessen the keen work ethic of those determined to succeed for the sake of their state. He was present at a remote site where a new compound was detonated. Not knowing what to expect, the group was stationed as far from the blast area as prudence dictated. He thought the distance excessive.

What followed made him thankful that they heeded the precautions. The location comprised of small ridges, gullies, and flat land and was totally devoid of any life signs. At the appointed time, the signal was given to initiate the arming process, which, when completed, left only the final step. Anxious looks betrayed the nervousness associated with birthing a process wrought with uncertainty or hoped for promise. The resultant detonation rivaled all the force that could be summoned by the mythical gods of Vulcar.

Legend had the entities of this realm unequal in causing devastation merely by glancing at a foe or by hurling javelins of frozen light. Obliteration would be total. Myth had become reality. Our agent and the others were flung to the ground and cast about like pebbles. The shock wave that proceeded the deafening roar left them numb and unprepared for the horrendous impact. Limbs were shattered, equipment trashed, and screams of anguish soon accompanied the pounding wave.

After what seemed like an eternity, silence became a vacuum of the mind. Coherent thought was momentarily suspended as supporting teams rushed to the site to give what aid they could. Their motivated speed tended to craw then completely halt as they gazed upon the carnage.

Transfixed, it would take only the abrupt and cajoling urging of their leaders to bring them back to some semblance of normalcy.

Other elements of the test were included in our agent's report, and he would remain with the ministry, perhaps acquiring more information on the test data. He was never heard from again, either because he was found out or more likely because subsequent events prevented it. With what we received, our specialists analyzed piece of data transmitted to us, dissecting the extent of the damage, power readings, and other indicators associated with the blast. While the potency of this weapon worried us greatly, we needed to know more, and this gave light to a course of speculation that at first was abhorrent but soon blossomed into a hideous revulsion on my part. Unrestrained I screamed, "Rel destroyed his own followers!"

This startled my comrades, who could not bring themselves to believe the annihilation was a deliberate act. Surely, it could have been a mishap. Angry at their stupidity, I lashed out at them. "An accident? Three enclaves separate and isolated, all cast into oblivion at the same moment. An accident?" I shouted again. That beast had justified all the animosity that resided within my being. My ranting eventually subsided, and shamefully I asked my colleagues to forgive me. Either through naivety or the firm belief that such a horrendous holocaust could never have been inflicted deliberately, they ignored the possibility of the latter. When informed of our conclusions, the Initiator paled, and he made a slight moaning sound. When first shown our agent's damning report, he refused to challenge Rel, and even if he could, he said, what leverage would he have? Indecisiveness and age had robbed our leader of his once-formidable attributes. He had embraced appeasement, and now the consequences would embrace him.

There was nothing we could do but mount what feeble defenses we could muster. My anger was so intense that the thought of ripping Rel apart was the only solace left to me. Members of the Emporium were instructed to go among the population to instill courage and hope, but the looks from our brethren showed how futile the gesture was. They had demanded peace at any price and now realized the folly of it all. They too were honest and sincere in opposing our arms development, but sincerity without reciprocity was an empty virtue.

Any strike upon our land was expected quickly, for what could stop this madman? As if to validate his superiority over us, he made us languish, anticipation working over raw nerves. Being so overwrought, many had killed, reacting to a threat generated only by frayed emotions. Eventually, the false respite ended with an air attack by converted civilian sky cars upon the districts near the border. The results corresponded to those describe in the testing reports but on a smaller scale. Refugees fled in horror from the approaching armies, if they could be called that. They constituted no more than armed rabble and lacked the discipline demanded of any true army. Nevertheless, they overwhelmed any and all in their path.

You reluctantly force the sheaves down upon the desk, and your mind absorbs the numbness that shrouds it. You are witnessing the death throes of what was once a culture preeminent over many that you had studied. The history of Earth had parallels that seemed to be replicated by this race. You recall the rise of Hitler and how he had shrewdly invoked the same rationale on his citizens that Rel did. Where Stalin had used brute force and total domination, he lacked the sophistication of his counterpart. Here, millions of miles from home, was a history lesson not different from our past and just as predictable. But where the good prevailed over the evil, there is no evidence that anything prevailed but obliteration. You almost want to cry, something that has eluded you for years. Not that there was no cause to cry. It was not in your nature to indulge in an emotional release. The one time that you did when you were three, your father held you in his arms and said, "Big boys don't cry." From that day forward, you shielded yourself behind a mental wall built to protect yourself from one of the most natural acts ingrained in us. Tears did not aid or stop the root cause of crying. At least that is what you convinced yourself to believe. You are tempted now to wonder if the death of this unique world would be to invite violating that self-imposed moratorium.

Surely those faced with injury, or worse, did they also cry? What a ludicrous thought. One of the basic instincts, if not the most important, is self-preservation. Drawn into this line of reasoning is a curious, hypothetical analogy. If what you believe is true, then a person attempting suicide by drowning would fight fiercely to live once this instinct kicks in. Knowing you may die can bring even the hardest among us to cry. You feel a sense of empathy with these unknown and yet not-so-unknown souls. And if the trickle of a tear down the side of your cheek confirms it, you allow it to pass without notice. "Big boys don't cry." Once again you grasp the sheaves, wanting to know and somehow reluctant to experience their dilemma. You recall watching a plane from your unit spinning out of control to the ground and its inevitable outcome but were too mesmerized not to look. Like a moth drawn to a flame, your flame was burning in your hands.

> Word reached the Emporium of the invaders' progress. Though without serious opposition,

their march was not nearly as rapid as would be supposed. Supply problems, insufficient training, and perhaps some soul searching contributed to a less-than-stellar campaign. Searching for a miracle, the Initiator contacted our clandestine research facility. The scientist who had been deemed our "savior" spoke with him and asked for an immediate audience to discuss the current situation. He had kept abreast of the dire reports received from the intelligence branch and had increased the speed of the fabrication of materials and testing.

A fortunate breakthrough had allowed his team to bypass several stages, and this in turn reduced the development cycle to the point where the construct was nearly complete. In fact, with some slight alterations, deployment could begin immediately. Standing alongside our leader, I observed a slight bent of his head upward, an almost imperceptible movement of his mouth. I did not question his actions but fully embraced them.

Considering the distance from the mountain retreat, the journey was made in quick order. With a heavy escort, the caravan made its way to our central logistics center and proceeded to a sealed area.

Under an almost religious scrutiny, the weapon was off loaded and kept shrouded to hide its configuration. Only the Initiator was allowed to see it, and while doing so, the scientist described its function and hoped-for result. When he emerged, a certain sadness draped across his haggard face.

Upon his shoulders he bore the weight that all leaders must feel when forced to defend their country but in this case it will be against those who were once part of this nation. Blood against blood. The agony was tearing him apart, as it would any father who saw his children at conflict with one another. Not to belabor him any more than necessary, and curious as to the conversation he had with the scientist, I sought to know how one weapon could ever hope to halt the invasion.

Returning to the Emporium and to his chambers, he divulged a startling scenario that would unfold with the activation of the device—that was his term for it, not wanting to address it as a weapon. I imagine it gave him some solace. Somehow, in a warped sense, the new meaning had a benign impact on his reasoning that only he could understand. The device would be taken to a location somewhere behind our initial lines and energized. Its field of coverage was almost the breath of the district where it was based, and its depth reached far beyond the border. Its major effect would be mass incapacitation, not necessarily death, which to some degree brought him comfort. Because of its great range and high mobility, it was believed that one device was all that was needed. We left the hall and journeyed to the command and communications center. Biding our time with tempered anxiety, we waited and waited for word from the forward base of operations.

It would be some time before anything was known, and we busied ourselves with reports from other sectors. It seemed the Western advance had bogged down, and perhaps, just perhaps, this erosion of invincibility would foment some second guessing by their commanders. If they were stopped, there would be no need for the device, a forlorn hope that was dashed as quickly as it was born. These impediments would not deter Rel, who, I fervently believed, would not hesitate to sacrifice as many of his forces that he thought necessary to triumph. Time is a cruel foe in the worst of circumstances, and these circumstances were far from ideal. An internal alarm shook us from our thoughts and riveted our attention to the viewer. The shrouded container housing the device hove into sight and was trundled to its point of operation. Like the small microbes that inhabit much of our soil and, to our chagrin, our domiciles, the crew swarmed over the dormant machine. Even with the shroud removed, not much could be made of the device. A protective opaque shield obscured its outline as did its coloration, a dark hue which reflected our mood.

The Initiator caught my glance, his eyes seemingly begging for absolution. His burden was one of office, yet he took it as a personal reflection of his failure to negotiate a coexistence. I was tempted to dismiss his overture when I recalled the overwhelming disgust I felt when he had canceled our programs. I quickly canceled the thought and nodded to him.

Summoned to the viewer by one of his aides, the Initiator exchanged words with the device's on-site commander. Formalities were dispensed with, and he was acquainted with the startup procedures. Pleading ignorance on the details, the Initiator gave permission to commence with the countdown. As each step was accompanied by a verbal reply and confirmation, my anxiety also increased with each phase. I scanned the viewer looking for a telltale sign that signaled the device's awakening. Slowly, from a pinpoint to its eventual prominence, a wavering glow surrounded the weapon accompanied by a high-pitch whining that must have been unbearable at the site. It was alive! If you could call a machine alive. Whatever you wish to call it, hope welled in my breast as I saw what could be our counterstrike against Rel. I turned to the Initiator, all thoughts of appeasement gone from my mind. We grasped each other with unconcealed joy, believing a great turn of events was at hand. With a searing abruptness, the commander's voice could be heard shouting orders. We turned to the screen and saw him pointing to the sky and yelling to his crew to man some defensive weaponry.

Descending from above were several sky cars that had been converted for military use by the West.

An attempt was made to take them out, but what we had was ineffective. I could hear the commander's staccato voice ordering his crew to take cover, all the while gesturing wildly at the intruders as if his anger could wipe them from the sky. We stared transfixed, unsure of what was happening. At its height, the machine's blossoming ball of light was accompanied by resonating pulse. Then, a descending object released by a sky car ploughed into the unit, which was obscured by an all-consuming fireball. The brightness blinded me, and when my vision returned, the viewer was dark. Efforts were made to restore communications, but nothing worked. Stunned is too mild to describe the reaction we all experienced. The Initiator did not move or speak. He had just witnessed our last and best hope destroyed. I will never forget his abject despair. Whether through deceit or a chance encounter, something we will never know, the aerial forces that struck not only eliminated our best hope of preservation but dealt a mortal blow to our sovereignty.

    Crestfallen and unconcerned for his own personal safety, the Initiator lamented on the fate of the personnel caught up in the attack. Continued attempts to reach them came to naught, and he was forced to concede that they well may have been lost. A contingent of security personnel sprang into action and hustled a reluctant Initiator from the post as well as myself and a few others. As we were placed into armored conveyances and driven away, I felt that safety would be illusory in light of what had transpired. The route to our next command post was a winding venture over a route destined to take us to the farthest reaches of our Eastern territories. Drawn and tired, sleep was an elusive commodity, not to mention the pangs of hunger relieved only partially by consuming a tasteless and dried offering. Originally created to sustain wilderness explorers, they had been requisitioned to feed our units on the border. Little could be done to establish a train of fresh food; we had no experience or time to devise one.

    Upon arriving at our new location, it reflected well on the ingenuity and concern of the base guard. A yawning aperture penetrated the rough facade of a small ridge, through which the convoy entered. Illumination had already been provided and temporary structures erected to provide comfort or working areas. Alighting from the convoy, personnel were directed to their assigned units, many scouring the interior with curiosity and some with a drawn resignation. The Initiator again sought to learn of the fate that had befallen his heroic soldiers, but again nothing. After setting up and pouring over what intelligence reports to be had, it appeared to all, from the least in command to the Initiator himself, that the unthinkable was to befall our glorious nation—total surrender. The will to resist was there, but not the means. The Initiator gathered the few members of the Emporium who had journeyed with us and instructed them to prepare a presentation of surrender to be tendered to Rel's government. There were no illusions as to what we could expect. Fueled by his unrelenting hatred for us, and only seeking to spare our populace, we accepted what harsh measures that would be meted out. Does providence dwell in anonymous homes, shining on those who had wished for it dearly but never truly expecting it? What occurred next initially seemed to bear out that axiom but would prove to be a bitter potion. Rushing to our group in a barely controlled state of mind, a communicator shattered protocol by foisting himself upon the Initiator in a stammering slur of words and had to be restrained and calmed before any sense could be made of his rantings.

 Brought to his senses but still unsteady, he related that contact had been restored to the base. What we learned was horrific and perplexing. A fortunate survivor, dazed and injured, said that the aerial assault decimated the surrounding area, and the device, though damaged, was still operational.

 This elicited a mass sigh of relief but not for long. He recounted a mass movement of forces toward our front, which became more discernible as the moments passed. A horde, now identified as the West's vanguard, emerged from a light mist, which conveyed a ghostly aura. The closer they came, the more belligerent the words and actions. With each step they became more hellish, with no constraint whatsoever. The device continued to pulse but without any deterrent effect upon them.

With a savagery only seen in the wilds of Ormac, where the Califor reigned supreme, those unfortunate to stand in the way were ripped to pieces. This revelation unnerved us. We comprehended that war could incite our worst passions, but this was beyond that. As the carnage continued, all contact to the base was lost. Subsequent efforts failed to reestablish the line. The silence that ensued cast into stark reality the fate that would befall us. Control over this machine of promise had completely been lost. It wouldn't be long before our time would come. Realizing the potential loss of our way of life, I could not allow myself to believe oblivion was the only alternative. With a defiant impulse, I approached the Initiator and pleaded that I be allowed to preserve in any manner I could the legacy of our history.

How we began, the hurdles overcome, all the elements that defined greatness. I would not surrender and cast into oblivion that which may never be again. He looked at me as a parent would to a child who had asked permission to ride his first pedicycle, a determined expression draping a young and pleading face.

"Go," he said and embraced me, both knowing it would be the last time. I turned, not wanting to look back, pain and emotion both battling for ascendancy. I left the headquarters with an aide and requested a personal conveyance.

Although my request to the Initiator seemed abrupt, and without prior thought, this was not the case. Many were the times I had authored short essays on various issues. I possessed some degree of literary skills, although my colleagues would jest that I should seek another occupation. Now there would be no need of critical acclaim, just the bare truth. To the southeast lay a city that existed so far into the past that none knew of its origin. Surveys and exploration could not satisfy our curiosity. I visited the site often, wondering who they were and why they were no more. The bleakness bred sadness for this must have been a notable race.

Concern for my friends never left me as I traveled through the lush meadows and gently rolling hills. A stream and its meandering course engendered a soothing effect upon me, as I paralleled its course. Eventually the ruins came into sight, and I could possibly be mistaken for a former resident, as I negotiated the different pathways with certainty. The debris gave no clue as to what form the constructs took. The sameness could dull the average onlooker but not those steeped in the art and science of skeletal study. My route was not random. Through my many excursions, I had come to recognize many features, lest I become lost, and using these as my guideposts I was able to explore confidently. One anomaly known to all who came here was the only intact structure that existed. If you are reading this account, I have no need to describe its features. What you will want to know is that this edifice predates the ruins themselves. According to scientific applications, no age can be determined, or for that matter who constructed it, since it does not conform to our physiology.

What our farsighted leaders observed was the ageless virtue of its beauty and design. So well founded as to be converted to any use, thought was given to create a national archive. The interior spaces were conveniently placed and accorded minimal problems in stocking our missives. Introduced to this marvel of engineering for studying scholars were tele-access units to allow them to retrieve or transmit any information. Not knowing what time was left to me, I hurriedly proceeded to record all the data that I retrieved from my home's auto-storage library. All this was our past history. Not being a historian, I still delighted in my own research of our society and therefore had accumulated an extensive tome. While these were relegated to the bland-colored containers, one more notable in color and size, containing my message, was chosen to arouse curiosity and interest.

My work is finished, and now I leave this lengthy reminder to impress upon you and others of its mystery and misery. I await my fate elsewhere so as not to contaminate this treasury of ideas and cherished memories. My time will eventually come, but may you profit from our mistakes and succeed by our accomplishments. All I can leave is what is before you. May the Giver yet intercede for us in our darkest moments.

Tau of the Emporium

You rest the last sheaf upon your lap, gazing at it as if to divine the ultimate fate of its author or his race. It's an unconscious act, for your mind reels at the tumbling sequences that speeds through your head. The end of Eden, as the serpent lures an unsuspecting victim into violating the forbidden decree.

You feel a surge of anger in that a miscreant and his ruinous ambition would lead to the demise of an incredible society. What further proof do you need than a world devoid of all life, animal, or otherwise. You slam your fist against an unyielding wall, the pain barely noticeable, your rage all-consuming. But pain cannot compete with disgust.

How could they let it slip away when generation after generation laid the building blocks of accomplishment?

Then again, it may not have been unavoidable. You recall Earth's history, which produced another manipulator, Cramer Furst. This fairly recent history revealed the extent in which he garnered the support from those whose wallets were bottomless and whose ethics were bankrupt. Using the same pattern of guile as Rel, he almost ignited a world war proving that the three previous ones accomplished nil. This near tragedy unseated him from power and led to draconian measures to eliminate a repetition. Only now do we find some of our lost liberties being restored. Having duplicated the sheave's contents by scanning, you place them back into the container and close the two halves with a finality that mirrors this world's fate. Returning to the cabinet, you gently replace the cylinder, triggering a sense of acute melancholy. Trying to find some solace, you recall Tau's last entry. Maybe others who find it will profit from his world's mistakes.

It is only fitting that his last testament serve as a beacon of light for those still fighting darkness. Gathering your gear, you head from the chamber and down the pathway that led you here. You turn for one last look, drinking in this last vestige of awe and wonder, questioning if any of this could ever be replicated, if their Giver existed as does my God, why not? The universe is vast, and so are all its secrets, enticing men to unravel them.

Reaching the entrance, you are delighted to see that there is what you may call daylight. By the darkness of the azure-blue sky, it will soon be dusk, making it a little tricky to return to the ship but not impossible.

As you head for the 'copter, your mind is still spinning from all that has happened to you while in the archive. What could cause an enlightened society to go off the deep end? What was the nature of the so-called device? Was it the panacea they thought it was? They, and for that matter, you will never know, especially since it was damaged in the attack. Suppose it wasn't damaged?

Would that have changed what occurred afterward? These thoughts and many others crowd your mind and make it difficult to preflight the 'copter. Can't chance a malfunction now and with little time remaining before you head home. Home! What a comforting thought after all this time away.

You guess it wasn't so much the time but the lack of companionship that weighed on you subconsciously.

This will be addressed in the briefing reports you will file after the mission. As you walk around the craft, there is a nagging sensation that tugs at you, as if you forgot something. It's not just a memory thing but a real pull on you. As you ponder the cause, you ascribe it to the atmosphere or the gravity, but you have been on planet long enough for this to have manifested itself earlier. You tense and hope some type of virus you could not detect before hasn't infected you.

Pulling out your immune detector from the medical pouch and giving your body the once-over, you're relieved to see a negative reading. That bit of relief can't overcome the concern you have for this unaccountable reaction. Determined to return to base, an irresistible urge overcomes you. Your eyes peer to the west and a small ridge. Since you approached from what would be the east, you could not tell what lay beyond it. If like the rest of the planet, probably nothing, but it seems as if the unknown impulse is from that direction. How and what can it be? Only one way to find out is to give in to the pull and follow along. Girding yourself for any possible confrontation, you unholster your archaic Model 1911 Browning .45 caliber semiautomatic and chamber a round. It's all that you have, but you may not need anything heavier, since one hit in a vital spot could spoil anyone's day—or night. You have to stop with the quips, but secretly it's these things that takes the edge off your nerves. Okay, you quit the stalling and trek toward the small rise. You'll probably laugh at some little thing that caused more nervousness than harm and will soon be on your way. At least that is what you tell yourself. You hope it's true.

You approach the rise and discover that it's steeper than it looked. Your first step causes you to slip to the ground. Not only is the gradient steeper, the loose rotten rock denies you a secure foothold. Again you attempt to gain traction but with limited success. It's one step forward and two backward. With sweat now complicating your trials, and hands scraped and bloodied, you finally conquer this mini Mt. Everest and reach the crest. Before you spans an expanse no different from the other areas you have seen. A mixture of flat land, hillocks, and small ravines. The source of your mystifying urge escapes you. Better to descend and quickly scout around before returning to your ship. You negotiate the descent only marginally better than the climb. Reaching the base of the hill, you strike out in the direction that seems to pull more strongly. Then you see it! A blueish pulsating glow, about three hundred meters distant. As you watch transfixed and alarmed, the intensity of its light increases, and the pulsating races faster and faster. Even as you feel mesmerized, a strange effect now seems to invade your mind. Thoughts of hatred, any type of hatred now permeates your being. You feel a hostility that has no rationale for being. While fighting this involuntary assault upon your psyche, you catch sight of a figure off to side that seems menacing. You swing your body in that direction and squeeze off three rounds.

It is only when you really focus on your assailant that you discover a pulverized rock formation. This is not like you! You would not have fired without assessing the danger, but in this instance, you disregarded your own fire discipline. Time and space dissolves into a matrix that strangles all sense of being. Again you try to reassert some control over what is happening to your mind and body.

You feel yourself slipping deeper and deeper into some dark chasm with steep walls that seem to close in on you, to crush you, to smother you. What the hell is this? Please, God, help me! It's the mental anguish more than physical pain that threatens to disable you, some diabolical force that defies explanation.

If it's of the mind, you stand a chance of escape, for through all the trials and errors you have had to face in your life, nothing could ever conquer your will to survive, and with a last supreme effort, you exert all that is left in you, a fight you must win or you may perish. You feel a definable lessening of the force as you maintain your struggle, and finally, with mind reeling and a sense of all-consuming fear, you swiftly turn and run back to the rise. The incentive to survive is a great spur to your efforts to scale the slope. Once past the crest, you plunge forward, pulse racing and sweat blinding your eyes.

Why were you acting so impulsively, and more importantly, why the animosity? No one would have recognized you if they saw your hostility, your blinding need to hurt someone, something. You run as if the devil himself were after you, and who could refute this after what you just experienced? Finally, you reach the 'copter, jump in, and without adjusting your harness, punch in auto liftoff and with increasing speed, head back to base. The short time it takes to return is filled with questions, questions, and more questions, with no plausible answers. What just happened? Why?

These are conjectures that only deepen your apprehensions as you allow a cool breeze to pass through the port aperture. Can it ever be explained, and if it could, would you or anyone else believe it?

What just happened is either the most monumental thing you've ever come up against or a curse or a mixture of both.

As the distance widens, your thoughts focus more sharply on the image of what you had seen and heard. Recounting what you could through the haze that had engulfed you, a familiar theme presents itself that would have been ordinarily overlooked. You think back to the sheaves that detailed the dilemma confronting the Eastern bloc and the creation of a mystery weapon that seemed to hold a promise of defense if not outright victory over Rel's forces. Mention was made of a pulsating entity, similar to the one you just encountered. Could there be a connec—no! It can't be, it just can't be, not after who knows how long ago this nightmare occurred. Startling as this conclusion is, it seems to fit in, however remote. As advanced as this race was, it would not be beyond their means to construct something of this nature, pressed as they were for some form of protection. If so, how can it still be functioning, and what was or is its operational capability beyond pulsing and glowing like it's Halloween? You may never know because, darn it, you're just not going back to find out, that's for sure. This and other thoughts cross your mind, unnerving you further to the point of almost losing it. You struggle to fend off this attack upon your sanity and only succeed by taking over the controls, manually hoping this concentration will help you to avoid an overload. Slowly, you foster a descending level of anxiety that brings a welcome sense of relief, thank God. With that, you sight the tip of your ship rising above the small hill before you, a sanctuary in this maelstrom of uncertainty.

Control over the 'copter is a little shaky, as well it would be. Your nerves still a little tender. You come in too hot and slam into the ground with a jarring crunch. Through sheer luck, the craft doesn't tip over, its rotors almost ripping into the gravelly surface. The shrapnel effect would have proven fatal. Hastily, you exit and run to the loading bay. This time, the old-fashioned way will not do, and you ascend to the control deck on an agonizingly slow lift. All hatches are locked down and the view screens activated. Your intentions are to blast off as quickly as possible, not knowing what to expect from whatever it was back there.

You care not a wit for the equipment that will be left behind; they served their purpose, most data having been transferred to the ship's storage banks. The risks are minimal but real. In the absence of a preflight check, you can only rely on the quality of the product you inhabit and trust that's sufficient—it has to be.

Anger surges through your veins, cursing the circumstances that force this premature departure. So much left behind and unanswered, other treasures that could have been uncovered. You mentally rail at the pulsating creation that's robbed you of this never-to-be-repeated experience. Strapped in and the control panel brought to your chest, a glance of all screens reveals no outside activity, no immediate danger, but that doesn't mean there is none. The ignition sequence is punched in, and your body tenses in anticipation of the jolt to come. One final look at the barren, unyielding, and unforgiving world of enigmas; who were they, what had they achieved in there long history, why did they destroy themselves, and more importantly, what was it that destroyed them? You may never know. The jolt catches you in midthought, and now all that occupies your mind is reading the instruments and assuring yourself that all systems are online and functioning. The ever-present physical discomforts attendant on launch repeat themselves as before, the pressure clawing at your body. The pain doesn't prevent you from glimpsing the last vestiges of this world and—what in the hell! No! No! It can't be! There, in the upper portion of the screen, a pulsating light! Oh my god! By the landmarks discernible at this altitude, you can tell that this thing is tracking you! Or at least your base. Your fears were not unwarranted, there was a danger.

You stare transfixed at the ominous sight and know that if not for your foresight in forcing a premature takeoff, you could very well have been in its grip again. Even so, through a wild imagination or some other explanation, you tend to feel that same inexplicable urge of hatred you felt before.

Is it real? You honestly can't say, so far removed from rational thought. Can it fly? Can it reach you? God forbid. Oh, God, please don't make it so. As the distance increases, so does the urge lessen, until finally, it's gone. Your body is completely soaked in the sweat of your fears. Unbuckling the straps, you roll off the command seat onto the deck, completely drained. You can't recall how long you lay there, only that you keep murmuring a prayer for deliverance, that God will protect you. Could anyone else have endured what you did and not go mad? Eventually, the discomfort from your gear forces a change in clothing, which does wonders.

As you fling the sodden garments down to the now-empty 'copter bay, you notice a nondescript package tucked behind the bulkhead. With all your chores and expectations during and after the flight, you never noticed it. Needing a distraction, you retrieve the parcel and rip off the wrapping. Removing the lid, you find a folded sheet of paper atop some items covered with a blanket of tissues.

The paper's message is handwritten, and you read it with a chuckle.

"Chief, where you're goin' is gonna be dry, so I left a little nip for you, along with some canned fruit that you like. I was gonna leave a butt or two but thought better of it. Oh, by the way, they didn't have Buttercrunch, so I got you Hershey's with almonds. Enjoy. Bring me back a souvenir. Sal."

This man should be the head of the psychology department, he is *so* good. Snatching the tissue, you uncover a pint bottle of Scotch and gulp down a healthy portion. Your body warms to the potent elixir's effects, and the respite is just what the doctor, or should you say, the sergeant ordered. There's a lot to sort through, but for now you go over the ship's internal feeds and controls, eliminating any errors you may find. The automatic settings take a great deal of worry off your mind as you calculate duration of the voyage back to Earth. A little house cleaning, a short nap, and then the prospect of a long, dull flight. Without the com unit, you can't alert your people to the dangers wrought upon you but also facing an isolation akin to a quarantine. Somehow, you have to make sense, if any sense exists, of what's back there. No movie producer or scriptwriter could have conjured up such a scenario, and then again, why not? You've seen too many sci-fis to dismiss any probabilities. Once home, you'll need a coherent report to support your observations. The data alone will not suffice as it only dealt with the scientific approach to the mission.

No, you'll need more than that or they'll think you cracked up, what with being cut off and being alone on the surface.

You lie on the deck with your head propped against the bunk and study vids of the terrain, the ruins of the city, and reading and rereading the recorded story from the archive. Point by point, you look for anything which could provide a basis for a rational conclusion. Time you have plenty of, smarts you're not sure of. If only you could transmit, garner help from the other end. Hours pass and no sensible argument can be made. Then a thought occurs that embraces the sci-fi mode. Why does it have to make sense? What if the answer is off the wall? Using that tact, you lay out a premise that can only be pieced together in jagged chunks, one segment rejected while another is installed. Reverting to pen and paper, the resulting pile of rejects rivals that left on the floor at the archive. Sucking on the end of a pen while in a pensive mood does nothing for the teeth and sours the taste buds. Think hard, what ends can you connect? A bare world, bereft of anything alive, plant or animal, is the first place to start. Then, how did it come to this? An empty world and the cause unknown. Good. Next, the discovery of an ancient and dead metropolis, offset by the existence of a solitary structure, said structure containing a personal narrative alluding to the end of days.

Very good. The challenge imposed on this society by a rabble rouser with the guile of a carnival shill. Getting there. An attempt to stave off defeat by creating a dominant weapon, which may have failed. Whoa, back up. The weapon was bombed, but there is only an inference that it was destroyed. Remember, it was described as glowing and pulsating when it was clobbered. And if the purpose was to disable or obliterate the enemy, why were they still attacking in spite of the continual output of energy? Something doesn't add up.

You scan the data over and over again, trying to discover that elusive clue that would put all the puzzle pieces together. Think. These were rabble that somehow became unstoppable scourges, when they were no different than their opposing brethren. Now go forward a little to the instance when you first encountered that pulsating blue light and how you felt transformed for the worse and only recovering when you fled from field. Bingo! It's only conjecture, but a darn good one. Suppose the damage done to the device changed its designed function and suppose that and the one you encountered are the same!

Even you find it difficult to accept this extrapolation, but as tenuous as it is, the possibility exists.

Trying to support this theory, you again examine all the points thus far and scrutinize them as thoroughly as a lawyer trying to close any and all loopholes in a contract.

What thread weaves all these facts together? Back and forth, over and over and…wait, of course. Overwhelmed by the magnitude of everything that's happened to you, it was easy to overlook a seemingly out-of-place indicator—behavior! Think about it, an army that seemed to gain inspiration at the same moment of a disabling attack upon a dominant weapon. Think also of the change in your feelings which became barbarian, something you know you are not. Yes, that has to be it! But that's not all. This thing didn't take sides. If it affected the attackers, it most certainly affected the defenders. And therein lies the almost unmistakable conclusion—they annihilated themselves! It has to be. And until it's destroyed, it will contaminate any who fall within its reach. Why no bodies? Remember that chunk of power bar? It was consumed by organic feasting microbes. My guess is that they had a grand banquet. As for the lack of settlements, save for the ruined city, you have no clue bearing on their disappearance. Maybe it was so long ago that they just crumbled to dust, but even you can't buy that logic. It's something you're destined never to know.

Okay, so maybe you don't have all the answers, such as how can it still be operating for who knows how long? Perhaps the damage allowed it to transform into what it is now and its longevity because of the sophistication of its construction. Energy wouldn't be a problem if its operation was fueled by solar power or some form of chemical or nuclear package. This you probably will never know either, but whatever its longevity, it's real. Which fuels another question, why was it stalking you?

Was it just its inherent nature to eliminate all and everything it came in contact with? Probably. But I think there has to be another reason, something you can't grasp at the moment, in the wake of your brilliant Sherlock Holmes assessment. Isn't this the way he wrapped up his cases, by smothering poor Dr. Watson with his step-by-step analysis of the dastardly deed and how he was able to thwart it with his insight? Holmes you're not, and you doubt you have done anything to thwart whatever it is you're supposed to thwart. Nonetheless, it lingers, waiting to tap you on the shoulder to say, "Hey, this is what it's all about." Okay, get some sleep, and tomorrow may bring some answers. The energy of the moment prevents a go-silently-into-the-night mode, the result being a thought-dominated, unsatisfying attempt at slumber.

Sleep is useless as the weight of confusion suffocates your prospective. My, how time seems to obey every position opposite your own. You want fast, you get slow and vice versa. In the days that follow, the helplessness of not being able to do more than just hoping to reach home weighs heavily. If what you surmised is even partially accurate, the danger to your world is grave and incalculable. That brilliantly conceived monstrosity musn't be underestimated and has to be contained somehow. You don't know how, but something has to be done to neutralize it, but with little scientific data to go on, it will be a long and maybe impossible haul.

Again, that troubling intuition nudges at you like a cat skirting your legs for attention. Why? Why did it come after you? You posed no threat to it; indeed, you were almost toast, but there's an answer, if only you can find it. Going over the data again only vindicates what you've already established.

If it's there, you can't find it. Heaven help us all. You take a much-needed a break to clear your thoughts. Jerry rigging the com unit is fruitless but helps to ease the feeling of hopelessness. Maybe a chance wire hookup or a random connection will breathe life into this pile of junk. No good. Nothing. You tinker halfheartedly, then, in an electrifying moment, your mind and body stiffen in unison, as the proverbial light bulb illuminates a path to discovery. The veil that cloaked your search for the answer, now parts.

What was only a nudge has now become more definitive and frightening, and if true, heaven really help us. You base this observation on a simple but overlooked incident. What were you feeling when you blasted off?

Anger!

Hostility!

Feelings you experienced when you first confronted that spawn from hell. That's got to be it. But you can't believe its design was a deliberate effort, something that would consume both friend and foe alike.

Its original purpose must have altered when it was bombed, causing it to evolve as the mind bender which confronted you. Those poor creatures never stood a chance, and neither will anyone else if it's not stopped. How powerful is this thing? A flash of genius rips across your mind—the portable telemetry unit carried in your field pack! Where is it? You fish through the mounds of clothing, MRE packs, and other minutia that litter the deck. Here it is! Great.

The unit was designed to record all types of waves, electronic, infrared, and x-ray, among others. Despite its size, the resultant data it can provide is staggering and may confirm your darkest fears. Plugged into the screening console, the read out of intensity and power levels is astounding. Considering the size of this weapon, how can such a relatively small device project so much raw energy? What you discover next almost knocks you off your seat. The waves emanating from the pulsing entity start on a low scale and then escalate to higher levels. This thing can control its own power? Is it sentient, artificial intelligence? You rub your eyes to clear the sweat and only succeed in stinging them. More bad news. The waves have a projection rate that does not diminish; however its strength can degrade over distance. Apparently, if the projection rate is increased, so does its strength, still subject to distance.

Okay, you guess that it supplies what it needs for any given circumstance and supports your previous belief that it has indeed reached out to you. Maybe the speed of the ship and the widening distance have diluted its output, saving you from a total takeover. You can only hope. And how far away is safe? Maybe not far enough as the readings provide another gloomy assessment. Even in its weakened state, the waves, when projected against a substantial body, will tend to build up, as each wave collides with the previous one. Think tsunami! Small waves that seem insignificant but maintain a steady accumulation, unleashing mountains of destructive water. If this is the case, has Earth been subjected to this phenomena? If so, for how long?

You don't laugh at this assumption, just as you can't laugh at what would have passed for science fiction not so long ago. Pondering Earth's history and the development of its people, were they the target to this curse? Most likely, but man is generally decent, with some weaker than others. Could this account for the rise of despots throughout history, Genghis Khan, Hitler, Stalin, Fürst, and others? Surely, not all evil could be laid at this doorstep, but enough so. At least that's what you think, and another thought crosses your now beleaguered mind: can it also implement acts of sabotage?

The near-fatal crash of your trainer, the wheel coming off your jeep, and the meltdown of your com system. Were these acts to forestall, if not prevent your mission? You can't be sure, but you're convinced that things don't happen by chance but by design. That assertion boils your blood. Well, pal, you scream, this guy isn't goin' down that easy! Do you hear me? Venting your frustration ignites a resolve to bury that monstrosity whatever the cost and in any way you can find to do so.

For now, you must survive, to warn Earth of the impending annihilation that may be visited upon its unsuspecting people. You step to the screen and peer into the darkness that conceals the bane of humanity. Once home, will there be enough time to spell out an incredible tale and convince those briefed that not a second must be lost? In order to facilitate this mind-boggling challenge, all data are assembled into the most concise package possible, removing all fat and only the bare but informative bones remaining. To sell it, your credibility has to be without one iota of contradiction, so immense and unbelievable the story. Would you believe it? You shake your head as if to partially answer that self-imposed query. Would you? You don't know. This honest opinion raises the hair on your neck. If you can't convince yourself, how in the world will you convince them. You bury your face into your scarred hands and murmur a plea of supplication. What man can't do, only God can.

The weeks drone by, one after the other, the beauty of the cosmos tempered by the burden you bear.

Trying to be the consummate professional expected of you, data is still being collected and collated as the ship's sensors and probes dutifully perform their tasks. You can still garner some measure of appreciation for various discoveries. One day they may unlock those mysteries of the universe that defy explanation. A glance at the chronometer revives a spirit of anticipation; soon the solar system and sol will be visible and then…Earth. The paths of the outward planets are crossed, bringing you closer and closer to home, blessed home. A final check of the readings, a little house cleaning and—*breep, breep, breep*. What the hell! The alarm comes from the far side of the deck, the side which controls the fuel system! With pounding heart, you race to the display console, pleading inwardly that this is an instrument malfunction. That plea is ignored when the status indicator for the fuel reserve reads *Empty! God, no! It can't be!*

But it is, a final rebuke in your efforts to reach home. How? Why? But that last thought dissolves with the image of the pulsating light reasserting itself in your consciousness. You fiend, you damn hellish fiend, what did I ever do to you? A question with a subtle answer.

You don't know how you know, but you do. To inflict punishment on you for what you discovered back there. A way to prevent the exposure that such a creature exists and its fear that an enlightened race will one day spell its doom. For millennia it spewed its evil force without letup, leaving a hapless society ravaged by its malevolence, unsuspecting the cause of their dilemma. And now Earth will never know.

The ship heads relentlessly toward that blue globe, its image growing larger on the screen. You wish you could shout to them, to warn them, and then you cry. "Big boys don't cry." *But, Dad, this is different, our world is going to die, and I can't do a thing to stop it.* For a moment, Dad seemed to be a real presence, and then he is gone. Was he there? Of course not, but you wanted so much to draw from his strength, to fight the fight of your life. Maybe that's all you needed and a renewed defiance emerges, something we all need at some time in our lives. But will it be enough?

You seek to find any means that will allow you to salvage victory, but to no avail. Soon, you will enter the atmosphere, and without the ionic engine thrusters to turn the ship into its landing position, the trajectory will be straight down. With nothing to slow it, the friction will start to generate tremendous heat, and eventually a breakup will occur. You feel weak but surprisingly calm at your impending demise. You've done all that could be done, and damn it, you won't leave this life a coward. The Earth now appears through the observation port, beautiful and unsuspecting.

A glistening sphere of life and vitality that will one day be extinguished. Heart heavy, you return to your bunk, where you lay your weary and tried body. Staring at the overhead, you whisper a final prayer to your creator and await the inevitable. Immediately you notice the suffocating heat that surprises you with its suddenness. Perhaps it will end quickly, no pain, no torment. Buffeting now rocks the craft in violent surges, the creaking of the metal signaling imminent destruction. The heat becomes unbearable, the gyrations increasing. All hope is abandoned. You surrender your will and consciousness to an all-consuming shroud of darkness, slipping more and more into a realm of deathly peace.

No! Damn it to hell, no! You won't make it that easy, not after all you've been through. Ripping away the mist you were so ready to surrender to, you glimpse a possible way out to your dilemma, scant but possible. Recalling the features of your ship and the many attributes that made it astounding in its creativity and resourcefulness, an overlooked section comes to mind. It never had the special attention that other sections did, only because you felt that it would never be needed. The data storage compartment, where all info that had been gathered during the moment of liftoff weeks before until your final flight home. You had peeked into the small confines as a cursory inspection, confident of its purpose to securely maintain all the data that it would receive and not giving it much thought afterward. Now it looms large as a means of survival, for if memory serves you correctly, it has a safety feature to protect the fount of wisdom it contains—ejection. The engineers had provided a means for which, in the case of imminent disaster, the compartment could be jettisoned and later retrieved. Boy, were they on the ball. Hurriedly, fighting against the suffocating heat and your fading consciousness, you stumble toward this island of salvation, hoping that it's not too late.

Your fingers recoil with pain as you activate the searing hatch panel and program a short countdown for ejection. For what seems like centuries, the entryway reveals itself and then comes the extreme effort to place yourself within its confines, for it was not truly designed for passengers. A repeat application on the panel eases the hatch shut and with it the hope of rescue, not only of its precious data, but of your being. The wait is interminable and then—nothing! Where is the surge of compression that accompanies separation from the ship? Nothing! Your heart sinks as rapidly as the temperature increases. That monster has reached out and ensured that it would not be revealed. It tortured you with possible salvation only to whip it away at the last moment. Your last effort has failed, and with this resignation, you allow the mist to close over you, dimly anticipating an uncertain appearance before your maker. Surprisingly, these last moments seem to be embraced with a cool feeling and then—nothing.

Time is meaningless if you are not aware of it, and how much of it has passed is elusive and inconsequential to those with no agendas or schedules to keep. But time does pass, regardless of the import or lack of it we put upon it. And then, you become aware of a subtle motion beside you. What a strange experience, as light stirs an awareness, and a fuzzy vision vies for your feeble attention.

It takes a while before you can acknowledge to yourself that what you see and feel is a presence of mind and body. A number of people are glancing and pointing, or whispering to one another, supposedly directed at or about you. Then a familiar face looms before you, confirming that you have not passed the portals of heaven. Sal, your stalwart aide and confidant.

"Chief, Chief, you're okay. At least I hope so. Talk to me. Tell me you're okay."

You detect a moist eye socket which he attempts to conceal by turning away and effecting as loud a honk as he can get with his hanky. Turning back to you, a nurse ushers him and other to the side as she checks your pulse and other vitals.

"Everyone out! He needs his rest!" she shouts, rivaling any general officer in an authoritative display of command. As they leave, Sal ducks into the bathroom, evading the attention of the nurse. When the room is clear and a decent interval of time has elapsed, the door slowly opens, and peering apprehensively about, as if not wishing to be seen or caught in some subversive act, an animated Sal rushes over to your side.

"Chief, I hope you're not mad at me, but I had to see you and know you're okay." His devotion has not waned a wit, as witness the deep concern carved into his brow. You reply in a cracked, raspy voice, motioning to him to pour you some water. He gently lifts your head and places the rim to your parched lips, careful to avoid spillage. Having gently swallowed a few sips, you start upward, and with an electrifying observation, shout, "Hey, I'm alive! How did I manage that?"

It's strange how the mind has difficulty picking up the strands of continuity when subjected to a traumatic experience. But still, the question is valid. How come you are alive?

"Sal, what happened, do you know?" you voice, remembering the last moments of consciousness on the ship.

"Chief, not being privy to all the goings-on around here, I finagled an acquaintance into keeping me up-to-date on the mission. Whenever a piece of info was received, I was notified because of"—here a slight redness crosses his face—"what I thought of you. Well, anyway, readings from the ship were constantly streaming in, not anything about your day-to-day exploration, but readings that showed the ship was operational and a few other things I couldn't understand.

"We did wonder why there was no radio communication from you and figured something must have happened to interfere with the signal getting through. As long as the readings kept up, we figured you'd be okay. Anyhow, what could we do?

"As the time for your departure grew nearer, we were mildly surprised when telemetry showed that you had abruptly taken off. We knew that because protocol was not followed, no automatic flight check.

"In other words, a blind liftoff. Boy, that got everyone's attention. I practically slept at the mission control room until they kicked me out. Again, my friend kept me informed. As the ship got closer to home, everyone became anxious, and then they blew a fuse when the power supply for the attitude thrusters showed zero on their panel. The damn tanks were empty. Zilch, nada. There should have been plenty left according to one of the staff. Talk about chaos, the place went nuts. Whatever they ran though the simulator to find a way to bring you home was a dud. Chief, I was beside myself and prayed for the first time in quite a while.

"Funny how we always go to the Big Guy when things are going south. Anyhow, my friend let me know that they picked up the ship entering the system and frantically tried to contact you, but no go. Hell, what are they paying these guys the big bucks for if they can't bring you in? Then, just as you hit the outer layer of atmosphere, a wave of excitement ran through the controllers. Yowwee! A signal from the ship indicating the data compartment ejection mode was energized. But nothing was happening. Now these guys finally earned their moola, when they began to send out an intensified override signal, at least that was what they called it, and repeatedly boosted the carrier wave.

"Man oh man, the place almost exploded when separation was confirmed. Of course, we could only guess if it was you who activated it in the first place, but let me tell you, Chief, I knew you'd be smart enough to think of a way outta that mess. Ground control tracked the capsule landing in the South Atlantic, and one of our missile subs was in the area close enough to pull you from the drink. Man, I love the Navy. Anyhow, after pulling you out, the damned capsule sank! Man oh man, was the director fit to be tied! The damned ingrate, he got you back, didn't he? I'm sure you can fill in a lot of the info they want, right, Chief?"

When he had said that, your mind races back and forth, and then you freeze, what info? What is he talking about? All you know is that you were ejected from your ship, but other than that…

Something's terribly wrong, something that snatches at your gut and indicates by feeling what you cannot put into words or even thought. You know that you were part of a mission, but what it was is something that eludes you. Why? Why can't you remember?

Sal sees the emptiness in your face, the confusion, and becomes visibly alarmed.

"Chief, what is it? Why do you look different? Are you okay?"

You respond that you just feel tired and that everything he has said needs to be digested. After all, coming back from an intrasolar mission isn't like a walk in the park. His features soften as he feels reassured, believing in you and trusting that soon you'll be your old self.

What he doesn't know is your own self-doubt, a doubt that you may not be able to reconcile with the void that resides in you. Maybe, just maybe, that a period of rest will jar something loose hanging in the back of your mind, lighting up that dark passageway that leads to revelation and relief. Sal asks if you need anything and implores, if not commands, you to call him if you need anything. Trusting that rest may be a better companion for you than himself, Sal squeezes your hand and leaves, glancing over his shoulder to reassure himself that you're okay. As the door closes, the quiet settles upon you like a blanket and generates a silent noise of its own. You remember dozing off in a lawn chair near the base highway lulled by the drone of the passing cars. It's only when traffic was absent that you felt that ping of silence which awakened you more so than a horn blown by an irate motorist. You shiver with the realization that for one of the few times in your life, you are scared!

Not of any physical harm, but that which you have no defense against, the assault upon your psyche. How can you lose a memory of what was your greatest adventure?

Your mind races to find an answer only to be worn down by repeated blanks, a wall that will not yield to repeated and desperate attempts to penetrate its secrets. Exhausted, your mind mercifully slips into a respite of sleep.

Occasionally, a flash of blue light sears your subconscious and then disappears. Your mind does not comprehend its presence but senses a threat, a threat you cannot rationally explain in your dream state. Your eyes open and looking at the clock realize that you have slept for some hours, which should have been refreshing, but a nagging suspicion hangs over you that all is not what it should be. Fading, but still lingering, is the image of the blue light that haunted your sleep. What part does it play with your predicament?

The next few days offer no improvement to your memory or disposition. Finally the doctor in charge sees no reason to keep you any further, and you are discharged. Ever-faithful Sal is there to drive you back to the base and the director of operations. After a few preliminary observances of protocol, you are stunned at what they propose. They had been informed of your unexpected memory lapse.

It is their opinion that nothing further could be gained by a continual effort to jar your memory. That avenue was considered and then rejected, the rationale being that a man of your training and experience would have been able to surmount this lapse by now. Further efforts toward this end would be futile losing valuable time for what they now propose to you.

A recovery effort succeeded in locating and retrieving the data capsule. A sense of relief you experience, engendered by the hope of knowing what your mission entailed is abruptly dashed when informed of the condition of the data-recording units. While in seemingly perfect operating condition, only fragments of information could be retrieved, tantalizing but inconclusive. It also seems that the bulk of the data had been mysteriously erased. Assuring them that this was not of your doing, and could not be explained, they then hit you with a knockout punch. Would you consider going back again? It takes a while for your mind to absorb the offer. Why me again, especially since many of the questions that were at the core of the mission were unanswered? It was significant to note that you had brought the ship to your destination and home again, a feat requiring an inordinate amount of skill. Their faith in your piloting abilities almost submerges the feeling of failure that has rested on your shoulders like a leaden yoke.

They convince you to accept the premise that although the data was almost nonexistent, there were enough teasers to prompt another exploration. You wonder why a second trip would be any more productive, not to mention expensive, considering the failure of the recovered data units to satisfy their thirst for alien enlightenment. In this day and age, they postured, today's breakthrough in any field of endeavor is measured in months or weeks, rendering any previous accomplishment obsolescent or outright obsolete.

Their energized explanation, like schoolboys creating wonders with an erector set, puts into prospective the plan they have conceived to revive the mission. Military intelligence being the core factor in protecting the nation from its enemies, tremendous strides had been accomplished in creating miraculous if not magical constructs of electronic surveillance, decryption, storage, you name it. With this enhanced capacity, newly acquired inputs would not be affected by any intrusion intended to compromise, distort, or to eliminate them. Trial after trial had proven this defensive segment to be highly effective. Not only that, any results obtained would not be nebulous or open to second guessing but would lay out exactly what had occurred. This was a quantum leap that would leave the pilot of the ship, as just that, a pilot. His visual observations, while contributory, would be relegated to a trivial input.

You sit there for a moment, mesmerized by this dangling carrot, and wonder if you're up to it. Having crossed open space to another orbiting body and returning to Earth, not fully remembering the greatest adventure in your life, you fumble for an answer, but not for long. Your innate sense of risk taking and of the challenges that had been your staple in life leads you to only one conclusion.

"I'll do it."

No sooner do those words leave your lips that you almost bit into them. Are you sure? Not knowing anything as to the origins of your memory loss raises a red flag, but you ignore it. Trying to rationalize your impulsive decision, you realize that an answer could be more confusing than the question. The mind is constantly at war when confronted with the challenges inherent in defining age-old riddles or newly discovered ones. Maybe it's the thought of unfinished business and not having failed at anything so serious that drives you to seek finality. Anyhow, the die is cast.

You're instructed to take some time off before prepping for the new mission. Time to rest and maybe to address the mystery of the blue light. You wonder if you should have related this anomaly to the director but counter with the thought that disclosure might have caused them to rescind their offer and scrubbed you for another candidate. Motioning to Sal with a nod of your head, both of you leave the ready room and exit the building.

"Where to, Chief? Want to grab a bite?" Sal intones as you scramble into the jeep. You decline in a somber and detached reply, your mind still adjusting to the path to which you have committed yourself. "How 'bout I take you back home and you can get some rest?" One thing that Sal doesn't lack is a sense of anticipation, and you nod in the affirmative. The jeep zooms from the lot in the carefully controlled mayhem Sal is noted for.

He respects your silence, and small talk is at a minimum, but you notice the fatherly concern he exhibits as he glances your way without being too obvious. What a great guy and friend. Arriving at your apartment, Sal mutters a few words of encouragement and waits for you to enter the building before screeching away, but not before barking a stark order to call him if needed. The elevator is thankfully empty, the silence compounding the slight apprehension you feel as the floors slip by, signaling their passage by the pinging of the floor indicator. A feeling of anticipation engulfs you as approach your apartment. It will be like seeing an old friend again, welcoming your return and ready to lavish its long-abandoned comforts which at one time seemed trivial and taken for granted.

Voice recognition allows access to the vestibule, where you dump your gear, after which a search of the fridge yields a cold brew. Slumping onto the living room sofa, the small repast slightly invigorates your solemn mood, and a certain clarity begins to dawn on you. The tiredness slips away, and your mind begins again to gather up the loose clues you have harbored in the hopes of lifting the shroud of darkness that has concealed the past. What did you do there, what did you see? Why must the most adventurous period of your life be a blank? Whatever the cause, it must have been exceedingly traumatic to have wrought such a profound effect. Will the second time be any different? You fervently hope so, but characteristically you will not allow this to deter you, for this mystery, worthy of a novelist, will and must be solved, if only to assuage your own concerns. The light of day yields to the encroachment of the evening's shadows, and you realize that you have pondered your dilemma for far too long. Perhaps a good night's sleep will change your fortunes, the least of which will be a refreshed body, if not mind. You rise slowly and pause for a moment, attracted by the sound of the city below coming to nocturnal life. Like a magnet, it draws you to the glass partition leading to the balcony, sliding open to reveal a view that has always been captivating. The sun is sinking rapidly as it has done countless times, accompanied by the street level noise wafting upward. And in the distance you will soon see another gleaming needle, pointing upward, pointing to a new adventure. You are reliving a moment that has been lived before. Moving closer to the balcony and surveying the panorama of the skies' beautiful array of emerging stars, you lower your head. It's a cool evening as you look over this teeming city of millions.

About the Author

The author retired from the Camden Police Department after twenty-seven years of service. He and his wife, Lynne, recently celebrated their fiftieth wedding anniversary. Their daughter, Jenn, and her husband, Bernie, have blessed them with three grandchildren, Maryn, Mason, and Madden. He is an avid model collector and builder, loves woodworking, and has done many pencil artworks. He recently dabbled in painting. He credits his family for their support in his writing efforts and gives thanks to God for the results.

CPSIA information can be obtained
at www.ICGtesting.com
Printed in the USA
BVHW071318011121
620441BV00004BA/16